American Short Stories

Fifth Editio[n]

Eugene Cu
Auburn Univers

Bert Hitch
Auburn Univers

Scott, Foresm
A Division of Sco
Glenview, Illino

Dedicated to the memory of our beloved colleague and chief, Walton R. Patrick (1909–1986), co-editor of this anthology from its inception in 1950 until his departure from us: . . .

"Nature [he] loved and next to nature, art
[He] warmed both hands before the fire of life;
It sank—and [he] was ready to depart."

Aaron Bohrod. Landscape Near Chicago. 1934. Oil on composition board. 24 x 32 inches. Collection of Whitney Museum of American Art. Purchase 34.13

Library of Congress Cataloging-in-Publication Data
American short stories / [edited by] Eugene Current-García, Bert Hitchcock.--5th ed.
p. cm.
ISBN 0-673-38568-X
1. Short stories, American. I. Current-García, Eugene.
II. Hitchcock, Bert.
PS648.S5A47 1990
813'.0108--dc20 89-34255
CIP

123456 — RRN — 949392919089

Preface

In several important ways this Fifth Edition of *American Short Stories* is a new departure for us—a memorial edition of two kinds. Our first concern was to make of it a volume worthy of the scholar and co-editor to whom we have dedicated it, our colleague Walton R. Patrick. To produce an anthology that would meet his standards, we wished also to fashion a broader memorial, a fifth edition resting on the traditional basis of four earlier ones but celebrating at the same time two full centuries of growth and development of short fiction in the United States from its primitive origins in 1789 to the present. As in previous editions, we have tried again to fulfill a dual purpose: first, to assemble here the best of the old and what we believe to be the most promising among more recent short stories by American authors, so as to illustrate the long evolution of the short story form that began appearing in Colonial magazines even before Washington Irving's advent; and, second, to provide students with an interesting potpourri of representative stories, each of which invites careful study and lively discussion in its own right.

The format of this new edition still bears the same basic pattern established in earlier ones: a chronological arrangement of stories keyed to the sequence of their authors' birth dates and grouped together within sectional divisions. But we have made significant changes in both the number and selection of stories within these groupings, notably in the fourth and fifth sections of this volume, which include fiction published since 1935. While four writers were dropped from the previous Section Four, three new ones have been selected to replace them, and eleven more writers have been added to fill the new Section Five; thus, more recent time is represented by twenty-six writers and stories as opposed to sixteen in the fourth edition.

Similarly, we have modified the selection and improved the variety and balance of older materials in the first three sections of this edition. Instead of offering two stories apiece for each of the five "masters" named in earlier editions (Poe, Hawthorne, James, Crane, and Faulkner), we now hold each of them to a single story and allow five other standard authors, hitherto omitted, to challenge their supremacy. Besides the two anonymous primitives in Section One, we have added an early detective tale by William Gilmore Simms and a Simon Suggs yarn by Johnson Jones Hooper; in Section Two we have dropped stories by Bret Harte, William Dean Howels, and Hamlin Garland, but added an amusing tale by Sarah Orne Jewett; and in Section Three we have added stories by William March, Zora Neale Hurston, and Jean Toomer to offset the loss of Ring Lardner's. Still other changes that we hope may further enhance the literary quality and appeal of works by standard authors include the substitution of Ambrose Bierce's "One Officer, One Man" for his "The Coup de Grâce"; Crane's "The Blue Hotel" for "The Open Boat"; O. Henry's "The Caballero's Way" for "A Madison Square Arabian Night"; Edith Wharton's "The Other Two" for "Roman Fever"; James Thurber's "The Secret Life of Walter Mitty" for "The Catbird Seat"; Hemingway's "Hills Like White Elephants" for "A Clean Well-Lighted Place"; and Steinbeck's "The Chrysanthemums" for his "Flight."

As compared with the forty-eight stories by forty-three writers contained in our fourth edition, there are fifty-seven stories and authors in the present volume, a net gain of nine new stories and fourteen authors. Together with the substitutions we noted, our revised fifth edition offers teachers and students alike a comprehensive, fresh sampling of some of the most impressive short stories published in the United States since the eighteenth century, more than a third of them written within the last few decades by authors who are still producing. We have prepared updated or new critical introductions for each of the five sections of these chronologically grouped stories and biographical headnotes for their individual authors. Together, the introductions and headnotes call attention to the shifting attitudes, manners, and modes of expression that, over the course of many decades, have altered the mores of American society and have been reflected in both the content and style (indeed, even the freedom of language usage) to be found in the developing short story form.

Essentially, the critical commentary on short fiction techniques discussed in the introductory material follows the same pattern as that of earlier editions; yet each segment of critical and biographical data has been carefully screened and modified, where necessary, in the light of recent scholarship. As before, we have carefully selected each story as a valid representation of its author's individual techniques, significant features of which we have tried, in each case, to relate to the specific story included in the text. We have made no attempt, however, to thrust our own judgments on the structure and meaning of the stories in the form of elaborate critical analyses because we believe that the interpretation and evaluation of these stories are best achieved through the give-and-take of class discussion between teachers and their students. The stories may thus be taken up in chronological order as examples of a sequentially developing form, or they may be rearranged under various other classifications and studied in any order that suits the teacher's preference.

As in all previous editions of this text, our task of choosing, assembling, and revising its contents has been pleasurably eased by the encouragement and valuable suggestions given us by various members of the staff of Scott, Foresman and Company, especially Marisa L. L'Heureux, Anne Smith, and Ann-Marie Buesing. Revision of the older critical introductions and author headnotes has been done mainly by Eugene Current-García; that of the modern and contemporary periods by Bert Hitchcock. Other aspects of revising this book, such as the selection of authors or the substitution of stories, were the result of much cooperative effort. We wish to acknowledge with special gratitude the suggestions of Stephen Gresham, Byron Hopkins, Vernon Hyles, and Lex Williford.

Eugene Current-García
Bert Hitchcock

Contents

SECTION ONE

Romanticism and the Beginnings

1789 – 1850

Although the short story as we know it today springs from a tradition buried in the distant past, it first appeared as a distinctive literary form in the United States about two centuries ago at a time when the young nation was becoming culturally self-conscious. In 1815, as the second war against England ended, Americans could boast of their military and political achievements and look forward confidently to a great economic future for their country, but their pride in these things was a bit dampened by the feeling that they had as yet no independent literary tradition. Ever since the Revolution, the patriotic desire to establish a native literature had spurred many an American into energetic, though largely amateurish writing of poetry, drama, and fiction. Yet, as late as 1820, their failure to impress foreign travelers and critics, who jeered at their lack of artistic development, could be summed up in Sydney Smith's contemptuous wisecrack: "In the four quarters of the globe, who reads an American book?" Significantly, the short story gave the first effective response to this paltry question, for Washington Irving's *The Sketch Book* (1820) proved that American writers could produce a literature that would command respect abroad.

A single book, however, even though a classic, does not make a literature. Long after 1820, the United States, while developing rapidly in other fields, continued to lag culturally behind Europe, its literature overshadowed by England's. To cut away its literary dependence upon England was especially difficult, first because Americans naturally kept on reading English books, and second because they had little time or monetary incentive to write many of their own, as both book publishers and magazinists filled their pages with the more popular English literary works (which they could pirate freely!) and often ignored the prior claims of American writers whom they would have had to pay. Nevertheless, during the brief period between 1820 and the 1850s, the short story flourished in America despite the nation's predominantly agrarian make-up: with no large cities and a rural population thinly scattered over a million square miles, Americans founded hundreds of literary periodicals, many of them sincerely dedicated to bringing the writings of their fellow citizens before the public. Among the most noteworthy of these were the *North American Review, Knickerbocker Magazine, Graham's,* and *Southern Literary Messenger.* Next to poetry, short fiction was perhaps most adaptable to magazine publication, and, as it quickly proved to be the most popular as well, the short story developed as a distinctive art form with extraordinary rapidity. By the 1850s, thousands of short stories had been written and published in America, and the technique of the short story had been raised to the highest level of nineteenth-century literary art.

Types of Magazine Short Fiction before 1820

Magazines began appearing in the Colonies as early as the 1740s, and the people who published them quickly took advantage of the opportunity to imitate popular English journals by borrowing the kinds of literary fare that English readers admired. Often without bothering to acknowledge their sources, many of the earliest American magazines simply reprinted excerpts from or amateurish imitations of the works of leading English writers such as Alexander Pope, Thomas Gray, Ben Jonson, and Laurence Sterne. By 1800, more than one hundred American magazines had sprung up, most of them surviving only a year or two, but leaving behind in their files nearly 500 pieces of short fiction; and these numbers increased dramatically during the next few decades as more and more magazines appeared on the scene. Lacking fixed principles of content, composition, and form, the earliest pieces of short fiction published in American magazines were usually anonymous adaptations of tales or anecdotes casually lifted from British or Continental magazines without reference to their authorship or point of origin. Many of these early narratives were mere anecdotal fragments such as sentimental sketches of girls gone astray or comic parodies or skits involving Indian or black dialogue. But many others were narratives of six to ten pages and more, revealing some effort to achieve individuality in composition, structure, and style. Since most of them are anonymous, it is almost impossible to determine whether any were original tales written by Americans; yet the presence in them of many native touches of character, setting, and speech, as well as local or regional references, suggests that a sizable proportion of these tales were of native American origin.

Whatever their sources, the growing numbers of these tales toward the end of the eighteenth century reveal an ironic paradox: on one hand, obviously, there is the increasing popular appeal of fiction; on the other hand, a vociferous clamor against it from pulpit and public rostrum. The make-up of this fiction—its themes, structure, tone, and emphasis—reflected the actions, interests, and aspirations, as well as the doubts and fears, the manners and morals, of a self-conscious, democratic society, a society emerging from its Puritan, colonial work ethic and responding to the winds of change both at home and abroad. Adjusting to new conditions and problems, Americans were seeking their identity as a nation in the very process of dramatizing their behavior under the guise of a moralistic self-examination; and the earliest tales thus fulfilled their purpose simply by appealing to an unsophisticated reading public eager to be amused, instructed, preached to, shocked, or titillated. Ironically, therefore, the more vigorously some Americans condemned fiction as a debaucher of youth and a waste of time, the more it was published and read. And the more it seemed to echo the tones of its harshest critics!

The prevailing movement in European literature at this time was the romantic revival, a movement in thought and expression embracing a sense of newness and wonder, which Americans found particularly appealing and quickly turned to their own uses. Though difficult to define precisely, Romanticism was characterized by: (1) an ardent interest in the emotions and the imagination and an awareness of the mystery, ecstasy, and yearning locked up in the human heart; (2) a fondness for the picturesque, exotic, and sensational manifestations of these feelings; (3) a belief in the greater goodness of simple, unspoiled humanity, and a humanitarian sympathy for the joys and sorrows of the common man; (4) a marked enthusiasm for external nature, the wilder and more primitive the better, since many romanticists tended to assume that nature in its pristine state taught unmistakable lessons of wisdom, beauty, and truth; (5) a fascination for remote times and places that possessed exotic charms in the form of picturesque legends, superstitions, and adventures; and (6) a tendency to manipulate all these materials so as to idealize both nature and human nature without too much regard for "truth to life." Romanticism, in short, implied a search for new realms of experience, a thirst for novelty, and a desire to live intensely.

In their efforts to dramatize such freewheeling urges as these and, at the same time, turn aside the wrath of outraged critics, the early tale writers often became pseudo-moralists themselves. To justify their role as storytellers, they wrote fiction that resembled the Biblical parables evoked by the clergy, combining under the cloak of sermonic truth-telling many a scandalous episode or sequence of events that could be luridly embroidered. Holding the mirror up to nature in the new world, they thus provided both moral guidance and heightened entertainment by ringing a familiar pattern of changes involving three prevalent themes: (1) sexual incontinence, its hazards and painful results; (2) rural virtue as opposed to urban vice; and (3) the vulnerability of unprotected individuals in a lawless, uncertain world. Under the first two of these headings many doleful tales focused upon the fatal effects of rape, seduction, fornication, marital infidelity, even incest; others stressed the virtues of the gospel of work, pointing out explicitly how satisfaction with one's humble status and honest daily toil in a quiet rural setting became the pathway to salvation, remote from the city-bred evils of luxury, idleness, and discontent, which, of course, led straight to perdition. Scores of admonitory titles can be cited to illustrate the popularity of these tales, as well as those of the third group, which dramatized the remaining social or psychological ills the harried colonist had to face: the threat of highway robbery, murder, kidnapping, slavery, piracy, or mass upheaval and violence. A few such titles from magazines of the 1780s and 1790s are self-explanatory: "The Exemplary Daughter," "Miseries of Idleness and Affluence," "The Pangs of Repentance," "The Progress of Vice," "The Imprudent Parents," "The Fatal Effects of Seduction," "The Repentant Prostitute," and "Treachery and Infidelity Punished."

Whatever the substance of these anonymous early tales—whether external violence and physical pain or remorse and emotional distress caused by misconduct, parental tyranny, or frustrated desires—their authors had to cope with the basic problem of achieving fictional validity. The writers' repeated claim that their stories were based on actual events implied a felt need to defend themselves against the charge of falsifying ("making things up") and to establish a connecting link between the palpable, external world of the senses and the inner world of the imagination. They were groping toward what Nathaniel Hawthorne would later call "a neutral territory, somewhere between the real world and fairyland, where the Actual and the Imaginary may meet, and each imbue itself with the nature of the other." Because these writers still lacked the formulae and the techniques for producing such a creative art form, they had to seek their "neutral ground" through a process of trial and error. They had to find ways of making the tale come alive as a convincing portrayal of lifelike human beings, acting and reacting believably in a believable situation and place. They had to suit the individual to the deed, to master the art of character motivation, and to arouse and maintain, from start to finish, the reader's mounting concern for a sequence of developments leading up to an unforeseen yet logical climax and an aesthetically satisfying denouement. And besides such basic structural problems as these, they also faced that of getting the story told in language appropriate to its tone, mood, atmosphere, and source of utterance: that is, the problem of style and point of view.

Few of the nation's earliest fiction writers had the professional skills needed to fulfill these aims. Many, perhaps, were but dimly aware of the need for them; for theories about the proper make-up and role of the short story did not emerge until the 1830s, when such writers as Edgar Allan Poe, Nathaniel Hawthorne, and William Gilmore Simms began to consider critically the basis of their own literary aims, particularly those involving significant distinctions between long and short fiction. Still, however crudely contrived most of these early tales would appear to an average reader today, the alert student can detect in them some interesting techniques designed to enthrall their own readers. Varied uses of the first-person narrative method, for example, were employed to evoke a suitably horrified response, as in the lugubriously remorseful letters presented in "Fatal Effects of Seduction" (1789) and "Melancholy Effects of Seduction" (1795); while in others, the spirit of Fielding rather than of Richardson probably accounted for the rollicking humor and sprightly dialogue provided in "The Fair Recluse" (1784), "Three Days After Marriage" (1789), and "Matrimonial Infidelity" (1789), which dealt with the same popular theme.

Among the best examples of competent craftsmanship in the treatment of marital infidelity, however, are the two tales reprinted here: "The Story of the Captain's Wife, and an Aged Woman" (1789) and "The Child of Snow" (1792). In both of these one finds a combined use of irony, novel detail, both realistic and fantastic, a matter-of-fact tone, and a touch of the macabre—all of which lead to remarkably contrasting conclusions. The earlier tale, attributed to the anonymous Ruri Colla, deals with the routine social problem of the long-absent seafaring husband and the lonely wife in terms of universal, psychologically genuine human yearning, frustration, and fulfillment. And equally shorn of moral preachment, the latter one works up the same standard materials, even more economically, to a much grimmer, bizarre end. Whoever their authors may have been, no superior talents than these would be evident in American short fiction until Poe and Hawthorne emerged forty years later.

The Development of an American Art Form

American writers naturally turned to popular European romantic literary types for inspiration and strove to convert them to the uses of American materials. Their efforts were often too slavishly imitative to be wholly successful, but they quickly demonstrated considerable originality in the short story, possibly because European romanticists had only begun to work out the techniques of this type of fiction when the Americans themselves began to experiment with it. In form the short tale was partly an outgrowth of the eighteenth-century sketch and periodical essay, and the possibilities of its development into a type of fiction distinct from the novel, yet containing most of the elements that gave the novel its strong popular appeal, were just coming to be realized when Irving took it up and fashioned it into a species of narrative that brought him immediate fame.

Nearly all the short tales in Irving's three most important volumes—*The Sketch Book, Bracebridge Hall,* and *Tales of a Traveller*—are the result of his borrowings from older European literatures. Even his most famous stories, "Rip Van Winkle" and "The Legend of Sleepy Hollow," are directly traceable to German legends that he found ready made during his travels on the continent. In refashioning the source materials of European legends, Irving simply followed the standard practice of most of his contemporaries, but the difference between their transparent imitations and his successful adaptations lay in his artistry, which made these old materials uniquely his own rather than obviously derivative.

Irving had both a professional attitude toward the materials of fiction and a highly developed skill in shaping them within a preconceived framework in order to produce a finished and pleasing work of art. He had a keen eye and ear for the significant details of everyday life and human character, the look on a face, the tone of a voice, the meaning of a certain gesture; he understood his own limitations as a writer and knew how to work within them to the best advantage in short units; and he possessed a feeling for words, knowing how to choose and combine sensuous imagery appealing to his readers' emotions. Irving's artistry may be summarized as the realization of a fundamental principle of art, later to be forcefully reaffirmed by Poe and James, that "manner" or execution rather than choice of subject matter is the criterion of a writer's worth. This principle is clearly set forth in the letter Irving wrote to his brother-in-law in 1824, explaining his refusal to attempt writing a novel:

> *. . . I fancy much of what I value myself upon in writing, escapes the observation of the great mass of my readers: who are intent more upon the story than the way in which it is told. For my part I consider a story merely as a frame on which to stretch my materials. It is the play of thought, and sentiments and language; the weaving in of characters, lightly yet expressively delineated; the familiar and faithful exhibition of senses in common life; and the half-concealed vein of humour that is often playing through the whole—these are among what I aim at, and upon which I felicitate myself in proportion as I think I succeed. . . .*
>
> *I have preferred adopting a mode of sketches and short tales rather than long works, because I chose to take a line of writing*

peculiar to myself; rather than fall into the manner or school of any other writer: and there is a constant activity of thought and nicety of execution required in writings of the kind, more than the world appears to imagine. . . .

However strongly later critics have objected to the looseness of structure implicit in Irving's idea that a story is merely a frame on which to stretch materials, none has ever questioned that an especial "nicety of execution" distinguishes the short story from longer forms of fiction. Irving's realization of this fact establishes him as our first conscious literary artist in the short story.

By twentieth-century standards of short story technique, however, even the best of Irving's stories betray faults that the critical reader may find disturbing. Action develops slowly, impeded by long passages of description and chatty editorial commentary, which the reader accustomed to the swifter pace of today's stories grudgingly tolerates or skips altogether. Besides lacking tension and that sense of "immediacy" that we have come to regard as almost necessary attributes to the short story, Irving's stories often betray an objectionable quality of languorous softness, most prominently displayed in such tearful tales as "The Broken Heart" and "The Pride of the Village." But the fact that Byron wept over "The Broken Heart" and pronounced it good is evidence that such softness was a characteristic of the romantic age in which Irving wrote.

No adverse criticism, however, can destroy the enduring values that Irving's contemporaries were quick to recognize in his work. The perfection of tone in his best stories, the pictorial quality of his prose, and the pervasive humor, subtly blended with a nostalgic, dreamlike atmosphere, coalesced in a style that a whole generation of younger writers sought to duplicate. Taking their cue from Irving's success with *The Sketch Book,* many of them tried to imitate both its style and methods, with the result that their stories often revealed even more obvious technical crudities and unevenness of form than were apparent in Irving's. But like him these writers were also striving to make vivid the characters, scenes, customs, and legends of American life. Among the most noteworthy of these minor contemporaries were William Austin, J. K. Paulding, R. H. Dana, James Hall, Catharine Sedgwick, Albert Pike, and A. B. Longstreet, men and women from widely scattered areas of the United States, yet all imbued with a common desire to capture in story form the charm and picturesqueness of their own communities. From the beginning, "local color," one of the chief virtues in such a tale as "Rip Van Winkle," has been a prominent motif in the development of the American short story.

The mounting popularity achieved by our earliest short story writers soon raised a problem—the commercialization and standardization of literary art—that has remained central in American literature down to the present, particularly in the short story. Professional authors in America have always had to meet the demands of a commercial market; at first they had to compete with pirated British authors for space in the magazines, and, if they hoped to succeed financially, they had to write the kind of stories that magazine editors would buy and publish. Commercialization of the short story came to the fore as early as the mid-1820s with the appearance of the annual or gift book, a new publishing phenomenon that created a wide vogue lasting more than a quarter century. An ornate volume containing a variety of literary fare, the gift book quickly proved both a popular and profitable medium for the distribution of short stories. The demand for stories kept pace with the burgeoning gift books, and as more and more publishers brought out many new editions of them between 1830 and 1850, shrewd authors who managed to place each year a number of their stories in several gift books could count on a moderate income from their efforts. While these annuals created a market for short stories and offered encouragement to even the most talented of our early writers (nearly thirty of Hawthorne's earliest stories first appeared in *The Token,* an annual published in Boston beginning in 1827), they also served to direct the course of the short story's development. The fact that gift book requirements were geared to a popular demand for frothy, romanticized treatment of such current interests and fads as pseudo-science, the Indians, hair-raising deaths and premature burials, unrequited love, and the great American rags-to-riches theme, necessarily brought about a certain degree of standardization in the product—or at least standardization skillfully blended with only enough novelty to meet and surpass competition.

Such literary conventions naturally resulted in a flood of ludicrously pretentious writing, which rapidly increased in volume as more and more writers strove to satisfy the almost insatiable demands of the American public for light literary entertainment. The success of the annuals prepared the way for the still greater success of "ladies' books," which offered a monthly instead of a yearly harvest. *Godey's Lady's Book,* founded in 1830, became the first of the great "slicks." This new magazine was so astutely tailored to fit the demands of its feminine audience that despite the swift growth of competition, it boasted, by 1836, the largest circulation of any monthly in the United States and continued to dominate the field for half a century. Fiction in the *Lady's Book* during its early years consisted largely of sentimental tales culled from British magazines and annuals. But financial success soon led to the bolder and more constructive policy of soliciting "original" American stories and paying their contributors the highest rates in the country, so long as they could satisfy its editor's plea for

> *... short, racy, spirited essays; stories and sketches that embody pages of narrative and sentiment in a single paragraph, and by a few bold touches paint rather than describe, the characters they exhibit for the instruction and entertainment of our readers.*[1]

Authors who could readily meet these demands, such as Nathaniel Parker Willis, quickly became the most popular. Willis's fabulous success (his yearly income during the early 1840s, when both Poe and Hawthorne were struggling desperately to earn a livelihood from writing, ranged between $8000 and $10,000) was due largely to his mass production of sentimental tales, "crowded with duels, intrigues, disguises, escapades, masked balls, lost heirs, and all the stock properties of the romancers' art."[2] Obviously a degeneration of Irving's style of writing, this sort of thing predominated in the annuals and ladies' magazines, with the result that not even Poe or Hawthorne could escape its influence altogether. The demands of the age help explain the lush, rococo quality in much of Poe's writing as well as the pale, fragile tint in some of Hawthorne's. At the same time, the movement toward sprightlier dialogue, faster action, purposeful description, and other such techniques of the short story was given impetus by the *Lady's Book,* as its remarkable success bred a host of imitators, all eager to exploit its materials and methods. The influence of the annuals and ladies' books was both bad and good, but they deserve acknowledgment for having occasionally published the work of the two greatest artists of the short story of their day, Hawthorne and Poe.

Toward an Aesthetics of Form

Long before Irving had ceased writing, Hawthorne and Poe emerged, almost simultaneously, to challenge and presently to surpass his preeminence. The publication of Hawthorne's *Twice-Told Tales* in 1837 emphatically proved that the young nation need no longer apologize for its literature, but if further proof were needed, Poe's short stories, appearing regularly during the 1830s and 1840s, supplied it. Like Irving, both Hawthorne and Poe were literary artists, but they differed markedly from each other—and from Irving—in that Hawthorne's stories, generally unfolding against a New England background, were often symbolical and almost always stressed a moral theme, while Poe's usually depended on no particular locality, generally avoided allegory, but revealed an extremely tight and unified construction, as well as an astonishing power

[1]Mrs. Sarah Josepha Hale, quoted in F. L. Pattee, *The Development of the American Short Story* (New York: Harper and Brothers, 1923), p. 71.
[2]Ibid, p. 80.

to evoke atmosphere. In the work of these two writers, the short story in America reached a high level of art, though the nation at large scarcely realized that fact.

Hawthorne's active career as a short story writer fell roughly into two periods of nearly equal length covering a span of about twenty-five years. The first period, sometimes called his "anonymous years," began with his graduation from Bowdoin College in 1825 and ended with the publication of his first noteworthy collection in 1837; the second ended shortly after the publication of *The Scarlet Letter* when, his fame now assured, Hawthorne issued in 1851 his last significant collection of tales, *The Snow Image and Other Twice-Told Tales.* By this time he had published over one hundred tales and sketches, including two other important volumes, his second series of *Twice-Told Tales* (1842) and *Mosses from an Old Manse* (1846).

To *The Snow Image* Hawthorne affixed a short preface that casts an oblique but penetrating light upon both the evolution of his own art and the status of the writing profession in New England during the formative years of his career. Looking back a quarter century from the vantage point of 1851, he could now survey his earliest efforts with cool detachment. The first twelve years of heartbreaking struggle and frustration, during which he had made at least three abortive attempts to publish a collection of tales, he quietly summarized with the simple statement that he had then been "the obscurest man of letters in America." He called attention to the slender success his first volume of stories achieved when it finally appeared in 1837 and modestly admitted that, although their reputation "was not such as would have gratified a craving desire for notoriety," the stories themselves "made no enemies." But neither had they taken the country by storm because, he now believed, they were too shadowy and insubstantial:

> *They have the pale tint of flowers that blossomed in too retired a shade,—the coolness of a meditative habit, which diffuses itself through the feeling and observation of every sketch. Instead of passion there is sentiment; and, even in what purport to be pictures of actual life, we have allegory, not always so warmly dressed in its habiliments of flesh and blood as to be taken into the reader's mind without a shiver.*

In this incisive self-criticism Hawthorne touched the core of the objections raised against his short stories by both his contemporaries and subsequent critics. As early as 1830, Samuel Goodrich, editor and publisher of the annual in which some of Hawthorne's earliest stories appeared anonymously, said that his tales were "too mystical to be popular"; and Poe repeated much the same charge in his famous review of *Twice-Told Tales* in 1842, when he found in them "a somewhat too general or prevalent *tone*—a tone of melancholy and mysticism." Hawthorne himself acknowledged this deficiency in confessing to Longfellow: "I have seen so little of the world that I have nothing but thin air to concoct my stories of, and it is not easy to give a lifelike semblance to such shadowy stuff." It was a weakness he felt he never fully overcame.

What Hawthorne and his critics alike meant by the terms "mystical" and "shadowy" was simply that his stories did not capture the surface texture of life in the way that Irving's did; for instead of working from human types or individuals whom he had observed, he usually began with an imagined problem or situation involving human destiny and then invented characters to fit it. Since he was more interested in human motives than in human actions, he chose to delve, like a modern psychologist, deep into the hidden springs of human nature rather than dwell lightly, like Irving and his imitators, upon the surface features of life. His stories, therefore, revealed a persistent quest for the "inner" meanings of human nature that made its surface action understandable. In following this path, Hawthorne was living up to his Puritan heritage; when he admitted that strong traits of his ancestors' grim nature had intertwined themselves with his own, he did not mean simply that he inherited a "New England conscience," but that he had been bequeathed their sense of a "calling"—the need, in this case, to confront and express the life of the mind. As a true scion of the Puritans he could not have been satisfied merely to portray externals of scene or character. But by rendering anew in nineteenth-century symbolic terms the grim moral vision of his forebears, he might reenact in the forms of romance the old truths of seventeenth-century Puritan religious thought. Thus, the moral idea or "truth" undergirding each of his stories and novels is often set forth in a manner analogous to that of the old seventeenth-century sermons, by means of signs and symbols, carefully selected and elaborated for the purpose of dramatizing a complex theme.

Only within recent years, as critics have begun to free themselves from the demand for purely realistic fiction and to appreciate the values of symbolic treatment, has it become apparent, first, that Hawthorne deliberately chose the symbolic in preference to the realistic because he wished to "manage his atmospherical medium [so] as to bring out or mellow the lights and deepen and enrich the shadows of the picture"; and second, that the recurrence of images signifying guilt, isolation, self-contemplation, and emotional frigidity, interwoven into the texture of his stories, was intended to dramatize the several basic themes that summarize his views and attitudes toward life. The most frequently noted of these themes are the inescapable presence in the world of evil as a positive force; the alienation or isolation of individuals from their fellow humans; the necessary dependence of the present upon the past;

and the interdependence of the intellect and the emotions in the make-up of a normal human being. Most of Hawthorne's significant stories offer variations upon one or another of these themes, although central to all of them is the conviction that life is essentially tragic, and that therefore "a loving heart is better than wisdom." The theme of isolation, for example, finds such frequent and varied embodiment in his stories that almost all his major characters are made to feel its influence. Similarly, the problem of guilt and its manifold effects in the lives of human beings is often rigorously confronted in his fiction. For, in direct contrast to the prevailing optimism of his age, Hawthorne felt deeply the ubiquitous presence of evil in the world and strove not only to penetrate its mystery but also to portray its corrosive influence. To most of the comforting beliefs of men like his friend Ralph Waldo Emerson—beliefs in the innate goodness of humans, in the assurance of moral lessons to be derived from nature, in the inevitable rightness of impulse and the virtue of self-reliant individualism—Hawthorne countered by depicting repeatedly in his stories the disastrous effects of pride and hardheartedness.

The problem of evaluating these stories, therefore, is not simply a question of deciding whether they are too "mystical" or too allegorical, as Poe and other contemporaries regarded them. It is rather the more complex question of determining whether and to what extent Hawthorne succeeded in fusing in them the worlds of fact and idea. He probably failed more often than he succeeded because he tended to neglect the visible, tangible surface of life that provides a necessary support for the inner spiritual realities informing it. He knew well enough that every story risks failure if it does not "possess enough physical substance to stand alone"; and although he reminded himself that "human nature craves a certain materialism," still he fixed his attention so unwaveringly upon those spiritual realities that he did not at times heed his own warning, with the result that many of his characters strike us as merely personified abstractions, neither their actions nor their speech possessing vitality enough to move us with the force of convincingly real persons. Moreover, many of his poorer tales betray weaknesses in structure and technique which indicate a lack of both power and effort. Some are mere fragmentary sketches, undeveloped outlines; others suffer from the conventions of the gift book trade for which they were written. A sprawling, imprecise, leisurely style and an overuse of the hackneyed devices of sentimental fiction—Gothic terrors, fiendlike villains, supernatural portents—are sufficiently prominent in these poorer tales to remind us that Hawthorne, like Poe, occasionally lowered his standards to thrill the crowds.

But Hawthorne's best stories succeeded in capturing with astonishing power both the inner and the outer reality of his subject. In "Young

Goodman Brown" and "Rappaccini's Daughter," clearly among the finest examples of his work, allegory is abundantly present too, but the important difference is in the spontaneity and control of its employment. It does not give the impression of having been groped and fumbled for; so skillfully blended are image and idea, meaning and form, that it would take longer to explain either story's total effectiveness than it does to tell the story. These and fifteen or twenty other stories of nearly equal quality were so powerfully wrought that Hawthorne's own generation and later ones barely recognized their explosive potentialities; whereas a generation like ours, nurtured on Freudian psychology and inured to the presence of evil in the modern world, is perhaps better prepared to accept and evaluate them. For all of them show unmistakable evidence of finished craftsmanship: the rounded development of a central theme; the evocation of a single, poignant mood; the economy and density of revelatory detail; the meaningful integration of parts; the detached, unobtrusive style; and the richness of imagery—all are evident in the voluminous critical commentary Hawthorne's fiction continues to inspire. Up to 1850, Hawthorne was still unsure of his medium, his grip on reality less firm than it might have been or than he wanted it to be. Yet from the beginning of his career, his stories demonstrated how the genius of Puritanism, when channeled into an unfamiliar realm of art, could develop into a rare growth altogether unlike that of the short story elsewhere in the United States.

No two contemporaries similarly dedicated to the creation of enduring literature could have been further apart than Hawthorne and Poe in background, training, and temperament: one, the typical offspring of a deep-rooted New England Puritan heritage; the other, rootless, erratic, brilliant, and psychologically insecure. Where the one was relatively democratic, the other was blatantly antidemocratic; where the one distrusted the claims of science, the other admired, perhaps above all else, the orderly processes of rational analysis. Interested almost exclusively in probing the nature and destiny of the human soul, Hawthorne had fashioned his art into a delicate instrument for that purpose. Determinedly opposed to didacticism, Poe was interested primarily in achieving brilliant effects and therefore studiously devoted his talent in the short story to the creation of novelty, variety, and surprise. In view of these basic differences in their character, it is not surprising that the works of the two present startling contrasts. Yet in several significant respects, their careers as short story writers followed parallel lines of development. Both began to experiment with the form at approximately the same time; both underwent preparatory periods of solitary study; both knew the bitterness of popular neglect and the pinch of penury, despite repeated efforts to suit their product to popular demand; and both persevered, despite repeated discouragement, in their devotion to literature.

Poe's earliest stories consisted of a group of sixteen, probably written between 1830 and 1835, which he hoped to publish as a volume entitled *Tales from the Folio Club*. But like Hawthorne, he had to draw what satisfaction he could at first from having the stories published separately in annuals and magazines like the *Courier* and the *Southern Literary Messenger*. As he became better known, he succeeded in publishing in 1840 a two-volume edition called *Tales of the Grotesque and Arabesque*, containing all but one of the twenty-six stories he had written up to that time; and again in 1845 he published another selected edition of twelve *Tales*. These were the only book-length collections of his stories issued during his lifetime, though he wrote in all nearly seventy prose tales and sketches.

From the beginning of his career, Poe clearly had his eye on the market and attempted to meet its demands by exploiting the sensational devices then current in popular magazine fiction. Chided in 1835 by the publisher of the *Messenger* for his questionable taste in "Berenice," he admitted frankly that some details in the story were "far too horrible"; but to him the question of taste was irrelevant, since "to be appreciated you must be *read*." He knew, or thought he knew, precisely what sorts of material would appeal to the public; and the variety of subject matter and treatment in his earliest stories indicates that he was striving to make his own appeal as broad as possible. "The ludicrous heightened into the grotesque: the fearful coloured into the horrible; the witty exaggerated into the burlesque: the singular wrought out into the strange and mystical"—these, said Poe, were the types of stories the public would buy; hence these he would write. His early stories, accordingly, were done in the popular Gothic manner of the time: they were morbid horror tales, full of the supernatural, of madness, premature burial, mutilation, and weird, unearthly scenes.

Such wildly outrageous fictions quickly appealed to masses of readers who perhaps failed to see beneath their surface level of action deeper and still deeper levels of satiric and ironic intent. Only within recent decades have critics begun to recognize that slyly concealed comic patterns of meaning lurking in these early tales enabled Poe to poke fun at both the writer and the audience, as well as at the types of Gothic fiction they admired. Obviously hoaxing his readers, even in supposedly "serious" stories, Poe's fiction is thus seen from this viewpoint as a precursor of the modern Theatre of the Absurd. For throughout his career, he worked in these ironically perverse, grotesque modes, combining in mocking burlesques ironic themes and modes of language "with ironies of plot and characterization in the creation of an absurd universe."[3] Thus, along with his success in editing several leading magazines, Poe's subsequent reputation in the field of the short story suggests that he had not only gauged his own public pretty accurately, but also bequeathed a formidable legacy of literary art for future generations of bemused readers and critics.

Poe's reputation rests, however, not only on his virtuosity as an artist, but also on his brilliance as a critic and theorist of the short story, for he was the first American writer who attempted to define its technical requirements. In critical essays published from time to time, he gradually evolved his aesthetic theory of *effect* based upon the principles of brevity and unity, the best known statement of which (as regards the development of the short story) occurs in his review of Hawthorne's *Twice-Told Tales*. Briefly, the three central ideas of his theory are these: (1) that since "unity of effect or impression" is of primary importance in any form of imaginative expression, the most effective poem or story is one that can be read at a single sitting; (2) that the short prose narrative, as exemplified by Hawthorne's tales, offers the greatest opportunity next to the poem for the exercise of artistic genius, provided the writer deliberately subordinates everything in his story—characters, incidents, style, and tone—to the bringing out of a single, preconceived effect; (3) that the prose tale may be made the vehicle for a greater variety of these effects than even the short poem. This abridgment of his theory makes clear that Poe's main concern focused sharply upon matters of design, proportion, composition; for what he meant by *effect* was largely the impact that a work of art would make upon the reader. Speaking of the artist's obligation and reward, he added:

> *If his very initial sentence tend not to the outbringing of this effect, then he has failed in his first step. In the whole composition there should be no word written, of which the tendency, direct or indirect, is not to the one pre-established design. And by such means, with such care and skill, a picture is at length painted which leaves in the mind of him who contemplates it with a kindred art, a sense of the fullest satisfaction.*

Given this dominant preoccupation with effect, one is not surprised to find Poe frankly praising Hawthorne's artistry, yet at the same time apparently misconstruing altogether Hawthorne's equally significant moral purpose. As both critic and artist, Poe's interest in the short story was that of the artist, not that of the moralist; but by insisting upon

[3] G.R. Thompson, ed. *Great Short Works of Edgar Allan Poe* (New York: Harper & Row, 1970), p. 45.

standards of literary excellence, calling attention repeatedly to the need for effective presentation, and demanding that the finished work of art be judged on its own merits rather than on its author's well-meant if unfulfilled intentions, he probably performed his greatest service to American literature.

Many former critics have argued that Poe's stories are little more than a tissue of cleverly wrought impressionistic effects—of horror, fear, melancholy, disgust, or analytical agility—and that his vaunted aesthetic theory is merely a means of rationalizing his own limitations as a literary artist. They admit his skill in the manipulation of incidents, his inventiveness in plot construction, and his vividness in the depiction of intense situations, but they find no evidence in his stories of an imaginative power to recreate life and human feeling through characters. His characters seem to them mere pawns in a game that Poe, the mastermind, plays with his audience. Today, however, Poe's apologists are more inclined to take at face value his declaration that the terror in his tales was "not of Germany but of the soul" and to probe beneath the surface of his work for clues to the meaning of his ambiguities, since almost invariably these ambiguities appear to be ironic reflections on humankind's perverse fate. Ultimately, the issue can perhaps be settled only by individual readers, who must decide for themselves whether Poe's fantasies and abnormalities, along with his morbid, narcissistic heroes, decadent damsels, and desperate narrators, are simply sensational Gothic devices, or whether they reflect genuine, deeply felt emotions. The problem is not easy, since even Poe's most unsympathetic critics grudgingly acknowledge the imaginative power in a few of his stories, such as "Ligeia," "William Wilson," "The Masque of the Red Death," and "The Fall of the House of Usher." Ruin and the disintegration of human life are the prevailing themes in these stories, and it is difficult to read any of them sympathetically and still affirm that Poe's own sense of suffering is not mirrored there, since much the same preoccupation with evil, the same "haunted mind" that troubled Hawthorne, hovers over them. Indeed, since recent studies have disclosed unsuspected levels of meaning artfully concealed beneath Poe's elaborate facades, perhaps all his stories—even his detective tales—should be read as allegories of dream experience and neurotic states of mind. However they are interpreted, Poe's impact upon our literature was that of an original creative force; the kinds of fiction he wrote—detective, pseudoscientific, lurid adventure—have become the staple of millions who have never heard of his theories.

During the 1840s and 1850s, many other American writers entered the field of short fiction, but the fact that the short story still went unrecognized as a distinct literary form was evident in the almost total neglect of Poe after his death, as well as in the prevailing notion that short fiction belonged chiefly to the popular ladies' books and magazines. The 1850s, in fact, became known as the "feminine fifties" as a result of the popularity of the sentimental, didactic fiction produced during that decade by a group of writers whom Hawthorne despairingly characterized as "a damned mob of scribbling women." The short story, therefore, struggled along with little purposeful guidance in the absence of any other first-rate practitioners except Herman Melville, whose *Piazza Tales* (1856) was virtually the only collection of short pieces of the decade which was fit to put beside those of Hawthorne and Poe. Melville treated symbolically in these tales a number of the powerfully tragic themes, such as the endless struggle between innocence and evil, the paradox in the dualism of human nature, and the pain of loss and despair suffered in the effort to reconcile ideals and worldly values, which he had developed more fully in such novels as *Moby Dick* and *Pierre.*

"Ruri Colla" *(nom de plume)*

The Story of the Captain's Wife, and an Aged Woman

There is not perhaps in the whole system of vices any one to which human nature is more prone, than this, *viz,* the censuring and condemning others for those very things which we practise ourselves; and it is no very uncommon thing to see a person suffer his resentment to rise to an exceeding high pitch against his neighbor for treating him, or only a suspicion that he has treated him, in the same way that he himself had before treated that very same person, and for which he has never felt himself disposed to make any kind of satisfaction; but this must be as wrong as it is common, for notwithstanding it is wrong in A to injure B, after that B has injured A, yet B has no right to entertain any resentment against A, when he has conducted in the same manner towards him, and has made him no kind of satisfaction therefor; or at least such a resentment must sit with an exceeding ill-grace on B, and prove the exceeding criminality of his conduct, it being what he most pointedly condemns himself. People would do well to consider before they are so lavish with their censures of others, to pause a moment and ask themselves this serious question, "do not I practise the same things myself, for which I am just going to load my neighbor with reproaches?" If this idea could be reduced to practise it would have two very good effects; one is, scandal would in a measure cease to be the topic of conversation; the other is, many people would leave off the practise of certain vices, that they might have the opportunity of exposing the follies of others.

I have nowhere met with a more striking instance of the above-mentioned vice than in the following narration, which I some years ago had

Ruri Colla, "The Story of the Captain's Wife, and an Aged Woman," *Gentleman and Ladies Town and Country Magazine,* October, November, 1789.

from a then aged clergyman of this Commonwealth, and which, though some parts of it appear of the incredible kind, yet he affirmed it to have been a fact, and that it took place while he was at his studies, before he entered on the work of the ministry, in one of the capital towns on the American continent, where he had his place of abode. The story I believe was never before committed to print, which consideration had induced me to insert it here.

A woman of the age of about twenty one years, the wife of a seacaptain (whose husband had been absent on a voyage a very considerable time longer than was expected he would have been gone when he left his home) began to be exceedingly anxious for his safety, and as a succession of days and weeks brought her no intelligence of him, she grew quite inconsolable. Day after day, she spent her time walking down on the different wharves, inquiring of all who had lately arrived, if they had any tidings from her husband. Fruitless were all her enquiries, which fixed a solemn gloom on her countenance.

One day as she was returning from her unavailing enquiries, she met an aged woman, who looking steadfastly in her face, said, "Child, what makes you appear so melancholy?" The afflicted woman told her it was the absence of her husband, whom she never expected to see more. The old woman perceiving the depth of her distress spoke smilingly to her, saying "Child be not so troubled; your husband is alive, he is well. In time he will return in safety. Follow my advice. Say nothing. You meet me on THAT wharf this evening a little before the close of daylight, and you shall see your husband, and be returned to this place before morning."

The woman was struck with amazement at this proposal, and though she gave but a small degree of credence to the assertion, yet her desire was so great to see him, that her wishes got the better of her belief, and she promised to meet the old woman accordingly: on which they parted, and the wife returned to her home.

After returning home she began to ruminate on what was past, and the whole appeared to her so strange, that she concluded to pay no regard to the appointment; yet when the time appointed came, her desires prevailed upon her to repair to the place appointed, where she no sooner arrived than she met the old woman with a half-bushel measure under her arm.

"Follow me," she said, and stepping between two stores to the back side of the wharf, she put the half-bushel into the water, which was immediately transformed to a sailboat, with the sails all standing. The old woman taking her by the hand, led her into the boat, they shoved off from the wharf, a smart breeze springing up. They soon lost sight of the town, the harbour, and the land. The consternation of the lady was such at this adventure, that she was nearly in suspension of ideas, but according to her best judgment, in about two hour's time they made an harbour, on which a fine town was situated. They landed at a wharf, and walked up a street about ten rods, when the old woman turning up to a door, said to the lady in a low voice, "Here child is your husband, in this house. Go in, you will find him—meet me two hours before day, at the boat."

The lady, full of astonishment, entered the house, where to her increased surprise, she beheld her husband, sitting at the table at supper. He cast his eyes upon her, and viewed her with the greatest degree of attention while eating his supper, during which his wife observed in his hand a knife and fork, of a very curious and singular form.

Supper being finished, he arose from the table and took a seat by her, saying "Woman, perhaps my conduct may appear odd, and perhaps offensive to you—but I trace in your countenance every feature of my wife. I therefore propose spending the night with you, if it is in my power to purchase the favour. I would wish therefore, you would inform me of your terms."

The lady, blushing, replied, "This is a negotiation which I am totally unacquainted with. Yet sir, if you will deliver me the curious knife and fork, with which you eat your supper, I will grant you your request."

He told her the knife and fork were of insignificant value indeed—he could not hesitate of giving her one hundred times the value of them. But the knife and fork he wished to keep, on account of an intimate friend, who had made a present of them. But the woman insisted they were her only terms, which if he did not mean to comply with, she hoped he would give her no more trouble on the occasion. He seeing she was determined, gave her the knife and fork, on which they retired.

At two or three hours before day, the husband falling asleep, she arose softly, left the house, and repaired to the boat, where she met the old woman. They entered on board, and in about two or three hours time they were at the wharf, from whence they first sailed, being then about half way between break of day, and the rising of the sun, from whence she returned to her house.

About seven months from this her husband returned into port, and before he reached his house some officious friend informed him of the pregnancy of his wife.

Words are scarcely capable of conveying an idea of the rage into which he flew on this occasion. He stamped and stormed like a madman, swearing by all that was great or good, that he would never let his eyes on her again—that a breach of the marriage covenant—that incontinency was a crime in its nature unpardonable, and which never could be forgiven, that he would as fast as possible make sale of his estate—leave his native country and return no more—that he would leave the unfaithful partner of his bed, to the free and full possession of her favorite, or else satisfy himself with the heart's blood of them both.

However, he took lodgings at a friend's house, and so vigilent was he, that his wife's [persistent] attempts to fall in his company, all proved fruitless. Day after day did she rack her inventions in fabricating schemes to bring herself into his company, but all to no kind of effect.

More than a week had transpired when she went to an uncle of his, and agreed with him to make an entertainment, and that her husband should be one of the guests, and she was to be there *incognito* until the guests had sat down at table. The guests were invited and accepted—the day arrived—the guests made their appearance, dinner was brought upon the table. Those who were bidden sat down.

It so happened that our sea-captain had a place set before him which was unaccompanied with a knife and fork. Notice was taken of it by the master of the feast, who called on a waiter to supply the Captain, when on a sudden from a door right behind him, issued his wife, and laid on his plate the remarkable knife and fork which she received of him in the *foreign port.*

The Captain seeing the knife and fork, recognized them in a moment, which summoned up nearly the whole mass of blood into his face, and by his looks there was the utmost danger of its bursting through his skin—from the vivid colour of the rose, his face assumed the lifeless colour of the lily, which again was changed to the blooming red, and thus alternating did his countenance assume different aspects.

It was some time before his confusion would admit of his speaking. At length he arose from the table, while the company neglected the plentiful provision which was made for them, to gaze upon the Captain, and turning round to his wife, he thus addressed her: "Pray, in the name of goodness, inform me where you procured this remarkable knife and fork."

"Do you wish," reply'd his wife, "I should satisfy your curiosity at this time?"

"Yes, by all means," reply'd he.

"Well, then," said the wife, "do you not remember that between seven and eight months ago, you, in a foreign port, parted with such a knife and fork to a woman, for the sake of her company a night?"

The Captain in confusion, after some hesitation, answered in the affirmative.

"Well," said the wife, "that woman was no other than she who addresses you." With that she gave them a relation of the whole adventure.

The Captain (whose confusion rather increased) stood motionless for a few moments, while the company was all attention. At length he broke silence, and thus addressed her: "Dear, loving, and much injured wife, with the deepest contrition I now make you my double acknowledgements, first, for the incontinence which I in my heart was actually guilty of towards you; and secondly, for my ill-usage of you for the false suspicion of a crime which I myself was in fact guilty of—I hope you will treat me in a different way from that in which I have conducted [myself] towards you, and overlook the real guilt which had proposed never to have acquitted you of. I am myself a guilty culprit, convicted by your own confessions—I lie wholly at your mercy, and I hope you will extend that clemency towards me which I deny'd to you."

The wife with a softness peculiar to herself, answered him. "Tho your conduct toward me, all things considered, has been rather hard-hearted, yet I have no disposition to act the same or unfeeling part towards you—you have my hearty forgiveness, since matters are as they are. And I hope from this you will not again take action yourself to divorce yourself from your wife without first examining whether she is guilty or not, and never hereafter to condemn another for these practices which you follow yourself."

The company was exceedingly pleased with her answer—another seat and place was provided. They all sat down and made a very merry, as well as a very good, dinner, after which they arose in good humor, each one repairing to his respective home—the Captain and his wife to theirs, and nothing more was said by either of them with regard to the unaccountable adventure of theirs.

Whether the foregoing relation was true in *fact*, or not, I pretend not to say, (tho' the character of the relater was well established in the moral world) yet it strongly enforces the observations made in the foregoing part of this paper, and everyone would do well to consider, that while he condemns others for those things which he practices himself, he cuts the same ridiculous and dispicable figure with the Captain, in the foregoing narrative; and that when at any time he has been exposing the vices of his neighbors, he should conclude with this observation, *I am the man;* and he may rest assured, that if he does not make the observation himself, those in company will not fail to do it, if they are acquainted with him.

Anonymous

The Child of Snow

An active and industrious merchant had occasion often to be abroad a considerable time together, in the pursuit of his traffic. During one of his voyages, which lasted for more than two years, it happened that his wife became enamoured of a young neighbor. Love, which is restrained with difficulty, soon brought them together; but they managed their affairs in so bungling a manner, that at the expiration of about nine months, the merchant's wife found herself for the first time a mother. The husband, on his return, was greatly surprised to find this acquisition to his family, and asked his wife to what accident they were indebted for it.

"Sir," said she, "I happened one day to be reclined above stairs, at the window, giving vent to my grief for your absence. It was in the winter season, and there was at the time a heavy fall of snow. As I cast up my streaming eyes to heaven, and heaved a sigh on thinking of you, a flake of snow accidentally made its way into my mouth, and I immediately found that I had conceived this child whom you now see."

The merchant on hearing this story, did not betray the least symptoms of discontent or ill humor. "Thanks be to God," said he, "I have wished for an heir, and he has sent me one. I am satisfied and thankful for his bounty." He indeed thenceforward, affected the most entire satisfaction, never offered the least reproach to his wife, but lived in the same good understanding with her as before. Nevertheless, this was all dissimulation—he had formed inwardly a resolution to be one day or another amply revenged.

The child, however, grew up, and had attained the age of fifteen, when the merchant, who was still occupied with his project of revenge, thought seriously of putting it into execution. "Wife," said he one day, "you must not be afflicted, if I once more take my leave of you for a time.

"The Child of Snow," *Massachusetts Magazine,* December, 1792.

I am going upon a long journey tomorrow, and I desire you will get ready my baggage, and that of my son: for I mean to take him with me, that he may acquire some knowledge of trading while he is young."

"Alas!" replied the mother, "I am much grieved to hear that you are going to take him abroad so soon; but since it is for your satisfaction and his advantage, I submit. God be with you both, and bring you back in safety." Matters being thus arranged, the merchant set off early next morning, and took the child of snow along with him.

It is needless to give the particulars of the journey, or an account of the countries through which he passed. It is enough to mention that on his arrival at Genoa, he found a Saracen merchant bound for Alexandria, to whom he sold the boy as a slave. Afterwards having settled his business affairs at leisure, he returned home.

The imagination of a hundred poets combined would not give you an adequate description of the distraction of the mother, when she saw the merchant return without her son. She tore her hair, and fell into a fit of frenzy. At length having recovered herself, she conjured her husband to tell her without reserve what had happened to the youth. The husband expected all this uproar: and therefore was not puzzled for an answer.

"Wife," said he, "one cannot arrive to my age, without having had experience in the world, to know the necessity of reconciling one's self to whatever may happen. For what do we gain by giving way to our affliction? Listen with fortitude to the misfortune that happened to us in the country [from] whence I come. Your son and myself were, on a sultry day, climbing up a steep and lofty mountain. It was about noon, the sun was vertical over our heads, and burned like fire. When, behold, on a sudden, your son began to dissolve, and melted before my eyes! I would have offered him assistance, but knew that it would be in vain: for I recollected that you told me he sprang out of a flake of snow."

The wife knew perfectly well the merchant's meaning. She durst not, however, break out, but was obliged to swallow the liquor which she had brewed.

Washington Irving

1783 – 1859

Washington Irving was born in New York City in 1783, the eleventh child of a prosperous merchant. A frail boy, he traveled abroad (1804–1806) to improve his health and further his education. Although he read for the law and was admitted to the bar in 1806, he soon abandoned any serious thought of making law his career, preferring instead to turn to writing. His first significant work, *Salmagundi* (1807–1808), written in collaboration with his brother William and James K. Paulding, drew some attention; but it was with his next work, *Diedrich Knickerbocker's* History of New York (1809), that he won literary recognition. He did not immediately follow up this success, however, being occupied during the next half-dozen years with such miscellaneous activities as lobbying in Washington for his brothers' hardware firm, editing the *Analectic Magazine,* and serving as an aide-de-camp to Governor Tompkins. In 1815, he went to England to work in the Liverpool branch of his brothers' firm, but its failure in 1818 caused him to resume writing, this time with the added incentive of earning a livelihood. The first result of his renewed effort, *The Sketch Book,* published serially in England and America in 1819–1820 and in book form in 1820, was an immediate success. Continuing his foreign residence, where he enjoyed the friendship of the leading European writers of the day, he exploited the popularity of *The Sketch Book* in later volumes of similar tales and sketches. When he finally returned to the United States in 1832, after seventeen years abroad, he was internationally famous. He continued an active literary career until his death in 1859, but devoted his energies principally to biographical and historical writing. Among other volumes of his tales and sketches are *Bracebridge Hall* (1822), *Tales of a Traveller* (1824), and *The Alhambra*

(1832). None of these equals *The Sketch Book* in merit or originality, so that in importance as well as in point of time, *The Sketch Book* is the initial landmark in the history of the American short story.

The first American writer to produce stories of genuine merit, Irving was also among the first to recognize the short story as a distinct form of literature. By insisting that the short tale required a "constant activity of thought and a nicety of execution" not reqired in a longer work and asserting that every sentence and every page "must have its merit," Irving showed an acute awareness of the artistry the short story demands. His manner of writing nevertheless permitted him to loiter over detail and infuse his own genial personality into his stories. Still, the appeal of his best stories, of which "Rip Van Winkle" is a leading example, remains fresh and vivid more than a century and a half after he wrote them.

Rip Van Winkle

a posthumous writing of Diedrich Knickerbocker

By Woden, God of Saxons,
From whence comes Wensday, that is Wodensday,
Truth is a thing that ever I will keep
Unto thylke day in which I creep into
My sepulchre—Cartwright

[The following Tale was found among the papers of the late Diedrich Knickerbocker, an old gentleman of New York, who was very curious in the Dutch history of the province, and the manners of the descendants from its primitive settlers. His historical researches, however, did not lie so much among books as among men; for the former are lamentably scanty on his favorite topics; whereas he found the old burghers, and still more their wives, rich in

"Rip Van Winkle" from *The Sketchbook* by Washington Irving, in *The Works of Washington Irving,* Vol. II (G. P. Putnam's, 1860).

that legendary lore so invaluable to true history. Whenever, therefore, he happened upon a genuine Dutch family, snugly shut up in its low-roofed farmhouse under a spreading sycamore, he looked upon it as a little clasped volume of black-letter, and studied it with the zeal of a book-worm.

The result of all these researches was a history of the province during the reign of the Dutch governors, which he published some years since. There have been various opinions as to the literary character of his work, and, to tell the truth, it is not a whit better than it should be. Its chief merit is its scrupulous accuracy, which indeed was a little questioned on its first-appearance, but has since been completely established; and it is now admitted into all historical collections as a book of unquestionable authority.

The old gentleman died shortly after the publication of his work, and now that he is dead and gone, it cannot do much harm to his memory to say that his time might have been much better employed in weightier labors. He, however, was apt to ride his hobby his own way; and though it did now and then kick up the dust a little in the eyes of his neighbors, and grieve the spirit of some friends, for whom he felt the truest deference and affection; yet his errors and follies are remembered "more in sorrow than in anger," and it begins to be suspected that he never intended to injure or offend. But however his memory may be appreciated by critics, it is still held dear by many folks whose good opinion is well worth having; particularly by certain biscuit-bakers, who have gone so far as to imprint his likeness on their new-year cakes; and have thus given him a chance for immortality, almost equal to the being stamped on a Waterloo Medal or a Queen Anne's Farthing.]

Whoever has made a voyage up the Hudson must remember the Kaatskill Mountains. They are a dismembered branch of the great Appalachian family, and are seen away to the west of the river, swelling up to a noble height, and lording it over the surrounding country. Every change of season, every change of weather, indeed, every hour of the day, produces some change in the magical hues and shapes of these mountains, and they are regarded by all the good wives, far and near, as perfect barometers. When the weather is fair and settled, they are clothed in blue and purple and print their bold outlines on the clear evening sky; but sometimes when the rest of the landscape is cloudless, they will gather a hood of gray vapors about their summits, which, in the last rays of the setting sun, will glow and light up like a crown of glory.

At the foot of these fairy mountains, the voyager may have descried the light smoke curling up from a village whose shingle-roofs gleam among the trees just where the blue tints of the upland melt away into the fresh green of the nearer landscape. It is a little village of great antiquity, having been founded by some of the Dutch colonists in the early times of the province, just about the beginning of the government of the good Peter Stuyvesant (may he rest in peace!), and there were some of the houses of the original settlers standing within a few years, built of small yellow bricks brought from Holland, having latticed windows and gable fronts, surmounted with weather-cocks.

In that same village, and in one of these very houses (which, to tell the precise truth, was sadly time-worn and weather-beaten) there lived many years since, while the country was yet a province of Great Britain, a simple good-natured fellow, of the name of Rip Van Winkle. He was a descendant of the Van Winkles who figured so gallantly in the chivalrous days of Peter Stuyvesant, and accompanied him to the siege of Fort Christina. He inherited, however, but little of the material character of his ancestors. I have observed that he was a simple good-natured man; he was, moreover, a kind neighbor, and an obedient, henpecked husband. Indeed, to the latter circumstance might be owing that meekness of spirit which gained him such universal popularity; for those men are most apt to be obsequious and conciliating abroad who are under the discipline of shrews at home. Their tempers, doubtless, are rendered pliant and malleable in the fiery furnace of domestic tribulation; and a curtain lecture is worth all the sermons in the world for teaching the virtues of patience and long-suffering. A termagant wife may, therefore, in some respects be considered a tolerable blessing; and if so, Rip Van Winkle was thrice blessed.

Certain it is, that he was a great favorite among all the good wives of the village, who, as usual with the amiable sex, took his part in all family squabbles; and never failed, whenever they talked those matters over in their evening gossipings, to lay all the blame on Dame Van Winkle. The children of the village, too, would shout with joy whenever he approached. He assisted at their sports, made their playthings, taught them to fly kites and shoot marbles, and told them long stories of ghosts, witches, and Indians. Whenever he went dodging about the village, he was surrounded by a troop of them, hanging on his skirts, clambering on his back, and playing a thousand tricks on him with impunity; and not a dog would bark at him throughout the neighborhood.

The great error in Rip's composition was an insuperable aversion to all kinds of profitable labor. It could not be from the want of assiduity or perseverance; for he would sit on a wet rock with a rod as long and heavy as a Tartar's lance and fish all day without a murmur even though he should not be encouraged by a single nibble. He would carry a fowling-piece on his shoulder for hours together, trudging through woods and swamps and up hill and down dale, to shoot a few squirrels or wild pigeons. He would never refuse to assist a neighbor, even in the roughest toil, and was a foremost man at all country frolics for husking Indian corn, or building stone-fences; the women of the village, too, used to employ him to run their errands and do such little odd jobs as their less obliging husbands would not do for them. In a word, Rip was ready to attend to anybody's business but his own; but as to doing family duty, and keeping his family in order, he found it impossible.

In fact, he declared it was of no use to work on his farm; it was the most pestilent little piece of ground in the whole country; every thing about it went wrong, and would go wrong, in spite of him. His fences were continually falling to pieces; his cow would either go astray or get among the cabbages; weeds were sure to grow quicker in his fields than anywhere else; the rain always made a point of setting in just as he had outdoor work to do; so that though his patrimonial estate had dwindled away under his management, acre by acre, until there was little more left than a mere patch of Indian corn and potatoes, yet it was the worst-conditioned farm in the neighborhood.

His children, too, were as ragged and wild as if they belonged to nobody. His son Rip, an urchin begotten in his own likeness, promised to inherit the habits, with the old clothes of his father. He was generally seen trooping like a colt at his mother's heels, equipped in a pair of his father's cast-off galligaskins, which he had much ado to hold up with one hand, as a fine lady does her train in bad weather.

Rip Van Winkle, however, was one of those happy mortals, of foolish, well-oiled dispositions, who take the world easy, eat white bread or brown, whichever can be got with least thought or trouble, and would rather starve on a penny than work for a pound. If left to himself, he would have whistled life away in perfect contentment; but his wife kept continually dinning in his ears about his idleness, his carelessness, and the ruin he was bringing on his family. Morning, noon, and night, her tongue was incessantly going, and everything he said or did was sure to produce a torrent of household eloquence. Rip had but one way of replying to all lectures of that kind, and that, by frequent use, had grown into a habit. He shrugged his shoulders, shook his head, cast up his eyes, but said nothing. This, however, always provoked a fresh volley from his wife; so that he was fain to draw off his forces, and take to the outside of the house—the only side which, in truth, belongs to a henpecked husband.

Rip's sole domestic adherent was his dog Wolf, who was as much henpecked as his master; for Dame Van Winkle regarded them as companions in idleness, and even looked upon Wolf with an evil eye, as the cause of his master's going so often astray. True it is, in all points of spirit befitting an honorable dog, he was as courageous an animal as ever scoured the woods—but what courage can withstand the ever-during and all-besetting terrors of a woman's tongue? The moment Wolf entered the house his crest fell, his tail drooped to the ground, or curled between his legs, he sneaked about with a gallows air, casting many a sidelong glance at Dame Van Winkle, and at the least flourish of a broomstick or ladle, he would fly to the door with yelping precipitation.

Times grew worse and worse with Rip Van Winkle as years of matrimony rolled on; a tart temper never mellows with age, and a sharp tongue is the only edged tool that grows keener with constant use. For a long while he used to console himself, when driven from home, by frequenting a kind of perpetual club of the sages, philosophers, and other idle personages of the village, which held its sessions on a bench before a small inn, designated by a rubicund portrait of His Majesty George the Third. Here they used to sit in the shade through a long lazy summer's day, talking listlessly over village gossip, or telling endless sleepy stories about nothing. But it would have been worth any statesman's money to have heard the profound discussions that sometimes took place when, by chance, an old newspaper fell into their hands from some passing traveller. How solemnly they would listen to the contents, as drawled out by Derrick Van Bummel, the schoolmaster, a dapper, learned little man, who was not to be daunted by the most gigantic word in the dictionary; and how sagely they would deliberate upon public events some months after they had taken place.

The opinions of this junto were completely controlled by Nicholas Vedder, a patriarch of the village, and landlord of the inn, at the door of which he took his seat from morning till night, just moving sufficiently to avoid the sun and keep in the shade of a large tree; so that the neighbors could tell the hour by his movements as accurately as by a sun-dial. It is true he was rarely heard to speak, but smoked his pipe incessantly. His adherents, however (for every great man has his adherents), perfectly understood him and knew how to gather his opinions. When anything that was read or related displeased him, he was observed to smoke his pipe vehemently, and to send forth short, frequent, and angry puffs; but when pleased, he would inhale the smoke slowly and tranquilly, and emit it in light and placid clouds; and sometimes, taking the pipe from his mouth, and letting the fragrant vapor curl about his nose, would gravely nod his head in token of perfect approbation.

From even this stronghold the unlucky Rip was at length routed by his termagant wife, who would suddenly break in upon the tranquility of the assemblage and call the members all to naught; nor was that august personage, Nicholas Vedder himself, sacred from the daring tongue of this terrible virago, who charged him outright with encouraging her husband in habits of idleness.

Poor Rip was at last reduced almost to despair; and his only alternative, to escape from the labor of the farm and clamor of his wife, was to take gun in hand and stroll away into the woods. Here he would sometimes seat himself at the foot of a tree and share the contents of his wallet with Wolf, with whom he sympathized as a fellow-sufferer in persecution. "Poor Wolf," he would say, "thy mistress leads thee a dog's life of it; but never mind, my lad, whilst I live thou shalt never want a friend to stand by thee!" Wolf would wag his tail, look wistfully in his master's face, and if dogs can feel pity, I verily believe he reciprocated the sentiment with all his heart.

In a long ramble of the kind on a fine autumnal day, Rip had unconsciously scrambled to one of the highest parts of the Kaatskill Mountains. He was after his favorite sport of squirrel shooting, and the still solitudes had echoed and reëchoed with the reports of his gun. Panting and fatigued, he threw himself, late in the afternoon, on a green knoll, covered with mountain herbage, that crowned the brow of a precipice. From an opening between the trees he could overlook all the lower country for many a mile of rich woodland. He saw at a distance the lordly Hudson, far, far below him, moving on its silent but majestic course, with the reflection of a purple cloud, or the sail of a lagging bark, here and there sleeping on its glassy bosom, and at last losing itself in the blue highlands.

On the other side he looked down into a deep mountain glen, wild, lonely, and shagged, the bottom filled with fragments from the impending cliffs and scarcely lighted by the reflected rays of the setting sun. For some time Rip lay musing on this scene; evening was gradually advancing; the mountains began to throw their long blue shadows over the valleys; he saw that it would be dark long before he could reach the village, and he heaved a heavy sigh when he thought of encountering the terrors of Dame Van Winkle.

As he was about to descend, he heard a voice from a distance, hallooing, "Rip Van Winkle! Rip Van Winkle!" He looked round, but could see nothing but a crow winging its solitary flight across the mountain. He thought his fancy must have deceived him, and turned again to descend, when he heard the same cry ring through the still evening air; "Rip Van Winkle! Rip Van Winkle!"—at the same time Wolf bristled up his back, and giving a low growl, skulked to his master's side, looking fearfully down into the glen. Rip now felt a vague apprehension stealing over him; he looked anxiously in the same direction, and perceived a strange figure slowly toiling up the rocks, and bending under the weight of something he carried on his back. He was surprised to see any human being in this lonely and unfrequented place; but supposing it to be someone of the neighborhood in need of his assistance, he hastened down to yield it.

On nearer approach he was still more surprised at the singularity of the stranger's appearance. He was a short, square-built old fellow, with thick bushy hair, and a grizzled beard. His dress was of the antique Dutch fashion: a cloth jerkin strapped round the waist, several pair of breeches, the outer one of ample volume, decorated with rows of buttons down the sides, and bunches at the knees. He bore on his shoulder a stout keg, that seemed full of liquor, and made signs for Rip to approach and assist him with the load. Though rather shy and distrustful of this new acquaintance, Rip complied with his usual alacrity; and mutually relieving one another, they clambered up a narrow gully, apparently the dry bed of a mountain torrent. As they ascended, Rip every now and then heard long rolling peals, like distant thunder, that seemed to issue out of a deep ravine, or rather cleft, between lofty rocks, toward which their rugged path conducted. He paused for an instant, but supposing it to be the muttering of one of those transient thunder-showers which often take place in mountain heights, he proceeded. Passing through the ravine, they came to a hollow like a small amphitheatre, surrounded by perpendicular precipices, over the brinks of which impending trees shot their branches, so that you only caught glimpses of the azure sky and the bright evening cloud. During the whole time Rip and his companion had labored on in silence; for though the former marvelled greatly what could be the object of carrying a keg of liquor up this wild mountain, yet there was something strange and incomprehensible about the unknown, that inspired awe and checked familiarity.

On entering the amphitheatre, new objects of wonder presented themselves. On a level spot in the center was a company of odd-looking personages playing at ninepins. They were dressed in a quaint outlandish fashion; some wore short doublets, others jerkins, with long knives in their belts, and most of them had enormous breeches of similar style with that of the guide's. Their visages, too, were peculiar: one had a large beard, broad face, and small piggish eyes: the face of another seemed to consist entirely of nose, and was surmounted by a white sugarloaf hat, set off with a little red cock's tail. They all had beards, of various shapes and colors. There was one who seemed to be the commander. He was a stout old gentleman, with a weather-beaten countenance; he wore a laced doublet, broad belt and hanger, high-crowned hat and feather, red stockings, and high-heeled shoes, with roses in them. The whole group reminded Rip of the figures in an old Flemish painting in the parlor of Dominie Van Shaick, the village parson, and which had been brought over from Holland at the time of the settlement.

What seemed particularly odd to Rip was, that though these folks were evidently amusing themselves, yet they maintained the gravest faces, the most mysterious silence, and were, withal, the most melancholy party of pleasure he had ever witnessed. Nothing interrupted the stillness of the scene but the noise of the balls, which, whenever they were rolled, echoed along the mountains like rumbling peals of thunder.

As Rip and his companion approached them, they suddenly desisted from their play, and stared at him with such fixed, statue-like gaze, and such strange, uncouth, lack-lustre countenances, that his heart turned within him, and his knees smote together. His companion now emptied the contents of the keg into large flagons, and made signs to him to wait upon the company. He obeyed with fear and trembling; they quaffed the liquor in profound silence, and then returned to their game.

By degrees Rip's awe and apprehension subsided. He even ventured, when no eye was fixed upon him, to taste the beverage, which he found had much of the flavor of excellent Hollands. He was naturally a thirsty soul and was soon tempted to repeat the draught. One taste provoked another; and he reiterated his visits to the flagon so often that at length his senses were overpowered, his eyes swam in his head, his head gradually declined, and he fell into a deep sleep.

On waking, he found himself on the green knoll whence he had first seen the old man of the glen. He rubbed his eyes. It was a bright, sunny morning. The birds were hopping and twittering among the bushes, and the eagle was wheeling aloft, and breasting the pure mountain breeze. "Surely," thought Rip, "I have not slept here all night." He recalled the occurrences before he fell asleep—the strange man with a keg of liquor, the mountain ravine, the wild retreat among the rocks, the wobegone party at ninepins, the flagon. "Oh! that flagon! that wicked flagon!" thought Rip. "What excuse shall I make to Dame Van Winkle?"

He looked round for his gun, but in place of the clean, well-oiled fowling-piece, he found an old firelock lying by him, the barrel incrusted with rust, the lock falling off, and the stock worm-eaten. He now suspected that the grave roisterers of the mountain had put a trick upon him, and, having dosed him with liquor, had robbed him of his gun. Wolf, too, had disappeared, but he might have strayed away after a squirrel or partridge. He whistled after him, and shouted his name, but all in vain; the echoes repeated his whistle and shout, but no dog was to be seen.

He determined to revisit the scene of the last evening's gambol, and if he met with any of the party, to demand his dog and gun. As he rose to walk, he found himself stiff in the joints, and wanting in his usual activity. "These mountain beds do not agree with me," thought Rip, "and if this frolic should lay me up with a fit of the rheumatism, I shall have a blessed time with Dame Van Winkle." With some difficulty he got down into the glen: he found the gully up which he and his companion had ascended the preceding evening; but to his astonishment a mountain stream was now foaming down it, leaping from rock to rock, and filling the glen with babbling murmurs. He, however, made shift to scramble up its sides, working his toilsome way through thickets of birch, sassafras, and witch-hazel, and sometimes tripped up or entangled by the wild grapevines that twisted their coils or tendrils from tree to tree, and spread a kind of network in his path.

At length he reached to where the ravine had opened through the cliffs to the amphitheatre; but no traces of such opening remained. The rocks presented a high, impenetrable wall, over which the torrent came tumbling in a sheet of feathery foam, and fell into a broad, deep basin, black from the shadows of the surrounding forest. Here, then, poor Rip was brought to a stand. He again called and whistled after his dog; he was only answered by the cawing of a flock of idle crows, sporting high in air about a dry tree that overhung a sunny precipice; and who, secure in their elevation, seemed to look down and scoff at the poor man's perplexities. What was to be done? The morning was passing away, and Rip felt famished for want of his breakfast. He grieved to give up his dog and gun; he dreaded to meet his wife; but it would not do to starve among the mountains. He shook his head, shouldered the rusty firelock, and, with a heart full of trouble and anxiety, turned his steps homeward.

As he approached the village he met a number of people, but none whom he knew, which somewhat surprised him, for he had thought himself acquainted with everyone in the country round. Their dress, too, was of a different fashion from that to which he was accustomed. They all stared at him with equal marks of surprise, and whenever they cast their eyes upon him, invariably stroked their chins. The constant recurrence of this gesture induced Rip, involuntarily, to do the same, when, to his astonishment, he found his beard had grown a foot long!

He had now entered the skirts of the village. A troop of strange children ran at his heels, hooting after him, and pointing at his gray beard. The dogs, too, not one of which he recognized for an old acquaintance, barked at him as he passed. The very village was altered; it was larger and more populous. There were rows of houses which he had never seen before, and those which had been his familiar haunts had disappeared. Strange names were over the doors—strange faces at the windows—everything was strange. His mind now misgave him; he began to doubt whether both he and the world around him were not bewitched. Surely this was his native village, which he had left but the day before. There stood the Kaatskill Mountains. There ran the silver Hudson at a distance. There was every hill and dale precisely as it had always been. Rip was sorely perplexed. "That flagon last night," thought he, "has addled my poor head sadly!"

It was with some difficulty that he found the way to his own house, which he approached with silent awe, expecting every moment to hear the shrill voice of Dame Van Winkle. He found the house gone to decay—the roof fallen in, the windows shattered, and the doors off the hinges. A half-starved dog that looked like Wolf was skulking about it.

Rip called him by name, but the cur snarled, showed his teeth, and passed on. This was an unkind cut indeed. "My very dog," sighed poor Rip, "has forgotten me!"

He entered the house, which, to tell the truth, Dame Van Winkle had always kept in neat order. It was empty, forlorn, and apparently abandoned. This desolateness overcame all his connubial fears. He called loudly for his wife and children. The lonely chambers rang for a moment with his voice, and then all again was silence.

He now hurried forth, and hastened to his old resort, the village inn. But it, too, was gone. A large, rickety wooden building stood in its place, with great gaping windows, some of them broken and mended with old hats and petticoats, and over the door was painted, "The Union Hotel, by Jonathan Doolittle." Instead of the great tree that used to shelter the quiet little Dutch inn of yore, there now was reared a tall naked pole, with something on the top that looked like a red night-cap, and from it was fluttering a flag on which was a singular assemblage of stars and stripes. All this was strange and incomprehensible. He recognized on the sign, however, the ruby face of King George, under which he had smoked so many a peaceful pipe; but even this was singularly metamorphosed. The red coat was changed for one of blue and buff, a sword was held in the hand instead of a sceptre, the head was decorated with a cocked hat, and underneath was painted in large characters, *General Washington.*

There was, as usual, a crowd of folk about the door, but none that Rip recollected. The very character of the people seemed changed. There was a busy, bustling, disputatious tone about it, instead of the accustomed phlegm and drowsy tranquility. He looked in vain for the sage Nicholas Vedder, with his broad face, double chin, and fair long pipe, uttering clouds of tobacco smoke instead of idle speeches; or Van Bummel, the schoolmaster, doling forth the contents of an ancient newspaper. In place of these, a lean, bilious-looking fellow, with his pockets full of handbills, was haranguing vehemently about rights of citizens, elections, members of Congress, liberty, Bunker's Hill, heroes of seventy-six, and other words, which were a perfect Babylonish jargon to the bewildered Van Winkle.

The appearance of Rip, with his long grizzled beard, his rusty fowling-piece, his uncouth dress, and an army of women and children at his heels, soon attracted the attention of the tavern politicians. They crowded round him, eyeing him from head to foot with great curiosity. The orator bustled up to him, and, drawing him partly aside, inquired on which side he voted. Rip stared in vacant stupidity. Another short but busy little fellow pulled him by the arm, and, rising on tiptoe, inquired in his ear, whether he was Federal or Democrat. Rip was equally at a loss to comprehend the question; when a knowing, self-important old gentleman, in a sharp cocked hat, made his way through the crowd, putting them to the right and left with his elbows as he passed, and planting himself before Van Winkle, with one arm akimbo, the other resting on his cane, his keen eyes and sharp hat penetrating, as it were, into his very soul, demanded in an austere tone, what brought him to the election with a gun on his shoulder, and a mob at his heels, and whether he meant to breed a riot in the village.

"Alas! gentlemen," cried Rip, somewhat dismayed, "I am a poor quiet man, a native of the place, and a loyal subject of the King. God bless him!"

Here a general shout burst from the bystanders. "A tory! a tory! a spy! a refugee! hustle him! away with him!" It was with great difficulty that the self-important man in the cocked hat restored order; and, having assumed a tenfold austerity of brow, demanded again of the unknown culprit what he came there for, and whom he was seeking. The poor man humbly assured him that he meant no harm, but merely came there in search of some of his neighbors, who used to keep about the tavern.

"Well, who are they? Name them."

Rip bethought himself a moment, and inquired, "Where's Nicholas Vedder?"

There was a silence for a little while, when an old man replied, in a thin, piping voice, "Nicholas Vedder! why, he is dead and gone these eighteen years! There was a wooden tombstone in the churchyard that used to tell all about him, but that's rotten and gone too."

"Where's Brom Dutcher?"

"Oh, he went off to the army in the beginning of the war; some say he was killed at the storming of Stony Point. Others say he was drowned in a squall at the foot of Antony's Nose. I don't know. He never came back again."

"Where's Van Bummel, the schoolmaster?"

"He went off to the wars, too, was a great militia general, and is now in Congress."

Rip's heart died away at hearing of these sad changes in his home and friends, and finding himself thus alone in the world. Every answer puzzled him, too, by treating such enormous lapses of time, and of matters which he could not understand: war, Congress, Stony Point; he had no courage to ask after any more friends, but cried out in despair, "Does nobody here know Rip Van Winkle?"

"Oh, Rip Van Winkle!" exclaimed two or three, "Oh, to be sure! that's Rip Van Winkle yonder, leaning against the tree."

Rip looked and beheld a precise counterpart of himself as he went up the mountain, apparently as lazy and certainly as ragged. The poor fellow was now completely confounded. He doubted his own identity, and whether he was himself or another man. In the midst of his bewilderment, the man in the cocked hat demanded who he was, and what was his name.

"God knows," exclaimed he, at wit's end; "I'm not myself. I'm somebody else. That's me yonder. No, that's somebody else got into my shoes. I was myself last night, but I fell asleep on the mountain, and they've changed my gun, and everything's changed, and I'm changed, and I can't tell what's my name, or who I am!"

The bystanders began now to look at each other, nod, wink significantly, and tap their fingers against their foreheads. There was a whisper, also, about securing the gun and keeping the old fellow from doing mischief, at the very suggestion of which the self-important man in the cocked hat retired with some precipitation. At this critical moment a fresh, comely woman pressed through the throng to get a peep at the gray-bearded man. She had a chubby child in her arms, which, frightened at his looks, began to cry. "Hush, Rip," cried she, "hush, you little fool; the old man won't hurt you."

The name of the child, the air of the mother, and tone of her voice, all awakened a train of recollections in his mind. What is your name, my good woman?" asked he.

"Judith Gardenier."

"And your father's name?"

"Ah, poor man, Rip Van Winkle was his name, but it's twenty years since he went away from home with his gun, and never has been heard of since. His dog came home without him; but whether he shot himself, or was carried away by the Indians, nobody can tell. I was then but a little girl."

Rip had but one question more to ask; but he put it with a faltering voice, "Where's your mother?"

"Oh, she too died but a short time since; she broke a bloodvessel in a fit of passion at a New England peddler."

There was a drop of comfort, at least, in this intelligence. The honest man could contain himself no longer. He caught his daughter and her child in his arms. "I am your father!" cried he. "Young Rip Van Winkle once—old Rip Van Winkle now! Does nobody know poor Rip Van Winkle?"

All stood amazed until an old woman, tottering out from among the crowd, put her hand to her brow, and peering under it in his face for a moment, exclaimed, "Sure enough! it is Rip Van Winkle. It is himself! Welcome home again, old neighbor. Why, where have you been these twenty long years?"

Rip's story was soon told, for the whole twenty years had been to him but one night. The neighbors stared when they heard it; some were seen to wink at each other and put their tongues in their cheeks; and the self-important man in the cocked hat, who, when the alarm was over, had returned to the field, screwed down the corners of his mouth and shook his head—upon which there was a general shaking of the head throughout the assemblage.

It was determined, however, to take the opinion of old Peter Vanderdonk, who was seen slowly advancing up the road. He was a descendant of the historian of that name, who wrote of the earliest accounts of the province. Peter was the most ancient inhabitant of the village and well versed in all the wonderful events and traditions of the neighborhood. He recollected Rip at once and corroborated his story in the most satisfactory manner. He assured the company that it was a fact, handed down from his ancestor the historian, that the Kaatskill Mountains had always been haunted by strange beings. That it was affirmed that the great Hendrick Hudson, the first discoverer of the river and country, kept a kind of vigil there every twenty years with his crew of the *Half Moon;* being permitted in this way to revisit the scenes of his enterprise and keep a guardian eye upon the river and the great city called by his name. That his father had once seen them in their old Dutch dresses playing at ninepins in a hollow of the mountain; and that he himself had heard, one summer afternoon, the sound of their balls, like distant peals of thunder.

To make a long story short, the company broke up and returned to the more important concerns of the election. Rip's daughter took him home to live with her; she had a snug, well-furnished house, and a stout, cheery farmer for a husband, whom Rip recollected for one of the urchins that used to climb upon his back. As to Rip's son and heir, who was the ditto of himself, seen leaning against the tree, he was employed to work on the farm, but evinced an hereditary disposition to attend to anything else but his business.

Rip now resumed his old walks and habits; he soon found many of his former cronies, though all rather the worse for wear and tear of time, and preferred making friends among the rising generation, with whom he soon grew into great favor.

Having nothing to do at home, and being arrived at that happy age when a man can be idle with impunity, he took his place once more on the bench at the inn door and was reverenced as one of the patriarchs of the village and a chronicler of the old times "before the war." It was some time before he could get into the regular track of gossip or could be made to comprehend the strange events that had taken place during his torpor. How that there had been a revolutionary war, that the country had thrown off the yoke of old England, and that, instead of being a subject of His Majesty George the Third, he was now a free citizen of the United States. Rip, in fact, was no politician; the changes of states and empires made but little impression on him, but there was one species of despotism under which he had long groaned, and that was petticoat government. Happily that was at an end; he had got his neck out of the yoke of matrimony, and could go in and out whenever he pleased without dreading the tyranny of Dame Van Winkle. Whenever her name was mentioned, however, he shook his head, shrugged his shoulders, and cast up his eyes; which might pass either for an expression of resignation to his fate, or joy at his deliverance.

He used to tell his story to every stranger that arrived at Mr. Doolittle's hotel. He was observed, at first, to vary on some points every time he told it, which was doubtless owing to his having so recently awaked. It at last settled down precisely to the tale I have related, and not a man, woman, or child in the neighborhood but knew it by heart. Some always pretended to doubt the reality of it, and insisted that Rip had been out of his head, and that this was one point on which he always remained flighty. The old Dutch inhabitants, however, almost universally gave it full credit. Even to this day they never hear a thunderstorm of a summer afternoon about the Kaatskill, but they say Hendrick Hudson and his crew are at their game of ninepins; and it is a common wish of all henpecked husbands in the neighborhood, when life hangs heavy on their hands, that they might have a quieting draught out of Rip Van Winkle's flagon.

Note

The foregoing Tale, one would suspect, had been suggested to Mr. Knickerbocker by a little German superstition about the Emperor Frederick der Rothbart, *and the Kypphäuser mountain: the subjoined note, however, which he had appended to the tale, shows that it is an absolute fact, narrated with his usual fidelity.*

"The story of Rip Van Winkle may seem incredible to many, but nevertheless I give it my full belief, for I know the vicinity of our old Dutch settlements to have been very subject to marvellous events and appearances. Indeed, I have heard many stranger stories than this, in the villages along the Hudson; all of which were too well authenticated to admit of a doubt. I have even talked with Rip Van Winkle myself, who, when last I saw him, was a very venerable old man, and so perfectly rational and consistent on every other point, that I think no conscientious person could refuse to take this into the bargain; nay, I have seen a certificate on the subject taken before a country justice and signed with a cross, in the justice's own handwriting. The story, therefore, is beyond the possibility of doubt.

"D. K."

Postscript

The following are travelling notes from a memorandum-book of Mr. Knickerbocker.

The Kaatsberg, or Catskill Mountains, have always been a region full of fable. The Indians considered them the abode of spirits, who influenced the weather, spreading sunshine or clouds over the landscape, and sending good or bad hunting-seasons. They were ruled by an old squaw spirit, said to be their mother. She dwelt on the highest peak of the Catskills, and had charge of the doors of day and night to open and shut them at the proper hour. She hung up the new moons in the skies, and cut up the old ones into stars. In times of drought, if properly propitiated, she would spin light summer clouds out of cobwebs and morning dew, and send them off from the crest of the mountain, flake by flake, like flakes of carded cotton, to float in the air; until, dissolved by the heat of the sun, they would fall in gentle showers, causing the grass to spring, the fruits to ripen, and the corn to grow an inch an hour. If displeased, however, she would brew up clouds black as ink, sitting in the midst of them like a bottle-bellied spider in the midst of its web; and when these clouds broke, woe betide the valleys!

In old times, say the Indian traditions, there was a kind of Manitou or Spirit, who kept about the wildest recesses of the Catskill Mountains, and took a mischievous pleasure in wreaking all kinds of evils and vexations upon the red men. Sometimes he would assume the form of a bear, a panther, or a deer, lead the bewildered hunter a weary chase through tangled forests and among ragged rocks; and then spring off with a loud ho! ho! leaving him aghast on the brink of a beetling precipice or raging torrent.

The favorite abode of this Manitou is still shown. It is a great rock or cliff on the loneliest part of the mountains, and, from the flowering vines which clamber about it, and the wild flowers which abound in its neighborhood, is known by the name of the Garden Rock. Near the foot of it is a small lake, the haunt of the solitary bittern, with water-snakes basking in the sun on the leaves of the pond-lilies which lie on the surface. This place was held in great awe by the Indians, insomuch that the boldest hunter would not pursue his game within its precincts. Once upon a time, however, a hunter who had lost his way, penetrated to the Garden Rock, where he beheld a number of gourds placed in the crotches of trees. One of these he seized and made off with it, but in the hurry of his retreat he let it fall among the rocks, when a great stream gushed forth, which washed him away and swept him down precipices, where he was dashed to pieces, and the stream made its way to the Hudson, and continues to flow to the present day; being the identical stream known by the name of the Kaaters-kill.

Nathaniel Hawthorne

1804 – 1864

Nathaniel Hawthorne was born in 1804, in Salem, Massachusetts, the son of a sea captain who died in Dutch Guiana when Nathaniel was four years old. Through the aid of an uncle, Hawthorne entered Bowdoin College, numbering among his friends there the poet Longfellow and Franklin Pierce, a future president of the United States. While still an undergraduate, he decided to follow writing as a profession, and upon receiving his degree in 1825, he returned to Salem, where he spent the next twelve years in a virtually monastic study of literature and of the history and legends of his native region, chiefly those of the Puritan era. During this period of literary apprenticeship, Hawthorne grew to maturity as a writer, for his first volume of stories, *Twice-Told Tales,* published in 1837, is obviously the work of a finished writer. This volume caused so little stir, however, that he worked on in semiobscurity, engaging in hack work and serving in various posts, such as surveyor of customs for the port of Salem from 1846 to 1849. The publication in 1850 of the novel *The Scarlet Letter* brought him some fame, and a campaign biography he wrote of his friend Pierce secured for him the appointment as consul in Liverpool, England. He held this post from 1853 to 1857 and continued to reside abroad until 1860, when he returned to live in Concord, Massachusetts, until his death four years later in 1864. The best of some 120 short tales and sketches he wrote are contained in *Twice-Told Tales* (first published in 1837 and expanded into a second series in 1842), *Mosses from an Old Manse* (1846), and *The Snow Image* (1851).

Unlike Irving, who was content if his writing kept "mankind in good humor with one another," Hawthorne wrote with a high seriousness of purpose, concerning himself primarily with fundamental problems of human character and conscience. The themes he embodied in his stories are often so complex and many-faceted in their symbolic development and allegory that his approach appears to sacrifice "the familiar and faithful exhibition of scenes in common life" as achieved by Irving and to present story situations and characters that are often more metaphorical than real or lifelike. At the same time, in his best stories, as the following one illustrates, he achieved a successful fusion of the symbolic and narrative levels so that the symbolism enriches the thematic structure of the stories without impeding their narrative appeal.

Young Goodman Brown

Young Goodman Brown came forth at sunset into the street at Salem village; but put his head back, after crossing the threshold, to exchange a parting kiss with his young wife. And Faith, as the wife was aptly named, thrust her own pretty head into the street, letting the wind play with the pink ribbons of her cap while she called to Goodman Brown.

"Dearest heart," whispered she, softly and rather sadly, when her lips were close to his ear, "prithee put off your journey until sunrise and sleep in your own bed to-night. A lone woman is troubled with such dreams and such thoughts that she's afeard of herself sometimes. Pray tarry with me this night, dear husband, of all nights in the year."

"My love and my Faith," replied young Goodman Brown, "of all nights in the year, this one must I tarry away from thee. My journey, as thou callest it, forth and back again, must needs be done 'twixt now and sunrise. What, my sweet, pretty wife, dost thou doubt me already, and we but three months married?"

"Then God bless you!" said Faith, with the pink ribbons; "and may you find all well when you come back."

"Young Goodman Brown" by Nathaniel Hawthorne, in *The Complete Works of Nathaniel Hawthorne* (Houghton Mifflin, 1883).

"Amen!" cried Goodman Brown. "Say thy prayers, dear Faith, and go to bed at dusk, and no harm will come to thee."

So they parted; and the young man pursued his way until, being about to turn the corner by the meeting-house, he looked back and saw the head of Faith still peeping after him with a melancholy air, in spite of her pink ribbons.

"Poor little Faith!" thought he, for his heart smote him. "What a wretch am I to leave her on such an errand! She talks of dreams, too. Methought as she spoke there was trouble in her face, as if a dream had warned her what work is to be done to-night. But no, no; 'twould kill her to think it. Well, she's a blessed angel on earth; and after this one night I'll cling to her skirts and follow her to heaven."

With this excellent resolve for the future, Goodman Brown felt himself justified in making more haste on his present evil purpose. He had taken a dreary road, darkened by all the gloomiest trees of the forest, which barely stood aside to let the narrow path creep through, and closed immediately behind. It was all as lonely as could be; and there is this peculiarity in such a solitude, that the traveller knows not who may be concealed by the innumerable trunks and the thick boughs overhead; so that with lonely footsteps he may yet be passing through an unseen multitude.

"There may be a devilish Indian behind every tree," said Goodman Brown to himself; and he glanced fearfully behind him as he added, "What if the devil himself should be at my very elbow!"

His head being turned back, he passed a crook of the road, and, looking forward again, beheld the figure of a man, in grave and decent attire, seated at the foot of an old tree. He arose at Goodman Brown's approach and walked onward side by side with him.

"You are late, Goodman Brown," said he. "The clock of the Old South was striking as I came through Boston, and that is full fifteen minutes agone."

"Faith kept me back a while," replied the young man, with a tremor in his voice, caused by the sudden appearance of his companion, though not wholly unexpected.

It was now deep dusk in the forest, and deepest in that part of it where these two were journeying. As nearly as could be discerned, the second traveller was about fifty years old, apparently in the same rank of life as Goodman Brown, and bearing a considerable resemblance to him, though perhaps more in expression than features. Still they might have been taken for father and son. And yet, though the elder person was as simply clad as the younger, and as simple in manner, too, he had an indescribable air of one who knew the world, and who would not have felt abashed at the governor's dinner table or in King William's court, were it possible that his affairs should call him thither. But the only thing about him that could be fixed upon as remarkable was his staff, which bore the likeness of a great black snake, so curiously wrought that it might almost be seen to twist and wriggle itself like a living serpent. This, of course, must have been an ocular deception, assisted by the uncertain light.

"Come, Goodman Brown," cried his fellow-traveller, "this is a dull pace for the beginning of a journey. Take my staff, if you are so soon weary."

"Friend," said the other, exchanging his slow pace for a full stop, "having kept covenant by meeting thee here, it is my purpose now to return whence I came. I have scruples touching the matter thou wot'st of."

"Sayest thou so?" replied he of the serpent, smiling apart. "Let us walk on, nevertheless, reasoning as we go; and if I convince thee not thou shalt turn back. We are but a little way in the forest yet."

"Too far! too far!" exclaimed the good man, unconsciously resuming his walk. "My father never went into the woods on such an errand, nor his father before him. We have been a race of honest men and good Christians since the days of the martyrs; and shall I be the first of the name of Brown that ever took this path and kept—"

"Such company, thou wouldst say," observed the elder person, interpreting his pause. "Well said, Goodman Brown! I have been as well acquainted with your family as with ever a one among the Puritans; and that's no trifle to say. I helped your grandfather, the constable, when he lashed the Quaker woman so smartly through the streets of Salem; and it was I that brought your father a pitch-pine knot, kindled at my own hearth, to set fire to an Indian village, in King Philip's war. They were my good friends, both; and many a pleasant walk have we had along this path, and returned merrily after midnight. I would fain be friends with you for their sake."

"If it be as thou sayest," replied Goodman Brown, "I marvel they never spoke of these matters; or, verily, I marvel not, seeing that the least rumor of the sort would have driven them from New England. We are a people of prayer, and good works to boot, and abide no such wickedness."

"Wickedness or not," said the traveller with the twisted staff, "I have a very general acquaintance here in New England. The deacons of many a church have drunk the communion wine with me; the selectmen of divers towns make me their chairman; and a majority of the Great and General Court are firm supporters of my interest. The governor and I, too—But these are state secrets."

"Can this be so?" cried Goodman Brown, with a stare of amazement at his undisturbed companion. "Howbeit, I have nothing to do with the governor and council; they have their own ways, and are no rule for a simple husbandman like me. But, were I to go on with thee, how should

I meet the eye of that good old man, our minister, at Salem village? Oh, his voice would make me tremble both Sabbath day and lecture day."

Thus far the elder traveller had listened with due gravity; but now burst into a fit of irrepressible mirth, shaking himself so violently that his snake-like staff actually seemed to wriggle in sympathy.

"Ha! ha! ha!" shouted he again and again; then composing himself, "Well, go on, Goodman Brown, go on; but, prithee, don't kill me with laughing."

"Well, then, to end the matter at once," said Goodman Brown, considerably nettled, "there is my wife, Faith. It would break her dear little heart; and I'd rather break my own."

"Nay, if that be the case," answered the other, "e'en go thy ways, Goodman Brown. I would not for twenty old women like the one hobbling before us that Faith should come to any harm."

As he spoke he pointed his staff at a female figure on the path, in whom Goodman Brown recognized a very pious and exemplary dame, who had taught him his catechism in youth, and was still his moral and spiritual adviser, jointly with the minister and Deacon Gookin.

"A marvel, truly, that Goody Cloyse should be so far in the wilderness at nightfall," said he. "But with your leave, friend, I shall take a cut through the woods until we have left this Christian woman behind. Being a stranger to you, she might ask whom I was consorting with and whither I was going."

"Be it so," said his fellow-traveller. "Betake you to the woods, and let me keep the path."

Accordingly the young man turned aside, but took care to watch his companion, who advanced softly along the road until he had come within a staff's length of the old dame. She, meanwhile, was making the best of her way, with singular speed for so aged a woman, and mumbling some indistinct words—a prayer, doubtless—as she went. The traveller put forth his staff and touched her withered neck with what seemed the serpent's tail.

"The devil!" screamed the pious old lady.

"Then Goody Cloyse knows her old friend?" observed the traveller, confronting her and leaning on his writhing stick.

"Ah, forsooth, and is it your worship indeed?" cried the good dame. "Yea, truly is it, and in the very image of my old gossip, Goodman Brown, the grandfather of the silly fellow that now is. But—would your worship believe it?—my broomstick hath strangely disappeared, stolen, as I suspect, by that unhanged witch, Goody Cory, and that, too, when I was all anointed with the juice of smallage, and cinquefoil, and wolf's bane—"

"Mingled with fine wheat and the fat of a new-born babe," said the shape of old Goodman Brown.

"Ah, your worship knows the recipe," cried the old lady, cackling aloud. "So, as I was saying, being all ready for the meeting, and no horse to ride on, I made up my mind to foot it; for they tell me there is a nice young man to be taken into communion to-night. But now your good worship will lend me your arm, and we shall be there in a twinkling."

"That can hardly be," answered her friend. "I may not spare you my arm, Goody Cloyse; but here is my staff, if you will."

So saying, he threw it down at her feet, where, perhaps, it assumed life, being one of the rods which its owner had formerly lent to the Egyptian magi. Of this fact, however, Goodman Brown could not take cognizance. He had cast up his eyes in astonishment, and, looking down again, beheld neither Goody Cloyse nor the serpentine staff, but his fellow-traveller alone, who waited for him as calmly as if nothing had happened.

"That old woman taught me my catechism," said the young man; and there was a world of meaning in this simple comment.

They continued to walk onward, while the elder traveller exhorted his companion to make good speed and persevere in the path, discoursing so aptly that his arguments seemed rather to spring up in the bosom of his auditor than to be suggested by himself. As they went, he plucked a branch of maple to serve for a walking stick, and began to strip it of the twigs and little boughs, which were wet with evening dew. The moment his fingers touched them they became strangely withered and dried up as with a week's sunshine. Thus the pair proceeded, at a good free pace, until suddenly, in a gloomy hollow of the road, Goodman Brown sat himself down on the stump of a tree and refused to go any farther.

"Friend," said he stubbornly, "my mind is made up. Not another step will I budge on this errand. What if a wretched old woman do choose to go to the devil when I thought she was going to heaven: is that any reason why I should quit my dear Faith and go after her?"

"You will think better of this by and by," said his acquaintance, composedly. "Sit here and rest yourself a while; and when you feel like moving again, there is my staff to help you along."

Without more words, he threw his companion the maple stick, and was as speedily out of sight as if he had vanished into the deepening gloom. The young man sat a few moments by the roadside, applauding himself greatly, and thinking with how clear a conscience he should meet the minister in his morning walk, nor shrink from the eye of good old Deacon Gookin. And what calm sleep would be his that very night, which was to have been spent so wickedly, but so purely and sweetly now, in the arms of Faith! Amidst these pleasant and praise-worthy meditations, Goodman Brown heard the tramp of horses along the road, and deemed it advisable to conceal himself within the verge of the forest, conscious of the guilty purpose that had brought him thither, though now so happily turned from it.

On came the hoof tramps and the voices of the riders, two grave old voices, conversing soberly as they drew near. These mingled sounds appeared to pass along the road, within a few yards of the young man's hiding-place; but, owing doubtless to the depth of the gloom at that particular spot, neither the travellers nor their steeds were visible. Though their figures brushed the small boughs by the wayside, it could not be seen that they intercepted, even for a moment, the faint gleam from the strip of bright sky athwart which they must have passed. Goodman Brown alternately crouched and stood on tiptoe, pulling aside the branches and thrusting forth his head as far as he durst without discerning so much as a shadow. It vexed him the more, because he could have sworn, were such a thing possible, that he recognized the voices of the minister and Deacon Gookin, jogging along quietly, as they were wont to do, when bound to some ordination or ecclesiastical council. While yet within hearing, one of the riders stopped to pluck a switch.

"Of the two, reverend sir," said the voice like the deacon's, "I had rather miss an ordination dinner than to-night's meeting. They tell me that some of our community are to be here from Falmouth and beyond, and others from Connecticut and Rhode Island, besides several of the Indian powwows, who, after their fashion, know almost as much deviltry as the best of us. Moreover, there is a goodly young woman to be taken into communion."

"Mighty well, Deacon Gookin!" replied the solemn old tones of the minister. "Spur up, or we shall be late. Nothing can be done, you know, until I get on the ground."

The hoofs clattered again; and the voices, talking so strangely in the empty air, passed on through the forest, where no church had ever been gathered or solitary Christian prayed. Whither, then, could these holy men be journeying so deep into the heathen wilderness? Young Goodman Brown caught hold of a tree for support, being ready to sink down on the ground, faint and overburdened with the heavy sickness of his heart. He looked up to the sky, doubting whether there really was a heaven above him. Yet there was the blue arch, and the stars brightening in it.

"With heaven above and Faith below, I will yet stand firm against the devil!" cried Goodman Brown.

While he still gazed upward into the deep arch of the firmament and had lifted his hands to pray, a cloud, though no wind was stirring, hurried across the zenith and hid the brightening stars. The blue sky was still visible, except directly overhead, where this black mass of cloud was sweeping swiftly northward. Aloft in the air, as if from the depths of the cloud, came a confused and doubtful sound of voices. Once the listener fancied that he could distinguish the accents of townspeople of his own, men and women, both pious and ungodly, many of whom he had met at the communion table, and had seen others rioting at the tavern. The next moment, so indistinct were the sounds, he doubted whether he had heard aught but the murmur of the old forest, whispering without a wind. Then came a stronger swell of those familiar tones, heard daily in the sunshine at Salem village, but never until now from a cloud of night. There was one voice, of a young woman, uttering lamentations, yet with an uncertain sorrow, and entreating for some favor, which, perhaps, it would grieve her to obtain; and all the unseen multitude, both saints and sinners, seemed to encourage her onward.

"Faith!" shouted Goodman Brown, in a voice of agony and desperation; and the echoes of the forest mocked him, crying, "Faith! Faith!" as if bewildered wretches were seeking her all through the wilderness.

The cry of grief, rage, and terror was yet piercing the night, when the unhappy husband held his breath for a response. There was a scream, drowned immediately in a louder murmur of voices, fading into far-off laughter, as the dark cloud swept away, leaving the clear and silent sky above Goodman Brown. But something fluttered lightly down through the air and caught on the branch of a tree. The young man seized it, and beheld a pink ribbon.

"My Faith is gone!" cried he, after one stupefied moment. "There is no good on earth; and sin is but a name. Come, devil; for to thee is this world given."

And, maddened with despair, so that he laughed loud and long, did Goodman Brown grasp his staff and set forth again, at such a rate that he seemed to fly along the forest path rather than to walk or run. The road grew wilder and drearier and more faintly traced, and vanished at length, leaving him in the heart of the dark wilderness, still rushing onward with the instinct that guides mortal man to evil. The whole forest was peopled with frightful sounds—the creaking of the trees, the howling of wild beasts, and the yell of Indians; while sometimes the wind tolled like a distant church bell, and sometimes gave a broad roar around the traveller, as if all Nature were laughing him to scorn. But he was himself the chief horror of the scene, and shrank not from its other horrors.

"Ha! ha! ha!" roared Goodman Brown when the wind laughed at him. "Let us hear which will laugh loudest. Think not to frighten me with your deviltry. Come witch, come wizard, come Indian pow-wow, come devil himself, and here comes Goodman Brown. You may as well fear him as he fear you."

In truth, all through the haunted forest there could be nothing more frightful than the figure of Goodman Brown. On he flew among the black pines, brandishing his staff with frenzied gestures, now giving vent to an inspiration of horrid blasphemy, and now shouting forth such laughter as set all the echoes of the forest laughing like demons around him. The fiend in his own shape is less hideous than when he rages in the breast of man. Thus sped the demoniac on his course, until, quivering among the trees, he saw a red light before him, as when the felled trunks and branches of a clearing have been set on fire, and throw up their lurid blaze against the sky, at the hour of midnight. He paused, in a lull of the tempest that had driven him onward, and heard the swell of what seemed a hymn, rolling solemnly from a distance with the weight of many voices. He knew the tune; it was a familiar one in the choir of the village meeting-house. The verse died heavily away, and was lengthened by a chorus, not of human voices, but of all the sounds of the benighted wilderness pealing in awful harmony together. Goodman Brown cried out, and his cry was lost to his own ear by its unison with the cry of the desert.

In the interval of silence he stole forward until the light glared full upon his eyes. At one extremity of an open space, hemmed in by the dark wall of the forest, arose a rock, bearing some rude, natural resemblance to an altar or a pulpit, and surrounded by four blazing pines, their tops aflame, their stems untouched, like candles at an evening meeting. The mass of foliage that had overgrown the summit of the rock was all on fire, blazing high into the night and fitfully illuminating the whole field. Each pendent twig and leafy festoon was in a blaze. As the red light arose and fell, a numerous congregation alternately shone forth, then disappeared in shadow, and again grew, as it were, out of the darkness, peopling the heart of the solitary woods at once.

"A grave and dark-clad company," quoth Goodman Brown.

In truth they were such. Among them, quivering to and fro between gloom and splendor, appeared faces that would be seen next day at the council board of the province, and others which, Sabbath after Sabbath, looked devoutly heavenward, and benignantly over the crowded pews, from the holiest pulpits in the land. Some affirm that the lady of the governor was there. At least there were high dames well known to her, and wives of honored husbands, and widows, a great multitude, and ancient maidens, all of excellent repute, and fair young girls, who trembled lest their mothers should espy them. Either the sudden gleams of light flashing over the obscure field bedazzled Goodman Brown, or he recognized a score of the church members of Salem village famous for their especial sanctity. Good old Deacon Gookin had arrived, and waited at the skirts of that venerable saint, his revered pastor. But, irreverently consorting with these grave, reputable, and pious people, these elders of the church, these chaste dames and dewy virgins, there were men of dissolute lives and women of spotted fame, wretches given over to all mean and filthy vice, and suspected even of horrid crimes. It was strange to see that the good shrank not from the wicked, nor were the sinners abashed by the saints. Scattered also among their palefaced enemies were the Indian priests, or powwows, who had often scared their native forest with more hideous incantations than any known to English witchcraft.

"But where is Faith?" thought Goodman Brown; and, as hope came into his heart, he trembled.

Another verse of the hymn arose, a slow and mournful strain, such as the pious love, but joined to words which expressed all that our nature can conceive of sin, and darkly hinted at far more. Unfathomable to mere mortals is the lore of fiends. Verse after verse was sung; and still the chorus of the desert swelled between like the deepest tone of a mighty organ; and with the final peal of that dreadful anthem there came a sound, as if the roaring wind, the rushing streams, the howling beasts, and every other voice of the unconcerted wilderness were mingling and according with the voice of guilty man in homage to the prince of all. The four blazing pines threw up a loftier flame, and obscurely discovered shapes and visages of horror on the smoke wreaths above the impious assembly. At the same moment the fire on the rock shot redly forth and formed a glowing arch above its base, where now appeared a figure. With reverence be it spoken, the figure bore no slight similitude, both in garb and manner, to some grave divine of the New England churches.

"Bring forth the converts!" cried a voice that echoed through the field and rolled into the forest.

At the word, Goodman Brown stepped forth from the shadow of the trees and approached the congregation, with whom he felt a loathful brotherhood by the sympathy of all that was wicked in his heart. He could have well-nigh sworn that the shape of his own dead father beckoned him to advance, looking downward from a smoke wreath, while a woman, with dim features of despair, threw out her hand to warn him back. Was it his mother? But he had no power to retreat one step, nor to resist, even in thought, when the minister and good old Deacon Gookin seized his arms and led him to the blazing rock. Thither came also the slender form of a veiled female, led between Goody Cloyse, that pious teacher of the catechism, and Martha Carrier, who had received the devil's promise to be queen of hell. A rampant hag was she. And there stood the proselytes beneath the canopy of fire.

"Welcome, my children," said the dark figure, "to the communion of your race. Ye have found thus young your nature and your destiny. My children, look behind you!"

They turned; and flashing forth, as it were, in a sheet of flame, the fiend worshippers were seen; the smile of welcome gleamed darkly on every visage.

"There," resumed the sable form, "are all whom ye have reverenced from youth. Ye deemed them holier than yourselves, and shrank from your own sin, contrasting it with their lives of righteousness and prayerful aspirations heavenward. Yet here are they all in my worshipping assembly. This night it shall be granted you to know their secret deeds: how hoary-bearded elders of the church have whispered wanton words to the young maids of their households; how many a woman, eager for widows' weeds, has given her husband a drink at bedtime and let him sleep his last sleep in her bosom; how beardless youths have made haste to inherit their fathers' wealth; and how fair damsels—blush not, sweet ones—have dug little graves in the garden, and bidden me, the sole guest, to an infant's funeral. By the sympathy of your human hearts for sin ye shall scent out all the places—whether in church, bedchamber, street, field, or forest—where crime has been committed, and shall exult to behold the whole earth one stain of guilt, one mighty blood spot. Far more than this. It shall be yours to penetrate, in every bosom, the deep mystery of sin, the fountain of all wicked arts, and which inexhaustibly supplies more evil impulses than human power—than my power at its utmost—can make manifest in deeds. And now, my children, look upon each other."

They did so; and, by the blaze of the hell-kindled torches, the wretched man beheld his Faith, and the wife her husband, trembling before that unhallowed altar.

"Lo, there ye stand, my children," said the figure, in a deep and solemn tone, almost sad with its despairing awfulness, as if his once angelic nature could yet mourn for our miserable race. "Depending upon one another's hearts, ye had still hoped that virtue were not all a dream. Now are ye undeceived. Evil is the nature of mankind. Evil must be your only happiness. Welcome again, my children, to the communion of your race."

"Welcome," repeated the fiend worshippers, in one cry of despair and triumph.

And there they stood, the only pair, as it seemed, who were yet hesitating on the verge of wickedness in this dark world. A basin was hollowed, naturally, in the rock. Did it contain water, reddened by the lurid light? or was it blood? or, perchance, a liquid flame? Herein did the shape of evil dip his hand and prepare to lay the mark of baptism upon their foreheads, that they might be partakers of the mystery of sin, more conscious of the secret guilt of others, both in deed and thought, than they could now be of their own. The husband cast one look at his pale wife, and Faith at him. What polluted wretches would the next glance show them to each other, shuddering alike at what they disclosed and what they saw!

"Faith! Faith!" cried the husband, "look up to heaven, and resist the wicked one."

Whether Faith obeyed he knew not. Hardly had he spoken when he found himself amid calm night and solitude, listening to a roar of the wind which died heavily away through the forest. He staggered against the rock, and felt it chill and damp; while a hanging twig, that had been all on fire, besprinkled his cheek with the coldest dew.

The next morning young Goodman Brown came slowly into the street of Salem village, staring around him like a bewildered man. The good old minister was taking a walk along the graveyard to get an appetite for breakfast and meditate his sermon, and bestowed a blessing, as he passed, on Goodman Brown. He shrank from the venerable saint as if to avoid an anathema. Old Deacon Gookin was at domestic worship, and the holy words of his prayer were heard through the open window. "What God doth the wizard pray to?" quoth Goodman Brown. Goody Cloyse, that excellent old Christian, stood in the early sunshine at her own lattice, catechizing a little girl who had brought her a pint of morning's milk. Goodman Brown snatched away the child as from the grasp of the fiend himself. Turning the corner by the meeting-house, he spied the head of Faith, with the pink ribbons, gazing anxiously forth, and bursting into such joy at sight of him that she skipped along the street and almost kissed her husband before the whole village. But Goodman Brown looked sternly and sadly into her face, and passed on without a greeting.

Had Goodman Brown fallen asleep in the forest and only dreamed a wild dream of a witch-meeting?

Be it so if you will; but, alas! it was a dream of evil omen for young Goodman Brown. A stern, a sad, a darkly meditative, a distrustful, if not a desperate man did he become from the night of that fearful dream. On the Sabbath day, when the congregation were singing a holy psalm, he could not listen because an anthem of sin rushed loudly upon his ear and drowned all the blessed strain. When the minister spoke from the pulpit with power and fervid eloquence, and, with his hand on the open Bible, of the sacred truths of our religion, and of saint-like lives and triumphant deaths, and of future bliss or misery unutterable, then did Goodman Brown turn pale, dreading lest the roof should thunder down upon the gray blasphemer and his hearers. Often, awaking suddenly at midnight, he shrank from the bosom of Faith; and at morning or eventide, when the family knelt down at prayer, he scowled and muttered to himself, and gazed sternly at his wife, and turned away. And when he had lived long, and was borne to his grave a hoary corpse, followed by Faith, an aged woman, and children and grandchildren, a goodly procession, besides neighbors not a few, they carved no hopeful verse upon his tombstone, for his dying hour was gloom.

William Gilmore Simms

1806 – 1870

William Gilmore Simms, one of America's most prolific romanticists, was born in Charleston, South Carolina, on April 17, 1806. Half-orphaned at two when his mother died in childbirth, he was reared and educated by his maternal grandmother, Jane (Mrs. Jacob) Gates; she not only gave him a home after his father left to seek fortune in the southwestern Mississippi territory, but also nourished his early love of literature by telling him exciting eyewitness tales of her own youth during the Revolution in South Carolina. At age eighteen, during an extended visit with his father, Simms also witnessed the equally fascinating aspects of frontier life, but by then he had already decided to cast his lot for a career at home. In 1826, upon returning to Charleston to pursue his law studies, he married Anne Giles, fathered a child and was admitted to the bar of South Carolina the following year, tried but failed to edit his first literary journal, and, by 1830, purchased half-interest in a newspaper, the *City Gazette,* and published several collections of poems. The same year his father's death also presaged a series of personal losses that would dramatically affect his subsequent career: when his young wife, his grandmother, and his partner all died in 1832, Simms turned with redoubled dedication to the writer's craft, striving to create on his own a literature firmly based on native American historical and cultural traditions and, in several critical journals he also edited, to encourage other writers to do likewise. A man of prodigious energy and much personal charm, Simms gained added prestige, influence, and the financial support of a beautiful plantation, which came with his second marriage in 1836 to Chevillete Roach; so that by 1850 he had published about fifty-three of the eighty-odd volumes of poetry and prose he produced altogether during his lifetime. Despite the sorrows and ruinous losses he suffered from the Civil War, he was still striving valiantly as a creative artist at the time of his death.

In the forty-five year span of his career Simms published about eighty short tales and sketches. He also left behind at least eight unfinished manuscripts of fiction and two finished but unpublished ones, which appeared in print for the first time in volume 5 of the new *Centennial Edition* of his *Works.* His most impressive short fiction pieces are those in the collection called *The Wigwam and the Cabin,* published originally in 1845 and republished in his revised, second edition in 1856. Six of these stories are concerned primarily with the activities of white frontiersmen; in five others the chief characters are Indians; and in the remaining two, slaves. In most of these tales, the interrelationships between whites and Indians or between whites and blacks are skillfully blended in highly suspenseful action involving violence, fraud, malice, deceit, and retribution. Although they are tales based on commonplace events, Simms recognized that the problem of the artist was to make these common events "appear in the right place, strike at the right time, and so adapt one fact to another, as to create mystery, awaken curiosity, inspire doubt as to the result, and bring about the catastrophe, by processes which shall be equally natural and unexpected." He met this problem most successfully in the stories for which he provided an eyewitness narrator, either named or implied, who could "breathe life" into the deeds recounted, as does the grandmother in "Grayling."

Grayling; or, "Murder Will Out"

CHAPTER I

The world has become monstrous matter-of-fact in latter days. We can no longer get a ghost story, either for love or money. The materialists have it all their own way; and even the little urchin, eight years old, instead of deferring with decent reverence to the opinions of his grandmamma, now stands up stoutly for his own. He believes in every "ology" but pneumatology. "Faust" and the "Old Woman of Berkeley" move his derision only, and he would laugh incredulously, if he dared, at the Witch of Endor. The whole armoury of modern reasoning is on his side; and, however he may admit at seasons that belief can scarcely be counted a matter of will, he yet puts his veto on all sorts of credulity. That cold-blooded demon called Science has taken the place of all the other demons. He has certainly cast out innumerable devils, however he may still spare the principal. Whether we are the better for his intervention is another question. There is reason to apprehend that in disturbing our human faith in shadows, we have lost some of those wholesome moral restraints which might have kept many of us virtuous, where the laws could not.

The effect, however, is much the more seriously evil in all that concerns the romantic. Our story-tellers are so resolute to deal in the real, the actual only, that they venture on no subjects the details of which are not equally vulgar and susceptible of proof. With this end in view, indeed, they too commonly choose their subjects among convicted felons, in order that they may avail themselves of the evidence which led to their conviction; and, to prove more conclusively their devoted adherence to nature and the truth, they depict the former not only in her condition of nakedness, but long before she has found out the springs of running water. It is to be feared that some of the coarseness of modern taste arises from the too great lack of that veneration which belonged to, and elevated to dignity, even the errors of preceding ages. A love of the marvellous belongs, it appears to me, to all those who love and cultivate either of the fine arts. I very much doubt whether the poet, the painter, the sculptor,

W. Gilmore Simms, "Grayling; Or, 'Murder Will Out,'" *The Wigwam and the Cabin.* NY: H. C. Armstrong & Son, 1882.

or the romancer, ever yet lived, who had not some strong bias—a leaning, at least,—to a belief in the wonders of the invisible world. Certainly, the higher orders of poets and painters, those who create and invent, must have a strong taint of the superstitious in their composition. But this is digressive, and leads us from our purpose.

It is so long since we have been suffered to see or hear of a ghost, that a visitation at this time may have the effect of novelty, and I propose to narrate a story which I heard more than once in my boyhood, from the lips of an aged relative, who succeeded, at the time, in making me believe every word of it; perhaps, for the simple reason that she convinced me she believed every word of it herself. My grandmother was an old lady who had been a resident of the seat of most frequent war in Carolina during the Revolution. She had fortunately survived the numberless atrocities which she was yet compelled to witness; and, a keen observer, with a strong memory, she had in store a thousand legends of that stirring period, which served to beguile me from sleep many and many a long winter night. The story which I propose to tell was one of these; and when I say that she not only devoutly believed it herself, but that it was believed by sundry of her contemporaries, who were themselves privy to such of the circumstances as could be known to third parties, the gravity with which I repeat the legend will not be considered very astonishing.

The revolutionary war had but a little while been concluded. The British had left the country; but peace did not imply repose. The community was still in that state of ferment which was natural enough to passions, not yet at rest, which had been brought into exercise and action during the protracted seven years' struggle through which the nation had just passed. The state was overrun by idlers, adventurers, profligates, and criminals. Disbanded soldiers, half-starved and reckless, occupied the highways,—outlaws, emerging from their hiding-places, skulked about the settlements with an equal sentiment of hate and fear in their hearts;—patriots were clamouring for justice upon the tories, those against whom the proofs were too strong for denial or evasion, buckled on their armour for a renewal of the struggle. Such being the condition of the country, it may easily be supposed that life and property lacked many of their necessary securities. Men generally travelled with weapons which were displayed on the smallest provocation; and few who could provide themselves with an escort ventured to travel any distance without one.

There was, about this time, said my grandmother, and while such was the condition of the country, a family of the name of Grayling, that lived somewhere upon the skirts of "Ninety-six" district. Old Grayling, the head of the family, was dead. He was killed in Buford's massacre. His wife was a fine woman, not so very old, who had an only son named James, and a little girl, only five years of age, named Lucy. James was but fourteen when his father was killed, and that event made a man of him. He went out with his rifle in company with Joel Sparkman, who was his mother's brother, and joined himself to Pickens's Brigade. Here he made as good a soldier as the best. He had no sort of fear. He was always the first to go forward; and his rifle was always good for his enemy's button at a long hundred yards. He was in several fights both with the British and tories; and just before the war was ended he had a famous brush with the Cherokees, when Pickens took their country from them. But though he had no fear, and never knew when to stop killing while the fight was going on, he was the most bashful of boys that I ever knew; and so kind-hearted that it was almost impossible to believe all we heard of his fierce doings when he was in battle. But they were nevertheless quite true for all his bashfulness.

Well, when the war was over, Joel Sparkman, who lived with his sister, Grayling, persuaded her that it would be better to move down into the low country. I don't know what reason he had for it, or what they proposed to do there. They had very little property, but Sparkman was a knowing man, who could turn his hand to a hundred things; and as he was a bachelor, and loved his sister and her children just as if they had been his own, it was natural that she should go with him wherever he wished. James, too, who was restless by nature—and the taste he had enjoyed of the wars had made him more so—he was full of it; and so, one sunny morning in April, their wagon started for the city. The wagon was only a small one, with two horses, scarcely larger than those that are employed to carry chickens and fruit to the market from the Wassamaws and thereabouts. It was driven by a negro fellow named Clytus, and carried Mrs. Grayling and Lucy. James and his uncle loved the saddle too well to shut themselves up in such a vehicle; and both of them were mounted on fine horses which they had won from the enemy. The saddle that James rode on,—and he was very proud of it,—was one that he had taken at the battle of Cowpens from one of Tarleton's own dragoons, after he had tumbled the owner. The roads at that season were excessively bad, for the rains of March had been frequent and heavy, the track was very much cut up, and the red clay gullies of the hills of "Ninety-six" were so washed that it required all shoulders, twenty times a day, to get the wagon-wheels out of the bog. This made them travel very slowly,—perhaps, not more than fifteen miles a day. Another cause for slow travelling was, the necessity of great caution, and a constant look-out for enemies both up and down the road. James and his uncle took it by turns to ride a-head, precisely as they did when scouting in war, but one of them always kept along with the wagon. They had gone on this way for two days, and saw nothing to trouble and alarm them. There were few persons on the high-road, and these seemed to the full as shy of them as they probably were of strangers. But just as they were about to camp, the evening of the second day, while they were splitting light-wood, and getting out the kettles and the frying-pan, a person rode up and joined them without much ceremony. He was a short thick-set man, somewhere between forty and fifty: had on very coarse and common garments, though he rode a fine black horse of remarkable strength and vigour. He was very civil of speech, though he had but little to say, and that little showed him to be a person without much education and with no refinement. He begged permission to make one of the encampment, and his manner was very respectful and even humble; but there was something dark and sullen in his face—his eyes, which were of light gray colour, were very restless, and his nose turned up sharply, and was very red. His forehead was excessively broad, and his eyebrows thick and shaggy—white hairs being freely mingled with the dark, both in them and upon his head. Mrs. Grayling did not like this man's looks, and whispered her dislike to her son; but James, who felt himself equal to any man, said, promptly—

"What of that, mother! we can't turn the stranger off and say 'no;' and if he means any mischief, there's two of us, you know."

The man had no weapons—none, at least, which were then visible; and deported himself in so humble a manner, that the prejudice which the party had formed against him when he first appeared, if it was not dissipated while he remained, at least failed to gain any increase. He was very quiet, did not mention an unnecessary word, and seldom permitted his eyes to rest upon those of any of the party, the females not excepted. This, perhaps, was the only circumstance, that, in the mind of Mrs. Grayling, tended to confirm the hostile impression which his coming had originally occasioned. In a little while the temporary encampment was put in a state equally social and warlike. The wagon was wheeled a little way into the woods, and off the road; the horses fastened behind it in such a manner that any attempt to steal them would be difficult of success, even were the watch neglectful which was yet to be maintained upon them. Extra guns, concealed in the straw at the bottom of the wagon, were kept well loaded. In the foreground, and between the wagon and the highway, a fire was soon blazing with a wild but cheerful gleam; and the worthy dame, Mrs. Grayling, assisted by the little girl, Lucy, lost no time in setting on the frying-pan, and cutting into slices the haunch of bacon, which they had provided at leaving home. James Grayling patrolled the woods, meanwhile for a mile or two round the encampment, while his uncle, Joel Sparkman, foot to foot with the stranger, seemed—if the absence of all care constitutes the supreme of human felicity—to realize the most perfect conception of mortal happiness. But Joel was very far from being the careless person that he seemed. Like an old soldier, he simply hung out false colours, and concealed his real timidity by an extra show of confidence and courage. He did not relish the stranger from the first, any more than his sister; and having subjected him to a searching examination, such as was considered, in those days of peril and suspicion, by no means inconsistent with becoming courtesy, he came rapidly to the conclusion that he was no better than he should be.

"You are a Scotchman, stranger," said Joel, suddenly drawing up his feet, and bending forward to the other with an eye like that of a hawk stooping over a covey of partridges. It was a wonder that he had not made the discovery before. The broad dialect of the stranger was not to be subdued; but Joel made slow stages and short progress in his mental journeyings. The answer was given with evident hesitation, but it was affirmative.

"Well, now, it's mighty strange that you should ha' fou't with us and not agin us," responded Joel Sparkman. "There was a precious few of the Scotch, and none that I knows on, saving yourself, perhaps,—that didn't go dead agin us, and for the tories, through thick and thin. That 'Cross Creek settlement' was a mighty ugly thorn in the sides of us whigs. It turned out a raal bad stock of varmints. I hope,—I reckon, stranger,—you aint from that part."

"No," said the other; "oh no! I'm from over the other quarter. I'm from the Duncan settlement above."

"I've hearn tell of that other settlement, but I never know'd as any of the men fou't with us. What gineral did you fight under? What Carolina gineral?"

"I was at Gum Swamp when General Gates was defeated;" was the still hesitating reply of the other.

"Well, I thank God, *I* warn't there, though I reckon things wouldn't ha' turned out quite so bad, if there had been a leetle sprinkling of Sumter's, or Pickens's, or Marion's men, among them two-legged critters that run that day. They did tell that some of the regiments went off without ever once emptying their rifles. Now, stranger, I hope you warn't among them fellows."

"I was not," said the other with something more of promptness.

"I don't blame a chap for dodging a bullet if he can, or being too quick for a bagnet, because, I'm thinking, a live man is always a better man than a dead one, or he can become so; but to run without taking a single crack at the inimy, is downright cowardice. There's no two ways about it, stranger."

This opinion, delivered with considerable emphasis, met with the ready assent of the Scotchman, but Joel Sparkman was not to be diverted, even by his own eloquence, from the object of his inquiry.

"But you ain't said," he continued, "who was your Carolina gineral. Gates was from Virginny, and he stayed a mighty short time when he come. You didn't run far at Camden, I reckon, and you joined the army ag'in, and come in with Greene? Was that the how?"

To this the stranger assented, though with evident disinclination.

"Then, mou'tbe, we sometimes went into the same scratch together? I was at Cowpens and Ninety-Six, and seen sarvice at other odds and eends, where there was more fighting than fun. I reckon you must have been at 'Ninety-Six,"—perhaps at Cowpens, too, if you went with Morgan?"

The unwillingness of the stranger to respond to these questions appeared to increase. He admitted, however, that he had been at "Ninety-Six," though, as Sparkman afterwards remembered, in this case, as in that of the defeat of Gates at Gum Swamp, he had not said on which side he had fought. Joel, as he discovered the reluctance of his guest to answer his questions, and perceived his growing doggedness, forbore to annoy him, but mentally resolved to keep a sharper look-out than ever upon his motions. His examination concluded with an inquiry, which, in the plaindealing regions of the south and south-west, is not unfrequently put first.

"And what mout be your name, stranger?"

"Macnab," was the steady response. "Sandy Macnab."

"Well, Mr. Macnab I see that my sister's got supper ready for us; so we mou't as well fall to upon the hoecake and bacon."

Sparkman rose while speaking, and led the way to the spot, near the wagon, where Mrs. Grayling had spread the feast. "We're pretty nigh on to the main road, here, but I reckon there's no great danger now. Besides, Jim Grayling keeps watch for us, and he's got two as good eyes in his head as any scout in the country, and a rifle that, after you once know how it shoots, 'twould do your heart good to hear its crack, if so be that twa'n't your heart that he drawed sight on. He's a perdigious fine shot, and as ready to shoot and fight as if he had a nateral calling that way."

"Shall we wait for him before we eat?" demanded Macnab, anxiously.

"By no sort o' reason, stranger," answered Sparkman. "He'll watch for us while we're eating, and after that I'll change shoes with him. So fall to, and don't mind what's a coming."

Sparkman had just broken the hoecake, when a distant whistle was heard.

"Ha! That's the lad now!" he exclaimed, rising to his feet. "He's on trail. He's got a sight of an inimy's fire, I reckon. 'Twon't be onreasonable, friend Macnab, to get our we'pons in readiness;" and, so speaking, Sparkman bid his sister get into the wagon, where the little Lucy had already placed herself, while he threw open the pan of his rifle, and turned the priming over with his finger. Macnab, meanwhile, had taken from his holsters, which he had before been sitting upon, a pair of horseman's pistols, richly mounted with figures in silver. These were large and long, and had evidently seen service. Unlike his companion, his proceedings occasioned no comment. What he did seemed a matter of habit, of which he himself was scarcely conscious. Having looked at his priming, he laid the instruments beside him without a word, and resumed the bit of hoecake which he had just before received from Sparkman. Meanwhile, the signal whistle, supposed to come from James Grayling, was repeated. Silence ensued then for a brief space, which Sparkman employed in perambulating the grounds immediately contiguous. At length, just as he had returned to the fire, the sound of a horse's feet was heard, and a sharp quick halloo from Grayling informed his uncle that all was right. The youth made his appearance a moment after accompanied by a stranger on horseback; a tall, fine-looking young man, with a keen flashing eye, and a voice whose lively clear tones, as he was heard approaching, sounded cheerily like those of a trumpet after victory. James Grayling kept along on foot beside the new-comer; and his hearty laugh, and free, glib, garrulous tones, betrayed to his uncle, long ere he drew nigh enough to declare the fact, that he had met unexpectedly with a friend, or, at least, an old acquaintance.

"Why, who have you got there, James?" was the demand of Sparkman, as he dropped the butt of his rifle upon the ground.

"Why, who do you think, uncle? Who but Major Spencer—our own major?"

"You don't say so!—what!—well! Li'nel Spencer, for sartin! Lord bless you, major, who'd ha' thought to see you in these parts; and jest mounted too, for all natur, as if the war was to be fou't over ag'in. Well, I'm raal glad to see you. I am, that's sartin!"

"And I'm very glad to see you, Sparkman," said the other, as he alighted from his steed, and yielded his hand to the cordial grasp of the other.

"Well, I knows that, major, without you saying it. But you've jest come in the right time. The bacon's frying, and here's the bread;—let's down upon our haunches in right good airnest, camp fashion, and make the most of what God gives us in the way of blessings. I reckon you don't mean to ride any further to-night, major?"

"No," said the person addressed, "not if you'll let me lay my heels at your fire. But who's in your wagon? My old friend, Mrs. Grayling, I suppose?"

"That's a true word, major," said the lady herself, making her way out of the vehicle with good humoured agility, and coming forward with extended hand.

"Really, Mrs. Grayling, I'm very glad to see you." And the stranger, with the blandness of a gentleman and the hearty warmth of an old neighbour, expressed his satisfaction at once more finding himself in the company of an old acquaintance. Their greetings once over, Major Spencer readily joined the group about the fire, while James Grayling—though with some reluctance—disappeared to resume his toils of the scout while the supper proceeded.

"And who have you here?" demanded Spencer, as his eye rested on the dark, hard features of the Scotchman. Sparkman told him all that he himself had learned of the name and character of the stranger, in a brief whisper, and in a moment after formally introduced the parties in this fashion—

"Mr. Macnab, Major Spencer. Mr. Macnab says he's true blue, major, and fou't at Camden, when General Gates run so hard to 'bring the d—d militia back.' He also fou't at Ninety-Six, and Cowpens—so I reckon we had as good as count him one of us."

Major Spencer scrutinized the Scotchman keenly—a scrutiny which the latter seemed very ill to relish. He put a few questions to him on the subject of the war, and some of the actions in which he allowed himself to have been concerned; but his evident reluctance to unfold himself—a reluctance so unnatural to the brave soldier who has gone through his toils honourably—had the natural effect of discouraging the young officer, whose sense of delicacy had not been materially impaired amid the rude jostlings of military life. But, though he forbore to propose any other questions to Macnab, his eyes continued to survey the features of his sullen countenance with curiosity and a strangely increasing interest. This he subsequently explained to Sparkman, when, at the close of supper, James Grayling came in, and the former assumed the duties of the scout.

"I have seen that Scotchman's face somewhere, Sparkman, and I'm convinced at some interesting moment; but where, when, or how, I cannot call to mind. The sight of it is even associated in my mind with something painful and unpleasant; where could I have seen him?"

"I don't somehow like his looks myself," said Sparkman, "and I mislists he's been rether more of a tory than a whig; but that's nothing to the purpose now; and he's at our fire, and we've broken hoecake together; so we cannot rake up the old ashes to make a dust with."

"No, surely not," was the reply of Spencer. "Even though we knew him to be a tory, that cause of former quarrel should occasion none now. But it should produce watchfulness and caution. I'm glad to see that you have not forgot your old business of scouting in the swamp."

"Kin I forget it, major?" demanded Sparkman, in tones which, though whispered, were full of emphasis, as he laid his ear to the earth to listen.

"James has finished supper, major—that's his whistle to tell me so; and I'll jest step back to make it cl'ar to him how we're to keep up the watch tonight."

"Count me in your arrangements, Sparkman, as I am one of you for the night," said the major.

"By no sort of means," was the reply. "The night must be shared between James and myself. Ef so be you wants to keep company with one or t'other of us, why, that's another thing, and, of course, you can do as you please."

"We'll have no quarrel on the subject, Joel," said the officer, good-naturedly, as they returned to the camp together.

CHAPTER II

The arrangements of the party were soon made. Spencer renewed his offer at the fire to take his part in the watch; and the Scotchman, Macnab, volunteered his services also; but the offer of the latter was another reason why that of the former should be declined. Sparkman was resolute to have everything his own way; and while James Grayling went out upon his lonely rounds, he busied himself in cutting bushes and making a sort of tent for the use of his late commander. Mrs. Grayling and Lucy slept in a wagon. The Scotchman stretched himself with little effort before the fire; while Joel Sparkman, wrapping himself up in his cloak, crouched under the wagon body, with his back resting partly against one of the wheels. From time to time he rose and thrust additional brands into the fire, looked up at the night, and round upon the little encampment, then sunk back to his perch and stole a few moments, at intervals, of uneasy sleep. The first two hours of the watch were over, and James Grayling was relieved. The youth, however, felt in no mood for sleep, and taking his seat by the fire, he drew from his pocket a little volume of Easy Reading Lessons, and by the fitful flame of the resinous light-wood, he prepared, in this rude manner, to make up for the precious time which his youth had lost of its legitimate employments, in the stirring events of the preceding seven years consumed in war. He was surprised at this employment by his late commander, who, himself sleepless, now emerged from the bushes and joined Grayling at the fire. The youth had been rather a favourite with Spencer. They had both been reared in the same neighbourhood, and the first military achievements of James had taken place under the eye, and had met the approbation of his officer. The difference of their ages was just such as to permit of the warm attachment of the lad without diminishing any of the reverence which should be felt by the inferior. Grayling was not more than seventeen, and Spencer was perhaps thirty-four—the very prime of manhood. They sat by the fire and talked of old times and told old stories with the hearty glee and good-nature of the young. Their mutual inquiries led to the revelation of their several objects in pursuing the present journey. Those of James Grayling were scarcely, indeed, to be considered his own. They were plans and purposes of his uncle, and it does not concern this narrative that we should know more of their nature than has already been revealed. But, whatever they were, they were as freely unfolded to his hearer as if the parties had been brothers, and Spencer was quite as frank in his revelations as his companion. He, too, was on his way to Charleston, from whence he was to take passage for England.

"I am rather in a hurry to reach town," he said, "as I learn that the Falmouth packet is preparing to sail for England in a few days, and I must go in her."

"For England, major!" exclaimed the youth with unaffected astonishment.

"Yes, James, for England. But why—what astonishes you?"

"Why, lord!" exclaimed the simple youth, "if they only knew there, as I do, what a cutting and slashing you did use to make among their red coats, I reckon they'd hang you to the first hickory."

"Oh, no! scarcely," said the other, with a smile.

"But I reckon you'll change your name, major?" continued the youth.

"No," responded Spencer, "if I did that, I should lose the object of my voyage. You must know, James, that an old relative has left me a good deal of money in England, and I can only get it by proving that I am Lionel Spencer; so you see I must carry my own name, whatever may be the risk."

"Well, major, you know best; but I do think if they could only have a guess of what you did among their sodgers at Hobkirk's and Cowpens, and Eutaw, and a dozen other places, they'd find some means of hanging you up, peace or no peace. But I don't see what occasion you have to be going cl'ar away to England for money, when you've got a sight of your own already."

"Not so much as you think for," replied the major, giving an involuntary and uneasy glance at the Scotchman, who was seemingly sound asleep on the opposite side of the fire. "There is, you know, but little money in the country at any time, and I must get what I want for my expenses when I reach Charleston. I have just enough to carry me there."

"Well, now, major, that's mighty strange. I always thought that you was about the best off of any man in our parts; but if you're strained so close, I'm thinking, major,—if so be you wouldn't think me too presumptuous,—you'd better let me lend you a guinea or so that I've got to spare, and you can pay me back when you get the English money."

And the youth fumbled in his bosom for a little cotton wallet, which, with its limited contents, was displayed in another instant to the eyes of the officer.

"No, no, James," said the other, putting back the generous tribute; "I have quite enough to carry me to Charleston, and when there I can easily get a supply from the merchants. But I thank you, my good fellow, for your offer. You *are* a good fellow, James, and I will remember you."

It is needless to pursue the conversation farther. The night passed away without any alarms, and at dawn of the next day the whole party was engaged in making preparation for a start. Mrs. Grayling was soon busy in getting breakfast in readiness. Major Spencer consented to remain with them until it was over; but the Scotchman, after returning thanks very civilly for his accommodation of the night, at once resumed his journey. His course seemed, like their own, to lie below; but he neither declared his route nor betrayed the least desire to know that of Spencer. The latter had no disposition to renew those inquiries from which the stranger seemed to shrink the night before, and he accordingly suffered him to depart with a quiet farewell, and the utterance of a good-natured wish, in which all the parties joined, that he might have a pleasant journey. When he was fairly out of sight, Spencer said to Sparkman,

"Had I liked that fellow's looks, nay, had I not positively disliked them, I should have gone with him. As it is, I will remain and share your breakfast."

The repast being over, all parties set forward; but Spencer, after keeping along with them for a mile, took his leave also. The slow wagon-pace at which the family travelled, did not suit the high-spirited cavalier; and it was necessary, as he assured them, that he should reach the city in two nights more. They parted with many regrets, as truly felt as they were warmly expressed; and James Grayling never felt the tedium of wagon travelling to be so severe as throughout the whole of that day when he separated from his favourite captain. But he was too stout-hearted a lad to make any complaint; and his dissatisfaction only showed itself in his unwonted silence, and an over-anxiety, which his steed seemed to feel in common with himself, to go rapidly ahead. Thus the day passed, and the wayfarers at its close had made a progress of some twenty miles from sun to sun. The same precautions marked their encampment this night as the last, and they rose in better spirits the next morning, the dawn of which was very bright and pleasant, and encouraging. A similar journey of twenty miles brought them to the place of bivouac as the sun went down; and they prepared as usual for their securities and supper. They found themselves on the edge of a very dense forest of pines and scrubby oaks, a portion of which was swallowed up in a deep bay—so called in the dialect of the country—a swamp-bottom, the growth of which consisted of mingled cypresses and bay-trees, with tupola, gum, and dense thickets of low stunted shrubbery, cane grass, and dwarf willows, which filled up every interval between the trees, and to the eye most effectually barred out every human intruder. This bay was chosen as the background for the camping party. Their wagon was wheeled into an area on a gently rising ground in front, under a pleasant shade of oaks and hickories, with a lonely pine rising loftily in occasional spots among them. Here the horses were taken out, and James Grayling prepared to kindle up a fire; but, looking for his axe, it was unaccountably missing, and after a fruitless search of half an hour, the party came to the conclusion that it had been left on the spot where they slept last night. This was a disaster, and, while they meditated in what manner to repair it, a negro boy appeared in sight, passing along the road at their feet, and driving before him a small herd of cattle. From him they learned that they were only a mile or two from a farmstead where an axe might be borrowed; and James, leaping on his horse, rode forward in the hope to obtain one. He found no difficulty in his quest; and, having obtained it from the farmer, who was also a tavern-keeper, he casually asked if Major Spencer had not stayed with him the night before. He was somewhat surprised when told that he had not.

"There was one man stayed with me last night," said the farmer, "but he didn't call himself a major, and didn't much look like one."

"He rode a fine sorrel horse,—tall, bright colour, with white fore foot, didn't he?" asked James.

"No, that he didn't! He rode a powerful black, coal black, and not a bit of white about him."

"That was the Scotchman! But I wonder the major didn't stop with you. He must have rode on. Isn't there another house near you, below?"

"Not one. There's ne'er a house either above or below for a matter of fifteen miles. I'm the only man in all that distance that's living on this road; and I don't think your friend could have gone below, as I should have seen him pass. I've been all day out there in that field before your eyes, clearing up the brush."

CHAPTER III

Somewhat wondering that the major should have turned aside from the track, though without attaching to it any importance at that particular moment, James Grayling took up the borrowed axe and hurried back to the encampment, where the toil of cutting an extra supply of light-wood to meet the exigencies of the ensuing night, sufficiently exercised his mind as well as his body, to prevent him from meditating upon the seeming strangeness of the circumstance. But when he sat down to his supper over the fire that he had kindled, his fancies crowded thickly upon him, and he felt a confused doubt and suspicion that something was to happen, he knew not what. His conjectures and apprehensions were without form, though not altogether void; and he felt a strange sickness and a sinking at the heart which was very unusual with him. He had, in short, that lowness of spirits, that cloudy apprehensiveness of soul which takes the form of presentiment, and makes us look out for danger even when the skies are without a cloud, and the breeze is laden, equally and only, with balm and music. His moodiness found no sympathy among his companions. Joel Sparkman was in the best of humours, and his mother was so cheery and happy, that when the thoughtful boy went off into the woods to watch, he could hear her at every moment breaking out into little catches of a country ditty, which the gloomy events of the late war had not yet obliterated from her memory.

"It's very strange!" soliloquized the youth, as he wandered along the edges of the dense bay or swamp-bottom, which we have passingly referred to,—"it's very strange what troubles me so! I feel almost frightened, and yet I know I'm not to be frightened easily, and I don't see anything in the woods to frighten me. It's strange the major didn't come along this road! Maybe he took another higher up that leads by a different settlement. I wish I had asked the man at the house if there's such another road. I reckon there must be, however, for where could the major have gone?"

The unphilosophical mind of James Grayling did not, in his farther meditations, carry him much beyond this starting point; and with its continual recurrence in soliloquy, he proceeded to traverse the margin of the bay, until he came to its junction with, and termination at, the high-road. The youth turned into this, and, involuntarily departing from it a moment after, soon found himself on the opposite side of the bay thicket. He wandered on and on, as he himself described it, without any power to restrain himself. He knew not how far he went; but, instead of maintaining his watch for two hours only, he was gone more than four; and, at length, a sense of weariness which overpowered him all of a sudden, caused him to seat himself at the foot of a tree, and snatch a few moments of rest. He denied that he slept in this time. He insisted to the last moment of his life that sleep never visited his eyelids that night,—that he was conscious of fatigue and exhaustion, but not drowsiness,—and that this fatigue was so numbing as to be painful, and effectually kept him from any sleep. While he sat thus beneath the tree, with a body weak and nerveless, but a mind excited, he knew not how or why, to the most acute degree of expectation and attention, he heard his name called by the well-known voice of his friend, Major Spencer. The voice called him three times,—"James Grayling!—James!—James Grayling!" before he could muster strength enough to answer. It was not courage he wanted,—of that he was positive, for he felt sure, as he said, that something had gone wrong, and he was never more ready to fight in his life than at that moment, could he have commanded the physical capacity; but his throat seemed dry to suffocation,—his lips effectually sealed up as if with wax, and when he did answer, the sounds seemed as fine and soft as the whisper of some child just born.

"Oh! major, is it you?"

Such, he thinks, were the very words he made use of in reply; and the answer that he received was instantaneous, though the voice came from some little distance in the bay, and his own voice he did not hear. He only knows what he meant to say. The answer was to this effect.

"It is, James!—It is your own friend, Lionel Spencer, that speaks to you; do not be alarmed when you see me! I have been shockingly murdered!"

James asserts that he tried to tell him that he would not be frightened, but his own voice was still a whisper, which he himself could scarcely hear. A moment after he had spoken, he heard something like a sudden breeze that rustled through the bay bushes at his feet, and his eyes were closed without his effort, and indeed in spite of himself. When he opened them, he saw Major Spencer standing at the edge of the bay, about twenty steps from him. Though he stood in the shade of a thicket, and there was no light in the heavens save that of the stars, he was yet enabled to distinguish perfectly, and with great ease, every lineament of his friend's face.

He looked very pale, and his garments were covered with blood; and James said that he strove very much to rise from the place where he sat and approach him;—"for, in truth," said the lad, "so far from feeling any fear, I felt nothing but fury in my heart; but I could not move a limb. My feet were fastened to the ground; my hands to my sides; and I could only bend forward and gasp. I felt as if I should have died with vexation that I could not rise; but a power which I could not resist, made me motionless, and almost speechless. I could only say, 'Murdered!'—and that one word I believe I must have repeated a dozen times.

" 'Yes, murdered!—murdered by the Scotchman who slept with us at your fire the night before last. James, I look to you to have the murderer brought to justice! James!—do you hear me, James?'

"These," said James, "I think were the very words, or near about the very words, that I heard; and I tried to ask the major to tell me how it was, and how I could do what he required; but I didn't hear myself speak, though it would appear that he did, for almost immediately after I had tried to speak what I wished to say, he answered me just as if I had said it. He told me that the Scotchman had waylaid, killed, and hidden him in that very bay; that his murderer had gone to Charleston; and that if I made haste to town, I would find him in the Falmouth packet, which was then lying in the harbour and ready to sail for England. He farther said that everything depended on my making haste,—that I must reach town by tomorrow night if I wanted to be in season, and go right on board the vessel and charge the criminal with the deed. 'Do not be afraid,' said he, when he had finished; 'be afraid of nothing, James, for God will help and strengthen you to the end.' When I heard all I burst into a flood of tears, and then I felt strong. I felt that I could talk, or fight, or do almost anything; and I jumped up to my feet, and was just about to run down to where the major stood, but, with the first step which I made forward, he was gone. I stopped and looked all around me, but I could see nothing; and the bay was just as black as midnight. But I went down to it, and tried to press in where I thought the major had been standing; but I couldn't get far, the brush and bay bushes were so close and thick. I was now bold and strong enough, and I called out, loud enough to be heard half a mile. I didn't exactly know what I called for, or what I wanted to learn, or I have forgotten. But I heard nothing more. Then I remembered the camp, and began to fear that something might have happened to mother and uncle, for I now felt, what I had not thought of before, that I had gone too far round the bay to be of much assistance, or indeed, to be in time for any, had they been suddenly attacked. Besides, I could not think how long I had been gone; but it seemed very late. The stars were shining their brightest, and the thin white clouds of morning were beginning to rise and run towards the west. Well, I bethought me of my course,—for I was a little bewildered and doubtful where I was; but, after a little thinking, I took the back track, and soon got a glimpse of the camp-fire, which was nearly burnt down; and by this I reckoned I was gone considerably longer than my two hours. When I got back into the camp, I looked under the wagon, and found uncle in a sweet sleep, and though my heart was full almost to bursting with what I had heard, and the cruel sight I had seen, yet I wouldn't waken him; and I beat about and mended the fire, and watched, and waited, until near daylight, when mother called to me out of the wagon, and asked who it was. This wakened my uncle, and then I up and told all that had happened, for if it had been to save my life, I couldn't have kept it in much longer. But though mother said it was very strange, Uncle Sparkman considered that I had been only dreaming; but he couldn't persuade me of it; and when I told him I intended to be off at daylight, just as the major had told me to do, and ride my best all the way to Charleston, he laughed, and said I was a fool. But I felt that I was no fool, and I was solemn certain that I hadn't been dreaming; and though both mother and he tried their hardest to make me put off going, yet I made up my mind to do it, and they had to give up. For, wouldn't I have been a pretty sort of a friend to the major, if, after what he told me, I could have stayed behind, and gone on only at a wagon-pace to look after the murderer! I dont think if I had done so that I should ever have been able to look a white man in the face again. Soon as the peep of day, I was on horseback. Mother was mighty sad, and begged me not to go, but Uncle Sparkman was mighty sulky, and kept calling me fool upon fool, until I was almost angry enough to forget that we were of blood kin. But all his talking did not stop me, and I reckon I was five miles on my way before he had his team in traces for a start. I rode as briskly as I could get on without hurting my nag. I had a smart ride of more than forty miles before me, and the road was very heavy. But it was a good two hours from sunset when I got into town, and the first question I asked of the people I met was, to show me where the ships were kept. When I got to the wharf they showed me the Falmouth packet, where she lay in the stream, ready to sail as soon as the wind should favour."

CHAPTER IV

James Grayling, with the same eager impatience which he has been suffered to describe in his own language, had already hired a boat to go on board the British packet, when he remembered that he had neglected all those means, legal and otherwise, by which alone his purpose might be properly effected. He did not know much about legal process, but he had common sense enough, the moment that he began to reflect on the subject, to know that some such process was necessary. This conviction produced another difficulty; he knew not in which quarter to turn for counsel and assistance; but here the boatman who saw his bewilderment, and knew by his dialect and dress that he was a back-countryman, came to his relief, and from him he got directions where to find the merchants with whom his uncle, Sparkman, had done business in former years. To them he went, and without circumlocution, told the whole story of his ghostly visitation. Even as a dream, which those gentlemen at once conjectured it to be, the story of James Grayling was equally clear and curious; and his intense warmth and the entire absorption, which the subject had effected, of his mind and soul, was such that they judged it not improper, at least to carry out the search of the vessel which he contemplated. It would certainly, they thought, be a curious coincidence—believing James to be a veracious youth—if the Scotchman should be found on board. But another test of his narrative was proposed by one of the firm. It so happened that the business agents of Major Spencer, who was well known in Charleston, kept their office but a few rods distant from their own; and to them all parties at once proceeded. But here the story of James was encountered by a circumstance that made somewhat against it. These gentlemen produced a letter from Major Spencer, intimating the utter impossibility of his coming to town for the space of a month, and expressing his regret that he should be unable to avail himself of the opportunity of the foreign vessel, of whose arrival in Charleston, and proposed time of departure, they had themselves advised him. They read the letter aloud to James and their brother merchants, and with difficulty suppressed their smiles at the gravity with which the former related and insisted upon the particulars of his vision.

"He has changed his mind," returned the impetuous youth; "he was on his way down, I tell you,—a hundred miles on his way,—when he camped with us. I know him well, I tell you, and talked with him myself half the night."

"At least," remarked the gentlemen who had gone with James, "it can do no harm to look into the business. We can procure a warrant for searching the vessel after this man, Macnab; and should he be found on board the packet, it will be a sufficient circumstance to justify the magistrates in detaining him, until we can ascertain where Major Spencer really is."

The measure was accordingly adopted, and it was nearly sunset before the warant was procured, and the proper officer in readiness. The impatience of a spirit so eager and so devoted as James Grayling, under these delays, may be imagined; and when in the boat, and on his way to the packet where the criminal was to be sought, his blood became so excited that it was with much ado he could be kept in his seat. His quick, eager action continually disturbed the trim of the boat, and one of his mercantile friends, who had accompanied him, with that interest in the affair which curiosity alone inspired, was under constant apprehension lest he would plunge overboard in his impatient desire to shorten the space which lay between. The same impatience enabled the youth, though never on shipboard before, to grasp the rope which had been flung at their approach, and to mount her sides with catlike agility. Without waiting to declare himself or his purpose, he ran from one side of the deck to the other, greedily staring, to the surprise of the officers, passengers, and seamen, in the faces of all of them, and surveying them with an almost offensive scrutiny. He turned away from the search with disappointment. There was no face like that of the suspected man among them. By this time, his friend, the merchant, with the sheriff's officer, had entered the vessel, and were in conference with the captain. Grayling drew nigh in time to hear the latter affirm that there was no man of the name of Macnab, as stated in the warrant, among his passengers or crew.

"He is—he must be!" exclaimed the impetuous youth. "The major never lied in his life, and couldn't lie after he was dead. Macnab is here—he is a Scotchman—"

The captain interrupted him—

"We have, young gentleman, several Scotchmen on board, and one of them is named Macleod—"

"Let me see him—which is he?" demanded the youth.

By this time, the passengers and a goodly portion of the crew were collected about the little party. The captain turned his eyes upon the group, and asked,

"Where is Mr. Macleod?"

"He is gone below—he is sick!" replied one of the passengers.

"That's he! That must be the man!" exclaimed the youth. "I'll lay my life that's no other than Macnab. He's only taken a false name."

It was now remembered by one of the passengers, and remarked, that Macleod had expressed himself as unwell, but a few moments before, and had gone below even while the boat was rapidly approaching the vessel. At this statement, the captain led the way into the cabin, closely followed by James Grayling and the rest.

"Mr. Macleod," he said, with a voice somewhat elevated, as he approached the berth of that person, "you are wanted on deck for a few moments."

"I am really too unwell, captain," replied a feeble voice from behind the curtain of the berth.

"It will be necessary," was the reply of the captain. "There is a warrant from the authorities of the town, to look after a fugitive from justice."

Macleod had already begun a second speech declaring his feebleness, when the fearless youth, Grayling, bounded before the captain and tore away, with a single grasp of his hand, the curtain which concealed the suspected man from their sight.

"It is he!" was the instant exclamation of the youth, as he beheld him. "It is he—Macnab, the Scotchman—the man that murdered Major Spencer!"

Macnab,—for it was he,—was deadly pale. He trembled like an aspen. His eyes were dilated with more than mortal apprehension, and his lips were perfectly livid. Still, he found strength to speak, and to deny the accusation. He knew nothing of the youth before him—nothing of Major Spencer—his name was Macleod, and he had never called himself by any other. He denied, but with great incoherence, everything which was urged against him.

"You must get up, Mr. Macleod," said the captain; "the circumstances are very much against you. You must go with the officer!"

"Will you give me up to my enemies?" demanded the culprit. "You are a countryman—a Briton. I have fought for the king, our master, against these rebels, and for this they seek my life. Do not deliver me into their bloody hands!"

"Liar!" exclaimed James Grayling—"Didn't you tell us at our own camp-fire that you were with us? that you were at Gates's defeat, and Ninety-Six?"

"But I didn't tell you," said the Scotchman, with a grin, "which side I was on!"

"Ha! remember that!" said the sheriff's officer. "He denied, just a moment ago, that he knew this young man at all; now he confesses that he did see and camp with him."

The Scotchman was aghast at the strong point which, in his inadvertence, he had made against himself; and his efforts to excuse himself, stammering and contradictory, served only to involve him more deeply in the meshes of his difficulty. Still he continued his urgent appeals to the captain of the vessel, and his fellow-passengers, as citizens of the same country, subjects to the same monarch, to protect him from those who equally hated and would destroy them all. In order to move their national prejudices in his behalf, he boasted of the immense injury which he had done, as a tory, to the rebel cause; and still insisted that the murder was only a pretext of the youth before him, by which to gain possession of his person, and wreak upon him the revenge which his own fierce performances during the war had naturally enough provoked. One or two of the passengers, indeed, joined with him in entreating the captain to set the accusers adrift and make sail at once; but the stout Englishman who was in command, rejected instantly the unworthy counsel. Besides, he was better aware of the dangers which would follow any such rash proceeding. Fort Moultrie, on Sullivan's Island, had been already refitted and prepared for an enemy; and he was lying, at that moment, under the formidable range of grinning teeth, which would have opened upon him, at the first movement, from the jaws of Castle Pinckney.

"No, gentlemen," said he, "you mistake your man. God forbid that I should give shelter to a murderer, though he were from my own parish."

"But I am no murderer," said the Scotchman.

"You look cursedly like one, however," was the reply of the captain. "Sheriff, take your prisoner."

The base creature threw himself at the feet of the Englishman, and clung, with piteous entreaties, to his knees. The latter shook him off, and turned away in disgust.

"Steward," he cried, "bring up this man's luggage."

He was obeyed. The luggage was brought up from the cabin and delivered to the sheriff's officer, by whom it was examined in the presence of all, and an inventory made of its contents. It consisted of a small new trunk, which, it afterwards appeared, he had bought in Charleston, soon after his arrival. This contained a few changes of raiment, twenty-six guineas in money, a gold watch, not in repair, and two pistols which he had shown while at Joel Sparkman's camp fire; but, with this difference, that the stock of one was broken off short just above the grasp, and the butt was entirely gone. It was not found among his chattels. A careful examination of the articles in his trunk did not result in anything calculated to strengthen the charge of his criminality; but there was not a single person present who did not feel as morally certain of his guilt as if the jury had already declared the fact. That night he slept—if he slept at all—in the common jail of the city.

CHAPTER V

His accuser, the warm-hearted and resolute James Grayling, did not sleep. The excitement, arising from mingling and contradictory emotions,—sorrow for his brave young commander's fate, and the natural exultation of a generous spirit at the consciousness of having performed, with signal success, an arduous and painful task combined to drive all pleasant slumbers from his eyes; and with the dawn he was again up and stirring, with his mind still full of the awful business in which he had been engaged. We do not care to pursue his course in the ordinary walks of the city, nor account for his employments during the few days which ensued, until, in consequence of a legal examination into the circumstances which anticipated the regular work of the sessions, the extreme excitement of the young accuser had been renewed. Macnab or Macleod,—and it is possible that both names were fictitious,—as soon as he recovered from his first terrors, sought the aid of an attorney—one of those acute, small chopping lawyers, to be found in almost every community, who are willing to serve with equal zeal the sinner and the saint, provided that they can pay with equal liberality. The prisoner was brought before the court under *habeas corpus,* and several grounds submitted by his counsel with the view to obtaining his discharge. It became necessary to ascertain, among the first duties of the state, whether Major Spencer, the alleged victim, was really dead. Until it could be established that a man should be imprisoned, tried, and punished for a crime, it was first necessary to show that a crime had been committed, and the attorney made himself exceedingly merry with the ghost story of young Grayling. In those days, however, the ancient Superstition was not so feeble as she has subsequently become. The venerable judge was one of those good men who had a decent respect for the faith and opinions of his ancestors; and though he certainly would not have consented to the hanging of Macleod under the sort of testimony which had been adduced, he yet saw enough, in all the circumstances, to justify his present detention. In the meantime, efforts were to be made, to ascertain the whereabouts of Major Spencer; though, were he even missing,—so the counsel for Macleod contended,—his death could be by no means assumed in consequence. To this the judge shook his head doubtfully. "'Fore God!" said he, "I would not have you to be too sure of that." He was an Irishman, and proceeded after the fashion of his country. The reader will therefore *bear* with his *bull.* "A man may properly be hung for murdering another, though the murdered man be not dead; ay, before God, even though he be actually unhurt and uninjured, while the murderer is swinging by the neck for the bloody deed!"

The judge,—who it must be understood was a real existence, and who had no small reputation in his day in the south,—proceeded to establish the correctness of his opinions by authorities and argument, with all of which, doubtlessly, the bar were exceedingly delighted; but, to provide them in this place would only be to interfere with our own progress. James Grayling, however, was not satisfied to wait the slow processes which were suggested for coming at the truth. Even the wisdom of the judge was lost upon him, possibly, for the simple reason that he did not comprehend it. But the ridicule of the culprit's lawyer stung him to the quick, and he muttered to himself, more than once, a determination "to lick the life out of that impudent chap's leather." But this was not his only resolve. There was one which he proceeded to put into instant execution, and that was to seek the body of his murdered friend in the spot where he fancied it might be found—namely, the dark and dismal bay where the spectre had made its appearance to his eyes.

The suggestion was approved—though he did not need this to prompt his resolution—by his mother and uncle, Sparkman. The latter determined to be his companion, and he was farther accompanied by the sheriff's officer who had arrested the suspected felon. Before daylight, on the morning after the examination before the judge had taken place, and when Macleod had been remanded to prison, James Grayling started on his journey. His fiery zeal received additional force at every added moment of delay, and his eager spurring brought him at an early hour after noon, to the neighbourhood of the spot through which his search was to be made. When his companions and himself drew nigh, they were all at a loss in which direction first to proceed. The bay was one of those massed forests, whose wall of thorns, vines, and close tenacious shrubs, seemed to defy invasion. To the eye of the townsman it was so forbidding that he pronounced it absolutely impenetrable. But James was not to be baffled. He led them round it, taking the very course which he had pursued the night when the revelation was made him; he showed them the very tree at whose foot he had sunk when the supernatural torpor—as he himself esteemed it—began to fall upon him; he then pointed out the spot, some twenty steps distant, at which the spectre made his appearance. To this spot they then proceeded in a body, and essayed an entrance, but were so discouraged by the difficulties at the outset that all, James not excepted, concluded that neither the murderer nor his victim could possibly have found entrance there.

But, lo! a marvel! Such it seemed, at the first blush, to all the party. While they stood confounded and indecisive, undetermined in which way to move, a sudden flight of wings was heard, even from the centre of the bay, at a little distance above the spot where they had striven for entrance. They looked up, and beheld about fifty buzzards—those notorious domestic vultures of the south—ascending from the interior of the bay, and perching along upon the branches of the loftier trees by which it was overhung. Even were the character of these birds less known, the particular business in which they had just then been engaged, was betrayed by huge gobbets of flesh which some of them had borne aloft in their flight, and still continued to rend with beak and bill, as they tottered upon the branches where they stood. A piercing scream issued from the lips of James Grayling as he beheld this sight, and strove to scare the offensive birds from their repast.

"The poor major! the poor major!" was the involuntary and agonized exclamation of the youth. "Did I ever think he would come to this!"

The search, thus guided and encouraged, was pressed with renewed diligence and spirit; and, at length, an opening was found through which it was evident that a body of considerable size had but recently gone. The branches were broken from the small shrub trees, and the undergrowth trodden into the earth. They followed this path, and, as is the case commonly with waste tracts of this description, the density of the growth diminished sensibly at every step they took, till they reached a little pond, which, though circumscribed in area, and full of cypresses, yet proved to be singularly deep. Indeed, it was an alligator-hole, where, in all probability, a numerous tribe of these reptiles had their dwelling. Here, on the edge of the pond, they discovered the object which had drawn the keen-sighted vultures to their feast, in the body of a horse, which James Grayling at once identified as that of Major Spencer. The carcass of the animal was already very much torn and lacerated. The eyes were plucked out, and the animal completely disembowelled. Yet, on examination, it was not difficult to discover the manner of his death. This had been effected by fire-arms. Two bullets had passed through his skull, just above the eyes, either of which must have been fatal. The murderer had led the horse to the spot, and committed the cruel deed where his body was found. The search was now continued for that of the owner, but for some time it proved ineffectual. At length, the keen eyes of James Grayling detected, amidst a heap of moss and green sedge that rested beside an overthrown tree, whose branches jutted into the pond, a whitish, but discoloured object, that did not seem native to the place. Bestriding the fallen tree, he was enabled to reach this object, which with a burst of grief, he announced to the distant party was the hand and arm of his unfortunate friend, the wristband of the shirt being the conspicuous object which had first caught his eye. Grasping this, he drew the corse, which had been thrust beneath the branches of the tree, to the surface; and with the assistance of his uncle, it was finally brought to the dry land. Here it underwent a careful examination. The head was very much disfigured; the skull was fractured in several places by repeated blows of some hard instrument, inflicted chiefly from behind. A closer inspection revealed a bullet-hole in the abdomen, the first wound, in all probability, which the unfortunate gentleman received, and by which he was, perhaps, tumbled from his horse. The blows on the head would seem to have been unnecessary, unless the murder—whose proceedings appeared to have been singularly deliberate,—was resolved upon making "assurance doubly sure." But, as if the watchful Providence had meant that nothing should be left doubtful which might tend to the complete conviction of the criminal, the constable stumbled upon the butt of the broken pistol which had been found in Macleod's trunk. This he picked up on the edge of the pond in which the corse had been discovered, and while James Grayling and his uncle, Sparkman, were engaged in drawing it from the water. The place where the fragment was discovered at once denoted the pistol as the instrument by which the final blows were inflicted. "'Fore God," said the judge to the criminal, as these proofs were submitted on the trial, "you may be a very innocent man after all, as, by my faith, I do think there have been many murderers before you; but you ought, nevertheless, to be hung as an example to all other persons who suffer such strong proofs of guilt to follow their innocent misdoings. Gentlemen of the jury, if this person, Macleod or Macnab, didn't murder Major Spencer, either you or I did; and you must now decide which of us it is! I say, gentlemen of the jury, either you, or I, or the prisoner at the bar, murdered this man; and if you have any doubts which of us it was, it is but justice and mercy that you should give the prisoner the benefit of your doubts; and so find your verdict. But, before God, should you find him not guilty, Mr. Attorney there can scarcely do anything wiser than to put us all upon trial for the deed."

The jury, it may be scarcely necessary to add, perhaps under certain becoming fears of an alternative such as his honour had suggested, brought in a verdict of "Guilty," without leaving the panel; and Macnab, *alias* Macleod, was hung at White Point, Charleston, somewhere about the year 178—.

"And here," said my grandmother, devoutly, "you behold a proof of God's watchfulness to see that murderer should not be hidden, and that the murderer should not escape. You see that he sent the spirit of the murdered man—since, by no other mode could the truth have been revealed—to declare the crime, and to discover the criminal. But for that ghost, Macnab would have got off to Scotland, and probably have been living to this very day on the money that he took from the person of the poor major."

As the old lady finished the ghost story, which, by the way, she had been tempted to relate for the fiftieth time in order to combat my father's ridicule of such superstitions, the latter took up the thread of the narrative.

"Now, my son," said he, "as you have heard all that your grandmother has to say on this subject, I will proceed to show you what you have to believe, and what not. It is true that Macnab murdered Spencer in the manner related; that James Grayling made the discovery and prosecuted the pursuit; found the body and brought the felon to justice; that Macnab suffered death, and confessed the crime; alleging that he was moved to do so, as well because of the money that he suspected Spencer to have in his possession, as because of the hate which he felt for a man who had been particularly bold and active in cutting up a party of Scotch loyalists to which he belonged, on the borders of North Carolina. But the appearance of the spectre was nothing more than the work of a quick imagination, added to a shrewd and correct judgment. James Grayling saw no ghost, in fact, but such as was in his own mind; and, though the instance was one of a most remarkable character, one of singular combination, and well depending circumstances, still, I think it is to be accounted for by natural and very simple laws."

The old lady was indignant.

"And how could he see the ghost just on the edge of the same bay where the murder had been committed, and where the body of the murdered man even then was lying?"

My father did not directly answer the demand, but proceeded thus:—

"James Grayling, as we know, mother, was a very ardent, impetuous, sagacious man. He had the sanguine, the race-horse temperament. He was generous, always prompt and ready, and one who never went backward. What he did, he did quickly, boldly, and thoroughly! He never shrank from trouble of any kind; nay, he rejoiced in the constant encounter with difficulty and trial; and his was the temper which commands and enthrals mankind. He felt deeply and intensely whatever occupied his mind, and when he parted from his friend he brooded over little else than their past communion and the great distance by which they were to be separated. The dull travelling wagon-gait at which he himself was compelled to go, was a source of annoyance to him; and he became sullen, all the day, after the departure of his friend. When, on the evening of the next day, he came to the house where it was natural to expect that Major Spencer would have slept the night before, and he learned the fact that no one stopped there but the Scotchman, Macnab, we see that he was struck with the circumstance. He mutters it over to himself, "Strange, where the major could have gone!" His mind then naturally reverts to the character of the Scotchman; to the opinions and suspicions which had been already expressed of him by his uncle, and felt by himself. They had all, previously, come to the full conviction that Macnab was, and had always been, a tory, in spite of his protestations. His mind next, and very naturally, reverted to the insecurity of the highways; the general dangers of travelling at that period; the frequency of crime, and the number of desperate men who were everywhere to be met with. The very employment in which he was then engaged, in scouting the woods for the protection of the camp, was calculated to bring such reflections to his mind. If these precautions were considered necessary for the safety of persons so poor, so wanting in those possessions which might prompt cupidity to crime, how much more necessary were precautions in the case of a wealthy gentleman like Major Spencer! He then remembered the conversation with the major at the camp-fire, when they fancied that the Scotchman was sleeping. How natural to think then, that he was all the while awake; and, if awake, he must have heard him speak of the wealth of his companion. True, the major, with more prudence than himself, denied that he had any money about him, more than would bear his expenses to the city; but such an assurance was natural enough to the lips of a traveller who knew the dangers of the country. That the man, Macnab, was not a person to be trusted, was the equal impression of Joel Sparkman and his nephew from the first. The probabilities were strong that he would rob and perhaps murder, if he might hope to do so with impunity; and as the youth made the circuit of the bay in the darkness and solemn stillness of the night, its gloomy depths and mournful shadows, naturally gave rise to such reflections as would be equally active in the mind of a youth, and of one somewhat familiar with the arts and usages of strife. He would see that the spot was just the one in which a practised partisan would delight to set an ambush for an unwary foe. There ran the public road, with a little sweep, around two-thirds of the extent of its dense and impenetrable thickets. The ambush could lie concealed, and at ten steps command the bosom of its victim. Here, then, you perceive that the mind of James Grayling, stimulated by an active and sagacious judgment, had by gradual and reasonable stages come to these conclusions: that Major Spencer was an object to tempt a robber; that the country was full of robbers; that Macnab was one of them; that this was the very spot in which a deed of blood could be most easily committed, and most easily concealed; and, one important fact, that gave strength and coherence to the whole, that Major Spencer had not reached a well-known point of destination, while Macnab had.

"With these thoughts, thus closely linked together, the youth forgets the limits of his watch and his circuit. This fact, alone, proves how active his imagination had become. It leads him forward, brooding more and more on the subject, until, in the very exhaustion of his body, he sinks down beneath a tree. He sinks down and falls asleep; and in his sleep, what before was plausible conjecture, becomes fact, and the creative properties of his imagination give form and vitality to all his fancies. These forms are bold, broad, and deeply coloured, in due proportion with the degree of force which they receive from probability. Here, he sees the image of his friend; but, you will remark—and this should almost conclusively satisfy any mind that all that he sees is the work of his imagination,—that, though Spencer tells him that he is murdered, and by Macnab, he does not tell him how, in what manner, or with what weapons. Though he sees him pale and ghostlike, he does not see, nor can he say, where his wounds are! He sees his pale features distinctly, and his garments are bloody. Now, had he seen the spectre in the true appearances of death, as he was subsequently found, he would not have been able to discern his features, which were battered, according to his own account, almost out of all shape of humanity, and covered with mud; while his clothes would have streamed with mud and water, rather than with blood."

"Ah!" exclaimed the old lady, my grandmother, "it's hard to make you believe anything that you don't see; you are like Saint Thomas in the Scriptures; but how do you propose to account for his knowing that the Scotchman was on board the Falmouth packet? Answer to that!"

"That is not a more difficult matter than any of the rest. You forget that in the dialogue which took place between James and Major Spencer at the camp, the latter told him that he was about to take passage for Europe in the Falmouth packet, which then lay in Charleston harbour, and was about to sail. Macnab heard all that."

"True enough, and likely enough," returned the old lady; "but, though you show that it was Major Spencer's intention to go to Europe in the Falmouth packet, that will not show that it was also the intention of the murderer."

"Yet what more probable, and how natural for James Grayling to imagine such a thing! In the first place he knew that Macnab was a Briton; he felt convinced that he was a tory; and the inference was immediate, that such a person would scarcely have remained long in a country where such characters laboured under so much odium, disfranchisement, and constant danger from popular tumults. The fact that Macnab was compelled to disguise his true sentiments, and affect those of the people against whom he fought so vindictively, shows what was his sense of the danger which he incurred. Now, it is not unlikely that Macnab was quite as well aware that the Falmouth packet was in Charleston, and about to sail, as Major Spencer. No doubt he was pursuing the same journey, with the same object, and had he not murdered Spencer, they would, very likely, have been fellow-passengers together to Europe. But, whether he knew the fact before or not, he probably heard it stated by Spencer while he seemed to be sleeping; and, even supposing that he did not then know, it was enough that he found this to be the fact on reaching the city. It was an after-thought to fly to Europe with his ill gotten spoils; and whatever may have appeared a politic course to the criminal, would be a probable conjecture in the mind of him by whom he was suspected. The whole story is one of strong probabilities which happened to be verified; and if proving anything, proves only that which we know—that James Grayling was a man of remarkably sagacious judgment, and quick, daring imagination. This quality of imagination, by the way, when possessed very strongly in connexion with shrewd common sense and well-balanced general faculties, makes that particular kind of intellect which, because of its promptness and powers of creation and combination, we call genius. It is genius only which can make ghosts, and James Grayling was a genius. He never, my son, saw any other ghosts than those of his own making!"

I heard my father with great patience to the end, though he seemed very tedious. He had taken a great deal of pains to destroy one of my greatest sources of pleasure. I need not add that I continued to believe in the ghost, and, with my grandmother, to reject the philosophy. It was more easy to believe the one than to comprehend the other.

Edgar Allan Poe

1809 – 1849

In part the victim of unfortunate circumstances and in part a prey to his own highly wrought sensibilities, Edgar Allan Poe lived a brief, troubled life. Born in Boston in 1809, the son of traveling theatrical parents, he was adopted after his mother's death by John Allan of Richmond, Virginia, in 1811. After attending school in England for two years (1818–1820) and in Richmond for another six years (1820–1825), he enrolled at the University of Virginia in 1826. His foster father, however, withdrew him from the university at the end of the first term, presumably because of the debts Poe had accumulated. He served two years in the army as an enlisted man and then entered the U.S. Military Academy at West Point, but deliberately secured his dismissal at the end of a year. Having been disowned by Allan, he was obliged to earn his own living; to do so he turned to writing as a profession, settling in Baltimore in 1831. In 1833, his "MS Found in a Bottle" won a prize, but, more important, it brought him recognition that resulted in his getting an editorial position on the *Southern Literary Messenger,* of which he became editor in 1835. In spite of the nationwide attention his reviews, poems, and stories drew to the magazine, he was dismissed as editor in 1837 because of his unstable temperament. Thereafter, while continuing to publish stories and poems, he held a succession of editorial positions on magazines in Philadelphia and New York, but the remaining years of his life were marred by his acute struggle with poverty, personal grief over the loss of his young wife, his alcoholism, and his frenetic affairs with other women. He died on October 7, 1849, four days after being picked up unconscious on the streets of Baltimore.

Until recent decades critics assigned Poe an important place in the development of the short story primarily because of the technical brilliance of his stories and because of his contribution to the critical theory of the form. He is important for both of these reasons, for no writer before or during his day constructed stories so economically or tightly unified as his, and no one else had developed as complete an aesthetic of the story as the one published in his 1842 review of Hawthorne's *Twice-Told Tales.* These earlier critics, however, took Poe's statements rather literally and pegged him simply as a master of the "story-of-effect," one designed solely to produce a powerful impact on the reader's mind rather than to make a significant commentary on the human predicament. It is now clear—or some recent critics think it is—that many of Poe's stories are psycho-moral allegories or symbolic dramas which explore the hidden depths of the human psyche. Viewed in this light, the issue in "The Cask of Amontillado" may be less that of how Montresor commits a "perfect" murder than what the crime has done to his mind.

The Cask of Amontillado

The thousand injuries of Fortunato I had borne as I best could, but when he ventured upon insult I vowed revenge. You, who so well know the nature of my soul, will not suppose, however, that I gave utterance to a threat. *At length* I would be avenged; this was a point definitely settled—but the very definitiveness with which it was resolved precluded the idea of risk. I must not only punish, but punish with impunity. A wrong is unredressed when retribution overtakes its redresser. It is equally unredressed when the avenger fails to make himself felt as such to him who has done the wrong.

It must be understood that neither by word nor deed had I given Fortunato cause to doubt my good will. I continued, as was my wont, to smile in his face, and he did not perceive that my smile *now* was at the thought of his immolation.

He had a weak point—this Fortunato—although in other regards he was a man to be respected and even feared. He prided himself on his

"The Cask of Amontillado" by Edgar Allan Poe, in *The Complete Works of Edgar Allan Poe,* ed. by James Harrison (Thomas Crowell, 1902).

connoisseurship in wine. Few Italians have the true virtuoso spirit. For the most part their enthusiasm is adopted to suit the time and opportunity, to practice imposture upon the British and Austrian *millionnaires*. In painting and gemmary, Fortunato, like his countrymen, was a quack, but in the matter of old wines he was sincere. In this respect I did not differ from him materially;—I was skillful in the Italian vintages myself, and bought largely whenever I could.

It was about dusk, one evening during the supreme madness of the carnival season, that I encountered my friend. He accosted me with excessive warmth, for he had been drinking much. The man wore motley. He had on a tight-fitting parti-striped dress, and his head was surmounted by the conical cap and bells. I was so pleased to see him that I thought I should never have done wringing his hand.

I said to him—"My dear Fortunato, you are luckily met. How remarkably well you are looking to-day. But I have received a pipe of what passes for Amontillado, and I have my doubts."

"How?" said he. "Amontillado? A pipe? Impossible! And in the middle of the carnival!"

"I have my doubts," I replied; "and I was silly enough to pay the full Amontillado price without consulting you in the matter. You were not to be found, and I was fearful of losing a bargain."

"Amontillado!"

"I have my doubts."

"Amontillado!"

"And I must satisfy them."

"Amontillado!"

"As you are engaged, I am on my way to Luchresi. If any one has a critical turn, it is he. He will tell me—"

"Luchresi cannot tell Amontillado from Sherry."

"And yet some fools will have it that his taste is a match for your own."

"Come, let us go."

"Whither?"

"To your vaults."

"My friend, no; I will not impose upon your good nature. I perceive you have an engagement. Luchresi—"

"I have no engagement;—come."

"My friend, no. It is not the engagement, but the severe cold with which I perceive you are afflicted. The vaults are insufferably damp. They are encrusted with nitre."

"Let us go, nevertheless. The cold is merely nothing. Amontillado! You have been imposed upon. And as for Luchresi, he cannot distinguish Sherry from Amontillado."

Thus speaking, Fortunato possessed himself of my arm; and putting on a mask of black silk and drawing a *roquelaire* closely about my person, I suffered him to hurry me to my palazzo.

There were no attendants at home; they had absconded to make merry in honour of the time. I had told them that I should not return until the morning, and had given them explicit orders not to stir from the house. These orders were sufficient, I well knew, to insure their immediate disappearance, one and all, as soon as my back was turned.

I took from their sconces two flambeaux, and giving one to Fortunato, bowed him through several suites of rooms to the archway that led into the vaults. I passed down a long and winding staircase, requesting him to be cautious as he followed. We came at length to the foot of the descent, and stood together on the damp ground of the catacombs of the Montresors.

The gait of my friend was unsteady, and the bells upon his cap jingled as he strode.

"The pipe?" said he.

"It is farther on," said I; "but observe the white web-work which gleams from these cavern walls."

He turned towards me, and looked into my eyes with two filmy orbs that distilled the rheum of intoxication.

"Nitre?" he asked, at length.

"Nitre," I replied. "How long have you had that cough?"

"Ugh! ugh! ugh!—ugh! ugh! ugh!—ugh! ugh! ugh!—ugh! ugh! ugh!—ugh! ugh! ugh!"

My poor friend found it impossible to reply for many minutes.

"It is nothing," he said, at last.

"Come," I said, with decision, "we will go back; your health is precious. You are rich, respected, admired, beloved; you are happy, as once I was. You are a man to be missed. For me it is no matter. We will go back; you will be ill, and I cannot be responsible. Besides, there is Luchresi—"

"Enough," he said; "the cough is a mere nothing; it will not kill me. I shall not die of a cough."

"True—true," I replied; "and, indeed, I had no intention of alarming you unnecessarily—but you should use all proper caution. A draught of this Medoc will defend us from the damps."

Here I knocked off the neck of a bottle which I drew from a long row of its fellows that lay upon the mould.

"Drink," I said, presenting him the wine.

He raised it to his lips with a leer. He paused and nodded to me familiarly, while his bells jingled.

"I drink," he said, "to the buried that repose around us."

"And I to your long life."

He again took my arm, and we proceeded.

"These vaults," he said, "are extensive."

"The Montresors," I replied, "were a great and numerous family."

"I forget your arms."

"A huge human foot d'or, in a field azure; the foot crushes a serpent rampant whose fangs are imbedded in the heel."

"And the motto?"

"Nemo me impune lacessit."

"Good!" he said.

The wine sparkled in his eyes and the bells jingled. My own fancy grew warm with the Medoc. We had passed through long walls of piled skeletons, with casks and puncheons intermingling, into the inmost recesses of the catacombs. I paused again, and this time I made bold to seize Fortunato by an arm above the elbow.

"The nitre!" I said; "see, it increases. It hangs like moss upon the vaults. We are below the river's bed. The drops of moisture trickle among the bones. Come, we will go back ere it is too late. Your cough—"

"It is nothing," he said; "let us go on. But first, another draught of the Medoc."

I broke and reached him a flagon of De Grâve. He emptied it at a breath. His eyes flashed with a fierce light. He laughed and threw the bottle upward with a gesticulation I did not understand.

I looked at him in surprise. He repeated the movement—a grotesque one.

"You do not comprehend?" he said.

"Not I," I replied.

"Then you are not of the brotherhood."

"How?"

"You are not of the masons."

"Yes, yes," I said; "yes, yes."

"You? Impossible! A mason?"

"A mason," I replied.

"A sign," he said, "a sign."

"It is this," I answered, producing from beneath the folds of my *roquelaire* a trowel.

"You jest," he exclaimed, recoiling a few paces. "But let us proceed to the Amontillado."

"Be it so," I said, replacing the tool beneath the cloak and again offering him my arm. He leaned upon it heavily. We continued our route in search of the Amontillado. We passed through a range of low arches, descended, passed on, and descending again, arrived at a deep crypt, in which the foulness of the air caused our flambeaux rather to glow than flame.

At the most remote end of the crypt there appeared another less spacious. Its walls had been lined with human remains, piled to the vault overhead, in the fashion of the great catacombs of Paris. Three sides of this interior crypt were still ornamented in this manner. From the fourth the bones had been thrown down, and lay promiscuously upon the earth, forming at one point a mound of some size. Within the wall thus exposed by the displacing of the bones, we perceived a still interior crypt or recess, in depth about four feet, in width three, in height six or seven. It seemed to have been constructed for no especial use within itself, but formed merely the interval between two of the colossal supports of the roof of the catacombs, and was backed by one of their circumscribing walls of solid granite.

It was in vain that Fortunato, uplifting his dull torch, endeavoured to pry into the depth of the recess. Its termination the feeble light did not enable us to see.

"Proceed," I said; "herein is the Amontillado. As for Luchresi—"

"He is an ignoramus," interrupted my friend, as he stepped unsteadily forward, while I followed immediately at his heels. In an instant he had reached the extremity of the niche, and finding his progress arrested by the rock, stood stupidly bewildered. A moment more and I had fettered him to the granite. In its surface were two iron staples, distant from each other about two feet, horizontally. From one of these depended a short chain, from the other a padlock. Throwing the links about his waist, it was but the work of a few seconds to secure it. He was too much astounded to resist. Withdrawing the key, I stepped back from the recess.

"Pass your hand," I said, "over the wall; you cannot help feeling the nitre. Indeed, it is *very* damp. Once more let me *implore* you to return. No? Then I must positively leave you. But I must first render you all the little attentions in my power."

"The Amontillado!" ejaculated my friend, not yet recovered from his astonishment.

"True," I replied; "the Amontillado."

As I said these words I busied myself among the pile of bones of which I have before spoken. Throwing them aside, I soon uncovered a quantity of building stone and mortar. With these materials and with the aid of my trowel, I began vigorously to wall up the entrance of the niche.

I had scarcely laid the first tier of the masonry when I discovered that the intoxication of Fortunato had in a great measure worn off. The earliest indication I had of this was a low moaning cry from the depth of the recess. It was *not* the cry of a drunken man. There was then a long and obstinate silence. I laid the second tier, and the third, and the fourth; and then I heard the furious vibrations of the chain. The noise lasted for several minutes, during which, that I might hearken to it with the more satisfaction, I ceased my labours and sat down upon the bones. When at last the clanking subsided, I resumed the trowel, and finished without interruption the fifth, the sixth, and the seventh tier. The wall was now nearly upon a level with my breast. I again paused, and holding the flambeaux over the mason-work, threw a few feeble rays upon the figure within.

A succession of loud and shrill screams, bursting suddenly from the throat of the chained form, seemed to thrust me violently back. For a brief moment I hesitated, I trembled. Unsheathing my rapier, I began to grope with it about the recess; but the thought of an instant reassured me. I placed my hand upon the solid fabric of the catacombs, and felt satisfied. I reapproached the wall. I replied to the yells of him who clamoured. I re-echoed, I aided, I surpassed them in volume and in strength. I did this, and the clamourer grew still.

It was now midnight, and my task was drawing to a close. I had completed the eighth, the ninth and the tenth tier. I had finished a portion of the last and the eleventh; there remained but a single stone to be fitted and plastered in. I struggled with its weight; I placed it partially in its destined position. But now there came from out the niche a low laugh that erected the hairs upon my head. It was succeeded by a sad voice, which I had difficulty in recognizing as that of the noble Fortunato. The voice said—

"Ha! ha! ha!—he! he! he!—a very good joke, indeed—an excellent jest. We will have many a rich laugh about it at the palazzo—he! he! he!—over our wine—he! he! he!"

"The Amontillado!" I said.

"He! he! he!—he! he! he!—yes, the Amontillado. But is it not getting late? Will not they be awaiting us at the palazzo, the Lady Fortunato and the rest? Let us be gone."

"Yes," I said, "let us be gone."

"For the love of God, Montresor!"

"Yes," I said, "for the love of God!"

But to these words I hearkened in vain for a reply. I grew impatient. I called aloud—

"Fortunato!"

No answer. I called again—

"Fortunato!"

No answer still. I thrust a torch through the remaining aperture and let it fall within. There came forth in return only a jingling of the bells. My heart grew sick—on account of the dampness of the catacombs. I hastened to make an end of my labour. I forced the last stone into its position; I plastered it up. Against the new masonry I re-erected the old rampart of bones. For the half of a century no mortal has disturbed them. *In pace requiescat!*

Johnson Jones Hooper

1815 – 1862

Johnson Jones Hooper, the sixth and youngest child of Charlotte De Berniere and Archibald Maclaine Hooper, was born in Wilmington, North Carolina, on June 9, 1815. While still a lad, young "Jonce" absorbed the basic principles of sound journalism by serving as a printer's devil in his father's newspaper, the *Cape Fear Recorder.* The family's straitened circumstances, however, kept him from following his older brothers to college; instead, at age twenty he moved to Chambers County, Alabama, to join his eldest brother, George, a practicing lawyer in the tiny frontier community of La Fayette. Within a few years Hooper had "read" enough law under his brother's supervision to be admitted to the bar; in 1839 he was appointed notary public and, the next year, census taker in the adjoining Tallapoosa County. Two years after completing the census he became editor, at age twenty-seven, of the *East Alabamian,* a weekly newspaper in La Fayette. Hooper's writings in that obscure little weekly soon brought him to the attention of William T. Porter, editor of the widely popular sportsmen's weekly, the *New York Spirit of the Times.* Beginning in 1843 with "Taking the Census in Alabama by a Chicken Man of 1840," Porter jubilantly reprinted Hooper's sketches in the *Spirit* as fast as they appeared, praising them repeatedly as each of those dealing with the outrageous adventures of Hooper's heroic rascal, Simon Suggs, succeeded one another. Through Porter's influence Hooper thus gained national recognition first in the *Spirit* and then redoubled fame when his first collection, *Some Adventures of Captain Simon Suggs, Late of the Tallapoosa Volunteers; Together with "Taking the Census," and Other Alabama Sketches, By a Country Editor,* was published by Carey and Hart of Philadelphia in 1845.

Hooper had several other books published during his lifetime while also editing newspapers elsewhere in Alabama and serving, shortly before his death, as secretary of the Provisional Congress of the Confederate States of America. But his literary fame, like Longstreet's, is firmly based on the humorous sketches in a single book and their influence on the works of other humorists. From the 1840s to the present, at least fifteen editions recounting the exploits of the notorious "Captain," who is at his best in outfoxing the fraudulent revivalist preachers at a frontier camp meeting, have delighted successive generations of readers and stimulated the creative instincts of many writers. Like an avatar, Suggs is reborn in Faulkner's Flem Snopes.

The Captain Attends a Camp-Meeting

Captain Suggs found himself as poor at the conclusion of the Creek war, as he had been at its commencement. Although no "arbitrary," "despotic," "corrupt," and "unprincipled" judge had fined him a thousand dollars for his proclamation of martial law at Fort Suggs, or the enforcement of its rules in the case of Mrs. Haycock; yet somehow—the thing is alike inexplicable to him and to us—the money which he had contrived, by various shifts to obtain, melted away and was gone forever. To a man like the Captain, of intense domestic affections, this state of destitution was most distressing. "He could stand it himself—didn't care a d—n for it, no way," he observed, "but the old woman and the children; *that* bothered him!"

As he sat one day, ruminating upon the unpleasant condition of his "financial concerns," Mrs. Suggs informed him that "the sugar and coffee was nigh about out," and that there were not "a dozen j'ints and middlins, *all put together,* in the smoke-house." Suggs bounced up on the

Johnson Jones Hooper, "The Captain Attends a Camp-Meeting."

instant, exclaiming, "D—n it! *somebody* must suffer!" But whether this remark was intended to convey the idea that he and his family were about to experience the want of the necessaries of life; or that some other, and as yet unknown individual should "suffer" to prevent that prospective exigency, must be left to the commentators, if perchance any of that ingenious class of persons should hereafter see proper to write notes for this history. It is enough for us that we give all the facts in this connection, so that ignorance of the subsequent conduct of Captain Suggs may not lead to an erroneous judgment in respect to his words.

Having uttered the exclamation we have repeated—and perhaps, hurriedly walked once or twice across the room—Captain Suggs drew on his famous old green-blanket overcoat, and ordered his horse, and within five minutes was on his way to a camp-meeting, then in full blast on Sandy creek, twenty miles distant, where he hoped to find amusement, at least. When he arrived there, he found the hollow square of the encampment filled with people, listening to the mid-day sermon and its dozen accompanying "exhortations." A half-dozen preachers were dispensing the word; the one in the pulpit, a meek-faced old man, of great simplicity and benevolence. His voice was weak and cracked, notwithstanding which, however, he contrived to make himself heard occasionally, above the din of the exhorting, the singing, and the shouting which were going on around him. The rest were walking to and fro, (engaged in the other exercises we have indicated), among the "mourners"—a host of whom occupied the seat set apart for their especial use—or made personal appeals to the mere spectators. The excitement was intense. Men and women rolled about on the ground, or lay sobbing or shouting in promiscuous heaps. More than all, the negroes sang and screamed and prayed. Several, under the influence of what is technically called "the jerks," were plunging and pitching about with convulsive energy. The great object of all seemed to be, to see who could make the greatest noise—

"And each—for madness ruled the hour—
Would try his own expressive power."

"Bless my poor old soul!" screamed the preacher in the pulpit; "ef yonder aint a squad in that corner that we aint got one outen yet! It'll never do"—raising his voice—"you must come outen that! Brother Fant, fetch up that youngster in the blue coat! I see the Lord's a-workin' upon him! Fetch him along—glory—yes!—hold to him!"

"Keep the thing warm!" roared a sensual seeming man, of stout mould and florid countenance, who was exhorting among a bevy of young women, upon whom he was lavishing caresses. "Keep the thing warm, breethring!—come to the Lord, honey!" he added, as he vigorously hugged one of the damsels he sought to save.

"Oh, I've got him!" said another in exulting tones, as he led up a gawky youth among the mourners—"I've got him—he tried to git off, but—ha! Lord!"—shaking his head as much as to say, it took a smart fellow to escape him—"ha! Lord!"—and he wiped the perspiration from his face with one hand, and with the other, patted his neophyte on the shoulder—"he couldn't do it! No! Then he tried to argy wi' me—but bless the Lord!—he couldn't do that nother! Ha! Lord! I tuk him, fust in the Old Testament—bless the Lord!—and I argyed him all thro' Kings—then I throwed him into Proverbs!—and from that, here we had it up and down, kleer down to the New Testament, and then I begun to see it work him!—then we got into Matthy, and from Matthy right straight along to Acts; and *thar* I throwed him! Y-e-s L-o-r-d!"—assuming the nasal twang and high pitch which are, in some parts, considered the perfection of rhetorical art—"Y-e-s L-o-r-d! and h-e-r-e he is! Now g-i-t down thar," addressing the subject, "and s-e-e ef the L-o-r-d won't do somethin' f-o-r you!" Having thus deposited his charge among the mourners, he started out, summarily to convert another soul!

"Gl-o-*ree!*" yelled a huge, greasy negro woman, as in a fit of the jerks, she threw herself convulsively from her feet, and fell "like a thousand of brick," across a diminutive old man in a little round hat, who was squeaking consolation to one of the mourners.

"Good Lord, have mercy!" ejaculated the little man earnestly and unaffectedly, as he strove to crawl from under the sable mass which was crushing him.

In another part of the square a dozen old women were singing. They were in a state of absolute ecstasy, as their shrill pipes gave forth,

"I rode on the sky,
Quite ondestified I,
And the moon it was under my feet!"

Near these last, stood a delicate woman in that hysterical condition in which the nerves are incontrollable, and which is vulgarly—and almost blasphemously—termed the "holy laugh." A hideous grin distorted her mouth, and was accompanied with a maniac's chuckle; while every muscle and nerve of her face twitched and jerked in horrible spasms.*

*The reader is requested to bear in mind, that the scenes described in this chapter are not *now* to be witnessed. Eight or ten years ago, all classes of population of the Creek country were very different from what they now are. Of course, no disrespect is intended to any denomination of Christians. We believe that camp-meetings are not peculiar to any church, though most usual in the Methodist—a denomination whose respectability in Alabama is attested by the fact, that *very many* of its worthy clergymen and lay members, hold honourable and profitable offices in the gift of the state legislature; of which, indeed, almost a controlling portion are themselves Methodists. [Author's note]

Amid all this confusion and excitement Suggs stood unmoved. He viewed the whole affair as a grand deception—a sort of "opposition line" running against his own, and looked on with a sort of professional jealousy. Sometimes he would mutter running comments upon what passed before him.

"Well now," said he, as he observed the full-faced brother who was "officiating" among the women, "that ere feller takes *my* eye!—thar he's been this half-hour, a-figurin amongst them galls, and's never said the fust word to nobody else. Wonder what's the reason these here preachers never hugs up the old, ugly women? Never seed one do it in my life—the sperrit never moves 'em that way! It's nater tho'; and the women, *they* never flocks round one o' the old dried-up breethring—bet two to one old splinter-legs thar,"—nodding at one of the ministers—"won't git a chance to say turkey to a good-looking gall to-day! Well! who blames 'em? Nater will be nater, all the world over; and I judge ef I was a preacher, I should save the purtiest souls fust, myself!"

While the Captain was in the middle of this conversation with himself, he caught the attention of the preacher in the pulpit, who inferring from an indescribable something about his appearance that he was a person of some consequence, immediately determined to add him at once to the church if it could be done; and to that end began a vigorous, direct personal attack.

"Breethring," he exclaimed, "I see yonder a man that's a sinner; I *know* he's a sinner! Thar he stands," pointing at Simon, "a missubble old crittur, with his head a-blossomin for the grave! A few more short years, and d-o-w-n he'll go to perdition, lessen the Lord have mer-cy on him! Come up here, you old hoary-headed sinner, a-n-d git down upon your knees, a-n-d put up your cry for the Lord to snatch you from the bottomless pit! You're ripe for the devil—you're b-o-u-n-d for hell, and the Lord only knows what'll become of you!"

"D—n it," thought Suggs, "*ef* I only had you down in the krick swamp for a minit or so, *I'd* show you who's *old! I'd* alter your tune *mighty* sudden, you sassy, 'saitful old rascal!" But he judiciously held his tongue and gave no utterance to the thought.

The attention of many having been directed to the Captain by the preacher's remarks, he was soon surrounded by numerous well-meaning, and doubtless very pious persons, each one of whom seemed bent on the application of his own particular recipe for the salvation of souls. For a long time the Captain stood silent, or answered the incessant stream of exhortation only with a sneer; but at length, his countenance began to give token of inward emotion. First his eye-lids twitched—then his upper lip quivered—next a transparent drop formed on one of his eye-lashes, and a similar one on the tip of his nose—and, at last, a sudden bursting of air from nose and mouth, told that Captain Suggs was overpowered by by his emotions. At the moment of the explosion, he made a feint as if to rush from the crowd, but he was in experienced hands, who well knew that the battle was more than half won.

"Hold to him!" said one—"it's a-workin in him as strong as a Dick horse!"

"Pour it into him," said another, "it'll all come right directly!"

"That's the way I love to see 'em do," observed a third; "when you begin to draw the water from their eyes, taint gwine to be long afore you'll have 'em on their knees!"

And so they clung to the Captain manfully, and half dragged, half led him to the mourner's bench; by which he threw himself down, altogether unmanned, and bathed in tears. Great was the rejoicing of the brethren, as they sang, shouted, and prayed around him—for by this time it had come to be generally known that the "convicted" old man was Captain Simon Suggs, the very "chief of sinners" in all that region.

The Captain remained grovelling in the dust during the usual time, and gave vent to even more than the requisite number of sobs, and groans, and heart-piercing cries. At length, when the proper time had arrived, he bounced up, and with a face radiant with joy, commenced a series of vaultings and tumblings, which "laid in the shade" all previous performances of the sort at that camp-meeting. The brethren were in ecstasies at this demonstrative evidence of completion of the work; and whenever Suggs shouted "Gloree!" at the top of his lungs, every one of them shouted it back, until the woods rang with echoes.

The effervescence having partially subsided, Suggs was put upon his pins to relate his experience, which he did somewhat in this style—first brushing the tear-drops from his eyes, and giving the end of his nose a preparatory wring with his fingers, to free it of the superabundant moisture:

"Friends," he said, "it don't take long to curry a short horse, accordin' to the old sayin', and I'll give you the pertícklers of the way I was 'brought to a knowledge' "—here the Captain wiped his eyes, brushed the tip of his nose and snuffled a little—"in less'n no time."

"Praise the Lord!" ejaculated a bystander.

"You see I come here full o' romancin' and devilment, and jist to make game of all the purceedins. Well, sure enough, I done so for some time, and was a-thinkin how I should play some trick—"

"Dear soul alive! *don't* he talk sweet!" cried an old lady in black silk—"Whar's John Dobbs? You Sukey!" screaming at a negro woman on the other side of the square—"ef you don't hunt up your mass John in a minute, and have him here to listen to this 'sperience. I'll tuck you up when I git home and give you a hundred and fifty lashes, madam!—see ef I don't! Blessed Lord!"—referring again to the Captain's relation—"aint it a *precious* 'scource!"

"I was jist a-thinkin' how I should play some trick to turn it all into redecule, when they began to come round me and talk. Long at fust I didn't mind it, but arter a little that brother"—pointing to the reverend gentlemen who had so successfully carried the unbeliever through the Old and New Testaments, and who Simon was convinced was the "big dog of the tanyard"—"that brother spoke a word that struck me kleen to the heart, and run all over me, like fire in dry grass—"

"*I–I–I* can bring 'em!" cried the preacher alluded to, in a tone of exultation—"Lord thou knows ef thy servant can't stir 'em up, nobody else needn't try—but the glory aint mine! I'm a poor worrum of the dust," he added, with ill-managed affectation.

"And so from that I felt somethin' a-pullin' me inside—"

"Grace! grace! nothin' but grace!" exclaimed one; meaning that "grace" had been operating in the Captain's gastric region.

"And then," continued Suggs, "I wanted to git off, but they hilt me, and bimeby I felt so missuble, I had to go yonder"—pointing to the mourners' seat—"and when I lay down thar it got wuss and wuss, and 'peared like somethin' was a-mashin' down on my back—"

"That was his load o' sin," said one of the brethren—"never mind, it'll tumble off presently; see ef it don't!" and he shook his head professionally and knowingly.

"And it kept a-gittin heavier and heavier, ontwell it looked like it might be a four year old steer, or a big pine log, or somethin' of that sort—"

"Glory to my soul," shouted Mrs. Dobbs, "it's the sweetest talk I *ever* hearn! You Sukey! aint you got John yit? never mind, my lady, *I*'ll settle wi' you!" Sukey quailed before the finger which her mistress shook at her.

"And arter awhile," Suggs went on, " 'peared like I fell into a trance, like, and I seed—"

"Now we'll git the good on it!" cried one of the sanctified.

"And I seed the biggest, longest, rip-roarenest, blackest, scaliest—" Captain Suggs paused, wiped his brow, and ejaculated "Ah, L-o-r-d!" so as to give full time for curiosity to become impatience to know what he saw.

"*Sarpent!* warn't it?" asked one of the preachers.

"No, not a sarpent," replied Suggs, blowing his nose.

"Do tell us *what* it war, soul alive!—whar *is* John?" said Mrs. Dobbs.

"Allegator!" said the Captain.

"Alligator!" replied every woman present, and screamed for very life.

Mrs. Dobbs' nerves were so shaken by the announcement, that after repeating the horrible word, she screamed to Sukey, "you Sukey, I say, you Su-u-ke-e-y! ef you let John come a-nigh this way, whar the dreadful alliga—shaw! what am I thinkin' 'bout? 'Twarn't nothin' but a vishin!"

"Well," said the Captain in continuation, "the allegator kept a-comin' and a-comin' to'ards me, with his great long jaws a-gapin' open like a ten-foot pair o' tailors' shears—"

"Oh! oh! oh! Lord! gracious above!" cried the women.

"SATAN!" was the laconic ejaculation of the oldest preacher present, who thus informed the congregation that it was the devil which had attacked Suggs in the shape of an alligator.

"And then I concluded the jig was up, 'thout I could block his game some way; for I seed his idee was to snap off my head—"

The women screamed again.

"So I fixed myself jist like I was purfectly willin' for him to take my head, and rather he'd do it as not"—here the women shuddered perceptibly—"and so I hilt my head straight out"—the Captain illustrated by elongating his neck—"and when he come up and was a gwine to *shet down* on it, I jist pitched in a big rock which choked him to death, and that minit I felt the weight slide off, and I had the best feelins—sorter like you'll have from *good* sperrits—any body ever had!"

"Didn't I *tell* you so? Didn't I *tell* you so?" asked the brother who had predicted the off-tumbling of the load of sin. "Ha, Lord! fool *who!* I've been *all* along thar!—yes, *all along thar!* and I know every inch of the way jist as good as I do the road home!"—and then he turned round and round, and looked at all, to receive a silent tribute to his superior penetration.

Captain Suggs was now the "lion of the day." Nobody could pray so well, or exhort so movingly, as "brother Suggs." Nor did his natural modesty prevent the proper performance of appropriate exercises. With the reverend Bela Bugg (him to whom, under providence, he ascribed his conversion), he was a most especial favourite. They walked, sang, and prayed together for hours.

"Come, come up; thar's room for all!" cried brother Bugg, in his evening exhortation. "Come to the 'seat,' and ef you won't pray yourselves, let *me* pray for you!"

"Yes!" said Simon, by way of assisting his friend; "it's a game that all can win at! Ante up! ante up, boys—friends I mean—don't back out!"

"Thar aint a sinner here," said Bugg, "no matter ef his soul's black as a nigger, but what thar's room for him!"

"No matter what sort of a hand you've got," added Simon in the fulness of his benevolence; "take stock! Here am *I*, the wickedest and blindest of sinners—has spent my whole life in the sarvice of the devil—has now come in on *narry pair* and won a *pile!*" and the Captain's face beamed with holy pleasure.

"D-o-n-'t be afeard!" cried the preacher; "come along! the meanest won't be turned away! humble yourselves and come!"

"No!" said Simon, still indulging in his favourite style of metaphor; "the bluff game aint played here! No runnin' of a body off! Every body holds four aces, and when you bet, you win!"

And thus the Captain continued, until the services were concluded, to assist in adding to the number at the mourners' seat; and up to the hour of retiring, he exhibited such enthusiasm in the cause, that he was unanimously voted to be the most efficient addition the church had made during that meeting.

The next morning, when the preacher of the day first entered the pulpit, he announced that "brother Simon Suggs," mourning over his past iniquities, and desirous of going to work in the cause as speedily as possible, would take up a collection to found a church in his own neighbourhood, at which he hoped to make himself useful as soon as he could prepare himself for the ministry, which the preacher didn't doubt, would be in a very few weeks, as brother Suggs was "a man of mighty good judge*ment,* and of *a great discorse.*" The funds were to be collected by "brother Suggs," and held in trust by brother Bela Bugg, who was the financial officer of the circuit, until some arrangement could be made to build a suitable house.

"Yes, breethring," said the Captain, rising to his feet; "I want to start a little 'sociation close to me, and I want you all to help. I'm mighty poor myself, as poor as any of you—don't leave breethring"—observing that several of the well-to-do were about to go off—"don't leave; ef you aint able to afford any thing, jist give us your blessin' and it'll be all the same!"

This insinuation did the business, and the sensitive individuals reseated themselves.

"It's mighty little of this world's goods I've got," resumed Suggs, pulling off his hat and holding it before him; "but I'll bury *that* in the cause any how," and he deposited his last five-dollar bill in the hat.

There was a murmur of approbation at the Captain's liberality throughout the assembly.

Suggs now commenced collecting, and very prudently attacked first the gentlemen who had shown a disposition to escape. These, to exculpate themselves from anything like poverty, contributed handsomely.

"Look here, breethring," said the Captain, displaying the banknotes thus received, "brother Snooks has drapt a five wi' me, and Brother Snodgrass a ten! In course 'taint expected that you *that aint as well off as them,* will give *as much;* let every one give *accordin'* to ther means."

This was another chain-shot that raked as it went!

"Who so low" as not to be able to contribute as much as Snooks and Snodgrass?

"Here's all the *small* money I've got about me," said a burly old fellow, ostentatiously handing to Suggs, over the heads of a half dozen, a ten dollar bill.

"That's what I call maganimus!" exclaimed the Captain; "that's the way *every* rich man ought to do!"

These examples were followed, more or less closely, by almost all present, for Simon had excited the pride of purse of the congregation, and a very handsome sum was collected in a very short time.

The reverend Mr. Bugg, as soon as he observed that our hero had obtained all that was to be had at that time, went to him and inquired what amount had been collected. The Captain replied that it was still uncounted, but that it couldn't be much under a hundred.

"Well, brother Suggs, you'd better count it and turn it over to me now. I'm goin' to leave presently."

"No!" said Suggs—"can't do it!"

"Why?—what's the matter?" inquired Bugg.

"It's got to be *prayed over,* fust!" said Simon, a heavenly smile illuminating his whole face.

"Well," replied Bugg, "less go one side and do it!"

"No!" said Simon, solemnly.

Mr. Bugg gave a look of inquiry.

"You see that krick swamp?" asked Suggs—"I'm gwine down in *thar,* and I'm gwine to lay this money down *so*"—showing how he would place it on the ground—"and I'm gwine to git on these here knees"—slapping the right one—"and I'm *n-e-v-e-r* gwine to quit the grit ontwell I feel it's got the blessin'! And nobody aint got to be thar but me!"

Mr. Bugg greatly admired the Captain's fervent piety, and bidding him God-speed, turned off.

Captain Suggs "struck for" the swamp sure enough, where his horse was already hitched. "Ef them fellers aint done to a cracklin," he muttered to himself as he mounted, "*I*'ll never bet on two pair agin! They're peart at the snap game, theyselves; but they're badly lewed this hitch! Well! Live and let live is a good old motter, and it's my sentiments adzactly!" And giving the spur to his horse, off he cantered.

Thomas Bangs Thorpe

1815 – 1878

Thomas Bangs Thorpe was born at Westfield, Connecticut, in 1815.[1] His family moved to New York City in 1818 where he completed his secondary schooling in the late 1820s. Having decided to become an artist, Thorpe began to study painting in 1830 in the studio of John Quidor, and within three years he achieved competence enough to exhibit his work at the National Academy of Design and to win praise from other artists. Financially unable to continue further study in Europe, in 1834 he enrolled at Wesleyan University in Middletown, Connecticut.

At Wesleyan Thorpe formed important friendships with several young men from Mississippi and Louisiana who urged him to visit the South to improve both his health and his chances for continuing his artistic career. Without earning his degree, in 1837 he traveled south, eventually settling in St. Francisville, where he spent several happy and productive years with his young bride, Maria Hinckley.

With portrait painting as his primary source of income, in 1839 Thorpe began publishing sketches and tales in William T. Porter's *Spirit of the Times.* His first effort, "Tom Owens, the Bee Hunter," was widely reprinted, and Porter encouraged him to write more tales and sketches based on his knowledge of the Southwestern frontier. During the next four years he published more than thirty such pieces in the *Spirit,* including his most famous tale, "The Big Bear of Arkansas" (1841). In order to support a growing family, he turned to newspaper editing in 1844, serving first as co-editor of a Vidalia, Louisiana,

[1]This headnote is indebted to Milton Rickles, *Thomas Bangs Thorpe: Humorist of the Old Southwest* (Baton Rouge: The Louisiana State University Press, 1962) to which the reader is referred for fuller details on Thorpe's life and career.

newspaper. He established and worked on various Southern newspapers for the next ten years, but returned to New York with his family in 1854 and wrote for magazines. When New Orleans fell to the Union forces in 1862, he came back to serve for nearly two years as a colonel in the occupation forces of the city. Returning once again to New York, he spent his last years there engaged in further literary activities and working in the New City Customs House. He died in 1878.

In addition to his three books on the Mexican War and a novel, *The Master's House: A Tale of Southern Life* (1854), Thorpe published two collections of sketches and tales: *The Mysteries of the Backwoods; or Sketches of the Southwest* (1846); and *The Hive of the Bee Hunter, A Repository of Sketches, Including Peculiar American Character, Scenery, and Rural Sports* (1854).

"The Big Bear of Arkansas" is a masterly example of the Old Southwest yarnspinners' art. It is a "framework" story, or a story within a story, the frame serving to stage the inside story and to introduce the narrator, Jim Doggett. Gradually, with questions and comments from his auditors, Doggett launches into his story of an "unhuntable" bear. The vivid contrast between the literary language of the frame and the racy vernacular speech of the narrator heightens the characterization of Doggett and at the same time contributes to the comic effect of the story.

The Big Bear of Arkansas

A steamboat on the Mississippi, frequently, in making her regular trips, carries between places varying from one to two thousand miles apart; and, as these boats advertise to land passengers and freight at "all intermediate landings," the heterogeneous character of the passengers of one of these up-country boats can scarcely be imagined by one who has never seen it with his own eyes.

"The Big Bear of Arkansas" by Thomas Bangs Thorpe first appeared in *The Spirit of the Times*, 1841.

Starting from New Orleans in one of these boats, you will find yourself associated with men from every State in the Union, and from every portion of the globe; and a man of observation need not lack for amusement or instruction in such a crowd, if he will take the trouble to read the great book of character so favorably opened before him.

Here may be seen, jostling together, the wealthy Southern planter and the pedler of tin-ware from New England—the Northern merchant and the Southern jockey—a venerable bishop, and a desperate gambler—the land speculator, and the honest farmer—professional men of all creeds and characters—Wolvereens, Suckers, Hoosiers, Buckeyes, and Corncrackers, beside a "plentiful sprinkling" of the half-horse and half-alligator species of men, who are peculiar to "old Mississippi," and who appear to gain a livelihood by simply going up and down the river. In the pursuit of pleasure or business, I have frequently found myself in such a crowd.

On one occasion, when in New Orleans, I had occasion to take a trip of a few miles up the Mississippi, and I hurried on board the well-known "high-pressure-and-beat-every-thing" steamboat "Invincible," just as the last note of the last bell was sounding; and when the confusion and bustle that is natural to a boat's getting under way had subsided, I discovered that I was associated in as heterogeneous a crowd as was ever got together. As my trip was to be of a few hours' duration only, I made no endeavors to become acquainted with my fellow-passengers, most of whom would be together many days. Instead of this, I took out of my pocket the "latest paper," and more critically than usual examined its contents; my fellow-passengers, at the same time, disposed of themselves in little groups.

While I was thus busily employed in reading, and my companions were more busily still employed, in discussing such subjects as suited their humors best, we were most unexpectedly startled by a loud Indian whoop, uttered in the "social hall," that part of the cabin fitted off for a bar; then was to be heard a loud crowing, which would not have continued to interest us—such sounds being quite common in that *place of spirits*—had not the hero of these windy accomplishments stuck his head into the cabin, and hallooed out, "Hurra for the Big B*e*ar of Arkansaw!"

Then might be heard a confused hum of voices, unintelligible, save in such broken sentences as "horse," "screamer," "lightning is slow," &c.

As might have been expected, this continued interruption, attracted the attention of every one in the cabin; all conversation ceased, and in the midst of this surprise, the "Big B*e*ar" walked into the cabin, took a chair, put his feet on the stove, and looking back over his shoulder, passed the general and familiar salute—"Strangers, how are you?"

He then expressed himself as much at home as if he had been at "the Forks of Cypress," and "prehaps a little more so."

Some of the company at this familiarity looked a little angry, and some astonished; but in a moment every face was wreathed in a smile. There was something about the intruder that won the heart on sight. He appeared to be a man enjoying perfect health and contentment; his eyes were as sparkling as diamonds, and good-natured to simplicity. Then his perfect confidence in himself was irresistibly droll.

"Prehaps," said he, "gentlemen," running on without a person interrupting, "prehaps you have been to New Orleans often; I never made *the first visit before,* and I don't intend to make another in a crow's life. I am thrown away in that ar place, and useless, that ar a fact. Some of the gentlemen thar called me *green*—well, prehaps I am, said I, *but I arn't so at home;* and if I ain't off my trail much, the heads of them perlite chaps themselves wern't much the hardest; for according to my notion, they were *real know-nothings,* green as a pumpkin-vine—couldn't, in farming, I'll bet, raise a crop of turnips; and as for shooting, they'd miss a barn if the door was swinging, and that, too, with the best rifle in the country. And then they talked to me 'bout hunting, and laughed at my calling the principal game in Arkansaw poker, and high-low-jack.

" 'Prehaps,' said I, 'you prefer checkers and roulette;' at this they laughed harder than ever, and asked me if I lived in the woods, and didn't know what *game* was?

"At this, I rather think *I* laughed.

" 'Yes,' I roared, and says, I, 'Strangers, if you'd ask me *how we got our meat* in Arkansaw, I'd a told you at once, and given you a list of varmints that would make a caravan, beginning with the bar, and ending off with the cat; that's *meat* though, not game.

"Game, indeed,—that's what city folks call it; and with them it means chippen-birds and shite-pokes; may be such trash live in my diggins, but I arn't noticed them yet: a bird anyway is too trifling. I never did shoot at but one, and I'd never forgiven myself for that, had it weighed less than forty pounds. I wouldn't draw a rifle on anything less heavy than that; and when I meet with another wild turkey of the same size, I will drap him."

"A wild turkey weighing forty pounds!" exclaimed twenty voices in the cabin at once.

"Yes, strangers, and wasn't it a whopper? You see, the thing was so fat that it couldn't fly far; and when he fell out of the tree, after I shot him, on striking the ground he bust open behind, and the way the pound gobs of tallow rolled out of the opening was perfectly beautiful."

"Where did all that happen?" asked a cynical-looking Hoosier.

"Happen! happened in Arkansaw: where else could it have happened, but in the creation State, the finishing-up country—a State where the *sile* runs down to the centre of the 'arth, and government gives you a title to every inch of it? Then its airs—just breathe them, and they will make you snort like a horse. It's a State without a fault, it is."

"Excepting mosquitoes," cried the Hoosier.

"Well, stranger, except them; for it ar a fact that they are rather *enormous,* and do push themselves in somewhat troublesome. But, stranger, they never stick twice in the same place; and give them a fair chance for a few months, and you will get as much above noticing them as an alligator. They can't hurt my feelings, for they lay under the skin; and I never knew but one case of injury resulting from them, and that was to a Yankee: and they take worse to foreigners, any how, than they do to natives. But the way they used that fellow up! first they punched him until he swelled up and busted; then he sup-per-a-ted, as the doctor called it, until he was as raw as beef; then, owing to the warm weather, he tuck the ager, and finally he tuck a steamboat and left the country. He was the only man that ever tuck mosquitoes at heart that I knowd of.

"But mosquitoes is natur, and I never find fault with her. If they ar large, Arkansaw is large, her varmints ar large, her trees ar large, her rivers ar large, and a small mosquito would be of no more use in Arkansaw than preaching in a cane-brake."

This knock-down argument in favor of big mosquitoes used the Hoosier up, and the logician started on a new track, to explain how numerous bear were in his "diggins," where he represented them to be "about as plenty as blackberries, and a little plentifuller."

Upon the utterance of this assertion, a timid little man near me inquired, if the bear in Arkansaw ever attacked the settlers in numbers.

"No," said our hero, warming with the subject, "no, stranger, for you see it ain't the natur of b*e*ar to go in droves; but the way they squander about in pairs and single ones is edifying.

"And then the way I hunt them—the old black rascals know the crack of my gun as well as they know a pig's squealing. They grow thin in our parts, it frightens them so, and they do take the noise dreadfully, poor things. That gun of mine is a perfect *epidemic among bear:* if not watched closely, it will go off as quick on a warm scent as my dog Bowieknife will: and then that dog—whew! why the fellow thinks that the world is full of b*e*ar, he finds them so easy. It's lucky he don't talk as well as think; for with his natural modesty, if he should suddenly learn how much he is acknowledged to be ahead of all other dogs in the universe, he would be astonished to death in two minutes.

"Strangers, that dog knows a b*e*ar's way as well as a horse-jockey knows a woman's: he always barks at the right time, bites at the exact place, and whips without getting a scratch.

"I never could tell whether he was made expressly to hunt b*e*ar, or whether b*e*ar was made expressly for him to hunt; any way, I believe they were ordained to go together as naturally as Squire Jones says a man and woman is, when he moralizes in marrying a couple. In fact, Jones once said, said he, 'Marriage according to law is a civil contract of divine origin; it's common to all countries as well as Arkansaw, and people take to it as naturally as Jim Doggett's Bowieknife takes to b*e*ar.' "

"What season of the year do your hunts take place?" inquired a gentlemanly foreigner, who, from some peculiarities of his baggage, I suspected to be an Englishman, on some hunting expedition, probably at the foot of the Rocky Mountains.

"The season for b*e*ar hunting, stranger," said the man of Arkansaw, "is generally all the year round, and the hunts take place about as regular. I read in history that varmints have their fat season, and their lean season. That is not the case in Arkansaw, feeding as they do upon the *spontenacious* productions of the sile, they have one continued fat season the year round; though in winter things in this way is rather more greasy than in summer, I must admit. For that reason b*e*ar with us run in warm weather, but in winter they only waddle.

"Fat, fat! its an enemy to speed; it tames every thing that has plenty of it. I have seen wild turkeys, from its influence, as gentle as chickens. Run a b*e*ar in this fat condition, and the way it improves the critter for eating is amazing; it sort of mixes the ile up with the meat, until you can't tell t'other from which. I've done this often.

"I recollect one perty morning in particular, of putting an old he fellow on the stretch, and considering the weight he carried, he run well. But the dogs soon tired him down, and when I came up with him wasn't he in a beautiful sweat—I might say fever; and then to see his tongue sticking out of his mouth a feet, and his sides sinking and opening like a bellows, and his cheeks so fat that he couldn't look cross. In this fix I blazed at him, and pitch me naked into a briar patch, if the steam didn't come out of the bullet-hole ten foot in a straight line. The fellow, I reckon, was made on the high-pressure system, and the lead sort of bust his biler."

"That column of steam was rather curious, or else the bear must have been very *warm,*" observed the foreigner, with a laugh.

"Stranger, as you observe, that b*e*ar was WARM, and the blowing off of the steam show'd it, and also how hard the varmint had been run. I have no doubt if he had kept on two miles farther his insides would have been stewed; and I expect to meet with a varmint yet of extra bottom, that will run himself into a skinfull of b*e*ar's grease: it is possible; much onlikelier things have happened."

"Whereabouts are these bears so abundant?" inquired the foreigner, with increasing interest.

"Why stranger, they inhabit the neighborhood of my settlement, one of the prettiest places on old Mississipp—a perfeet location, and no mistake; a place that had some defects until the river made the cut-off' at 'Shirt-tail bend,' and that remedied the evil, as it brought my cabin on the edge of the river—a great advantage in wet weather, I assure you, as you can now roll a barrel of whiskey into my yard in high water from a boat, as easy as falling off a log. It's a great improvement, as toting it by land in a jug, as I used to do, *evaporated* it too fast, and it became expensive.

"Just stop with me, stranger, a month or two, or a year, if you like, and you will appreciate my place. I can give you plenty to eat; for beside hog and hominy, you can have b*e*ar-ham, and b*e*ar-sausages, and a mattrass of b*e*ar-skins to sleep on, and a wildcat-skin, pulled off hull, stuffed with cornshucks, for a pillow. That bed would put you to sleep if you had the rheumatics in every joint in your body. I call that ar bed, a *quietus.*

"Then look at my 'pre-emption'—the government ain't got another like it to dispose of. Such timber, and such bottom land,—why you can't preserve anything natural you plant in it unless you pick it young, things thar will grow out of shape so quick.

"I once planted in those diggins a few potatoes and beets; they took a fine start, and after that, an ox team couldn't have kept them from growing. About that time I went off to old Kaintuck on business, and did not hear from them things in three months, when I accidentally stumbled on a fellow who had drapped in at my place, with an idea of buying me out.

" 'How did you like things?' said I.

" 'Pretty well,' said he; 'the cabin is convenient, and the timber land is good; but that bottom land ain't worth the first red cent.' "

" 'Why?' said I.

" ' 'Cause,' said he.

" ' 'Cause what?' said I.

" ' 'Cause it's full of cedar stumps and Indian mounds, and *can't be cleared.*'

" 'Lord,' said I, 'them ar "cedar stumps" is beets, and them ar "Indian mounds" tater hills.'

"As I had expected, the crop was overgrown and useless: the sile is too rich, *and planting in Arkansaw is dangerous.*

"I had a good-sized sow killed in that same bottom land. The old thief stole an ear of corn, and took it down to eat where she slept at night. Well, she left a grain or two on the ground, and lay down on them: before morning the corn shot up, and the percussion killed her dead. I don't plant any more: natur intended Arkansaw for a hunting ground, and I go according to natur."

The questioner, who had thus elicited the description of our hero's settlement, seemed to be perfectly satisfied, and said no more; but the

"Big Bear of Arkansaw" rambled on from one thing to another with a volubility perfectly astonishing, occasionally disputing with those around him, particularly with a "live Sucker" from Illinois, who had the daring to say that our Arkansaw friend's stories "smelt rather tall."

The evening was nearly spent by the incidents we have detailed; and conscious that my own association with so singular a personage would probably end before morning, I asked him if he would not give me a description of some particular bear hunt; adding, that I took great interest in such things, though I was no sportsman. The desire seemed to please him, and he squared himself round towards me, saying, that he could give me an idea of a bear hunt that was never beat in this world, or in any other. His manner was so singular, that half of his story consisted in his excellent way of telling it, the great peculiarity of which was, the happy manner he had of emphasizing the prominent parts of his conversations. As near as I can recollect, I have italicized the words, and given the story in his own way.

"Stranger," said he, "in bear hunts *I am numerous,* and which particular one, as you say, I shall tell, puzzles me.

"There was the old she devil I shot at the Hurricane last fall—then there was the old hog thief I popped over at the Bloody Crossing, and then—Yes, I have it! I will give you an idea of a hunt, in which the greatest bear was killed that ever lived, *none excepted;* about an old fellow that I hunted, more or less, for two or three years; and if that ain't a *particular bear hunt,* I ain't got one to tell.

"But in the first place, stranger, let me say, I am pleased with you, because you ain't ashamed to gain information by asking and listening; and that's what I say to Countess's pups every day when I'm home; and I have got great hopes of them ar pups, because they are continually *nosing* about; and though they stick it sometimes in the wrong place, they gain experience any how, and may learn something useful to boot.

"Well, as I was saying about this big bear, you see when I and some more first settled in our region, we were drivin to hunting naturally; we soon liked it, and after that we found it an easy matter to make the thing our business. One old chap who had pioneered 'afore us, gave us to understand that we had settled in the right place. He dwelt upon its merits until it was affecting, and showed us, to prove his assertions, more scratches on the bark of the sassafras trees, than I ever saw chalk marks on a tavern door 'lection time.

" 'Who keeps that ar reckoning?' said I.

" 'The bear,' said he.

" 'What for?' said I.

" 'Can't tell,' said he; 'but so it is: the bear bite the bark and wood too, at the highest point from the ground they can reach, and you can tell, by the marks,' said he, 'the length of the bear to an inch.'

" 'Enough,' said I; 'I've learned something here a'ready, and I'll put it in practice.'

"Well, stranger, just one month from that time I killed a bear, and told its exact length before I measured it, by those very marks; and when I did that, I swelled up considerable—I've been a prouder man ever since.

"So I went on, larning something every day, until I was reckoned a buster, and allowed to be decidedly the best bear hunter in my district; and that is a reputation as much harder to earn than to be reckoned first man in Congress, as an iron ramrod is harder than a toadstool.

"Do the varmints grow over-cunning by being fooled with by greenhorn hunters, and by this means get troublesome, they send for me, as a matter of course; and thus I do my own hunting, and most of my neighbors'. I walk into the varmints though, and it has become about as much the same to me as drinking. It is told in two sentences—

"A bear is started, and he is killed.

"The thing is somewhat monotonous now—I know just how much they will run, where they will tire, how much they will growl, and what a thundering time I will have in getting their meat home. I could give you the history of the chase with all the particulars at the commencement, I know the signs so well—*Stranger, I'm certain.* Once I met with a match, though, and I will tell you about it; for a common hunt would not be worth relating.

"On a fine fall day, long time ago, I was trailing about for bear, and what should I see but fresh marks on the sassafras trees, about eight inches above any in the forests that I knew of. Says I, 'Them marks is a hoax, or it indicates the d——t bear that was ever grown.' In fact, stranger, I couldn't believe it was real, and I went on. Again I saw the same marks, at the same height, and *I knew the thing lived.* That conviction came home to my soul like an earthquake.

"Says I, 'Here is something a-purpose for me: that bear is mine, or I give up the hunting business.' The very next morning, what should I see but a number of buzzards hovering over my corn-field. 'The rascal has been there,' said I, 'for that sign is certain'; and, sure enough, on examining, I found the bones of what had been as beautiful a hog the day before, as was ever raised by a Buckeye. Then I tracked the critter out of the field to the woods, and all the marks he left behind, showed me that he was *the bear.*

"Well, stranger, the first fair chase I ever had with that big critter, I saw him no less than three distinct times at a distance; the dogs run him over eighteen miles and broke down, my horse gave out, and I was as nearly used up as a man can be, made on *my* principle, *which is patent.*

"Before this adventure, such things were unknown to me as possible; but, strange as it was, that bear got me used to it before I was done with him; for he got so at last, that he would leave me on a long chase *quite easy*. How he did it, I never could understand.

"That a bear runs at all, is puzzling; but how this one could tire down and bust up a pack of hounds and a horse, that were used to overhauling everything they started after in no time, was past my understanding. Well, stranger, that bear finally got so sassy, that he used to help himself to a hog off my premises whenever he wanted one; the buzzards followed after what he left, and so, between *bear and buzzard,* I rather think I got *out of pork.*

"Well, missing that bear so often took hold of my vitals, and I wasted away. The thing had been carried too far, and it reduced me in flesh faster than an ager. I would see that bear in every thing I did: *he hunted me,* and that, too, like a devil, which I began to think he was.

"While in this shaky fix, I made preparations to give him a last brush, and be done with it. Having completed everything to my satisfaction, I started at sunrise, and to my great joy, I discovered from the way the dogs run, that they were near him. Finding his trail was nothing, for that had become as plain to the pack as a turnpike road.

"On we went, and coming on an open country, what should I see but the bear very leisurely ascending a hill, and the dogs close at his heels, either a match for him this time in speed, or else he did not care to get out of their way—I don't know which. But wasn't he a beauty, though! I loved him like a brother.

"On he went, until he came to a tree, the limbs of which formed a crotch about six feet from the ground. Into this crotch he got and seated himself, the dogs yelling all around it; and there he sat eyeing them as quiet as a pond in low water.

"A greenhorn friend of mine, in company, reached shooting distance before me, and blazed away, hitting the critter in the centre of his forehead. The bear shook his head as the ball struck it, and then walked down from that tree, as gently as a lady would from a carriage.

" 'Twas a beautiful sight to see him do that—he was in such a rage, that he seemed to be as little afraid of the dogs as if they had been sucking pigs; and the dogs warn't slow in making a ring around him at a respectful distance, I tell you; even Bowieknife himself, stood off. Then the way his eyes flashed!—why the fire of them would have singed a cat's hair; in fact, that bear was in a *wrath all over.* Only one pup came near him, and he was brushed out so totally with the bear's left paw, that he entirely disappeared; and that made the old dogs more cautious still. In the mean time, I came up, and taking deliberate aim, as a man should do, at his side, just back of his foreleg, *if my gun did not snap,* call me a coward, and I won't take it personal.

"Yes, stranger, *it snapped,* and I could not find a cap about my person. While in this predicament, I turned round to my fool friend—'Bill,' says

I, 'you're an ass—you're a fool—you might as well have tried to kill that bear by barking the tree under his belly, as to have done it by hitting him in the head. Your shot has made a tiger of him; and blast me, if a dog gets killed or wounded when they come to blows, I will stick my knife into your liver, I will——.' My wrath was up. I had lost my caps, my gun had snapped, the fellow with me had fired at the bear's head, and I expected every moment to see him close in with the dogs and kill a dozen of them at least. In this thing I was mistaken; for the bear leaped over the ring formed by the dogs, and giving a fierce growl, was off—the pack, of course, in full cry after him. The run this time was short, for coming to the edge of a lake, the varmint jumped in, and swam to a little island in the lake, which it reached, just a moment before the dogs.

" 'I'll have him now,' said I, for I had found my caps in the *lining of my coat*—so, rolling a log into the lake, I paddled myself across to the island, just as the dogs had cornered the bear in a thicket. I rushed up and fired—at the same time the critter leaped over the dogs and came within three feet of me, running like mad; he jumped into the lake, and tried to mount the log I had just deserted, but every time he got half his body on it, it would roll over and send him under; the dogs, too, got around him, and pulled him about, and finally Bowieknife clenched with him, and they sunk into the lake together.

"Stranger, about this time I was excited, and I stripped off my coat, drew my knife, and intended to have taken a part with Bowieknife myself, when the bear rose to the surface. But the varmint staid under—Bowieknife came up alone, more dead than alive, and with the pack came ashore.

" 'Thank God!' said I, 'the old villain has got his deserts at last.'

"Determined to have the body, I cut a grape-vine for a rope, and dove down where I could see the bear in the water, fastened my rope to his leg, and fished him, with great difficulty, ashore. Stranger, may I be chawed to death by young alligators, if the thing I looked at wasn't a *she bear, and not the old critter after all.*

"The way matters got mixed on that island was onaccountably curious, and thinking of it made me more than ever convinced that I was hunting the devil himself. I went home that night and took to my bed—the thing was killing me. The entire team of Arkansaw in bear-hunting acknowledged himself used up, and the fact sunk into my feelings as a snagged boat will in the Mississippi. I grew as cross as a bear with two cubs and a sore tail. The thing got out 'mong my neighbors, and I was asked how come on that individ-u-al that never lost a bear when once started? and if that same individ-u-al didn't wear telescopes when he turned a she-bear, of ordinary size, into an old he one, a little larger than a horse?

" 'Prehaps,' said I, 'friends'—getting wrathy—'prehaps you want to call somebody a liar?'

" 'Oh, no,' said they, 'we only heard of such things being *rather common* of late, but we don't believe one word of it; oh, no,'—and then they would ride off, and laugh like so many hyenas over a dead nigger.

"It was too much, and I determined to catch that bear, go to Texas, or die,—and I made my preparations accordin'.

"I had the pack shut up and rested. I took my rifle to pieces, and iled it.

"I put caps in every pocket about my person, *for fear of the lining*.

"I then told my neighbors, that on Monday morning—naming the day—I would start THAT BEAR, and bring him home with me, or they might divide my settlement among them, the owner having disappeared.

"Well, stranger, on the morning previous to the great day of my hunting expedition, I went into the woods near my house, taking my gun and Bowieknife along, just *from habit,* and there sitting down, also from habit, what should I see, getting over my fence, but *the bear!* Yes, the old varmint was within a hundred yards of me, and the way he walked *over that fence*—stranger; he loomed up like a *black mist,* he seemed so large, and he walked right towards me.

"I raised myself, took deliberate aim, and fired. Instantly the varmint wheeled, gave a yell, and *walked through the fence,* as easy as a falling tree would through a cobweb.

"I started after, but was tripped up by my inexpressibles, which, either from habit or the excitement of the moment, were about my heels, and before I had really gathered myself up, I heard the old varmint groaning, like a thousand sinners, in a thicket near by, and, by the time I reached him, he was a corpse.

"Stranger, it took five niggers and myself to put that carcass on a mule's back, and old long-ears waddled under his load, as if he was foundered in every leg of his body; and with a common whopper of a bear, he would have trotted off, and enjoy himself.

" 'Twould astonish you to know how big he was: I made a *bedspread of his skin,* and the way it used to cover my bear mattress, and leave several feet on each side to tuck up, would have delighted you. It was, in fact, a creation bear, and if it had lived in Samson's time, and had met him in a fair fight, he would have licked him in the twinkling of a dice-box.

"But, stranger, I never liked the way I hunted him, *and missed him.* There is something curious about it, that I never could understand,—and I never was satisfied at his giving in *so easy at last.* Perhaps he had heard of my preparations to hunt him the next day, so he jist guv up, like Captain Scott's coon, to save his wind to grunt with in dying; but that ain't likely. My private opinion is, that that bear was an *unhuntable bear, and died when his time come.*"

When this story was ended, our hero sat some minutes with his auditors, in a grave silence; I saw there was a mystery to him connected with the bear whose death he had just related, that had evidently made a strong impression on his mind. It was also evident that there was some superstitious awe connected with the affair,—a feeling common with all "children of the wood," when they meet with any thing out of their every-day experience.

He was the first one, however, to break the silence, and, jumping up, he asked all present to "liquor" before going to bed,—a thing which he did, with a number of companions, evidently to his heart's content.

Long before day, I was put ashore at my place of destination, and I can only follow with the reader, in imagination, our Arkansas friend, in his adventures at the "Forks of Cypress," on the Mississippi.

SECTION TWO

Changing Currents and Maturing Forms

1850 – 1900

The decade of the 1850s provided a cultural watershed in the nation's development, bringing into focus a series of divisive forces that threatened to destroy the Union in the 1860s. The most ominous of these forces was the split between the slaveholding states of the South and the so-called free states of the North, a fundamentally irreconcilable clash between opposing ideologies, which began with the nation's founding and grew more intense as new states were brought into the Union from the West. To maintain an uneasy balance of power in Washington between Northern and Southern states, the political compromises of 1820 and 1850, involving the admission of both slave and free states, postponed the inevitable showdown, but also exacerbated the passions of citizens on both sides of the Mason-Dixon Line.

North and South, this increasing bitterness was reflected in the literature of the period, which became increasingly tendentious, didactic, and sentimental. Harriet Beecher Stowe's *Uncle Tom's Cabin* (1852), for example, became a rallying cry for Northern abolitionists, but it was also vigorously attacked by a host of Southern writers, including William Gilmore Simms and Thomas Bangs Thorpe, who sought to portray Southern slavery in a more favorable light. Not surprisingly, few of them could avoid defending the South's image in terms as outrageously exaggerated as those employed by their opponents. Thus, the quality of literary art suffered in the 1850s, even among America's foremost writers. During the war years of the early 1860s, its development virtually came to a standstill, although signs of a resurgence of power could be seen in several of the shorter works that Herman Melville produced, notably "Benito Cereno," "Bartleby, the Scrivener," "The Encantadas," "Billy Budd, Foretopman," and *The Confidence Man* (1857). Each of these would stir the imagination of scholars, critics, poets, and dramatists both in his era and in ours more than a century later.

The impact of the Civil War upon the United States was so powerful that after 1865 virtually a new nation came into being, and so numerous were the changes wrought by the war's aftermath that the basic patterns of thought and expression in the generation between 1860 and 1900 necessarily contrasted sharply with those of the preceding one. The dislocations and disillusionments produced in the defeated South, for example, kept that area depressed for over thirty years, creating almost insurmountable political, social, and economic problems, particularly in regard to race relations and civil rights. Elsewhere in the country, equally pressing problems arose, though from other causes, as three significant forces, operating concurrently, changed the face and the psychology of the nation more rapidly and more radically than ever before. As an outgrowth of the North's victory and the post-war expansion of its industrial system, great railroad lines spanned the continent, filling its vast empty spaces in the West with a polyglot multitude of European immigrants who had been lured there by the promise of land, wealth, and political freedom. The westward movement, reaching the climax of its surge in this period, thus became one of the dominant forces in reshaping national life. No less significant, a second force engendered by industrial growth was the rapid mass movement of population, both native and foreign, from farms to cities, creating a new American phenomenon—the metropolis—with its motley social fabric and its extremes of wealth and poverty symbolized by the skyscraper and the slum tenement.

From Romanticism to Realism

As a result of this increasing mechanization and urbanization, new tensions, reflected first in the nation's changing mores and ultimately in its cultural expression, produced a gradual but decisive shift in the basic assumptions of the age. In place of the older romantic optimism founded on the assumption of the individual's central significance and infinite progress in a world of moral values, there began to appear now a more critical, realistic mood, as the pressures of modern society, economic warfare, and the power of the machine made people less certain of their destinies. This drift toward a pessimistic determinism was further accelerated by a third important force, the rapid advance of scientific knowledge, particularly in geology and biology, which profoundly modified peoples' understanding of life and undermined their former certainties. For out of the welter of this new knowledge emerged the concepts of evolution, natural selection, and scientific materialism, which effectively destroyed the foundations of an older belief in nature as the visible manifestation of an indwelling, benevolent spiritual reality. Thus, science and industrialism, by changing America's thinking and living habits, prepared the way for a gradual shift in the prevailing national outlook from romanticism to realism.

As reflected in the literature of the period, this shift of emphasis from a romantic to a realistic interpretation of life was achieved only after much wrangling over the ultimate purpose of literature; for the romantic impulse persisted far into the new era, and romantic themes and moods continued to influence, often to dominate, American writing. At bottom, the issue between romanticism and realism was a philosophic conflict over the basic purpose and function of literature. The romantic believed that literature should idealize life by emphasizing its more picturesque or desirable features, while the realist tried to give a faithful representation of all the prosaic facts of actuality exactly as they appear to the senses. Between these two extreme views lay many varying attitudes concerning the proper use of the materials of fiction and the most appropriate techniques for rendering them artistically; but since most authors kept on writing for cash, not for the ideals of art, the vast majority of short stories in the popular magazines remained as before on the "boy-meets-girl" level of mass entertainment. Rather than venture too far afield, the popular magazines then as now tended to perpetuate the standardized romantic devices because these had proved to be the most profitable literary commodity, while the controversy over realism raged mainly among the few artists and critics who took literature seriously. Nevertheless, a gradually developing tendency to present life with greater fidelity to the facts of actual experience could be discerned, even at the popular level, in several types of stories that gained currency during the period. Though the movement toward pure realism was exceedingly slow, it became evident first in the regional "local color" stories, acquired new technical precision in the "well-made" story, and reached its fullest development before 1900 in the type of psychological fiction based on ethical problems that was written by William Dean Howells and Henry James.

Variants of Local Color

Of these three types, the first furnished the greatest variety of stories and was decidedly the most popular, as well as the least realistic. Elements of local color writing, which may be defined loosely as the representation in fiction of the distinctive features, customs, and modes of life in a particular area or locality, were present even in Washington Irving's stories; but as a type that dominated American fiction from 1870 to 1890, these local color stories grew out of two distinct streams of earlier romantic fiction—the comic tall tales of the Western frontier and the genteel, didactic stories of the antebellum East and South—which were fused by Bret Harte and others in the 1860s. Tracing its source to A. B. Longstreet's *Georgia Scenes* (1835), the first stream sprang naturally out of the free, unregulated life of the back country and in most respects presented a striking contrast to the refined product of the Eastern seaboard. For the high-mindedness, correct behavior, and polite tone of the latter, it substituted a frankly unethical, amoral tone and glorified in vigorous, gusty language the rough features of frontier life. Its heroes were braggarts, "bully boys," and rascals, whose exploits, modeled upon the fabulous deeds of Davy Crockett and Mike Fink, furnished the materials for the yarn-spinning talents of writers like Johnson Jones Hooper, T. B. Thorpe, J. G. Baldwin, and George Washington Harris. In the main, the stories written by these people discarded the rhetorical "literary" manner of conventional fiction and adopted in its place a method derived from the old folk tale, namely, the device of placing within the story a narrator who recounted in his or her own untutored but racy speech the principal events of the story. Called mock oral tales because they were written adaptations of yarns that were told or might have been told by fireside yarnspinners, these stories, though often crudely contrived, delighted a vast audience, chiefly masculine. Since they flouted the established conventions of polite literature, they usually drew censure rather than encouragement from the literary critics of their day and consequently flourished mainly on the subliterary level of newspapers and sports magazines. Recent scholars, however, have found in their authentic American types and indigenous backwoods idiom some of the myth-making sources of a native literary tradition—the "Big Bear" or tall-tale tradition—from which Mark Twain, O. Henry, William Faulkner, and others have drawn models and inspiration.

Less readily discernible in its early development, the second stream of local color writing came down through the work of such writers as Catharine Sedgwick in New England and William Gilmore Simms in South Carolina, who had consciously employed the scenes and legends of their respective localities as background for the romantic action of their characters. These decorous, didactic tales gradually acquired further realistic touches from other writers in the 1840s and 1850s, notably Harriet Beecher Stowe, but remained relatively undistinguished until the merger between them and the uninhibited, amoral Southwestern yarns produced a type of local color story that marked a decisive turning point in the history of the American short story. Credit for bringing about this union belongs largely to Bret Harte, who took hold of the more picturesque materials and methods of frontier humor and rendered them more palatable for sedate Eastern appetites. The stories he wrote for California periodicals in the 1860s gained nationwide fame when they appeared later in his small volume *The Luck of Roaring Camp and Other Sketches* (1870) and thus bridged the gap between East and West, giving impetus to a trend that had already begun. Harte's achievement may be explained in part by his awareness of the importance of humor in the short story and in part by his skill in exploiting it, together with irony and sentiment, through his compression of incident and terseness of phrase.

In the wake of Harte's success, but not necessarily in imitation of his methods, scores of writers, including G. W. Cable, Mary E. Wilkins Freeman, Sarah Orne Jewett, Mary Murfree, Kate Chopin, Joel Chandler Harris, and Thomas Nelson Page, fashioned the trend of the local color story. Quaintness of scene, character, dialect, and local customs, carefully purged of their grosser elements, thus became a staple in the short story from 1870 to 1900, as the nation was deluged with stories about life in the hinterland. Realistic only in externals, these stories were more like folk idylls than truthful representations of events in the contemporary scene, for an air of nostalgia pervaded most of them, as if their writers were seeking to preserve a bygone era that was being destroyed by the expanding industrialism of the post-war period. This is not to say that post-war local colorists altogether ignored the problems and conditions that their own society had to cope with, but rather that they tended to mask their concern over these matters by placing the action of their stories in earlier times and softening its harshness through romanticized coloration and picturesqueness of speech, settings, and dress. Thus, although both Cable and Harris voiced strongly sympathetic attitudes toward the plight of suppressed blacks in the South during the 1880s and 1890s, the fiction they wrote dealing with race relations bore a predominantly nostalgic flavor of sweet reasonableness. Similarly, even the early stories of Charles Chesnutt dealt so gently and humorously with the "color line" that most white readers who enjoyed them in the *Atlantic Monthly* and other northern magazines failed to recognize their author as the first important black literary artist in America. By the 1890s, however, the local color story had run its course. Having become fully as standardized as the sentimental romances that Hawthorne had condemned thirty years before, it elicited both the scorn of the "veritists" and the sarcasm of bored editors who had grown surfeited with the reign of dialect in "corrupt English." Before the vein played out, however, the many writers of local color stories had clearly demonstrated as never before how handily the short story form could make use of them. It is hardly coincidental, therefore, that at the peak of its local color vogue the short story was officially "discovered" by writers and critics who now resurrected Poe's theories and reapplied them.

The writers most prominently associated with this rediscovery of the short story were Thomas Bailey Aldrich, H. C. Bunner, and Brander Matthews, who formulated anew in 1885 the so-called laws governing the form and for the first time used the term "short-story" to designate it. These laws, though apparently new at the time, were merely Poe's principles rephrased and extended; but more significant than the mere restating of the principles were the new technical effects these writers produced. Their "well-made" story was interesting chiefly for its emphasis on technique, the consciousness of form implicit in it, rather than for its subject matter, which was realistic only to the extent that representative individuals from two or three social groups could be identified in it. Stories of this type ranged in content and tone all the way from the light foolery of Frank Stockton's "The Lady, or the Tiger?" to the tartly ironic cross purpose of Thomas Bailey Aldrich's "Two Bites at a Cherry"; yet all shared a quality that was new to the fiction of the time, a deliberate concern over the manner of presenting the story most effectively. To achieve their aims, leading writers applied to the rich body of American materials being exploited by the local colorists methods originally adapted from Poe by two French artists like Alphonse Daudet and Guy De Maupassant. Ingenuity in contrived situations and dexterity in manipulated incidents, along with compression, vivacity, and wit in characterization, became the hallmarks of the "well-made" story—as opposed to the somewhat greater emphasis placed on setting and dialect in the local color story. The chief emphasis of the "well-made" story lay upon a carefully worked out pattern of events moving swiftly toward a sharp climax and sudden denouement, with suspense as the *sine qua non*. Aldrich's "Marjorie Daw," an ingenious tale dating from the 1870s, served as the model for similarly contrived stories by Matthews, Stockton, and Bunner; the amusing twist of surprise at the end was the supreme mark of dexterity that inspired them. Such stories were less numerous during this period than the local color variety, partly because they required greater skill to bring off successfully and partly, perhaps, because at first their relatively sophisticated make-up lacked the broad democratic appeal of local color stories. However, as more and more writers caught on to the trickery and artifice needed to produce sharp, dramatic effects, and paid less and less attention to characterization and theme, the type degenerated into the standardized "plot story," which dominated the popular magazines of succeeding generations.

The Major Realists

Since the full flowering of realism depends on the truthful protrayal of individual human character, the foremost realists will be those who have imaginatively created the largest number of the most fully realized individuals. By this criterion, the short story form is almost ruled out of consideration in the ultimate reaches of realism because its limited scope prevents the writer from developing even in one character the multitudinous minutiae required to set that character apart from all other individuals, let alone enabling the writer to create a social pattern of such individuals. For this reason the three major writers of the period, Twain, Howells, and James, owe their reputation as realists to their novels rather than to their short stories. It would be hard to find within any five-year span three greater American masterpieces of realistic fiction than James's *The Portrait of a Lady* (1881), Twain's *Adventures of Huckleberry Finn* (1884), and Howells's *The Rise of Silas Lapham* (1885); but while all three of their authors figure prominently in the rise of realism, neither Twain nor Howells devoted much attention to the short story. Twain was altogether too dynamic a figure to be roped and branded by a single tag. He was humorist, realist, local colorist, romanticist, and satirist all in one, and thus uniquely representative of the America of his time. And although Howells became the high priest of realism, persuasively codifying its criteria in his *Criticism and Fiction* (1891) and vigorously championing its cause during his long editorial career, as a practicing realist he is remembered chiefly for his thirty-odd novels, which showed a deepening interest in human character—particularly in character confronted with ethical problems. James, on the other hand, gave virtually as much study and care to the art of the short story as to that of the novel. Beginning in the 1860s and working steadily for forty years, he produced an imposing number of stories of such finished artistry that his reputation as a craftsman still stands preeminently high.

James, however, has never been a popular writer, even to the extent that Poe and Hawthorne were popular in their day; for the problem he set himself, to create flawless stories embodying and dramatizing the subtlest of psychological conflicts, proved to be too fastidious an aim for the general public. James regarded fiction as a form of art and the writer of fiction as an artist, whose obligation was to create a nearly perfect illusion of life. To do this would be to produce stories whose form and substance were inseparably fused and indistinguishable from each other. Going beyond terms like realism and romanticism, he argued that the imaginative writer should strive to catch the color and texture of life and convert "the very pulses of the air into revelations"; for only by such means could he hope to achieve in story form a work of art that would be "a living thing, all one and continuous, like any other organism." In his own efforts to achieve such a harmonious union of meaning and form, James's short stories, though less rich in texture than his novels, often show him at his best, besides offering sharper insights into the underlying purpose of his art. This purpose, like Hawthorne's, is the revelation of some psychological truth hidden beneath the surface facts of life in the motives and actions of the human mind and heart. Having posited a world in which moral values are not merely of primary but almost of exclusive importance, James's major interest did not center upon the obvious clashes of temperament and passion that go on all about us in everyday experience; it centered rather upon the undisclosed reasons that cause highly civilized men and women to think and act in certain ways when confronted with inescapable moral problems. His heroes and heroines, accordingly, do not strive for the ordinary prizes of everyday life—money, glory, prestige—but instead for the much greater prizes of self-realization and the preservation of their individual integrity, which can only be won by submitting to the most rigorous of tests and making difficult decisions entirely on their own responsibility. This was the essential reality of life as James saw it. To create a faithful illusion of it in fiction that his readers would be compelled to accept as meaningful and interesting, he gradually worked out a method that managed to convey dramatically both the external action involved in a complex experience and the inner significance of that action.

In order that readers might get the feeling of looking directly at a significant bit of life unfolding before their eyes, everything that happened in the story and the meaning of everything that happened was to be presented from a single point of view, or center of revelation. Ordinarily, this center of revelation was fixed in the mind of one of the characters who, at the outset of the story, possessed no more knowledge of the situation that was about to develop than did the reader. Thus the readers, as though standing directly behind this observing character, would discover for themselves both the events occurring before their eyes and the complex implications of those events in the same way as the observer because there would be no gratuitous information about them supplied during the story's unfolding, no help from the author, explaining the meaning of this or that character's real intentions in saying or doing a certain thing. Every turn of events must fall logically within the range of this observing character's impressions; every meaning and every evaluation must grow organically out of his or her own process of discovery. By means of this method, James could direct the course of the story entirely from behind the scenes and achieve simultaneously both an objective presentation of situations, characters, and events and a subjective evaluation of their significance. It not only preserved the illusion of reality, but also communicated with the fullest immediacy every sensation evoked by the experience.

To achieve both the illusion and the fullness of lifelike situations, James strove constantly to design plots packed with significant incidents, yet firmly contained within a shapely, uncluttered form, so that his short stories might become "like the hard shining sonnet, one of the most indestructible forms of composition in general use." For him, therefore, the writing of every story posed the problem of reconciling the opposing thrusts of matter and form, and in his efforts to deal with this problem he worked out another dramatic technique—the "scenic" method—which has since become a standard feature of serious contemporary fiction. Many of his stories are comparable to stage plays in that their most significant action occurs in a series of scenes that bring several characters face to face with the problem at hand, and it is thus conveyed to the reader through the dialogue. Essentially the same method is employed by Ernest Hemingway in "The Killers," in which nearly all the climactic tension is developed and communicated through several conversations, although the clipped, monosyllabic dialogue of Hemingway's lowbrow characters is quite different from the elaborate conversational fencing of James's refined sophisticates. More than any other single element, perhaps, this circumlocutory quality of James's style, which becomes so involved in his "later manner" that many readers find it disturbing, has severely restricted his audience to a small circle of enthusiasts. Once this difficulty of style is mastered, however, there is little tendency to question either the permanence of James's artistic achievement or the importance of his contribution to the development of fiction in the short story. For his best stories are perennially absorbing, capable of being reread many times with profit and amusement; moveover, his technical innovations, such as the restricted point of view and the subjective inner drama, have remained standard in the serious fiction of today. Virtually every significant writer of the twentieth century owes something to his craftsmanship.

The fiction of Howells and James, with its emphasis on the highest ideals of both ethical motivation and artistic craftsmanship, brought more sharply into focus than ever before the cleavage in American fiction between serious art for the few and standardized entertainment for the many. While the popular magazine story remained essentially the same rehash of old formulas, the work of serious artists continued developing experimentally from the point to which James, Howells, and Twain had brought the realism of their day. This development proceeded in two parallel paths: first, the artists' increasing concern over socioeconomic problems, which extended the concept of realism into the realm of social protest, and second, their reaction against the genteel formalism and exclusiveness in the art of the older realists. Toward the end of the century, both these lines of development, as reflected in the works of serious younger writers, led to a bold new kind of fiction that, as we shall see, stretched the concept of realism far beyond the limits prescribed for it by Howells and James.

The Later Realists

To understand this shift of emphasis one needs to know something of the vast changes occurring in the United States in the closing years of the nineteenth century. As the nation prepared to enter fully into the age of the machine, its phenomenal growth brought sharply into focus all the problems common to an urban industrial society. During these years, as the population nearly doubled again and the ranks of migrants from farms to factories were swelled, the nation's predominantly rural and agricultural image rapidly changed to that of a great industrial power, its new strength symbolized in the relatively easy triumph of the Spanish-American War. At the close of the old century, the United States had emerged from relative isolation and self-centeredness to a position of involvement and eventual leadership in the affairs of the whole world. Inevitably, the vast expansion in all lines of activity that accounted for these fundamental changes made itself felt directly and indirectly in the work of American writers, augmenting on the one hand the volume of their product and requiring on the other a reassessment of their values. With the advent of the five- and ten-cent weekly magazines, supported by advertising and brightened by modern methods of printing and illustration, the reading public in America multiplied, and the demand for short fiction increased accordingly. A mass market was created for the short story, just as it was for the automobile, and both products became increasingly standardized. The financial rewards to successful writers in this highly competitive field kept pace with its growth, so that in time the author whose stories appeared regularly in *Collier's* or the *Saturday Evening Post* could flaunt the income of a bank president. But more and more American writers were forced to choose whether they would serve art or mammon, for the price of success in the popular commercial field was an inflexible pattern of writing that led eventually to sterility. Thus, the struggle to reconcile these conflicting pressures, to maintain high standards of craftsmanship and artistic integrity despite the lure of profit in mass entertainment, has been one of the most characteristic phenomena in twentieth-century American literature.

Above the level of sheer entertainment, the serious fiction of this period reflected the stresses and strains of modern life in other ways, taking on deeper tones of pessimism and determinism as well as extending the implications of realism to include harsher and more unpleasant aspects of life than earlier realists had cared to investigate. Realism, in short, developed a tendency to pry beneath the smiling surface of the average that Howells had characterized as typical of America and to expose to view conditions that he and James in particular had preferred to leave unexplored. In its progress toward the ultimate extreme of unabashed frankness, realism thus passed through two further stages, one growing out of the other. The first stage, identifiable in the fiction of social and economic protest, may be seen at its best, perhaps, in the early stories of Hamlin Garland, with their emphasis on the injustices suffered by Midwestern farmers in the 1880s under the tyranny of corporate ownership, or in Howells's later novels, which attempt to dramatize specific instances of industrial strife, such as railway strikes and lockouts. The second stage introduced into American fiction a new literary movement called *naturalism,* which long remained a disturbing yet highly provocative force in modern literature.

An offshoot of modern scientific inquiry, naturalism promulgated a concept of humanity and its relation to nature and society totally different from the older view of the nineteenth century and thus became responsible for changing both the content and the form of contemporary prose fiction. In place of the artistic and moral standards of the earlier period, which were grounded in a philosophy of optimistic idealism, naturalism substituted a set of standards based on a skeptical, deterministic view of the universe. Under the older system of belief, carefully plotted stories emphasizing moral and spiritual themes—beauty, faith, ethical purpose—were the norm, since the universe itself had been conceived of as a divine and purposeful plan, in which human actions were inspired by divine motives and judged on the basis of "free will" choice between good and evil. Stressing the moral conduct of the individual, such stories could be made to dramatize conflicts that proceeded logically to a climax and resolution consistent with the accepted moral code for distinguishing between right and wrong: Goodness, truth, and beauty might be made triumphant, evil and ugliness suppressed, because God's eternal verities were believed to work out that way. From the naturalistic point of view, however, any such attempt to recreate divinely inspired patterns of human behavior in literature became meaningless, as the naturalist saw the universe itself as a purposeless complex of blind forces, a vast mechanism of which humanity is a very insignificant part. Far from being accountable for their actions, individuals in a naturalistic world have no control whatever over their destinies but must follow the inexorable pattern designed for them by their heredity and environment. Their actions might be interpreted in terms of these controlling factors, but since "free will" has nothing to do with their behavior, to propose moral judgments on it or to label some individuals good and some bad would be patently absurd. Strictly speaking, there can be neither heroes nor villains in naturalistic fiction, since there are no longer any spiritual values for differentiating between them.

Having thrown overboard the traditional ideals of human conduct, the naturalists therefore sought and found new modes of expression for the patterns of behavior they regarded as significant. Pretending to take a detached, scientific view of life (like that of a chemist or biologist examining matter under a microscope), they analyzed individuals' actions on the basis of the inner, biological forces or the external social and economic forces controlling them. Like the scientist, too, they believed *all* life to be equally significant and therefore determined to examine all the facts, the unlovely and ignoble, the revolting and the coarse, as well as those that had heretofore been socially acceptable. Naturalism, in short, refused to recognize the sacredness of old taboos, literary or otherwise, with the result that the form as well as the content of modern prose fiction was torn apart and subjected to all manner of experimentation. Whereas formerly the characters in fiction could be defined as consistent human beings, acting in accordance with the normal human patterns of behavior common to their station in life, they were now presented as mere fragmentary bundles of impressions, delusions, or frustrations, victims of the outer forces of industrialism or the inner forces of biological necessity. And since individuals had ceased to be whole persons and were no longer regarded as responsible agents of society, the methods of recreating them in fiction became widely exploratory, varying in each case with the writer's own preconceptions as to which were the facets of their personalities most deserving of portrayal. For some writers, such portrayal meant a relatively objective presentation of men and women driven by their impulses into open violation of social conventions; for others, it implied a subjective study of the mazes of the human mind itself. But whether predominantly objective or subjective in method, the new fiction brushed aside all restraints as irrelevant, becoming by turns bold, reckless, brutal, cynical, bawdy, tender, and sympathetic. Accordingly, the most obvious effect of naturalism in American fiction was to make readers more intensely aware of the animalistic side of human nature than they had ever been before; and as a result, the guardians of traditional morality, clamoring from pulpit and editorial page, denounced the more extreme naturalists as pornographers and sensation mongers. From the artistic point of view, however, a more important effect of naturalism, too often ignored by conventional moralists, is apparent in the increased vigor, honesty, and sensitivity that characterize the serious short story today as compared with that of 1900. Because of the influence of naturalism, few areas of American life have been left unexplored and no realms of being can any longer be regarded unworthy of creative representation, for the philosophy of naturalism has broadened the scope and deepened the perception of living American writers, regardless of whether they subscribe to its basic tenets or not.

In the short story, the first steps toward the goal of a franker realism were taken in the 1890s by Hamlin Garland and Mary E. Wilkins

Freeman, whose work represented a new, if not very daring, departure from the conventional local color fiction of that era. Garland consciously rebelled against the implications of this type of writing and the restrictions imposed by the genteel tradition upon its realism, a term he scorned and tried to replace by the word "veritism." Feeling that both the local colorists and the genteel realists had falsified or sentimentalized the American scene, especially that part of it which he knew best, the raw, unlovely Midwestern prairies of his youth, he was determined to tell the truth about it. He remembered that life, not as a picturesque round of pastoral episodes engaged in by happy farming folk, but as a heroically tragic, almost futile struggle against great odds. Endless, profitless drudgery, grinding poverty, loneliness, and the abuses of grasping landlords and monopolies—these were the characteristics of rural life on the plains that Garland felt impelled to exhibit, "not as the summer boarder or the young lady novelist sees it—but as the working farmer endures it."

What his "veritism" did for the local color portrayal of the Middle West, Freeman's art accomplished for New England, though with less emphasis upon social protest. Her forte was depicting the granitic characters of ordinary New England village folk in a style as flinty as their own lives. During a long career, she wrote well over two hundred stories, most of them characterized by careful workmanship, sincerity, and sympathetic insight into human motives; but like Garland, her fame rests primarily upon the achievement of her first two collections, *A Humble Romance and Other Stories* (1887) and *A New England Nun and Other Stories* (1891). The distinctive qualities of the fifty-odd stories in these volumes are of two sorts: their accuracy of portraiture, aided by an abundant use of dialect, which is skillfully employed as a dramatic characterizing device, and their incisive presentation of those ineradicable vestiges among New Englanders of the Puritan inner life, its inhibitions and smouldering passions, as well as its rigidly Old Testament standards of loyalty, honor, and integrity. Thus, they record with quiet effectiveness the somber side of a declining civilization, which yet clung tenaciously to old values and mores.

During the same decade of the 1890s, the work of two other writers, Ambrose Bierce and Stephen Crane, demonstrated even more clearly than that of Garland or Freeman how the infusion of naturalistic attitudes and methods was deepening the tone of the short story and turning its course into newer paths. Bierce gathered much of his material from Civil War experiences, working it up somewhat in the manner of Poe with an eye toward achieving sensational, melodramatic effects. So mordant was the bitterness of these stories, however, that magazines of that day refused to print them. Physical suffering and death, unrelieved by any saving grace of pathos but accentuated rather by a kind of sardonic diablerie, comprised their major substance; and Bierce's chief concern appeared to be a pitiless, almost sadistic revelation of human weaknesses. Many of the stories in his two collections, *In the Midst of Life* (1891) and *Can Such Things Be?* (1893), show the touch of a skilled craftsman. His ability to bring into focus many carefully chosen details that lead swiftly but inexorably toward a horrifying revelation points unmistakably back to Poe, while the sudden, ironic surprise of his endings and the economy of his method point forward to O. Henry.

A similarly mordant attitude toward human nature and the forces controlling its destiny colored and conditioned the work of Crane, the more significant artist of the two. As seen in his two best collections of stories, *The Open Boat and Other Tales of Adventure* (1898) and *The Monster and Other Stories* (1899), life represented to him an endless series of ironic contradictions, which he strove to recreate objectively through the medium of symbol and paradox. There were seldom any plots of the conventional sort in his stories, just as there were no heroic figures, no leaders or ideal types. Often nameless, his characters, like Bierce's, are frequently defeated in an unequal struggle against the superior force of an indifferent universe; but the question of how they face up to this struggle at a moment of crisis is their story. Moreover, while Bierce's mannerisms and his unvariedly sardonic tone make his treatment of similar materials seem contrived, Crane's intensity of vision and his determination to keep aloof from his characters impart to his best stories that illusion of actuality that James described as "a direct impression of life." His achievement of this illusion is due to his style, a seemingly loose collection of brilliant fragments that, on closer inspection, turns out to be based on a carefully patterned arrangement of images and symbols disclosing interrelated meanings that add up to a convincing recreation of experience. Crane did not attempt either to paint the whole scene with all its documentary minutiae or to tailor the situation and events into a "well-made" plot; instead, he presented the total experience in terms of those fragmentary portions of it that his characters were able to comprehend, often dimly or mistakenly, at any given moment. By minimizing the importance of plot construction and at the same time suggesting the inscrutable complexity of a universe in which human beings are helplessly involved, Crane become one of the first naturalists in American literature, blazing a trail for such later writers as Theodore Dreiser, John Dos Passos, and James T. Farrell. But in his use of precise, colorful imagery, as well as in his economy and respect for point of view, he also pointed the way toward the widely varied styles of writers such as Willa Cather and Ernest Hemingway. By viture of both temperament and technique, therefore, Crane revealed a closer affinity with diverse twentieth-century writers than any other artist of his time.

Herman Melville

1819 – 1891

Herman Melville was born in New York City in 1819, the son of fairly well-to-do parents. For a time he attended the Albany Academy, but in 1834, two years after his father had died bankrupt, he left school to support himself and aid the family income by working in a bank, clerking in his brother's fur and cap store, shipping as cabin boy on a merchantman bound for Liverpool, and teaching school. In 1841, he shipped out as a seaman on the *Acushnet,* a whaler bound for the South Seas, thereby initiating a series of colorful adventures that took him into many faraway corners of the world and provided him with material he later used extensively in his works. Dissatisfied with the hardships of life aboard a whaler, Melville deserted the *Acushnet* at Nukahiva, in the Marquesas Islands, in July 1842, and lived for a month among the cannibals in Typee Valley. After escaping from Typee on an Australian ship, which he deserted at Papeete in September 1842, Melville worked as a field laborer in Tahiti and studied the native life of that island. He left Tahiti on a whaler, reached Honolulu, and there on August 7, 1843, enlisted as a seaman on the frigate *United States,* on which he served until he received his discharge at Boston in October 1844.

With the enlarged knowledge of the world gained through these experiences he returned to New York and, encouraged by Evert and George Duyckinck, editors of the *Literary World* (1847–53), recognized as "the best literary magazine of its time," began his literary career. In quick succession, he published *Typee* (1846), concerned with his adventures in Typee Valley; *Omoo* (1847), based on his experiences in Tahiti; *Mardi* (1849), an allegorical novel, laid in a fictional archipelago in the South Seas; *Redburn* (1849), an account of his merchant seaman experiences; *White-Jacket* (1850), a depiction of life aboard a man-of-war; and *Moby Dick* (1851), his masterpiece, the symbolic narrative of a mad captain's pursuit of a white whale. His earlier works, particularly those dealing with exotic native life, were very successful, but his popularity began to wane after *Moby Dick,* and his next two novels, *Pierre* (1852) and *Israel Potter* (1855), added little to his contemporary fame. With the publication of *Piazza Tales* in 1856, a volume containing the finest pieces of his short fiction, and of the *Confidence Man* in 1857, he virtually stopped writing prose, turning instead to poetry. Unsuccessful in his efforts to earn a living as a lecturer or to secure a consulship, he became an outdoor customs inspector in New York in 1863 and lived there until his death in 1891.

"Bartleby" is perhaps not only the finest but also the most complex short story Melville wrote. On the first and simplest level, the story may be interpreted as an allegory of Melville's personal situation as a writer in the early 1850s (see Hugh W. Hetherington, *Melville and His Reviewers,* pp. 265–271). On a second and more general level, it may be taken as a symbolic commentary on the plight of artists in a democratic, materialistic society, which forces artists to conform to (or copy) the literary fashions popular in their day or risk the possibility of their works becoming "dead letters." But the concluding words of the story, "Ah, Bartleby! Ah, humanity," suggest that on a third and still more significant level, it may be viewed as a commentary on the human predicament itself with Bartleby standing for all people rather than for Melville in particular or for the artist in general. The specific nature of the commentary the story makes on humanity is a provocative question, the answer to which must be sought in terms not only of Bartleby but also of the attorney-narrator, an equally important character, through whose sensibility Bartleby, the other characters, and the whole pattern of strange events are presented.

Bartleby, the Scrivener

A Story of Wall Street

I am a rather elderly man. The nature of my avocations, for the last thirty years, has brought me into more than ordinary contact with what would seem an interesting and somewhat singular set of men, of whom, as yet, nothing, that I know of, has ever been written—I mean, the law-copyists, or scriveners. I have known very many of them, professionally and privately, and, if I pleased, could relate divers histories, at which good-natured gentlemen might smile, and sentimental souls might weep. But I waive the biographies of all other scriveners, for a few passages in the life of Bartleby, who was a scrivener, the strangest I ever saw, or heard of. While, of other law-copyists, I might write the complete life, of Bartleby nothing of that sort can be done. I believe that no materials exist for a full and satisfactory biography of this man. It is an irreparable loss to literature. Bartleby was one of those beings of whom nothing is ascertainable, except from the original sources, and, in his case, those are very small. What my own astonished eyes saw of Bartleby, *that* is all I know of him, except, indeed, one vague report, which will appear in the sequel.

Ere introducing the scrivener, as he first appeared to me, it is fit I make some mention of myself, my *employés*, my business, my chambers, and general surroundings; because some such description is indispensable to an adequate understanding of the chief character about to be presented. Imprimis: I am a man who, from his youth upwards, has been filled with a profound conviction that the easiest way of life is the best. Hence, though I belong to a profession proverbially energetic and nervous, even to turbulence, at times, yet nothing of that sort have I ever suffered to invade my peace. I am one of those unambitious lawyers who never address a jury, or in any way draw down public applause; but, in the cool tranquillity of a snug retreat, do a snug business among rich men's bonds, and mortgages, and title-deeds. All who know me, consider me an eminently *safe* man. The late John Jacob Astor, a personage little given to poetic enthusiasm, had no hesitation in pronouncing my first grand point to be prudence; my next, method. I do not speak it in vanity, but simply record the fact, that I was not unemployed in my profession by the late John Jacob Astor; a name which, I admit, I love to repeat; for

"Bartleby, the Scrivener" by Herman Melville, from *The Piazza Tales* (G. P. Putnam's, 1856).

it hath a rounded and orbicular sound to it, and rings like unto bullion. I will freely add, that I was not insensible to the late John Jacob Astor's good opinion.

Some time prior to the period at which this little history begins, my avocations had been largely increased. The good old office, now extinct in the State of New York, of a Master in Chancery, had been conferred upon me. It was not a very arduous office, but very pleasantly remunerative. I seldom lose my temper; much more seldom indulge in dangerous indignation at wrongs and outrages; but I must be permitted to be rash here, and declare that I consider the sudden and violent abrogation of the office of Master in Chancery, by the new Constitution, as a—premature act; inasmuch as I had counted upon a life-lease of the profits, whereas I only received those of a few short years. But this is by the way.

My chambers were up stairs, at No.—Wall Street. At one end, they looked upon the white wall of the interior of a spacious sky-light shaft, penetrating the building from top to bottom.

This view might have been considered rather tame than otherwise, deficient in what landscape painters call "life." But, if so, the view from the other end of my chambers offered, at least, a contrast, if nothing more. In that direction, my windows commanded an unobstructed view of a lofty brick wall, black by age and everlasting shade; which wall required no spy-glass to bring out its lurking beauties, but, for the benefit of all near-sighted spectators, was pushed up to within ten feet of my window panes. Owing to the great height of the surrounding buildings, and my chambers being on the second floor, the interval between this wall and mine not a little resembled a huge square cistern.

At the period just preceding the advent of Bartleby, I had two persons as copyists in my employment, and a promising lad as an officeboy. First, Turkey; second, Nippers; third, Ginger Nut. These may seem names, the like of which are not usually found in the Directory. In truth, they were nicknames, mutually conferred upon each other by my three clerks, and were deemed expressive of their respective persons or characters. Turkey was a short, pursy Englishman, of about my own age—that is, somewhere not far from sixty. In the morning, one might say, his face was of a fine florid hue, but after twelve o'clock, meridian—his dinner hour—it blazed like a grate full of Christmas coals; and continued blazing—but, as it were, with a gradual wane—till six o'clock, P.M., or thereabouts; after which, I saw no more of the proprietor of the face, which, gaining its meridian with the sun, seemed to set with it, to rise, culminate, and decline the following day, with the like regularity and undiminished glory. There are many singular coincidences I have known in the course of my life, not the least among which was the fact, that, exactly when Turkey displayed his fullest beams from his red and radiant countenance, just then, too, at that critical moment, began the daily period when I considered his business capacities as seriously disturbed for the remainder of the twenty-four hours. Not that he was absolutely idle, or averse to business then; far from it. The difficulty was, he was apt to be altogether too energetic. There was a strange, inflamed, flurried, flighty recklessness of activity about him. He would be incautious in dipping his pen into his inkstand. All his blots upon my documents were dropped there after twelve o'clock, meridian. Indeed, not only would he be reckless, and sadly given to making blots in the afternoon, but, some days, he went further, and was rather noisy. At such times, too, his face flamed with augmented blazonry, as if cannel coal had been heaped on anthracite. He made an unpleasant racket with his chair; spilled his sand-box; in mending his pens, impatiently split them all to pieces, and threw them on the floor in a sudden passion; stood up, and leaned over his table, boxing his papers about in a most indecorous manner, very sad to behold in an elderly man like him. Nevertheless, as he was in many ways a most valuable person to me, and all the time before twelve o'clock, meridian, was the quickest, steadiest creature, too, accomplishing a great deal of work in a style not easily to be matched—for these reasons, I was willing to overlook his eccentricities, though, indeed, occasionally, I remonstrated with him. I did this very gently, however, because, though the civilist, nay, the blandest and most reverential of men in the morning, yet, in the afternoon, he was disposed, upon provocation, to be slightly rash with his tongue—in fact, insolent. Now, valuing his morning services as I did, and resolved not to lose them—yet, at the same time, made uncomfortable by his inflamed ways after twelve o'clock—and being a man of peace, unwilling by my admonitions to call forth unseemly retorts from him, I took upon me, one Saturday noon (he was always worse on Saturdays) to hint to him, very kindly, that, perhaps, now that he was growing old, it might be well to abridge his labors; in short, he need not come to my chambers after twelve o'clock, but, dinner over, had best go home to his lodgings, and rest himself till tea-time. But no; he insisted upon his afternoon devotions. His countenance became intolerably fervid, as he oratorically assured me—gesticulating with a long ruler at the other end of the room—that if his services in the morning were useful, how indispensable, then, in the afternoon?

"With submission, sir," said Turkey, on this occasion, "I consider myself your right-hand man. In the morning I but marshal and deploy my columns; but in the afternoon I put myself at their head, and gallantly charge the foe, thus"—and he made a violent thrust with the ruler.

"But the blots, Turkey," intimated I.

"True; but, with submission, sir, behold these hairs! I am getting old. Surely, sir, a blot or two of a warm afternoon is not to be severely urged against gray hairs. Old age—even if it blot the page—is honorable. With submission, sir, we *both* are getting old."

This appeal to my fellow-feeling was hardly to be resisted. At all events, I saw that go he would not. So, I made up my mind to let him stay, resolving, nevertheless, to see to it that, during the afternoon, he had to do with my less important papers.

Nippers, the second on my list, was a whiskered, sallow, and, upon the whole, rather piratical-looking young man, of about five-and-twenty. I always deemed him the victim of two evil powers—ambition and indigestion. The ambition was evinced by a certain impatience of the duties of a mere copyist, an unwarrantable usurpation of strictly professional affairs, such as the original drawing up of legal documents. The indigestion seemed betokened in an occasional nervous testiness and grinning irritability, causing the teeth to audibly grind together over mistakes committed in copying; unnecessary maledictions, hissed, rather than spoken, in the heat of business; and especially by a continual discontent with the height of the table where he worked. Though of a very ingenious, mechanical turn, Nippers could never get this table to suit him. He put chips under it, blocks of various sorts, bits of pasteboard, and at last went so far as to attempt an exquisite adjustment, by final pieces of folded blottingpaper. But no invention would answer. If, for the sake of easing his back, he brought the table lid at a sharp angle well up towards his chin, and wrote there like a man using the steep roof of a Dutch house for his desk, then he declared that it stopped the circulation of his arms. If now he lowered the table to his waistbands, and stooped over it in writing, then there was a sore aching in his back. In short, the truth of the matter was, Nippers knew not what he wanted. Or, if he wanted anything, it was to be rid of a scrivener's table altogether. Among the manifestations of his diseased ambition was a fondness he had for receiving visits from certain ambiguous-looking fellows in seedy coats, whom he called his clients. Indeed, I was aware that not only was he, at times, considerable of a ward-politician, but he occasionally did a little business at the Justices' courts, and was not unknown on the steps of the Tombs. I have good reasons to believe, however, that one individual who called upon him at my chambers, and who, with a grand air, he insisted was his client, was no other than a dun, and the alleged title-deed, a bill. But, with all his failings, and the annoyances he caused me, Nippers, like his compatriot Turkey, was a very useful man to me; wrote a neat, swift hand; and, when he chose, was not deficient in a gentlemanly sort of deportment. Added to this, he always dressed in a gentlemanly sort of way; and so, incidentally, reflected credit upon my chambers. Whereas, with respect to Turkey, I had much ado to keep him from being a reproach to me. His clothes were apt to look oily, and smell of eating-houses. He wore his pantaloons very loose and baggy in summer. His coats were execrable; his hat not to be handled. But while the hat was a thing of indifference to me, inasmuch as his natural civility and deference, as a dependent Englishman, always led him to doff it the moment he entered the room, yet his coat was another matter. Concerning his coats, I reasoned with him; but with no effect. The truth was, I suppose, that a man with so small an income could not afford to sport such a lustrous face and a lustrous coat at one and the same time. As Nippers once observed, Turkey's money went chiefly for red ink. One winter day, I presented Turkey with a highly respectable looking coat of my own—a padded gray coat, of a most comfortable warmth, and which buttoned straight up from the knee to the neck. I thought Turkey would appreciate the favor, and abate his rashness and obstreperousness of afternoons. But no; I verily believe that buttoning himself up in so downy and blanket-like a coat had a pernicious effect on him—upon the same principle that too much oats are bad for horses. In fact, precisely as a rash, restive horse is said to feel his oats, so Turkey felt his coat. It made him insolent. He was a man whom prosperity harmed.

Though, concerning the self-indulgent habits of Turkey, I had my own private surmises, yet, touching Nippers, I was well persuaded that, whatever might be his faults in other respects, he was, at least, a temperate young man. But, indeed, nature herself seemed to have been his vintner, and, at his birth, charged him so thoroughly with an irritable, brandy-like disposition, that all subsequent potations were needless. When I consider how, amid the stillness of my chambers, Nippers would sometimes impatiently rise from his seat, and stooping over his table, spread his arms wide apart, seize the whole desk, and move it, and jerk it, with a grim, grinding motion on the floor, as if the table were a perverse voluntary agent, intent on thwarting and vexing him, I plainly perceive that, for Nippers, brandy-and-water were altogether superfluous.

It was fortunate for me that, owing to its peculiar cause—indigestion—the irritability and consequent nervousness of Nippers were mainly observable in the morning, while in the afternoon he was comparatively mild. So that, Turkey's paroxysms only coming on about twelve o'clock, I never had to do with their eccentricities at one time. Their fits relieved each other, like guards. When Nippers's was on, Turkey's was off; and *vice versa*. This was a good natural arrangement, under the circumstances.

Ginger Nut, the third on my list, was a lad, some twelve years old. His father was a car-man, ambitious of seeing his son on the bench instead of a cart, before he died. So he sent him to my office, as student at law, errand-boy, cleaner and sweeper, at the rate of one dollar a week. He had a little desk to himself, but he did not use it much. Upon inspection, the drawer exhibited a great array of the shells of various sorts of nuts. Indeed, to this quick-witted youth, the whole noble science of the law was contained in a nutshell. Not the least among the employments of Ginger Nut, as well as one which he discharged with the most alacrity, was his duty as cake and apple purveyor for Turkey and Nippers. Copying law-papers being proverbially a dry, husky sort of business, my two scriveners were fain to moisten their mouths very often with Spitzenbergs, to be had at the numerous stalls nigh the Custom House and Post Office. Also, they sent Ginger Nut very frequently for that peculiar cake—small, flat, round, and very spicy—after which he had been named by them. Of a cold morning, when business was but dull, Turkey would gobble up scores of these cakes, as if they were mere wafers—indeed, they sell them at the rate of six or eight for a penny—the scrape of his pen blending with the crunching of the crisp particles in his mouth. Rashest of all the fiery afternoon blunders and flurried rashnesses of Turkey, was his once moistening a ginger-cake between his lips, and clapping it on to a mortgage, for a seal. I came within an ace of dismissing him then. But he mollified me by making an oriental bow, and saying—

"With submission, sir, it was generous of me to find you in stationery on my own account."

Now my original business—that of a conveyancer and title hunter, and drawer-up of recondite documents of all sorts—was considerably increased by receiving the Master's office. There was now great work for scriveners. Not only must I push the clerks already with me, but I must have additional help.

In answer to my advertisement, a motionless young man one morning stood upon my office threshold, the door being open, for it was summer. I can see that figure now—pallidly neat, pitiably respectable, incurably forlorn! It was Bartleby.

After a few words touching his qualifications, I engaged him, glad to have among my corps of copyists a man of so singularly sedate an aspect, which I thought might operate beneficially upon the flighty temper of Turkey, and the fiery one of Nippers.

I should have stated before that ground glass folding-doors divided my premises into two parts, one of which was occupied by my scriveners, the other by myself. According to my humor, I threw open these doors, or closed them. I resolved to assign Bartleby a corner by the folding-doors, but on my side of them, so as to have this quiet man within easy call, in case any trifling thing was to be done. I placed his desk close up to a small side-window in that part of the room, a window which originally had afforded a lateral view of certain grimy backyards and bricks, but which, owing to subsequent erections, commanded at present no view at all, though it gave some light. Within three feet of the panes was a wall, and the light came down from far above, between two lofty buildings, as from a very small opening in a dome. Still further to a satisfactory arrangement, I procured a high green folding screen, which might entirely isolate Bartleby from my sight, though not remove him from my voice. And thus, in a manner, privacy and society were conjoined.

At first, Bartleby did an extraordinary quantity of writing. As if long famishing for something to copy, he seemed to gorge himself on my documents. There was no pause for digestion. He ran a day and night line, copying by sun-light and by candle-light. I should have been quite delighted with his application, had he been cheerfully industrious. But he wrote on silently, palely, mechanically.

It is, of course, an indispensable part of a scrivener's business to verify the accuracy of his copy, word by word. Where there are two or more scriveners in an office, they assist each other in this examination, one reading from the copy, the other holding the original. It is a very dull, wearisome, and lethargic affair. I can readily imagine that, to some sanguine temperaments, it would be altogether intolerable. For example, I cannot credit that the mettlesome poet, Byron, would have contentedly sat down with Bartleby to examine a law document of, say five hundred pages, closely written in a crimpy hand.

Now and then, in the haste of business, it had been my habit to assist in comparing some brief document myself, calling Turkey or Nippers for this purpose. One object I had, in placing Bartleby so handy to me behind the screen, was to avail myself of his services on such trivial occasions. It was on the third day, I think, of his being with me, and before any necessity had arisen for having his own writing examined, that, being much hurried to complete a small affair I had in hand, I abruptly called to Bartleby. In my haste and natural expectancy of instant compliance, I sat with my head bent over the original on my desk, and my right hand sideways, and somewhat nervously extended with the copy, so that, immediately upon emerging from his retreat, Bartleby might snatch it and proceed to business without the least delay.

In this very attitude did I sit when I called to him, rapidly stating what it was I wanted him to do—namely, to examine a small paper with me. Imagine my surprise, nay, my consternation, when, without moving from his privacy, Bartleby, in a singularly mild, firm voice, replied, "I would prefer not to."

I sat awhile in perfect silence, rallying my stunned faculties. Immediately it occurred to me that my ears had deceived me, or Bartleby had entirely misunderstood my meaning. I repeated my request in the clearest tone I could assume; but in quite as clear a one came the previous reply, "I would prefer not to."

"Prefer not to," echoed I, rising in high excitement, and crossing the room with a stride. "What do you mean? Are you moonstruck? I want you to help me compare this sheet here—take it," and I thrust it towards him.

"I would prefer not to," said he.

I looked at him steadfastly. His face was leanly composed; his gray eye dimly calm. Not a wrinkle of agitation rippled him. Had there been the least uneasiness, anger, impatience, or impertinence in his manner; in other words, had there been any thing ordinarily human about him, doubtless I should have violently dismissed him from the premises. But as it was, I should have as soon thought of turning my pale plaster-of-paris bust of Cicero out of doors. I stood gazing at him awhile, as he went on with his writing, and then reseated myself at my desk. This is very strange, thought I. What had one best do? But my business hurried me. I concluded to forget the matter for the present, reserving it for my future leisure. So, calling Nippers from the other room, the paper was speedily examined.

A few days after this, Bartleby concluded four lengthy documents, being quadruplicates of a week's testimony taken before me in my High Court of Chancery. It became necessary to examine them. It was an important suit, and great accuracy was imperative. Having all things arranged, I called Turkey, Nippers, and Ginger Nut from the next room, meaning to place the four copies in the hands of my four clerks, while I should read from the original. Accordingly, Turkey, Nippers, and Ginger Nut had taken their seats in a row, each with his document in his hand, when I called to Bartleby to join this interesting group.

"Bartleby! quick, I am waiting."

I heard a slow scrape of his chair legs on the uncarpeted floor, and soon he appeared standing at the entrance of his hermitage.

"What is wanted?" said he, mildly.

"The copies, the copies," said I, hurriedly. "We are going to examine them. There—" and I held towards him the fourth quadruplicate.

"I would prefer not to," he said, and gently disappeared behind the screen.

For a few moments I was turned into a pillar of salt, standing at the head of my seated column of clerks. Recovering myself, I advanced towards the screen, and demanded the reason for such extraordinary conduct.

"*Why* do you refuse?"

"I would prefer not to."

With any other man I should have flown outright into a dreadful passion, scorned all further words, and thrust him ignominiously from my presence. But there was something about Bartleby that not only strangely disarmed me, but, in a wonderful manner, touched and disconcerted me. I began to reason with him.

"These are your own copies we are about to examine. It is labor saving to you, because one examination will answer for your four papers. It is common usage. Every copyist is bound to help examine his copy. Is it not so? Will you not speak? Answer!"

"I prefer not to," he replied in a flutelike tone. It seemed to me that, while I had been addressing him, he carefully revolved every statement that I made; fully comprehended the meaning; could not gainsay the irresistible conclusion; but, at the same time, some paramount consideration prevailed with him to reply as he did.

"You are decided, then, not to comply with my request—a request made according to common usage and common sense?"

He briefly gave me to understand, that on that point my judgment was sound. Yes: his decision was irreversible.

It is not seldom the case that, when a man is browbeaten in some unprecedented and violently unreasonable way, he begins to stagger in his own plainest faith. He begins, as it were, vaguely to surmise that, wonderful as it may be, all the justice and all the reason is on the other side. Accordingly, if any disinterested persons are present, he turns to them for some reinforcement for his own faltering mind.

"Turkey," said I, "what do you think of this? Am I not right?"

"With submission, sir," said Turkey in his blandest tone, "I think that you are."

"Nippers," said I, "what do *you* think of it?"

"I think I should kick him out of the office."

(The reader of nice perceptions will here perceive that, it being morning, Turkey's answer is couched in polite and tranquil terms, but Nippers replies in ill-tempered ones. Or, to repeat a previous sentence, Nippers's ugly mood was on duty, and Turkey's off.)

"Ginger Nut," said I, willing to enlist the smallest suffrage in my behalf, "what do *you* think of it?"

"I think, sir, he's a little *luny,*" replied Ginger Nut, with a grin.

"You hear what they say," said I, turning towards the screen, "come forth and do your duty."

But he vouchsafed no reply. I pondered a moment in sore perplexity. But once more business hurried me. I determined again to postpone the consideration of this dilemma to my future leisure. With a little trouble we made out to examine the papers without Bartleby, though at every page or two Turkey deferentially dropped his opinion, that this proceeding was quite out of the common; while Nippers, twitching in his chair with a dyspeptic nervousness, ground out, between his teeth, occasional hissing maledictions against the stubborn oaf behind the screen. And for his (Nippers's) part, this was the first and the last time he would do another man's business without pay.

Meanwhile Bartleby sat in his hermitage, oblivious to everything but his own peculiar business there.

Some days passed, the scrivener being employed upon another lengthy work. His late remarkable conduct led me to regard his ways narrowly. I observed that he never went to dinner; indeed, that he never went anywhere. As yet I had never, of my personal knowledge, known him to be outside of my office. He was a perpetual sentry in the corner. At about eleven o'clock though, in the morning, I noticed that Ginger Nut would advance toward the opening in Bartleby's screen, as if silently beckoned thither by a gesture invisible to me where I sat. The boy would then leave the office, jingling a few pence, and reappear with a handful of ginger-nuts, which he delivered in the hermitage, receiving two of the cakes for his trouble.

He lives, then, on ginger-nuts, thought I; never eats a dinner, properly speaking; he must be a vegetarian, then; but no; he never eats even vegetables; he eats nothing but ginger-nuts. My mind then ran on in reveries concerning the probable effects upon the human constitution of living entirely on ginger-nuts. Ginger-nuts are so called, because they contain ginger as one of their peculiar constituents, and the final flavoring one. Now, what was ginger? A hot, spicy thing. Was Bartleby hot and spicy? Not at all. Ginger, then, had no effect upon Bartleby. Probably he preferred it should have none.

Nothing so aggravates an earnest person as a passive resistance. If the individual so resisted be of a not inhumane temper, and the resisting one perfectly harmless in his passivity, then, in the better moods of the former, he will endeavor charitably to construe to his imagination what proves impossible to be solved by his judgment. Even so, for the most part, I regarded Bartleby and his ways. Poor fellow! thought I, he means no mischief; it is plain he intends no insolence; his aspect sufficiently evinces that his eccentricities are involuntary. He is useful to me. I can get along with him. If I turn him away, the chances are he will fall in with some less-indulgent employer, and then he will be rudely treated, and perhaps driven forth miserably to starve. Yes. Here I can cheaply purchase a delicious self-approval. To befriend Bartleby; to humor him in his strange willfulness, will cost me little or nothing, while I lay up in my soul what will eventually prove a sweet morsel for my conscience. But this mood was not invariable with me. The passiveness of Bartleby sometimes irritated me. I felt strangely goaded on to encounter him in new opposition—to elicit some angry spark from him answerable to my own. But, indeed, I might as well have essayed to strike fire with my knuckles against a bit of Windsor soap. But one afternoon the evil impulse in me mastered me, and the following little scene ensued:

"Bartleby," said I, "when those papers are all copied, I will compare them with you."

"I would prefer not to."

"How? Surely you do not mean to persist in that mulish vagary?"

No answer.

I threw open the folding-doors near by, and, turning upon Turkey and Nippers, exclaimed:

"Bartleby a second times says, he won't examine his papers. What do you think of it, Turkey?"

It was afternoon, be it remembered. Turkey sat glowing like a brass boiler; his bald head steaming; his hands reeling among his blotted papers.

"Think of it?" roared Turkey; "I think I'll just step behind his screen, and black his eyes for him!"

So saying, Turkey rose to his feet and threw his arms into a pugilistic position. He was hurrying away to make good his promise, when I detained him, alarmed at the effect of incautiously rousing Turkey's combativeness after dinner.

"Sit down, Turkey," said I, "and hear what Nippers has to say. What do you think of it, Nippers? Would I not be justified in immediately dismissing Bartleby?"

"Excuse me, that is for you to decide, sir. I think his conduct quite unusual, and, indeed, unjust, as regards Turkey and myself. But it may only be a passing whim."

"Ah," exclaimed I, "you have strangely changed your mind, then—you speak very gently of him now."

"All beer," cried Turkey; "gentleness is effects of beer—Nippers and I dined together to-day. You see how gentle *I* am, sir. Shall I go and black his eyes?"

"You refer to Bartleby, I suppose. No, not to-day, Turkey," I replied; "pray, put up your fists."

I closed the doors, and again advanced towards Bartleby. I felt additional incentives tempting me to my fate. I burned to be rebelled against again. I remembered that Bartleby never left the office.

"Bartleby," said I, "Ginger Nut is away; just step around to the Post Office, won't you?" (it was but a three minutes' walk), "and see if there is anything for me."

"I would prefer not to."

"You *will* not?"

"I *prefer* not."

I staggered to my desk, and sat there in a deep study. My blind inveteracy returned. Was there any other thing in which I could procure myself to be ignominiously repulsed by this lean, penniless wight?—my hired clerk? What added thing is there, perfectly reasonable, that he will be sure to refuse to do?

"Bartleby!"

No answer.

"Bartleby," in a louder tone.

No answer.

"Bartleby," I roared.

Like a very ghost, agreeably to the laws of magical invocation, at the third summons, he appeared at the entrance of his hermitage.

"Go to the next room, and tell Nippers to come to me."

"I prefer not to," he respectfully and slowly said, and mildly disappeared.

"Very good, Bartleby," said I, in a quiet sort of serenely-severe, self-possessed tone, intimating the unalterable purpose of some terrible retribution very close at hand. At the moment I half intended something of the kind. But upon the whole, as it was drawing towards my dinner-hour, I thought it best to put on my hat and walk home for the day, suffering much from perplexity and distress of mind.

Shall I acknowledge it? The conclusion of this whole business was, that it soon became a fixed fact of my chambers, that a pale young scrivener, by the name of Bartleby, had a desk there; that he copied for me at the usual rate of four cents a folio (one hundred words); but he was permanently exempt from examining the work done by him, that duty being transferred to Turkey and Nippers, out of compliment, doubtless, to their superior acuteness; moreover, said Bartleby was never, on any account, to be dispatched on the most trivial errand of any sort; and that even if entreated to take upon him such a matter, it was generally understood that he would "prefer not to"—in other words, that he would refuse point-blank.

As days passed on, I became considerably reconciled to Bartleby. His steadiness, his freedom from all dissipation, his incessant industry (except when he chose to throw himself into a standing revery behind his screen), his great stillness, his unalterableness of demeanor under all circumstances, made him a valuable acquisition. One prime thing was this—*he was always there*—first in the morning, continually through the day, and the last at night. I had a singular confidence in his honesty. I felt my most precious papers perfectly safe in his hands. Sometimes, to be sure, I could not, for the very soul of me, avoid falling into sudden spasmodic passions with him. For it was exceeding difficult to bear in mind all the time those strange peculiarities, privileges, and unheard-of exemptions, forming the tacit stipulations on Bartleby's part under which he remained in my office. Now and then, in the eagerness of dispatching pressing business, I would inadvertently summon Bartleby, in a short, rapid tone, to put his finger, say, on the incipient tie of a bit of red tape with which I was about compressing some papers. Of course, from behind the screen the usual answer, "I prefer not to," was sure to come; and then, how could a human creature, with the common infirmities of our nature, refrain from bitterly exclaiming upon such perverseness—such unreasonableness? However, every added repulse of this sort which I received only tended to lessen the probability of my repeating the inadvertence.

Here it must be said, that according to the custom of most legal gentlemen occupying chambers in densely-populated law buildings, there were several keys to my door. One was kept by a woman residing in the attic, which person weekly scrubbed and daily swept and dusted my apartments. Another was kept by Turkey for convenience sake. The third I sometimes carried in my own pocket. The fourth I knew not who had.

Now, one Sunday morning I happened to go to Trinity Church, to hear a celebrated preacher, and finding myself rather early on the ground I thought I would walk round to my chambers for a while. Luckily I had my key with me; but upon applying it to the lock, I found it resisted by something inserted from the inside. Quite surprised, I called out; when to my consternation a key was turned from within; and thrusting his lean visage at me, and holding the door ajar, the apparition of Bartleby appeared, in his shirt sleeves, and otherwise in a strangely tattered *déshabillé,* saying quietly that he was sorry, but he was deeply engaged just then, and—preferred not admitting me at present. In a brief word or two, he moreover added, that perhaps I had better walk round the block two or three times, and by that time he would probably have concluded his affairs.

Now, the utterly unsurmised appearance of Bartleby, tenanting my law-chambers of a Sunday morning, with his cadaverously gentlemanly *nonchalance,* yet withal firm and self-possessed, had such a strange effect upon me, that incontinently I slunk away from my own door, and did as desired. But not without sundry twinges of impotent rebellion against the mild effrontery of this unaccountable scrivener. Indeed, it was his wonderful mildness chiefly, which not only disarmed me, but unmanned me, as it were. For I consider that one, for the time, is somehow unmanned when he tranquilly permits his hired clerk to dictate to him, and order him away from his own premises. Furthermore, I was full of uneasiness as to what Bartleby could possibly be doing in my office in his shirt sleeves, and in an otherwise dismantled condition of a Sunday morning. Was anything amiss going on? Nay, that was out of the question. It was not to be thought of for a moment that Bartleby was an immoral person. But what could he be doing there?—copying? Nay again, whatever might be his eccentricities, Bartleby was an eminently decorous person. He would be the last man to sit down to his desk in any state approaching nudity. Besides, it was Sunday; and there was something about Bartleby that forbade the supposition that he would by any secular occupation violate the proprieties of the day.

Nevertheless, my mind was not pacified; and full of a restless curiosity, at last I returned to the door. Without hindrance I inserted the key, opened it, and entered. Bartleby was not to be seen. I looked round anxiously, peeped behind his screen; but it was very plain that he was gone. Upon more closely examining the place, I surmised that for an indefinite period Bartleby must have eaten, dressed, and slept in my office, and that, too, without plate, mirror, or bed. The cushioned seat of a ricketty old sofa in one corner bore the faint impress of a lean, reclining form. Rolled away under his desk, I found a blanket; under the empty grate, a blacking box and brush; on a chair, a tin basin, with soap and a ragged towel; in a newspaper a few crumbs of ginger-nuts and a morsel of cheese. Yes, thought I, it is evident enough that Bartleby has been making his home here, keeping bachelor's hall all by himself. Immediately then the thought came sweeping across me, what miserable friendlessness and loneliness are here revealed! His poverty is great; but his solitude, how horrible! Think of it. Of a Sunday, Wall Street is deserted as Petra; and every night of every day it is an emptiness. This building, too, which of weekdays hums with industry and life, at nightfall echoes with sheer vacancy, and all through Sunday is forlorn. And here Bartleby makes his home; sole spectator of a solitude which he has seen all populous—a sort of innocent and transformed Marius brooding among the ruins of Carthage!

For the first time in my life a feeling of overpowering stinging melancholy seized me. Before, I had never experienced aught but a not unpleasing sadness. The bond of a common humanity now drew me irresistibly to gloom. A fraternal melancholy! For both I and Bartleby were sons of Adam. I remembered the bright silks and sparkling faces I had seen that day, in gala trim, swan-like sailing down the Mississippi of Broadway; and I contrasted them with the pallid copyist, and thought to myself, Ah, happiness courts the light, so we deem the world is gay; but misery hides aloof, so we deem that misery there is none. These sad fancyings—chimeras, doubtless, of a sick and silly brain—led on to other and more special thoughts, concerning the eccentricities of Bartleby. Presentiments of strange discoveries hovered round me. The scrivener's pale form appeared to me laid out, among uncaring strangers, in its shivering winding sheet.

Suddenly I was attracted to Bartleby's closed desk, the key in open sight left in the lock.

I mean no mischief, seek the gratification of no heartless curiosity, thought I; besides, the desk is mine, and its contents, too, so I will make bold to look within. Everything was methodically arranged, the papers smoothly placed. The pigeon holes were deep, and removing the files of documents, I groped into their recesses. Presently I felt something there, and dragged it out. It was an old bandanna handkerchief, heavy and knotted. I opened it, and saw it was a savings' bank.

I now recalled all the quiet mysteries which I had noted in the man. I remembered that he never spoke but to answer; that, though at intervals he had considerable time to himself, yet I had never seen him reading—

no, not even a newspaper; that for long periods he would stand looking out, at his pale window behind the screen, upon the dead brick wall; I was quite sure he never visited any refectory or eating house; while his pale face clearly indicated that he never drank beer like Turkey, or tea and coffee even, like other men; that he never went anywhere in particular that I could learn; never went out for a walk, unless, indeed, that was the case at present; that he had declined telling who he was, or whence he came, or whether he had any relatives in the world; that though so thin and pale, he never complained of ill health. And more than all, I remembered a certain unconscious air of pallid—how shall I call it?—of pallid haughtiness, say, or rather an austere reserve about him, which had positively awed me into my tame compliance with his eccentricities, when I had feared to ask him to do the slightest incidental thing for me, even though I might know, from his long-continued motionlessness, that behind his screen he must be standing in one of those deadwall reveries of his.

Revolving all these things, and coupling them with the recently discovered fact, that he made my office his constant abiding place and home, and not forgetful of his morbid moodiness; revolving all these things, a prudential feeling began to steal over me. My first emotions had been those of pure melancholy and sincerest pity; but just in proportion as the forlornness of Bartleby grew and grew to my imagination, did that same melancholy merge into fear, that pity into repulsion. So true it is, and so terrible, too, that up to a certain point the thought or sight of misery enlists our best affections; but, in certain special cases, beyond that point it does not. They err who would assert that invariably this is owing to the inherent selfishness of the human heart. It rather proceeds from a certain hopelessness of remedying excessive and organic ill. To a sensitive being, pity is not seldom pain. And when at last it is perceived that such pity cannot lead to effectual succor, common sense bids the soul be rid of it. What I saw that morning persuaded me that the scrivener was the victim of innate and incurable disorder. I might give alms to his body; but his body did not pain him; it was his soul that suffered, and his soul I could not reach.

I did not accomplish the purpose of going to Trinity Church that morning. Somehow, the things I had seen disqualified me for the time from church-going. I walked homeward, thinking what I would do with Bartleby. Finally, I resolved upon this—I would put certain calm questions to him the next morning, touching his history, etc., and if he declined to answer them openly and unreservedly (and I supposed he would prefer not), then to give him a twenty dollar bill over and above whatever I might owe him, and tell him his services were no longer required; but that if in any other way I could assist him, I would be happy to do so, especially if he desired to return to his native place, wherever that might be, I would willingly help to defray the expenses. Moreover, if, after reaching home, he found himself at any time in want of aid, a letter from him would be sure of a reply.

The next morning came.

"Bartleby," said I, gently calling to him behind his screen.

No reply.

"Bartleby," said I, in a still gentler tone, "come here; I am not going to ask you to do anything you would prefer not to do—I simply wish to speak to you."

Upon this he noiselessly slid into view.

"Will you tell me, Bartleby, where you were born?"

"I would prefer not to."

"Will you tell me *anything* about yourself?"

"I would prefer not to."

"But what reasonable objection can you have to speak to me? I feel friendly towards you."

He did not look at me while I spoke, but kept his glance fixed upon my bust of Cicero, which, as I then sat, was directly behind me, some six inches above my head.

"What is your answer, Bartleby?" said I, after waiting a considerable time for a reply, during which his countenance remained immovable, only there was the faintest conceivable tremor of the white attenuated mouth.

"At present I prefer to give no answer," he said, and retired into his hermitage.

It was rather weak in me I confess, but his manner, on this occasion, nettled me. Not only did there seem to lurk in it a certain calm disdain, but his perverseness seemed ungrateful, considering the undeniable good usage and indulgence he had received from me.

Again I sat ruminating what I should do. Mortified as I was at his behavior, and resolved as I had been to dismiss him when I entered my office, nevertheless I strangely felt something superstitious knocking at my heart, and forbidding me to carry out my purpose, and denouncing me for a villain if I dared to breathe one bitter word against this forlornest of mankind. At last, familiarly drawing my chair behind his screen, I sat down and said: "Bartleby, never mind, then, about revealing your history; but let me entreat you, as a friend, to comply as far as may be with the usages of this office. Say now, you will help examine papers to-morrow or next day: in short, say now, that in a day or two you will begin to be a little reasonable:—say so, Bartleby."

"At present I would prefer not to be a little reasonable," was his mildly cadaverous reply.

Just then the folding-doors opened, and Nippers approached. He seemed suffering from an unusually bad night's rest, induced by severer indigestion than common. He overhead those final words of Bartleby.

"*Prefer not*, eh?" gritted Nippers—"I'd *prefer* him, if I were you, sir," addressing me—"I'd *prefer* him; I'd give him preferences, the stubborn mule! What is it, sir, pray, that he *prefers* not to do now?"

Bartleby moved not a limb.

"Mr. Nippers," said I, "I'd prefer that you would withdraw for the present."

Somehow, of late, I had got into the way of involuntarily using this word "prefer" upon all sorts of not exactly suitable occasions. And I trembled to think that my contact with the scrivener had already and seriously affected me in a mental way. And what further and deeper aberration might it not yet produce? This apprehension had not been without efficacy in determining me to summary measures.

As Nippers, looking very sour and sulky, was departing, Turkey blandly and deferentially approached.

"With submission, sir," said he, "yesterday I was thinking about Bartleby here, and I think that if he would but prefer to take a quart of good ale every day, it would do much towards mending him, and enabling him to assist in examining his papers."

"So you have got the word, too," said I, slightly excited.

"With submission, what word, sir?" asked Turkey, respectfully crowding himself into the contracted space behind the screen, and by so doing, making me jostle the scrivener. "What word, sir?"

"I would prefer to be left alone here," said Bartleby, as if offended at being mobbed in his privacy.

"*That's* the word, Turkey," said I—"*that's* it."

"Oh, *prefer?* oh yes—queer word. I never use it myself. But, sir, as I was saying, if he would but prefer—"

"Turkey," interrupted I, "you will please withdraw."

"Oh certainly, sir, if you prefer that I should."

As he opened the folding-door to retire, Nippers at his desk caught a glimpse of me, and asked whether I would prefer to have a certain paper copied on blue or white. He did not in the least roguishly accent the word "prefer." It was plain that it involuntarily rolled from his tongue. I thought to myself, surely I must get rid of a demented man, who already has in some degree turned the tongues, if not the heads of myself and clerks. But I thought it prudent not to break the dismission at once.

The next day I noticed that Bartleby did nothing but stand at his window in his dead-wall revery. Upon asking him why he did not write, he said that he had decided upon doing no more writing.

"Why, how now? what next?" exclaimed I, "do no more writing?"

"No more."

"And what is the reason?"

"Do you not see the reason for yourself?" he indifferently replied.

I looked steadfastly at him, and perceived that his eyes looked dull and glazed. Instantly it occurred to me, that his unexampled diligence in copying by his dim window for the first few weeks of his stay with me might have temporarily impaired his vision.

I was touched. I said something in condolence with him. I hinted that of course he did wisely in abstaining from writing for a while; and urged him to embrace that opportunity of taking wholesome exercise in the open air. This, however, he did not do. A few days after this, my other clerks being absent, and being in a great hurry to dispatch certain letters by the mail, I thought that, having nothing else earthly to do, Bartleby would surely be less inflexible than usual, and carry these letters to the post-office. But he blankly declined. So, much to my inconvenience, I went myself.

Still added days went by. Whether Bartleby's eyes improved or not, I could not say. To all appearance, I thought they did. But when I asked him if they did, he vouchsafed no answer. At all events, he would do no copying. At last, in reply to my urgings, he informed me that he had permanently given up copying.

"What!" exclaimed I; "suppose your eyes should get entirely well—better than ever before—would you not copy then?"

"I have given up copying," he answered, and slid aside.

He remained as ever, a fixture in my chamber. Nay—if that were possible—he became still more of a fixture than before. What was to be done? He would do nothing in the office; why should he stay there? In plain fact, he had now become a millstone to me, not only useless as a necklace, but afflictive to bear. Yet I was sorry for him. I speak less than truth when I say that, on his own account, he occasioned me uneasiness. If he would but have named a single relative or friend, I would instantly have written, and urged their taking the poor fellow away to some convenient retreat. But he seemed alone, absolutely alone in the universe. A bit of wreck in the mid Atlantic. At length, necessities connected with my business tyrannized over all other considerations. Decently as I could, I told Bartleby that in six days' time he must unconditionally leave the office. I warned him to take measures, in the interval, for procuring some other abode. I offered to assist him in his endeavor, if he himself would but take the first step towards a removal. "And when you finally quit me; Bartleby," added I, "I shall see that you go not away entirely unprovided. Six days from this hour, remember."

At the expiration of that period, I peeped behind the screen, and lo! Bartleby was there.

I buttoned up my coat, balanced myself; advanced slowly towards him, touched his shoulder, and said, "The time has come; you must quit this place; I am sorry for you; here is money; but you must go."

"I would prefer not," he replied, with his back still towards me.

"You *must.*"

He remained silent.

Now I had an unbounded confidence in this man's common honesty. He had frequently restored to me sixpences and shillings carelessly dropped upon the floor, for I am apt to be very reckless in such shirt-button affairs. The proceeding, then, which followed will not be deemed extraordinary.

"Bartleby," said I, "I owe you twelve dollars on account; here are thirty-two; the odd twenty are yours—Will you take it?" and I handed the bills towards him.

But he made no motion.

"I will leave them here, then," putting them under a weight on the table. Then taking my hat and cane and going to the door, I tranquilly turned and added—"After you have removed your things from these offices, Bartleby, you will of course lock the door—since every one is now gone for the day but you—and if you please, slip your key underneath the mat, so that I may have it in the morning. I shall not see you again; so good-by to you. If, hereafter, in your new place of abode, I can be of any service to you, do not fail to advise me by letter. Good-by, Bartleby, and fare you well."

But he answered not a word; like the last column of some ruined temple, he remained standing mute and solitary in the middle of the otherwise deserted room.

As I walked home in a pensive mood, my vanity got the better of my pity. I could not but highly plume myself on my masterly management in getting rid of Bartleby. Masterly I call it, and such it must appear to any dispassionate thinker. The beauty of my procedure seemed to consist in its perfect quietness. There was no vulgar bullying, no bravado of any sort, no choleric hectoring, and striding to and fro across the apartment, jerking out vehement commands for Bartleby to bundle himself off with his beggarly traps. Nothing of the kind. Without loudly bidding Bartleby depart—as an inferior genius might have done—I *assumed* the ground that depart he must; and upon that assumption built all I had to say. The more I thought over my procedure, the more I was charmed with it. Nevertheless, next morning, upon awakening, I had my doubts. I had somehow slept off the fumes of vanity. One of the coolest and wisest hours a man has, is just after he awakes in the morning. My procedure seemed as sagacious as ever—but only in theory. How it would prove in practice—there was the rub. It was truly a beautiful thought to have assumed Bartleby's departure; but, after all, that assumption was simply my own, and none of Bartleby's. The great point was, not whether I had assumed that he would quit me, but whether he would prefer so to do. He was more a man of preferences than assumptions.

After breakfast, I walked down town, arguing the probabilities *pro* and *con*. One moment I thought it would prove a miserable failure, and Bartleby would be found all alive in my office as usual; the next moment it seemed certain that I should find his chair empty. And so I kept veering about. At the corner of Broadway and Canal Street, I saw quite an excited group of people standing in earnest conversation.

"I'll take odds he doesn't," said a voice as I passed.

"Doesn't go?—done!" said I; "put up your money."

I was instinctively putting my hand in my pocket to produce my own, when I remembered that this was an election day. The words I had overheard bore no reference to Bartleby, but to the success or non-success of some candidate for the mayoralty. In my intent frame of mind, I had, as it were, imagined that all Broadway shared in my excitement, and were debating the same question with me. I passed on, very thankful that the uproar of the street screened my momentary absent-mindedness.

As I had intended, I was earlier than usual at my office door. I stood listening for a moment. All was still. He must be gone. I tried the knob. The door was locked. Yes, my procedure had worked to a charm; he indeed must be vanished. Yet a certain melancholy mixed with this; I was almost sorry for my brilliant success. I was fumbling under the door mat for the key, which Bartleby was to have left there for me, when accidentally my knee knocked against a panel, producing a summoning sound, and in response a voice came to me from within—"Not yet; I am occupied."

It was Bartleby.

I was thunderstruck. For an instant I stood like the man who, pipe in mouth, was killed one cloudless afternoon long ago in Virginia, by summer lightning; at his own warm open window he was killed, and remained leaning out there upon the dreamy afternoon, till some one touched him, when he fell.

"Not gone!" I murmured at last. But again obeying that wondrous ascendancy which the inscrutable scrivener had over me, and from which ascendancy, for all my chafing, I could not completely escape, I slowly went down stairs and out into the street, and while walking round the block, considered what I should next do in this unheard-of perplexity. Turn the man out by an actual thrusting I could not; to drive him away by calling him hard names would not do; calling in the police was an unpleasant idea; and yet, permit him to enjoy his cadaverous triumph over me—this, too, I could not think of. What was to be done? or, if nothing could be done, was there anything further that I could *assume* in the matter? Yes, as before I had prospectively assumed that Bartleby would depart, so now I might retrospectively assume that departed he was. In the legitimate carrying out of this assumption, I might enter my office in a great hurry, and pretending not to see Bartleby at all, walk straight against him as if he were air. Such a proceeding would in a singular degree have the appearance of a home-thrust. It was hardly possible that Bartleby could withstand such an application of the doctrine of assumptions. But upon second thoughts the success of the plan seemed rather dubious. I resolved to argue the matter over with him again.

"Bartleby," said I, entering the office, with a quietly severe expression, "I am seriously displeased. I am pained, Bartleby. I had thought better of you. I had imagined you of such a gentlemanly organization, that in any delicate dilemma a slight hint would suffice—in short, an assumption. But it appears I am deceived. Why," I added, unaffectedly starting, "you have not even touched that money yet," pointing to it, just where I had left it the evening previous.

He answered nothing.

"Will you, or will you not, quit me?" I now demanded in a sudden passion, advancing close to him.

"I would prefer *not* to quit you," he replied, gently emphasizing the *not*.

"What earthly right have you to stay here? Do you pay any rent? Do you pay my taxes? Or is this property yours?"

He answered nothing.

"Are you ready to go on and write now? Are your eyes recovered? Could you copy a small paper for me this morning? or help examine a few lines? or step round to the post-office? In a word, will you do anything at all, to give a coloring to your refusal to depart the premises?"

He silently retired into his hermitage.

I was now in such a state of nervous resentment that I thought it but prudent to check myself at present from further demonstrations. Bartleby and I were alone. I remembered the tragedy of the unfortunate Adams and the still more unfortunate Colt in the solitary office of the latter; and how poor Colt, being dreadfully incensed by Adams, and imprudently permitting himself to get wildly excited, was at unawares hurried into his fatal act—an act which certainly no man could possibly deplore more than the actor himself. Often it had occurred to me in my ponderings upon the subject that had that altercation taken place in the public street, or at a private residence, it would not have terminated as it did. It was the circumstance of being alone in a solitary office, up stairs, of a building entirely unhallowed by humanizing domestic associations—an uncarpeted office, doubtless, of a dusty, haggard sort of appearance—this it must have been, which greatly helped to enhance the irritable desperation of the hapless Colt.

But when this old Adam of resentment rose in me and tempted me concerning Bartleby, I grappled him and threw him. How? Why, simply be recalling the divine injunction: "A new commandment give I unto you, that ye love one another." Yes, this it was that saved me. Aside from higher considerations, charity often operates as a vastly wise and prudent principle—a great safeguard to its possessor. Men have committed murder for jealousy's sake, and anger's sake, and hatred's sake, and selfishness' sake, and spiritual pride's sake; but no man, that ever I heard of, ever committed a diabolical murder for sweet charity's sake. Mere self-interest, then, if no better motive can be enlisted, should, especially with high-tempered men, prompt all beings to charity and philanthropy. At any rate, upon the occasion in question, I strove to drown my exasperated feelings towards the scrivener by benevolently construing his conduct. Poor fellow, poor fellow! thought I, he don't mean anything, and besides, he has seen hard times, and ought to be indulged.

I endeavored, also, immediately to occupy myself, and at the same time to confront my despondency. I tried to fancy, that in the course of the morning, at such time as might prove agreeable to him, Bartleby, of his own free accord, would emerge from his hermitage and take up some decided line of march in the direction of the door. But no. Half-past twelve o'clock came; Turkey began to glow in the face, overturn his inkstand, and become generally obstreperous; Nippers abated down into quietude and courtesy; Ginger Nut munched his noon apple; and Bartleby remained standing at his window in one of his profoundest dead-wall reveries. Will it be credited? Ought I to acknowledge it? That afternoon I left the office without saying one further word to him.

Some days now passed, during which, at leisure intervals I looked a little into "Edwards on the Will," and "Priestley on Necessity." Under the circumstances, those books induced a salutary feeling. Gradually I slid into the persuasion that these troubles of mine, touching the scrivener, had been all predestinated from eternity, and Bartleby was billeted upon me for some mysterious purpose of an allwise Providence, which it was not for a mere mortal like me to fathom. Yes, Bartleby, stay there behind your screen, thought I; I shall persecute you no more; you are harmless and noiseless as any of these old chairs; in short, I never feel so private as when I know you are here. At last I see it, I feel it; I penetrate to the predestinated purpose of my life. I am content. Others may have loftier parts to enact; but my mission in this world, Bartleby, is to furnish you with office-room for such period as you may see fit to remain.

I believe that this wise and blessed frame of mind would have continued with me, had it not been for the unsolicited and uncharitable remarks obtruded upon me by my professional friends who visited the rooms. But thus it often is, that the constant friction of illiberal minds wears out at last the best resolves of the more generous. Though to be sure, when I reflected upon it, it was not strange that people entering my office should be struck by the peculiar aspect of the unaccountable Bartleby, and so be tempted to throw out some sinister observations concerning him. Sometimes an attorney, having business with me, and calling at my office, and finding no one but the scrivener there, would undertake to obtain some sort of precise information from him touching my whereabouts; but without heeding his idle talk, Bartleby would remain standing immovable in the middle of the room. So after contemplating him in that position for a time, the attorney would depart, no wiser than he came.

Also, when a reference was going on, and the room full of lawyers and witnesses, and business driving fast, some deeply-occupied legal gentleman present, seeing Bartleby wholly unemployed, would request him to run round to his (the legal gentleman's) office and fetch some papers for him. Thereupon, Bartleby would tranquilly decline, and yet remain idle as before. Then the lawyer would give a great stare, and turn to me. And what could I say? At last I was made aware that all through the circle of my professional acquaintance, a whisper of wonder was running round, having reference to the strange creature I kept at my office. This worried me very much. And as the idea came upon me of his possibly turning out a long-lived man, and keep occupying my chambers, and denying my authority; and perplexing my visitors; and scandalizing my professional reputation; and casting a general gloom over the premises; keeping soul and body together to the last upon his savings (for doubtless he spent but half a dime a day), and in the end perhaps outlive me, and claim possession of my office by right of his perpetual occupancy: as all these dark anticipations crowded upon me more and more, and my friends continually intruded their relentless remarks upon the apparition in my room; a great change was wrought in me. I resolved to gather all my faculties together, and forever rid me of this intolerable incubus.

Ere resolving any complicated project, however, adapted to this end, I first simply suggested to Bartleby the propriety of his permanent departure. In a calm and serious tone, I commended the idea to his careful and mature consideration. But, having taken three days to meditate upon it, he apprised me, that his original determination remained the same; in short, that he still preferred to abide with me.

What shall I do? I now said to myself, buttoning up my coat to the last button. What shall I do? what ought I to do? what does conscience say I *should* do with this man, or, rather, ghost. Rid myself of him, I must; go, he shall. But how? You will not thrust him, the poor, pale, passive mortal—you will not thrust such a helpless creature out of your door? you will not dishonor yourself by such cruelty? No, I will not, I cannot do that. Rather would I let him live and die here, and then mason up his remains in the wall. What, then, will you do? For all your coaxing, he will not budge. Bribes he leaves under your own paper-weight on your table; in short, it is quite plain that he prefers to cling to you.

Then something severe, something unusual most be done. What! surely you will not have him collared by a constable, and commit his innocent pallor to the common jail? And upon what ground could you procure such a thing to be done?—a vagrant, is he? What! he a vagrant, a wanderer, who refuses to budge? It is because he will *not* be a vagrant, then, that you seek to count him *as* a vagrant. That is too absurd. No visible means of support: there I have him. Wrong again: for indubitably he *does* support himself, and that is the only unanswerable proof that any man can show of his possessing the means so to do. No more, then. Since he will not quit me, I must quit him. I will change my offices; I will move elsewhere, and give him fair notice, that if I find him on my new premises I will then proceed against him as a common trespasser.

Acting accordingly, next day I thus addressed him: "I find these chambers too far from the City Hall; the air is unwholesome. In a word, I propose to remove my offices next week, and shall no longer require your services. I tell you this now, in order that you may seek another place."

He made no reply; and nothing more was said.

On the appointed day I engaged carts and men, proceeded to my chambers, and, having but little furniture, everything was removed in a few hours. Throughout, the scrivener remained standing behind the screen, which I directed to be removed the last thing. It was withdrawn; and, being folded up like a huge folio, left him the motionless occupant of a naked room. I stood in the entry watching him a moment, while something from within me upbraided me.

I re-entered, with my hand in my pocket—and—and my heart in my mouth.

"Good-by, Bartleby; I am going—good-by, and God some way bless you; and take that," slipping something in his hand. But it dropped upon the floor, and then—strange to say—I tore myself from him whom I had so longed to be rid of.

Established in my new quarters, for a day or two I kept the door locked, and started at every footfall in the passages. When I returned to my rooms, after a little absence, I would pause at the threshold for an instant, and attentively listen, ere applying my key. But these fears were needless. Bartleby never came nigh me.

I thought all was going well, when a perturbed-looking stranger visited me, inquiring whether I was the person who had recently occupied rooms at No.—Wall Street.

Full of forebodings, I replied that I was.

"Then, sir," said the stranger, who proved a lawyer, "you are responsible for the man you left there. He refuses to do any copying; he refuses to do anything; he says he prefers not to; and he refuses to quit the premises."

"I am very sorry, sir" said I, with assumed tranquillity, but an inward tremor, "but, really, the man you allude to is nothing to me—he is no relation or apprentice of mine, that you should hold me responsible for him."

"In mercy's name, who is he?"

"I certainly cannot inform you. I know nothing about him. Formerly I employed him as a copyist; but he has done nothing for me now for some time past."

"I shall settle him, then—good morning, sir."

Several days passed, and I heard nothing more; and, though I often felt a charitable prompting to call at the place and see poor Bartleby, yet a certain squeamishness, of I know not what, withheld me.

All is over with him, but this time, thought I, at last, when, through another week, no further intelligence reached me. But, coming to my room the day after, I found several persons waiting at my door in a high state of nervous excitement.

"That's the man—here he comes," cried the foremost one, whom I recognized as the lawyer who had previously called upon me alone.

"You must take him away, sir, at once," cried a portly person among them, advancing upon me, and whom I knew to be the landlord of No.—Wall Street. "These gentlemen, my tenants, cannot stand it any longer; Mr. B——," pointing to the lawyer, "has turned him out of his room, and he now persists in haunting the building generally, sitting upon the banisters of the stairs by day, and sleeping in the entry by night. Everybody is concerned; clients are leaving the offices; some fears are entertained of a mob; something you must do, and that without delay."

Aghast at this torrent, I fell back before it, and would fain have locked myself in my new quarters. In vain I persisted that Bartleby was nothing to me—no more than to anyone else. In vain—I was the last person known to have anything to do with him, and they held me to the terrible account. Fearful, then, of being exposed in the papers (as one person present obscurely threatened), I considered the matter, and, at length, said, that if the lawyer would give me a confidential interview with the scrivener, in his (the lawyer's) own room, I would, that afternoon, strive my best to rid them of the nuisance they complained of.

Going up stairs to my old haunt, there was Bartleby silently sitting upon the banister at the landing.

"What are you doing here, Bartleby?" said I.

"Sitting upon the banister," he mildly replied.

I motioned him into the lawyer's room, who then left us.

"Bartleby," said I, "are you aware that you are the cause of great tribulation to me, by persisting in occupying the entry after being dismissed from the office?"

No answer.

"Now one of two things must take place. Either you must do something, or something must be done to you. Now what sort of business would you like to engage in? Would you like to re-engage in copying for some one?"

"No; I would prefer not to make any change."

"Would you like a clerkship in a dry-goods store?"

"There is too much confinement about that. No, I would not like a clerkship; but I am not particular."

"Too much confinement," I cried, "why, you keep yourself confined all the time!"

"I would prefer not to take a clerkship," he rejoined, as if to settle that little item at once.

"How would a bar-tender's business suit you? There is no trying of the eye-sight in that."

"I would not like it at all; though, as I said before, I am not particular."

His unwonted wordiness inspirited me. I returned to the charge.

"Well, then, would you like to travel through the country collecting bills for merchants? That would improve your health."

"No, I would prefer to be doing something else."

"How, then, would going as a companion to Europe, to entertain some young gentleman with your conversation—how would that suit you?"

"Not at all. It does not strike me that there is anything definite about that. I like to be stationary. But I am not particular."

"Stationary you shall be, then," I cried, now losing all patience, and, for the first time in all my exasperating connection with him, fairly flying into a passion. "If you do not go away from these premises before night, I shall feel bound—indeed, I *am* bound—to—to—to quit the premises myself!" I rather absurdly concluded, knowing not with what possible threat to try to frighten his immobility into compliance. Despairing of all further efforts, I was precipitately leaving him, when a final thought occurred to me—one which had not been wholly unindulged before.

"Bartleby," said I, in the kindest tone I could assume under such exciting circumstances, "will you go home with me now—not to my office, but my dwelling—and remain there till we can conclude upon some convenient arrangement for you at our leisure? Come, let us start now, right away."

"No: at present I would prefer not to make any change at all."

I answered nothing; but, effectually dodging every one by the suddenness and rapidity of my flight, rushed from the building, ran up Wall Street towards Broadway, and, jumping into the first omnibus, was soon removed from pursuit. As soon as tranquillity returned, I distinctly perceived that I had now done all that I possibly could, both in respect to the demands of the landlord and his tenants, and with regard to my own desire and sense of duty, to benefit Bartleby, and shield him from rude persecution. I now strove to be entirely care-free and quiescent; and my conscience justified me in the attempt; though, indeed, it was not so successful as I could have wished. So fearful was I of being again hunted out by the incensed landlord and his exasperated tenants, that, surrendering my business to Nippers, for a few days, I drove about the upper part of the town and through the suburbs, in my rockaway; crossed over to Jersey City and Hoboken, and paid fugitive visits to Manhattanville and Astoria. In fact, I almost lived in my rockaway for the time.

When again I entered my office, lo, a note from the landlord lay upon the desk. I opened it with trembling hands. It informed me that the writer had sent to the police, and had Bartleby removed to the Tombs as a vagrant. Moreover, since I knew more about him than any one else, he wished me to appear at that place, and make a suitable statement of the facts. These tidings had a conflicting effect upon me. At first I was indignant; but, at last, almost approved. The landlord's energetic, summary disposition, had led him to adopt a procedure which I do not think I would have decided upon myself; and yet, as a last resort, under such peculiar circumstances, it seemed the only plan.

As I afterwards learned, the poor scrivener, when told that he must be conducted to the Tombs, offered not the slightest obstacle, but, in his pale, unmoving way, silently acquiesced.

Some of the compassionate and curious bystanders joined the party; and headed by one of the constables arm in arm with Bartleby, the silent procession filed its way through all the noise, and heat, and joy of the roaring thoroughfares at noon.

The same day I received the note, I went to the Tombs, or, to speak more properly, the Halls of Justice. Seeking the right officer, I stated the purpose of my call, and was informed that the individual I described was, indeed, within. I then assured the functionary that Bartleby was a perfectly honest man, and greatly to be compassionated, however unaccountably eccentric. I narrated all I knew, and closed by suggesting the idea of letting him remain in as indulgent confinement as possible, till something less harsh might be done—though, indeed, I hardly knew what. At all events, if nothing else could be decided upon, the alms-house must receive him. I then begged to have an interview.

Being under no disgraceful charge, and quite serene and harmless in all ways, they had permitted him freely to wander about the prison, and, especially, in the inclosed grass-platted yards thereof. And so I found him there, standing all alone in the quietest of the yards, his face towards a high wall, while all around, from the narrow slits of the jail windows, I thought I saw peering out upon him the eyes of murderers and thieves.

"Bartleby!"

"I know you," he said, without looking around—"and I want nothing to say to you."

"It was not I that brought you here, Bartleby," said I, keenly pained at his implied suspicion. "And to you, this should not be so vile a place. Nothing reproachful attaches to you by being here. And see, it is not so sad a place as one might think. Look, there is the sky, and here is the grass."

"I know where I am," he replied, but would say nothing more, and so I left him.

As I entered the corridor again, a broad meat-like man, in an apron, accosted me, and jerking his thumb over his shoulder, said—"Is that your friend?"

"Yes."

"Does he want to starve? If he does, let him live on the prison fare, that's all."

"Who are you?" asked I, not knowing what to make of such an unofficially speaking person in such a place.

"I am the grub-man. Such gentlemen as have friends here, hire me to provide them with something good to eat."

"Is this so?" said I, turning to the turnkey.

He said it was.

"Well, then," said I, slipping some silver into the grub-man's hands (for so they called him), "I want you to give particular attention to my friend there; let him have the best dinner you can get. And you must be as polite to him as possible."

"Introduce me, will you?" said the grub-man, looking at me with an expression which seemed to say he was all impatience for an opportunity to give a specimen of his breeding.

Thinking it would prove of benefit to the scrivener, I acquiesced; and, asking the grub-man his name, went up with him to Bartleby.

"Bartleby, this is a friend; you will find him very useful to you."

"Your sarvant, sir, your sarvant," said the grub-man, making a low salutation behind his apron. "Hope you find it pleasant here, sir; nice grounds—cool apartments—hope you'll stay with us sometimes—try to make it agreeable. What will you have for dinner to-day?"

"I prefer not to dine to-day," said Bartleby, turning away. "It would disagree with me; I am unused to dinners." So saying, he slowly moved to the other side of the inclosure, and took up a position fronting the dead-wall.

"How's this?" said the grub-man, addressing me with a stare of astonishment. "He's odd, ain't he?"

"I think he is a little deranged," said I sadly.

"Deranged? deranged is it? Well, now, upon my word I thought that friend of yourn was a gentleman forger; they are always pale and genteel-like, them forgers. I can't help pity 'em—can't help it, sir. Did you know Monroe Edwards?" he added, touchingly, and paused. Then, laying his hand piteously on my shoulder, sighed, "he died of consumption at Sing-Sing. So you weren't acquainted with Monroe?"

"No, I was never socially acquainted with any forgers. But I cannot stop longer. Look to my friend yonder. You will not lose by it. I will see you again."

Some few days after this, I again obtained admission to the Tombs, and went through the corridors in quest of Bartleby; but without finding him.

"I saw him coming from his cell not long ago," said a turnkey, "may be he's gone to loiter in the yards."

So I went in that direction.

"Are you looking for the silent man?" said another turnkey, passing me. "Yonder he lies—sleeping in the yard there. 'Tis not twenty minutes since I saw him lie down."

The yard was entirely quiet. It was not accessible to the common prisoners. The surrounding walls, of amazing thickness, kept off all sounds behind them. The Egyptian character of the masonry weighed upon me with its gloom. But a soft imprisoned turf grew under foot. The heart of the eternal pyramids, it seemed, wherein, by some strange magic, through the clefts, grass-seed, dropped by birds, had sprung.

Strangely huddled at the base of the wall, his knees drawn up, and lying on his side, his head touching the cold stones, I saw the wasted Bartleby. But nothing stirred. I paused; then went close up to him; stooped over, and saw that his dim eyes were open; otherwise he seemed profoundly sleeping. Something prompted me to touch him. I felt his hand, when a tingling shiver ran up my arm and down my spine to my feet.

The round face of the grub-man peered upon me now. "His dinner is ready. Won't he dine to-day, either? Or does he live without dining?"

"Lives without dining," said I, and closed the eyes.

"Eh!—He's asleep, aint he?"

"With kings and counselors," murmured I.

There would seem little need for proceeding further in this history. Imagination will readily supply the meagre recital of poor Bartleby's interment. But, ere parting with the reader, let me say, that if this little narrative has sufficiently interested him, to awaken curiosity as to who

Bartleby was, and what manner of life he led prior to the present narrator's making his acquaintance, I can only reply, that in such curiosity I fully share, but am wholly unable to gratify it. Yet here I hardly know whether I should divulge one little item of rumor, which came to my ear a few months after the scrivener's decease. Upon what basis it rested, I could never ascertain; and hence, how true it is I cannot now tell. But, inasmuch as this vague report has not been without a certain suggestive interest to me, however sad, it may prove the same with some others; and so I will briefly mention it. The report was this: that Bartleby had been a subordinate clerk in the Dead Letter Office at Washington, from which he had been suddenly removed by a change in the administration. When I think over this rumor, hardly can I express the emotions which seize me. Dead letters! does it not sound like dead men? Conceive a man by nature and misfortune prone to a pallid hopelessness, can any business seem more fitted to heighten it than that of continually handling those dead letters, and assorting them for the flames? For by the cart-load they are annually burned. Sometimes from out the folded paper the pale clerk takes a ring—the finger it was meant for, perhaps, moulders in the grave; a bank-note sent in swift charity—he whom it would relieve, nor eats nor hungers any more; pardon for those who died despairing; hope for those who died unhoping; good tidings for those who died stifled by unrelieved calamities. On errands of life, these letters speed to death.

Ah, Bartleby! Ah, humanity!

Samuel Langhorne Clemens (Mark Twain)

1835 – 1910

In his thoroughly American viewpoint, subject matter, and style, Mark Twain (Samuel Langhorne Clemens) reflects the influence of the frontier tradition, with which he was closely associated in his early life. Born in Florida, Missouri, in 1835, he was taken at the age of four to Hannibal, a town on the banks of the Mississippi River. There, in daily contact with the colorful life moving along the Mississippi, he attended school, learned to be a printer by serving a two-year apprenticeship in a local newspaper shop, and worked for three years on his brother Orion's newspaper, *The Western Union.* In 1853, at the age of eighteen, he left Hannibal to earn his living as a tramp printer, working on newspapers in New York, Pennsylvania, and Ohio. In 1857, lured by adventure and the possibility of a quick fortune, he set out for South America but got no farther than New Orleans. Having met Horace Bixby, a famous steamboat pilot, he served an apprenticeship under him and eventually became a pilot on the Mississippi. When the Civil War closed the Mississippi River to traffic in 1861 and ended Twain's career as a pilot, he traveled west to Nevada, where he resumed newspaper work as a reporter, first on a Virginia City newspaper and later on one in San Francisco. Soon acquiring recognition for his humorous tales and sketches and encouraged in his literary efforts by Bret Harte, he published his first volume in 1867, *The Celebrated Jumping Frog of Calaveras County, and Other Sketches.* His second work, *Innocents Abroad* (1869), based on an excursion to Europe and the Holy Land, won him wide acclaim. He married Olivia Langdon of New York in 1870, settled in Hartford, Connecticut, and began to pursue the brilliant literary career opening to him. For the next forty years, until his death in 1910, besides engaging in many side adventures—such as platform lecturing, sponsoring inventions, and owning a publishing company—Twain wrote such significant and popular works as *Roughing It* (1872), *The Gilded Age* (1873), *The Adventures of Tom Sawyer* (1876), *A Tramp Abroad* (1880), *Adventures of Huckleberry Finn* (1884), and *A Connecticut Yankee in King Arthur's Court* (1889). Among his other important volumes of short fiction, in addition to *The Jumping Frog* collection, are *Tom Sawyer Abroad, Tom Sawyer, Detective, and Other Stories* (1896), and *The Man that Corrupted Hadleyburg and Other Stories and Essays* (1900). *The Complete Short Stories of Mark Twain,* edited by Charles Neider (1957), brings together sixty pieces that show the scope and diversity of Twain's achievement in short fiction.

In no branch of the story-telling art did Twain exhibit more skill than in his handling of the technique of the frontier oral tale, as the story that follows illustrates.

The Notorious Jumping Frog of Calaveras County

In compliance with the request of a friend of mine, who wrote me from the East, I called on good-natured, garrulous old Simon Wheeler, and inquired after my friend's friend, Leonidas W. Smiley, as requested to do, and I hereunto append the result. I have a lurking suspicion that *Leonidas* W. Smiley is a myth; that my friend never knew such a personage; and that he only conjectured that if I asked old Wheeler about him, it would remind him of his infamous *Jim* Smiley, and he would go to work and bore me to death with some exasperating reminiscence of him as long

"The Notorious Jumping Frog of Calaveras County" by Mark Twain, from *The Celebrated Jumping Frog of Calaveras County and Other Sketches* (C. H. Webb, 1867).

and as tedious as it should be useless to me. If that was the design, it succeeded.

I found Simon Wheeler dozing comfortably by the bar-room stove of the dilapidated tavern in the decayed mining camp of Angel's, and I noticed that he was fat and bald-headed, and had an expression of winning gentleness and simplicity upon his tranquil countenance. He roused up, and gave me good day. I told him that a friend of mine had commissioned me to make some inquiries about a cherished companion of his boyhood named *Leonidas* W. Smiley—*Rev. Leonidas* W. Smiley, a young minister of the Gospel, who he had heard was at one time a resident of Angel's Camp. I added that if Mr. Wheeler could tell me anything about this Rev. Leonidas W. Smiley, I would feel under many obligations to him.

Simon Wheeler backed me into a corner and blockaded me there with his chair, and then sat down and reeled off the monotonous narrative which follows this paragraph. He never smiled, he never frowned, he never changed his voice from the gentle-flowing key to which he tuned his initial sentence, he never betrayed the slightest suspicion of enthusiasm; but all through the interminable narrative there ran a vein of impressive earnestness and sincerity, which showed me plainly that, so far from his imagining that there was anything ridiculous or funny about his story, he regarded it as a really important matter, and admired its two heroes as men of transcendent genius in *finesse*. I let him go on in his own way, and never interrupted him once.

"Rev. Leonidas W. H'm, Reverend Le—well, there was a feller here once by the name of *Jim* Smiley, in the winter of '49—or maybe it was the spring of '50—I don't recollect exactly, somehow, though what makes me think it was one or the other is because I remember the big flume warn't finished when he first come to the camp; but anyway, he was the curiousest man about always betting on anything that turned up you ever see, if he could get anybody to bet on the other side; and if he couldn't he'd change sides. Any way that suited the other man would suit *him*—any way just so's he got a bet, *he* was satisfied. But still he was lucky, uncommon lucky; he most always come out winner. He was always ready and laying for a chance; there couldn't be no solit'ry thing mentioned but that feller'd offer to bet on it, and take ary side you please, as I was just telling you. If there was a horse-race, you'd find him flush or you'd find him busted at the end of it; if there was a dog-fight, he'd bet on it; if there was a cat-fight, he'd bet on it; if there was a chicken-fight, he'd bet on it; why, if there was two birds setting on a fence, he would bet you which one would fly first; or if there was a camp-meeting, he would be there reg'lar to bet on Parson Walker, which he judged to be the best exhorter about here, and so he was too, and a good man. If he even sees a straddle-bug start to go anywheres, he would bet you how long it would take him to get to—to wherever he was going to, and if you took him up, he would foller that straddle-bug to Mexico but what he would find out where he was bound for and how long he was on the road. Lots of the boys here has seen that Smiley, and can tell you about him. Why, it never made no difference to *him*—he'd bet on *any* thing—the dangdest feller. Parson Walker's wife laid very sick once, for a good while, and it seemed as if they warn't going to save her; but one morning he come in, and Smiley up and asked him how she was, and he said she was considerable better—thank the Lord for his inf'nite mercy—and coming onso smart that with the blessing of Prov'dence she'd get well yet; and Smiley, before he thought, says, 'Well, I'll resk two-and-a-half she don't anyway.'

"Thish-yer Smiley had a mare—the boys called her the fifteen-minute nag, but that was only in fun, you know, because of course she was faster than that—and he used to win money on that horse, for all she was so slow and always had the asthma, or the distemper, or the consumption, or something of that kind. They used to give her two or three hundred yards' start, and then pass her under way; but always at the fag end of the race she'd get excited and desperate like, and come cavorting and straddling up, and scattering her legs around limber, sometimes in the air, and sometimes out to one side among the fences, and kicking up m-o-r-e dust and raising m-o-r-e racket with her coughing and sneezing and blowing her nose—and *always* fetch up at the stand just about a neck ahead, as near as you could cipher it down.

"And he had a little small bull-pup, that to look at him you'd think he warn't worth a cent but to set around and look ornery and lay for a chance to steal something. But as soon as money was up on him he was a different dog; his under-jaw'd begin to stick out like the fo'castle of a steamboat, and his teeth would uncover and shine like the furnaces. And a dog might tackle him and bully-rag him, and bite him, and throw him over his shoulder two or three times, and Andrew Jackson—which was the name of the pup—Andrew Jackson would never let on but what *he* was satisfied, and hadn't expected nothing else—and the bets being doubled and doubled on the other side all the time, till the money was all up; and then all of a sudden he would grab that other dog jest by the j'int of his hind leg and freeze to it—not chaw, you understand, but only just grip and hang on till they throwed up the sponge, if it was a year. Smiley always come out winner on that pup, till he harnessed a dog once that didn't have no hind legs, because they'd been sawed off in a circular saw, and when the thing had gone along far enough, and the money was all up, and he come to make a snatch for his pet holt, he see in a minute how he'd been imposed on, and how the other dog had him in the door, so to speak, and he 'peared surprised, and then he looked sorter discouraged-like, and didn't try no more to win the fight, and so he got shucked out bad. He give Smiley a look, as much as to say his heart was broke, and it was *his* fault, for putting up a dog that hadn't no hind legs for him to take holt of, which was his main dependence in a fight, and then he limped off a piece and laid down and died. It was a good pup, was that Andrew Jackson, and would have made a name for hisself if he'd lived, for the stuff was in him and he had genius—I know it, because he hadn't no opportunities to speak of, and it don't stand to reason that a dog could make such a fight as he could under them circumstances if he hadn't no talent. It always makes me feel sorry when I think of that last fight of his'n, and the way it turned out.

"Well, thish-yer Smiley had rat-terriers, and chicken cocks, and tomcats and all them kind of things, till you couldn't rest, and you couldn't fetch nothing for him to bet on but he'd match you. He ketched a frog one day, and took him home, and said he cal'lated to educate him; and so he never done nothing for three months but set in his back yard and learn that frog to jump. And you bet you he *did* learn him, too. He'd give him a little punch behind, and the next minute you'd see that frog whirling in the air like a doughnut—see him turn one summerset, or maybe a couple, if he got a good start, and come down flat-footed and all right, like a cat. He got him up so in the matter of ketching flies, and kep' him in practice so constant, that he'd nail a fly every time as fur as he could see him. Smiley said all a frog wanted was education, and he could do 'most anything—and I believe him. Why, I've seen him set Dan'l Webster down here on this floor—Dan'l Webster was the name of the frog—and sing out, 'Flies, Dan'l, flies!' and quicker'n you could wink he'd spring straight up and snake a fly off'n the counter there, and flop down on the floor ag'in as solid as a gob of mud, and fall to scratching the side of his head with his hind foot as indifferent as if he hadn't no idea he'd been doin' any more'n any frog might do. You never see a frog so modest and straightfor'ard as he was, for all he was so gifted. And when it come to fair and square jumping on a dead level, he could get over more ground at one straddle than any animal of his breed you ever see. Jumping on a dead level was his strong suit, you understand; and when it come to that, Smiley would ante up money on him as long as he had a red. Smiley was monstrous proud of his frog, and well he might be, for fellers that had traveled and been everywheres, all said he laid over any frog that ever *they* see.

"Well, Smiley kep' the beast in a little lattice box, and he used to fetch him down-town sometimes and lay for a bet. One day a feller—a stranger in the camp, he was—come acrost him with his box, and says:

" 'What might it be that you've got in the box?'

"And Smiley says, sorter indifferent-like, 'It might be a parrot, or it might be a canary, maybe, but it ain't—it's only just a frog.'

"And the feller took it, and looked at it careful, and turned it round this way and that, and says, 'H'm—so 'tis. Well, what's *he* good for?'

" 'Well,' Smiley says, easy and careless, 'he's good enough for *one* thing, I should judge—he can outjump any frog in Calaveras County.'

"The feller took the box again, and took another long, particular look, and give it back to Smiley, and says, very deliberate, 'Well,' he says, 'I don't see no p'ints about that frog that's any better'n any other frog.'

" 'Maybe you don't,' Smiley says. 'Maybe you understand frogs and maybe you don't understand 'em; maybe you've had experience, and maybe you ain't only a amature, as it were. Anyways, I've got *my* opinion, and I'll resk forty dollars that he can outjump any frog in Calaveras County.'

"And the feller studied a minute, and then says, kinder sad-like 'Well, I'm only a stranger here, and I ain't got no frog; but if I had a frog, I'd bet you.'

"And then Smiley says, 'That's all right—that's all right—if you'll hold my box a minute, I'll go and get you a frog.' And so the feller took the box, and put up his forty dollars along with Smiley's, and set down to wait.

"So he set there a good while thinking and thinking to himself, and then he got the frog out and prized his mouth open and took a teaspoon and filled him full of quail-shot—filled him pretty near up to his chin—and set him on the floor. Smiley he went to the swamp and slopped around in the mud for a long time, and finally he ketched a frog, and fetched him in, and give him to this feller, and says:

" 'Now, if you're ready, set him alongside of Dan'l, with his fore paws just even with Dan'l's, and I'll give the word.' Then he says, 'One—two—three—*git!*' and him and the feller touched up the frogs from behind, and the new frog hopped off lively, but Dan'l give a heave, and hysted up his shoulders—so—like a Frenchman, but it warn't no use—he couldn't budge; he was planted as solid as a church, and he couldn't no more stir than if he was anchored out. Smiley was a good deal surprised, and he was disgusted too, but he didn't have no idea what the matter was, of course.

"The feller took the money and started away; and when he was going out at the door, he sorter jerked his thumb over his shoulder—so—at Dan'l, and says again, very deliberate, 'Well,' he says, '*I* don't see no p'ints about that frog that's any better'n any other frog.'

"Smiley he stood scratching his head and looking down at Dan'l a long time, and at last he says, 'I do wonder what in the nation that frog throw'd off for—I wonder if there ain't something the matter with him—he 'pears to look mighty baggy, somehow.' And he ketched Dan'l by the nap of the neck, and hefted him, and says, 'Why blame my cats if he don't weigh five pound!' and turned him upside down and he belched out a double handful of shot. And then he see how it was, and he was the maddest man—he set the frog down and took out after that feller, but he never ketched him. And—"

[Here Simon Wheeler heard his name called from the front yard, and got up to see what was wanted.] And turning to me as he moved away, he said: "Just set where you are, stranger, and rest easy—I ain't going to be gone a second."

But, by your leave, I did not think that a continuation of the history of the enterprising vagabond *Jim* Smiley would be likely to afford me much information concerning the Rev. *Leonidas* W. Smiley, and so I started away.

At the door I met the sociable Wheeler returning, and he buttonholed me and recommended:

"Well, thish-yer Smiley had a yaller one-eyed cow that didn't have no tail, only just a short stump like a bannanner, and—"

However, lacking both time and inclination, I did not wait to hear about the afflicted cow, but took my leave.

Ambrose Bierce

1842 – 1914

Born in Ohio, in 1842, the son of a poor farmer and the youngest in a family of nine children, Ambrose Bierce grew up with little formal schooling. He enlisted in the Ninth Indiana Volunteers in 1861 and, during his four-year period of service, took part in some of the bloodiest campaigns of the Civil War, an experience which provided him with material he later used in his stories and probably was responsible for his bitter outlook on life. After the war, Bierce, like Twain and Harte, served for a time as a newspaper reporter in San Francisco. In 1871, he married Mary Ellen Day and the following year took up residence in England, where he joined the staff of *Fun,* contribued to *Hood's Comic Almanac,* and published three volumes of sketches, *The Fiend's Delight* (1872), *Nuggets and Dust Panned Out in California* (1872), and *Cobwebs from an Empty Skull* (1874), works so biting and sardonic in tone that critics called him "Bitter Bierce." Returning to California in 1876 because of poor health, he contributed a column entitled "Prattle" to the San Francisco *Examiner* and, by virtue of his acid wit, soon gained an important place among the writers of the Pacific Coast. In 1891, he published a volume of short stories, *Tales of Soldiers and Civilians* (retitled *In the Midst of Life),* and in 1893, a second volume, *Can Such Things Be?* His best stories are included among the fifty pieces in these two volumes.

Continuing in journalistic work as a Washington correspondent for Hearst's New York *American* (1897) and as a contributor to Hearst's *Cosmopolitan Magazine* (1905–1909), he also published a number of books of a miscellaneous nature, such as *Fantastic Fables* (1899), *The Cynic's Word Book* (1906), and *Antepenultimata* (1909). Personal suffering caused by the death of one son in 1899, of the second in

1901, and by divorce from his wife in 1904 deepened his long-evident pessimism and resulted ultimately in his settling his affairs in 1913 and disappearing into Mexico. Although there is no authentic information concerning his fate, it is presumed that he died in Mexico in 1914.

In his use of horror and the supernatural, as well as in his finished technique, Bierce resembles Poe; there, however, the resemblance stops, for Poe is a romantic and Bierce not merely a realist but a sardonic pessimist, who seems to delight in showing what sorry, terror-ridden creatures humans are and in how many ways they can be dismembered by fate. Writing to create a powerful effect, Bierce uses such devices as the surprise ending, the double reversal of the situation, and coincidence. Even though Bierce's extensive use of these devices results in artificiality, he is often able to construct a story that "explodes" in the last several lines and stuns the reader with a sudden, horrible revelation.

One Officer, One Man

Captain Graffenreid stood at the head of his company. The regiment was not engaged. It formed a part of the front line-of-battle, which stretched away to the right with a visible length of nearly two miles through the open ground. The left flank was veiled by woods; to the right also the line was lost to sight, but it extended many miles. A hundred yards in rear was a second line; behind this, the reserve brigades and divisions in column. Batteries of artillery occupied the spaces between and crowned the low hills. Groups of horsemen—generals with their staffs and escorts, and field officers of regiments behind the colors—broke the regularity of the lines and columns. Numbers of these figures of interest had field-glasses at their eyes and sat motionless, stolidly scanning the country in front;

"One Officer, One Man" by Ambrose Bierce from *The Complete Short Stories of Ambrose Bierce*. Published by Doubleday, a division of Bantam, Doubleday, Dell Publishing Group, Inc.

others came and went at a slow canter, bearing orders. There were squads of stretcher-bearers, ambulances, wagon-trains with ammunition, and officers' servants in rear of all—of all that was visible—for still in rear of these, along the roads, extended for many miles all that vast multitude of non-combatants who with their various *impedimenta* are assigned to the inglorious but important duty of supplying the fighters' many needs.

An army in line-of-battle awaiting attack, or prepared to deliver it, presents strange contrasts. At the front are precision, formality, fixity, and silence. Toward the rear these characteristics are less and less conspicuous and finally, in point of space, are lost altogether in confusion, motion and noise. The homogeneous becomes heterogeneous. Definition is lacking; repose is replaced by an apparently purposeless activity; harmony vanishes in hubbub, form in disorder. Commotion everywhere and ceaseless unrest. The men who do not fight are never ready.

From his position at the right of his company in the front rank, Captain Graffenreid had an unobstructed outlook toward the enemy. A half-mile of open and nearly level ground lay before him, and beyond it an irregular wood, covering a slight acclivity; not a human being anywhere visible. He could imagine nothing more peaceful than the appearance of that pleasant landscape with its long stretches of brown fields over which the atmosphere was beginning to quiver in the heat of the morning sun. Not a sound came from forest or field—not even the barking of a dog or the crowing of a cock at the half-seen plantation house on the crest among the trees. Yet every man in those miles of men knew that he and death were face to face.

Captain Graffenreid had never in his life seen an armed enemy, and the war in which his regiment was one of the first to take the field was two years old. He had had the rare advantage of a military education, and when his comrades had marched to the front he had been detached for administrative service at the capital of his State, where it was thought that he could be most useful. Like a bad soldier he protested, and like a good one obeyed. In close official and personal relations with the governor of his State, and enjoying his confidence and favor, he had firmly refused promotion and seen his juniors elevated above him. Death had been busy in his distant regiment; vacancies among the field officers had occurred again and again; but from a chivalrous feeling that war's rewards belonged of right to those who bore the storm and stress of battle he had held his humble rank and generously advanced the fortunes of others. His silent devotion to principle had conquered at last: he had been relieved of his hateful duties and ordered to the front, and now, untried by fire, stood in the van of battle in command of a company of hardy veterans, to whom he had been only a name, and that name a by-word.

By none—not even by those of his brother officers in whose favor he had waived his rights—was his devotion to duty understood. They were too busy to be just; he was looked upon as one who had shirked his duty, until forced unwillingly into the field. Too proud to explain, yet not too insensible to feel, he could only endure and hope.

Of all the Federal Army on that summer morning none had accepted battle more joyously than Anderton Graffenreid. His spirit was buoyant, his faculties were riotous. He was in a state of mental exaltation and scarcely could endure the enemy's tardiness in advancing to the attack. To him this was opportunity—for the result he cared nothing. Victory or defeat, as God might will; in one or in the other he should prove himself a soldier and a hero; he should vindicate his right to the respect of his men and the companionship of his brother officers—to the consideration of his superiors. How his heart leaped in his breast as the bugle sounded the stirring notes of the "assembly"! With what a light tread, scarcely conscious of the earth beneath his feet, he strode forward at the head of his company, and how exultingly he noted the tactical dispositions which placed his regiment in the front line! And if perchance some memory came to him of a pair of dark eyes that might take on a tenderer light in reading the account of that day's doings, who shall blame him for the unmartial thought or count it a debasement of soldierly ardor?

Suddenly, from the forest a half-mile in front—apparently from among the upper branches of the trees, but really from the ridge beyond—rose a tall column of white smoke. A moment later came a deep, jarring explosion, followed—almost attended—by a hideous rushing sound that seemed to leap forward across the intervening space with inconceivable rapidity, rising from whisper to roar with too quick a gradation for attention to note the successive stages of its horrible progression! A visible tremor ran along the lines of men; all were startled into motion. Captain Graffenreid dodged and threw up his hands to one side of his head, palms outward. As he did so he heard a keen, ringing report, and saw on a hillside behind the line a fierce roll of smoke and dust—the shell's explosion. It had passed a hundred feet to his left! He heard, or fancied he heard, a low, mocking laugh and turning in the direction whence it came saw the eyes of his first lieutenant fixed upon him with an unmistakable look of amusement. He looked along the line of faces in the front ranks. The men were laughing. At him? The thought restored the color to his bloodless face—restored too much of it. His cheeks burned with a fever of shame.

The enemy's shot was not answered: the officer in command at that exposed part of the line had evidently no desire to provoke a cannonade. For the forbearance Captain Graffenreid was conscious of a sense of gratitude. He had not known that the flight of a projectile was a phenomenon of so appalling character. His conception of war had already undergone a profound change, and he was conscious that his new feeling was manifesting itself in visible perturbation. His blood was boiling in his veins; he had a choking sensation and felt that if he had a command to give it would be inaudible, or at least unintelligible. The hand in which he held his sword trembled; the other moved automatically, clutching at various parts of his clothing. He found a difficulty in standing still and fancied that his men observed it. Was it fear? He feared it was.

From somewhere away to the right came, as the wind served, a low, intermittent murmur like that of ocean in a storm—like that of a distant railway train—like that of wind among the pines—three sounds so nearly alike that the ear, unaided by the judgment, cannot distinguish them one from another. The eyes of the troops were drawn in that direction; the mounted officers turned their field-glasses that way. Mingled with the sound was an irregular throbbing. He thought it, at first, the beating of his fevered blood in his ears; next, the distant tapping of a bass drum.

"The ball is opened on the right flank," said an officer.

Captain Granffenreid understood: the sounds were musketry and artillery. He nodded and tried to smile. There was apparently nothing infectious in the smile.

Presently a light line of blue smoke-puffs broke out along the edge of the wood in front, succeeded by a crackle of rifles. There were keen, sharp hissings in the air, terminating abruptly with a thump near by. The man at Captain Graffenreid's side dropped his rifle; his knees gave way and he pitched awkwardly forward, falling upon his face. Somebody shouted "Lie down!" and the dead man was hardly distinguishable from the living. It looked as if those few rifle-shots had slain ten thousand men. Only the field officers remained erect; their concession to the emergency consisted in dismounting and sending their horses to the shelter of the low hills immediately in rear.

Captain Graffenreid lay alongside the dead man, from beneath whose breast flowed a little rill of blood. It had a faint, sweetish odor that sickened him. The face was crushed into the earth and flattened. It looked yellow already, and was repulsive. Nothing suggested the glory of a soldier's death nor mitigated the loathsomeness of the incident. He could not turn his back upon the body without facing away from his company.

He fixed his eyes upon the forest, where all again was silent. He tried to imagine what was going on there—the lines of troops forming to attack, the guns being pushed forward by hand to the edge of the open. He fancied he could see their black muzzles protruding from the undergrowth, ready to deliver their storm of missiles—such missiles as the one whose shriek had so unsettled his nerves. The distension of his eyes became painful; a mist seemed to gather before them; he could no longer see across the field, yet would not withdraw his gaze lest he see the dead man at his side.

The fire of battle was not now burning very brightly in this warrior's soul. From inaction had come introspection. He sought rather to analyze his feelings than distinguish himself by courage and devotion. The result was profoundly disappointing. He covered his face with his hands and groaned aloud.

The hoarse murmur of battle grew more and more distinct upon the right; the murmur had, indeed, become a roar, the throbbing, a thunder. The sounds had worked round obliquely to the front; evidently the enemy's left was being driven back, and the propitious movement to move against the salient angle of his line would soon arrive. The silence and mystery in front were ominous; all felt that they boded evil to the assailants.

Behind the prostrate lines sounded the hoofbeats of galloping horses; the men turned to look. A dozen staff officers were riding to the various brigade and regimental commanders, who had remounted. A moment more and there was a chorus of voices, all uttering out of time the same words—"Attention, battalion!" The men sprang to their feet and were aligned by the company commanders. They awaited the word "Forward"—awaited, too, with beating hearts and set teeth the gusts of lead and iron that were to smite them at their first movement in obedience to that word. The word was not given; the tempest did not break out. The delay was hideous, maddening! It unnerved like a respite at the guillotine.

Captain Graffenreid stood at the head of his company, the dead man at his feet. He heard the battle on the right—rattle and crash of musketry, ceaseless thunder of cannon, desultory cheers of invisible combatants. He marked ascending clouds of smoke from distant forests. He noted the sinister silence of the forest in front. These contrasting extremes affected the whole range of his sensibilities. The strain upon his nervous organization was insupportable. He grew hot and cold by turns. He panted like a dog, and then forgot to breathe until reminded by vertigo.

Suddenly he grew calm. Glancing downward, his eyes had fallen upon his naked sword, as he held it, point to earth. Foreshortened to his view, it resembled somewhat, he thought, the short heavy blade of the ancient Roman. The fancy was full of suggestion, malign, fateful, heroic!

The sergeant in the rear rank, immediately behind Captain Graffenreid, now observed a strange sight. His attention drawn by an uncommon movement made by the captain—a sudden reaching forward of the hands and their energetic withdrawal, throwing the elbows out, as in pulling an oar—he saw spring from between the officer's shoulders a bright point of metal which prolonged itself outward, nearly a half-arm's length—a blade! It was faintly streaked with crimson, and its point approached so near to the sergeant's breast, and with so quick a movement, that he shrank backward in alarm. That moment Captain Graffenreid pitched heavily forward upon the dead man and died.

A week later the major-general commanding the left corps of the Federal Army submitted the following official report:

"SIR: I have the honor to report, with regard to the action of the 19th inst., that owing to the enemy's withdrawal from my front to reinforce his beaten left, my command was not seriously engaged. My loss was as follows: Killed, one officer, one man."

Henry James

1843 – 1916

Henry James believed that fiction should present a serious, truthful, but dramatically interesting view of life, and he dedicated a lifetime of theory and practice toward showing how this aim might best be fulfilled. His critical theories and their successful embodiment in his fiction were not widely appreciated in his own day, but they have now so pervaded the method of our fiction today that few writers have failed to profit directly or indirectly from them.

From early childhood on, James enjoyed the advantages of wealth, leisure, extensive travel, and freedom to cultivate the arts. Born in New York City in 1843, he also enjoyed a vigorously intellectual family atmosphere, stimulated by the interests and friends of his father, Henry, Sr., and his elder brother, William, a noted psychologist and philosopher. To cultivate his children as future citizens of the world possessing a thoroughly cosmopolitan outlook, the father took his family abroad in 1855, where for the next three years, young James continued his eclectic education and began his long study of European culture. From 1862 to 1864, he attended the Harvard Law School but with little aim of entering law as a profession, for already literature was becoming his consuming passion. He had begun contributing reviews and short stories to the *Nation,* the *Atlantic Monthly,* and by 1871, with the publication of *A Passionate Pilgrim* and *Watch and Ward,* he was well embarked on his professional career. Feeling that America was too young and raw to provide the fiction writer with proper materials, in 1876 James took up residence in England, where he continued to live, with only occasional visits to America, until his death in 1916. An astute student of Hawthorne and Balzac and of his great European contemporaries, Ivan Turgenev, Guy De Maupassant,

Gustave Flaubert, Alphonse Daudet, and Emile Zola, he sought to achieve perfection in his own work with the result that throughout his long writing career he steadily grew in power and skill. In addition to his volumes of criticism, his plays, and his many novels, he wrote numerous short stories, some of the most significant collections of which are *The Lesson of the Master* (1892), *The Real Thing and Other Tales* (1893), *The Soft Side* (1900), and *The Better Sort* (1903). All the stories James wrote have been collected in *The Complete Tales of Henry James,* edited by Leon Edel in twelve volumes (Lippincott, 1962-64).

"Europe" is a typically vintage James story that dramatizes two of his favorite theories: (1) the constant struggle of the artist to recreate or transform real life into an art form through (2) a process that can be carried out successfully only when the actual is transmuted by the artistic imagination. "Europe" illustrates James's theme concerning the artist's vision into the heart of a tragic tangle of human relationships. To grasp its complexity, the reader must pay close attention so as not to lose the story line.

"Europe"

1

"Our feeling is, you know, that Becky *should* go." That earnest little remark comes back to me, even after long years, as the first note of something that began, for my observation, the day I went with my sister-in-law to take leave of her good friends. It's a memory of the American time, which revives so at present—under some touch that doesn't signify—that it rounds itself off as an anecdote. That walk to say good-bye was the beginning; and the end, so far as I enjoyed a view of it, was not till long after; yet even the end also appears to me now as of the old days. I went, in those days, on occasion, to see my sister-in-law, in whose affairs, on my brother's death, I had had to take a helpful hand. I continued to go indeed after these little matters were straightened out,

"Europe" by Henry James, from *The Soft Side* (Macmillan, 1900).

for the pleasure, periodically, of the impression—the change to the almost pastoral sweetness of the good Boston suburb from the loud longitudinal New York. It was another world, with other manners, a different tone, a different taste; a savour nowhere so mild, yet so distinct, as in the square white house—with the pair of elms, like gigantic wheat-sheaves, in front, the rustic orchard not far behind, the old-fashioned door-lights, the big blue-and-white jars on the porch, the straight bricked walk from the high gate—that enshrined the extraordinary merit of Mrs. Rimmle and her three daughters.

These ladies were so much of the place and the place so much of themselves that from the first of their being revealed to me I felt that nothing else at Brookbridge much mattered. They were what, for me, at any rate, Brookbridge had most to give: I mean in the way of what it was naturally strongest in, the thing we called in New York the New England expression, the air of Puritanism reclaimed and refined. The Rimmles had brought this down to a wonderful delicacy. They struck me even then—all four almost equally—as very ancient and very earnest, and I think theirs must have been the house in all the world in which "culture" first came to the aid of morning calls. The head of the family was the widow of a great public character—as public characters were understood at Brookbridge—whose speeches on anniversaries formed a part of the body of national eloquence spouted in the New England schools by little boys covetous of the most marked, though perhaps the easiest, distinction. He was reported to have been celebrated, and in such fine declamatory connexions that he seemed to gesticulate even from the tomb. He was understood to have made, in his wife's company, the tour of Europe at a date not immensely removed from that of the battle of Waterloo. What was the age then of the bland firm antique Mrs. Rimmle at the period of her being first revealed to me? That's a point I'm not in a position to determine—I remember mainly that I was young enough to regard her as having reached the limit. And yet the limit for Mrs. Rimmle must have been prodigiously extended; the scale of its extension is in fact the very moral of this reminiscence. She was old, and her daughters were old, but I was destined to know them all as older. It was only by comparison and habit that—however much I recede—Rebecca, Maria and Jane were the "young ladies."

I think it was felt that, though their mother's life, after thirty years of widowhood, had had a grand backward stretch, her blandness and firmness—and this in spite of her extreme physical fraility—would be proof against any surrender not overwhelmingly justified by time. It had appeared, years before, at a crisis of which the waves had not even yet quite subsided, a surrender not justified by anything nameable, that she should go to Europe with her daughters and for her health. Her health was supposed to require constant support; but when it had at that period tried conclusions with the idea of Europe it was not the idea of Europe that had been insidious enough to prevail. She hadn't gone, and Becky, Maria and Jane hadn't gone, and this was long ago. They still merely floated in the air of the visit achieved, with such introductions and such acclamations, in the early part of the century; they still, with fond glances at the sunny parlour-walls, only referred, in conversation, to divers pictorial and other reminders of it. The Miss Rimmles had quite been brought up on it, but Becky, as the most literary, had most mastered the subject. There were framed letters—tributes to their eminent father—suspended among the mementoes, and of two or three of these, the most foreign and complimentary, Becky had executed translations that figured beside the text. She knew already, through this and other illumination, so much about Europe that it was hard to believe for her in that limit of adventure which consisted only of her having been twice to Philadelphia. The others hadn't been to Philadelphia, but there was a legend that Jane had been to Saratoga. Becky was a short stout fair person with round serious eyes, a high forehead, the sweetest neatest enunciation, and a miniature of her father—"done in Rome"—worn as a breastpin. She had written the life, she had edited the speeches, of the original of this ornament, and now at last, beyond the seas, she was really to tread in his footsteps.

Fine old Mrs. Rimmle, in the sunny parlour and with a certain austerity of cap and chair—though with a gay new "front" that looked like rusty brown plush—had had so unusually good a winter that the question of her sparing two members of her family for an absence had been threshed as fine, I could feel, as even under that Puritan roof, any case of conscience had ever been threshed. They were to make their dash while the coast, as it were, was clear, and each of the daughters had tried—heroically, angelically and for the sake of each of her sisters—not to be one of the two. What I encountered that first time was an opportunity to concur with enthusiasm in the general idea that Becky's wonderful preparation would be wasted if she were the one to stay with their mother. Their talk of Becky's preparation (they had a sly old-maidish humour that was as mild as milk) might have been of some mixture, for application somewhere, that she kept in a precious bottle. It had been settled at all events that, armed with this concoction and borne aloft by their introductions, she and Jane were to start. They were wonderful on their introductions, which proceeded naturally from their mother and were addressed to the charming families that in vague generations had so admired vague Mr. Rimmle. Jane, I found at Brookbridge, had to be described, for want of other description, as the pretty one, but it wouldn't have served to identify her unless you had seen the others. *Her* preparation was only this figment of her prettiness—only, that is, unless one took into account something that, on the spot, I silently divined: the lifelong secret passionate ache of her little rebellious desire. They were all growing old in the yearning to go, but Jane's yearning was the sharpest. She struggled with it as people at Brookbridge mostly struggled with what they liked, but fate, by threatening to prevent what she *dis*liked and what was therefore duty—which was to stay at home instead of Maria—had bewildered her, I judged, not a little. It was she who, in the words I have quoted, mentioned to me Becky's case and Becky's affinity as the clearest of all. Her mother moreover had on the general subject still more to say.

"I positively desire, I really quite insist that they shall go," the old lady explained to us from her stiff chair. "We've talked about it so often, and they've had from me so clear an account—I've amused them again and again with it—of what's to be seen and enjoyed. If they've had hitherto too many duties to leave, the time seems to have come to recognise that there are also many duties to *seek*. Wherever we go we find them—I always remind the girls of that. There's a duty that calls them to those wonderful countries, just as it called, at the right time, their father and myself—if it be only that of laying-up for the years to come the same store of remarkable impressions, the same wealth of knowledge and food for conversation as, since my return, I've found myself so happy to possess." Mrs. Rimmle spoke of her return as of something of the year before last, but the future of her daughters was somehow, by a different law, to be on the scale of great vistas, of endless after-tastes. I think that, without my being quite ready to say it, even this first impression of her was somewhat upsetting; there was a large placid perversity, a grim secrecy of intention, in her estimate of the ages.

"Well, I'm so glad you don't delay it longer," I said to Miss Becky before we withdrew. "And whoever should go," I continued in the spirit of the sympathy with which the good sisters had already inspired me, "I quite feel, with your family, you know, that *you* should. But of course I hold that every one should." I suppose I wished to attenuate my solemnity; there was, however, something in it I couldn't help. It must have been a faint foreknowledge.

"Have you been a great deal yourself?" Miss Jane, I remembered, enquired.

"Not so much but that I hope to go a good deal more. So perhaps we shall meet," I encouragingly suggested.

I recall something—something in the nature of susceptibility to encouragement—that is brought into the more expressive brown eyes to which Miss Jane mainly owed it that she was the pretty one. "Where, do you think?"

I tried to think. "Well, on the Italian lakes—Como, Bellaggio, Lugano." I liked to say the names to them.

"'Sublime, but neither bleak nor bare—nor misty are the mountains there!'" Miss Jane softly breathed, while her sister looked at her as if her acquaintance with the poetry of the subject made her the most interesting feature of the scene she evoked.

But Miss Becky presently turned to me. "Do you know everything—?"

"Everything?"

"In Europe."

"Oh yes," I laughed, " and one or two things even in America."

The sisters seemed to me furtively to look at each other. "Well, you'll have to be quick—to meet *us,*" Miss Jane resumed.

"But surely when you're once there you'll stay on."

"Stay on?"—they murmured it simultaneously and with the oddest vibration of dread as well as of desire. It was if they had been in presence of a danger and yet wished me, who "knew everything," to torment them with still more of it.

Well, I did my best. "I mean it will never do to cut it short."

"No, that's just what I keep saying," said brilliant Jane. "It would be better in that case not to go."

"Oh don't talk about not going—at this time!" It was none of my business, but I felt shocked and impatient.

"No, not at *this* time!" broke in Miss Maria, who, very red in the face, had joined us. Poor Miss Maria was known as the flushed one; but she was not flushed—she only had an unfortunate surface. The third day after this was to see them embark.

Miss Becky, however, desired as little as any one to be in any way extravagant. "It's only the thought of our mother," she explained.

I looked a moment at the old lady, with whom my sister-in-law was engaged. "Well—your mother's magnificent."

"*Isn't* she magnificent?"—they eagerly took it up.

She *was*—I could reiterate it with sincerity, though I perhaps mentally drew the line when Miss Maria again risked, as a fresh ejaculation: "I think she's better than Europe!"

"Maria!" they both, at this, exclaimed with a strange emphasis: it was as if they feared she had suddenly turned cynical over the deep domestic drama of their casting of lots. The innocent laugh with which she answered them gave the measure of her cynicism.

We separated at last, and my eyes met Mrs. Rimmle's as I held for an instant her aged hand. It was doubtless only my fancy that her calm cold look quietly accused me of something. Of what *could* it accuse me? Only, I thought, of thinking.

2

I left Brookbridge the next day, and for some time after that had no occasion to hear from my kinswoman; but when she finally wrote there was a passage in her letter that affected me more than all the rest. "Do you know the poor Rimmles never, after all, 'went'? The old lady, at the eleventh hour, broke down; everything broke down, and all of *them* on top of it, so that the dear things are with us still. Mrs. Rimmle, the night after our call, had, in the most unexpected manner, a turn for the worse—something in the nature (though they're rather mysterious about it) of a seizure; Becky and Jane felt it—dear devoted stupid angels that they are—heartless to leave her at such a moment, and Europe's indefinitely postponed. However, they think they're still going—or *think* they think it—when she's better. They also think—or think they think—that she *will* be better. I certainly pray she may." So did I—quite fervently. I was conscious of a real pang—I didn't know how much they had made me care.

Late that winter my sister-in-law spent a week in New York; when almost my first enquiry on meeting her was about the health of Mrs. Rimmle.

"Oh she's rather bad—she really is, you know. It's not surprising that at her age she should be infirm."

"Then what the deuce *is* her age?"

"I can't tell you to a year—but she's immensely old."

"That of course I saw," I replied—"unless you literally mean so old that the records have been lost."

My sister-in-law thought. "Well, I believe she wasn't positively young when she married. She lost three or four children before these women were born."

We surveyed together a little, on this, the "dark backward." "And they were born, I gather, *after* the famous tour? Well then, as the famous tour was in a manner to celebrate—wasn't it?—the restoration of the Bourbons—" I considered, I gasped. "My dear child, what on earth do you make her out?"

My relative, with her Brookbridge habit, transferred her share of the question to the moral plane—turned it forth to wander, by implication at least, in the sandy desert of responsibility. "Well, you know, we all immensely admire her."

"You can't admire her more than I do. She's awful."

My converser looked at me with a certain fear. "She's *really* ill."

"Too ill to get better?"

"Oh no—we hope not. Because then they'll be able to go."

"And *will* they go if she should?"

"Oh the moment they should be quite satisfied. I mean *really,*" she added.

I'm afraid I laughed at her—the Brookbridge "really" was a thing so by itself. "But if she shouldn't get better?" I went on.

"Oh don't speak of it! They want so to go."

"It's a pity they're so infernally good," I mused.

"No—don't say that. It's what keeps them up."

"Yes, but isn't it what keeps *her* up too?"

My visitor looked grave. "Would you like them to kill her?"

I don't know that I was then prepared to say I should—though I believe I came very near it. But later on I burst all bounds, for the subject grew and grew. I went again before the good sisters ever did—I mean I went to Europe. I think I went twice, with a brief interval, before my fate again brought round for me a couple of days at Brookbridge. I had been there repeatedly, in the previous time, without making the acquaintance of the Rimmles; but now that I had had the revelation I couldn't have it too much, and the first request I preferred was to be taken again to see them. I remember well indeed the scruple I felt—the real delicacy—about betraying that *I* had, in the pride of my power, since our other meeting, stood, as their phrase went, among romantic scenes; but they were themselves the first to speak of it, and what moreover came home to me was that the coming and going of their friends in general—Brookbridge itself having even at that period one foot in Europe—was such as to place constantly before them the pleasure that was only postponed. They were thrown back after all on what the situation, under a final analysis, had most to give—the sense that, as every one kindly said to them and they kindly said to every one, Europe would keep. Every one felt for them so deeply that their own kindness in alleviating every one's feelings was really what came out most. Mrs. Rimmle was still in her stiff chair and in the sunny parlour, but if *she* made no scruple of introducing the Italian lakes my heart sank to observe that she dealt with them, as a topic, not in the least in the leave-taking manner in which Falstaff babbled of green fields.

I'm not sure that after this my pretexts for a day or two with my sister-in-law weren't apt to be a mere cover for another glimpse of these particulars: I at any rate never went to Brookbridge without an irrepressible eagerness for our customary call. A long time seems to me thus to have passed, with glimpses and lapses, considerable impatience and still more pity. Our visits indeed grew shorter, for, as my companion said, they were more and more of a strain. It finally struck me that the good sisters even shrank from me a little as from one who penetrated their consciousness in spite of himself. It was as if they knew where I thought they ought to be, and were moved to deprecate at last, by a systematic silence of that hemisphere, the criminality I fain would fix on them. They were full instead—as with the instinct of throwing dust in my eyes—of little pathetic hypocrisies about Brookbridge interests and delights. I dare say that as time went on my deeper sense of their situation came practically to rest on my companion's report of it. I certainly think I recollect every word we ever exchanged about them, even if I've lost the thread of the special occasions. The impression they made on me after each interval always broke out with extravagance as I walked away with her.

"*She* may be as old as she likes—I don't care. It's the fearful age the 'girls' are reaching that constitutes the scandal. One shouldn't pry into such matters, I know; but the years and the chances are really going. They're all growing old together—it will presently be too late; and their mother meanwhile perches over them like a vulture—what shall I call it?—calculating. Is she waiting for them successively to drop off? She'll survive them each and all. There's something too remorseless in it."

"Yes, but what do you want her to do? If the poor thing *can't* die she can't. Do you want her to take poison or to open a blood-vessel? I dare say she'd prefer to go."

"I beg your pardon," I must have replied; "you daren't say anything of the sort. If she'd prefer to go she *would* go. She'd feel the propriety, the decency, the necessity of going. She just prefers *not* to go. She prefers to stay and keep up the tension, and her calling them 'girls' and talking of the good time they'll still have is the mere conscious mischief of a subtle old witch. They won't have *any* time—there isn't any time to have! I mean there's, on her own part, no real loss of measure or of perspective in it. She *knows* she's a hundred and ten, and she takes a cruel pride in it."

My sister-in-law differed with me about this; she held that the old woman's attitude was an honest one and that her magnificent vitality, so great in spite of her infirmities, made it inevitable she should attribute youth to persons who had come into the world so much later. "Then suppose she should die?"—so my fellow student of the case always put it to me.

"Do you mean while her daughters are away? There's not the least fear of that—not even if at the very moment of their departure she should be *in extremis*. They'd find her all right on their return."

"But think how they'd feel not to have been with her!"

"That's only, I repeat, on the unsound assumption. If they'd only go to-morrow—literally make a good rush for it—they'll be with her when they come back. That will give them plenty of time." I'm afraid I even heartlessly added that if she *should*, against every probability, pass away in their absence they wouldn't have to come back at all—which would be just the compensation proper to their long privation. And then Maria would come out to join the two others, and they would be—though but for the too scanty remnant of their career—as merry as the day is long.

I remained ready, somehow, pending the fulfilment of that vision, to sacrifice Maria; it was only over the urgency of the case for the others respectively that I found myself balancing. Sometimes it was for Becky I thought the tragedy deepest—sometimes, and in quite a different manner, I thought it most dire for Jane. It was Jane after all who had most sense of life. I seemed in fact dimly to descry in Jane a sense—as yet undescribed by herself or by any one—of all sorts of queer things. Why didn't *she* go? I used desperately to ask; why didn't she make a bold personal dash for it, strike up a partnership with some one or other of the travelling spinsters in whom Brookbridge more and more abounded? Well, there came a flash for me at a particular point of the grey middle desert: my correspondent was able to let me know that poor Jane at last *had* sailed. She had gone of a sudden—I liked my sister-in-law's view of suddenness—with the kind Hathaways, who had made an irresistible grab at her and lifted her off her feet. They were going for the summer and for Mr. Hathaway's health, so that the opportunity was perfect and it was impossible not to be glad that something very like physical force had finally prevailed. This was the general feeling at Brookbridge, and I might imagine what Brookbridge had been brought to from the fact that, at the very moment she was hustled off, the doctor, called to her mother at the peep of dawn, had considered that *he* at least must stay. There had been real alarm—greater than ever before; it actually did seem as if this time the end had come. But it was Becky, strange to say, who, though fully recognising the nature of the crisis, had kept the situation in hand and insisted upon action. This, I remember, brought back to me a discomfort with which I had been familiar from the first. One of the two had sailed, and I was sorry it wasn't the other. But if it had been the other I should have been equally sorry.

I saw with my eyes that very autumn what a fool Jane would have been if she had again backed out. Her mother had of course survived the peril of which I had heard, profiting by it indeed as she had profited by every other; she was sufficiently better again to have come downstairs. It was there that, as usual, I found her, but with a difference of effect produced somehow by the absence of one of the girls. It was as if, for the others, though they hadn't gone to Europe, Europe had come to them: Jane's letters had been so frequent and so beyond even what could have been hoped. It was the first time, however, that I perceived on the old woman's part a certain failure of lucidity. Jane's flight was clearly the great fact with her, but she spoke of it as if the fruit had now been plucked and the parenthesis closed. I don't know what sinking sense of still further physical duration I gathered, as a menace, from this first hint of her confusion of mind.

"My daughter has been; my daughter has been—" She kept saying it, but didn't say where; that seemed unnecessary, and she only repeated the words to her visitors with a face that was all puckers and yet now, save in so far as it expressed an ineffaceable complacency, all blankness. I think she rather wanted us to know how little she had stood in the way. It added to something—I scarce knew what—that I found myself desiring to extract privately from Becky. As our visit was to be of the shortest my opportunity—for one of the young ladies always came to the door with us—was at hand. Mrs. Rimmle, as we took leave, again sounded her phrase, but she added this time: "I'm so glad she's going to have always—"

I knew so well what she meant that, as she again dropped, looking at me queerly and becoming momentarily dim, I could help her out. "Going to have what *you* have?"

"Yes, yes—my privilege. Wonderful experience," she mumbled. She bowed to me a little as if I would understand. "She has things to tell."

I turned, slightly at a loss, to Becky. "She has then already arrived?"

Becky was at that moment looking a little strangely at her mother, who answered my question. "She reached New York this morning—she comes on to-day."

"Oh then—!" But I let the matter pass as I met Becky's eye—I saw there was a hitch somewhere. It was not she but Maria who came out with us; on which I cleared up the question of their sister's reappearance.

"Oh no, not to-night," Maria smiled; "that's only the way mother puts it. We shall see her about the end of November—the Hathaways are so indulgent. They kindly extend their tour."

"For *her* sake? How sweet of them!" my sister-in-law exclaimed.

I can see our friend's plain mild old face take on a deeper mildness, even though a higher colour, in the light of the open door. "Yes, it's for Jane they prolong it. And do you know what they write?" She gave us time, but is was too great a responsibility to guess. "Why that it has brought her out."

"Oh, I knew it *would!*" my companion sympathetically sighed.

Maria put it more strongly still. "They say we wouldn't know her."

This sounded a little awful, but it was after all what I had expected.

3

My correspondent in Brookbridge came to me that Christmas, with my niece, to spend a week; and the arrangement had of course been prefaced by an exchange of letters, the first of which from my sister-in-law scarce took space for acceptance of my invitation before going on to say: "The Hathaways are back—but without Miss Jane!" She presented in a few words the situation thus created at Brookbridge, but was not yet, I gathered, fully in possession of the other one—the situation created in "Europe" by the presence there of that lady. The two together, however that might be, demanded, I quickly felt, all my attention, and perhaps my impatience to receive my relative was a little sharpened by my desire for the whole story. I had it at last, by the Christmas fire, and I may say without reserve that it gave me all I could have hoped for. I listened eagerly, after which I produced the comment: "Then she simply refused—"

"To budge from Florence? Simply. She had it out there with the poor Hathaways, who felt responsible for her safety, pledged to restore her to her mother's, to her sisters' hands, and showed herself in a light, they mention under their breath, that made their dear old hair stand on end. Do you know what, when they first got back, they said of her—at least it was *his* phrase—to two or three people?"

I thought for a moment. "That she had 'tasted blood'?"

My visitor fairly admired me. "How clever of you to guess! It's exactly what he did say. She appeared—she continues to appear, it seems—in a new character."

I wondered a little. "But that's exactly—don't you remember?—what Miss Maria reported to us from them; that we 'wouldn't know her.' "

My sister-in-law perfectly remembered. "Oh yes—she broke out from the first. But when they left her she was worse."

"Worse?"

"Well, different—different from anything she ever *had* been or—for that matter—had had a chance to be." My reporter hung fire a moment, but presently faced me. "Rather strange and free and obstreperous."

"Obstreperous?" I wondered again.

"Peculiarly so, I inferred, on the question of not coming away. She wouldn't hear of it and, when they spoke of her mother, said she had given her mother up. She had thought she should like Europe, but didn't know she should like it so much. They had been fools to bring her if they expected to take her away. She was going to see what she could—she hadn't yet seen half. The end of it at any rate was that they had to leave her alone."

I seemed to see it all—to see even the scared Hathaways. "So she *is* alone?"

"She told them, poor thing, it appears, and in a tone they'll never forget, that she was in any case quite old enough to be. She cried—she quite went on—over not having come sooner. That's why the only way for her," my companion mused, "*is,* I suppose, to stay. They wanted to put her with some people or other—to find some American family. But she says she's on her own feet."

"And she's still in Florence?"

"No—I believe she was to travel. She's bent on the East."

I burst out laughing. "Magnificent Jane! It's most interesting. Only I feel that I distinctly *should* 'know' her. To my sense, always, I must tell you, she had it in her."

My relative was silent a little. "So it now appears Becky always felt."

"And yet pushed her off? Magnificent Becky!"

My companion met my eyes a moment. "You don't know the queerest part. I mean the way it has *most* brought her out."

I turned it over; I felt I should like to know—to that degree indeed that, oddly enough, I jocosely disguised my eagerness. "You don't mean she has taken to drink?"

My visitor had a dignity—and yet had to have a freedom. "She has taken to flirting."

I expressed disappointment. "Oh she took to *that* long ago. Yes," I declared at my kinswoman's stare, "she positively flirted—with *me!*"

The stare perhaps sharpened. "Then you flirted with *her?*"

"How else could I have been as sure as I wanted to be? But has she means?"

"Means to flirt?"—my friend looked an instant as if she spoke literally. "I don't understand about the means—though of course they have something. But I have my impression," she went on. "I think that Becky—" It seemed almost too grave to say.

But *I* had no doubts. "That Becky's backing her?"

She brought it out. "Financing her."

"Stupendous Becky! So that morally then—"

"Becky's quite in sympathy. But isn't it too odd?" my sister-in-law asked.

"Not in the least. Didn't we know, as regards Jane, that Europe was to bring her out? Well, it has also brought out Rebecca."

"It has indeed!" my companion indulgently sighed. "So what would it do if she were there?"

"I should like immensely to see. And we *shall* see."

"Do you believe then she'll still go?"

"Certainly. She *must.*"

But my friend shook it off. "She won't."

"She shall!" I retorted with a laugh. But the next moment I said: "And what does the old woman say?"

"To Jane's behaviour? Not a word—never speaks of it. She talks now much less than she used—only seems to wait. But it's my belief she thinks."

"And—do you mean—knows?"

"Yes, knows she's abandoned. In her silence there she takes it in."

"It's her way of making Jane pay?" At this, somehow, I felt more serious. "Oh dear, dear—she'll disinherit her!"

When in the following June I went on to return my sister-in-law's visit the first object that met my eyes in her little white parlour was a figure that, to my stupefaction, presented itself for the moment as that of Mrs. Rimmle. I had gone to my room after arriving and had come down when dressed; the apparition I speak of had arisen in the interval. Its ambiguous character lasted, however, but a second or two—I had taken Becky for her mother because I knew no one but her mother of that extreme age. Becky's age was quite startling; it had made a great stride, though, strangely enough, irrecoverably seated as she now was in it, she had a wizened brightness that I had scarcely yet seen in her. I remember indulging on this occasion in two silent observations: one on the article of my not having hitherto been conscious of her full resemblance to the old lady, and the other to the effect that, as I had said to my sister-in-law at Christmas, "Europe," even as reaching her only through Jane's sensibilities, had really at last brought her out. She was in fact "out" in a manner of which this encounter offered to my eyes a unique example: it was the single hour, often as I had been at Brookbridge, of my meeting her elsewhere than in her mother's drawing-room. I surmise that, besides being adjusted to her more marked time of life, the garments she wore abroad, and in particular her little plain bonnet, presented points of resemblance to the close sable sheath and the quaint old head-gear that, in the white house behind the elms, I had from far back associated with the eternal image in the stiff chair. Of course I immediately spoke of Jane, showing an interest and asking for news; on which she answered me with a smile, but not at all as I had expected.

"*Those* are not really the things you want to know—where she is, whom she's with, how she manages and where she's going next—oh no!" And the admirable woman gave a laugh that was somehow both light and sad—sad, in particular, with a strange long weariness. "What you do want to know is when she's coming back."

I shook my head very kindly, but out of a wealth of experience that, I flattered myself, was equal to Miss Becky's. "I do know it. Never."

Miss Becky exchanged with me at this a long deep look. "Never."

We had, in silence, a little luminous talk about it, at the end of which she seemed to have told me the most interesting things. "And how's your mother?" I then enquired.

She hesitated, but finally spoke with the same serenity. "My mother's all right. You see she's not alive."

"Oh Becky!" my sister-in-law pleadingly interjected.

But Becky only addressed herself to me. "Come and see if she is. *I* think she isn't—but Maria perhaps isn't so clear. Come at all events and judge and tell me."

It was a new note, and I was a little bewildered. "Ah but I'm not a doctor!"

"No, thank God—you're not. That's why I ask you." And now she said good-bye.

I kept her hand a moment. "*You're* more alive than ever!"

"I'm very tired." She took it with the same smile, but for Becky it was much to say.

"Not alive," the next day, was certainly what Mrs. Rimmle looked when, arriving in pursuit of my promise, I found her, with Miss Maria, in her usual place. Though wasted and shrunken she still occupied her high-backed chair with a visible theory of erectness, and her intensely aged face—combined with something dauntless that belonged to her very presence and that was effective even in this extremity—might have been that of some immemorial sovereign, of indistinguishable sex, brought forth to be shown to people in disproof of the rumour of extinction. Mummified and open-eyed she looked at me, but I had no impression that she made me out. I had come this time without my sister-in-law, who had frankly pleaded to me—which also, for a daughter of Brookbridge, was saying much—that the house had grown too painful. Poor Miss Maria excused Miss Becky on the score of her not being well—and that, it struck me, was saying most of all. The absence of the others gave the occasion a different note; but I talked with Miss Maria for five minutes and recognized that—save for her saying, of her own movement, anything about Jane—she now spoke as if her mother had lost hearing or sense, in fact both, alluding freely and distinctly, though indeed favourably, to her condition. "She has expected your visit and much enjoys it," my entertainer said, while the old woman, soundless and motionless, simply fixed me without expression. Of course there was little to keep me; but I became aware as I rose to go that there was more than I had supposed.

On my approaching her to take leave Mrs. Rimmle gave signs of consciousness. "Have you heard about Jane?"

I hesitated, feeling a responsibility, and appealed for direction to Maria's face. But Maria's face was troubled, was turned altogether to her mother's. "About her life in Europe?" I then rather helplessly asked.

The old lady fronted me on this in a manner that made me feel silly. "Her life?"—and her voice, with this second effort, came out stronger. "Her death, if you please."

"Her death?" I echoed, before I could stop myself, with the accent of deprecation.

Miss Maria uttered a vague sound of pain, and I felt her turn away, but the marvel of her mother's little unquenched spark still held me. "Jane's dead. We've heard," said Mrs. Rimmle. "We've found from—

where is it we've heard from?" She had quite revived—she appealed to her daughter.

The poor old girl, crimson, rallied to her duty. "From Europe."

Mrs. Rimmle made at us both a little grim inclination of the head. "From Europe." I responded, in silence, by a deflexion from every rigour, and, still holding me, she went on: "And now Rebecca's going."

She had gathered by this time such emphasis to say it that again, before I could help myself, I vibrated in reply. "To Europe—now?" It was as if for an instant she had made me believe it.

She only stared at me, however, from her wizened mask; then her eyes followed my companion. "Has she gone?"

"Not yet, mother." Maria tried to treat it as a joke, but her smile was embarrassed and dim.

"Then where is she?"

"She's lying down."

The old woman kept up her hard queer gaze, but directing it after a minute at me. "She's going."

"Oh some day!" I foolishly laughed; and on this I got to the door, where I separated from my younger hostess, who came no further.

Only, as I held the door open, she said to me under cover of it and very quietly: "It's poor mother's idea."

I saw—it was her idea. Mine was—for some time after this, even after I had returned to New York and to my usual occupations—that I should never again see Becky. I had seen her for the last time, I believed, under my sister-in-law's roof, and in the autumn it was given to me to hear from that fellow admirer that she had succumbed at last to the situation. The day of the call I have just described had been a date in the process of her slow shrinkage—it was literally the first time she had, as they said at Brookbridge, given up. She had been ill for years, but the other state of health in the contemplation of which she had spent so much of her life had left her till too late no margin for heeding it. The power of attention came at last simply in the form of the discovery that it *was* too late; on which, naturally, she had given up more and more. I had heard indeed, for weeks before, by letter, how Brookbridge had watched her do so; in consequence of which the end found me in a manner prepared. Yet in spite of my preparation there remained with me a soreness, and when I was next—it was some six months later—on the scene of her martyrdom I fear I replied with an almost rabid negative to the question put to me in due course by my kinswoman. "Call on them? Never again!"

I went none the less the very next day. Everything was the same in the sunny parlour—everything that most mattered, I mean: the centenarian mummy in the high chair and the tributes, in the little frames on the walls, to the celebrity of its late husband. Only Maria Rimmle was different; if Becky, on my last seeing her, had looked as old as her mother,

Maria—save that she moved about—looked older. I remember she moved about, but I scarce remember what she said; and indeed what was there to say? When I risked a question, however, she found a reply.

"But *now* at least—?" I tried to put it to her suggestively.

At first she was vague. " 'Now'?"

"Won't Miss Jane come back?"

Oh the headshake she gave me! "Never." It positively pictured to me, for the instant, a well-preserved woman, a rich ripe *seconde jeunesse* by the Arno.

"Then that's only to make more sure of your finally joining her."

Maria Rimmle repeated her headshake. "Never."

We stood so a moment bleakly face to face; I could think of no attenuation that would be particularly happy. But while I tried I heard a hoarse gasp that fortunately relieved me—a signal strange and at first formless from the occupant of the high-backed chair. "Mother wants to speak to you," Maria then said.

So it appeared from the drop of the old woman's jaw, the expression of her mouth opened as if for the emission of sound. It was somehow difficult for me to seem to sympathise without hypocrisy, but, so far as a step nearer could do that, I invited communication. "Have you heard where Becky's gone?" the wonderful witch's white lips then extraordinarily asked.

It drew from Maria, as on my previous visits, an uncontrollable groan, and this in turn made me take time to consider. As I considered, however, I had an inspiration. "To Europe?"

I must have adorned it with a strange grimace, but my inspiration had been right. "To Europe," said Mrs. Rimmle.

Sarah Orne Jewett

1849 – 1909

Sarah Orne Jewett, the daughter of a country doctor, was born in 1849 in South Berwick, Maine, where she spent nearly the whole sixty years of her life. Educated chiefly at home, she frequently accompanied her father as he made professional calls in rural homes, and she soon became intimately acquainted with the desiccated farming and seaport life of the countryside around South Berwick. She was inspired by Harriet Beecher Stowe's local color stories of the country folk of Maine, and, still in her teens, she determined to record the life of the Maine region she knew. In 1869 her first story was accepted for publication in the *Atlantic Monthly.* Working slowly and carefully, she continued publishing in the *Atlantic,* and by the 1880s, her work had won the acclaim of such influential critics as Lowell, James, and Howells. During her extensive career, she published about fifteen volumes of stories, novels, and sketches, as well as numerous children's books. Her most important short story collections are *Deephaven* (1877), *Old Friends and New* (1879), *A White Heron and Other Stories* (1886), *A Native of Winby and Other Tales* (1893), *The Country of the Pointed Firs* (1896), and *The Queen's Twin and Other Stories* (1899). *The Best Stories of Sarah Orne Jewett,* a collection edited by Willa Cather in 1925, contains the finest of Jewett's work.

By dwelling on a decaying past, emphasizing the picturesque, and avoiding the coarse and unpleasant, Jewett's artistry is more closely allied to the tradition of local color fiction represented by Washington Irving than to the more robust one represented by the works of Hooper, Thorpe, Harte, and Twain. But in her depiction of simple, earthy people grappling with life's fundamental problems, her realistic if sometimes overindulgent character portrayals, her accurate use of dialect, and her close-to-nature settings, she anticipates Willa Cather, on whom she exerted a direct and profound influence.

Jewett gives less emphasis in her stories to plot and plot development than do most local colorists; instead, she focuses attention primarily on a character or group of characters, and such action or plot development that one finds in her stories serves mainly to reveal the minds and personalities of her characters against their localized background. As a result, the gripping suspense and sharp dramatic effects seen in the stories by Poe or Bierce are missing in hers; but she offsets their customary methods of provoking suspense by arousing interest in her character contrasts, economical descriptive detail, and a graceful, sustained style. If her stories are the less dramatic, they nevertheless often produce a more complex and durable effect than showier stories. The effect of "The Courting of Sister Wisby," for example, is remarkable in being at one and the same time ironic, sympathetic, and, in a quiet way, rather humorous, too.

The Courting of Sister Wisby

All the morning there had been an increasing temptation to take an out-door holiday, and early in the afternoon the temptation outgrew my power of resistance. A far-away pasture on the long southwestern slope of a high hill was persistently present to my mind, yet there seemed to be no particular reason why I should think of it. I was not sure that I wanted anything from the pasture, and there was no sign, except the temptation, that the pasture wanted anything of me. But I was on the farther side of as many as three fences before I stopped to think again where I was going, and why.

Sarah Orne Jewett, "The Courting of Sister Wisby," *Tales of New England.* Freeport, NY: Books For Libraries Press, 1894.

There is no use in trying to tell another person about that afternoon unless he distinctly remembers weather exactly like it. No number of details concerning an Arctic ice-blockade will give a single shiver to a child of the tropics. This was one of those perfect New England days in late summer, when the spirit of autumn takes a first stealthy flight, like a spy, through the ripening country-side, and, with feigned sympathy for those who droop with August heat, puts her cool cloak of bracing air about leaf and flower and human shoulders. Every living thing grows suddenly cheerful and strong; it is only when you catch sight of a horror-stricken little maple in swampy soil,—a little maple that has second sight and foreknowledge of coming disaster to her race,—only then does a distrust of autumn's friendliness dim your joyful satisfaction.

In midwinter there is always a day when one has the first foretaste of spring; in late August there is a morning when the air is for the first time autumn like. Perhaps it is a hint to the squirrels to get in their first supplies for the winter hoards, or a reminder that summer will soon end, and everybody had better make the most of it. We are always looking forward to the passing and ending of winter, but when summer is here it seems as if summer must always last. As I went across the fields that day, I found myself half lamenting that the world must fade again, even that the best of her budding and bloom was only a preparation for another spring-time, for an awakening beyond the coming winter's sleep.

The sun was slightly veiled; there was a chattering group of birds, which had gathered for a conference about their early migration. Yet, oddly enough, I heard the voice of a belated bobolink, and presently saw him rise from the grass and hover leisurely, while he sang a brief tune. He was much behind time if he were still a housekeeper; but as for the other birds, who listened, they cared only for their own notes. An old crow went sagging by, and gave a croak at his despised neighbor, just as a black reviewer croaked at Keats: so hard it is to be just to one's contemporaries. The bobolink was indeed singing out of season, and it was impossible to say whether he really belonged most to this summer or to the next. He might have been delayed on his northward journey; at any rate, he had a light heart now, to judge from his song, and I wished that I could ask him a few questions,—how he liked being the last man among the bobolinks, and where he had taken singing lessons in the South.

Presently I left the lower fields, and took a path that led higher, where I could look beyond the village to the northern country mountainward. Here the sweet fern grew, thick and fragrant, and I also found myself heedlessly treading on pennyroyal. Near by, in a field corner, I long ago made a most comfortable seat by putting a stray piece of board and bit of rail across the angle of the fences. I have spent many a delightful hour there, in the shade and shelter of a young pitch-pine and a wild-cherry tree, with a lovely outlook toward the village, just far enough away beyond the green slopes and tall elms of the lower meadows. But that day I still had the feeling of being outward bound, and did not turn aside nor linger. The high pasture land grew more and more enticing.

I stopped to pick some blackberries that twinkled at me like beads among their dry vines, and two or three yellow-birds fluttered up from the leaves of a thistle, and then came back again, as if they had complacently discovered that I was only an overgrown yellow-bird, in strange disguise but perfectly harmless. They made me feel as if I were an intruder, though they did not offer to peck at me, and we parted company very soon. It was good to stand at last on the great shoulder of the hill. The wind was coming in from the sea, there was a fine fragrance from the pines, and the air grew sweeter every moment. I took new pleasure in the thought that in a piece of wild pasture land like this one may get closest to Nature, and subsist upon what she gives of her own free will. There have been no drudging, heavy-shod ploughmen to overturn the soil, and vex it into yielding artificial crops. Here one has to take just what Nature is pleased to give, whether one is a yellow-bird or a human being. It is very good entertainment for a summer wayfarer, and I am asking my reader now to share the winter provision which I harvested that day. Let us hope that the small birds are also faring well after their fashion, but I give them an anxious thought while the snow goes hurrying in long waves across the buried fields, this windy winter night.

I next went farther down the hill, and got a drink of fresh cool water from the brook, and pulled a tender sheaf of sweet flag beside it. The mossy old fence just beyond was the last barrier between me and the pasture which had sent an invisible messenger earlier in the day, but I saw that somebody else had come first to the rendezvous: there was a brown gingham cape-bonnet and a sprigged shoulder-shawl bobbing up and down, a little way off among the junipers. I had taken such uncommon pleasure in being alone that I instantly felt a sense of disappointment; then a warm glow of pleasant satisfaction rebuked my selfishness. This could be no one but dear old Mrs. Goodsoe, the friend of my childhood and fond dependence of my maturer years. I had not seen her for many weeks, but here she was, out on one of her famous campaigns for herbs, or perhaps just returning from a blueberrying expedition. I approached with care, so as not to startle the gingham bonnet; but she heard the rustle of the bushes against my dress, and looked up quickly, as she knelt, bending over the turf. In that position she was hardly taller than the luxuriant junipers themselves.

"I'm a-gittin' in my mulleins," she said briskly, "an' I've been thinking o' you these twenty times since I come out o' the house. I begun to believe you must ha' forgot me at last."

"I have been away from home," I explained. "Why don't you get in your pennyroyal too? There's a great plantation of it beyond the next fence but one."

"Pennyr'yal!" repeated the dear little old woman, with an air of compassion for inferior knowledge; "'tain't the right time, darlin'. Pennyr'yal's too rank now. But for mulleins this day is prime. I've got a dreadful graspin' fit for 'em this year; seems if I must be goin' to need 'em extry. I feel like the squirrels must when they know a hard winter's comin'." And Mrs. Goodsoe bent over her work again, while I stood by and watched her carefully cut the best full-grown leaves with a clumsy pair of scissors, which might have served through at least half a century of herb-gathering. They were fastened to her apron-strings by a long piece of list.

"I'm going to take my jack-knife and help you," I suggested, with some fear of refusal. "I just passed a flourishing family of six or seven heads that must have been growing on purpose for you."

"Now be keerful, dear heart," was the anxious response; "choose 'em well. There's odds in mulleins same's there is in angels. Take a plant that's all run up to stalk, and there ain't but little goodness in the leaves. This one I'm at now must ha' been stepped on by some creatur' and blighted of its bloom, and the leaves is han'some! When I was small I used to have a notion that Adam an' Eve must a took mulleins fer their winter wear. Ain't they just like flannel, for all the world? I've had experience, and I know there's plenty of sickness might be saved to folks if they'd quit horse-radish and such fiery, exasperating things, and use mullein drarves in proper season. Now I shall spread these an' dry 'em nice on my spare floor in the garrit, an' come to steam 'em for use along in the winter there'll be the vally of the whole summer's goodness in 'em, sartin." And she snipped away with the dull scissors, while I listened respectfully, and took great pains to have my part of the harvest present a good appearance.

"This is most too dry a head," she added presently, a little out of breath. "There! I can tell you there's win'rows o' young doctors, bilin' over with book-larnin', that is truly ignorant of what to do for the sick, or how to p'int out those paths that well people foller toward sickness. Book-fools I call 'em, them young men, an' some on 'em never'll live to know much better, if they git to be Methuselahs. In my time every middle-aged woman, who had brought up a family, had some proper ideas o' dealin' with complaints. I won't say but there was some fools amongst *them,* but I'd rather take my chances, unless they'd forsook herbs and gone to dealin' with patent stuff. Now my mother really did sense the use of herbs and roots. I never see anybody that come up to her. She was a meek-looking woman, but very understandin', mother was."

"Then that's where you learned so much yourself, Mrs. Goodsoe," I ventured to say.

"Bless your heart, I don't hold a candle to her; 't is but little I can recall of what she used to say. No, her l'arnin' died with her," said my friend, in a self-depreciating tone. "Why, there was as many as twenty kinds of roots alone that she used to keep by her, that I forget the use of; an' I'm sure I shouldn't know where to find the most of 'em, any. There was an herb"—*airb,* she called it—"an herb called master-wort, that she used to get way from Pennsylvany; and she used to think everything of noble-liverwort, but I never could seem to get the right effects from it as she could. Though I don't know as she ever really did use masterwort where somethin' else wouldn't a served. She had a cousin married out in Pennsylvany that used to take pains to get it to her every year or two, and so she felt 't was important to have it. Some set more by such things as come from a distance, but I rec'lect mother always used to maintain that folks was meant to be doctored with the stuff that grew right about 'em; 't was sufficient, an' so ordered. That was before the whole population took to livin' on wheels, the way they do now. 'T was never my idee that we was meant to know what's goin' on all over the world to once. There's goin' to be some sort of a set-back one o' these days, with these telegraphs an' things, an' letters comin' every hand's turn, and folks leavin' their proper work to answer 'em. I may not live to see it. 'T was allowed to be difficult for folks to git about in old times, or to git word across the country, and they stood in their lot an' place, and were n't all just alike, either, same as pine-spills."

We were kneeling side by side now, as if in penitence for the march of progress, but we laughed as we turned to look at each other.

"Do you think it did much good when everybody brewed a cracked quart mug of herb-tea?" I asked, walking away on my knees to a new mullein.

"I've always lifted my voice against the practice, far 's I could," declared Mrs. Goodsoe; "an' I won't deal out none o' the herbs I save for no such nonsense. There was three houses along our road,—I call no names,—where you couldn't go into the livin' room without findin' a mess o' herb-tea drorin' on the stove or side o' the fireplace, winter or summer, sick or well. One was thoroughwut, one would be camomile, and the other, like as not, yellow dock; but they all used to put in a little new rum to git out the goodness, or keep it from spilin'." (Mrs. Goodsoe favored me with a knowing smile.) "Land, how mother used to laugh! But, poor creaturs, they had to work hard, and I guess it never done 'em a mite o' harm; they was all good herbs. I wish you could hear the quawkin' there used to be when they was indulged with a case o' sickness. Everybody would collect from far an' near; you'd see 'em coming along the road and across the pastures then; everybody clamorin' that nothin' wouldn't do no kind o' good but her choice o' teas or drarves to the feet. I wonder there was a babe lived to grow up in the whole lower part o' the town; an' if nothin' else 'peared to ail 'em, word was passed about that 't was likely Mis' So-and So's last young one was goin' to be foolish. Land, how they'd gather! I know one day the doctor come to Widder Peck's and the house was crammed so 't he could scercely git inside the door; and he says, just as polite, 'Do send for some of the neighbors!' as if there wa'n't a soul to turn to, right or left. You'd ought to seen 'em begin to scatter."

"But don't you think the cars and telegraphs have given people more to interest them, Mrs. Goodsoe? Don't you believe people's lives were narrower then, and more taken up with little things?" I asked, unwisely, being a product of modern times.

"Not one mite, dear," said my companion stoutly. "There was as big thoughts then as there is now; these times was born o' them. The difference is in folks themselves; but now, instead o' doin' their own housekeepin' and watchin' their own neighbors,—though that was carried to excess,—they git word that a niece's child is ailin' the other side o' Massachusetts, and they drop everything and git on their best clothes, and off they jiggit in the cars. 'Tis a bad sign when folks wears out their best clothes faster 'n they do their every-day ones. The other side o' Massachusetts has got to look after itself by rights. An' besides that, Sunday-keepin' 's all gone out o' fashion. Some lays it to one thing an' some another, but some o' them old ministers that folks are all a-sighin' for did preach a lot o' stuff that wa'n't nothin' but chaff; 't wa'n't the word o' God out o' either Old Testament or New. But everybody went to meetin' and heard it, and come home, and was set to fightin' with their next door neighbor over it. Now I'm a believer, and I try to live a Christian life, but I'd as soon hear a surveyor's book read out, figgers an' all, as try to get any simple truth out o' most sermons. It's them as is most to blame."

"What was the matter that day at Widow Peck's?" I hastened to ask, for I knew by experience that the good, clear-minded soul beside me was apt to grow unduly vexed and distressed when she contemplated the state of religious teaching.

"Why, there wa'n't nothin' the matter, only a gal o' Miss Peck's had met with a dis'pintment and had gone into screechin' fits. 'T was a rovin' creatur' that had come along hayin' time, and he'd gone off an' forsook her betwixt two days; nobody ever knew what become of him. Them Pecks was 'Good Lord, anybody!' kind o' gals, and took up with whoever they could get. One of 'em married Heron, the Irishman; they lived in that little house that was burnt this summer, over on the edge o' the plains. He was a good-hearted creatur', with a laughin' eye and a clever word for everybody. He was the first Irishman that ever came this way, and we was all for gettin' a look at him, when he first used to go by.

Mother's folks was what they call Scotch-Irish, though; there was an old race of 'em settled about here. They could foretell events, some on 'em, and had the second sight. I know folks used to say mother's grandmother had them gifts, but mother was never free to speak about it to us. She remembered her well, too."

"I suppose that you mean old Jim Heron, who was such a famous fiddler?" I asked with great interest, for I am always delighted to know more about the rustic hero, parochial Orpheus that he must have been!

"Now, dear heart, I suppose you don't remember him, do you?" replied Mrs. Goodsoe, earnestly. "Fiddle! He'd about break your heart with them tunes of his, or else set your heels flying up the floor in a jig, though you was minister o' the First Parish and all wound up for a funeral prayer. I tell ye there ain't no tunes sounds like them used to. It used to seem to me summer nights when I was comin' along the plains road, and he set by the window playin', as if there was a bewitched human creatur' in that old red fiddle o' his. He could make it sound just like a woman's voice tellin' somethin' over and over, as if folks could help her out o' her sorrows if she could only make 'em understand. I've set by the stone-wall and cried as if my heart was broke, and dear knows it wa'n't in them days. How he would twirl off them jigs and dance tunes! He used to make somethin' han'some out of 'em in fall an' winter, playin' at huskins and dancin' parties; but he was unstiddy by spells, as he got along in years, and never knew what it was to be forehanded. Everybody felt bad when he died; you couldn't help likin' the creatur'. He'd got the gift—that's all you could say about it.

"There was a Mis' Jerry Foss, that lived over by the brook bridge, on the plains road, that had lost her husband early, and was left with three child'n. She set the world by 'em, and was a real pleasant, ambitious little woman, and was workin' on as best she could with that little farm, when there come a rage o' scarlet fever, and her boy and two girls was swept off and laid dead within the same week. Every one o' the neighbors did what they could, but she'd had no sleep since they was taken sick, and after the funeral she set there just like a piece o' marble, and would only shake her head when you spoke to her. They all thought her reason would go; and 't would certain, if she couldn't have shed tears. An' one o' the neighbors—'t was like mother's sense, but it might have been somebody else—spoke o' Jim Heron. Mother an' one or two o' the women that knew her best was in the house with her. 'T was right in the edge o' the woods and some of us younger ones was over by the wall on the other side of the road where there was a couple of old willows,—I remember just how the brook damp felt; and we kept quiet 's we could, and some other folks come along down the road, and stood waitin' on the little bridge, hopin' somebody'd come out, I suppose, and they'd git news. Everybody was wrought up, and felt a good deal for her, you know. By an' by Jim Heron come stealin' right out o' the shadows an' set down on the doorstep, an' 't was a good while before we heard a sound; then, oh, dear me! 't was what the whole neighborhood felt for that mother all spoke in notes, an' they told me afterwards, that Mis' Foss's face changed in a minute, and she come right over an' got into my mother's lap,—she was a little woman,—an' laid her head down, and there she cried herself into a blessed sleep. After awhile one o' the other women stole out an' told the folks, and we all went home. He only played that one tune.

"But there!" resumed Mrs. Goodsoe, after a silence, during which my eyes were filled with tears. "His wife always complained that the fiddle made her nervous. She never 'peared to think nothin' o' poor Heron after she'd once got him."

"That's often the way," said I, with harsh cynicism, though I had no guilty person in my mind at the moment; and we went straying off, not very far apart, up through the pasture. Mrs. Goodsoe cautioned me that we must not get so far off that we could not get back the same day. The sunshine began to feel very hot on our backs, and we both turned toward the shade. We had already collected a large bundle of mullein leaves, which were carefully laid into a clean, calico apron, held together by the four corners, and proudly carried by me, though my companion regarded them with anxious eyes. We sat down together at the edge of the pine woods, and Mrs. Goodsoe proceeded to fan herself with her limp cape-bonnet.

"I declare, how hot it is! The east wind's all gone again," she said. "It felt so cool this forenoon that I overburdened myself with as thick a petticoat as any I've got. I'm despri't afeared of having a chill, now that I ain't so young as once. I hate to be housed up."

"It's only August, after all," I assured her unnecessarily, confirming my statement by taking two peaches out of my pocket, and laying them side by side on the brown pine needles between us.

"Dear sakes alive!" exclaimed the old lady, with evident pleasure. "Where did you get them, now? Doesn't anything taste twice better out-o'-doors? I ain't had such a peach for years. Do le's keep the stones, an' I'll plant 'em; it only takes four year for a peach pit to come to bearing, an' I guess I'm good for four year, 'thout I meet with some accident."

I could not help agreeing, or taking a fond look at the thin little figure, and her wrinkled brown face and kind, twinkling eyes. She looked as if she had properly dried herself, by mistake, with some of her mullein leaves, and was likely to keep her goodness, and to last the longer in consequence. There never was a truer, simple-hearted soul made out of the old-fashioned country dust than Mrs. Goodsoe. I thought, as I looked away from her across the wide country, that nobody was left in any of the farm-houses so original, so full of rural wisdom and reminiscence, so really able and dependable, as she. And nobody had made better use of her time in a world foolish enough to sometimes under-value medicinal herbs.

When we had eaten our peaches we still sat under the pines, and I was not without pride when I had poked about in the ground with a little twig, and displayed to my crony a long fine root, bright yellow to the eye, and a wholesome bitter to the taste.

"Yis, dear, goldthread," she assented indulgently. "Seems to me there's more of it than anything except grass an' hardhack. Good for canker, but no better than two or three other things I can call to mind; but I always lay in a good wisp of it, for old times' sake. Now, I want to know why you should a bit it, and took away all the taste o' your nice peach? I was just thinkin' what a han'some entertainment we've had. I've got so I 'sociate certain things with certain folks, and goldthread was somethin' Lizy Wisby could n't keep house without, no ways whatever. I believe she took so much it kind o' puckered her disposition."

"Lizy Wisby?" I repeated inquiringly.

"You knew her, if ever, by the name of Mis' Deacon Brimblecom," answered my friend, as if this were only a brief preface to further information, so I waited with respectful expectation. Mrs. Goodsoe had grown tired out in the sun, and a good story would be an excuse for sufficient rest. It was a most lovely place where we sat, halfway up the long hillside; for my part, I was perfectly contented and happy. "You've often heard of Deacon Brimblecom?" she asked, as if a great deal depended upon his being properly introduced.

"I remember him," said I. "They called him Deacon Brimfull, you know, and he used to go about with a witch-hazel branch to show people where to dig wells."

"That's the one," said Mrs. Goodsoe, laughing. "I didn't know's you could go so far back. I'm always divided between whether you can remember everything I can, or are only a babe in arms."

"I have a dim recollection of there being something strange about their marriage," I suggested, after a pause, which began to appear dangerous. I was so much afraid the subject would be changed.

"I can tell you all about it," I was quickly answered. "Deacon Brimblecom was very pious accordin' to his lights in his early years. He lived way back in the country then, and there come a rovin' preacher along, and set everybody up that way all by the ears. I've heard the old folks talk it over, but I forget most of his doctrine, except some of his followers was persuaded they could dwell among the angels while yet on airth, and this Deacon Brimfull, as you call him, felt sure he was called by the voice of a spirit bride. So he left a good, deservin' wife he had, an' four children, and built him a new house over to the other side of the land he'd had from his father. They didn't take much pains with the buildin', because they expected to be translated before long, and then the spirit brides and them folks was goin' to appear and divide up the airth amongst 'em, and the world's folks and on-believers was goin' to serve 'em or be sent to torments. They had meetins about in the school-houses, an' all sorts o' goins on; some on 'em went crazy, but the deacon held on to what wits he had, an' by an' by the spirit bride didn't turn out to be much of a housekeeper, an' he had always been used to good livin', so he sneaked home ag'in. One o' mother's sisters married up to Ash Hill, where it all took place; that's how I come to have the particulars."

"Then how did he come to find his Eliza Wisby?" I inquired. "Do tell me the whole story; you've got mullein leaves enough."

"There's all yisterday's at home, if I haven't," replied Mrs. Goodsoe. "The way he come a-courtin' o' Sister Wisby was this: she went a-courtin' o' him.

"There was a spell he lived to home, and then his poor wife died, and he had a spirit bride in good earnest, an' the child'n was placed about with his folks and hers, for they was both out o' good families; and I don't know what come over him, but he had another pious fit that looked for all the world like the real thing. He had n't no family cares, and he lived with his brother's folks, and turned his land in with theirs. He used to travel to every meetin' an' conference that was within reach of his old sorrel hoss's feeble legs; he j'ined the Christian Baptists that was just in their early prime, and he was a great exhorter, and got to be called deacon, though I guess he wa'n't deacon, 'less it was for a spare hand when deacon timber was scercer 'n usual. An' one time there was a four days' protracted meetin' to the church in the lower part of the town. 'T was a real solemn time; something more'n usual was goin' forward, an' they collected from the whole country round. Women folks liked it, an' the men too; it give 'em a change, an' they was quartered round free, same as conference folks now. Some on 'em, for a joke, sent Silas Brimblecom up to Lizy Wisby's, though she'd give out she could n't accommodate nobody, because of expectin' her cousin's folks. Everybody knew 't was a lie; she was amazin' close considerin' she had plenty to do with. There was a streak that wa'n't just right somewheres in Lizy's wits, I always thought. She was very kind in case o' sickness, I'll say that for her.

"You know where the house is, over there on what they call Windy Hill? There the deacon went, all unsuspectin', and 'stead o' Lizy's resentin' of him she put in her own hoss, and they come back together to evenin' meetin'. She was prominent among the sect herself, an' he bawled and talked, and she bawled and talked, an' took up more 'n the time allotted in the exercises, just as if they was showin' off to each other what they was able to do at expoundin'. Everybody was laughin' at 'em after the meetin' broke up, and that next day an' the next, an' all through, they was constant, and seemed to be havin' a beautiful occasion. Lizy had always give out she scorned the men, but when she got a chance at a particular one 't was altogether different, and the deacon seemed to please her somehow or 'nother, and—There! you don't want to listen to this old stuff that's past an' gone?"

"Oh yes, I do," said I.

"I run on like a clock that's onset her striking hand," said Mrs. Goodsoe mildly. "Sometimes my kitchen timepiece goes on half the forenoon, and I says to myself the day before yisterday I would let it be a warnin', and keep it in mind for a check on my own speech. The next news that was heard was that the deacon an' Lizy—well, opinions differed which of 'em had spoke first, but them fools settled it before the protracted meetin' was over, and give away their hearts before he started for home. They considered 't would be wise, though, considerin' their short acquaintance, to take one another on trial a spell; 't was Lizy's notion, and she asked him why he wouldn't come over and stop with her till spring, and then, if they both continued to like, they could git married any time 't was convenient. Lizy, she come and talked it over with mother, and mother disliked to offend her, but she spoke pretty plain; and Lizy felt hurt, an' thought they was showin' excellent judgment, so much harm come from hasty unions and folks comin' to a realizin' sense of each other's failin's when 't was too late.

"So one day our folks saw Deacon Brimfull a-ridin' by with a gre't coopful of hens in the back o' his wagon, and bundles o' stuff tied on top and hitched to the exes underneath; and he riz a hymn just as he passed the house, and was speedin' the old sorrel with a willer switch. 'T was most Thanksgivin' time, an' sooner 'n she expected him. New Year's was the time she set; but he thought he'd better come while the roads was fit for wheels. They was out to meetin' together Thanksgivin' Day, an' that used to be a gre't season for marryin'; so the young folks nudged each other, and some on' 'em ventured to speak to the couple as they come down the aisle. Lizy carried it off real well; she wa'n't afraid o' what nobody said or thought, and so home they went. They'd got out her yaller sleigh and her hoss; she never would ride after the deacon's poor old creatur', and I believe it died long o' the winter from stiffenin' up.

"Yes," said Mrs. Goodsoe emphatically, after we had silently considered the situation for a short space of time,—"yes, there was consider'ble talk, now I tell you! The raskil boys pestered 'em just about to death for a while. They used to collect up there an' rap on the winders, and they'd turn out all the deacon's hens 'long at nine o'clock 'o night, and chase 'em all over the dingle; an' one night they even lugged the pig right out o' the sty, and shoved it into the back entry, an' run for their lives. They'd stuffed its mouth full o' somethin', so it could n't squeal till it got there. There wa'n't a sign o' nobody to be seen when Lizy hasted out with the light, and she an' the deacon had to persuade the creatur' back as best they could; 't was a cold night, and they said it took 'em till towards mornin'. You see the deacon was just the kind of a man that a hog wouldn't budge for; it takes a masterful man to deal with a hog. Well, there was no end to the works nor the talk, but Lizy left 'em pretty much alone. She did 'pear kind of dignified about it, I must say!"

"And then, were they married in the spring?"

"I was tryin' to remember whether it was just before Fast Day or just after," responded my friend, with a careful look at the sun, which was nearer the west than either of us had noticed. "I think likely 't was along in the last o' April, any way some of us looked out o' the window one Monday mornin' early, and says, 'For goodness' sake! Lizy's sent the deacon home again!' His old sorrel havin' passed away, he was ridin' in Ezry Welsh's hoss-cart, with his hen-coop and more bundles than he had when he come, and he looked as meechin' as ever you see. Ezry was drivin', and he let a glance fly swiftly round to see if any of us was lookin' out; an' then I declare if he did n't have the malice to turn right in towards the barn, where he see my oldest brother, Joshuay, an' says he real natural, 'Joshuay, just step out with your wrench. I believe I hear my kingbolt rattlin' kind o' loose.' Brother, he went out an' took in the sitooation, an' the deacon bowed kind of stiff. Joshuay was so full o' laugh, and Ezry Welsh, that they could n't look one another in the face. There wa'n't nothing ailed the kingbolt, you know, an' when Josh riz up he says, 'Goin' up country for a spell, Mr. Brimblecom?'

" 'I be,' says the deacon, lookin' dreadful mortified and cast down.

" 'Ain't things turned out well with you an' Sister Wisby?' says Joshuay. 'You had ought to remember that the woman is the weaker vessel.'

" 'Hang her, let her carry less sail, then!' the deacon bu'st out, and he stood right up an' shook his fist there by the hen-coop, he was so mad; an' Ezry's hoss was a young creatur', an' started up an set the deacon right over backwards into the chips. We did n't know but he 'd broke his neck; but when he see the women folks runnin' out, he jumped up quick as a cat, an' clim' into the cart, an' off they went. Ezry said he told him that he couldn't git along with Lizy, she was so fractious in thundery weather; if there was a rumble in the daytime she must go right to bed an' screech, and if 't was night she must git right up an' go an' call him out of a sound sleep. But everybody knew he's never a gone home unless she'd sent him.

"Somehow they made it up agin right away, him an' Lizy, and she had him back. She'd been countin' all along on not havin' to hire nobody to work about the gardin an' so on, an' she said she wa'n't goin' to let him have a whole winter's board for nothin'. So the old hens was moved back, and they was married right off fair an' square, an' I don't know but they got along well as most folks. He brought his youngest girl down to live with 'em after a while, an' she was a real treasure to Lizy; everybody spoke well o' Phebe Brimblecom. The deacon got over his pious fit, and there was consider'ble work in him if you kept right after him. He was an amazin' cider-drinker, and he airnt the name you know him by in his latter days. Lizy never trusted him with nothin' but she kep' him well. She left everything she owned to Phebe, when she died, 'cept somethin' to satisfy the law. There, they're all gone now: seems to me sometimes, when I get thinkin', as if I'd lived a thousand years!"

I laughed, but I found that Mrs. Goodsoe's thoughts had taken a serious turn.

"There, I come by some old graves down here in the lower edge of the pasture," she said as we rose to go. "I couldn't help thinking how I should like to be laid right out in the pasture ground, when my time comes; it looked sort o' comfortable, and I have ranged these slopes so many summers. Seems as if I could see right up through the turf and tell when the weather was pleasant, and get the goodness o' the sweet fern. Now, dear, just hand me my apernful o' mulleins out o' the shade. I hope you won't come to need none this winter, but I'll dry some special for you."

"I'm going home by the road," said I, "or else by the path across the meadows, so I will walk as far as the house with you. Are n't you pleased with my company?" for she demurred at my going the least bit out of the way.

So we strolled toward the little gray house, with our plunder of mullein leaves slung on a stick which we carried between us. Of course I went in to make a call, as if I had not seen my hostess before; she is the last maker of muster-gingerbread, and before I came away I was kindly measured for a pair of mittens.

"You'll be sure to come an' see them two peach-trees after I get 'em well growin'?" Mrs. Goodsoe called after me when I had said good-by, and was almost out of hearing down the road.

Kate Chopin
1851 – 1904

Kate O'Flaherty Chopin began writing only in her thirties and died in her early fifties. As a result, by comparison with such contemporaries as Sarah Orne Jewett and Mary E. Wilkins Freeman, she produced but a small body of fiction—only two volumes of short stories and two novels. Slender as her contribution to short fiction is, it nevertheless illustrates the progressive development of the post-war local color movement into nearly every distinctive phase of American life, including the problem of miscegenation, which earlier local colorists were loath to touch. In their best vein, her stories show that the technique of the "well-made" story could be used in depicting materials as peculiar to a specific locality as the bayou country of Louisiana.

Of French and Irish ancestry, Kate O'Flaherty was born in 1851 in St. Louis, Missouri. A wide reader from early youth, she received her educational training at the Sacred Heart Convent, from which she graduated in 1868. Two years later, she married Oscar Chopin, a native of Louisiana, who took her to live in New Orleans, where he was a cotton broker. She and her husband participated in the social life of that exotic city, despite the responsibilities of a steadily growing family, which ultimately numbered six children—five boys and a girl. When her husband gave up his cotton brokerage business to manage a large plantation he owned on the Red River in central Louisiana, the family relocated there, and the writer was thus brought to the section of the country which was to provide her with the distinctive settings and characters of her stories. Her husband died in 1882, and feeling herself unable to assume the responsibilities of operating the plantation, she sold it and returned to St. Louis with her six children.

Encouraged to write by friends who had admired her letters, she first produced an amateurish novel, *At Fault* (1890). Then she began publishing skillfully written stories in *Century* and *Harper's* magazines. Two collections soon appeared: *Bayou Folk* (1894) and *A Night in Acadie* (1897). Her final work, *The Awakening* (1899), a novel, received unfavorable critical notices because of its treatment of mixed marriage and adultery. She died suddenly in 1904.

It seems evident that the title Chopin chose for this story was meant to convey a double meaning—one referring to the storm occurring outside the house; the other to the one inside. Chopin was clearly in advance of her times in the candor with which she treated sex in her fiction. But the current revival of interest in her work depends less on this—or any other single theme—than it does on her integrity and her artistry as a writer.

The Storm

A Sequel to "The 'Cadian Ball"

The leaves were so still that even Bibi thought it was going to rain. Bobinôt, who was accustomed to converse on terms of perfect equality with his little son, called the child's attention to certain sombre clouds that were rolling with sinister intention from the west, accompanied by a sullen, threatening roar. They were at Friedheimer's store and decided to remain there till the storm had passed. They sat within the door on two empty kegs. Bibi was four years old and looked very wise.

"Mama'll be 'fraid, yes," he suggested with blinking eyes.

"She'll shut the house. Maybe she got Sylvie helpin' her this evenin'," Bobinôt responded reassuringly.

"No; she ent got Sylvie. Sylvie was helpin' her yistiday," piped Bibi.

"A Respectable Woman" by Kate Chopin, from *A Night in Acadie* (Way & Williams, 1897).

Bobinôt arose and going across to the counter purchased a can of shrimps, of which Calixta was very fond. Then he returned to his perch on the keg and sat stolidly holding the can of shrimps while the storm burst. It shook the wooden store and seemed to be ripping great furrows in the distant field. Bibi laid his little hand on his father's knee and was not afraid.

II

Calixta, at home, felt no uneasiness for their safety. She sat at a side window sewing furiously on a sewing machine. She was greatly occupied and did not notice the approaching storm. But she felt very warm and often stopped to mop her face on which the perspiration gathered in beads. She unfastened her white sacque at the throat. It began to grow dark, and suddenly realizing the situation she got up hurriedly and went about closing windows and doors.

Out on the small front gallery she had hung Bobinôt's Sunday clothes to air and she hastened out to gather them before the rain fell. As she stepped outside, Alcée Laballière rode in at the gate. She had not seen him very often since her marriage, and never alone. She stood there with Bobinôt's coat in her hands, and the big rain drops began to fall. Alcée rode his horse under the shelter of a side projection where the chickens had huddled and there were plows and a harrow piled up in the corner.

"May I come and wait on your gallery till the storm is over, Calixta?" he asked.

"Come 'long in, M'sieur Alcée."

His voice and her own startled her as if from a trance, and she seized Bobinôt's vest. Alcée, mounting to the porch, grabbed the trousers and snatched Bibi's braided jacket that was about to be carried away by a sudden gust of wind. He expressed an intention to remain outside, but it was soon apparent that he might as well have been out in the open: the water beat in upon the boards in driving sheets, and he went inside, closing the door after him. It was even necessary to put something beneath the door to keep the water out.

"My! what a rain! It's good two years sence it rain' like that," exclaimed Calixta as she rolled up a piece of bagging and Alcée helped her to thrust it beneath the crack.

She was a little fuller of figure than five years before when she married; but she had lost nothing of her vivacity. Her blue eyes still retained their melting quality; and her yellow hair, dishevelled by the wind and rain, kinked more stubbornly than ever about her ears and temples.

The rain beat upon the low, shingled roof with a force and clatter that threatened to break an entrance and deluge them there. They were in the dining room—the sitting room—the general utility room. Adjoining was her bed room, with Bibi's couch along side her own. The door stood open, and the room with its white, monumental bed, its closed shutters, looked dim and mysterious.

Alcée flung himself into a rocker and Calixta nervously began to gather up from the floor the lengths of a cotton sheet which she had been sewing.

"If this keeps up, *Dieu sait* if the levees goin' to stan' it!" she exclaimed.

"What have you got to do with the levees?"

"I got enough to do! An' there's Bobinôt with Bibi out in that storm—if he only didn' left Friedheimer's!"

"Let us hope, Calixta, that Bobinôt's got sense enough to come in out of a cyclone."

She went and stood at the window with a greatly disturbed look on her face. She wiped the frame that was clouded with moisture. It was stiflingly hot. Alcée got up and joined her at the window, looking over her shoulder. The rain was coming down in sheets obscuring the view of far-off cabins and enveloping the distant wood in a gray mist. The playing of the lightning was incessant. A bolt struck a tall chinaberry tree at the edge of the field. It filled all visible space with a blinding glare and the crash seemed to invade the very boards they stood upon.

Calixta put her hands to her eyes, and with a cry, staggered backward. Alcée's arm encircled her, and for an instant he drew her close and spasmodically to him.

"Bonté!" she cried, releasing herself from his encircling arm and retreating from the window, "the house'll go next! If I only knew w'ere Bibi was!" She would not compose herself; she would not be seated. Alcée clasped her shoulders and looked into her face. The contact of her warm, palpitating body when he had unthinkingly drawn her into his arms, had aroused all the old-time infatuation and desire for her flesh.

"Calixta," he said, "don't be frightened. Nothing can happen. The house is too low to be struck, with so many tall trees standing about. There! aren't you going to be quiet? say, aren't you?" He pushed her hair back from her face that was warm and steaming. Her lips were as red and moist as pomegranate seed. Her white neck and a glimpse of her full, firm bosom disturbed him powerfully. As she glanced up at him the fear in her liquid blue eyes had given place to a drowsy gleam that unconsciously betrayed a sensuous desire. He looked down into her eyes and there was nothing for him to do but to gather her lips in a kiss. It reminded him of Assumption.

"Do you remember—in Assumption, Calixta?" he asked in a low voice broken by passion. Oh! she remembered; for in Assumption he had kissed her and kissed and kissed her; until his senses would well nigh fail, and to save her he would resort to a desperate flight. If she was not an immaculate dove in those days, she was still inviolate; a passionate creature whose very defenselessness had made her defense, against which his honor forbade him to prevail. Now—well, now—her lips seemed in a manner free to be tasted, as well as her round, white throat and her whiter breasts.

They did not heed the crashing torrents, and the roar of the elements made her laugh as she lay in his arms. She was a revelation in that dim, mysterious chamber; as white as the couch she lay upon. Her firm, elastic flesh that was knowing for the first time its birthright, was like a creamy lily that the sun invites to contribute its breath and perfume to the undying life of the world.

The generous abundance of her passion, without guile or trickery, was like a white flame which penetrated and found response in depths of his own sensuous nature that had never yet been reached.

When he touched her breasts they gave themselves up in quivering ecstasy, inviting his lips. Her mouth was a fountain of delight. And when he possessed her, they seemed to swoon together at the very borderland of life's mystery.

He stayed cushioned upon her, breathless, dazed, enervated, with his heart beating like a hammer upon her. With one hand she clasped his head, her lips lightly touching his forehead. The other hand stroked with a soothing rhythm his muscular shoulders.

The growl of the thunder was distant and passing away. The rain beat softly upon the shingles, inviting them to drowsiness and sleep. But they dared not yield.

The rain was over; and the sun was turning the glistening green world into a palace of gems. Calixta, on the gallery, watched Alcée ride away. He turned and smiled at her with a beaming face; and she lifted her pretty chin in the air and laughed aloud.

III

Bobinôt and Bibi, trudging home, stopped without at the cistern to make themselves presentable.

"My! Bibi, w'at will yo' mama say! You ought to be ashame'. You oughtn' put on those good pants. Look at 'em! An' that mud on yo' collar! How you got that mud on yo' collar, Bibi? I never saw such a boy!" Bibi was the picture of pathetic resignation. Bobinôt was the embodiment of serious solicitude as he strove to remove from his own person and his son's the signs of their tramp over heavy roads and through wet fields. He scraped the mud off Bibi's bare legs and feet with a stick and carefully removed all traces from his heavy brogans. Then, prepared for the worst—the meeting with an over-scrupulous housewife, they entered cautiously at the back door.

Calixta was preparing supper. She had set the table and was dripping coffee at the hearth. She sprang up as they came in.

"Oh, Bobinôt! You back! My! but I was uneasy. W'ere you been during the rain? An' Bibi? he ain't wet? he ain't hurt?" She had clasped Bibi and was kissing him effusively. Bobinôt's explanations and apologies which he had been composing all along the way, died on his lips as Calixta felt him to see if he were dry, and seemed to express nothing but satisfaction at their safe return.

"I brought you some shrimps, Calixta," offered Bobinôt, hauling the can from his ample side pocket and laying it on the table.

"Shrimps! Oh, Bobinôt! you too good fo' anything!" and she gave him a smacking kiss on the cheek that resounded. *"J'vous réponds,* we'll have a feas' to night! umph-umph!"

Bobinôt and Bibi began to relax and enjoy themselves, and when the three seated themselves at table they laughed much and so loud that anyone might have heard them as far away as Laballière's.

IV

Alcée Laballière wrote to his wife, Clarisse, that night. It was a loving letter, full of tender solicitude. He told her not to hurry back, but if she and the babies liked it at Biloxi, to stay a month longer. He was getting on nicely; and though he missed them, he was willing to bear the separation a while longer—realizing that their health and pleasure were the first things to be considered.

V

As for Clarisse, she was charmed upon receiving her husband's letter. She and the babies were doing well. The society was agreeable; many of her old friends and acquaintances were at the bay. And the first free breath since her marriage seemed to restore the pleasant liberty of her maiden days. Devoted as she was to her husband, their intimate conjugal life was something which she was more than willing to forego for a while.

So the storm passed and every one was happy.

Mary E. Wilkins Freeman

1852 – 1930

Mary E. Wilkins Freeman, like her contemporary Sarah Orne Jewett, won distinction for her portrayal of simple New England folk. However, beyond restricting her characters primarily to one region, she has little in common with Jewett or other local colorists of her period. Although meticulous in her use of dialect and localized mannerisms, she is less concerned in her stories with these character externals than with the internal ones of mind, heart, and conscience. Further, she stresses the pinched souls and the drabness of the lives of her people. As a result, the local color element in her work, so far as it may be considered present at all, exists not for its own sake but rather as an organic part of her materials. Finally, she seldom gives way to the temptation besetting some local colorists to substitute the appeal of subject matter for sound workmanship: The finished artistry of her best stories compares favorably with that of such masters as Hawthorne and Poe.

Mary Wilkins was born in 1852, in Randolph, Massachusetts, a town near Boston, and spent much of her life there among people still touched by the lengthening shadow of Puritanism. A frail child, she received most of her education at home, isolating herself among her books for many formative years, in somewhat the fashion of Hawthorne. Her first published work, light poems in the *vers de société* vein, appeared in the *Century Magazine* in 1881; but in 1883, when her father's death confronted her with the necessity of earning a livelihood, she began to write short stories. Within four years, she demonstrated her competency in this field by writing thirty stories for leading magazines and by publishing her first volume, *A Humble Romance and Other Stories* (1887); but it was not until the appearance of her second volume, *A New England Nun and Other Stories,* in 1891, that her stories won wide critical recognition. Shortly before her marriage in 1902 to Dr. C. M. Freeman and their move to Metuchen, New Jersey, she turned her attention to other types of literature, and, during the latter part of her writing career, published twelve novels, in addition to one play and two volumes of poetry. That she never lost interest in the short story—clearly the field for which her talent was best fitted—is apparent from the fact that during her lifetime she published the amazing total of nearly two hundred and fifty stories. It is further remarkable that a collection appearing as late in her career as 1918, *Edgewater People,* has in it stories fully as good as those in earlier volumes.

Characteristically, as in "A New England Nun," her stories center on one dominant character facing a major crisis in life, and they are told with a minimum of exposition and description but in such a manner as to reveal the character's personality. The detached objectivity, compression, and irony of her method are suggestive of the French master, Guy de Maupassant.

A New England Nun

It was late in the afternoon, and the light was waning. There was a difference in the look of the tree shadows out in the yard. Somewhere in the distance cows were lowing and a little bell was tinkling; now and then a farm-wagon tilted by, and the dust flew; some blue-shirted laborers with shovels over their shoulders plodded past; little swarms of flies were dancing up and down before the people's faces in the soft air. There seemed to be a gentle stir arising over everything for the mere sake of subsidence—a very premonition of rest and hush and night.

This soft diurnal commotion was over Louisa Ellis also. She had been

"A New England Nun" by Mary E. Wilkins Freeman, from *A New England Nun and Other Stories* (Harper & Brothers, 1891).

peacefully sewing at her sitting-room window all the afternoon. Now she quilted her needle carefully into her work, which she folded precisely, and laid in a basket with her thimble and thread and scissors. Louisa Ellis could not remember that ever in her life she had mislaid one of these little feminine appurtenances, which had become, from long use and constant association, a very part of her personality.

Louisa tied a green apron round her waist, and got out a flat straw hat with a green ribbon. Then she went into the garden with a little blue crockery bowl, to pick some currants for her tea. After the currants were picked she sat on the back door-step and stemmed them, collecting the stems carefully in her apron, and afterward throwing them into the hen-coop. She looked sharply at the grass beside the step to see if any had fallen there.

Louisa was slow and still in her movements; it took her a long time to prepare her tea; but when ready it was set forth with as much grace as if she had been a veritable guest to her own self. The little square table stood exactly in the centre of the kitchen, and was covered with a starched linen cloth whose border pattern of flowers glistened. Louisa had a damask napkin on her tea-tray, where were arranged a cut-glass tumbler full of teaspoons, a silver cream-pitcher, a china sugar-bowl, and one pink china cup and saucer. Louisa used china every day—something which none of her neighbors did. They whispered about it among themselves. Their daily tables were laid with common crockery, their sets of best china stayed in the parlor closet, and Louisa Ellis was no richer nor better bred than they. Still she would use the china. She had for her supper a glass dish full of sugared currants, a plate of little cakes, and one of light white biscuits. Also a leaf or two of lettuce, which she cut up daintily. Louisa was very fond of lettuce, which she raised to perfection in her little garden. She ate quite heartily, though in a delicate, pecking way; it seemed almost surprising that any considerable bulk of the food should vanish.

After tea she filled a plate with nicely baked thin corn-cakes, and carried them out into the back-yard.

"Cæsar!" she called. "Cæsar! Cæsar!"

There was a little rush, and the clank of a chain, and a large yellow-and-white dog appeared at the door of his tiny hut, which was half hidden among the tall grasses and flowers. Louisa patted him and gave him the corn-cakes. Then she returned to the house and washed the tea-things, polishing the china carefully. The twilight had deepened; the chorus of the frogs floated in at the open window wonderfully loud and shrill, and once in a while a long sharp drone from a tree-toad pierced it. Louisa took off her green gingham apron, disclosing a shorter one of pink-and-white print. She lighted her lamp, and sat down again with her sewing.

In about half an hour Joe Dagget came. She heard his heavy step on the walk, and rose and took off her pink-and-white apron. Under that was still another—white linen with a little cambric edging on the bottom; that was Louisa's company apron. She never wore it without her calico sewing apron over it unless she had a guest. She had barely folded the pink and white one with methodical haste and laid it in a table-drawer when the door opened and Joe Dagget entered.

He seemed to fill up the whole room. A little yellow canary that had been asleep in his green cage at the south window woke up and fluttered wildly, beating his little yellow wings against the wires. He always did so when Joe Dagget came into the room.

"Good-evening," said Louisa. She extended her hand with a kind of solemn cordiality.

"Good-evening, Louisa," returned the man, in a loud voice.

She placed a chair for him, and they sat facing each other, with the table between them. He sat bolt-upright, toeing out his heavy feet squarely, glancing with a good-humored uneasiness around the room. She sat gently erect, folding her slender hands in her white-linen lap.

"Been a pleasant day," remarked Dagget.

"Real pleasant," Louisa assented softly, "Have you been haying?" she asked, after a little while.

"Yes, I've been haying all day, down in the ten-acre lot. Pretty hot work."

"It must be."

"Yes, it's pretty hot work in the sun."

"Is your mother well to-day?"

"Yes, mother's pretty well."

"I suppose Lily Dyer's with her now?"

Dagget colored. "Yes, she's with her," he answered, slowly.

He was not very young, but there was a boyish look about his large face. Louisa was not quite as old as he, her face was fairer and smoother, but she gave people the impression of being older.

"I suppose she's a good deal of help to your mother." she said, further.

"I guess she is; I don't know how mother'd get along without her," said Dagget, with a sort of embarrassed warmth.

"She looks like a real capable girl. She's pretty-looking too," remarked Louisa.

"Yes, she is pretty fair looking."

Presently Dagget began fingering the books on the table. There was a square red autograph album, and a Young Lady's Gift-Book which had belonged to Louisa's mother. He took them up one after the other and opened them; then laid them down again, the album on the Gift-Book.

Louisa kept eyeing them with mild uneasiness. Finally she rose and changed the position of the books, putting the album underneath. That was the way they had been arranged in the first place.

Dagget gave an awkward little laugh. "Now what difference did it make which book was on top?" said he.

Louisa looked at him with a deprecating smile. "I always keep them that way," murmured she.

"You do beat everything," said Dagget, trying to laugh again. His large face was flushed.

He remained about an hour longer, then rose to take leave. Going out, he stumbled over a rug, and trying to recover himself, hit Louisa's work-basket on the table, and knocked it on the floor.

He looked at Louisa, then at the rolling spools; he ducked himself awkwardly toward them, but she stopped him. "Never mind," said she; "I'll pick them up after you're gone."

She spoke with a mild stiffness. Either she was a little disturbed, or his nervousness affected her, and made her seem constrained in her effort to reassure him.

When Joe Dagget was outside he drew in the sweet evening air with a sigh, and felt much as an innocent and perfectly well-intentioned bear might after his exit from a china shop.

Louisa, on her part, felt much as the kind-hearted, long-suffering owner of the china shop might have done after the exit of the bear.

She tied on the pink, then the green apron, picked up all the scattered treasures and replaced them in her work-basket, and straightened the rug. Then she set the lamp on the floor, and began sharply examining the carpet. She even rubbed her fingers over it, and looked at them.

"He's tracked in a good deal of dust," she murmured. "I thought he must have."

Louisa got a dust-pan and brush, and swept Joe Dagget's track carefully.

If he could have known it, it would have increased his perplexity and uneasiness, although it would not have disturbed his loyalty in the least. He came twice a week to see Louisa Ellis, and every time, sitting there in her delicately sweet room, he felt as if surrounded by a hedge of lace. He was afraid to stir lest he should put a clumsy foot or hand through the fairy web, and he had always the consciousness that Louisa was watching fearfully lest he should.

Still the lace and Louisa commanded perforce his perfect respect and patience and loyalty. They were to be married in a month, after a singular courtship which had lasted for a matter of fifteen years. For fourteen out of the fifteen years the two had not once seen each other, and they had seldom exchanged letters. Joe had been all those years in Australia, where he had gone to make his fortune, and where he had stayed until he made it. He would have stayed fifty years if it had taken so long, and come home feeble and tottering, or never come home at all, to marry Louisa.

But the fortune had been made in the fourteen years, and he had come home now to marry the woman who had been patiently and unquestioningly waiting for him all that time.

Shortly after they were engaged he had announced to Louisa his determination to strike out into new fields, and secure a competency before they should be married. She had listened and assented with the sweet serenity which never failed her, not even when her lover set forth on that long and uncertain journey. Joe, buoyed up as he was by his sturdy determination, broke down a little at the last, but Louisa kissed him with a mild blush, and said good-by.

"It won't be for long," poor Joe had said, huskily; but it was for fourteen years.

In that length of time much had happened. Louisa's mother and brother had died, and she was all alone in the world. But greatest happening of all—a subtle happening which both were too simple to understand—Louisa's feet had turned into a path, smooth maybe under a calm, serene sky, but so straight and unswerving that it could only meet a check at the grave, and so narrow that there was no room for any one at her side.

Louisa's first emotion when Joe Dagget came home (he had not apprised her of his coming) was consternation, although she would not admit it to herself, and he never dreamed of it. Fifteen years ago she had been in love with him—at least she considered herself to be. Just at that time, gently acquiescing with and falling into the natural drift of girlhood, she had seen marriage ahead as a reasonable feature and a probable desirability of life. She had listened with calm docility to her mother's views upon the subject. Her mother was remarkable for her cool sense and sweet, even temperament. She talked wisely to her daughter when Joe Dagget presented himself, and Louisa accepted him with no hesitation. He was the first lover she had ever had.

She had been faithful to him all these years. She had never dreamed of the possibility of marrying any one else. Her life, especially for the last seven years, had been full of a pleasant peace, she had never felt discontented nor impatient over her lover's absence; still she had always looked forward to his return and their marriage as the inevitable conclusion of things. However, she had fallen into a way of placing it so far in the future that it was almost equal to placing it over the boundaries of another life.

When Joe came she had been expecting him, and expecting to be married for fourteen years, but she was as much surprised and taken aback as if she had never thought of it.

Joe's consternation came later. He eyed Louisa with an instant confirmation of his old admiration. She had changed but little. She still kept her pretty manner and soft grace, and was, he considered, every whit as attractive as ever. As for himself, his stent was done; he had his face turned away from fortune-seeking, and the old winds of romance whistled as loud and sweet as ever through his ears. All the song which he had been wont to hear in them was Louisa; he had for a long time a loyal belief that he heard it still, but finally it seemed to him that although the winds sang always that one song, it had another name. But for Louisa the wind had never more than murmured; now it had gone down, and everything was still. She listened for a little while with half-wistful attention; then she turned quietly away and went to work on her wedding clothes.

Joe had made some extensive and quite magnificent alterations in his house. It was the old homestead; the newly-married couple would live there, for Joe could not desert his mother, who refused to leave her old home. So Louisa must leave hers. Every morning, rising and going about among her neat maidenly possessions, she felt as one looking her last upon the faces of dear friends. It was true that in a measure she could take them with her, but, robbed of their old environments, they would appear in such new guises that they would almost cease to be themselves. Then there were some peculiar features of her happy solitary life which she would probably be obliged to relinquish altogether. Sterner tasks than these graceful but half-needless ones would probably devolve upon her. There would be a large house to care for; there would be company to entertain; there would be Joe's rigorous and feeble old mother to wait upon; and it would be contrary to all thrifty village traditions for her to keep more than one servant. Louisa had a little still, and she used to occupy herself pleasantly in summer weather with distilling the sweet aromatic essences from roses and peppermint and spearmint. By-and-by her still must be laid away. Her store of essences was already considerable, and there would be no time for her to distil for the mere pleasure of it. Then Joe's mother would think it foolishness; she had already hinted her opinion in the matter. Louisa dearly loved to sew a linen seam, not always for use, but for the simple, mild pleasure which she took in it. She would have been loath to confess how more than once she had ripped a seam for the mere delight of sewing it together again. Sitting at her window during long sweet afternoons, drawing her needle gently through the dainty fabric, she was peace itself. But there was small chance of such foolish comfort in the future. Joe's mother, domineering, shrewd old matron that she was even in her old age, and very likely even Joe himself, with his honest masculine rudeness, would laugh and frown down all these pretty but senseless old maiden ways.

Louisa had almost the enthusiasm of an artist over the mere order and cleanliness of her solitary home. She had throbs of genuine triumph at the sight of the window-panes which she had polished until they shone like jewels. She gloated gently over her orderly bureau-drawers, with their exquisitely folded contents redolent with lavender and sweet clover and very purity. Could she be sure of the endurance of even this? She had visions, so startling that she half repudiated them as indelicate, of coarse masculine belongings strewn about in endless litter; of dust and disorder arising necessarily from a coarse masculine presence in the midst of all this delicate harmony.

Among her forebodings of disturbance, not the least was with regard to Cæsar. Cæsar was a veritable hermit of a dog. For the greater part of his life he had dwelt in his secluded hut, shut out from the society of his kind and all innocent canine joys. Never had Cæsar since his early youth watched at a woodchuck's hole; never had he known the delights of a stray bone at a neighbor's kitchen door. And it was all on account of a sin committed when hardly out of his puppyhood. No one knew the possible depth of remorse of which this mild-visaged, altogether innocent-looking old dog might be capable; but whether or not he had encountered remorse, he had encountered a full measure of righteous retribution. Old Cæsar seldom lifted up his voice in a growl or a bark; he was fat and sleepy; there were yellow rings which looked like spectacles around his dim old eyes; but there was a neighbor who bore on his hand the imprint of several of Cæsar's sharp white youthful teeth, and for that he had lived at the end of a chain, all alone in a little hut, for fourteen years. The neighbor, who was choleric and smarting with the pain of his wound, had demanded either Cæsar's death or complete ostracism. So Louisa's brother, to whom the dog had belonged, had built him his little kennel and tied him up. It was now fourteen years since, in a flood of youthful spirits, he had inflicted that memorable bite, and with the exception of short excursions, always at the end of the chain, under the strict guardianship of his master or Louisa, the old dog had remained a close prisoner. It is doubtful if, with his limited ambition, he took much pride in the fact, but it is certain that he was possessed of considerable cheap fame. He was regarded by all the children in the village and by many adults as a very monster of ferocity. St. George's dragon could hardly have surpassed in evil repute Louisa Ellis's old yellow dog. Mothers charged their children with solemn emphasis not to go too near him, and the children listened and believed greedily, with a fascinated appetite for terror, and ran by Louisa's house stealthily, with many sidelong glances at the terrible dog. If perchance he sounded a hoarse bark, there was a panic. Wayfarers chancing into Louisa's yard eyed him with respect, and inquired if the chain were stout. Cæsar at large might have seemed a very ordinary dog, and excited no comment whatever; chained, his reputation overshadowed him, so that he lost his own proper outlines and looked darkly vague and enormous. Joe Dagget, however, with his good-humored sense and shrewdness, saw him as he was. He strode valiantly up to him and patted him on the head, in spite of Louisa's soft clamor of warning, and even attempted to set him loose. Louisa grew so alarmed that he desisted, but kept announcing his opinion in the matter quite forcibly at intervals. "There ain't a better-natured dog in town," he would say, "and it's downright cruel to keep him tied up there. Some day I'm going to take him out."

Louisa had very little hope that he would not, one of these days, when their interests and possessions should be more completely fused in one. She pictured to herself Cæsar on the rampage through the quiet and unguarded village. She saw innocent children bleeding in his path. She was herself very fond of the old dog, because he had belonged to her dead brother, and he was always very gentle with her; still she had great faith in his ferocity. She always warned people not to go too near him. She fed him on ascetic fare of corn-mush and cakes, and never fired his dangerous temper with heating and sanguinary diet of flesh and bones. Louisa looked at the old dog munching his simple fare, and thought of her approaching marriage and trembled. Still no anticipation of disorder and confusion in lieu of sweet peace and harmony, no forebodings of Cæsar on the rampage, no wild fluttering of her little yellow canary, were sufficient to turn her a hair's breadth. Joe Dagget had been fond of her and working for her all these years. It was not for her, whatever came to pass, to prove untrue and break his heart. She put the exquisite little stitches into her wedding-garments, and the time went on till it was only a week before her wedding-day. It was a Tuesday evening, and the wedding was to be a week from Wednesday.

There was a full moon that night. About nine o'clock Louisa strolled down the road a little way. There were harvest-fields on either hand, bordered by low stone walls. Luxuriant clumps of bushes grew beside the wall, and trees—wild cherry and old apple trees—at intervals. Presently Louisa sat down on the wall and looked about her with mildly sorrowful reflectiveness. Tall shrubs of blueberry and meadow-sweet, all woven together and tangled with blackberry vines and horse-briers, shut her in on either side. She had a little clear space between them. Opposite her, on the other side of the road, was a spreading tree; the moon shone between its boughs, and the leaves twinkled like silver. The road was bespread with a beautiful shifting dapple of silver and shadow; the air was full of a mysterious sweetness. "I wonder if it's wild grapes?" murmured Louisa. She sat there some time. She was just thinking of rising, when she heard footsteps and low voices, and remained quiet. It was a lonely place, and she felt a little timid. She thought she would keep still in the shadow and let the persons, whoever they might be, pass her.

But just before they reached her the voices ceased, and the footsteps. She understood that their owners had also found seats upon the stone wall. She was wondering if she could not steal away unobserved, when the voice broke the stillness. It was Joe Dagget's. She sat still and listened.

The voice was announced by a loud sigh, which was as familiar as itself. "Well," said Dagget, "you've made up your mind, then, I suppose?"

"Yes," returned another voice; "I'm going day after to-morrow."

"That's Lily Dyer," thought Louisa to herself. The voice embodied itself in her mind. She saw a girl tall and full-figured, with a firm, fair face, looking fairer and firmer in the moonlight, her strong yellow hair braided in a close knot. A girl full of a calm rustic strength and bloom, with a masterful way which might have beseemed a princess. Lily Dyer was a favorite with the village folk; she had just the qualities to arouse the admiration. She was good and handsome and smart. Louisa had often heard her praises sounded.

"Well," said Joe Dagget, "I ain't got a word to say."

"I don't know what you could say," returned Lily Dyer.

"Not a word to say," repeated Joe, drawing out the words heavily. Then there was a silence. "I ain't sorry," he began at last, "that that happened yesterday—that we kind of let on how we felt to each other. I guess it's just as well we knew. Of course I can't do anything any different. I'm going right on an' get married next week. I ain't going back on a woman that's waited for me fourteen years, an' break her heart."

"If you should jilt her to-morrow, I wouldn't have you," spoke up the girl, with sudden vehemence.

"Well, I ain't going to give you the chance," said he; "but I don't believe you would, either."

"You'd see I wouldn't. Honor's honor, an' right's right. An' I'd never think anything of any man that went against 'em for me or any other girl; you'd find that out, Joe Dagget."

"Well, you'll find out fast enough that I ain't going against 'em for you or any other girl," returned he. Their voices sounded almost as if they were angry with each other. Louisa was listening eagerly.

"I'm sorry you feel as if you must go away," said Joe, "but I don't know but it's best.

"Of course it's best. I hope you and I have got common-sense."

"Well, I suppose you're right." Suddenly Joe's voice got an undertone of tenderness. "Say, Lily," he said, "I'll get along well enough myself, but I can't bear to think— You don't suppose you're going to fret much about it?"

"I guess you'll find out I sha'n't fret much over a married man."

"Well, I hope you won't—I hope you won't, Lily. God knows I do. And—I hope—one of these days—you'll—come across somebody else—"

"I don't see any reason why I shouldn't." Suddenly her tone changed. She spoke in a sweet, clear voice, so loud that she could have been heard across the street. "No, Joe Dagget," said she, "I'll never marry any other man as long as I live. I've got good sense, an' I ain't going to break my heart nor make a fool of myself; but I'm never going to be married, you can be sure of that. I ain't that sort of a girl to feel this way twice."

Louisa heard an exclamation and a soft commotion behind the bushes; then Lily spoke again—the voice sounded as if she had risen. "This must be put a stop to," said she. "We've stayed here long enough. I'm going home."

Louisa sat there in a daze, listening to their retreating steps. After a while she got up and slunk softly home herself. The next day she did her housework methodically; that was as much a matter of course as breathing; but she did not sew on her wedding-clothes. She sat at her window and meditated. In the evening Joe came. Louisa Ellis had never known that she had any diplomacy in her, but when she came to look for it that night she found it, although meek of its kind, among her little feminine weapons. Even now she could hardly believe that she had heard aright, and that she would not do Joe a terrible injury should she break her troth-plight. She wanted to sound him without betraying too soon her own inclinations in the matter. She did it successfully, and they finally came to an understanding; but it was a difficult thing, for he was as afraid of betraying himself as she.

She never mentioned Lily Dyer. She simply said that while she had no cause of complaint against him, she had lived so long in one way that she shrank from making a change.

"Well, I never shrank, Louisa," said Dagget. "I'm going to be honest enough to say that I think maybe it's better this way; but if you'd wanted to keep on, I'd have stuck to you till my dying day. I hope you know that."

"Yes, I do," said she.

That night she and Joe parted more tenderly than they had done for a long time. Standing in the door, holding each other's hands, a last great wave of regretful memory swept over them.

"Well, this ain't the way we've thought it was all going to end, is it, Louisa?" said Joe.

She shook her head. There was a little quiver on her placid face.

"You let me know if there's ever anything I can do for you," said he. "I ain't ever going to forget you, Louisa." Then he kissed her, and went down the path.

Louisa, all alone by herself that night, wept a little, she hardly knew why; but the next morning, on waking, she felt like a queen who, after fearing lest her domain be wrested away from her, sees it firmly insured in her possession.

Now the tall weeds and grasses might cluster around Cæsar's little hermit hut, the snow might fall on its roof year in and year out, but he never would go on a rampage through the unguarded village. Now the little canary might turn itself into a peaceful yellow ball night after night, and have no need to wake and flutter with wild terror against its bars. Louisa could sew linen seams, and distil roses, and dust and polish and fold away in lavender, as long as she listed. That afternoon she sat with her needle-work at the window, and felt fairly steeped in peace. Lily Dyer, tall and erect and blooming, went past; but she felt no qualm. If Louisa Ellis had sold her birthright she did not know it, the taste of the pottage was so delicious, and had been her sole satisfaction for so long. Serenity and placid narrowness had become to her as the birthright itself. She gazed ahead through a long reach of future days strung together like pearls in a rosary, every one like the other, and all smooth and flawless and innocent, and her heart went up in thankfulness. Outside was the fervid summer afternoon; the air was filled with the sounds of the busy harvest of men and birds and bees; there were halloos, metallic clatterings, sweet calls, and long hummings. Louisa sat, prayerfully numbering her days, like an uncloistered nun.

Charles W. Chesnutt
1858 – 1932

One of the most significant developments in the American short story during the twentieth century has been the emergence of many talented black writers such as Jean Toomer, Richard Wright, Langston Hughes, Zora Neale Hurston, Ralph Ellison, James Baldwin, Ernest Gaines, Lorraine Hansberry, and Cyrus Colter, to name only a few. By virtue of being the first important black story writer, Charles W. Chesnutt stands chronologically at the head of this group, but his importance does not rest alone on historical grounds. Despite the marked differences between his fictional themes and structures and those used by later black writers, he wrote stories of merit that entitle him to a respectable rank not only in the tradition of black literature but in the broader stream of American literature.

Born in 1858, in Cleveland, Ohio, Chesnutt was the son of free blacks who had moved from North Carolina to Cleveland two years before his birth. His father, Andrew Chesnutt, served during the Civil War as a teamster in the Union Army and decided to remain in North Carolina after the war to be near his aged father, his family joining him there in 1866. Charles, who had begun his education in the Cleveland public schools, then entered the newly established Howard school in Fayetteville, North Carolina. While still in his teens, however, he left school to become a teacher himself in rural schools in North Carolina and South Carolina, but he continued his education thereafter by independent reading and study. In 1877, he became assistant principal of the Normal School in Fayetteville, established to train teachers for black schools. The next year, he married Susan Perry, a teacher in the school and the daughter of a local business owner; and in 1880, he became principal of the Normal School. In 1883, dissatisfied with his restricted status as a black in the South, Chesnutt moved to New York, and then to Cleveland, where he worked for a railroad and read law in the office of Judge Samuel E. Williamson, eventually becoming a well-established member of the legal profession in Cleveland. In the meantime, following an interest held since his youth, he turned to writing, first publishing "Uncle Peter's House" in 1885 in the Cleveland *News and Herald* and thereafter appearing with some regularity in the *Atlantic Monthly.* Subsequently, as his stories in various periodicals continued to draw favorable critical attention, he published two collections, *The Conjure Woman* (1899) and *The Wife of His Youth and Other Stories of The Color Line* (also in 1899); three novels, *The House Behind The Cedars* (1900), *The Marrow of Tradition* (1901), and *The Colonel's Dream* (1905); and one nonfiction work, a biography of Frederick Douglass (1899). For some unexplained reason, he stopped writing in 1905 and lived out his life quietly in Cleveland. He died in 1932.

Even though "The Passing of Grandison" deals with the conventional antebellum slave and his typically aristocratic, wealthy owner, it is written in a mockingly good-humored vein which suggests that the relationship existing between slave and master may not always have fitted the stereotyped viewpoint found in the books written by white story-tellers and historians.

The Passing of Grandison

I

When it is said that it was done to please a woman, there ought perhaps to be enough said to explain anything; for what a man will not do to please a woman is yet to be discovered. Nevertheless, it might be well to state a few preliminary facts to make it clear why young Dick Owens tried to run one of his father's negro men off to Canada.

"The Passing of Grandison" by Charles Chesnutt, from *The Wife of His Youth and Other Stories of the Color Line* (Houghton Mifflin, 1899).

In the early fifties, when the growth of anti-slavery sentiment and the constant drain of fugitive slaves into the North had so alarmed the slaveholders of the border States as to lead to the passage of the Fugitive Slave Law, a young white man from Ohio, moved by compassion for the sufferings of a certain bondman who happened to have a "hard master," essayed to help the slave to freedom. The attempt was discovered and frustrated; the abductor was tried and convicted for slave-stealing, and sentenced to a term of imprisonment in the penitentiary. His death, after the expiration of only a small part of the sentence, from cholera contracted while nursing stricken prisoners, lent to the case a melancholy interest that made it famous in anti-slavery annals.

Dick Owens had attended the trial. He was a youth of about twenty-two, intelligent, handsome, and amiable, but extremely indolent, in a graceful and gentlemanly way; or, as old Judge Fenderson put it more than once, he was lazy as the Devil—a mere figure of speech, of course, and not one that did justice to the Enemy of Mankind. When asked why he never did anything serious, Dick would good-naturedly reply, with a well-modulated drawl, that he didn't have to. His father was rich; there was but one other child, an unmarried daughter, who because of poor health would probably never marry, and Dick was therefore heir presumptive to a large estate. Charity Lomax had shamed him into studying law, but notwithstanding an hour or so a day spent at Old Judge Fenderson's office, he did not make remarkable headway in his legal studies.

"What Dick needs," said the judge, who was fond of tropes, as became a scholar, and of horses, as was befitting a Kentuckian, "is the whip of necessity, or the spur of ambition. If he had either, he would soon need the snaffle to hold him back."

But all Dick required, in fact, to prompt him to the most remarkable thing he accomplished before he was twenty-five, was a mere suggestion from Charity Lomax. The story was never really known to but two persons until after the war, when it came out because it was a good story and there was no particular reason for its concealment.

Young Owens had attended the trial of this slave-stealer, or martyr,—either or both,—and, when it was over, had gone to call on Charity Lomax, and, while they sat on the veranda after sundown, had told her all about the trial. He was a good talker, as his career in later years disclosed, and described the proceedings very graphically.

"I confess," he admitted, "that while my principles were against the prisoner, my sympathies were on his side. It appeared that he was of good family, and that he had an old father and mother, respectable people, dependent upon him for support and comfort in their declining years. He had been led into the matter by pity for a negro whose master ought to have been run out of the county long ago for abusing his slaves. If it had been merely a question of old Sam Briggs's negro, nobody would have cared anything about it. But father and the rest of them stood on the principle of the thing, and told the judge so, and the fellow was sentenced to three years in the penitentiary."

Miss Lomax had listened with lively interest.

"I've always hated old Sam Briggs," she said emphatically, "ever since the time he broke a negro's leg with a piece of cordwood. When I hear of a cruel deed it makes the Quaker blood that came from my grandmother assert itself. Personally I wish that all Sam Briggs's negroes would run away. As for the young man, I regard him as a hero. He dared something for humanity. I could love a man who would take such chances for the sake of others."

"Could you love me, Charity, if I did something heroic?"

"You never will, Dick. You're too lazy for any use. You'll never do anything harder than playing cards or fox-hunting."

"Oh, come now, sweetheart! I've been courting you for a year, and it's the hardest work imaginable. Are you never going to love me?" he pleaded.

His hand sought hers, but she drew it back beyond his reach.

"I'll never love you, Dick Owens, until you have done something. When that time comes, I'll think about it."

"But it takes so long to do anything worth mentioning, and I don't want to wait. One must read two years to become a lawyer, and work five more to make a reputation. We shall both be gray by then."

"Oh, I don't know," she rejoined. "It doesn't require a lifetime for a man to prove that he is a man. This one did something, or at least tried to."

"Well, I'm willing to attempt as much as any other man. What do you want me to do, sweetheart? Give me a test."

"Oh, dear me!" said Charity, "I don't care what you *do,* so you do *something*. Really, come to think of it, why should I care whether you do anything or not?"

"I'm sure I don't know why you should, Charity," rejoined Dick humbly, "for I'm aware that I'm not worthy of it."

"Except that I do hate," she added, relenting slightly, "to see a really clever man so utterly lazy and good for nothing."

"Thank you, my dear; a word of praise from you has sharpened my wits already. I have an idea! Will you love me if *I* run a negro off to Canada?"

"What nonsense!" said Charity scornfully. "You must be losing your wits. Steal another man's slave, indeed, while you father owns a hundred!"

"Oh, there'll be no trouble about that," responded Dick lightly; "I'll run off one of the old man's; we've got too many anyway. It may not be quite as difficult as the other man found it, but it will be just as unlawful, and will demonstrate what I am capable of."

"Seeing's believing," replied Charity. "Of course, what you are talking about now is merely absurd. I'm going away for three weeks, to visit my aunt in Tennessee. If you're able to tell me, when I return, that you've done something to prove your quality, I'll—well, you may come and tell me about it."

II

Young Owens got up about nine o'clock next morning, and while making his toilet put some questions to his personal attendant, a rather bright looking young mulatto of about his own age.

"Tom," said Dick.

"Yas, Mars Dick," responded the servant.

"I'm going on a trip North. Would you like to go with me?"

Now, if there was anything that Tom would have liked to make, it was a trip North. It was something he had long contemplated in the abstract, but had never been able to muster up sufficient courage to attempt in the concrete. He was prudent enough, however, to dissemble his feelings.

"I wouldn't min' it, Mars Dick, ez long ez you'd take keer er me an' fetch me home all right."

Tom's eyes belied his words, however, and his young master felt well assured that Tom needed only a good opportunity to make him run away. Having a comfortable home, and a dismal prospect in case of failure, Tom was not likely to take any desperate chances; but young Owens was satisfied that in a free State but little persuasion would be required to lead Tom astray. With a very logical and characteristic desire to gain his end with the least necessary expenditure of effort, he decided to take Tom with him, if his father did not object.

Colonel Owens had left the house when Dick went to breakfast, so Dick did not see his father till luncheon.

"Father," he remarked casually to the colonel, over the fried chicken, "I'm feeling a trifle run down. I imagine my health would be improved somewhat by a little travel and change of scene."

"Why don't you take a trip North?" suggested his father. The colonel added to paternal affection a considerable respect for his son as the heir of a large estate. He himself had been "raised" in comparative poverty, and had laid the foundations of his fortune by hard work; and while he despised the ladder by which he had climbed, he could not entirely forget it, and unconsciously manifested, in his intercourse with his son, some of the poor man's deference toward the wealthy and well-born.

"I think I'll adopt your suggestion, sir," replied the son, "and run up to New York; and after I've been there awhile I may go on to Boston for a week or so. I've never been there, you know."

"There are some matters you can talk over with my factor in New York," rejoined the colonel, "and while you are up there among the Yankees, I hope you'll keep your eyes and ears open to find out what the rascally abolitionists are saying and doing. They're becoming altogether too active for our comfort, and entirely too many ungrateful niggers are running away. I hope the conviction of that fellow yesterday may discourage the rest of the breed. I'd just like to catch any one trying to run off one of my darkeys. He'd get short shrift; I don't think any Court would have a chance to try him."

"They are a pestiferous lot," assented Dick, "and dangerous to our institutions. But say, father, if I go North I shall want to take Tom with me."

Now, the colonel, while a very indulgent father, had pronounced views on the subject of negroes, having studied them, as he often said, for a great many years, and, as he asserted oftener still, understanding them perfectly. It is scarcely worth while to say, either, that he valued more highly than if he had inherited them the slaves he had toiled and schemed for.

"I don't think it safe to take Tom up North," he declared, with promptness and decision. "He's a good enough boy, but too smart to trust among those low-down abolitionists. I strongly suspect him of having learned to read, though I can't imagine how. I saw him with a newspaper the other day, and while he pretended to be looking at a woodcut, I'm almost sure he was reading the paper. I think it by no means safe to take him."

Dick did not insist, because he knew it was useless. The colonel would have obliged his son in any other matter, but his negroes were the outward and visible sign of his wealth and station, and therefore sacred to him.

"Whom do you think it safe to take?" asked Dick. "I suppose I'll have to have a body-servant."

"What's the matter with Grandison?" suggested the colonel. "He's handy enough, and I reckon we can trust him. He's too fond of good eating, to risk losing his regular meals; besides, he's sweet on your mother's maid, Betty, and I've promised to let 'em get married before long. I'll have Grandison up, and we'll talk to him. Here, you boy Jack," called the colonel to a yellow youth in the next room who was catching flies and pulling their wings off to pass the time, "go down to the barn and tell Grandison to come here."

"Grandison," said the colonel, when the negro stood before him, hat in hand.

"Yas, marster."

"Haven't I always treated you right?"

"Yas, marster."

"Haven't you always got all you wanted to eat?"

"Yas, marster."

"And as much whiskey and tobacco as was good for you, Grandison?"

"Y-a-s, marster."

"I should just like to know, Grandison, whether you don't think yourself a great deal better off than those poor free negroes down by the plank road, with no kind master to look after them and no mistress to give them medicine when they're sick and—and"—

"Well, I sh'd jes' reckon I is better off, suh, dan dem low-down free niggers, suh! Ef anybody ax 'em who dey b'long ter, dey has ter say nobody, er e'se lie erbout it. Anybody ax me who I b'longs ter, I ain't got no 'casion ter be shame' ter tell 'em, no, suh, 'deed I ain', suh!"

The colonel was beaming. This was true gratitude, and his feudal heart thrilled at such appreciative homage. What cold-blooded, heartless monsters they were who would break up this blissful relationship of kindly protection on the one hand, of wise subordination and loyal dependence on the other! The colonel always became indignant at the mere thought of such wickedness.

"Grandison," the colonel continued, "your young master Dick is going North for a few weeks, and I am thinking of letting him take you along. I shall send you on this trip, Grandison, in order that you may take care of your young master. He will need some one to wait on him, and no one can ever do it so well as one of the boys brought up with him on the old plantation. I am going to trust him in your hands, and I'm sure you'll do your duty faithfully, and bring him back home safe and sound—to old Kentucky."

Grandison grinned. "Oh yas, marster, I'll take keer er young Mars Dick."

"I want to warn you, though, Grandison," continued the colonel impressively, "against these cussed abolitionists, who try to entice servants from their comfortable homes and their indulgent masters, from the blue skies, the green fields, and the warm sunlight of their southern home, and send them away off yonder to Canada, a dreary country, where the woods are full of wildcats and wolves and bears, where the snow lies up to the eaves of the houses for six months of the year, and the cold is so severe that it freezes your breath and curdles your blood; and where, when runaway niggers get sick and can't work, they are turned out to starve and die, unloved and uncared for. I reckon, Grandison, that you have too much sense to permit yourself to be led astray by any such foolish and wicked people."

" 'Deed, suh, I would n'low none er dem cussed, low-down abolitioners ter come nigh me, suh. I'd—I'd—would I be 'lowed ter hit 'em, suh?"

"Certainly, Grandison," replied the colonel, chuckling, "hit 'em as hard as you can. I reckon they'd rather like it. Begad, I believe they would! It would serve 'em right to be hit by a nigger!"

"Er ef I didn't hit 'em, suh," continued Grandison reflectively, "I'd tell Mars Dick, en *he'd* fix 'em. He'd smash de face off'n 'em, suh, I jes' knows he would."

"Oh yes, Grandison, your young master will protect you. You need fear no harm while he is near."

"Dey wont try ter steal me, will dey, marster?" asked the negro, with sudden alarm.

"I don't know, Grandison," replied the colonel, lighting a fresh cigar. "They're a desperate set of lunatics, and there's no telling what they may resort to. But if you stick close to your young master, and remember always that he is your best friend, and understands your real needs, and has your true interests at heart, and if you will be careful to avoid strangers who try to talk to you, you'll stand a fair chance of getting back to your home and your friends. And if you please your master Dick, he'll buy you a present, and a string of beads for Betty to wear when you and she get married in the fall."

"Thanky, marster, thanky, suh," replied Grandison, oozing gratitude at every pore; "you is a good marster, to be sho', suh; yas, 'deed you is. You kin jes' bet me and Mars Dick gwine git 'long jes' lack I wuz own boy ter Mars Dick. En it won't be my fault ef he don' want me fer his boy all de time, w'en we come back home ag'in."

"All right, Grandison, you may go now. You needn't work any more to-day, and here's a piece of tobacco for you off my own plug."

"Thanky, marster, thanky, marster! You is de bes' marster any nigger ever had in dis worl'." And Grandison bowed and scraped and disappeared round the corner, his jaws closing around a large section of the colonel's best tobacco.

"You may take Grandison," said the colonel to his son. "I allow he's abolitionist-proof."

III

Richard Owens, Esq., and servant, from Kentucky, registered at the fashionable New York hostelry for Southerners in those days, a hotel where an atmosphere congenial to Southern institutions was sedulously maintained. But there were negro waiters in the dining room, and mulatto bell-boys, and Dick had no doubt that Grandison, with the native gregariousness and garrulousness of his race, would foregather and palaver with them sooner or later, and Dick hoped that they would speedily inoculate him with the virus of freedom. For it was not Dick's intention to say anything to his servant about his plan to free him, for obvious reasons. To mention one of them, if Grandison should go away, and by legal process be recaptured, his young master's part in the matter would doubtless become known, which would be embarrassing to Dick, to say the least. If, on the other hand, he should merely give Grandison sufficient latitude, he had no doubt he would eventually lose him. For while not exactly skeptical about Grandison's perfervid loyalty, Dick had been a somewhat keen observer of human nature, in his own indolent way, and based his expectations upon the force of the example and argument that his servant could scarcely fail to encounter. Grandison should have a fair chance to become free by his own initiative; if it should become necessary to adopt other measures to get rid of him, it would be time enough to act when the necessity arose; and Dick Owens was not the youth to take needless trouble.

The young master renewed some acquaintances and made others, and spent a week or two very pleasantly in the best society of the metropolis, easily accessible to a wealthy, well-bred young Southerner, with proper introductions. Young women smiled on him, and young men of convivial habits pressed their hospitalities; but the memory of Charity's sweet, strong face and clear blue eyes made him proof against the blandishments of the one sex and the persuasions of the other. Meanwhile he kept Grandison supplied with pocket-money, and left him mainly to his own devices. Every night when Dick came in he hoped he might have to wait upon himself, and every morning he looked forward with pleasure to the prospect of making his toilet unaided. His hopes, however, were doomed to disappointment, for every night when he came in Grandison was on hand with a bootjack, and a nightcap mixed for his young master as the colonel had taught him to mix it, and every morning Grandison appeared with his master's boots blacked and his clothes brushed, and laid his linen out for the day.

"Grandison," said Dick one morning, after finishing his toilet, "this is the chance of your life to go around among your own people and see how they live. Have you met any of them?"

"Yas, suh, I's seen some of 'em. But I don' keer nuffin fer 'em, suh. Dey're diffe'nt f'm de niggers down ou' way. Dey 'lows dey're free, but dey ain' got sense 'nuff ter know dey ain' half as well off as dey would be down Souf, whar dey'd be 'preciated."

When two weeks had passed without any apparent effect of evil example upon Grandison, Dick resolved to go on to Boston, where he thought the atmosphere might prove more favorable to his ends. After he had been at the Revere House for a day or two without losing Grandison, he decided upon slightly different tactics.

Having ascertained from a city directory the addresses of several well-known abolitionists, he wrote them each a letter something like this:—

> *Dear Friend and Brother:—*
>
> *A wicked slaveholder from Kentucky, stopping at the Revere House, has dared to insult the liberty-loving people of Boston by bringing his slave into their midst. Shall this be tolerated? Or shall steps be taken in the name of liberty to rescue a fellow-man from bondage? For obvious reasons I can only sign myself,*
>
> *A Friend of Humanity.*

That his letter might have an opportunity to prove effective, Dick made it a point to send Grandison away from the hotel on various errands. On one of these occasions Dick watched him for quite a distance down the street. Grandison had scarcely left the hotel when a long-haired, sharp-featured man came out behind him, followed him, soon overtook him, and kept along beside him until they turned the next corner. Dick's hopes were roused by this spectacle, but sank correspondingly when Grandison returned to the hotel. As Grandison said nothing about the encounter, Dick hoped there might be some self-consciousness behind his unexpected reticence, the results of which might develop later on.

But Grandison was on hand again when his master came back to the hotel at night, and was in attendance again in the morning, with hot water, to assist at his master's toilet. Dick sent him on further errands from day to day, and upon one occasion came squarely up to him—inadvertently of course—while Grandison was engaged in conversation with a young white man in clerical garb. When Grandison saw Dick approaching, he edged away from the preacher and hastened toward his master, with a very evident expression of relief on his countenance.

"Mars Dick," he said, "dese yer abolitioners is jes' pesterin' de life out er me tryin' ter git me ter run away. I don' pay no 'tention ter 'em, but dey riles me so sometimes dat I'm feared I'll hit some of 'em some er dese days, an' dat mought git me inter trouble. I ain' said nuffin' ter you 'bout it, Mars Dick, fer I didn' wanter 'sturb yo' min'; but I don' like it, suh; no, suh, I don'! Is we gwine back home 'fo' long, Mars Dick?"

"We'll be going back soon enough," replied Dick somewhat shortly, while he inwardly cursed the stupidity of a slave who could be free and would not, and registered a secret vow that if he were unable to get rid of Grandison without assassinating him, and were therefore compelled to take him back to Kentucky, he would see that Grandison got a taste of an article of slavery that would make him regret his wasted opportunities. Meanwhile he determined to tempt his servant yet more strongly.

"Grandison," he said next morning, "I'm going away for a day or two, but I shall leave you here. I shall lock up a hundred dollars in this drawer and give you the key. If you need any of it, use it and enjoy yourself,—spend it all if you like,—for this is probably the last chance you'll have for some time to be in a free State, and you'd better enjoy your liberty while you may."

When he came back a couple of days later and found the faithful Grandison at his post, and the hundred dollars intact, Dick felt seriously annoyed. His vexation was increased by the fact that he could not express his feelings adequately. He did not even scold Grandison; how could he, indeed, find fault with one who so sensibly recognized his true place in the economy of civilization, and kept it with such touching fidelity?

"I can't say a thing to him," groaned Dick. "He deserves a leather medal, made out of his own hide tanned. I reckon I'll write to father and let him know what a model servant he has given me."

He wrote his father a letter which made the colonel swell with pride and pleasure. "I really think," the colonel observed to one of his friends, "that Dick ought to have the nigger interviewed by the Boston papers, so that they may see how contented and happy our darkeys really are."

Dick also wrote a long letter to Charity Lomax, in which he said, among other things, that if she knew how hard he was working, and under what difficulties, to accomplish something serious for her sake, she would no longer keep him in suspense, but overwhelm him with love and admiration.

Having thus exhausted without result the more obvious methods of getting rid of Grandison, and diplomacy having also proved a failure, Dick was forced to consider more radical measures. Of course he might run away himself, and abandon Grandison, but this would be merely to leave him in the United States, where he was still a slave, and where, with his notions of loyalty, he would speedily be reclaimed. It was necessary, in order to accomplish the purpose of his trip to the North, to leave Grandison permanently in Canada, where he would be legally free.

"I might extend my trip to Canada," he reflected, "but that would be too palpable. I have it! I'll visit Niagara Falls on the way home, and lose him on the Canada side. When he once realizes that he is actually free, I'll warrant that he'll stay."

So the next day saw them westward bound, and in due course of time, by the somewhat slow conveyances of the period, they found themselves at Niagara. Dick walked and drove about the Falls for several days, taking Grandison along with him on most occasions. One morning they stood on the Canadian side, watching the wild whirl of the waters below them.

"Grandison," said Dick, raising his voice above the roar of the cataract, "do you know where you are now?"

"I's wid you, Mars Dick; dat's all I keers."

"You are now in Canada, Grandison, where your people go when they run away from their masters. If you wished, Grandison, you might walk away from me this very minute, and I could not lay my hand upon you to take you back."

Grandison looked around uneasily.

"Let's go back ober de ribber, Mars Dick. I's feared I'll lose you ovuh heah, an' den I won' hab no marster, an' won't nebber be able to git back home no mo'."

Discouraged, but not yet hopeless, Dick said, a few minutes later,—

"Grandison, I'm going up the road a bit, to the inn over yonder. You stay here until I return. I'll not be gone a great while."

Grandison's eyes opened wide and he looked somewhat fearful.

"Is dey any er dem dadblasted abolitioners roun' heah, Mars Dick?"

"I don't imagine that there are," replied his master, hoping there might be. "But I'm not afraid of *your* running away, Grandison. I only wish I were," he added to himself.

Dick walked leisurely down the road to where the whitewashed inn, built of stone, with true British solidity, loomed up through the trees by the roadside. Arrived there he ordered a glass of ale and a sandwich, and took a seat at a table by a window, from which he could see Grandison in the distance. For a while he hoped that the seed he had sown might have fallen on fertile ground, and that Grandison, relieved from the restraining power of a master's eye, and finding himself in a free country, might get up and walk away; but the hope was vain, for Grandison remained faithfully at his post, awaiting his master's return. He had seated himself on a broad flat stone, and, turning his eyes away from the grand and awe-inspiring spectacle that lay close at hand, was looking anxiously toward the inn where his master sat cursing his ill-timed fidelity.

By and by a girl came into the room to serve his order, and Dick very naturally glanced at her; and as she was young and pretty and remained in attendance, it was some minutes before he looked for Grandison. When he did so his faithful servant had disappeared.

To pay his reckoning and go away without the change was a matter quickly accomplished. Retracing his footsteps toward the Falls, he saw, to his great disgust, as he approached the spot where he had left Grandison, the familiar form of his servant stretched out on the ground, his face to the sun, his mouth open, sleeping the time away, oblivious alike to the grandeur of the scenery, the thunderous roar of the cataract, or the insidious voice of sentiment.

"Grandison," soliloquized his master, as he stood gazing down at his ebony encumbrance, "I do not deserve to be an American citizen; I ought not to have the advantages I possess over you; and I certainly am not worthy of Charity Lomax, if I am not smart enough to get rid of you. I have an idea! You shall yet be free, and I will be the instrument of your deliverance. Sleep on, faithful and affectionate servitor, and dream of the blue grass and the bright skies of Old Kentucky, for it is only in your dreams that you will ever see them again!"

Dick retraced his footsteps towards the inn. The young woman chanced to look out of the window and saw the handsome young gentleman she had waited on a few minutes before, standing in the road a short distance away, apparently engaged in earnest conversation with a colored man employed as hostler for the inn. She thought she saw something pass from the white man to the other, but at that moment her duties called her away from the window, and when she looked out again the young gentleman had disappeared, and the hostler, with two other young men of the neighborhood, one white and one colored, were walking rapidly towards the Falls.

IV

Dick made the journey homeward alone, and as rapidly as the conveyances of the day would permit. As he drew near home his conduct in going back without Grandison took on a more serious aspect than it had borne at any previous time, and although he had prepared the colonel by a letter sent several days ahead, there was still the prospect of a bad quarter of an hour with him; not, indeed, that his father would upbraid him, but he was likely to make searching inquiries. And notwithstanding the vein of quiet recklessness that had carried Dick through his preposterous scheme, he was a very poor liar, having rarely had occasion or inclination to tell anything but the truth. Any reluctance to meet his father was more than offset, however, by a stronger force drawing him homeward, for Charity Lomax must long since have returned from her visit to her aunt in Tennessee.

Dick got off easier than he had expected. He told a straight story, and a truthful one, so far as it went.

The colonel raged at first, but rage soon subsided into anger, and anger moderated into annoyance, and annoyance into a sort of garrulous sense of injury. The colonel thought he had been hardly used; he had trusted this negro, and he had broken faith. Yet, after all, he did not blame Grandison so much as he did the abolitionists, who were undoubtedly at the bottom of it.

As for Charity Lomax, Dick told her, privately of course, that he had run his father's man, Grandison, off to Canada, and left him there.

"Oh, Dick," she had said with shuddering alarm, "what have you done? If they knew it they'd send you to the penitentiary, like they did that Yankee."

"But they don't know it," he had replied seriously; adding, with an injured tone, "you don't seem to appreciate my heroism like you did that of the Yankee; perhaps it's because I wasn't caught and sent to the penitentiary. I thought you wanted me to do it."

"Why, Dick Owens!" she exclaimed. "You know I never dreamed of any such outrageous proceeding.

"But I presume I'll have to marry you," she concluded, after some insistence on Dick's part, "if only to take care of you. You are too reckless for anything; and a man who goes chasing all over the North, being entertained by New York and Boston society and having negroes to throw away, needs some one to look after him."

"It's a most remarkable thing," replied Dick fervently, "that your views correspond exactly with my profoundest convictions. It proves beyond question that we were made for one another."

They were married three weeks later. As each of them had just returned from a journey, they spent their honeymoon at home.

A week after the wedding they were seated, one afternoon, on the piazza of the colonel's house, where Dick had taken his bride, when a negro from the yard ran down the lane and threw open the big gate for the colonel's buggy to enter. The colonel was not alone. Beside him, ragged and travel-stained, bowed with weariness, and upon his face a haggard look that told of hardship and privation, sat the lost Grandison.

The colonel alighted at the steps.

"Take the lines, Tom," he said to the man who had opened the gate, "and drive round to the barn. Help Grandison down,—poor devil, he's so stiff he can hardly move!—and get a tub of water and wash him and rub him down, and feed him, and give him a big drink of whiskey, and then let him come round and see his young master and his new mistress."

The colonel's face wore an expression compounded of joy and indignation,—joy at the restoration of a valuable piece of property; indignation for reasons he proceeded to state.

"It's astounding, the depths of depravity the human heart is capable of! I was coming along the road three miles away, when I heard some one call me from the roadside. I pulled up the mare, and who should come out of the woods but Grandison. The poor nigger could hardly crawl along, with the help of a broken limb. I was never more astonished in my life. You could have knocked me down with a feather. He seemed pretty far gone,—he could hardly talk above a whisper,—and I had to give him a mouthful of whiskey to brace him up so he could tell his story. It's just as I thought from the beginning, Dick; Grandison had no notion of running away; he knew when he was well off, and where his friends were. All the persuasions of abolition liars and runaway niggers did not move him. But the desperation of those fanatics knew no bounds; their guilty consciences gave them no rest. They got the notion somehow that Grandison belonged to a nigger-catcher, and had been brought North as a spy to help capture ungrateful runaway servants. They actually kidnaped him—just think of it!—and gagged him and bound him and threw him rudely into a wagon, and carried him into the gloomy depths of a Canadian forest, and locked him in a lonely hut, and fed him on bread and water for three weeks. One of the scoundrels wanted to kill him, and persuaded the others that it ought to be done; but they got to quarreling about how they should do it, and before they had their minds made up Grandison escaped, and, keeping his back steadily to the North Star, made his way, after suffering incredible hardships, back to the old plantation, back to his master, his friends, and his home. Why, it's as good as one of Scott's novels! Mr. Simms or some other one of our Southern authors ought to write it up."

"Don't you think, sir," suggested Dick, who had calmly smoked his cigar throughout the colonel's animated recital, "that the kidnaping yarn sounds a little improbable? Isn't there some more likely explanation?"

"Nonsense, Dick; it's the gospel truth! Those infernal abolitionists are capable or anything—everything! Just think of their locking the poor, faithful nigger up, beating him, kicking him, depriving him of his liberty, keeping him on bread and water for three long, lonesome weeks, and he all the time pining for the old plantation!"

There were almost tears in the colonel's eyes at the picture of Grandison's sufferings that he conjured up. Dick still professed to be slightly skeptical, and met Charity's severely questioning eye with bland unconsciousness.

The colonel killed the fatted calf for Grandison, and for two or three weeks the returned wanderer's life was a slave's dream of pleasure. His fame spread throughout the county, and the colonel gave him a permanent place among the house servants, where he could always have him conveniently at hand to relate his adventures to admiring visitors.

About three weeks after Grandison's return the colonel's faith in sable humanity was rudely shaken, and its foundation almost broken up. He came near losing his belief in the fidelity of the negro to his master,—the servile virtue most highly prized and most sedulously cultivated by the colonel and his kind. One Monday morning Grandison was missing. And not only Grandison, but his wife, Betty the maid; his mother, aunt Eunice; his father, uncle Ike; his brothers, Tom and John, and his little sister Elsie, were likewise absent from the plantation; and a hurried search and inquiry in the neighborhood resulted in no information as to their whereabouts. So much valuable property could not be lost without an effort to recover it, and the wholesale nature of the transaction carried consternation to the hearts of those whose ledgers were chiefly bound in black. Extremely energetic measures were taken by the colonel and his friends. The fugitives were traced, and followed from point to point, on their northward run through Ohio. Several times the hunters were close upon their heels, but the magnitude of the escaping party begot unusual vigilance on the part of those who sympathized with the fugitives, and strangely enough, the underground railroad seemed to have had its tracks cleared and signals set for this particular train. Once, twice, the colonel thought he had them, but they slipped through his fingers.

One last glimpse he caught of his vanishing property, as he stood, accompanied by a United States marshal, on a wharf at a port on the south shore of Lake Erie. On the stern of a small steamboat which was receding rapidly from the wharf, with nose pointing toward Canada, there stood a group of familiar dark faces, and the look they cast backward was not one of longing for the fleshpots of Egypt. The colonel saw Grandison point him out to one of the crew of the vessel, who waved his hand derisively toward the colonel. The latter shook his fist impotently—and the incident was closed.

Stephen Crane

1871 – 1900

Despite the relatively small body of fiction Stephen Crane published, he nevertheless holds a significant position in the development of the American short story. His best stories are noteworthy not only for their excellence, but also for their highly individualized style and structure. Coming as it does at the end of the nineteenth century, his work thus forecasts one of the new directions story technique would take during the twentieth century.

Within a lifetime briefer than Poe's—twenty-nine years from his birth in Newark, New Jersey, in 1871 to his death from tuberculosis in Badenweiler, Germany, in 1900—Crane pursued an equally intensive literary career, remarkable for its varied achievements. After three years of preparatory school at Claverack College, near Hudson, New York, a year of college training at Lafayette College, and a second year at Syracuse University, he went to New York, where he became a reporter. Soon, his literary aims having transcended journalism, he wrote a short novel, *Maggie: A Girl of the Streets,* which was so frankly naturalistic in viewpoint, language, and treatment of sex that it failed to sell even after Crane published it at his own expense in 1893 and reputedly employed persons to flourish it on streetcars. His next novel, however, *The Red Badge of Courage* (1895), a vividly impressionistic study of battle psychology that artfully concealed his lack of wartime experience, not only found a publisher but also established his reputation. During his last five years, Crane's activities included writing for a syndicate and reporting the Greco-Turkish and Spanish-American Wars. Added to these experiences were his marriage to Cora Taylor, residence in England, and the frequent publication of new novels, poems, and stories. His most important short stories appear in *The Little Regiment and Other Episodes of the American War* (1896), *The Open Boat and Other Tales* (1898), *The Monster and Other Stories* (1899), and *Whilomville Stories* (1900).

Crane's flair for bold metaphor and vivid, precise phrasing is as clearly evident in "The Blue Hotel" as in such better known stories of his as "The Bride Comes to Yellow Sky" and "The Open Boat"; yet it reveals subtle differences in the ironic effects evoked by its phrasing and imagery. Here the dramatic irony is neither basically comic as in "The Bride" nor altogether tragically grim as in "The Open Boat"; it seems rather like a bizarre combination of both extremes. Thus, in the course of the story the confrontation between the terrified Swede and the other card players becomes perplexing to both the Easterner and the cowboy—and, perhaps, equally so to each of us as well.

The Blue Hotel

I

The Palace Hotel at Fort Romper was painted a light blue, a shade that is on the legs of a kind of heron, causing the bird to declare its position against any background. The Palace Hotel, then, was always screaming and howling in a way that made the dazzling winter landscape of Nebraska seem only a grey swampish hush. It stood alone on the prairie, and when the snow was falling the town two hundred yards away was not visible. But when the traveller alighted at the railway station he was obliged to pass the Palace Hotel before he could come upon the company of low clapboard houses which composed Fort Romper, and it was not to be thought that any traveller could pass the Palace Hotel without looking at it. Pat Scully, the proprietor, had proved himself a master of strategy when he chose his paints. It is true that on clear days, when the great transcontinental expresses, long lines of swaying Pullmans, swept

"The Blue Hotel" by Stephen Crane, from *Stephen Crane: An Omnibus* (Alfred A. Knopf, 1898).

through Fort Romper, passengers were overcome at the sight, and the cult that knows the brown-reds and the subdivisions of the dark greens of the East expressed shame, pity, horror, in a laugh. But to the citizens of this prairie town and to the people who would naturally stop there, Pat Scully had performed a feat. With this opulence and splendour, these creeds, classes, egotisms, that streamed through Romper on the rails day after day, they had no colour in common.

As if the displayed delights of such a blue hotel were not sufficiently enticing, it was Scully's habit to go every morning and evening to meet the leisurely trains that stopped at Romper and work his seductions upon any man that he might see wavering, gripsack in hand.

One morning, when a snow-crusted engine dragged its long string of freight cars and its one passenger coach to the station, Scully performed the marvel of catching three men. One was a shaky and quick-eyed Swede, with a great shining cheap valise; one was a tall bronzed cowboy, who was on his way to a ranch near the Dakota line; one was a little silent man from the East, who didn't look it, and didn't announce it. Scully practically made them prisoners. He was so nimble and merry and kindly that each probably felt it would be the height of brutality to try to escape. They trudged off over the creaking board sidewalks in the wake of the eager little Irishman. He wore a heavy fur cap squeezed tightly down on his head. It caused his two red ears to stick out stiffly, as if they were made of tin.

At last, Scully, elaborately, with boisterous hospitality, conducted them through the portals of the blue hotel. The room which they entered was small. It seemed to be merely a proper temple for an enormous stove, which, in the centre, was humming with godlike violence. At various points on its surface the iron had become luminous and glowed yellow from the heat. Beside the stove Scully's son Johnnie was playing High-Five with an old farmer who had whiskers both grey and sandy. They were quarrelling. Frequently the old farmer turned his face toward a box of sawdust—coloured brown from tobacco juice—that was behind the stove, and spat with an air of great impatience and irritation. With a loud flourish of words Scully destroyed the game of cards, and bustled his son upstairs with part of the baggage of the new guests. He himself conducted them to three basins of the coldest water in the world. The cowboy and the Easterner burnished themselves fiery red with this water, until it seemed to be some kind of metal-polish. The Swede, however, merely dipped his fingers gingerly and with trepidation. It was notable that throughout this series of small ceremonies the three travellers were made to feel that Scully was very benevolent. He was conferring great favours upon them. He handed the towel from one to another with an air of philanthropic impulse.

Afterward they went to the first room, and, sitting about the stove, listened to Scully's officious clamour at his daughters, who were preparing the midday meal. They reflected in the silence of experienced men who tread carefully amid new people. Nevertheless, the old farmer, stationary, invincible in his chair near the warmest part of the stove, turned his face from the sawdust-box frequently and addressed a glowing commonplace to the strangers. Usually he was answered in short but adequate sentences by either the cowboy or the Easterner. The Swede said nothing. He seemed to be occupied in making furtive estimates of each man in the room. One might have thought that he had the sense of silly suspicion which comes to guilt. He resembled a badly frightened man.

Later, at dinner, he spoke a little, addressing his conversation entirely to Scully. He volunteered that he had come from New York, where for ten years he had worked as a tailor. These facts seemed to strike Scully as fascinating, and afterward he volunteered that he had lived at Romper for fourteen years. The Swede asked about the crops and the price of labour. He seemed barely to listen to Scully's extended replies. His eyes continued to rove from man to man.

Finally, with a laugh and a wink, he said that some of these Western communities were very dangerous; and after his statement he straightened his legs under the table, tilted his head, and laughed again, loudly. It was plain that the demonstration had no meaning to the others. They looked at him wondering and in silence.

II

As the men trooped heavily back into the front room, the two little windows presented views of a turmoiling sea of snow. The huge arms of the wind were making attempts—mighty, circular, futile—to embrace the flakes as they sped. A gate-post like a still man with a blanched face stood aghast amid this profligate fury. In a hearty voice Scully announced the presence of a blizzard. The guests of the blue hotel, lighting their pipes, assented with grunts of lazy masculine contentment. No island of the sea could be exempt in the degree of this little room with its humming stove. Johnnie, son of Scully, in a tone which defined his opinion of his ability as a card-player, challenged the old farmer of both grey and sandy whiskers to a game of High-Five. The farmer agreed with a contemptuous and bitter scoff. They sat close to the stove, and squared their knees under a wide board. The cowboy and the Easterner watched the game with interest. The Swede remained near the window, aloof, but with a countenance that showed signs of an inexplicable excitement.

The play of Johnnie and the grey-beard was suddenly ended by another quarrel. The old man arose while casting a look of heated scorn at his adversary. He slowly buttoned his coat, and then stalked with fabulous dignity from the room. In the discreet silence of all the other men the Swede laughed. His laughter rang somehow childish. Men by this time had begun to look at him askance, as if they wished to inquire what ailed him.

A new game was formed jocosely. The cowboy volunteered to become the partner of Johnnie, and they all then turned to ask the Swede to throw in his lot with the little Easterner. He asked some questions about the game, and, learning that it wore many names, and that he had played it when it was under an alias, he accepted the invitation. He strode toward the men nervously, as if he expected to be assaulted. Finally, seated, he gazed from face to face and laughed shrilly. This laugh was so strange that the Easterner looked up quickly, the cowboy sat intent and with his mouth open, and Johnnie paused, holding the cards with still fingers.

Afterward there was a short silence. Then Johnnie said, "Well, let's get at it. Come on now!" They pulled their chairs forward until their knees were bunched under the board. They began to play, and their interest in the game caused the others to forget the manner of the Swede.

The cowboy was a board-whacker. Each time that he held superior cards he whanged them, one by one, with exceeding force, down upon the improvised table, and took the tricks with a glowing air of prowess and pride that sent thrills of indignation into the hearts of his opponents. A game with a board-whacker in it is sure to become intense. The countenances of the Easterner and the Swede were miserable whenever the cowboy thundered down his aces and kings, while Johnnie, his eyes gleaming with joy, chuckled and chuckled.

Because of the absorbing play none considered the strange ways of the Swede. They paid strict heed to the game. Finally, during a lull caused by a new deal, the Swede suddenly addressed Johnnie: "I suppose there have been a good many men killed in this room." The jaws of the others dropped and they looked at him.

"What in hell are you talking about?" said Johnnie.

The Swede laughed again his blatant laugh, full of a kind of false courage and defiance. "Oh, you know what I mean all right," he answered.

"I'm a liar if I do!" Johnnie protested. The card was halted, and the men stared at the Swede. Johnnie evidently felt that as the son of the proprietor he should make a direct inquiry. "Now, what might you be drivin' at, mister?" he asked. The Swede winked at him. It was a wink full of cunning. His fingers shook on the edge of the board. "Oh, maybe you think I have been to nowheres. Maybe you think I'm a tenderfoot?"

"I don't know nothin' about you," answered Johnnie, "and I don't give a damn where you've been. All I got to say is that I don't know what you're driving at. There hain't never been nobody killed in this room."

The cowboy, who had been steadily gazing at the Swede, then spoke: "What's wrong with you, mister?"

Apparently it seemed to the Swede that he was formidably menaced. He shivered and turned white near the corners of his mouth. He sent an appealing glance in the direction of the little Easterner. During these moments he did not forget to wear his air of advanced pot-valour. "They say they don't know what I mean," he remarked mockingly to the Easterner.

The latter answered after prolonged and cautious reflection. "I don't understand you," he said, impassively.

The Swede made a movement then which announced that he thought he had encountered treachery from the only quarter where he had expected sympathy, if not help. "Oh, I see you are all against me. I see—"

The cowboy was in a state of deep stupefaction. "Say," he cried, as he tumbled the deck violently down upon the board, "say, what are you gittin' at, hey?"

The Swede sprang up with the celerity of a man escaping from a snake on the floor. "I don't want to fight!" he shouted. "I don't want to fight!"

The cowboy stretched his long legs indolently and deliberately. His hands were in his pockets. He spat into the sawdust-box. "Well, who the hell thought you did?" he inquired.

The Swede backed rapidly toward a corner of the room. His hands were out protectingly in front of his chest, but he was making an obvious struggle to control his fright. "Gentlemen," he quavered, "I suppose I am going to be killed before I can leave this house! I suppose I am going to be killed before I can leave this house!" In his eyes was the dying-swan look. Through the windows could be seen the snow turning blue in the shadow of dusk. The wind tore at the house, and some loose thing beat regularly against the clapboards like a spirit tapping.

A door opened, and Scully himself entered. He paused in surprise as he noted the tragic attitude of the Swede. Then he said, "What's the matter here?"

The Swede answered him swiftly and eagerly: "These men are going to kill me."

"Kill you!" ejaculated Scully. "Kill you! What are you talkin'?"

The Swede made the gesture of a martyr.

Scully wheeled sternly upon his son. "What is this, Johnnie?"

The lad had grown sullen. "Damned if I know," he answered. "I can't make no sense to it." He began to shuffle the cards, fluttering them together with an angry snap. "He says a good many men have been killed in this room, or something like that. And he says he's goin' to be killed here too. I don't know what ails him. He's crazy, I shouldn't wonder."

Scully then looked for explanation to the cowboy, but the cowboy simply shrugged his shoulders.

"Kill you?" said Scully again to the Swede. "Kill you? Man, you're off your nut."

"Oh, I know," burst out the Swede. "I know what will happen. Yes, I'm crazy—yes. Yes, of course, I'm crazy—yes. But I know one thing—" There was a sort of sweat of misery and terror upon his face. "I know I won't get out of here alive."

The cowboy drew a deep breath, as if his mind was passing into the last stages of dissolution. "Well, I'm doggoned," he whispered to himself.

Scully wheeled suddenly and faced his son. "You've been troublin' this man!"

Johnnie's voice was loud with its burden of grievance. "Why, good Gawd, I ain't done nothin' to 'im."

The Swede broke in. "Gentlemen, do not disturb yourselves. I will leave this house. I will go away, because"—he accused them dramatically with his glance—"because I do not want to be killed."

Scully was furious with his son. "Will you tell me what is the matter, you young divil? What's the matter, anyhow? Speak out!"

"Blame it!" cried Johnnie in despair, "don't I tell you I don't know? He—he says we want to kill him, and that's all I know. I can't tell what ails him."

The Swede continued to repeat: "Never mind, Mr. Scully; never mind. I will leave this house. I will go away, because I do not wish to be killed. Yes, of course, I am crazy—yes. But I know one thing! I will go away. I will leave this house. Never mind, Mr. Scully; never mind. I will go away."

"You will not go 'way." said Scully. "You will not go 'way until I hear the reason of this business. If anybody has troubled you I will take care of him. This is my house. You are under my roof, and I will not allow any peaceable man to be troubled here." He cast a terrible eye upon Johnnie, the cowboy, and the Easterner.

"Never mind, Mr. Scully; never mind. I will go away. I do not wish to be killed." The Swede moved toward the door which opened upon the stairs. It was evidently his intention to go at once for his baggage.

"No, no," shouted Scully peremptorily; but the white-faced man slid by him and disappeared. "Now," said Scully severely, "what does this mane?"

Johnnie and the cowboy cried together: "Why, we didn't do nothin' to 'im!"

Scully's eyes were cold. "No," he said, "you didn't?"

Johnnie swore a deep oath. "Why, this is the wildest loon I ever see. We didn't do nothin' at all. We were jest sittin' here playin' cards, and he—"

The father suddenly spoke to the Easterner. "Mr. Blanc," he asked, "what has these boys been doin'?"

The Easterner reflected again. "I didn't see anything wrong at all," he said at last, slowly.

Scully began to howl. "But what does it mane?" He stared ferociously at his son. "I have a mind to lather you for this, me boy."

Johnnie was frantic. "Well, what have I done?" he bawled at his father.

III

"I think you are tongue-tied," said Scully finally to his son, the cowboy, and the Easterner; and at the end of this scornful sentence he left the room.

Upstairs the Swede was swiftly fastening the straps of his great valise. Once his back happened to be half turned toward the door, and, hearing a noise there, he wheeled and sprang up, uttering a loud cry. Scully's wrinkled visage showed grimly in the light of the small lamp he carried. This yellow effulgence, streaming upward, coloured only his prominent features, and left his eyes, for instance, in mysterious shadow. He resembled a murderer.

"Man! man!" he exclaimed, "have you gone daffy?"

"Oh no! Oh, no!" rejoined the other. "There are people in this world who know pretty nearly as much as you do—understand?"

For a moment they stood gazing at each other. Upon the Swede's deathly pale cheeks were two spots brightly crimson and sharply edged, as if they had been carefully painted. Scully placed the light on the table and sat himself on the edge of the bed. He spoke ruminatively. "By cracky, I never heard of such a thing in my life. It's a complete muddle. I can't, for the soul of me, think how you ever got this idea into your head." Presently he lifted his eyes and asked: "And did you sure think they were going to kill you?"

The Swede scanned the old man as if he wished to see into his mind. "I did," he said at last. He obviously suspected that this answer might precipitate an outbreak. As he pulled on a strap his whole arm shook, the elbow wavering like a bit of paper.

Scully banged his hand impressively on the footboard of the bed. "Why, man, we're goin' to have a line of ilictric street-cars in this town next spring."

" 'A line of electric street-cars,' " repeated the Swede, stupidly.

"And," said Scully, "there's a new railroad goin' to be built down from Broken Arm to here. Not to mintion the four churches and the smashin' big brick school-house. Then there's the big factory, too. Why, in two years Romper'll be a met-tro-*pol*-is."

Having finished the preparation of his baggage, the Swede straightened himself. "Mr. Scully," he said, with sudden hardihood, "how much do I owe you?"

"You don't owe me anythin'," said the old man, angrily.

"Yes, I do," retorted the Swede. He took seventy-five cents from his pocket and tendered it to Scully; but the latter snapped his fingers in disdainful refusal. However, it happened that they both stood gazing in a strange fashion at three silver pieces on the Swede's open palm.

"I'll not take your money," said Scully at last. "Not after what's been goin' on here." Then a plan seemed to strike him. "Here," he cried, picking up his lamp and moving toward the door. "Here! Come with me a minute."

"No," said the Swede, in overwhelming alarm.

"Yes," urged the old man. "Come on! I want you to come and see a picter—just across the hall—in my room."

The Swede must have concluded that his hour was come. His jaw dropped and his teeth showed like a dead man's. He ultimately followed Scully across the corridor, but he had the step of one hung in chains.

Scully flashed the light high on the wall of his own chamber. There was revealed a ridiculous photograph of a little girl. She was leaning against a balustrade of gorgeous decoration, and the formidable bang to her hair was prominent. The figure was as graceful as an upright sled-stake, and, withal, it was of the hue of lead. "There," said Scully, tenderly, "that's the picter of my little girl that died. Her name was Carrie. She had the purtiest hair you ever saw! I was that fond of her, she—"

Turning then, he saw that the Swede was not contemplating the picture at all, but, instead, was keeping keen watch on the gloom in the rear.

"Look, man!" cried Scully, heartily. "That's the picter of my little gal that died. Her name was Carrie. And then here's the picter of my oldest boy, Michael. He's a lawyer in Lincoln, an' doin' well. I gave that boy a grand eddication, and I'm glad for it now. He's a fine boy. Look at 'im now. Ain't he bold as blazes, him there in Lincoln, An honoured an' respicted gintleman! An honoured and respicted gintleman," concluded Scully with a flourish. And, so saying, he smote the Swede jovially on the back.

The Swede faintly smiled.

"Now," said the old man, "there's only one more thing." He dropped suddenly to the floor and thrust his head beneath the bed. The Swede could hear his muffled voice. "I'd keep it under me piller if it wasn't for that boy Johnnie. Then there's the old woman— Where is it now? I never put it twice in the same place. Ah, now come out with you!"

Presently he backed clumsily from under the bed, dragging with him an old coat rolled into a bundle. "I've fetched him," he muttered. Kneeling on the floor, he unrolled the coat and extracted from its heart a large yellow-brown whisky-bottle.

His first manœuvre was to hold the bottle up to the light. Reassured, apparently, that nobody had been tampering with it, he thrust it with a generous movement toward the Swede.

The weak-kneed Swede was about to eagerly clutch this element of strength, but he suddenly jerked his hand away and cast a look of horror upon Scully.

"Drink," said the old man affectionately. He had risen to his feet, and now stood facing the Swede.

There was a silence. Then again Scully said: "Drink!"

The Swede laughed wildly. He grabbed the bottle, put it to his mouth; and as his lips curled absurdly around the opening and his throat worked, he kept his glance, burning with hatred, upon the old man's face.

IV

After the departure of Scully the three men, with the cardboard still upon their knees, preserved for a long time an astounded silence. Then Johnnie said: "That's the doddangedest Swede I ever see."

"He ain't no Swede," said the cowboy, scornfully.

"Well, what is he then?" cried Johnnie. "What is he then?"

"It's my opinion," replied the cowboy deliberately, "he's some kind of a Dutchman." It was a venerable custom of the country to entitle as Swedes all light-haired men who spoke with a heavy tongue. In consequence the idea of the cowboy was not without its daring. "Yes, sir," he repeated. "It's my opinion this feller is some kind of a Dutchman."

"Well, he says he's a Swede, anyhow," muttered Johnnie, sulkily. He turned to the Easterner: "What do you think, Mr. Blanc?"

"Oh, I don't know," replied the Easterner.

"Well, what do you think makes him act that way?" asked the cowboy.

"Why, he's frightened." The Easterner knocked his pipe against a rim of the stove. "He's clear frightened out of his boots."

"What at?" cried Johnnie and the cowboy together.

"Oh, I don't know, but it seems to me this man has been reading dime novels, and he thinks he's right out in the middle of it—the shootin' and stabbin' and all."

"But," said the cowboy, deeply scandalized, "this ain't Wyoming, ner none of them places. This is Nebrasker."

"Yes," added Johnnie, "an' why don't he wait till he gits *out West*?"

The travelled Easterner laughed. "It isn't different there even—not in these days. But he thinks he's right in the middle of hell."

Johnnie and the cowboy mused long.

"It's awful funny," remarked Johnnie at last.

"Yes," said the cowboy. "This is a queer game. I hope we don't git snowed in, because then we'd have to stand this here man bein' around with us all the time. That wouldn't be no good."

"I wish pop would throw him out," said Johnnie.

Presently they heard a loud stamping on the stairs, accompanied by ringing jokes in the voice of old Scully and laughter, evidently from the Swede. The men around the stove stared vacantly at each other. "Gosh!" said the cowboy. The door flew open, and old Scully, flushed and anecdotal, came into the room. He was jabbering at the Swede, who followed him, laughing bravely. It was the entry of two roisterers from a banquet hall.

"Come now," said Scully sharply to the three seated men, "move up and give us a chance at the stove." The cowboy and the Easterner obediently sidled their chairs to make room for the new-comers. Johnnie, however, simply arranged himself in a more indolent attitude, and then remained motionless.

"Come! Git over, there," said Scully.

"Plenty of room on the other side of the stove," said Johnnie.

"Do you think we want to sit in the draught?" roared the father.

But the Swede here interposed with a grandeur of confidence. "No, no. Let the boy sit where he likes," he cried in a bullying voice to the father.

"All right! All right!" said Scully, deferentially. The cowboy and the Easterner exchanged glances of wonder.

The five chairs were formed in a crescent about one side of the stove. The Swede began to talk; he talked arrogantly, profanely, angrily. Johnnie, the cowboy, and the Easterner maintained a morose silence, while old Scully appeared to be receptive and eager, breaking in constantly with sympathetic ejaculations.

Finally the Swede announced that he was thirsty. He moved in his chair, and said that he would go for a drink of water.

"I'll git it for you," cried Scully at once.

"No," said the Swede, contemptuously. "I'll get it for myself." He arose and stalked with the air of an owner off into the executive parts of the hotel.

As soon as the Swede was out of hearing Scully sprang to his feet and whispered intensely to the others: "Upstairs he thought I was tryin' to poison 'im."

"Say," said Johnnie, "this makes me sick. Why don't you throw 'im out in the snow?"

"Why, he's all right now," declared Scully. "It was only that he was from the East, and he thought this was a tough place. That's all. He's all right now."

The cowboy looked with admiration upon the Easterner. "You were straight," he said. "You were on to that there Dutchman."

"Well," said Johnnie to his father, "he may be all right now, but I don't see it. Other time he was scared, but now he's too fresh."

Scully's speech was always a combination of Irish brogue and idiom, Western twang and idiom, and scraps of curiously formal diction taken from the story-books and newspapers. He now hurled a strange mass of language at the head of his son. "What do I keep? What do I keep? What do I keep?" he demanded, in a voice of thunder. He slapped his knee impressively, to indicate that he himself was going to make reply, and that all should heed. "I keep a hotel," he shouted. "A hotel, do you mind? A guest under my roof has sacred privileges. He is to be intimidated by none. Not one word shall he hear that would prijudice him in favour of goin' away. I'll not have it. There's no place in this here town where they can say they iver took in a guest of mine because he was afraid to stay here." He wheeled suddenly upon the cowboy and the Easterner. "Am I right?"

"Yes, Mr. Scully," said the cowboy, "I think you're right."

"Yes, Mr. Scully," said the Easterner, "I think you're right."

V

At six-o'clock supper, the Swede fizzed like a fire-wheel. He sometimes seemed on the point of bursting into riotous song, and in all his madness he was encouraged by old Scully. The Easterner was encased in reserve; the cowboy sat in wide-mouthed amazement, forgetting to eat, while Johnnie wrathily demolished great plates of food. The daughters of the house, when they were obliged to replenish the biscuits, approached as warily as Indians, and, having succeeded in their purpose, fled with ill-concealed trepidation. The Swede domineered the whole feast, and he gave it the appearance of a cruel bacchanal. He seemed to have grown suddenly taller; he gazed, brutally disdainful, into every face. His voice rang through the room. Once when he jabbed out harpoon-fashion with his fork to pinion a biscuit, the weapon nearly impaled the hand of the Easterner, which had been stretched quietly out for the same biscuit.

After supper, as the men filed toward the other room, the Swede smote Scully ruthlessly on the shoulder. "Well, old boy, that was a good, square meal." Johnnie looked hopefully at his father; he knew that shoulder was tender from an old fall; and, indeed, it appeared for a moment as if Scully was going to flame out over the matter, but in the end he smiled a sickly smile and remained silent. The others understood from his manner that he was admitting his responsibility for the Swede's new view-point.

Johnnie, however, addressed his parent in an aside. "Why don't you license somebody to kick you downstairs?" Scully scowled darkly by way of reply.

When they were gathered about the stove, the Swede insisted on another game of High-Five. Scully gently deprecated the plan at first, but the Swede turned a wolfish glare upon him. The old man subsided, and the Swede canvassed the others. In his tone there was always a great threat. The cowboy and the Easterner both remarked indifferently that they would play. Scully said that he would presently have to go to meet the 6.58 train, and so the Swede turned menacingly upon Johnnie. For a moment their glances crossed like blades, and then Johnnie smiled and said, "Yes, I'll play."

They formed a square, with the little board on their knees. The Easterner and the Swede were again partners. As the play went on, it was noticeable that the cowboy was not board-whacking as usual. Meanwhile, Scully, near the lamp, had put on his spectacles and, with an appearance curiously like an old priest, was reading a newspaper. In time he went out to meet the 6.58 train, and, despite his precautions, a gust of polar wind whirled into the room as he opened the door. Besides scattering cards, it chilled the players to the marrow. The Swede cursed frightfully. When Scully returned, his entrance disturbed a cosy and friendly scene. The Swede again cursed. But presently they were once more intent, their heads bent forward and their hands moving swiftly. The Swede had adopted the fashion of board-whacking.

Scully took up his paper and for a long time remained immersed in matters which were extraordinarily remote from him. The lamp burned badly, and once he stopped to adjust the wick. The newspaper, as he turned from page to page, rustled with a slow and comfortable sound. Then suddenly he heard three terrible words: "You are cheatin'!"

Such scenes often prove that there can be little of dramatic import in environment. Any room can present a tragic front; any room can be comic. This little den was now hideous as a torture-chamber. The new faces of the men themselves had changed it upon the instant. The Swede held a huge fist in front of Johnnie's face, while the latter looked steadily over it into the blazing orbs of his accuser. The Easterner had grown pallid; the cowboy's jaw had dropped in that expression of bovine amazement which was one of his important mannerisms. After the three words, the first sound in the room was made by Scully's paper as it floated forgotten to his feet. His spectacles had also fallen from his nose, but by a clutch he had saved them in air. His hand, grasping the spectacles, now remained poised awkwardly and near his shoulder. He stared at the card-players.

Probably the silence was while a second elapsed. Then, if the floor had been suddenly twitched out from under the men they could not have moved quicker. The five had projected themselves headlong toward a common point. It happened that Johnnie, in rising to hurl himself upon the Swede, had stumbled slightly because of his curiously instinctive care for the cards and the board. The loss of the moment allowed time for the arrival of Scully, and also allowed the cowboy time to give the Swede a great push which sent him staggering back. The men found tongue together, and hoarse shouts of rage, appeal, or fear burst from every throat. The cowboy pushed and jostled feverishly at the Swede, and the Easterner and Scully clung wildly to Johnnie; but through the smoky air, above the swaying bodies of the peace-compellers, the eyes of the two warriors ever sought each other in glances of challenge that were at once hot and steely.

Of course the board had been overturned, and now the whole company of cards was scattered over the floor, where the boots of the men trampled the fat and painted kings and queens as they gazed with their silly eyes at the war that was waging above them.

Scully's voice was dominating the yells. "Stop now! Stop, I say! Stop, now—"

Johnnie, as he struggled to burst through the rank formed by Scully and the Easterner, was crying, "Well, he says I cheated! He says I cheated! I won't allow no man to say I cheated! If he says I cheated, he's a —— ——!"

The cowboy was telling the Swede, "Quit, now! Quit, d'ye hear—"

The screams of the Swede never ceased: "He did cheat! I saw him! I saw him—"

As for the Easterner, he was importuning in a voice that was not heeded: "Wait a moment, can't you? Oh, wait a moment. What's the good of a fight over a game of cards? Wait a moment—"

In this tumult no complete sentences were clear. "Cheat"—"Quit"—"He says"—these fragments pierced the uproar and rang out sharply. It was remarkable that, whereas Scully undoubtedly made the most noise, he was the least heard of any of the riotous band.

Then suddenly there was a great cessation. It was as if each man had paused for breath; and although the room was still lighted with the anger of men, it could be seen that there was no danger of immediate conflict, and at once Johnnie, shouldering his way forward, almost succeeded in confronting the Swede. "What did you say I cheated for? What did you say I cheated for? I don't cheat, and I won't let no man say I do!"

The Swede said, "I saw you! I saw you!"

"Well," cried Johnnie, "I'll fight any man what says I cheat!"

"No, you won't," said the cowboy. "Not here."

"Ah, be still, can't you?" said Scully, coming between them.

The quiet was sufficient to allow the Easterner's voice to be heard. He was repeating, "Oh, wait a moment, can't you? What's the good of a fight over a game of cards? Wait a moment!"

Johnnie, his red face appearing above his father's shoulder, hailed the Swede again. "Did you say I cheated?"

The Swede showed his teeth. "Yes."

"Then," said Johnnie, "we must fight."

Yes, fight," roared the Swede. He was like a demoniac. "Yes, fight!" I'll show you what kind of a man I am! I'll show you who you want to fight! Maybe you think I can't fight! Maybe you think I can't! I'll show you, you skin, you card-sharp! Yes, you cheated! You cheated! You cheated!"

"Well, let's go at it, then, mister," said Johnnie, coolly.

The cowboy's brow was beaded with sweat from his efforts in intercepting all sorts of raids. He turned in despair to Scully. "What are you goin' to do now?"

A change had come over the Celtic visage of the old man. He now seemed all eagerness; his eyes glowed.

"We'll let them fight," he answered, stalwartly. "I can't put up with it any longer. I've stood this damned Swede till I'm sick. We'll let them fight."

VI

The men prepared to go out of doors. The Easterner was so nervous that he had great difficulty in getting his arms into the sleeves of his new leather coat. As the cowboy drew his fur cap down over his ears his hands trembled. In fact, Johnnie and old Scully were the only ones who displayed no agitation. These preliminaries were conducted without words.

Scully threw open the door. "Well, come on," he said. Instantly a terrific wind caused the flame of the lamp to struggle at its wick, while a puff of black smoke sprang from the chimney-top. The stove was in mid-current of the blast, and its voice swelled to equal the roar of the storm. Some of the scarred and bedabbled cards were caught up from the floor and dashed helplessly against the farther wall. The men lowered their heads and plunged into the tempest as into a sea.

No snow was falling, but great whirls and clouds of flakes, swept up from the ground by the frantic winds, were streaming southward with the speed of bullets. The covered land was blue with the sheen of an unearthly satin, and there was no other hue save where, at the low, black railway station—which seemed incredibly distant—one light gleamed like a tiny jewel. As the men floundered into a thigh-deep drift, it was known that the Swede was bawling out something. Scully went to him, put a hand on his shoulder, and projected an ear. "What's that you say?" he shouted.

"I say," bawled the Swede again, "I won't stand much show against this gang. I know you'll all pitch on me."

Scully smote him reproachfully on the arm. "Tut, man!" he yelled. The wind tore the words from Scully's lips and scattered them far alee.

"You are all a gang of—" boomed the Swede, but the storm also seized the remainder of this sentence.

Immediately turning their backs upon the wind, the men had swung around a corner to the sheltered side of the hotel. It was the function of the little house to preserve here, amid this great devastation of snow, an irregular V-shape of heavily encrusted grass, which crackled beneath the feet. One could imagine the great drifts piled against the windward side. When the party reached the comparative peace of this spot it was found that the Swede was still bellowing.

"Oh, I know what kind of a thing this is!" I know you'll all pitch on me. I can't lick you all!"

Scully turned upon him panther-fashion. "You'll not have to whip all of us. You'll have to whip my son Johnnie. An' the man what troubles you durin' that time will have me to dale with."

The arrangements were swiftly made. The two men faced each other, obedient to the harsh commands of Scully, whose face, in the subtly luminous gloom, could be seen set in the austere impersonal lines that are pictured on the countenances of the Roman veterans. The Easterner's teeth were chattering, and he was hopping up and down like a mechanical toy. The cowboy stood rock-like.

The contestants had not stripped off any clothing. Each was in his ordinary attire. Their fists were up, and they eyed each other in a calm that had the elements of leonine cruelty in it.

During this pause, the Easterner's mind, like a film, took lasting impressions of three men—the iron-nerved master of the ceremony; the Swede, pale, motionless, terrible; and Johnnie, serene yet ferocious, brutish yet heroic. The entire prelude had in it a tragedy greater than the tragedy of action, and this aspect was accentuated by the long, mellow cry of the blizzard, as it sped the tumbling and wailing flakes into the black abyss of the south.

"Now!" said Scully.

The two combatants leaped forward and crashed together like bullocks. There was heard the cushioned sound of blows, and of a curse squeezing out from between the tight teeth of one.

As for the spectators, the Easterner's pent-up breath exploded from him with a pop of relief, absolute relief from the tension of the preliminaries. The cowboy bounded into the air with a yowl. Scully was immovable as from supreme amazement and fear at the fury of the fight which he himself had permitted and arranged.

For a time the encounter in the darkness was such a perplexity of flying arms that it presented no more detail than would a swiftly revolving wheel. Occasionally a face, as if illumined by a flash of light, would shine out, ghastly and marked with pink spots. A moment later, the men might have been known as shadows, if it were not for the involuntary utterance of oaths that came from them in whispers.

Suddenly a holocaust of warlike desire caught the cowboy, and he bolted forward with the speed of a broncho. "Go it, Johnnie! go it! Kill him! Kill him!"

Scully confronted him. "Kape back," he said; and by this glance the cowboy could tell that this man was Johnnie's father.

To the Easterner there was a monotony of unchangeable fighting that was an abomination. This confused mingling was eternal to his sense, which was concentrated in a longing for the end, the priceless end. Once the fighters lurched near him, and as he scrambled hastily backward he heard them breathe like men on the rack.

"Kill him, Johnnie! Kill him! Kill him! Kill him!" the cowboy's face was contorted like one of those agony masks in museums.

"Keep still," said Scully, icily.

Then there was a sudden loud grunt, incomplete, cut short, and Johnnie's body swung away from the Swede and fell with sickening heaviness to the grass. The cowboy was barely in time to prevent the mad Swede from flinging himself upon his prone adversary. "No, you don't," said the cowboy, interposing an arm. "Wait a second."

Scully was at his son's side. "Johnnie! Johnnie, me boy!" His voice had a quality of melancholy tenderness. "Johnnie! Can you go on with it?" He looked anxiously down into the bloody pulpy face of his son.

There was a moment of silence, and then Johnnie answered in his ordinary voice, "Yes, I—it—yes."

Assisted by his father he struggled to his feet. "Wait a bit now till you git your wind," said the old man.

A few paces away the cowboy was lecturing the Swede. "No, you don't! Wait a second!"

The Easterner was plucking at Scully's sleeve. "Oh, this is enough," he pleased. "This is enough! Let it go as it stands. This is enough!"

"Bill," said Scully, "git out of the road." The cowboy stepped aside. "Now." The combatants were actuated by a new caution as they advanced toward collision. They glared at each other, and then the Swede aimed a lightning blow that carried with it his entire weight. Johnnie was evidently half stupid from weakness, but he miraculously dodged, and his fist sent the overbalanced Swede sprawling.

The cowboy, Scully, and the Easterner burst into a cheer that was like a chorus of triumphant soldiery, but before its conclusion the Swede had scuffled agilely to his feet and come in berserk abandon at his foe. There was another perplexity of flying arms, and Johnnie's body again swung away and fell, even as a bundle might fall from a roof. The Swede instantly staggered to a little wind-waved tree and leaned upon it, breathing like an engine, while his savage and flame-lit eyes roamed from face to face as the men bent over Johnnie. There was a splendour of isolation in his situation at this time which the Easterner felt once when, lifting his eyes from the man on the ground, he beheld that mysterious and lonely figure, waiting.

"Are you any good yet, Johnnie?" asked Scully in a broken voice.

The son gasped and opened his eyes languidly. After a moment he answered, "No—I ain't—any good—any—more." Then, from shame and bodily ill, he began to weep, the tears furrowing down through the blood-stains on his face. "He was too—too—too heavy for me."

Scully straightened and addressed the waiting figure. "Stranger," he said, evenly, "it's all up with our side." Then his voice changed into that vibrant huskiness which is commonly the tone of the most simple and deadly announcements. "Johnnie is whipped."

Without replying, the victor moved off on the route to the front door of the hotel.

The cowboy was formulating new and unspellable blasphemies. The Easterner was startled to find that they were out in a wind that seemed to come direct from the shadowed arctic floes. He heard again the wail of the snow as it was flung to its grave in the south. He knew now that all this time the cold had been sinking into him deeper and deeper, and he wondered that he had not perished. He felt indifferent to the condition of the vanquished man.

"Johnnie, can you walk?" asked Scully.

"Did I hurt—hurt him any?" asked the son.

"Can you walk, boy? Can you walk?"

Johnnie's voice was suddenly strong. There was a robust impatience in it. "I asked you whether I hurt him any!"

"Yes, yes, Johnnie," answered the cowboy, consolingly; "he's hurt a good deal."

They raised him from the ground, and as soon as he was on his feet he went tottering off, rebuffing all attempts at assistance. When the party rounded the corner they were fairly blinded by the pelting of the snow. It burned their faces like fire. The cowboy carried Johnnie through the drift to the door. As they entered, some cards again rose from the floor and beat against the wall.

The Easterner rushed to the stove. He was so profoundly chilled that he almost dared to embrace the glowing iron. The Swede was not in the room. Johnnie sank into a chair and, folding his arms on his knees, buried his face in them. Scully, warming one foot and then the other at a rim of the stove, muttered to himself with Celtic mournfulness. The cowboy had removed his fur cap, and with a dazed and rueful air he was running one hand through his tousled locks. From overhead they could hear the creaking of boards, as the Swede tramped here and there in his room.

The sad quiet was broken by the sudden flinging open of a door that led toward the kitchen. It was instantly followed by an inrush of women. They precipitated themselves upon Johnnie amid a chorus of lamentation. Before they carried their prey off to the kitchen, there to be bathed and harangued with that mixture of sympathy and abuse which is a feat of their sex, the mother straightened herself and fixed old Scully with an eye of stern reproach. "Shame be upon you, Patrick Scully!" she cried. "Your own son, too. Shame be upon you!"

"There, now! Be quiet, now!" said the old man, weakly.

"Shame be upon you, Patrick Scully!" The girls, rallying to this slogan, sniffed disdainfully in the direction of those trembling accomplices, the cowboy and the Easterner. Presently they bore Johnnie away, and left the three men to dismal reflection.

VII

"I'd like to fight this here Dutchman myself," said the cowboy, breaking a long silence.

Scully wagged his head sadly. "No, that wouldn't do. It wouldn't be right. It wouldn't be right."

"Well, why wouldn't it?" argued the cowboy. "I don't see no harm in it."

"No," answered Scully, with mournful heroism. "It wouldn't be right. It was Johnnie's fight, and now we mustn't whip the man just because he whipped Johnnie."

"Yes, that's true enough," said the cowboy; "but—he better not get fresh with me, because I couldn't stand no more of it."

"You'll not say a word to him," commanded Scully, and even then they heard the tread of the Swede on the stairs. His entrance was made theatric. He swept the door back with a bang and swaggered to the middle of the room. No one looked at him. "Well," he cried, insolently, at Scully, "I s'pose you'll tell me now how much I owe you?"

The old man remained stolid. "You don't owe me nothin'."

"Huh!" said the Swede, "huh! Don't owe 'im nothin'."

The cowboy addressed the Swede. "Stranger, I don't see how you come to be so gay around here."

Old Scully was instantly alert. "Stop!" he shouted, holding his hand forth, fingers upward. "Bill, you shut up!"

The cowboy spat carelessly into the sawdust-box. "I didn't say a word, did I?" he asked.

"Mr. Scully," called the Swede, "how much do I owe you?" It was seen that he was attired for departure, and that he had his valise in his hand.

"You don't owe me nothin'," repeated Scully in the same imperturbable way.

"Huh!" said the Swede. "I guess you're right. I guess if it was any way at all, you'd owe me somethin'. That's what I guess." He turned to the cowboy. " 'Kill him! Kill him! Kill him!' " he mimicked, and then guffawed victoriously. " 'Kill him!' " He was convulsed with ironical humour.

But he might have been jeering the dead. The three men were immovable and silent, staring with glassy eyes at the stove.

The Swede opened the door and passed into the storm, giving one derisive glance backward at the still group.

As soon as the door was closed, Scully and the cowboy leaped to their feet and began to curse. They trampled to and fro, waving their arms and smashing into the air with their fists. "Oh, but that was a hard minute!" wailed Scully. "That was a hard minute! Him there leerin' and scoffin'! One bang at his nose was worth forty dollars to me that minute! How did you stand it, Bill?"

"How did I stand it?" cried the cowboy in a quivering voice. "How did I stand it? Oh!"

The old man burst into sudden brogue. "I'd loike to take that Swade," he wailed, "and hould 'im down on a shtone flure and bate 'im to a jelly wid a shtick!"

The cowboy groaned in sympathy. "I'd like to git him by the neck and ha-ammer him"—he brought his hand down on a chair with noise like a pistol-shot—"hammer that there Dutchman until he couldn't tell himself from a dead coyote!"

"I'd bate 'im until he—"

"I'd show *him* some things—"

And then together they raised a yearning, fanatic cry—"Oh-o-oh! if we only could—"

"Yes!"

"Yes!"
"And then I'd—"
"O-o-oh!"

VIII

The Swede, tightly gripping his valise, tacked across the face of the storm as if he carried sails. He was following a line of little naked, grasping trees which, he knew, must mark the way of the road. His face, fresh from the pounding of Johnnie's fists, felt more pleasure than pain in the wind and the driving snow. A number of square shapes loomed upon him finally, and he knew them as the houses of the main body of the town. He found a street and made travel along it, leaning heavily upon the wind whenever, at a corner, a terrific blast caught him.

He might have been in a deserted village. We picture the world as thick with conquering and elate humanity, but here, with the bugles of the tempest pealing, it was hard to imagine a peopled earth. One viewed the existence of man then as a marvel, and conceded a glamour of wonder to these lice which were caused to cling to a whirling, fire-smitten, ice-locked, disease-stricken, space-lost bulb. The conceit of man was explained by this storm to be the very engine of life. One was a coxcomb not to die in it. However, the Swede found a saloon.

In front of it an indomitable red light was burning, and the snowflakes were made blood-colour as they flew through the circumscribed territory of the lamp's shining. The Swede pushed open the door of the saloon and entered. A sanded expanse was before him, and at the end of it four men sat about a table drinking. Down one side of the room extended a radiant bar, and its guardian was leaning upon his elbows listening to the talk of the men at the table. The Swede dropped his valise upon the floor and, smiling fraternally upon the barkeeper, said, "Gimme some whisky, will you?" The man placed a bottle, a whisky-glass, and a glass of ice-thick water upon the bar. The Swede poured himself an abnormal portion of whisky and drank it in three gulps. "Pretty bad night," remarked the bartender, indifferently. He was making the pretension of blindness which is usually a distinction of his class; but it could have been seen that he was furtively studying the half-erased blood-stains on the face of the Swede. "Bad night," he said again.

"Oh, it's good enough for me," replied the Swede, hardily, as he poured himself some more whisky. The barkeeper took his coin and manœuvred it through its reception by the highly nickelled cash-machine. A bell rang; a card labelled "20 cts." had appeared.

"No," continued the Swede, "this isn't too bad weather. It's good enough for me."

"So?" murmured the barkeeper, languidly.

The copious drams made the Swede's eyes swim, and he breathed a trifle heavier. "Yes, I like this weather. I like it. It suits me." It was apparently his design to impart a deep significance to these words.

"So?" murmured the bartender again. He turned to gaze dreamily at the scroll-like birds and bird-like scrolls which had been drawn with soap upon the mirrors in back of the bar.

"Well, I guess I'll take another drink," said the Swede, presently. "Have something?"

"No, thanks; I'm not drinkin'," answered the bartender. Afterward he asked, "How did you hurt your face?"

The Swede immediately began to boast loudly. "Why, in a fight. I thumped the soul out of a man down here at Scully's hotel."

The interest of the four men at the table was at last aroused.

"Who was it?" said one.

"Johnnie Scully," blustered the Swede. "Son of the man what runs it. He will be pretty near dead for some weeks, I can tell you. I made a nice thing of him, I did. He couldn't get up. They carried him in the house. Have a drink?"

Instantly the men in some subtle way encased themselves in reserve. "No, thanks," said one. The group was of curious formation. Two were prominent local business men; one was the district attorney; and one was a professional gambler of the kind known as "square." But a scrutiny of the group would not have enabled an observer to pick the gambler from the men of more reputable pursuits. He was, in fact, a man so delicate in manner, when among people of fair class, and so judicious in his choice of victims, that in the strictly masculine part of the town's life he had come to be explicitly trusted and admired. People called him a thoroughbred. The fear and contempt with which his craft was regarded were undoubtedly the reason why his quiet dignity shone conspicuous above the quiet dignity of men who might be merely hatters, billiard-markers, or grocery clerks. Beyond an occasional unwary traveller who came by rail, this gambler was supposed to prey solely upon reckless and senile farmers, who, when flush with good crops, drove into town in all the pride and confidence of an absolutely invulnerable stupidity. Hearing at times in circuitous fashion of the despoilment of such a farmer, the important men of Romper invariably laughed in contempt of the victim, and if they thought of the wolf at all, it was with a kind of pride at the knowledge that he would never dare think of attacking their wisdom and courage. Besides, it was popular that this gambler had a real wife and two real children in a neat cottage in a suburb, where he led an exemplary home life; and when any one even suggested a discrepancy in his character, the crowd immediately vociferated descriptions of this virtuous family circle. Then men who led exemplary home lives, and men who did not lead exemplary home lives, all subsided in a bunch, remarking that there was nothing more to be said.

However, when a restriction was placed upon him—as, for instance, when a strong clique of members of the new Pollywog Club refused to permit him, even as a spectator, to appear in the rooms of the organization—the candour and gentleness with which he accepted the judgment disarmed many of his foes and made his friends more desperately partisan. He invariably distinguished between himself and a respectable Romper man so quickly and frankly that his manner actually appeared to be a continual broadcast compliment.

And one must not forget to declare the fundamental fact of his entire position in Romper. It is irrefutable that in all affairs outside his business, in all matters that occur eternally and commonly between man and man, this thieving card-player was so generous, so just, so moral, that, in a contest, he could have put to flight the consciences of nine tenths of the citizens of Romper.

And so it happened that he was seated in this saloon with the two prominent local merchants and the district attorney.

The Swede continued to drink raw whisky, meanwhile babbling at the barkeeper and trying to induce him to indulge in potations. "Come on. Have a drink. Come on. What—no? Well, have a little one, then. By gawd, I've whipped a man to-night, and I want to celebrate. I whipped him good, too. Gentlemen," the Swede cried to the men at the table, "have a drink?"

"Ssh!" said the barkeeper.

The group at the table, although furtively attentive, had been pretending to be deep in talk, but now a man lifted his eyes toward the Swede and said, shortly, "Thanks. We don't want any more."

At this reply the Swede ruffled out his chest like a rooster. "Well," he exploded, "it seems I can't get anybody to drink with me in this town. Seems so, don't it? Well!"

"Ssh!" said the barkeeper.

"Say," snarled the Swede, "don't you try to shut me up. I won't have it. I'm a gentleman, and I want people to drink with me. And I want 'em to drink with me now. *Now*—do you understand?" He rapped the bar with his knuckles.

Years of experience had calloused the bartender. He merely grew sulky. "I hear you," he answered.

"Well," cried the Swede, "listen hard then. See those men over there? Well, they're going to drink with me, and don't you forget it. Now you watch."

"Hi!" yelled the barkeeper, "this won't do!"

"Why won't it?" demanded the Swede. He stalked over to the table, and by chance laid his hand upon the shoulder of the gambler. "How about this?" he asked wrathfully. "I asked you to drink with me."

The gambler simply twisted his head and spoke over his shoulder. "My friend, I don't know you."

"Oh, hell!" answered the Swede, "come and have a drink."

"Now, my boy," advised the gambler, kindly, "take your hand off my shoulder and go 'way and mind your own business." He was a little, slim man, and it seemed strange to hear him use this tone of heroic patronage to the burly Swede. The other men at the table said nothing.

"What! You won't drink with me, you little dude? I'll make you, then! I'll make you!" The Swede had grasped the gambler frenziedly at the throat, and was dragging him from his chair. The other men sprang up. The barkeeper dashed around the corner of his bar. There was a great tumult, and then was seen a long blade in the hand of the gambler. It shot forward, and a human body, this citadel of virtue, wisdom, power, was pierced as easily as if it had been a melon. The Swede fell with a cry of supreme astonishment.

The prominent merchants and the district attorney must have at once tumbled out of the place backward. The bartender found himself hanging limply to the arm of a chair and gazing into the eyes of a murderer.

"Henry," said the latter, as he wiped his knife on one of the towels that hung beneath the bar rail, "you tell 'em where to find me. I'll be home, waiting for 'em." Then he vanished. A moment afterward the barkeeper was in the street dinning through the storm for help and, moreover, companionship.

The corpse of the Swede, alone in the saloon, had its eyes fixed upon a dreadful legend that dwelt atop of the cash-machine: "This registers the amount of your purchase."

IX

Months later, the cowboy was frying pork over the stove of a little ranch near the Dakota line, when there was a quick thud of hoofs outside, and presently the Easterner entered with the letters and the papers.

"Well," said the Easterner at once, "the chap that killed the Swede has got three years. Wasn't much, was it?"

"He has? Three years?" The cowboy poised his pan of pork, while he ruminated upon the news. "Three years. That ain't much."

"No. It was a light sentence," replied the Easterner as he unbuckled his spurs. "Seems there was a good deal of sympathy for him in Romper."

"If the bartender had been any good," observed the cowboy, thoughtfully, "he would have gone in and cracked that there Dutchman on the head with a bottle in the beginnin' of it and stopped all this here murderin'."

"Yes, a thousand things might have happened," said the Easterner, tartly.

The cowboy returned his pan of pork to the fire, but his philosophy continued. "It's funny, ain't it? If he hadn't said Johnnie was cheatin' he'd be alive this minute. He was an awful fool. Game played for fun, too. Not for money. I believe he was crazy."

"I feel sorry for that gambler," said the Easterner.

"Oh, so do I," said the cowboy. "He don't deserve none of it for killin' who he did."

"The Swede might not have been killed if everything had been square."

"Might not have been killed?" exclaimed the cowboy. "Everythin' square? Why, when he said that Johnnie was cheatin' and acted like such a jackass? And then in the saloon he fairly walked up to git hurt?" With these arguments the cowboy browbeat the Easterner and reduced him to rage.

"You're a fool!" cried the Easterner, viciously. "You're a bigger jackass than the Swede by a million majority. Now let me tell you one thing. Let me tell you something. Listen! Johnnie *was* cheating!"

"'Johnnie,'" said the cowboy, blankly. There was a minute of silence, and then he said, robustly, "Why, no. The game was only for fun."

"Fun or not," said the Easterner, "Johnnie was cheating. I saw him. I know it. I saw him. And I refused to stand up and be a man. I let the Swede fight it out alone. And you—you were simply puffing around the place and wanting to fight. And then old Scully himself! We are all in it! This poor gambler isn't even a noun. He is kind of an adverb. Every sin is the result of a collaboration. We, five of us, have collaborated in the murder of this Swede. Usually there are from a dozen to forty women really involved in every murder, but in this case it seems to be only five men—you, I, Johnnie, old Scully; and that fool of an unfortunate gambler came merely as a culmination, the apex of a human movement, and gets all the punishment."

The cowboy, injured and rebellious, cried out blindly into this fog of mysterious theory: "Well, I didn't do anythin', did I?"

SECTION THREE

Maturation and Renewal

1900 – 1935

During the first half of the twentieth century, the pace and patterns of life in the United States altered even more radically than they had throughout all the previous course of the nation's history. To grasp imaginatively the implications of such drastic changes one might focus momentarily on a few specific events that shattered old concepts and reshaped the thinking, actions, and values of millions of Americans. The Wright brothers' first successful flight in 1903, for example, signalized for good and ill in future decades the seemingly limitless possibilities of air transport; while the sinking of the *Lusitania* in 1915 and the Japanese attack on Pearl Harbor in 1941 galvanized the nation into action, turning its massive industrial energies toward the conduct of two world wars, the second one to be climaxed by the atomic bombing of Hiroshima, an act of human destructiveness that still haunts the minds of men and women everywhere. Analogous if less spectacular events could be cited in other areas of American endeavor that also contributed in part to the kaleidoscopic developments in twentieth-century American society, and that may be seen reflected in a bewildering variety of ways in the creative literature they helped to inspire. Thus, in striking contrast to the dramatic activity and prosperity engendered by America's participation in the two great wars, there were the after-effects of the New York Stock Market crash of 1929: a decade of economic depression that not only brought suffering and privation to a majority of American families, but also led to the questioning of many accepted standards and aspirations and to the significant reorganization of many American institutions. Inevitably, these conflicting forces, abetted by influences from abroad such as the breakdown of established regimes and the rise of Communism and Fascism in Europe, also found varied and contrasting expression in twentieth-century American fiction.

The Legacy of Henry James

As the nation entered the twentieth century, however, the most striking developments to be anticipated in the forms and techniques of short fiction writing reflected trends already established. The enormous expansion in magazine circulation (in 1905 about 6000 magazines were being published as compared with a mere 700 in 1865) provided an impetus toward the further refinement of two distinct but traditional types of short fiction: the popular story intended primarily as a means of light entertainment for a mass audience, and the story with more limited appeal—but more durable quality—intended as a work of fine art. By 1900, Henry James, as we have seen, stood preeminent among literary artists of the latter sort; and during the ensuing decade he even surpassed his earlier achievements by producing more than a dozen of the subtlest and most profound stories he ever wrote. Probing deeper and deeper into intricacies of consciousness confronting problems of the psyche, stories like "The Beast in the Jungle," "The Jolly Corner," and "The Beldonald Holbein" are worked out with extreme care, the details in their situations and forwarding action inserted like colorful threads in an unfolding tapestry, and their ultimate resolutions and revelations derived as a seemingly inevitable result of manifest cause and effect relationships, rather than sheer happenstance or artificially contrived tricks of fate. Thus, it is not surprising that work of this caliber, though lacking broad popular appeal, not only captured the imagination of serious younger writers of the 1900s who hoped to match its artistry in their own stories, but has also withstood the erosion of time and the tireless efforts of critics and scholars to encompass and interpret it.

But, if the vast reading public of that by-gone era knew little of and cared less for the merits of James's fiction, it had its own literary folk hero—O. Henry—whose popularity both in the United States and throughout the world has also survived despite the swift decline of his literary reputation among the critics since the 1920s. For while James created works of art for the few, O. Henry wrote for and has been loved by the millions, many of whom may not even know his real name, William Sydney Porter. Between 1900 and his death in 1910 he produced nearly 300 stories for mass circulation weeklies, most of them based on an obviously contrived plot formula taken over from his predecessors among the local colorists and fabricators of the "well-made" story. Part of their appeal lay in the seemingly endless variations played upon stock situations involving familiar urban and rural types—policemen, rogues, con men, clerks, cowboys, shopgirls, actresses, housewives, millionaires, southern planters, etc.—but part also in the breezy, familiar manner of their telling, a manner distinctively individualized yet broadly representative. For besides the narrator's voice in O. Henry's stories, the voices of many recognizable Americans, native and naturalized, speak through them, generally with a pervasive brand of humor which, though often gauche, flippant, slangy, and outrageously pun-laden, is also thoroughly American. Moreover, despite the essential unreality, the transparency of manipulated action based on coincidence and trickery leading to a predictably "surprise" ending, the typical O. Henry story suffuses a basic human warmth or sympathy for the common joys and sorrows of mankind that appeals to the romanticist in everyone.

In the world of O. Henry's fiction there is accordingly a strong element of romanticism that is seldom encountered in James's world; for instead of grappling seriously with moral problems in society or probing the depths of human psychology, his two-dimensional characters tend to romanticize alike both the rich and the poor. So it is understandable that this sort of story quickly lost favor among younger writers steeped in the mood of postwar disillusionment of the 1920s, whereas James's techniques continued to influence their narrative methods, even though they tended to avoid his manner and subject matter in order to cover the broader human scene introduced by O. Henry.

Among the first group of serious younger artists who took their cue from James's methods, yet proceeded to develop traditional realistic stories in their own distinctive ways, two emerged at nearly the same time—Edith Wharton and Willa Cather. Both shared James's concern for sensitive artistry, seeking to capture nuances of human emotion through carefully selected descriptive and narrative touches and firmly controlled management of dramatic scenes, situations, dialogue, and point of view. Both likewise shared his preference, at least initially, for dealing with problems and relationships peculiar to the upper levels of society, for example, those of artists and their associates among the leisured rich. Yet each developed a style distinctly different from his and from each other's.

Although Edith Wharton as an eager young author wisely took James's advice to "do" in her fiction the exclusive New York society to which she belonged, she later protested vigorously—and justifiably—against the assumption that her stories merely echoed his. In a long career extending from the 1890s until her death in 1937, she published eighty-six stories, most of them bearing the stamp of her own personality and many of them excellent examples of classically finished form. As one of her most perceptive critics has noted, Wharton did not significantly modify the short story form as others such as Joyce and Hemingway were doing during her lifetime; but what she did accomplish in adhering to principles of narrative technique borrowed from James was a seemingly effortless rendering of a situation which, in her best stories, "is gradually revealed in all its complexity and finality. What we know at the end . . . is not so much how some problem got resolved, but the full nature, usually the insurmountable nature of the problem itself."[1] Such deftness, applied repeatedly to problems involving marriage, infidelity, divorce, adultery, and illegitimacy (problems that we now know reflect the anguish of her own personal life) poignantly reveals a broad range of psychological insights into the anxieties, frustrations, and moral dilemmas with which men and women have to contend in their inter-relationships, both in and out of marriage. Repeatedly too these insights are devastatingly conveyed in terms of the simplest response to a query, the slightest shift of emphasis in designating a gesture, mannerism, or tone of voice. The pervasive influence of James's aesthetic principles is revealed in Wharton's most brilliant efforts.

For Willa Cather, however, James's influence was perhaps even stronger—at least during the formative period of her career. As an undergraduate at the University of Nebraska in the 1890s, she had found in him "the perfect writer," and when she left there shortly after graduation, determined to establish her own reputation as a literary artist, it was James's single-minded devotion to the art of fiction that set the standards for her achievement. By 1905, she had published more than thirty stories in various magazines, but she would allow only seven of them to appear in her first collection, *The Troll Garden,* and of the nearly twenty more written during the next fifteen years, she included only four in her second collection, *Youth and the Bright Medusa,* published in 1920. Thus, the eleven stories in these two collections, all echoing related Jamesian motifs concerning the plight of the artist at bay in a hostile or indifferent bourgeois society, were all that she wished to let stand as representative of her finest efforts in the short story until the publication of her third small collection, *Obscure Destinies,* in 1932. In all, Willa Cather produced about sixty stories during her lifetime, but she reckoned as adequate only a handful bearing the unmistakable stamp of James's lofty aims.

Yet, in their style and substance most of Cather's stories were even less imitative of James's than were those of Edith Wharton. Rather, they reflected the inspiration and encouragement she had drawn early in her career from the writings of Sarah Orne Jewett, whom she idolized throughout her lifetime. To a less noticeable degree, they reflected also the emerging naturalists' concern for the unsung heroism of ordinary Americans seeking fulfillment of their potential whatever their role in society, whether rural or urban. Thus, in the early 1900s, when only drawing room fiction was considered fashionable "and the only charac-

[1] R.W.B. Lewis (ed.) *The Collected Short Stories of Edith Wharton,* 2 vols. (New York: Scribners, 1968), Introduction, Vol. I, pp. vii–viii.

ters worth reading about were smart people or clever people,"[2] it was not James, but Jewett, whose stories about the lives of simple people close to their native soil revitalized Cather's creative energies and refocused her fictional endeavor. Thereafter both her novels and stories drew increasingly upon her personal experiences and memories of Nebraska and the West as well as upon those of her editorial career in Pittsburgh and New York. But because of her fastidious self-criticism, the range and variety of her achievement in the short story have not as yet received the critical attention they deserve; for, overshadowed by her brilliant successes in the nine or ten novels published between 1913 and 1935, most of the stories she produced during the peak years of her career, as well as many of the ones published earlier, were forgotten almost as rapidly as the magazine issues they appeared in were cast aside. And so the tendency until recently has been to assume that her short stories merited little close study, since she herself had repudiated most of them. During the past decade, however, as successive scholarly editions have brought to light all of Willa Cather's previously uncollected stories, a reassessment of their values has begun which recognizes that many bear favorable comparison with the best that were being written in the United States before the 1930s. Consequently, although "Paul's Case" still remains an early favorite, students of the modern American short story may now discover that neither this story nor the later "Neighbor Rosicky" marked the limits of her accomplishment; recently published collections such as the one entitled *Uncle Valentine and Other Stories: Willa Cather's Uncollected Short Fiction 1915–1929* show that her range and scope in the genre were no less impressive than her rival, Edith Wharton's.

The Impact of Naturalism

Despite their unqualified devotion to the art of fiction and the generally high level of their stories, however, neither Wharton nor Cather exerted a strong influence among their contemporaries. Whether justifiably or not, their writings were associated with the moribund tradition of genteel realism sponsored by Howells and James, rather than with the surging tide of naturalism initiated by Crane, Frank Norris, and Jack London that swept new modes of fiction to the fore in the period of World War I. Accordingly, among the writers whose work left a deeper impress in directing the course of contemporary fiction, Theodore Dreiser and Sherwood Anderson became the standard-bearers of the new naturalism,

[2]"My First Novels," in *Willa Cather on Writing* (New York: Knopf, 1949), p. 93.

the one for his massive handling of detail and the other for his sensitive analysis of personality.

Dreiser saw life as a gigantic but utterly purposeless struggle in which men and women are all "more or less pawns . . . moved about like chessmen by circumstances over which [they] have no control." Everyone, he felt, was driven by a love of power or a desire for self-realization through sexual or artistic achievement, but for most, even the strongest, either defeat or frustration was to be the inevitable goal of all their striving. In Dreiser's world, a grim, humorless place, the race is always to the swift and the battle to the mighty; but while he depicts with scrupulous honesty and a mass of convincing detail the dominance of strong-willed characters over their weaker or less fortunate competitors, their triumph offers no grounds for exultation, since it is achieved at the expense of the many who fail. For these, Dreiser manifests a deep, abiding pity, buttressed by his dogged accumulation of objective facts, which leave little to the reader's imagination to surmise or misinterpret. As a result, Dreiser's primary virtues, honesty, sincerity, and a massive power of expression, cannot be effaced by what is regarded by some critics as the clumsiest style in modern American prose. The sensitive reader is often annoyed by his tortured, ungrammatical sentences, his inelegant, cliche-ridden phrasing, his pointless repetitions and undiscriminating choice of detail. Yet despite these artistic flaws—serious enough to have sunk any lesser writer—the overall effect of Dreiser's stories is profoundly moving.

A more conscious artist than Dreiser, Anderson likewise accepted to a certain extent the naturalistic interpretation of modern industrial society as a huge swindle in which sensitive individuals are tricked and robbed, their normal instincts distorted by the artificial restraints and materialistic standards of their environment. But where Dreiser tended to dramatize the outer scene of conflict responsible for these frustrations, Anderson sought instead to objectify the inner warpings of the personality produced within individuals by the clash between their urges and the mores of their society. To present this inner experience dramatically Anderson felt that he must find a new form that would avoid the artificiality of the obviously plotted story, for he was certain that "there were no plot short stories ever lived in any life I had known anything about." In his search for a form he was aided and encouraged by Gertrude Stein, who showed him how form, through the skillful selection and arrangement of words in common speech, might be made to grow "out of the materials of the tale and the teller's reaction to them."

The first noteworthy result of this discovery was *Winesburg, Ohio* (1919), a collection of interrelated stories hailed by many critics as a landmark in the development of the contemporary American short story, not so much because of the radical departure from traditional forms that

Anderson thought he had achieved in it, but rather because it revitalized and combined older methods of storytelling that had fallen into disuse. In the *Winesburg* stories Anderson revived the methods employed by Hawthorne and Melville in their efforts to probe the recesses of the human mind, but he made those methods more flexible by combining with them a technique similar to that of the apparently artless narrator device in the frontier "mock oral" tale. In Anderson's best stories, therefore, the quality of the narrator's personality and the way he tells a remembered experience are as important to the total effect as the events he has to tell. As the narrator begins to tell his story, he often confesses a mixed feeling of oppressiveness and bewilderment, and as he proceeds in the telling he may have to pause occasionally to reassure himself that his recollection of the events is correct, that his mind has control of their significance. But Anderson himself, the creative mind outside the story, does have this control; what results as the story unfolds is a complex structure developing along several different levels at the same time: the events themselves, the feelings and memory of the narrator who recalls his involvement in them, and the underlying related significance of all three that, though present for the reader, lies outside the narrator's awareness. Unfortunately, Anderson could not keep such a firm grip as this on his medium; but in a few of his later stories, such as "The Egg" and "Death in the Woods," he did fulfill the promise of his early hopes.

Whatever their limitations, Dreiser and Anderson stand together with Crane as pioneer figures whose efforts to liberate American fiction from the shackles of conventional attitudes and methods encouraged the widespread experimentation in form and technique that has characterized the last seventy years of the short story's development and kept it vigorously alive as an art form. Their efforts were all the more noteworthy in that they had to overcome persistent, often violent, opposition, for up to 1920 and beyond, both the tenets and the exponents of naturalism were bitterly assailed in the United States. And yet, even though few present-day writers can be ticketed as naturalists pure and simple, the pervasive influence of this movement is still visible in the work of many. As new experiences arising from the widespread violence and suffering of contemporary life have brought a new awareness of impending chaos to larger numbers of the reading public, the extreme attitudes and the sensationalism for which our early naturalists were censured no longer seem quite so abnormal, while the methods they devised for expressing themselves have been quietly appropriated, even by our popular writers.

The new insights that Dreiser and Anderson brought to the writing of fiction, however, were but a foretaste of the dramatic developments that lay ahead. In the aftermath of World War I, as the attitudes and mores of American society altered sharply and established conventions, beliefs, and inhibitions gave way to new fashions in dress, manners, and personal conduct, a virtual explosion of new modes and new voices clamored to express these changes. The 1920s, aptly named the "jazz age" by F. Scott Fitzgerald, thus became an exciting period of revolt and experimentation, with Americans in virtually all walks of life reacting vigorously to new ideas and influences, both foreign and domestic. On the level of popular culture, the mass media, radio, and the movies, mirroring vividly all facets of the American dream, opened up for delighted millions the glamorous worlds of movie stars and millionaires, gangsters and tycoons; while on a more intellectual level, fresh currents of thought from abroad provided further stimuli to serious young artists and writers, many of whom absorbed them directly as Parisian expatriates. Among the most important of these foreign influences, the ideas and methods of Sigmund Freud in the field of psychoanalysis probably exerted the strongest impact, particularly in the new literary treatment of sexual relationships, although anthropological studies such as Sir James Fraser's *The Golden Bough* and the politico-economic theories of Karl Marx likewise played a significant role in reshaping the course of postwar American literature.

Renaissances and Innovations

Out of the ferment of ideas and events generated by these and other influences, there sprang forth in the 1920s an astonishing literary flowering comparable to but more widely scattered than that of the 1830s and 1840s. For this twentieth-century literary renaissance was not restricted to one or two areas or to a single class of writers; rather it became a series of rebirths involving new ethnic groups of writers seldom heard from before—immigrants and blacks, for example—as well as young men and women from the South and West whose cultural heritage antedated the Civil War. But whether as individuals or members of group movements, most of these new writers responded vigorously, if with varying degrees of depth and technical competence, to the many problems posed by rapid social and industrial change. A sharpened critical awareness of the disparity between what America might become and was becoming inspired among many of them a reassessment of traditional values and ideals, as well as a search for new methods of interpreting the present in the light of the past. As a result, the new fiction, along with poetry and drama, received bold and massive transformation in content and form—a process in which the short story abundantly shared. But however shocking, indeed often repulsive, much of the new fiction at first appeared to be to established tastes nurtured in the genteel tradition, it did not focus attention on the violent and sensational aspects of human behavior merely for the sake of repudiating that tradition or, as was often charged, of drawing attention to itself. Instead, the new fiction of the 1920s and 1930s often implied a keenly critical re-examination of the nature and function of literature itself. If not merely for refined, leisured entertainment, what was fiction for? In a swiftly changing technological age, what should serious fiction writers write about as they surveyed the diminishing role of the individual, and how should they write about it in order to register forcibly their meaning and tone of voice? This feeling that individuals, while becoming more and more submerged in the mass, had lost or were losing their identities and importance as persons, doubtless accounted for much of the sensationalism as well as the violence and sordidness, presented in the new fiction.

Among the various other short story writers who, besides Dreiser and Anderson, confronted these problems with significant finesse in the 1920s, the names of Conrad Aiken, Ring Lardner, F. Scott Fitzgerald, and Wilbur Daniel Steel first come to mind. Of the four, Steele's reputation has suffered most from the erosion of changing tastes, although ironically he was regarded as the finest of story tellers in that decade. A superb craftsman and winner of many "firsts" in the annual O. Henry awards, he was a master of the "well made" plotted story in which setting, situation, conflict, climax, and dénouement were almost flawlessly combined to arouse suspense and totally absorb the reader emotionally. And yet, for all his inventiveness, Steele's situations and plots began losing their appeal in the 1930s so that even the best of his stories, as he recognized himself, went out of fashion and are seldom now anthologized. With two or three notable exceptions, Aiken's stories have suffered a similar fate, though he too, like Steele, wrote many dealing with problems of madness and the unconscious that made a strong impact at the time they appeared. The difference between the two writers' work in this vein, however, is that Aiken's stories reflect an intense involvement in Freudian psychoanalysis; and this may help to explain why his two most brilliant successes, "Mr. Arcularis" and "Silent Snow, Secret Snow," are still frequently anthologized, for both are richly complex studies of the human mind under intense stress.

A somewhat larger number of both Lardner's and Fitzgerald's stories still receive favorable critical notice, possibly because they capture more successfully, though in vastly different styles, the special flavor of their period. An ex-sportswriter turned yarnspinner, Lardner penetrated the shams of the entertainment world with the force of a laser beam, sardonically exposing the vulgarity and pretentiousness of baseball players, pugilists, theater producers, and small-minded professional braggarts of various other sorts. By and large, the people he depicted are uniformly superficial, their attitudes and behavior often blatantly uninspiring; yet they become memorably alive and hilariously amusing as a result of Lardner's uncanny skill in presenting them through their own modes of expression. Even though many of his stories are obviously contrived, the humor and pathos combined in their brilliantly rendered voice tones and rhythms are still fresh after more than fifty years. Lardner at his best indelibly etched a portion of American society for all time.

Fitzgerald did too, but for a very different portion of that society and, for the most part, with very different skills and methods. In Fitzgerald's world one meets the sorts of individuals he himself associated with during successive stages of his career—upper middle class suburbanites, wealthy Yale and Princeton alumni, stockbrokers, doctors, lawyers, artists, Paris expatriates, Hollywood directors, and their assorted wives and girlfriends—most of whom he portrays with detached irony and a depth of understanding. The major themes binding them together are concerned with the futility of lost opportunities, wasted talents, and romantic dreams of an irrecoverable past, as suggested in the titles he chose for several of his collections—*Tales of the Jazz Age, All the Sad Young Men,* and *Taps at Reveille*—and for some of his most memorable stories such as "Babylon Revisited," "The Rich Boy," "The Diamond as Big as the Ritz," "Crazy Sunday," and "Winter Dreams." In the characters and action of his masterpiece, *The Great Gatsby,* these themes are brilliantly articulated, as indeed they are in a half dozen or so of his finest short stories, which dramatize the same basic moral idea: namely, the corrupting influence of the lure and possession of money—the American Dream. Himself a victim of that dream, Fitzgerald wrote over a hundred short stories, churning them out regularly at an increasingly lucrative rate in the late 1920s, yet desperately suffering from the deterioration of both his family life and his own creative powers. Ironically, however, both his triumphs and defeats were then miraculously epitomized in one of his greatest stories, "Babylon Revisited," written in 1931.

Unfortunately, Fitzgerald's success as a writer of stories for the commercial market worked against his lifelong desire to achieve permanent fame as a serious literary artist in that genre. And though he continued to produce for the popular magazines in the 1930s, he, like Steele, realized that his type of story even at its best had been superseded by the work of a greater artist—Ernest Hemingway. By that time, the famous Hemingway "style," which had appeared as early as 1923, had become the vogue: A totally new combination of narrative techniques—tight, compressed, clear, vivid, and deceptively "simple" on the surface—it was a method comparable to that of modern lyric poetry, and it became a major influence in reshaping the form and substance of the modern short story.

Although Hemingway's world is a pretty brutal one, in which primary emphasis falls on the need of individuals to grasp whatever self-satisfaction they can while they can, his stories reveal a strong undercurrent of compassion and admiration for the characters he created, together with an equally strong determination not to parade these feelings but to convey them cleanly and directly (without "cheating," as he put it, meaning void of lofty preachments) in terms of sharp reactions to physical sensations. In Hemingway's stories one finds almost no concern for the ordinary practical situations of business and family life, possibly because he regarded these as merely ancillary means toward the more urgent business of seizing whatever joy and comfort the moment may afford in a universe devoid of meaning. Determined throughout most of his career to write only what he really felt, not what he was supposed or expected to feel, Hemingway demonstrated his scorn for sham and hypocrisy by reducing life to its barest terms and judging it implicitly on the basis of primary emotions—love, hate, fear, hunger, thirst, pain, sexual desire. With simplicity and truth as his double aim, he thus created a world in which morality is measured, not by conventional standards, but in these same primary terms ("I know only that what is moral is what you feel good after"); and he peopled this world with characters whose worth is apparent by what they leave unsaid in the presence of fundamental situations involving love, danger, physical suffering, and death. To maintain one's courage, dignity, and integrity; to keep a "stiff upper lip" against overwhelming pressures; to salvage something of basic human value out of a messy universe, if only one's self-respect—these are the distinguishing marks of Hemingway's heroes from the young Nick Adams on through the whole series of bullfighters, soldiers, big game hunters, and artists to the aged Spanish tippler in "A Clean, Well-Lighted Place."

In a style stripped to the bone and cunningly contrived to dramatize this attitude of tight-lipped suppression of feeling, ironic understatement and simple but subtle repetitions furnish the keynotes. Hemingway has reduced everything in his stories—description, narrative, exposition, characterization, dialogue—to the status of the simple predication. Subordinate clauses and modifications, the language of logic and intellectual sophistication, are seldom used, for Hemingway's aim is to record brusquely yet sensitively the behavior and speech of people who are, for the most part, either nonintellectual or anti-intellectual. Hence the tone and idiom of these characters, their vocabulary as well as their syntax, flavor the narrative portions no less than the dialogue of the story. Their speech is colloquial and gutsy, their dialogue, lean and bare; the things they talk about are few and commonplace and undeveloped. Yet these things are set forth in subtly varied rhythms, suggesting varied implications woven into the tone and texture of a casual remark, which heighten the mood or emotion and intensify the effect desired. As a result, in the best of Hemingway's stories powerful irony, pathos, terror, and despair are forcefully and dramatically conveyed with few overt hints from author or narrator. Thus, it is not surprising that many other short story writers promptly took to Hemingway's methods and tried to apply them, not too successfully, to their own purposes. Nor is it surprising that, given the limitations of his vision—"his glorification of the self and of personal intuition . . . the ultimate in the American dream of self-validating identity"[3]—an inevitable reassessment of his values has occurred, dimming considerably the heroic image he had created for himself by the 1940s.

The Harlem Renaissance

Concurrently with the rise of Hemingway's fame—which actually emanated from Paris—another significant cultural movement was vibrantly awakening in New York in the 1920s—the Harlem Renaissance. Involving music, poetry, and social criticism, as well as fiction, the Harlem Renaissance reflected an exhilarating revival of consciousness among black Americans of their own racial heritage and individual identities as members of a society still strongly attuned to the mores, ambitions, and prejudices of its dominant white members. Though the initial thrust of this movement had begun as early as the 1880s, its primary impetus came some twenty-odd years later from the intellectual conflict represented by the two powerful black leaders Booker T. Washington and W. E. B. DuBois; but its full impact within the nation at large would not be felt until the dramatic events of the civil rights movement in the 1960s and the consequent proliferation of "black studies" courses within many prestigious "white" universities. As long as Washington's conciliatory policy of black subserviency held sway, black writers and artists were disadvantaged; for, in order to be heard at all outside their own community, their performance, as in the case of Charles Chestnutt's stories, would have to be shaped to suit a white audience, emphasizing all the old stereotypes of blacks as humble suppliants at the whites' footstool. But with the acceptance of DuBois's doctrine of the Talented Tenth, the founding of the NAACP and its publicity organ, *The Crisis*, in 1910 opened the door for black intellectuals to express themselves vociferously so as to be heard and taken seriously, on their own terms, by the dominant white publishing houses. As one of their leading writers, Arna Bontemps, later recalled, in the 1920s "The Walls of Jericho were toppling . . . [but] We had never dreamed that it would happen so soon."

[3]Cleanth Brooks, R. P. Warren, and R. W. B. Lewis, *American Literature* (New York: St. Martin's, 1973), Vol. 2, p. 2268.

With an exuberance suggested in the familiar Biblical image, black writers in that decade and the next expressed their newly awakened sense of racial pride voluminously and in an impressive diversity of forms, poetic and fictional. Understandably, the bulk of their writing must be characterized as protest literature, since one of their chief aims, as shown in Claude McKay's poem "If We Must Die," was to present blacks in militant confrontation with whites. Yet much, indeed most of their fiction, its overtones of protest notwithstanding, embodied an effort to depict the facts of black life in America rather than simply to propagandize their political woes. And this effort, as evidenced in such minor classics as Jean Toomer's *Cane,* Louis Fisher's *The Walls of Jericho,* Arna Bontemps's *Black Thunder,* and Langston Hughes's *The Ways of White Folks,* revealed a wealth of diversified talents and techniques. In order to avoid the old nineteenth-century stereotypes of blacks as comics or pathetic buffoons, the tendency in these stories was to depict the new blacks as intensely emotional, romantic, pugnacious, even violent individuals, leading bizarre lives in exotic settings, rather than to focus on the more humdrum, realistic struggles of their everyday existence. But a similar charge, as we have seen, can also be made of Hemingway's typical heroes; like Hemingway, these black writers were also presenting Negro life as they saw it, not as they were expected to. Moreover, in dramatizing their protests against white society, they spoke in distinctively individual tones and voices: Fisher, satirically; Toomer, lyrically; McKay, stridently; and Hughes, perhaps the most influential as he was certainly the most prolific, ironically and whimsically. The black writers of the Harlem Renaissance thus prepared the way for black artists after them to achieve the recognition they have earned in the United States today.

Protest Voices in the Great Depression

During the Depression decade of the 1930s many more white and black writers added their voices to the swelling chorus of social protest, employing a variety of situations and methods in their concerted attacks against the evils of poverty and unemployment in both urban and rural settings. With shrill Marxist overtones, the short story accordingly became a vehicle for proletarian fiction as writers like Nelson Algren, James T. Farrell, John Dos Passos, Albert Halper, and others sought to dramatize the violence and degradation of metropolitan life; while Erskine Caldwell, John Steinbeck, and William Saroyan exploited in their fiction some of the shocking social conditions prevalent among rural poor whites and blacks in the South or migrant fruit pickers, Hispanics, and other ethnic groups in the Far West. Caldwell, a prolific writer, was perhaps more successful than others in this group because in depicting the bestiality, ignorance, cruelty, and perversion of backwoods Georgia "white trash" he managed, in a number of memorable stories such as "Big Buck," "Daughter," "Saturady Afternoon," and "Kneel to the Rising Sun," to make the outrageous behavior of these degenerates seem both horrifying and ludicrous at the same time. And yet, despite the powerful impact felt on a first reading, even the best of these stories—like those of Ambrose Bierce—quickly lose their original shock value and melodramatic appeal. With the passing of time and the mitigation of social conditions that inspired them (for example, the widespread lynching of blacks), their frankly propagandist element of social protest tends to overshadow their aesthetic merit. Much the same criticism can also be made of the several hundred stories in which Farrell recorded, almost like social case histories, the empty, sordid lives of ordinary Chicago individuals, though a more serious deficiency is evident in the sameness and imitativeness of their structure. Too often, echoes from the works of Hemingway, Anderson, and Dreiser resound in the stories of both writers.

Though less deserving of this charge, Steinbeck's and Saroyan's stories have likewise lost some of the luster they once possessed, for they too focus largely on characters and events that no longer seem quite so memorable or compelling as they once did. Still, since both wrote primarily about life in California, their native state, the settings and situations in their best stories can still impart an appealingly distinctive regional flavor of rugged mountains and lush valleys and of the folk whose heritage brought them there. Steinbeck, though much less prolific, was the more versatile artist of the two, not only with respect to his superior inventiveness in creating characters of some depth and credibility, but also in his evocation of mood and atmosphere through vividly realized settings, symbolic imagery, and suspenseful action. Moreover, though his stories focus primarily on the lives of ordinary working people—the Salinas Valley farm laborers, ranchers, and townsfolk among whom he grew up—they are less obviously proletarian than psychological dramas of human conflicts and frustrations involving husbands and wives, parents and children, employers and laborers. There is thus an enduring appeal in the love-hate family relationships worked out in such stories as "The Murder," "The White Quail," "The Chrysanthemums," "The Leader of the People," and others in Steinbeck's major collections, *The Long Valley* and *The Red Pony*. Saroyan's hundreds of loosely written stories and sketches, on the other hand, are often both quixotically charming and irritating at the same time. Since a vast majority are concerned with the author's own personal idiosyncrasies and/or the antics of his inexhaustible tribe of Armenian relatives, the law of diminishing returns tends to reduce their effectiveness. But among all the proletarian fiction of the 1930s, perhaps no more poignant treatment of the loneliness and suffering of the dispossessed, or of the solidarity of family love, can be found than in Saroyan's two most impressive collections, *The Daring Young Man on the Flying Trapeze* and *My Name Is Aram*. Together, Steinbeck and Saroyan did much to humanize the dry automata of proletarian fiction.

The Southern Renaissance

The last and in many ways the most impressive literary revival that sprang up in the 1920s was a phenomenon that came to be known eventually as the Southern Renaissance. Among the factors contributing to the distinctiveness of this movement were its relatively modest, unspectacular origins, its quiet but steady growth during the 1930s and 1940s despite the lack of any powerfully organized supportive group or program, its fundamentally critical and philosophical implications, its longevity—and by no means least, the astonishing variety of first-rate literary talents it inspired as well as the equally astonishing body of literature they produced. The beginnings of the Southern Renaissance can be traced to a small group of young poets and teachers who, under the leadership of John Crowe Ransom at Vanderbilt University in the mid-1920s, attempted to create out of the traditions of their southern past a new kind of poetry more relevant to twentieth-century conditions of life in the South, as they saw them, than the genteel sentimentalities of earlier southern writing. Calling themselves the Fugitives, the group sought to flee from worn out modes of expression, yet wished at the same time to celebrate and to adhere to those antebellum southern traditions that they felt to be durable and valid: love of the land, the natural beauty and peace of rural surroundings as opposed to the noise and bustle of crowded cities, the quality of strong ancestral ties and family relationships, the sense of belonging to a community of kindred souls, and so on.

Besides Ransom, the Fugitive group included Donald Davidson, Allen Tate, Andrew Lytle, Robert Penn Warren, and others, several of them destined to achieve national recognition in their separate careers as poets, critics, and fiction writers. In 1930, however, when the group issued a collection of essays entitled *I'll Take My Stand,* it was promptly derided outside the South as a reactionary agrarian manifesto intended to undermine the political and industrial foundations of America; overlooked in the hue and cry inspired by its social criticism was the fact that these young writers were once again raising the fundamental issue of what a viable literature is supposed to be and do. They were proclaiming a spiritual renewal of faith in the humanistic ideals of their region's past, invoking and reinterpreting that past as a means of interpreting the present creatively in poetry and fiction. In isolated pockets elsewhere other young southern writers such as Thomas Wolfe, T. S. Stribling, Caroline Gordon, Katherine Anne Porter, and William Faulkner were similarly inspired with much the same Proustian fervor, so that by the end of the 1930s a vigorous flowering of southern literature had come about. Far transcending the narrow regional limitations of its local color antecedents, it was a movement, moreover, still vibrantly flourishing as the works of still younger writers fed its growth in the decades beyond World War II.

Much of the fiction written by these leading twentieth-century southerners is both powerful and finely crafted, but beyond a doubt the most distinguished in both respects, particularly in the short story, is the work of William Faulkner and Katherine Anne Porter. Faulkner's preeminence in modern fiction, however, results not so much from his technical versatility as from the boldness of his creative imagination. Yoknapatawpha County, Mississippi—"Area, 2400 Square Miles: Population, Whites, 6298; Negroes, 9313: William Faulkner, Sole Owner & Proprietor"—is his own imagined world, a microcosm of individuals who lived fully in their own right, their lives elaborately documented with genealogical evidence, but who also serve, like stones in a mosaic, the purpose of a grand design. There is thus a symbolic value in this "legend of the South," which some critics have interpreted as a commentary on the contrast between an older way of life based on a code of traditional values and disciplines and a modern one in which those values and disciplines have been lost sight of, a commentary that might well be extended beyond the borders of the South and applied to the modern world as a whole. And there is in it likewise a deeply felt tragic theme, intricately bound up with the lives and relationships of these men and women, both whites and blacks: It is a theme of virtually Biblical proportions and significance involving the timeless myths of race conflict and of humanity's perennial struggle to fulfill its destiny on earth and to rid itself of ancestral guilt.

To embody his theme in dramatic human action Faulkner created whole families of individual characters—Sartorises, Sutpens, Compsons, McCaslins, Edmondses, MacCallums, Bundrens, Snopeses, Beauchamps—who are so completely delineated and so exhaustively explored from one story to another that the casual reader may often despair of mastering their complexities. The fact that characters in one story will reappear at different stages of their lives and under different guises in other stories, and that cryptic references are made in one story to situations and events lying outside the context of that story but clarified in others, necessarily leads to the mystification of readers who are not acquainted with the whole panorama of Faulkner's unfolding legend. A major obstacle of this sort, for example, is presented in "A Rose for Emily," which might be misread as a mere horror tale of the sort Bierce produced in "The Coup de Grâce"; for, unless readers carefully note the narrator's subtle reference to the passing of time—and especially to the community's changing attitude toward Emily over a long period—they may have some difficulty orienting themselves within the environment and period of the story. And they may very likely miss the depth and complexity of Faulkner's vision—the very meaning of the story—whereas those who are familiar with Faulkner's patterned world will recognize that Miss Emily's triumphant pride and independence are among the values that all his heroic figures share, including both blacks and whites like the runaway slave Tomey's Turl and his two remarkable owners, Uncle Buck and Uncle Buddy, in "was."

Many other obstacles are strewn in the reader's path because Faulkner, an incorrigible experimenter, developed numerous methods for conveying his narratives, as well as a style that is sometimes so heavily freighted with poetic imagery or psychological speculation that one cannot easily thread one's way through the seeming chaos of his syntax. And yet, for all the difficulties he raises, Faulkner is indeed an enchanting storyteller, who knows how to fascinate his readers with the implied promise of some breathless disclosure to come, and to keep them guessing what it will be. In some stories he accomplishes this purpose by the fairly conventional method of characters objectively presented within the framework of a tightly organized plot leading up to a shocking climax, as in "A Rose for Emily." In others he renders the narrative entirely in terms of the mental processes of the characters themselves, making such daring use of the stream-of-consciousness technique that even the disorganized impulses of idiots or imbeciles become organic parts of the story. And in still others he employs an episodic method that is unified by means of what has been called the "sense of a voice," a narrator who remembers and tells the story as it was told to him but who is not present in the story as a narrator in the formal sense. Like Henry James, Faulkner often demands a great deal from his readers, expects them to become as fully absorbed in the reading as Faulkner himself was in the writing of the story; and more often than not careful readers are amply rewarded for their pains.

Whatever the technique employed, the best of Faulkner's stories have the quality of being lived and remembered experiences that combine a feeling of mingled compassion, pride, love, and understanding of and for the people and the land he is a part of. For too long a time Faulkner was misunderstood and misrepresented as a kind of literary psychopath, diabolically serving forth a witches' brew compounded of nightmare horrors, sexual abnormalities, violence, bloodshed, and mental derangement. The horror in Faulkner—psychological horror—is certainly there, as it is in the work of Poe, Hawthorne, Melville, and James; but it is balanced by a species of rich, earthy humor, which became more and more mellow in Faulkner's later stories. No one can read attentively all the episodes in *The Hamlet* or *Go Down, Moses* and fail to catch this strain in his writing. The humor of "was" is of the essence of Mark Twain and the frontier tradition in American literature, just as the horror of violence and decadence in "A Rose for Emily" is of the essence of Poe. The one deserves as much emphasis as the other, for the right key to an understanding of Faulkner must be sought in two of his favorite words—"doom" and "endure." Echoing throughout his stories and reemphasized in his Nobel Prize speech, as well as in numerous utterances made during his tenure as artist in residence at the University of Virginia, they symbolize his deeply tragic, ambivalent view of humanity and help to explain why his works are so powerful.

The tragic view is also abundantly evident in the stories of Katherine Anne Porter, but its presentation there is so distinctively different that no one would ever confuse her style with Faulkner's, even though their themes and methods are sometimes similar. Whereas Faulkner's expansive prose often appears to sprawl, Porter's almost invariably suggests restraint, subtle control, and impeccable selectivity. An uncompromising perfectionist, she belongs among that small group of serious writers who will release nothing for publication that they feel has not satisfied the highest standards of art. Her work accordingly gives the impression of having been shaped with extraordinary patience and attention to minute detail, scene by scene and incident by incident painstakingly enriched until all the parts have been cunningly and precisely fitted together and every phrase has been made to yield the utmost in poetic suggestiveness. Because such great devotion to the principles of craftsmanship exacts a high price in the limitation of one's output (Porter has said that her first published story, "María Concepción," was "rewritten fifteen or sixteen times" before she was satisfied with it), she produced scarcely more than half a dozen volumes and a scattering of occasional pieces in a career of more than forty years. And she had to wait until the 1960s to achieve the widespread acclaim—ironically on the basis of an inferior work, *The Ship of Fools*—that her consummate artistry had deserved many years before.

The nearly flawless quality of Porter's best stories springs from a balanced combination of several elements, chiefly characterizations, settings, point-of-view, and symbolic imagery, which are so carefully interrelated that no one is overemphasized at the expense of others. In the title story of her first collection, "Flowering Judas," for example, although the basic theme of betrayal and the conflict between the two principals involved in it are quite explicitly rendered, the full meaning of their relationship is enriched by a wealth of subtly suggestive ironies and overtones clothed in religious symbolism; so that both the characterizations of Laura and Braggioni, as well as the implications of their involvement in the Mexican revolution and the flavor of the very atmosphere they breathe, are all conveyed in a uniformly moving drama. The artistry supporting this story, which many critics uphold as one of the supreme examples of modern short fiction, is also apparent in its structure, wherein the external events of a single day are imperceptibly woven into the fabric of remembered background experiences focused in the mind of a single character. Repeatedly Porter employed this method of telescoping past and present, linking together the inner and outer reality through a modified stream-of-consciousness technique, as in "The Jilting of Granny Weatherall" and numerous other semi-autobiographical stories dealing with successive stages in the life of Miranda, their central character. It is in these, "Pale Horse, Pale Rider," "Old Mortality," "The Grave," and several others that one finds the richest expression of her feeling for family and tradition in the South.

The fiction written by William Faulkner and Katherine Anne Porter brought to a fitting climax one phase of the twentieth-century literary renaissance in both the South and the nation. As America prepared to enter another world conflict, its leading writers and their younger contemporaries faced a new, uncertain future.

William Sydney Porter (O. Henry)

1862 – 1910

William Sydney Porter, better known as O. Henry, was born in Greensboro, North Carolina, in 1862. Virtually orphaned at three, he was reared and educated by a maiden aunt who encouraged his bent toward literature and drawing. At fifteen, he began working as an apprentice in his uncle's drug store and became a licensed pharmacist in 1881. The following year he went to Texas, where he remained for fourteen years, drifting through a variety of experiences in both the cattle country and the booming towns of Austin, Houston, and San Antonio. After his marriage in 1886 he held a number of jobs—draftsman, bank teller, newspaper columnist—but in 1894 he began publishing sketches and tales in his own comic weekly, *The Rolling Stone,* and later in his column for the *Houston Daily Post.*

Indicted for the embezzlement of bank funds, Porter fled to Central America in 1896. The next year he was tried and sentenced to imprisonment in the federal penitentiary at Columbus, Ohio. During his term there his fabulous career as O. Henry, the unknown author of popular magazine fiction, began. Upon his release from prison in 1901 he went to New York City and soon became the most famous short story writer of his day. Writing with amazing speed, he produced about 250 stories for the New York *Sunday World* and other magazines between 1902 and his death in 1910. All but a handful of these appeared in collections bearing such familiar titles as *Cabbages and Kings* (1904), *The Four Million* (1906), *The Trimmed Lamp* (1907), *The Voice of the City* (1908), and *Roads of Destiny* (1909). Most of them have been translated into many languages and reprinted in hundreds of editions.

Writing frankly to make money, O. Henry shaped his stories to meet the ephemeral demands of mass-circulation periodicals, his purpose being, as he put it, to please "Mr. Everybody." But the enormous popularity of his method has been due to something more than its mere formula, which substituted technical tricks for the more demanding task of revealing character in conflict and action. In this sense, O. Henry's work marks the culmination of the story-of-effect tradition begun by Poe and refined by many other writers, notably De Maupassant. Sleight-of-hand plot jugglery; a crackling style with a punch in nearly every line; humor and wit combined with sentimentality; a racing, breathless narrative tempo; and, of course, the surprising reversal or twist at the climax—all such devices, used to the fullest by O. Henry, are plainly visible in a typical story such as "The Caballero's Way," the most melodramatic of his many stories about the Southwest. Its hero—the unflappable Cisco Kid—is another of his many contributions to the legendary figures of contemporary American television and motion pictures. However impalpable his plots or transparent his formulae, there is a pervasive quality in O. Henry's best stories that stamps him as an original, a minor classic whom the literate masses of the world have taken to heart and refuse to outgrow.

The Caballero's Way

The Cisco Kid had killed six men in more or less fair scrimmages, had murdered twice as many (mostly Mexicans), and had winged a larger number whom he modestly forbore to count. Therefore a woman loved him.

The Kid was twenty-five, looked twenty; and a careful insurance company would have estimated the probable time of his demise at, say, twenty-six. His habitat was anywhere between the Frio and the Rio Grande. He killed for the love of it—because he was quick-tempered—to avoid arrest—for his own amusement—any reason that came to his mind

O. Henry, "The Caballero's Way," *Heart of the West.* NY: Doubleday, Page & Company, 1904.

would suffice. He had escaped capture because he could shoot five-sixths of a second sooner than any sheriff or ranger in the service, and because he rode a speckled roan horse that knew every cow-path in the mesquite and pear thickets from San Antonio to Matamoras.

Tonia Perez, the girl who loved the Cisco Kid, was half Carmen, half Madonna, and the rest—oh, yes, a woman who is half Carmen and half Madonna can always be something more—the rest, let us say, was humming-bird. She lived in a grass-roofed *jacal* near a little Mexican settlement at the Lone Wolf Crossing of the Frio. With her lived a father or grandfather, a lineal Aztec, somewhat less than a thousand years old, who herded a hundred goats and lived in a continuous drunken dream from drinking *mescal.* Back of the *jacal* a tremendous forest of bristling pear, twenty feet high at its worst, crowded almost to its door. It was along the bewildering maze of this spinous thicket that the speckled roan would bring the Kid to see his girl. And once, clinging like a lizard to the ridge-pole, high up under the peaked grass roof, he had heard Tonia, with her Madonna face and Carmen beauty and humming-bird soul, parley with the sheriff's posse, denying knowledge of her man in her soft *mélange* of Spanish and English.

One day the adjutant-general of the State, who is, *ex officio,* commander of the ranger forces, wrote some sarcastic lines to Captain Duval of Company X, stationed at Laredo, relative to the serene and undisturbed existence led by murderers and desperadoes in the said captain's territory.

The captain turned the colour of brick dust under his tan, and forwarded the letter, after adding a few comments, per ranger Private Bill Adamson, to ranger Lieutenant Sandridge, camped at a water hole on the Nueces with a squad of five men in preservation of law and order.

Lieutenant Sandridge turned a beautiful *couleur de rose* through his ordinary strawberry complexion, tucked the letter in his hip pocket, and chewed off the ends of his gamboge moustache.

The next morning he saddled his horse and rode alone to the Mexican settlement at the Lone Wolf Crossing of the Frio, twenty miles away.

Six feet two, blond as a Viking, quiet as a deacon, dangerous as a machine gun, Sandridge moved among the *Jacales,* patiently seeking news of the Cisco Kid.

Far more than the law, the Mexicans dreaded the cold and certain vengeance of the lone rider that the ranger sought. It had been one of the Kid's pastimes to shoot Mexicans "to see them kick": if he demanded from them moribund Terpsichorean feats, simply that he might be entertained, what terrible and extreme penalties would be certain to follow should they anger him! One and all they lounged with upturned palms and shrugging shoulders, filling the air with *"quien sabes"* and denials of the Kid's acquaintance.

But there was a man named Fink who kept a store at the Crossing—a man of many nationalities, tongues, interests, and ways of thinking.

"No use to ask them Mexicans," he said to Sandridge. "They're afraid to tell. This *hombre* they call the Kid—Goodall is his name, ain't it?—he's been in my store once or twice. I have an idea you might run across him at—but I guess I don't keer to say, myself. I'm two seconds later in pulling a gun than I used to be, and the difference is worth thinking about. But this Kid's got a half-Mexican girl at the Crossing that he comes to see. She lives in that *jacal* a hundred yards down the arroyo at the edge of the pear. Maybe she—no, I don't suppose she would, but that *jacal* would be a good place to watch, anyway."

Sandridge rode down to the *jacal* of Perez. The sun was low, and the broad shade of the great pear thicket already covered the grass-thatched hut. The goats were enclosed for the night in a brush corral near by. A few kids walked the top of it, nibbling the chaparral leaves. The old Mexican lay upon a blanket on the grass, already in a stupor from his mescal, and dreaming, perhaps, of the nights when he and Pizarro touched glasses to their New World fortunes—so old his wrinkled face seemed to proclaim him to be. And in the door of the *jacal* stood Tonia. And Lieutenant Sandridge sat in his saddle staring at her like a gannet agape at a sailorman.

The Cisco Kid was a vain person, as all eminent and successful assassins are, and his bosom would have been ruffled had he known that at a simple exchange of glances two persons, in whose minds he had been looming large, suddenly abandoned (at least for the time) all thought of him.

Never before had Tonia seen such a man as this. He seemed to be made of sunshine and blood-red tissue and clear weather. He seemed to illuminate the shadow of the pear when he smiled, as though the sun were rising again. The men she had known had been small and dark. Even the Kid, in spite of his achievements, was a stripling no larger than herself, with black, straight hair and a cold, marble face that chilled the noonday.

As for Tonia, though she sends description to the poorhouse, let her make a millionaire of your fancy. Her blue-black hair, smoothly divided in the middle and bound close to her head, and her large eyes full of the Latin melancholy, gave her the Madonna touch. Her motions and air spoke of the concealed fire and the desire to charm that she had inherited from the *gitanas* of the Basque province. As for the humming-bird part of her, that dwelt in her heart; you could not perceive it unless her bright red skirt and dark blue blouse gave you a symbolic hint of the vagarious bird.

The newly lighted sun-god asked for a drink of water. Tonia brought it from the red jar hanging under the brush shelter. Sandridge considered it necessary to dismount so as to lessen the trouble of her ministrations.

I play no spy; nor do I assume to master the thoughts of any human heart; but I assert, by the chronicler's right, that before a quarter of an hour had sped, Sandridge was teaching her how to plait a six-strand rawhide stake-rope, and Tonia had explained to him that were it not for her little English book that the peripatetic *padre* had given her and the little crippled *chivo,* that she fed from a bottle, she would be very, very lonely indeed.

Which leads to a suspicion that the Kid's fences needed repairing, and that the adjutant-general's sarcasm had fallen upon unproductive soil.

In his camp by the water hole Lieutenant Sandridge announced and reiterated his intention of either causing the Cisco Kid to nibble the black loam of the Frio country prairies or of haling him before a judge and jury. That sounded business-like. Twice a week he rode over to the Lone Wolf Crossing of the Frio, and directed Tonia's slim, slightly lemon-tinted fingers among the intricacies of the slowly growing lariata. A six-strand plait is hard to learn and easy to teach.

The ranger knew that he might find the Kid there at any visit. He kept his armament ready, and had a frequent eye for the pear thicket at the rear of the *jacal.* Thus he might bring down the kite and the humming-bird with one stone.

While the sunny-haired ornithologist was pursuing his studies the Cisco Kid was also attending to his professional duties. He moodily shot up a saloon in a small cow village on Quintana Creek, killed the town marshal (plugging him neatly in the centre of his tin badge), and then rode away, morose and unsatisfied. No true artist is uplifted by shooting an aged man carrying an old-style .38 bulldog.

On his way the Kid suddenly experienced the yearning that all men feel when wrong-doing loses its keen edge of delight. He yearned for the woman he loved to reassure him that she was his in spite of it. He wanted her to call his bloodthirstiness bravery and his cruelty devotion. He wanted Tonia to bring him water from the red jar under the brush shelter, and tell him how the *chivo* was thriving on the bottle.

The Kid turned the speckled roan's head up the ten-mile pear flat that stretches along the Arroyo Hondo until it ends at the Lone Wolf Crossing of the Frio. The roan whickered; for he had a sense of locality and direction equal to that of a belt-line street-car horse; and he knew he would soon be nibbling the rich mesquite grass at the end of a forty-foot stake-rope while Ulysses rested his head in Circe's straw-roofed hut.

More weird and lonesome than the journey of an Amazonian explorer is the ride of one through a Texas pear flat. With dismal monotony and startling variety the uncanny and multiform shapes of the cacti lift their twisted trunks, and fat, bristly hands to encumber the way. The demon plant, appearing to live without soil or rain, seems to taunt the parched traveller with its lush grey greenness. It warps itself a thousand times about what look to be open and inviting paths, only to lure the rider into blind and impassable spind-defended "bottoms of the bag," leaving him to retreat, if he can, with the points of the compass whirling in his head.

To be lost in the pear is to die almost the death of the thief on the cross, pierced by nails and with grotesque shapes of all the fiends hovering about.

But it was not so with the Kid and his mount. Winding, twisting, circling, tracing the most fantastic and bewildering trail ever picked out, the good roan lessened the distance to the Lone Wolf Crossing with every coil and turn that he made.

While they fared the Kid sang. He knew but one tune and sang it, as he knew but one code and lived it, and but one girl and loved her. He was a single-minded man of conventional ideas. He had a voice like a coyote with bronchitis, but whenever he chose to sing his song he sang it. It was a conventional song of the camps and trail, running at its beginning as near as may be to these words:

Don't you monkey with my Lulu girl
Or I'll tell you what I'll do—

and so on. The roan was inured to it, and did not mind.

But even the poorest singer will, after a certain time, gain his own consent to refrain from contributing to the world's noises. So the Kid, by the time he was within a mile or two of Tonia's *jacal,* had reluctantly allowed his song to die away—not because his vocal performance had become less charming to his own ears, but because his laryngeal muscles were aweary.

As though he were in a circus ring the speckled roan wheeled and danced through the labyrinth of pear until at length his rider knew by certain landmarks that the Lone Wolf Crossing was close at hand. Then, where the pear was thinner, he caught sight of the grass roof of the *jacal* and the hackberry tree on the edge of the arroyo. A few yards farther the Kid stopped the roan and gazed intently through the prickly openings. Then he dismounted, dropped the roan's reins, and proceeded on foot, stooping and silent, like an Indian. The roan, knowing his part, stood still, making no sound.

The Kid crept noiselessly to the very edge of the pear thicket and reconnoitered between the leaves of a clump of cactus.

Ten yards from his hiding-place, in the shade of the *jacal,* sat his Tonia calmly plaiting a rawhide lariat. So far she might surely escape condemnation; women have been known, from time to time, to engage in more mischievous occupations. But if all must be told, there is to be added that her head reposed against the broad and comfortable chest of a tall red-and-yellow man, and that his arm was about her, guiding her nimble small fingers that required so many lessons at the intricate six-strand plait.

Sandridge glanced quickly at the dark mass of pear when he heard a slight squeaking sound that was not altogether unfamiliar. A gun-scabbard will make that sound when one grasps the handle of a six-shooter suddenly. But the sound was not repeated; and Tonia's fingers needed close attention.

And then, in the shadow of death, they began to talk of their love; and in the still July afternoon every word they uttered reached the ears of the Kid.

"Remember, then," said Tonia, "you must not come again until I send for you. Soon he will be here. A *vaquero* at the *tienda* said to-day he saw him on the Guadalupe three days ago. When he is that near he always comes. If he comes and finds you here he will kill you. So, for my sake, you must come no more until I send you the word."

"All right," said the ranger. "And then what?"

"And then," said the girl, "you must bring your men here and kill him. If not, he will kill you."

"He ain't a man to surrender, that's sure," said Sandridge. "It's kill or be killed for the officer that goes up against Mr. Cisco Kid."

"He must die," said the girl. "Otherwise there will not be any peace in the world for thee and me. He has killed many. Let him so die. Bring your men, and give him no chance to escape."

"You used to think right much of him," said Sandridge.

Tonia dropped the lariat, twisted herself around, and curved a lemon-tinted arm over the ranger's shoulder.

"But then," she murmured in liquid Spanish, "I had not beheld thee, thou great, red mountain of a man! And thou art kind and good, as well as strong. Could one choose him, knowing thee? Let him die; for then I will not be filled with fear by day and night lest he hurt thee or me."

"How can I know when he comes?" asked Sandridge.

"When he comes," said Tonia, "he remains two days, sometimes three. Gregorio, the small son of old Luisa, the *lavandera*, has a swift pony. I will write a letter to thee and send it by him, saying how it will be best to come upon him. By Gregorio will the letter come. And bring many men with thee, and have much care, oh, dear red one, for the rattlesnake is not quicker to strike than is *'El Chivato,'* as they call him, to send a ball from his *pistola*."

"The Kid's handy with his gun, sure enough," admitted Sandridge, "but when I come for him I shall come alone. I'll get him by myself or not at all. The Cap wrote one or two things to me that make me want to do the trick without any help. You let me know when Mr. Kid arrives, and I'll do the rest."

"I will send you the message by the boy Gregorio," said the girl. "I knew you were braver than that small slayer of men who never smiles. How could I ever have thought I cared for him?"

It was time for the ranger to ride back to his camp on the water hole. Before he mounted his horse he raised the slight form of Tonia with one arm high from the earth for a parting salute. The drowsy stillness of the torpid summer air still lay thick upon the dreaming afternoon. The smoke from the fire in the *jacal,* where the *frijoles* blubbered in the iron pot, rose straight as a plumb-line above the clay-daubed chimney. No sound or movement disturbed the serenity of the dense pear thicket ten yards away.

When the form of Sandridge had disappeared, loping his big dun down the steep banks of the Frio crossing, the Kid crept back to his own horse, mounted him, and rode back along the tortuous trail he had come.

But not far. He stopped and waited in the silent depths of the pear until half an hour had passed. And then Tonia heard the high, untrue notes of his unmusical singing coming nearer and nearer; and she ran to the edge of the pear to meet him.

The Kid seldom smiled; but he smiled and waved his hat when he saw her. He dismounted, and his girl sprang into his arms. The Kid looked at her fondly. His thick, black hair clung to his head like a wrinkled mat. The meeting brought a slight ripple of some undercurrent of feeling to his smooth, dark face that was usually as motionless as a clay mask.

"How's my girl?" he asked, holding her close.

"Sick of waiting so long for you, dear one," she answered. "My eyes are dim with always gazing into that devil's pincushion through which you come. And I can see into it such a little way, too. But you are here, beloved one, and I will not scold. *Que mal muchacho!* not to come to see your *alma* more often. Go in and rest, and let me water your horse and stake him with the long rope. There is cool water in the jar for you."

The Kid kissed her affectionately.

"Not if the court knows itself do I let a lady stake my horse for me," said he. "But if you'll run in, *chica,* and throw a pot of coffee together while I attend to the *caballo,* I'll be a good deal obliged."

Besides his marksmanship the Kid had another attribute for which he admired himself greatly. He was *muy caballero,* as the Mexicans express it, where the ladies were concerned. For them he had always gentle words and consideration. He could not have spoken a harsh word to a woman. He might ruthlessly slay their husbands and brothers, but he could not have laid the weight of a finger in anger upon a woman. Wherefore many of that interesting division of humanity who had come under the spell of his politeness declared their disbelief in the stories circulated about Mr. Kid. One shouldn't believe everything one heard, they said. When confronted by their indignant men folk with proof of the *caballero's* deeds of infamy, they said maybe he had been driven to it, and that he knew how to treat a lady, anyhow.

Considering this extremely courteous idiosyncrasy of the Kid and the pride that he took in it, one can perceive that the solution of the problem that was presented to him by what he saw and heard from his hiding-place in the pear that afternoon (at least as to one of the actors) must have been obscured by difficulties. And yet one could not think of the Kid overlooking little matters of that kind.

At the end of the short twilight they gathered around a supper of *frijoles*, goat steaks, canned peaches, and coffee, by the light of a lantern in the *jacal*. Afterward, the ancestor, his flock corralled, smoked a cigarette and became a mummy in a grey blanket. Tonia washed the few dishes while the Kid dried them with the flour-sacking towel. Her eyes shone; she chatted volubly of the inconsequent happenings of her small world since the Kid's last visit; it was as all his other home-comings had been.

Then outside Tonia swung in a grass hammock with her guitar and sang sad *canciones de amor.*

"Do you love me just the same, old girl?" asked the Kid, hunting for his cigarette papers.

"Always the same, little one," said Tonia, her dark eyes lingering upon him.

"I must go over to Fink's," said the Kid, rising, "for some tobacco. I thought I had another sack in my coat. I'll be back in a quarter of an hour."

"Hasten," said Tonia, "and tell me—how long shall I call you my own this time? Will you be gone again to-morrow, leaving me to grieve, or will you be longer with your Tonia?"

"Oh, I might stay two or three days this trip," said the Kid, yawning. "I've been on the dodge for a month, and I'd like to rest up."

He was gone half an hour for his tobacco. When he returned Tonia was still lying in the hammock.

"It's funny," said the Kid, "how I feel. I feel like there was somebody lying behind every bush and tree waiting to shoot me. I never had mullygrubs like them before. Maybe it's one of them presumptions. I've got half a notion to light out in the morning before day. The Guadalupe country is burning up about that old Dutchman I plugged down there."

"You are not afraid—no one could make my brave little one fear."

"Well, I haven't been usually regarded as a jackrabbit when it comes to scrapping; but I don't want a posse smoking me out when I'm in your *jacal*. Somebody might get hurt that oughtn't to."

"Remain with your Tonia; no one will find you here."

The Kid looked keenly into the shadows up and down the arroyo and toward the dim lights of the Mexican village.

"I'll see how it looks later on," was his decision.

At midnight a horseman rode into the rangers' camp, blazing his way by noisy "halloes" to indicate a pacific mission. Sandridge and one or two others turned out to investigate the row. The rider announced himself to be Domingo Sales, from the Lone Wolf Crossing. He bore a letter for Señor Sandridge. Old Luisa, the *lavandera,* had persuaded him to bring it, he said, her son Gregorio being too ill of a fever to ride.

Sandridge lighted the camp lantern and read the letter. These were its words:

> *Dear One:* He has come. Hardly had you ridden away when he came out of the pear. When he first talked he said he would stay three days or more. Then as it grew later he was like a wolf or a fox, and walked about without rest, looking and listening. Soon he said he must leave before daylight when it is dark and stillest. And then he seemed to suspect that I be not true to him. He looked at me so strange that I am frightened. I swear to him that I love him, his own Tonia. Last of all he said I must prove to him I am true. He thinks that even now men are waiting to kill him as he rides from my house. To escape he says he will dress in my clothes, my red skirt and the blue waist I wear and the brown mantilla over the head, and thus ride away. But before that he says that I must put on his clothes, his *pantalones* and *camisa* and hat, and ride away on his horse from the *jacal* as far as the big road beyond the crossing and back again. This before he goes, so he can tell if I am true and if men are hidden to shoot him. It is a terrible thing. An hour before daybreak this is to be. Come, my dear one, and kill this man and take me for your Tonia. Do not try to take hold of him alive, but kill him quickly. Knowing all, you should do that. You must come long before the time and hide yourself in the little shed near the *jacal* where the wagon and saddles are kept. It is dark in there. He will wear my red skirt and blue waist and brown mantilla. I send you a hundred kisses. Come surely and shoot quickly and straight.
>
> THINE OWN TONIA.

Sandridge quickly explained to his men the official part of the missive. The rangers protested against his going alone.

"I'll get him easy enough," said the lieutenant. "The girl's got him trapped. And don't even think he'll get the drop on me."

Sandridge saddled his horse and rode to the Lone Wolf Crossing. He tied his big dun in a clump of brush on the arroyo, took his Winchester from its scabbard, and carefully approached the Perez *jacal.* There was only the half of a high moon drifted over by ragged, milk-white gulf clouds.

The wagon-shed was an excellent place for ambush; and the ranger got inside it safely. In the black shadow of the brush shelter in front of the *jacal* he could see a horse tied and hear hiim impatiently pawing the hard-trodden earth.

He waited almost an hour before two figures came out of the *jacal.* One, in man's clothes, quickly mounted the horse and galloped past the wagon-shed toward the crossing and village. And then the other figure, in skirt, waist, and mantilla over its head, stepped out into the faint moonlight, gazing after the rider. Sandridge thought he would take his chance then before Tonia rode back. He fancied she might not care to see it.

"Throw up your hands," he ordered loudly, stepping out of the wagon-shed with his Winchester at his shoulder.

There was a quick turn of the figure, but no movement to obey, so the ranger pumped in the bullets—one—two—three—and then twice more; for you never could be too sure of bringing down the Cisco Kid. There was no danger of missing at ten paces, even in that half moonlight.

The old ancestor, asleep on his blanket, was awakened by the shots. Listening further, he heard a great cry from some man in mortal distress or anguish, and rose up grumbling at the disturbing ways of moderns.

The tall, red ghost of a man burst into the *jacal,* reaching one hand, shaking like a *tule* reed, for the lantern hanging on its nail. The other spread a letter on the table.

"Look at this letter, Perez," cried the man. "Who wrote it?"

"Ah, Dios! it is Señor Sandridge," mumbled the old man, approaching. "*Pues, señor,* that letter was written by *'El Chivato,'* as he is called—by the man of Tonia. They say he is a bad man; I do not know. While Tonia slept he wrote the letter and sent it by this old hand of mine to Domingo Sales to be brought to you. Is there anything wrong in the letter? I am very old; and I did not know. *Valgame Dios!* it is a very foolish world; and there is nothing in the house to drink—nothing to drink."

Just then all that Sandridge could think of to do was to go outside and throw himself face downward in the dust by the side of his humming-bird, of whom not a feather fluttered. He was not a *caballero* by instinct, and he could not understand the niceties of revenge.

A mile away the rider who had ridden past the wagon-shed struck up a harsh, untuneful song, the words of which began:

Don't you monkey with my Lulu girl
Or I'll tell you what I'll do—

Edith Wharton

1862 – 1937

Edith Wharton's literary reputation has suffered somewhat because she has been widely regarded as a disciple of Henry James rather than an original writer entitled to high artistic rank in her own right. James did exert a profound influence on her writing, but less as a model to be imitated in shaping specific fictional methods and themes than as a guiding spirit encouraging her to set a high standard in her work and to write about phases of life she knew well. In the critical reassessment of her achievement which is underway now, she is emerging as a writer who not only had a vision and artistic craft of her own, but as one who also deserves recognition as an important social historian, having left in her fiction a dramatic record of the sweeping social changes that occurred during her era.

Born in New York City in 1862, the third and youngest child of George and Lucretia Jones, Wharton enjoyed from childhood the advantage of belonging to an established, wealthy family. She was educated by private tutors and by periodic travel and residence in Europe. She developed early a passion for literary expression and published at her own expense a collection of juvenile verse in 1875, when she was only 13 years of age. Ten years later she began publishing poems in *Scribner's* but soon turned to prose fiction and published in 1899 her first collection of stories, *The Greater Inclination.* In the meantime, in 1885 she had married Edward Wharton whose unstable health motivated the couple to settle in Paris in 1905. When her marriage ended in divorce in 1913, she continued to reside in France, dividing her residence between a villa located in the outskirts of Paris and another in southern France. She died in 1937. During her long career, she published at intervals up to the last year of her life ten other collections of stories as well as sixteen novels. Among the honors her fiction earned her were a Pulitzer Prize in 1920, an Honorary Doctor of Letters degree from Yale University in 1923, and election to the Academy of Arts and Letters in 1930. Despite the fact that her literary position depends more on her best novels such as *The House of Mirth* (1905), *The Custom of the Country* (1913), and *The Age of Innocence* (1920) than on her stories, she made a significant contribution to the short story.

"The Other Two," one of the earliest short stories among the nearly eighty Wharton published, has been justifiably pronounced "the most nearly perfect story" she ever produced. It is very carefully constructed, leading up to a surprise ending that Poe or O. Henry might well have admired. But its primary effect arises from character depiction in a dramatically unfolding situation (which James also admired) rather than from the final snapper.

The Other Two

I

Waythorn, on the drawing-room hearth, waited for his wife to come down to dinner.

It was their first night under his own roof, and he was surprised at his thrill of boyish agitation. He was not so old, to be sure—his glass gave him little more than the five-and-thirty years to which his wife confessed—but he had fancied himself already in the temperate zone; yet here he was listening for her step with a tender sense of all it symbolised, with some old trail of verse about the garlanded nuptial door-posts floating through his enjoyment of the pleasant room and the good dinner just beyond it.

They had been hastily recalled from their honeymoon by the illness of Lily Haskett, the child of Mrs. Waythorn's first marriage. The little

Edith Wharton, *The Descent of Man and Other Stories.* New York: Charles Scribner's Sons, 1904.

girl, at Waythorn's desire, had been transferred to his house on the day of her mother's wedding, and the doctor, on their arrival, broke the news that she was ill with typhoid, but declared that all the symptoms were favourable. Lily could show twelve years of unblemished health, and the case promised to be a light one. The nurse spoke as reassuringly, and after a moment of alarm Mrs. Waythorn had adjusted herself to the situation. She was very fond of Lily—her affection for the child had perhaps been her decisive charm in Waythorn's eyes—but she had the perfectly balanced nerves which her little girl had inherited, and no woman ever wasted less tissue in unproductive worry. Waythorn was therefore quite prepared to see her come in presently, a little late because of a last look at Lily, but as serene and well-appointed as if her good-night kiss had been laid on the brow of health. Her composure was restful to him; it acted as ballast to his somewhat unstable sensibilities. As he pictured her bending over the child's bed he thought how soothing her presence must be in illness: her very step would prognosticate recovery.

His own life had been a gray one, from temperament rather than circumstance, and he had been drawn to her by the unperturbed gaiety which kept her fresh and elastic at an age when most women's activities are growing either slack or febrile. He knew what was said about her; for, popular as she was, there had always been a faint undercurrent of detraction. When she had appeared in New York, nine or ten years earlier, as the pretty Mrs. Haskett whom Gus Varick had unearthed somewhere—was it in Pittsburg or Utica?—society, while promptly accepting her, had reserved the right to cast a doubt on its own indiscrimination. Enquiry, however, established her undoubted connection with a socially reigning family, and explained her recent divorce as the natural result of a runaway match at seventeen; and as nothing was known of Mr. Haskett it was easy to believe the worst of him.

Alice Haskett's remarriage with Gus Varick was a passport to the set whose recognition she coveted, and for a few years the Varicks were the most popular couple in town. Unfortunately the alliance was brief and stormy, and this time the husband had his champions. Still, even Varick's stanchest supporters admitted that he was not meant for matrimony, and Mrs. Varick's grievances were of a nature to bear the inspection of the New York courts. A New York divorce is in itself a diploma of virtue, and in the semi-widowhood of this second separation Mrs. Varick took on an air of sanctity, and was allowed to confide her wrongs to some of the most scrupulous ears in town. But when it was known that she was to marry Waythorn there was a momentary reaction. Her best friends would have preferred to see her remain in the rôle of the injured wife, which was as becoming to her as crape to a rosy complexion. True, a decent time had elapsed, and it was not even suggested that Waythorn had supplanted his predecessor. People shook their heads over him, however, and one grudging friend, to whom he affirmed that he took the step with his eyes open, replied oracularly: "Yes—and with your ears shut."

Waythorn could afford to smile at these innuendoes. In the Wall Street phrase, he had "discounted" them. He knew that society has not yet adapted itself to the consequences of divorce, and that till the adaptation takes place every woman who uses the freedom the law accords her must be her own social justification. Waythorn had an amused confidence in his wife's ability to justify herself. His expectations were fulfilled, and before the wedding took place Alice Varick's group had rallied openly to her support. She took it all imperturbably: she had a way of surmounting obstacles without seeming to be aware of them, and Waythorn looked back with wonder at the trivialities over which he had worn his nerves thin. He had the sense of having found refuge in a richer, warmer nature than his own, and his satisfaction, at the moment, was humourously summed up in the thought that his wife, when she had done all she could for Lily, would not be ashamed to come down and enjoy a good dinner.

The anticipation of such enjoyment was not, however, the sentiment expressed by Mrs. Waythorn's charming face when she presently joined him. Though she had put on her most engaging teagown she had neglected to assume the smile that went with it, and Waythorn thought he had never seen her look so nearly worried.

"What is it?" he asked. "Is anything wrong with Lily?"

"No; I've just been in and she's still sleeping." Mrs. Waythorn hesitated. "But something tiresome has happened."

He had taken her two hands, and now perceived that he was crushing a paper between them.

"This letter?"

"Yes—Mr. Haskett has written—I mean his lawyer has written."

Waythorn felt himself flush uncomfortably. He dropped his wife's hands.

"What about?"

"About seeing Lily. You know the courts—"

"Yes, yes," he interrupted nervously.

Nothing was known about Haskett in New York. He was vaguely supposed to have remained in the outer darkness from which his wife had been rescued, and Waythorn was one of the few who were aware that he had given up his business in Utica and followed her to New York in order to be near his little girl. In the days of his wooing, Waythorn had often met Lily on the doorstep, rosy and smiling, on her way "to see papa."

"I am so sorry," Mrs. Waythorn murmured.

He roused himself. "What does he want?"

"He wants to see her. You know she goes to him once a week."

"Well—he doesn't expect her to go to him now, does he?"

"No—he has heard of her illness; but he expects to come here."

"*Here?*"

Mrs. Waythorn reddened under his gaze. They looked away from each other.

"I'm afraid he has the right. . . . You'll see. . . . " She made a proffer of the letter.

Waythorn moved away with a gesture of refusal. He stood staring about the softly lighted room, which a moment before had seemed so full of bridal intimacy.

"I'm so sorry," she repeated. "If Lily could have been moved—"

"That's out of the question," he returned impatiently.

"I suppose so."

Her lip was beginning to tremble, and he felt himself a brute.

"He must come, of course," he said. "When is—his day?"

"I'm afraid—to-morrow."

"Very well. Send a note in the morning."

The butler entered to announce dinner.

Waythorn turned to his wife. "Come—you must be tired. It's beastly, but try to forget about it," he said, drawing her hand through his arm.

"You're so good, dear. I'll try," she whispered back.

Her face cleared at once, and as she looked at him across the flowers, between the rosy candle-shades, he saw her lips waver back into a smile.

"How pretty everything is!" she sighed luxuriously.

He turned to the butler. "The champagne at once, please. Mrs. Waythorn is tired."

In a moment or two their eyes met above the sparkling glasses. Her own were quite clear and untroubled: he saw that she had obeyed his injunction and forgotten.

II

Waythorn, the next morning, went down town earlier than usual. Haskett was not likely to come till the afternoon, but the instinct of flight drove him forth. He meant to stay away all day—he had thoughts of dining at his club. As his door closed behind him he reflected that before he opened it again it would have admitted another man who had as much right to enter it as himself, and the thought filled him with a physical repugnance.

He caught the "elevated" at the employees' hour, and found himself crushed between two layers of pendulous humanity. At Eighth Street the man facing him wriggled out, and another took his place. Waythorn glanced up and saw that it was Gus Varick. The men were so close together that it was impossible to ignore the smile of recognition on Varick's handsome overblown face. And after all—why not? They had always been on good terms, and Varick had been divorced before Waythorn's attentions to his wife began. The two exchanged a word on the perennial grievance of the congested trains, and when a seat at their side was miraculously left empty the instinct of self-preservation made Waythorn slip into it after Varick.

The latter drew the stout man's breath of relief. "Lord—I was beginning to feel like a pressed flower." He leaned back, looking unconcernedly at Waythorn. "Sorry to hear that Sellers is knocked out again."

"Sellers?" echoed Waythorn, starting at his partner's name.

Varick looked surprised. "You didn't know he was laid up with the gout?"

"No. I've been away—I only got back last night." Waythorn felt himself reddening in anticipation of the other's smile.

"Ah—yes; to be sure. And Sellers's attack came on two days ago. I'm afraid he's pretty bad. Very awkward for me, as it happens, because he was just putting through a rather important thing for me."

"Ah?" Waythorn wondered vaguely since when Varick had been dealing in "important things." Hitherto he had dabbled only in the shallow pools of speculation, with which Waythorn's office did not usually concern itself.

It occurred to him that Varick might be talking at random, to relieve the strain of their propinquity. That strain was becoming momentarily more apparent to Waythorn, and when, at Cortlandt Street, he caught sight of an acquaintance and had a sudden vision of the picture he and Varick must present to an initiated eye, he jumped up with a muttered excuse.

"I hope you'll find Sellers better," said Varick civilly, and he stammered back: "If I can be of any use to you—" and let the departing crowd sweep him to the platform.

At his office he heard that Sellers was in fact ill with the gout, and would probably not be able to leave the house for some weeks.

"I'm sorry it should have happened so, Mr. Waythorn," the senior clerk said with affable significance. "Mr. Sellers was very much upset at the idea of giving you such a lot of extra work just now."

"Oh, that's no matter," said Waythorn hastily. He secretly welcomed the pressure of additional business, and was glad to think that, when the day's work was over, he would have to call at his partner's on the way home.

He was late for luncheon, and turned in at the nearest restaurant instead of going to his club. The place was full, and the waiter hurried him to the back of the room to capture the only vacant table. In the cloud of cigar-smoke Waythorn did not at once distinguish his neighbours: but presently, looking about him, he saw Varick seated a few feet off. This time, luckily, they were too far apart for conversation, and Varick, who faced another way, had probably not even seen him; but there was an irony in their renewed nearness.

Varick was said to be fond of good living, and as Waythorn sat despatching his hurried luncheon he looked across half enviously at the other's leisurely degustation of his meal. When Waythorn first saw him he had been helping himself with critical deliberation to a bit of Camembert at the ideal point of liquifaction, and now, the cheese removed, he was just pouring his *café double* from its little two-storied earthen pot. He poured slowly, his ruddy profile bent above the task, and one beringed white hand steadying the lid of the coffee-pot; then he stretched his other hand to the decanter of cognac at his elbow, filled a liqueur-glass, took a tentative sip, and poured the brandy into his coffee-cup.

Waythorn watched him in a kind of fascination. What was he thinking of—only of the flavour of the coffee and the liqueur? Had the morning's meeting left no more trace in his thoughts than on his face? Had his wife so completely passed out of his life that even this odd encounter with her present husband, within a week after her remarriage, was no more than an incident in his day? And as Waythorn mused, another idea struck him: had Haskett ever met Varick as Varick and he had just met? The recollection of Haskett perturbed him, and he rose and left the restaurant, taking a circuitous way out to escape the placid irony of Varick's nod.

It was after seven when Waythorn reached home. He thought the footman who opened the door looked at him oddly.

"How is Miss Lily?" he asked in haste.

"Doing very well, sir. A gentleman—"

"Tell Barlow to put off dinner for half an hour," Waythorn cut him off, hurrying upstairs.

He went straight to his room and dressed without seeing his wife. When he reached the drawing-room she was there, fresh and radiant. Lily's day had been good; the doctor was not coming back that evening.

At dinner Waythorn told her of Sellers's illness and of the resulting complications. She listened sympathetically, adjuring him not to let himself be over-worked, and asking vague feminine questions about the routine of the office. Then she gave him the chronicle of Lily's day; quoted the nurse and doctor, and told him who had called to inquire. He had never seen her more serene and unruffled. It struck him, with a curious pang, that she was very happy in being with him, so happy that she found a childish pleasure in rehearsing the trivial incidents of her day.

After dinner they went to the library, and the servant put the coffee and liqueurs on a low table before her and left the room. She looked singularly soft and girlish in her rosy pale dress, against the dark leather of one of his bachelor armchairs. A day earlier the contrast would have charmed him.

He turned away now, choosing a cigar with affected deliberation.

"Did Haskett come?" he asked, with his back to her.

"Oh, yes—he came."

"You didn't see him, of course?"

She hesitated a moment. "I let the nurse see him."

That was all. There was nothing more to ask. He swung round toward her, applying a match to his cigar. Well, the thing was over for a week, at any rate. He would try not to think of it. She looked up at him, a trifle rosier than usual, with a smile in her eyes.

"Ready for your coffee, dear?"

He leaned against the mantelpiece, watching her as she lifted the coffee-pot. The lamplight struck a gleam from her bracelets and tipped her soft hair with brightness. How light and slender she was, and how each gesture flowed into the next! She seemed a creature all compact of harmonies. As the thought of Haskett receded, Waythorn felt himself yielding again to the joy of possessorship. They were his, those white hands with their flitting motions, his the light haze of hair, the lips and eyes. . . .

She set down the coffee-pot, and reaching for the decanter of cognac, measured off a liqueur-glass and poured it into his cup.

Waythorn uttered a sudden exclamation.

"What is the matter?" she said, startled.

"Nothing; only—I don't take cognac in my coffee."

"Oh, how stupid of me," she cried.

Their eyes met, and she blushed a sudden agonised red.

III

Ten days later, Mr. Sellers, still house-bound, asked Waythorn to call on his way down town.

The senior partner, with his swaddled foot propped up by the fire, greeted his associate with an air of embarrassment.

"I'm sorry, my dear fellow; I've got to ask you to do an awkward thing for me."

Waythorn waited, and the other went on, after a pause apparently given to the arrangement of his phrases: "The fact is, when I was knocked out I had just gone into a rather complicated piece of business for—Gus Varick."

"Well?" said Waythorn, with an attempt to put him at his ease.

"Well—it's this way: Varick came to me the day before my attack. He had evidently had an inside tip from somebody, and had made about a hundred thousand. He came to me for advice, and I suggested his going in with Vanderlyn."

"Oh, the deuce!" Waythorn exclaimed. He saw in a flash what had happened. The investment was an alluring one, but required negotiation. He listened quietly while Sellers put the case before him, and, the statement ended, he said: "You think I ought to see Varick?"

"I'm afraid I can't as yet. The doctor is obdurate. And this thing can't wait. I hate to ask you, but no one else in the office knows the ins and outs of it."

Waythorn stood silent. He did not care a farthing for the success of Varick's venture, but the honour of the office was to be considered, and he could hardly refuse to oblige his partner.

"Very well," he said, "I'll do it."

That afternoon, apprised by telephone, Varick called at the office. Waythorn, waiting in his private room, wondered what the others thought of it. The newspapers, at the time of Mrs. Waythorn's marriage, had acquainted their readers with every detail of her previous matrimonial ventures, and Waythorn could fancy the clerks smiling behind Varick's back as he was ushered in.

Varick bore himself admirably. He was easy without being undignified, and Waythorn was conscious of cutting a much less impressive figure. Varick had no experience of business, and the talk prolonged itself for nearly an hour while Waythorn set forth with scrupulous precision the details of the proposed transaction.

"I'm awfully obliged to you," Varick said as he rose. "The fact is I'm not used to having much money to look after, and I don't want to make an ass of myself—" He smiled, and Waythorn could not help noticing that there was something pleasant about his smile. "It feels uncommonly queer to have enough cash to pay one's bills. I'd have sold my soul for it a few years ago!"

Waythorn winced at the allusion. He had heard it rumoured that a lack of funds had been one of the determining causes of the Varick separation, but it did not occur to him that Varick's words were intentional. It seemed more likely that the desire to keep clear of embarrassing topics had fatally drawn him into one. Waythorn did not wish to be outdone in civility.

"We'll do the best we can for you," he said. "I think this is a good thing you're in."

"Oh, I'm sure it's immense. It's awfully good of you—" Varick broke off, embarrassed. "I suppose the thing's settled now—but if—"

"If anything happens before Sellers is about, I'll see you again," said Waythorn quietly. He was glad, in the end, to appear the more self-possessed of the two.

The course of Lily's illness ran smooth, and as the days passed Waythorn grew used to the idea of Haskett's weekly visit. The first time the day came round, he stayed out late, and questioned his wife as to the visit on his return. She replied at once that Haskett had merely seen the nurse downstairs, as the doctor did not wish any one in the child's sick-room till after the crisis.

The following week Waythorn was again conscious of the recurrence of the day, but had forgotten it by the time he came home to dinner. The crisis of the disease came a few days later, with a rapid decline of fever, and the little girl was pronounced out of danger. In the rejoicing which ensued the thought of Haskett passed out of Waythorn's mind, and one afternoon, letting himself into the house with a latch-key, he went straight to his library without noticing a shabby hat and umbrella in the hall.

In the library he found a small effaced-looking man with a thinnish gray beard sitting on the edge of a chair. The stranger might have been a piano-tuner, or one of those mysteriously efficient persons who are summoned in emergencies to adjust some detail of the domestic machinery. He blinked at Waythorn through a pair of gold-rimmed spectacles and said mildly: "Mr. Waythorn, I presume? I am Lily's father."

Waythorn flushed. "Oh—" he stammered uncomfortably. He broke off, disliking to appear rude. Inwardly he was trying to adjust the actual Haskett to the image of him projected by his wife's reminiscences. Waythorn had been allowed to infer that Alice's first husband was a brute.

"I am sorry to intrude," said Haskett, with his over-the-counter politeness.

"Don't mention it," returned Waythorn, collecting himself. "I suppose the nurse has been told?"

"I presume so. I can wait," said Haskett. He had a resigned way of speaking, as though life had worn down his natural powers of resistance.

Waythorn stood on the threshold, nervously pulling off his gloves.

"I'm sorry you've been detained. I will send for the nurse," he said; and as he opened the door he added with an effort: "I'm glad we can give you a good report of Lily." He winced as the *we* slipped out, but Haskett seemed not to notice it.

"Thank you, Mr. Waythorn. It's been an anxious time for me."

"Ah, well, that's past. Soon she'll be able to go to you." Waythorn nodded and passed out.

In his own room he flung himself down with a groan. He hated the womanish sensibility which made him suffer so acutely from the grotesque chances of life. He had known when he married that his wife's former husbands were both living, and that amid the multiplied contacts of modern existence there were a thousand chances to one that he would run against one or the other, yet he found himself as much disturbed by his brief encounter with Haskett as though the law had not obligingly removed all difficulties in the way of their meeting.

Waythorn sprang up and began to pace the room nervously. He had not suffered half as much from his two meetings with Varick. It was Haskett's presence in his own house that made the situation so intolerable. He stood still, hearing steps in the passage.

"This way, please," he heard the nurse say. Haskett was being taken upstairs, then: not a corner of the house but was open to him. Waythorn dropped into another chair, staring vaguely ahead of him. On his dressing-table stood a photograph of Alice, taken when he had first known her. She was Alice Varick then—how fine and exquisite he had thought her! Those were Varick's pearls about her neck. At Waythorn's instance they had been returned before her marriage. Had Haskett ever given her any trinkets—and what had become of them, Waythorn wondered? He realised suddenly that he knew very little of Haskett's past or present situation; but from the man's appearance and manner of speech he could reconstruct with curious precision the surroundings of Alice's first marriage. And it startled him to think that she had, in the background of her life, a phase of existence so different from anything with which he had connected her. Varick, whatever his faults, was a gentleman, in the conventional, traditional sense of the term: the sense which at that moment seemed, oddly enough, to have most meaning to Waythorn. He and Varick had the same social habits, spoke the same language, understood the same allusions. But this other man . . . it was grotesquely uppermost in Waythorn's mind that Haskett had worn a made-up tie attached with an elastic. Why should that ridiculous detail symbolise the whole man? Waythorn was exasperated by his own paltriness, but the fact of the tie expanded, forced itself on him, became as it were the key to Alice's past. He could see her, as Mrs. Haskett, sitting in a "front parlour" furnished in plush, with a pianola, and a copy of "Ben Hur" on the centre-table. He could see her going to the theatre with Haskett—or perhaps even to a "Church Sociable"—she in a "picture hat" and Haskett in a black frock-coat, a little creased, with the made-up tie on an elastic. On the way home they would stop and look at the illuminated shop-windows, lingering over the photographs of New York actresses. On Sunday afternoons Haskett would take her for a walk, pushing Lily ahead of them in a white enamelled perambulator, and Waythorn had a vision of the people they would stop and talk to. He could fancy how pretty Alice must have looked, in a dress adroitly constructed from the hints of a New York fashion-paper, and how she must have looked down on the other women, chafing at her life, and secretly feeling that she belonged in a bigger place.

For the moment his foremost thought was one of wonder at the way in which she had shed the phase of existence which her marriage with Haskett implied. It was as if her whole aspect, every gesture, every inflection, every allusion, were a studied negation of that period of her life. If she had denied being married to Haskett she could hardly have stood more convicted of duplicity than in this obliteration of the self which had been his wife.

Waythorn started up, checking himself in the analysis of her motives. What right had he to create a fantastic effigy of her and then pass judgment on it? She had spoken vaguely of her first marriage as unhappy, had hinted, with becoming reticence, that Haskett had wrought havoc among her young illusions. . . . It was a pity for Waythorn's peace of mind that Haskett's very inoffensiveness shed a new light on the nature of those illusions. A man would rather think that his wife has been brutalised by her first husband than that the process has been reversed.

IV

"Mr. Waythorn, I don't like that French governess of Lily's."

Haskett, subdued and apologetic, stood before Waythorn in the library, revolving his shabby hat in his hand.

Waythorn, surprised in his armchair over the evening paper, stared back perplexedly at his visitor.

"You'll excuse my asking to see you," Haskett continued. "But this is my last visit, and I thought if I could have a word with you it would be a better way than writing to Mrs. Waythorn's lawyer."

Waythorn rose uneasily. He did not like the French governess either; but that was irrelevant.

"I am not so sure of that," he returned stiffly; "but since you wish it I will give your message to—my wife." He always hesitated over the possessive pronoun in addressing Haskett.

The latter sighed. "I don't know as that will help much. She didn't like it when I spoke to her."

Waythorn turned red. "When did you see her?" he asked.

"Not since the first day I came to see Lily—right after she was taken sick. I remarked to her than that I didn't like the governess."

Waythorn made no answer. He remembered distinctly that, after that first visit, he had asked his wife if she had seen Haskett. She had lied to him then, but she had respected his wishes since; and the incident cast a curious light on her character. He was sure she would not have seen Haskett that first day if she had divined that Waythorn would object, and the fact that she did not divine it was almost as disagreeable to the latter as the discovery that she had lied to him.

"I don't like the woman," Haskett was repeating with mild persistency. "She ain't straight, Mr. Waythorn—she'll teach the child to be underhand. I've noticed a change in Lily—she's too anxious to please—and she don't always tell the truth. She used to be the straightest child, Mr. Waythorn—" He broke off, his voice a little thick. "Not but what I want her to have a stylish education," he ended.

Waythorn was touched. "I'm sorry, Mr. Haskett; but frankly, I don't quite see what I can do."

Haskett hesitated. Then he laid his hat on the table, and advanced to the hearth-rug, on which Waythorn was standing. There was nothing aggressive in his manner, but he had the solemnity of a timid man resolved on a decisive measure.

"There's just one thing you can do, Mr. Waythorn," he said. "You can remind Mrs. Waythorn that, by the decree of the courts, I am entitled to have a voice in Lily's bringing up." He paused, and went on more deprecatingly: "I'm not the kind to talk about enforcing my rights, Mr. Waythorn. I don't know as I think a man is entitled to rights he hasn't known how to hold on to; but this business of the child is different. I've never let go there—and I never mean to."

The scene left Waythorn deeply shaken. Shame-facedly, in indirect ways, he had been finding out about Haskett; and all that he had learned was favorable. The little man, in order to be near his daughter, had sold out his share in a profitable business in Utica, and accepted a modest clerkship in a New York manufacturing house. He boarded in a shabby street and had few acquaintances. His passion for Lily filled his life. Waythorn felt that this exploration of Haskett was like groping about with a dark-lantern in his wife's past; but he saw now that there were recesses his lantern had not explored. He had never enquired into the exact circumstances of his wife's first matrimonial rupture. On the surface all had been fair. It was she who had obtained the divorce, and the courts had given her the child. But Waythorn knew how many ambiguities such a verdict might cover. The mere fact that Haskett retained a right over his daughter implied an unsuspected compromise.

Waythorn was an idealist. He always refused to recognise unpleasant contingencies till he found himself confronted with them, and then he saw them followed by a spectral train of consequences. His next days were thus haunted, and he determined to try to lay the ghosts by conjuring them up in his wife's presence.

When he repeated Haskett's request a flame of anger passed over her face; but she subdued it instantly and spoke with a slight quiver of outraged motherhood.

"It is very ungentlemanly of him," she said.

The word grated on Waythorn. "That is neither here nor there. It's a bare question of rights."

She murmured: "It's not as if he could ever be a help to Lily—"

Waythorn flushed. This was even less to his taste. "The question is," he repeated, "what authority has he over her?"

She looked downward, twisting herself a little in her seat. "I am willing to see him—I thought you objected," she faltered.

In a flash he understood that she knew the extent of Haskett's claims. Perhaps it was not the first time she had resisted them.

"My objecting has nothing to do with it," he said coldly; "if Haskett has a right to be consulted you must consult him."

She burst into tears, and he saw that she expected him to regard her as a victim.

Haskett did not abuse his rights. Waythorn had felt miserably sure that he would not. But the governess was dismissed, and from time to time the little man demanded an interview with Alice. After the first outburst she accepted the situation with her usual adaptability. Haskett had once reminded Waythorn of the piano-tuner, and Mrs. Waythorn, after a month or two, appeared to class him with that domestic familiar. Waythorn could not but respect the father's tenacity. At first he had tried to cultivate the suspicion that Haskett might be "up to" something, that he had an object in securing a foothold in the house. But in his heart Waythorn was sure of Haskett's single-mindedness; he even guessed in the latter a mild contempt for such advantages as his relation with the Waythorns might offer. Haskett's sincerity of purpose made him invulnerable, and his successor had to accept him as a lien on the property.

Mr. Sellers was sent to Europe to recover from his gout, and Varick's affairs hung on Waythorn's hands. The negotiations were prolonged and complicated; they necessitated frequent conferences between the two men, and the interests of the firm forbade Waythorn's suggesting that his client should transfer his business to another office.

Varick appeared well in the transaction. In moments of relaxation his coarse streak appeared, and Waythorn dreaded his geniality; but in the office he was concise and clear-headed, with a flattering deference to Waythorn's judgment. Their business relations being so affably established, it would have been absurd for the two men to ignore each other in society. The first time they met in a drawing-room, Varick took up their intercourse in the same easy key, and his hostess's grateful glance obliged Waythorn to respond to it. After that they ran across each other frequently, and one evening at a ball Waythorn, wandering through the remoter rooms, came upon Varick seated beside his wife. She coloured a little, and faltered in what she was saying; but Varick nodded to Waythorn without rising, and the latter strolled on.

In the carriage, on the way home, he broke out nervously: "I didn't know you spoke to Varick."

Her voice trembled a little. "It's the first time—he happened to be standing near me; I didn't know what to do. It's so awkward, meeting everywhere—and he said you had been very kind about some business."

"That's different," said Waythorn.

She paused a moment. "I'll do just as you wish," she returned pliantly. "I thought it would be less awkward to speak to him when we meet."

Her pliancy was beginning to sicken him. Had she really no will of her own—no theory about her relation to these men? She had accepted Haskett—did she mean to accept Varick? It was "less awkward," as she had said, and her instinct was to evade difficulties or to circumvent them. With sudden vividness Waythorn saw how the instinct had developed. She was "as easy as an old shoe"—a shoe that too many feet had worn. Her elasticity was the result of tension in too many different directions. Alice Haskett—Alice Varick—Alice Waythorn—she had been each in turn, and had left hanging to each name a little of her privacy, a little of her personality, a little of the inmost self where the unknown god abides.

"Yes—it's better to speak to Varick," said Waythorn wearily.

V

The winter wore on, and society took advantage of the Waythorns' acceptance of Varick. Harassed hostesses were grateful to them for bridging over a social difficulty, and Mrs. Waythorn was held up as a miracle of good taste. Some experimental spirits could not resist the diversion of throwing Varick and his former wife together, and there were those who thought he found a zest in the propinquity. But Mrs. Waythorn's conduct remained irreproachable. She neither avoided Varick nor sought him out. Even Waythorn could not but admit that she had discovered the solution of the newest social problem.

He had married her without giving much thought to that problem. He had fancied that a woman can shed her past like a man. But now he saw that Alice was bound to hers both by the circumstances which forced her into continued relation with it, and by the traces it had left on her nature. With grim irony Waythorn compared himself to a member of a syndicate. He held so many shares in his wife's personality and his predecessors were his partners in the business. If there had been any element of passion in the transaction he would have felt less deteriorated by it. The fact that Alice took her change of husbands like a change of weather reduced the situation to mediocrity. He could have forgiven her for blunders, for excesses; for resisting Haskett, for yielding to Varick; for anything but her acquiescence and her tact. She reminded him of a juggler tossing knives; but the knives were blunt and she knew they would never cut her.

And then, gradually, habit formed a protecting surface for his sensibilities. If he paid for each day's comfort with the small change of his illusions, he grew daily to value the comfort more and set less store upon the coin. He had drifted into a dulling propinquity with Haskett and Varick and he took refuge in the cheap revenge of satirising the situation. He even began to reckon up the advantages which accrued from it, to ask himself if it were not better to own a third of a wife who knew how to make a man happy than a whole one who had lacked opportunity to acquire the art. For it *was* an art, and made up, like all others, of concessions, eliminations and embellishments; of lights judiciously thrown and shadows skilfully softened. His wife knew exactly how to manage the lights, and he knew exactly to what training she owed her skill. He even tried to trace the source of his obligations, to discriminate between the influences which had combined to produce his domestic happiness: he perceived that Haskett's commonness had made Alice worship good breeding, while Varick's liberal construction of the marriage bond had taught her to value the conjugal virtues; so that he was directly indebted to his predecessors for the devotion which made his life easy if not inspiring.

From this phase he passed into that of complete acceptance. He ceased to satirise himself because time dulled the irony of the situation and the joke lost its humour with its sting. Even the sight of Haskett's hat on the hall table had ceased to touch the springs of epigram. The hat was often seen there now, for it had been decided that it was better for Lily's father to visit her than for the little girl to go to his boarding-house. Waythorn, having acquiesced in this arrangement, had been surprised to find how little difference it made. Haskett was never obtrusive, and the few visitors who met him on the stairs were unaware of his identity. Waythorn did not know how often he saw Alice, but with himself Haskett was seldom in contact.

One afternoon, however, he learned on entering that Lily's father was waiting to see him. In the library he found Haskett occupying a chair in his usual provisional way. Waythorn always felt grateful to him for not leaning back.

"I hope you'll excuse me, Mr. Waythorn," he said rising. "I wanted to see Mrs. Waythorn about Lily, and your man asked me to wait here till she came in."

"Of course," said Waythorn, remembering that a sudden leak had that morning given over the drawing-room to the plumbers.

He opened his cigar-case and held it out to his visitor, and Haskett's acceptance seemed to mark a fresh stage in their intercourse. The spring evening was chilly, and Waythorn invited his guest to draw up his chair to the fire. He meant to find an excuse to leave Haskett in a moment; but he was tired and cold, and after all the little man no longer jarred on him.

The two were enclosed in the intimacy of their blended cigar-smoke when the door opened and Varick walked into the room. Waythorn rose abruptly. It was the first time that Varick had come to the house, and the surprise of seeing him, combined with the singular inopportuneness of his arrival, gave a new edge to Waythorn's blunted sensibilities. He stared at his visitor without speaking.

Varick seemed too preoccupied to notice his host's embarrassment.

"My dear fellow," he exclaimed in his most expansive tone, "I must apologise for tumbling in on you in this way, but I was too late to catch you down town, and so I thought—"

He stopped short, catching sight of Haskett, and his sanguine colour deepened to a flush which spread vividly under his scant blond hair. But in a moment he recovered himself and nodded slightly. Haskett returned the bow in silence, and Waythorn was still groping for speech when the footman came in carrying a tea-table.

The intrusion offered a welcome vent to Waythorn's nerves. "What the deuce are you bringing this here for?" he said sharply.

"I beg your pardon, sir, but the plumbers are still in the drawing-room, and Mrs. Waythorn said she would have tea in the library." The footman's perfectly respectful tone implied a reflection on Waythorn's reasonableness.

"Oh, very well," said the latter resignedly, and the footman proceeded to open the folding tea-table and set out its complicated appointments. While this interminable process continued the three men stood motionless, watching it with a fascinated stare, till Waythorn, to break the silence, said to Varick: "Won't you have a cigar?"

He held out the case he had just tendered to Haskett, and Varick helped himself with a smile. Waythorn looked about for a match, and finding none, proffered a light from his own cigar. Haskett, in the background, held his ground mildly, examining his cigar-tip now and then, and stepping forward at the right moment to knock its ashes into the fire.

The footman at last withdrew, and Varick immediately began: "If I could just say half a word to you about this business—"

"Certainly," stammered Waythorn; "in the dining-room—"

But as he placed his hand on the door it opened from without, and his wife appeared on the threshold.

She came in fresh and smiling, in her street dress and hat, shedding a fragrance from the boa which she loosened in advancing.

"Shall we have tea in here, dear?" she began; and then she caught sight of Varick. Her smile deepened, veiling a slight tremor of surprise.

"Why, how do you do?" she said with a distinct note of pleasure.

As she shook hands with Varick she saw Haskett standing behind him. Her smile faded for a moment, but she recalled it quickly, with a scarcely perceptible side-glance at Waythorn.

"How do you do, Mr. Haskett?" she said, and shook hands with him a shade less cordially.

The three men stood awkwardly before her, till Varick, always the most self-possessed, dashed into an explanatory phrase.

"We—I had to see Waythorn a moment on business," he stammered, brick-red from chin to nape.

Haskett stepped forward with his air of mild obstinacy. "I am sorry to intrude; but you appointed five o'clock—" he directed his resigned glance to the time-piece on the mantel.

She swept aside their embarrassment with a charming gesture of hospitality.

"I'm so sorry—I'm always late; but the afternoon was so lovely." She stood drawing off her gloves, propitiatory and graceful, diffusing about her a sense of ease and familiarity in which the situation lost its grotesqueness. "But before talking business," she added brightly, "I'm sure every one wants a cup of tea."

She dropped into her low chair by the tea-table, and the two visitors, as if drawn by her smile, advanced to receive the cups she held out.

She glanced about for Waythorn, and he took the third cup with a laugh.

Willa Cather

1873 – 1947

Willa Cather's fiction embraces the literary aims of both the past and the emerging twentieth century. In her use of local color and her concern with life on the frontier, she continued the development of two major phases of nineteenth-century fiction; in her approach to the interpretation of character through heredity and environment and the avoidance in her best stories of technical clichés, she adopted the new modes of the twentieth century. To this fusion of the old and new, she brought a sincerity and clarity of artistic vision that raised her work to a level of major importance.

Willa Cather was born near Winchester, Virginia, but in 1882, her father, Charles Cather, moved the family to a farm near Red Cloud, Nebraska, where she grew to be closely identified with the immigrant homesteaders struggling to establish themselves in a new way of life on the bleak prairies. After attending the preparatory school of the University of Nebraska, she entered the University, concentrating on English and classical literature and vigorously committing herself to writing for the student newspaper, editing the senior yearbook, and submitting articles to the Nebraska *State Journal.* After her graduation in 1895, she spent one year as associate editor of the Lincoln *Courier* and then went to Pittsburgh, first to write for the *Leader* and later to teach English in the Allegheny High School. She was soon contributing stories and poems to *Cosmopolitan, McClure's Magazine, Lippincott's Magazine,* and other periodicals. In 1903, she published a volume of verse, *April Twilights,* and two years later, her first collection of stories, *The Troll Garden.* From 1906 to 1912, she was on the staff of *McClure's Magazine,* and while serving for several years as managing editor traveled widely in Europe and the Southwestern states.

With the publication of her first and not too praiseworthy novel, *Alexander's Bridge,* in 1912, she retired from editorial work to devote her full energies to writing. In her next novel, *O Pioneers!* (1913), she—to use her own words—"hit the home pasture" by turning back to the Nebraska farm-immigrant life she had known in her youth. The heroic toil of these western pioneers and the equally heroic earlier struggles of frontier priests in the Southwest provided the inspiration for most of her later fiction. Among the best of her other novels are *My Ántonia* (1918), *A Lost Lady* (1923), *The Professor's House* (1925), and *Death Comes for the Archbishop* (1927). In addition to *The Troll Garden,* she published only two other collections of short stories, *Youth and the Bright Medusa* (1920) and *Obscure Destinies* (1932).

Cather was not as fully committed to literary naturalism as Dreiser was, but "Paul's Case" nevertheless is as thoroughly naturalistic as any story Dreiser ever wrote. The story embodies the concept that human fate is determined by the interplay between inherited or inward traits and environment or outward circumstances. When the inward and outward forces are in conflict, as they usually are in naturalistic fiction, the character is doomed to suffer tragic consequences.

Paul's Case

A Study in Temperament

It was Paul's afternoon to appear before the faculty of the Pittsburgh High School to account for his various misdemeanours. He had been suspended a week ago, and his father had called the Principal's office and confessed his perplexity about his son. Paul entered the faculty room suave and smiling. His clothes were a trifle outgrown and the tan velvet on the collar of his open overcoat was frayed and worn; but for all that there was something of the dandy about him, and he wore an opal pin in

"Paul's Case" by Willa Cather, from *The Troll Garden,* McClure Phillips & Co., 1905.

his neatly knotted black four-in-hand, and a red carnation in his buttonhole. This latter adornment the faculty somehow felt was not properly significant of the contrite spirit befitting a boy under the ban of suspension.

Paul was tall for his age and very thin, with high, cramped shoulders and a narrow chest. His eyes were remarkable for a certain hysterical brilliancy and he continually used them in a conscious, theatrical sort of way, peculiarly offensive in a boy. The pupils were abnormally large, as though he were addicted to belladonna, but there was a glassy glitter about them which that drug does not produce.

When questioned by the Principal as to why he was there, Paul stated, politely enough, that he wanted to come back to school. This was a lie, but Paul was quite accustomed to lying; found it, indeed, indispensable for overcoming friction. His teachers were asked to state their respective charges against him, which they did with such a rancour and aggrievedness as evinced that this was not a usual case. Disorder and impertinence were among the offences named, yet each of his instructors felt that it was scarcely possible to put into words the real cause of the trouble, which lay in a sort of hysterically defiant manner of the boy's; in the contempt which they all knew he felt for them, and which he seemingly made not the least effort to conceal. Once, when he had been making a synopsis of a paragraph at the blackboard, his English teacher had stepped to his side and attempted to guide his hand. Paul had started back with a shudder and thrust his hands violently behind him. The astonished woman could scarcely have been more hurt and embarrassed had he struck at her. The insult was so involuntary and definitely personal as to be unforgettable. In one way and another, he had made all his teachers, men and women alike, conscious of the same feeling of physical aversion. In one class he habitually sat with his hand shading his eyes; in another he always looked out of the window during the recitation; in another he made a running commentary on the lecture, with humorous intention.

His teachers felt this afternoon that his whole attitude was symbolized by his shrug and his flippantly red carnation flower, and they fell upon him without mercy, his English teacher leading the pack. He stood through it smiling, his pale lips parted over his white teeth. (His lips were continually twitching, and he had a habit of raising his eyebrows that was contemptuous and irritating to the last degree.) Older boys than Paul had broken down and shed tears under that baptism of fire, but his set smile did not once desert him, and his only sign of discomfort was the nervous trembling of the fingers that toyed with the buttons of his overcoat, and an occasional jerking of the other hand that held his hat. Paul was always smiling, always glancing about him, seeming to feel that people might be watching him and trying to detect something. This conscious expression, since it was as far as possible from boyish mirthfulness, was usually attributed to insolence or "smartness."

As the inquisition proceeded, one of his instructors repeated an impertinent remark of the boy's, and the Principal asked him whether he thought that a courteous speech to have made a woman. Paul shrugged his shoulders slightly and his eyebrows twitched.

"I don't know," he replied. "I didn't mean to be polite or impolite, either. I guess it's a sort of way I have of saying things regardless."

The Principal, who was a sympathetic man, asked him whether he didn't think that a way it would be well to get rid of. Paul grinned and said he guessed so. When he was told that he could go, he bowed gracefully and went out. His bow was but a repetition of the scandalous red carnation.

His teachers were in despair, and his drawing master voiced the feeling of them all when he declared there was something about the boy which none of them understood. He added: "I don't really believe that smile of his comes altogether from insolence; there's something sort of haunted about it. The boy is not strong, for one thing. I happen to know that he was born in Colorado, only a few months before his mother died out there of a long illness. There is something wrong about the fellow."

The drawing master had come to realize that, in looking at Paul, one saw only his white teeth and the forced animation of his eyes. One warm afternoon the boy had gone to sleep at his drawing-board, and his master had noted with amazement what a white, blue-veined face it was; drawn and wrinkled like an old man's about the eyes, the lips twitching even in his sleep, and stiff with a nervous tension that drew them back from his teeth.

His teachers left the building dissatisfied and unhappy; humiliated to have felt so vindictive toward a mere boy, to have uttered this feeling in cutting terms, and to have set each other on, as it were, in the grewsome game of intemperate reproach. Some of them remembered having seen a miserable street cat set at bay by a ring of tormentors.

As for Paul, he ran down the hill whistling the Soldiers' Chorus from *Faust* looking wildly behind him now and then to see whether some of his teachers were not there to writhe under his light-heartedness. As it was now late in the afternoon and Paul was on duty that evening as usher at Carnegie Hall, he decided that he would not go home to supper. When he reached the concert hall the doors were not yet open and, as it was chilly outside, he decided to go up into the picture gallery—always deserted at this hour—where there were some of Raffelli's gay studies of Paris streets and an airy blue Venetian scene or two that always exhilarated him. He was delighted to find no one in the gallery but the old guard, who sat in one corner, a newspaper on his knee, a black patch over one eye and the other closed. Paul possessed himself of the place and walked confidently up and down, whistling under his breath. After a while he sat down before a blue Rico and lost himself. When he bethought him to look at his watch, it was after seven o'clock, and he rose with a start and ran downstairs, making a face at Augustus, peering out from the cast-room, and an evil gesture at the Venus of Milo as he passed her on the stairway.

When Paul reached the ushers' dressing-room half-a-dozen boys were there already, and he began excitedly to tumble into his uniform. It was one of the few that at all approached fitting, and Paul thought it very becoming—though he knew that the tight, straight coat accentuated his narrow chest, about which he was exceedingly sensitive. He was always considerably excited while he dressed, twanging all over to the tuning of the strings and the preliminary flourishes of the horns in the music-room; but to-night he seemed quite beside himself, and he teased and plagued the boys until, telling him that he was crazy, they put him down on the floor and sat on him.

Somewhat calmed by his suppression, Paul dashed out to the front of the house to seat the early comers. He was a model usher; gracious and smiling he ran up and down the aisles; nothing was too much trouble for him; he carried messages and brought programmes as though it were his greatest pleasure in life, and all the people in his section thought him a charming boy, feeling that he remembered and admired them. As the house filled, he grew more and more vivacious and animated, and the colour came to his cheeks and lips. It was very much as though this were a great reception and Paul were the host. Just as the musicians came out to take their places, his English teacher arrived with checks for the seats which a prominent manufacturer had taken for the season. She betrayed some embarrassment when she handed Paul the tickets, and a *hauteur* which subsequently made her feel very foolish. Paul was startled for a moment, and had the feeling of wanting to put her out; what business had she here among all these fine people and gay colours? He looked her over and decided that she was not appropriately dressed and must be a fool to sit downstairs in such togs. The tickets had probably been sent her out of kindness, he reflected as he put down a seat for her, and she had about as much right to sit there as he had.

When the symphony began Paul sank into one of the rear seats with a long sigh of relief, and lost himself as he had done before the Rico. It was not that symphonies, as such, meant anything in particular to Paul, but the first sigh of the instruments seemed to free some hilarious and potent spirit within him; something that struggled there like the Genius in the bottle found by the Arab fisherman. He felt a sudden zest of life; the lights danced before his eyes and the concert hall blazed into unimaginable splendour. When the soprano soloist came on, Paul forgot even the nastiness of his teacher's being there and gave himself up to the peculiar stimulus such personages always had for him. The soloist chanced to be a German woman, by no means in her first youth, and the mother of many children; but she wore an elaborate gown and a tiara, and above all she had that indefinable air of achievement, that world-shine upon her, which, in Paul's eyes, made her a veritable queen of Romance.

After a concert was over Paul was always irritable and wretched until he got to sleep, and to-night he was even more than usually restless. He had the feeling of not being able to let down, of its being impossible to give up this delicious excitement which was the only thing that could be called living at all. During the last number he withdrew and, after hastily changing his clothes in the dressing-room, slipped out to the side door where the soprano's carriage stood. Here he began pacing rapidly up and down the walk, waiting to see her come out.

Over yonder the Schenley, in its vacant stretch, loomed big and square through the fine rain, the windows of its twelve stories glowing like those of a lighted card-board house under a Christmas tree. All the actors and singers of the better class stayed there when they were in the city, and a number of the big manufacturers of the place lived there in the winter. Paul had often hung about the hotel, watching the people go in and out, longing to enter and leave schoolmasters and dull care behind him forever.

At last the singer came out, accompanied by the conductor, who helped her into her carriage and closed the door with a cordial *auf wiedersehen* which set Paul to wondering whether she were not an old sweetheart of his. Paul followed the carriage over to the hotel, walking so rapidly as not to be far from the entrance when the singer alighted and disappeared behind the swinging glass doors that were opened by a negro in a tall hat and a long coat. In the moment that the door was ajar, it seemed to Paul that he, too, entered. He seemed to feel himself go after her up the steps, into the warm, lighted building, into an exotic, tropical world of shiny, glistening surfaces and basking ease. He reflected upon the mysterious dishes that were brought into the dining-room, the green bottles in buckets of ice, as he had seen them in the supper party pictures of the *Sunday World* supplement. A quick gust of wind brought the rain down with sudden vehemence, and Paul was startled to find that he was still outside in the slush of the gravel driveway; that his boots were letting in the water and his scanty overcoat was clinging wet about him; that the lights in front of the concert hall were out, and that the rain was driving in sheets between him and the orange glow of the windows above him. There it was, what he wanted—tangibly before him, like the fairy world of a Christmas pantomime, but mocking spirits stood guard at the doors, and, as the rain beat in his face, Paul wondered whether he were destined always to shiver in the black night outside, looking up at it.

He turned and walked reluctantly toward the car tracks. The end had to come sometime; his father in his night-clothes at the top of the stairs, explanations that did not explain, hastily improvised fictions that were forever tripping him up, his upstairs room and its horrible yellow wall-paper, the creaking bureau with the greasy plush collar-box, and over his painted wooden bed the pictures of George Washington and John Calvin, and the framed motto, "Feed my Lambs," which had been worked in red worsted by his mother.

Half an hour later, Paul alighted from his car and went slowly down one of the side streets off the main thoroughfare. It was a highly respectable street, where all the houses were exactly alike, and where business men of moderate means begot and reared large families of children, all of whom went to Sabbath-school and learned the shorter catechism, and were interested in arithmetic; all of whom were as exactly alike as their homes, and of a piece with the monotony in which they lived. Paul never went up Cordelia Street without a shudder of loathing. His home was next the house of the Cumberland minister. He approached it to-night with the nerveless sense of defeat, the hopeless feeling of sinking back forever into ugliness and commonness that he had always had when he came home. The moment he turned into Cordelia Street he felt the waters close above his head. After each of these orgies of living, he experienced all the physical depression which follows a debauch; the loathing of respectable beds, of common food, of a house penetrated by kitchen odours; a shuddering repulsion for the flavourless, colourless mass of every-day existence; a morbid desire for cool things and soft lights and fresh flowers.

The nearer he approached the house, the more absolutely unequal Paul felt to the sight of it all; his ugly sleeping chamber; the cold bathroom with the grimy zinc tub, the cracked mirror, the dripping spiggots; his father, at the top of the stairs, his hairy legs sticking out from his nightshirt, his feet thrust into carpet slippers. He was so much later than usual that there would certainly be inquiries and reproaches. Paul stopped short before the door. He felt that he could not be accosted by his father to-night; that he could not toss again on that miserable bed. He would not go in. He would tell his father that he had no car fare, and it was raining so hard he had gone home with one of the boys and stayed all night.

Meanwhile, he was wet and cold. He went around to the back of the house and tried one of the basement windows, found it open, raised it cautiously, and scrambled down the cellar wall to the floor. There he stood, holding his breath, terrified by the noise he had made, but the floor above him was silent, and there was no creak on the stairs. He found a soap-box, and carried it over to the soft ring of light that streamed from the furnace door, and sat down. He was horribly afraid of rats, so he did not try to sleep, but sat looking distrustfully at the dark, still terrified lest he might have awakened his father. In such reactions, after one of the experiences which made days and nights out of the dreary blanks of the calendar, when his senses were deadened, Paul's head was always singularly clear. Suppose his father had heard him getting in at the window and had come down and shot him for a burglar? Then, again, suppose his father had come down, pistol in hand, and he had cried out in time to save himself, and his father had been horrified to think how nearly he had killed him? Then, again, suppose a day should come when his father would remember that night, and wish there had been no warning cry to stay his hand? With this last supposition Paul entertained himself until daybreak.

The following Sunday was fine; the sodden November chill was broken by the last flash of autumnal summer. In the morning Paul had to go to church and Sabbath-school, as always. On seasonable Sunday afternoons the burghers of Cordelia Street always sat out on their front "stoops," and talked to their neighbours on the next stoop, or called to those across the street in neighbourly fashion. The men usually sat on gay cushions placed upon the steps that led down to the sidewalk, while the women, in their Sunday "waists," sat in rockers on the cramped porches, pretending to be greatly at their ease. The children played in the streets; there were so many of them that the place resembled the recreation grounds of a kindergarten. The men on the steps—all in their shirt sleeves, their vests unbuttoned—sat with their legs well apart, their stomachs comfortably protruding, and talked of the prices of things, or told anecdotes of the sagacity of their various chiefs and overlords. They occasionally looked over the multitude of squabbling children, listening affectionately to their high-pitched, nasal voices, smiling to see their own proclivities reproduced in their offspring, and interspersed their legends of the iron kings with remarks about their sons' progress at school, their grades in arithmetic, and the amounts they had saved in their toy banks.

On this last Sunday of November, Paul sat all the afternoon on the lowest step of his "stoop," staring into the street, while his sisters, in their rockers, were talking to the minister's daughters next door about how many shirt-waists they had made in the last week, and how many waffles some one had eaten at the last church supper. When the weather was warm, and his father was in a particularly jovial frame of mind, the girls made lemonade, which was always brought out in a red-glass pitcher, ornamented with forget-me-nots in blue enamel. This the girls thought very fine, and the neighbours always joked about the suspicious colour of the pitcher.

To-day Paul's father sat on the top step, talking to a young man who shifted a restless baby from knee to knee. He happened to be the young man who was daily held up to Paul as a model, and after whom it was his father's dearest hope that he would pattern. This young man was of a ruddy complexion, with a compressed, red mouth, and faded, near-sighted eyes, over which he wore thick spectacles, with gold bows that curved about his ears. He was clerk to one of the magnates of a great steel corporation, and was looked upon in Cordelia Street as a young man with a future. There was a story that, some five years ago—he was now barely twenty-six—he had been a trifle dissipated but in order to curb his appetites and save the loss of time and strength that a sowing of wild oats might have entailed, he had taken his chief's advice, oft reiterated to his employees, and at twenty-one had married the first woman whom he could persuade to share his fortunes. She happened to be an angular school-mistress, much older than he, who also wore thick glasses, and who had now borne him four children, all near-sighted, like herself.

The young man was relating how his chief, now cruising the Mediterranean, kept in touch with all the details of the business, arranging his office hours on his yacht just as though he were at home, and "knocking off work enough to keep two stenographers busy." His father told, in turn, the plan his corporation was considering, of putting in an electric railway plant at Cairo. Paul snapped his teeth; he had an awful apprehension that they might spoil it all before he got there. Yet he rather liked to hear these legends of the iron kings, that were told and retold on Sundays and holidays; these stories of palaces in Venice, yachts on the Mediterranean, and high play at Monte Carlo appealed to his fancy, and he was interested in the triumphs of these cash boys who had become famous, though he had no mind for the cash-boy stage.

After supper was over, and he had helped to dry the dishes, Paul nervously asked his father whether he could go to George's to get some help in his geometry, and still more nervously asked for car fare. This latter request he had to repeat, as his father, on principle, did not like to hear requests for money, whether much or little. He asked Paul whether he could not go to some boy who lived nearer, and told him that he ought not to leave his school work until Sunday; but he gave him the dime. He was not a poor man, but he had a worthy ambition to come up in the world. His only reason for allowing Paul to usher was, that he thought a boy ought to be earning a little.

Paul bounded upstairs, scrubbed the greasy odour of the dish-water from his hands with the ill-smelling soap he hated, and then shook over his fingers a few drops of violet water from the bottle he kept hidden in his drawer. He left the house with his geometry conspicuously under his arm, and the moment he got out of Cordelia Street and boarded a downtown car, he shook off the lethargy of two deadening days, and began to live again.

The leading juvenile of the permanent stock company which played at one of the downtown theatres was an acquaintance of Paul's, and the boy had been invited to drop in at the Sunday-night rehearsals whenever he could. For more than a year Paul had spent every available moment loitering about Charley Edwards's dressing-room. He had won a place among Edwards's following not only because the young actor, who could not afford to employ a dresser, often found him useful, but because he recognized in Paul something akin to what churchmen term "vocation."

It was at the theatre and at Carnegie Hall that Paul really lived; the rest was but a sleep and a forgetting. This was Paul's fairy tale, and it had for him all the allurement of a secret love. The moment he inhaled the gassy, painty, dusty odour behind the scenes, he breathed like a prisoner set free, and felt within him the possibility of doing or saying splendid, brilliant, poetic things. The moment the cracked orchestra beat out the overture from *Martha* or jerked at the serenade from *Rigoletto,* all stupid and ugly things slid from him, and his senses were deliciously, yet delicately fired.

Perhaps it was because, in Paul's world, the natural nearly always wore the guise of ugliness, that a certain element of artificiality seemed to him necessary in beauty. Perhaps it was because his experience of life elsewhere was so full of Sabbath-school picnics, petty economies, wholesome advice as to how to succeed in life, and the unescapable odours of cooking, that he found this existence so alluring, these smartly-clad men and women so attractive, that he was so moved by these starry apple orchards that bloomed perennially under the lime-light.

It would be difficult to put it strongly enough how convincingly the stage entrance of that theatre was for Paul the actual portal of Romance. Certainly none of the company ever suspected it, least of all Charley Edwards. It was very like the old stories that used to float about London of fabulously rich Jews, who had subterranean halls there, with palms, and fountains, and soft lamps and richly apparelled women who never saw the disenchanting light of London day. So, in the midst of that smoke-palled city, enamoured of figures and grimy toil, Paul had his secret temple, his wishing carpet, his bit of blue-and-white Mediter-ranean shore bathed in perpetual sunshine.

Several of Paul's teachers had a theory that his imagination had been perverted by garish fiction, but the truth was that he scarcely ever read at all. The books at home were not such as would either tempt or corrupt a youthful mind, and as for reading the novels that some of his friends urged upon him—well, he got what he wanted much more quickly from music; any sort of music, from an orchestra to a barrel organ. He needed only the spark, the indescribable thrill that made his imagination master of his senses, and he could make plots and pictures enough of his own. It was equally true that he was not stage struck—not, at any rate, in the usual acceptation of that expression. He had no desire to become an actor, any more than he had to become a musician. He felt no necessity to do any of these things; what he wanted was to see, to be in the atmosphere, float on the wave of it, to be carried out, blue league after blue league, away from everything.

After a night behind the scenes, Paul found the school-room more than ever repulsive; the bare floors and naked walls; the prosy men who never wore frock coats, or violets in their buttonholes; the women with their dull gowns, shrill voices, and pitiful seriousness about prepositions that govern the dative. He could not bear to have the other pupils think, for a moment, that he took these people seriously; he must convey to them that he considered it all trivial, and was there only by way of a jest, anyway. He had autograph pictures of all the members of the stock company which he showed his classmates, telling them the most incredible stories of his familiarity with these people, of his acquaintance with the soloists who came to Carnegie Hall, his suppers with them and the flowers he sent them. When these stories lost their effect, and his audience grew listless, he became desperate and would bid all the boys good-bye, announcing that he was going to travel for awhile; going to Naples, to Venice, to Egypt. Then, next Monday, he would slip back, conscious and nervously smiling; his sister was ill, and he should have to defer his voyage until spring.

Matters went steadily worse with Paul at school. In the itch to let his instructors know how heartily he despised them and their homilies, and how thoroughly he was appreciated elsewhere, he mentioned once or twice that he had no time to fool with theorems; adding—with a twitch of the eyebrows and a touch of that nervous bravado which so perplexed them—that he was helping the people down at the stock company; they were old friends of his.

The upshot of the matter was that the Principal went to Paul's father, and Paul was taken out of school and put to work. The manager at Carnegie Hall was told to get another usher in his stead; the doorkeeper at the theatre was warned not to admit him to the house; and Charley Edwards remorsefully promised the boy's father not to see him again.

The members of the stock company were vastly amused when some of Paul's stories reached them—especially the women. They were hardworking women, most of them supporting indigent husbands or brothers, and they laughed rather bitterly at having stirred the boy to such fervid and florid inventions. They agreed with the faculty and with his father that Paul's was a bad case.

The east-bound train was ploughing through a January snow-storm; the dull dawn was beginning to show grey when the engine whistled a mile out of Newark. Paul started up from the seat where he had lain curled in uneasy slumber, rubbed the breath-misted window glass with his hand, and peered out. The snow was whirling in curling eddies above the white bottom lands, and the drifts lay already deep in the fields and along the fences, while here and there the long dead grass and dried weed stalks protruded black above it. Lights shown from the scattered houses, and a gang of labourers who stood beside the track waved their lanterns.

Paul had slept very little, and he felt grimy and uncomfortable. He had made the all-night journey in a day coach, partly because he was ashamed, dressed as he was, to go into a Pullman, and partly because he was afraid of being seen there by some Pittsburgh business man, who might have noticed him in Denny & Carson's office. When the whistle awoke him, he clutched quickly at his breast pocket, glancing about him with an uncertain smile. But the little, clay-bespattered Italians were still sleeping, the slatternly women across the aisle were in open-mouthed oblivion, and even the crumby, crying babies were for the nonce stilled. Paul settled back to struggle with his impatience as best he could.

When he arrived at the Jersey City station, he hurried through his breakfast, manifestly ill at ease and keeping a sharp eye about him. After he reached the Twenty-third Street station, he consulted a cabman, and had himself driven to a men's furnishing establishment that was just opening for the day. He spent upward of two hours there, buying with endless reconsidering and great care. His new street suit he put on in the fitting-room; the frock coat and dress clothes he had bundled into the cab with his linen. Then he drove to a hatter's and a shoe house. His next errand was at Tiffany's, where he selected his silver and a new scarf-pin. He would not wait to have his silver marked, he said. Lastly, he stopped at a trunk shop on Broadway, and had his purchases packed into various travelling bags.

It was a little after one o'clock when he drove up to the Waldorf, and after settling with the cabman, went into the office. He registered from Washington; said his mother and father had been abroad, and that he had come down to await the arrival of their steamer. He told his story plausibly and had no trouble, since he volunteered to pay for them in advance, in engaging his rooms; a sleeping-room, sitting-room and bath.

Not once, but a hundred times Paul had planned this entry into New York. He had gone over every detail of it with Charley Edwards, and in his scrap book at home there were pages of description about New York hotels, cut from the Sunday papers. When he was shown to his sitting-room on the eighth floor, he saw at a glance that everything was as it should be; there was but one detail in his mental picture that the place did not realize, so he rang for the bell boy and sent him down for flowers. He moved about nervously until the boy returned, putting away his new linen and fingering it delightedly as he did so. When the flowers came, he put them hastily into water, and then tumbled into a hot bath. Presently he came out of his white bath-room, resplendent in his new silk underwear, and playing with the tassels of his red robe. The snow was whirling so fiercely outside his windows that he could scarcely see across the street, but within the air was deliciously soft and fragrant. He put the violets and jonquils on the taboret beside the couch, and threw himself down, with a long sigh, covering himself with a Roman blanket. He was thoroughly tired; he had been in such haste, he had stood up to such a strain, covered so much ground in the last twenty-four hours, that he wanted to think how it had all come about. Lulled by the sound of the wind, the warm air, and the cool fragrance of the flowers, he sank into deep, drowsy retrospection.

It had been wonderfully simple; when they had shut him out of the theatre and concert hall, when they had taken away his bone, the whole thing was virtually determined. The rest was a mere matter of opportunity. The only thing that at all surprised him was his own courage—for he realized well enough that he had always been tormented by fear, a sort of apprehensive dread that, of late years, as the meshes of the lies he had told closed about him, had been pulling the muscles of his body tighter and tighter. Until now, he could not remember the time when he had not been dreading something. Even when he was a little boy, it was always there—behind him, or before, or on either side. There had always been the shadowed corner, the dark place into which he dared not look, but from which something seemed always to be watching him—and Paul had done things that were not pretty to watch, he knew.

But now he had a curious sense of relief, as though he had at last thrown down the gauntlet to the thing in the corner.

Yet it was but a day since he had been sulking in the traces; but yesterday afternoon that he had been sent to the bank with Denny & Carson's deposit, as usual—but this time he was instructed to leave the book to be balanced. There was above two thousand dollars in checks, and nearly a thousand in the bank notes which he had taken from the book and quietly transferred to his pocket. At the bank he had made out a new deposit slip. His nerves had been steady enough to permit of his returning to the office, where he had finished his work and asked for a full day's holiday to-morrow, Saturday, giving a perfectly reasonable pretext. The bank book, he knew, would not be returned before Monday or Tuesday, and his father would be out of town for the next week. From the time he slipped the bank notes into his pocket until he boarded the night train for New York, he had not known a moment's hesitation. It was not the first time Paul had steered through treacherous waters.

How astonishingly easy it had all been; here he was, the thing done; and this time there would be no awakening, no figure at the top of the stairs. He watched the snow flakes whirling by his window until he fell asleep.

When he awoke, it was three o'clock in the afternoon. He bounded up with a start; half of one of his precious days gone already! He spent more than an hour in dressing, watching every stage of his toilet carefully in the mirror. Everything was quite perfect; he was exactly the kind of boy he had always wanted to be.

When he went downstairs, Paul took a carriage and drove up Fifth Avenue toward the Park. The snow had somewhat abated; carriages and tradesmen's wagons were hurrying soundlessly to and fro in the winter twilight; boys in woollen mufflers were shovelling off the doorsteps; the avenue stages made fine spots of colour against the white street. Here and there on the corners were stands, with whole flower gardens blooming under glass cases, against the sides of which the snow flakes stuck and melted; violets, roses, carnations, lilies of the valley—somehow vastly more lovely and alluring that they blossomed thus unnaturally in the snow. The Park itself was a wonderful stage winter-piece.

When he returned, the pause of the twilight had ceased, and the tune of the streets had changed. The snow was falling faster, lights streamed from the hotels that reared their dozen stories fearlessly up into the storm, defying the raging Atlantic winds. A long, black stream of carriages poured down the avenue, intersected here and there by other streams, tending horizontally. There were a score of cabs about the entrance of his hotel, and his driver had to wait. Boys in livery were running in and out of the awning stretched across the sidewalk, up and down the red velvet carpet laid from the door to the street. Above, about, within it all was the rumble and roar, and hurry and toss of thousands of human beings as hot for pleasure as himself, and on every side of him towered the glaring affirmation of the omnipotence of wealth.

The boy set his teeth and drew his shoulders together in a spasm of realization; the plot of all dramas, the text of all romances, the nerve-stuff of all sensations was whirling about him like the snow flakes. He burnt like a faggot in a tempest.

When Paul went down to dinner, the music of the orchestra came floating up the elevator shaft to greet him. His head whirled as he stepped into the thronged corridor, and he sank back into one of the chairs against the wall to get his breath. The lights, the chatter, the perfumes, the bewildering medley of colour—he had, for a moment, the feeling of not being able to stand it. But only for a moment; these were his own people, he told himself. He went slowly about the corridors, through the writing-rooms, smoking-rooms, reception-rooms, as though he were exploring the chambers of an enchanted palace, built and peopled for him alone.

When he reached the dining-room he sat down at a table near a window. The flowers, the white linen, the many-coloured wine glasses, the gay toilettes of the women, the low popping of corks, the undulating repetitions of the *Blue Danube* from the orchestra, all flooded Paul's dream with bewildering radiance. When the roseate tinge of his champagne was added—that cold, precious, bubbling stuff that creamed and foamed in his glass—Paul wondered that there were honest men in the world at all. This was what all the world was fighting for, he reflected; this was what all the struggle was about. He doubted the reality of his past. Had he ever known a place called Cordelia Street, a place where fagged-looking business men got on the early car; mere rivets in a machine they seemed to Paul,—sickening men with combings of children's hair always hanging to their coats, and the smell of cooking in their clothes. Cordelia Street—Ah! that belonged to another time and country; had he not always been thus, had he not sat here night after night, from as far back as he could remember, looking pensively over just such shimmering textures, and slowly twirling the stem of a glass like this one between his thumb and middle finger? He rather thought he had.

He was not in the least abashed or lonely. He had no especial desire to meet or to know any of these people; all he demanded was the right to look on and conjecture, to watch the pageant. The mere stage properties were all he contended for. Nor was he lonely later in the evening, in his loge at the Metropolitan. He was now entirely rid of his nervous misgivings, of his forced aggressiveness, of the imperative desire to show himself different from his surroundings. He felt now that his surroundings explained him. Nobody questioned the purple; he had only to wear it passively. He had only to glance down at his attire to reassure himself that here it would be impossible for any one to humiliate him.

He found it hard to leave his beautiful sitting-room to go to bed that night, and sat long watching the raging storm from his turret window. When he went to sleep it was with the lights turned on in his bedroom; partly because of his old timidity, and partly so that, if he should wake in the night, there would be no wretched moment of doubt, no horrible suspicion of yellow wall-paper, or of Washington and Calvin above his bed.

Sunday morning the city was practically snowbound. Paul breakfasted late, and in the afternoon he fell in with a wild San Francisco boy, a freshman at Yale, who said he had run down for a "little flyer" over Sunday. The young man offered to show Paul the night side of the town, and the two boys went out together after dinner, not returning to the hotel until seven o'clock the next morning. They had started out in the confiding warmth of a champagne friendship, but their parting in the elevator was singularly cool. The freshman pulled himself together to make his train, and Paul went to bed. He awoke at two o'clock in the afternoon, very thirsty and dizzy, and rang for ice-water, coffee, and the Pittsburgh papers.

On the part of the hotel management, Paul excited no suspicion. There was this to be said for him, that he wore his spoils with dignity and in no way made himself conspicuous. Even under the glow of his wine he was never boisterous, though he found the stuff like a magician's wand for wonder-building. His chief greediness lay in his ears and eyes, and his excesses were not offensive ones. His dearest pleasures were the grey winter twilights in his sitting-room; his quiet enjoyment of his flowers, his clothes, his wide divan, his cigarette and his sense of power. He could not remember a time when he had felt so at peace with himself. The mere release from the necessity of petty lying, lying every day and every day, restored his self-respect. He had never lied for pleasure, even at school; but to be noticed and admired, to assert his difference from other Cordelia Street boys; and he felt a good deal more manly, more honest, even, now that he had no need for boastful pretensions, now that he could, as his actor friends used to say, "dress the part." It was characteristic that remorse did not occur to him. His golden days went by without a shadow, and he made each as perfect as he could.

On the eighth day after his arrival in New York, he found the whole affair exploited in the Pittsburgh papers, exploited with a wealth of detail which indicated that local news of a sensational nature was at a low ebb. The firm of Denny & Carson announced that the boy's father had refunded the full amount of the theft, and that they had no intention of prosecuting. The Cumberland minister had been interviewed, and expressed his hope of yet reclaiming the motherless lad, and his Sabbath-school teacher declared that she would spare no effort to that end. The rumour had reached Pittsburgh that the boy had been seen in a New York hotel, and his father had gone East to find him and bring him home.

Paul had just come in to dress for dinner; he sank into a chair, weak to the knees, and clasped his head in his hands. It was to be worse than jail, even; the tepid waters of Cordelia Street were to close over him finally and forever. The grey monotony stretched before him in hopeless, unrelieved years; Sabbath-school, Young People's Meeting, the yellow-papered room, the damp dish-towels; it all rushed back upon him with a sickening vividness. He had the old feeling that the orchestra had suddenly stopped, the sinking sensation that the play was over. The sweat broke out on his face, and he sprang to his feet, looked about him with his white, conscious smile, and winked at himself in the mirror. With something of the old childish belief in miracles with which he had so often gone to class, all his lessons unlearned, Paul dressed and dashed whistling down the corridor to the elevator.

He had no sooner entered the dining-room and caught the measure of the music than his remembrance was lightened by his old elastic power of claiming the moment, mounting with it, and finding it all sufficient. The glare and glitter about him, the mere scenic accessories had again, and for the last time, their old potency. He would show himself that he was game, he would finish the thing splendidly. He doubted, more than ever, the existence of Cordelia Street, and for the first time he drank his wine recklessly. He was not, after all, one of those fortunate beings born to the purple, was he not still himself and in his own place? He drummed a nervous accompaniment to the Pagliacci music and looked about him, telling himself over and over that it had paid.

He reflected drowsily, to the swell of the music and the chill sweetness of his wine, that he might have done it more wisely. He might have caught an outbound steamer and been well out of their clutches before now. But the other side of the world had seemed too far away and too uncertain then; he could not have waited for it; his need had been too sharp. If he had to choose over again, he would do the same thing to-morrow. He looked affectionately about the dining-room, now gilded with a soft mist. Ah, it had paid indeed!

Paul was awakened next morning by a painful throbbing in his head and feet. He had thrown himself across the bed without undressing, and had slept with his shoes on. His limbs and hands were lead heavy, and his tongue and throat were parched and burnt. There came upon him one of those fateful attacks of clear-headedness that never occurred except when he was physically exhausted and his nerves hung loose. He lay still and closed his eyes and let the tide of things wash over him.

His father was in New York; "stopping at some joint or other," he told himself. The memory of successive summers on the front stoop fell upon him like a weight of black water. He had not a hundred dollars left; and he knew now, more than ever, that money was everything, the wall that stood between all he loathed and all he wanted. The thing was winding itself up; he had thought of that on his first glorious day in New York, and had even provided a way to snap the thread. It lay on his dressing-table now; he had got it out last night when he came blindly up from dinner, but the shiny metal hurt his eyes, and he disliked the looks of it.

He rose and moved about with a painful effort, succumbing now and again to attacks of nausea. It was the old depression exaggerated; all the world had become Cordelia Street. Yet somehow he was not afraid of anything, was absolutely calm; perhaps because he had looked into the dark corner at last and knew. It was bad enough, what he saw there, but somehow not so bad as his long fear of it had been. He saw everything clearly now. He had a feeling that he had made the best of it, that he had lived the sort of life he was meant to live, and for half an hour he sat staring at the revolver. But he told himself that was not the way, so he went downstairs and took a cab to the ferry.

When Paul arrived at Newark, he got off the train and took another cab, directing the driver to follow the Pennsylvania tracks out of the town. The snow lay heavy on the roadways and had drifted deep in the open fields. Only here and there the dead grass or dried weed stalks projected, singularly black, above it. Once well into the country, Paul dismissed the carriage and walked, floundering along the tracks, his mind a medley of irrelevant things. He seemed to hold in his brain an actual picture of everything he had seen that morning. He remembered every feature of both his drivers, of the toothless old woman from whom he had bought the red flowers in his coat, the agent from whom he had got his ticket, and all of his fellow-passengers on the ferry. His mind, unable to cope with vital matters near at hand, worked feverishly and deftly at sorting and grouping these images. They made for him a part of the ugliness of the world, of the ache in his head, and the bitter burning on his tongue. He stooped and put a handful of snow into his mouth as he walked, but that, too, seemed hot. When he reached a little hillside, where the tracks ran through a cut some twenty feet below him, he stopped and sat down.

The carnations in his coat were drooping with the cold, he noticed; their red glory all over. It occurred to him that all the flowers he had seen in the glass cases that first night must have gone the same way, long before this. It was only one splendid breath they had, in spite of their brave mockery at the winter outside the glass; and it was a losing game in the end, it seemed, this revolt against the homilies by which the world is run. Paul took one of the blossoms carefully from his coat and scooped a little hole in the snow, where he covered it up. Then he dozed a while, from his weak condition, seemingly insensible to the cold.

The sound of an approaching train awoke him, and he started to his feet, remembering only his resolution, and afraid lest he should be too late. He stood watching the approaching locomotive, his teeth chattering, his lips drawn away from them in a frightened smile; once or twice he glanced nervously sidewise, as though he were being watched. When the right moment came, he jumped. As he fell, the folly of his haste occurred to him with merciless clearness, the vastness of what he had left undone. There flashed through his brain, clearer than ever before, the blue of Adriatic water, the yellow of Algerian sands.

He felt something strike his chest, and that his body was being thrown swiftly through the air, on and on, immeasurably far and fast, while his limbs were gently relaxed. Then, because the picture making mechanism was crushed, the disturbing visions flashed into black, and Paul dropped back into the immense design of things.

Sherwood Anderson

1876 – 1941

Sherwood Anderson shared with other writers of the early twentieth century a conviction that the short story, under the aegis of the popular magazine, had become standardized in technique, a "plot" story, written by formula. Objecting to the "plot notion" and to arbitrary rules of any kind, Anderson cultivated artistic freedom in his method of writing. As a result of its unconventionality in technique and subject matter, his first collection, *Winesburg, Ohio,* was roundly criticized on its appearance in 1919 but now stands as a landmark in the short story's development.

Although Anderson became a professional writer relatively late in life, after a career in business, his predisposition for storytelling probably dated from his early childhood in Camden, Ohio, his birthplace (1876), where he heard his imaginative, jack-of-all-trades father enthrall country listeners with tall tales. Compelled to earn his own way without the benefit of much schooling, he successively worked as newsboy, farm laborer, stable boy, factory hand, and copywriter in an advertising office. Service as a soldier during the Spanish-American War stimulated him to enlarge his horizons, and he enrolled in the Wittenberg Academy in Springfield, Ohio. Through the acquaintanceship he formed in his one term there with a friendly editor, he secured a position as copywriter and solicitor in a Chicago advertising agency. From copywriting, he soon branched out into articles and attempts at fiction, but he was yet far from being a professional writer. Resigning from the agency in 1906, he entered business for himself, first as president of a mail-order store in Cleveland and next as part owner and manager of a paint factory in

Elyria, Ohio. In 1912, no longer able to continue business in the daytime and writing at night, he left his factory, returned to Chicago, and supported himself by advertising work again while he entered seriously into his writing career. His first novels, *Windy McPherson's Son* (1916) and *Marching Men* (1917), and a volume of poetry, *Mid-American Chants* (1918), brought him some attention, but wide recognition came only with *Winesburg, Ohio* (1919) and such later works as *Poor White* (1920) and, particularly, *Dark Laughter* (1925). In addition to *Winesburg,* his most important story collections are *Triumph of the Egg* (1921), *Horses and Men* (1923), and *Death in the Woods and Other Stories* (1933). He published various other works before his death in 1941.

Anderson's chief objection to the "plot notion" was that the compulsion on the writer to make his characters fit a mechanical scheme of action inevitably resulted in a false, distorted presentation of life. Rather than plot, the writer should concentrate on *form*—"an altogether more elusive and difficult thing to come at." "Form," he said, "grew out of the materials of the tale and the teller's reaction to them," by which he meant that each story is a highly individualistic problem incapable of being solved by any set technical formula. His way of attempting to realize the elusiveness of form may be profitably studied in "Death in the Woods," which he considered his best story.

Death in the Woods

She was an old woman and lived on a farm near the town in which I lived. All country and small-town people have seen such old women, but no one knows much about them. Such an old woman comes into town driving an old worn-out horse or she comes afoot carrying a basket. She may own

"Death in the Woods" by Sherwood Anderson. Published in *American Mercury*, September 1926.

a few hens and have eggs to sell. She brings them in a basket and takes them to a grocer. There she trades them in. She gets some salt pork and some beans. Then she gets a pound or two of sugar and some flour.

Afterwards she goes to the butcher's and asks for some dog-meat. She may spend ten or fifteen cents, but when she does she asks for something. Formerly the butchers gave liver to any one who wanted to carry it away. In our family we were always having it. Once one of my brothers got a whole cow's liver at the slaughter-house near the fairgrounds in our town. We had it until we were sick of it. It never cost a cent. I have hated the thought of it ever since.

The old farm woman got some liver and a soup-bone. She never visited with any one, and as soon as she got what she wanted she lit out for home. It made quite a load for such an old body. No one gave her a lift. People drive right down a road and never notice an old woman like that.

There was such an old woman who used to come into town past our house one Summer and Fall when I was a young boy and was sick with what was called inflammatory rheumatism. She went home later carrying a heavy pack on her back. Two or three large gaunt-looking dogs followed at her heels.

The old woman was nothing special. She was one of the nameless ones that hardly any one knows, but she got into my thoughts. I have just suddenly now, after all these years, remembered her and her husband and son in a small unpainted house on the bank of a small creek four miles from town.

The husband and son were a tough lot. Although the son was but twenty-one, he had already served a term in jail. It was whispered about that the woman's husband stole horses and ran them off to some other county. Now and then, when a horse turned up missing, the man had also disappeared. No one ever caught him. Once, when I was loafing at Tom Whitehead's livery-barn, the man came there and sat on the bench in front. Two or three other men were there, but no one spoke to him. He sat for a few minutes and then got up and went away. When he was leaving he turned around and stared at the men. There was a look of defiance in his eyes. "Well, I have tried to be friendly. You don't want to talk to me. It has been so wherever I have gone in this town. If, some day, one of your fine horses turns up missing, well, then what?" He did not say anything actually. "I'd like to bust one of you on the jaw," was about what his eyes said. I remember how the look in his eyes made me shiver.

The old man belonged to a family that had had money once. His name was Jake Grimes. It all comes back clearly now. His father, John Grimes, had owned a sawmill when the country was new, and had made money. Then he got to drinking and running after women. When he died there wasn't much left.

Jake blew in the rest. Pretty soon there wasn't any more lumber to cut and his land was nearly all gone.

He got his wife off a German farmer, for whom he went to work one June day in the wheat harvest. She was a young thing then and scared to death. You see, the farmer was up to something with the girl—she was, I think, a bound girl and his wife had her suspicions. She took it out on the girl when the man wasn't around. Then, when the wife had to go off to town for supplies, the farmer got after her. She told young Jake that nothing really ever happened, but he didn't know whether to believe it or not.

He got her pretty easy himself, the first time he was out with her. He wouldn't have married her if the German farmer hadn't tried to tell him where to get off. He got her to go riding with him in his buggy one night when he was threshing on the place, and then he came for her the next Sunday night.

She managed to get out of the house without her employer's seeing, but when she was getting into the buggy he showed up. It was almost dark, and he just popped up suddenly at the horse's head. He grabbed the horse by the bridle and Jake got out his buggy-whip.

They had it out all right! The German was a tough one. Maybe he didn't care whether his wife knew or not. Jake hit him over the face and shoulders with the buggy-whip, but the horse got to acting up and he had to get out.

Then the two men went for it. The girl didn't see it. The horse started to run away and went nearly a mile down the road before the girl got him stopped. Then she managed to tie him to a tree beside the road. (I wonder how I know all this. It must have stuck in my mind from small-town tales when I was a boy.) Jake found her there after he got through with the German. She was huddled up in the buggy seat, crying, scared to death. She told Jake a lot of stuff, how the German had tried to get her, how he chased her once into the barn, how another time, when they happened to be alone in the house together, he tore her dress open clear down the front. The German, she said, might have got her that time if he hadn't heard his old woman drive in at the gate. She had been off to town for supplies. Well, she would be putting the horse in the barn. The German managed to sneak off to the fields without his wife seeing. He told the girl he would kill her if she told. What could she do? She told a lie about ripping her dress in the barn when she was feeding the stock. I remember now that she was a bound girl and did not know where her father and mother were. Maybe she did not have any father. You know what I mean.

Such bound children were often enough cruelly treated. They were children who had no parents, slaves really. There were very few orphan homes then. They were legally bound into some home. It was a matter of pure luck how it came out.

II

She married Jake and had a son and daughter, but the daughter died.

Then she settled down to feed stock. That was her job. At the German's place she had cooked the food for the German and his wife. The wife was a strong woman with big hips and worked most of the time in the fields with her husband. She fed them and fed the cows in the barn, fed the pigs, the horses and the chickens. Every moment of every day, as a young girl, was spent feeding something.

Then she married Jake Grimes and he had to be fed. She was a slight thing, and when she had been married for three or four years, and after the two children were born, her slender shoulders became stooped.

Jake always had a lot of big dogs around the house, that stood near the unused sawmill near the creek. He was always trading horses when he wasn't stealing something and had a lot of poor bony ones about. Also he kept three or four pigs and a cow. They were all pastured in the few acres left of the Grimes place and Jake did little enough work.

He went into debt for a threshing outfit and ran it for several years, but it did not pay. People did not trust him. They were afraid he would steal the grain at night. He had to go a long way off to get work and it cost too much to get there. In the Winter he hunted and cut a little firewood, to be sold in some nearby town. When the son grew up he was just like the father. They got drunk together. If there wasn't anything to eat in the house when they came home the old man gave his old woman a cut over the head. She had a few chickens of her own and had to kill one of them in a hurry. When they were all killed she wouldn't have any eggs to sell when she went to town, and then what would she do?

She had to scheme all her life about getting things fed, getting the pigs fed so they would grow fat and could be butchered in the Fall. When they were butchered her husband took most of the meat off to town and sold it. If he did not do it first the boy did. They fought sometimes and when they fought the old woman stood aside trembling.

She had got the habit of silence anyway—that was fixed. Sometimes, when she began to look old—she wasn't forty yet—and when the husband and son were both off, trading horses or drinking or hunting or stealing, she went around the house and the barnyard muttering to herself.

How was she going to get everything fed?—that was her problem. The dogs had to be fed. There wasn't enough hay in the barn for the horses and the cow. If she didn't feed the chickens how could they lay eggs? Without eggs to sell how could she get things in town, things she had to have to keep the life of the farm going? Thank heaven, she did not have to feed her husband—in a certain way. That hadn't lasted long after their marriage and after the babies came. Where he went on his long trips she did not know. Sometimes he was gone from home for weeks, and after the boy grew up they went off together.

They left everything at home for her to manage and she had no money. She knew no one. No one ever talked to her in town. When it was Winter she had to gather sticks of wood for her fire, had to try to keep the stock fed with very little grain.

The stock in the barn cried to her hungrily, the dogs followed her about. In the Winter the hens laid few enough eggs. They huddled in the corners of the barn and she kept watching them. If a hen lays an egg in the barn in the Winter and you do not find it, it freezes and breaks.

One day in Winter the old woman went off to town with a few eggs and the dogs followed her. She did not get started until nearly three o'clock and the snow was heavy. She hadn't been feeling very well for several days and so she went muttering along, scantily clad, her shoulders stooped. She had an old grain bag in which she carried her eggs, tucked away down in the bottom. There weren't many of them, but in Winter the price of eggs is up. She would get a little meat in exchange for the eggs, some salt pork, a little sugar, and some coffee perhaps. It might be the butcher would give her a piece of liver.

When she had got to town and was trading in her eggs the dogs lay by the door outside. She did pretty well, got the things she needed, more than she had hoped. Then she went to the butcher and he gave her some liver and some dog-meat.

It was the first time any one had spoken to her in a friendly way for a long time. The butcher was alone in his shop when she came in and was annoyed by the thought of such a sick-looking old woman out on such a day. It was bitter cold and the snow, that had let up during the afternoon, was falling again. The butcher said something about her husband and her son, swore at them, and the old woman stared at him, a look of mild surprise in her eyes as he talked. He said that if either the husband or the son were going to get any of the liver or the heavy bones with scraps of meat hanging to them that he had put into the grain bag, he'd see him starve first.

Starve, eh? Well, things had to be fed. Men had to be fed, and horses that weren't any good but maybe could be traded off, and the poor thin cow that hadn't given any milk for three months.

Horses, cows, pigs, dogs, men.

III

The old woman had to get back before darkness came if she could. The dogs followed at her heels, sniffing at the heavy grain bag she had fastened on her back. When she got to the edge of town she stopped by a fence and tied the bag on her back with a piece of rope she had carried in her dress-pocket for just that purpose. It was hard when she had to crawl over fences and once she fell over and landed in the snow. The dogs went frisking about. She had to struggle to get to her feet again, but she made it. The point of climbing over the fences was that there was a short cut over a hill and through a woods. She might have gone around by the road, but it was a mile farther that way. She was afraid she couldn't make it. And then, besides, the stock had to be fed. There was a little hay left and a little corn. Perhaps her husband and son would bring some home when they came. They had driven off in the only buggy the Grimes family had, a rickety thing, a rickety horse hitched to the buggy, two other rickety horses led by halters. They were going to trade horses, get a little money if they could. They might come home drunk. It would be well to have something in the house when they came back.

The son had an affair on with a woman at the county seat, fifteen miles away. She was a rough enough woman, a tough one. Once, in the Summer, the son had brought her to the house. Both she and the son had been drinking. Jake Grimes was away and the son and his woman ordered the old woman about like a servant. She didn't mind much; she was used to it. Whatever happened she never said anything. That was her way of getting along. She had managed that way when she was a young girl at the German's and ever since she had married Jake. That time her son brought his woman to the house they stayed all night, sleeping together just as though they were married. It hadn't shocked the old woman, not much. She had got past being shocked early in life.

With the pack on her back she went painfully along across an open field, wading in the deep snow, and got into the woods.

There was a path, but it was hard to follow. Just beyond the top of the hill, where the woods was thickest, there was a small clearing. Had some one once thought of building a house there? The clearing was as large as a building lot in town, large enough for a house and a garden. The path ran along the side of the clearing, and when she got there the old woman sat down to rest at the foot of a tree.

It was a foolish thing to do. When she got herself placed, the pack against the tree's trunk, it was nice, but what about getting up again? She worried about that for a moment and then quietly closed her eyes.

She must have slept for a time. When you are about so cold you can't get any colder. The afternoon grew a little warmer and the snow came thicker than ever. Then after a time the weather cleared. The moon even came out.

There were four Grimes dogs that had followed Mrs. Grimes into town, all tall gaunt fellows. Such men as Jake Grimes and his son always keep just such dogs. They kick and abuse them, but they stay. The Grimes dogs, in order to keep from starving, had to do a lot of foraging for themselves, and they had been at it while the old woman slept with her back to the tree at the side of the clearing. They had been chasing rabbits in the woods and in adjoining fields and in their ranging had picked up three other farm dogs.

After a time all the dogs came back to the clearing. They were excited about something. Such nights, cold and clear and with a moon, do things to dogs. It may be that some old instinct, come down from the time when they were wolves, and ranged the woods in packs on Winter nights, comes back into them.

The dogs in the clearing, before the old woman, had caught two or three rabbits and their immediate hunger had been satisfied. They began to play, running in circles in the clearing. Round and round they ran, each dog's nose at the tail of the next dog. In the clearing, under the snow-laden trees and under the wintry moon they made a strange picture, running thus silently, in a circle their running had beaten in the soft snow. The dogs made no sound. They ran around and around in the circle.

It may have been that the old woman saw them doing that before she died. She may have awakened once or twice and looked at the strange sight with dim old eyes.

She wouldn't be very cold now, just drowsy. Life hangs on a long time. Perhaps the old woman was out of her head. She may have dreamed of her girlhood at the German's, and before that, when she was a child and before her mother lit out and left her.

Her dreams couldn't have been very pleasant. Not many pleasant things had happened to her. Now and then one of the Grimes dogs left the running circle and came to stand before her. The dog thrust his face to her face. His red tongue was hanging out.

The running of the dogs may have been a kind of death ceremony. It may have been that the primitive instinct of the wolf, having been aroused in the dogs by the night and the running, made them somehow, afraid.

"Now we are no longer wolves. We are dogs, the servants of men. Keep alive, man! When man dies we become wolves again." When one of the dogs came to where the old woman sat with her back against the tree and thrust his nose close to her face he seemed satisfied and went back to run with the pack. All the Grimes dogs did it at some time during the evening, before she died. I knew all about it afterward, when I grew to be a man, because once in a woods in Illinois, on another Winter night, I saw a pack of dogs act just like that. The dogs were waiting for me to die as they had waited for the old woman that night when I was a child, but when it happened to me I was a young man and had no intention whatever of dying.

The old woman died softly and quietly. When she was dead and when one of the Grimes dogs had come to her and had found her dead all the dogs stopped running.

They gathered about her.

Well, she was dead now. She had fed the Grimes dogs when she was alive, what about now?

There was the pack on her back, the grain bag containing the piece of salt pork, the liver the butcher had given her, the dog-meat, the soup bones. The butcher in town, having been suddenly overcome with a feeling of pity, had loaded her grain bag heavily. It had been a big haul for the old woman.

It was a big haul for the dogs now.

IV

One of the Grimes dogs sprang suddenly out from among the others and began worrying the pack on the old woman's back. Had the dogs really been wolves that one would have been the leader of the pack. What he did, all the others did.

All of them sank their teeth into the grain bag the old woman had fastened with ropes to her back.

They dragged the old woman's body out into the open clearing. The worn-out dress was quickly torn from her shoulders. When she was found, a day or two later, the dress had been torn from her body clear to the hips, but the dogs had not touched her body. They had got the meat out of the grain bag, that was all. Her body was frozen stiff when it was found, and the shoulders were so narrow and the body so slight that in death it looked like the body of some charming young girl.

Such things happened in towns of the Middle West, on farms near town, when I was a boy. A hunter out after rabbits found the old woman's body and did not touch it. Something, the beaten round path in the little snow-covered clearing, the silence of the place, the place where the dogs had worried the body trying to pull the grain bag away or tear it open—something startled the man and he hurried off to town.

I was in Main Street with one of my brothers who was town newsboy and who was taking the afternoon papers to the stores. It was almost night.

The hunter came into a grocery and told his story. Then he went into a hardware-shop and into a drugstore. Men began to gather on the sidewalks. Then they started out along the road to the place in the woods.

My brother should have gone on about his business of distributing papers but he didn't. Every one was going to the woods. The undertaker went and the town marshal. Several men got on a dray and rode out to where the path left the road and went into the woods, but the horses weren't very sharply shod and slid about on the slippery roads. They made no better time than those of us who walked.

The town marshal was a large man whose leg had been injured in the Civil War. He carried a heavy cane and limped rapidly along the road. My brother and I followed at his heels, and as we went other men and boys joined the crowd.

It had grown dark by the time we got to where the old woman had left the road but the moon had come out. The marshal was thinking there might have been a murder. He kept asking the hunter questions. The hunter went along with his gun across his shoulders, a dog following at his heels. It isn't often a rabbit hunter has a chance to be so conspicuous. He was taking full advantage of it, leading the procession with the town marshal. "I didn't see any wounds. She was a beautiful young girl. Her face was buried in the snow. No, I didn't know her." As a matter of fact, the hunter had not looked closely at the body. He had been frightened. She might have been murdered and some one might spring out from behind a tree and murder him. In a woods, in the late afternoon, when the trees are all bare and there is white snow on the ground, when all is silent, something creepy steals over the mind and body. If something strange or uncanny has happened in the neighborhood all you think about is getting away from there as fast as you can.

The crowd of men and boys had got to where the old woman had crossed the field and went, following the marshal and the hunter, up the slight incline and into the woods.

My brother and I were silent. He had his bundle of papers in a bag slung across his shoulder. When he got back to town he would have to go on distributing his papers before he went home to supper. If I went along, as he had no doubt already determined I should, we would both be late. Either mother or our older sister would have to warm our supper.

Well, we would have something to tell. A boy did not get such a chance very often. It was lucky we just happened to go into the grocery when the hunter came in. The hunter was a country fellow. Neither of us had ever seen him before.

Now the crowd of men and boys had got to the clearing. Darkness comes quickly on such Winter nights, but the full moon made everything clear. My brother and I stood near the tree, beneath which the old woman had died.

She did not look old, lying there in that light, frozen and still. One of the men turned her over in the snow and I saw everything. My body trembled with some strange mystical feeling and so did my brother's. It might have been the cold.

Neither of us had ever seen a woman's body before. It may have been the snow, clinging to the frozen flesh, that made it look so white and lovely, so like marble. No woman had come with the party from town; but one of the men, he was the town blacksmith, took off his overcoat and spread it over her. Then he gathered her into his arms and started off to town, all the others following silently. At that time no one knew who she was.

V

I had seen everything, had seen the oval in the snow, like a miniature race-track, where the dogs had run, had seen how the men were mystified, had seen the white bare young-looking shoulders, had heard the whispered comments of the men.

The men were simply mystified. They took the body to the undertaker's, and when the blacksmith, the hunter, the marshal and several others had got inside they closed the door. If father had been there perhaps he could have got in, but we boys couldn't.

I went with my brother to distribute the rest of his papers and when we got home it was my brother who told the story.

I kept silent and went to bed early. It may have been I was not satisfied with the way he told it.

Later, in the town, I must have heard other fragments of the old woman's story. She was recognized the next day and there was an investigation.

The husband and son were found somewhere and brought to town and there was an attempt to connect them with the woman's death, but it did not work. They had perfect enough alibis.

However, the town was against them. They had to get out. Where they went I never heard.

I remember only the picture there in the forest, the men standing about, the naked girlish-looking figure, face down in the snow, the tracks made by the running dogs and the clear cold Winter sky above. White fragments of clouds were drifting across the sky. They went racing across the little open space among the trees.

The scene in the forest had become for me, without my knowing it, the foundation for the real story I am now trying to tell. The fragments, you see, had to be picked up slowly, long afterwards.

Things happened. When I was a young man I worked on the farm of a German. The hired-girl was afraid of her employer. The farmer's wife hated her.

I saw things at that place. Once later, I had a half-uncanny, mystical adventure with dogs in an Illinois forest on a clear, moon-lit Winter night. When I was a schoolboy, and on a Summer day, I went with a boy friend out along a creek some miles from town and came to the house where the old woman had lived. No one had lived in the house since her death. The doors were broken from the hinges; the window lights were all broken. As the boy and I stood in the road outside, two dogs, just roving farm dogs no doubt, came running around the corner of the house. The dogs were tall, gaunt fellows and came down to the fence and glared through at us, standing in the road.

The whole thing, the story of the old woman's death, was to me as I grew older like music heard from far off. The notes had to be picked up slowly one at a time. Something had to be understood.

The woman who died was one destined to feed animal life. Anyway, that is all she ever did. She was feeding animal life before she was born, as a child, as a young woman working on the farm of the German, after she married, when she grew old and when she died. She fed animal life in cows, in chickens, in pigs, in horses, in dogs, in men. Her daughter had died in childhood and with her one son she had no articulate relations. On the night when she died she was hurrying homeward, bearing on her body food for animal life.

She died in the clearing in the woods and even after her death continued feeding animal life.

You see it is likely that, when my brother told the story, that night when we got home and my mother and sister sat listening, I did not think he got the point. He was too young and so was I. A thing so complete has its own beauty.

I shall not try to emphasize the point. I am only explaining why I was dissatisfied then and have been ever since. I speak of that only that you may understand why I have been impelled to try to tell the simple story over again.

Katherine Anne Porter

1890 – 1980

Despite having published only a relatively small body of fiction, Katherine Anne Porter holds a preeminent rank among the many brilliant writers who have contributed significantly to the development of the American short story during the twentieth century. One of the finest prose stylists in American literature, past or present, she wrote with the utmost economy and compactness, extending through metaphorical language and symbolism the meaning of what was actually stated on the page.

Porter was born in 1890 in Indian Creek, Texas, near San Antonio, the daughter of Harrison Boone and Mary Alice Porter. She received her education in small southern schools for girls, supplementing her formal training by extensive reading. Although from her earliest youth she wanted to write fiction, she entered her professional career by way of journalism and miscellaneous writing. For a time she was a news reporter in Dallas and later in Denver, but after an illness interrupted her newspaper work, she traveled in the United States and many foreign countries, supporting herself by book reviewing, articles, and hack writing of various kinds. She first began publishing stories in *Century, Transition, New Masses, Scribner's,* and *Hound and Horn,* and her first collection, *Flowering Judas* (1930), reissued in 1935 with four additional stories, was of such merit that critics acclaimed her as one of the most talented short story writers of the day. She continued to hold this position on the basis of the equally high merit of other collections which appeared at intervals: *Hacienda* (1934), *Pale Horse, Pale Rider* (1939), and *The Leaning Tower and Other Stories* (1944). Periodically she continued to travel and lived in different parts of the United States, Europe, and Mexico; her cosmopolitanism is reflected in her acute understanding of the various groups portrayed in her fiction, notably in her novel *The Ship of Fools* (1962). She died in 1980.

Some critics regard "The Grave" as a "lyric" short story. As the term suggests, this type of story bears a structural kinship to the lyric poem in that it presents a character in a dramatic situation rather than through a developing plot, the author's intention being less that of telling a story than dramatizing an idea or state of mind, as the poem does. This kind of story also employs symbolic detail, figurative language, imagery, and other structural devices traditionally more closely associated with the manner and method of poetry than with that of prose.

The Grave

The grandfather, dead for more than thirty years, had been twice disturbed in his long repose by the constancy and possessiveness of his widow. She removed his bones first to Louisiana and then to Texas as if she had set out to find her own burial place, knowing well she would never return to the places she had left. In Texas she set up a small cemetery in a corner of her first farm, and as the family connection grew, and oddments of relations came over from Kentucky to settle, it contained at last about twenty graves. After the grandmother's death, part of her land was to be sold for the benefit of certain of her children, and the cemetery happened to lie in the part set aside for sale. It was necessary to take up the bodies and bury them again in the family plot in the big new public cemetery, where the grandmother had been buried. At last her husband was to lie beside her for eternity, as she had planned.

The familiy cemetery had been a pleasant small neglected garden of tangled rose bushes and ragged cedar trees and cypress, the simple flat stones rising out of uncropped sweet-smelling wild grass. The graves were lying open and empty one burning day when Miranda and her brother Paul, who often went together to hunt rabbits and doves, propped their twenty-two Winchester rifles carefully against the rail fence, climbed over and explored among the graves. She was nine years old and he was twelve.

They peered into the pits all shaped alike with such purposeful accuracy, and looking at each other with pleased adventurous eyes, they said in solemn tones: "These were graves!" trying by words to shape a special, suitable emotion in their minds, but they felt nothing except an agreeable thrill of wonder: they were seeing a new sight, doing something they had not done before. In them both there was also a small disappointment at the entire commonplaceness of the actual spectacle. Even if it had once contained a coffin for years upon years, when the coffin was gone a grave was just a hole in the ground. Miranda leaped into the pit that had held her grandfather's bones. Scratching around aimlessly and pleasurably as any young animal, she scooped up a lump of earth and weighed it in her palm. It had a pleasantly sweet, corrupt smell, being mixed with cedar needles and small leaves, and as the crumbs fell apart, she saw a silver dove no larger than a hazel nut, with spread wings and a neat fan-shaped tail. The breast had a deep round hollow in it. Turning it up to the fierce sunlight, she saw that the inside of the hollow was cut in little whorls. She scrambled out, over the pile of loose earth that had fallen back into one end of the grave, calling to Paul that she had found something, he must guess what . . . His head appeared smiling over the rim of another grave. He waved a closed hand at her. "I've got something too!" They ran to compare treasures, making a game of it, so many guesses each, all wrong, and a final showdown with opened palms. Paul had found a thin wide gold ring carved with intricate flowers and leaves. Miranda was smitten at sight of the ring and wished to have it. Paul seemed more impressed by the dove. They made a trade, with some little bickering. After he had got the dove in his hand, Paul said, "Don't you know what this is? This is a screw head for a *Coffin!* . . . I'll bet nobody else in the world has one like this!"

Miranda glanced at it without covetousness. She had the gold ring on her thumb; it fitted perfectly. "Maybe we ought to go now," she said, "maybe one of the niggers 'll see us and tell somebody." They knew the land had been sold, the cemetery was no longer theirs, and they felt like trespassers. They climbed back over the fence, slung their rifles loosely under their arms—they had been shooting at targets with various kinds of firearms since they were seven years old—and set out to look for the rabbits and doves or whatever small game might happen along. On these expeditions Miranda always followed at Paul's heels along the path, obeying instructions about handling her gun when going through fences; learning how to stand it up properly so it would not slip and fire unexpectedly; how to wait her time for a shot and not just bang away in the air without looking, spoiling shots for Paul, who really could hit things if given a chance. Now and then, in her excitement at seeing birds whizz up suddenly before her face, or a rabbit leap across her very toes, she lost her head, and almost without sighting she flung her rifle up and pulled the trigger. She hardly ever hit any sort of mark. She had no proper sense of hunting at all. Her brother would be often completely disgusted with her. "You don't care whether you get your bird or not," he said. "That's no way to hunt." Miranda could not understand his indignation. She had seen him smash his hat and yell with fury when he had missed his aim. "What I like about shooting," said Miranda, with exasperating inconsequence, "is pulling the trigger and hearing the noise."

"Then, by golly," said Paul, "whyn't you go back to the range and shoot at bulls-eyes?

"I'd just as soon," said Miranda, "only like this, we walk around more."

"Well, you just stay behind and stop spoiling my shots," said Paul, who, when he made a kill, wanted to be certain he had made it. Miranda, who alone brought down a bird once in twenty rounds, always claimed as her own any game thay got when they fired at the same moment. It was tiresome and unfair and her brother was sick of it.

"Now, the first dove we see, or the first rabbit, is mine," he told her. "And the next will be yours. Remember that and don't get smarty."

"What about snakes?" asked Miranda idly. "Can I have the first snake?"

Waving her thumb gently and watching her gold ring glitter, Miranda lost interest in shooting. She was wearing her summer roughing outfit: dark blue overalls, a light blue shirt, a hired-man's straw hat, and thick brown sandals. Her brother had the same outfit except his was a sober hickory-nut color. Ordinarily Miranda preferred her overalls to any other dress, though it was making rather a scandal in the countryside, for the year was 1903, and in the back country the law of female decorum had teeth in it. Her father had been criticized for letting his girls dress like boys and go careering around astride barebacked horses. Big sister Maria, the really independent and fearless one, in spite of her rather affected ways, rode at a dead run with only a rope knotted around her horse's nose. It was said the motherless family was running down, with the Grandmother no longer there to hold it together. It was known that she had discriminated against her son Harry in her will, and that he was in straits about money. Some of his old neighbors reflected with vicious satisfaction that now he would probably not be so stiffnecked, nor have any more high-stepping horses either. Miranda knew this, though she could not say how. She had met along the road old women of the kind who smoked corn-cob pipes, who had treated her grandmother with most sincere respect. They slanted their gummy old eyes side-ways at the granddaughter and said, "Ain't you ashamed of yoself, Missy? It's aginst the Scriptures to dress like that. Whut yo Pappy thinkin about?" Miranda, with her powerful social sense, which was like a fine set of antennae radiating from every pore of her skin, would feel ashamed because she knew well it was rude and ill-bred to shock anybody, even bad-tempered old crones, though she had faith in her father's judgment and was perfectly comfortable in the clothes. Her father had said, "They're just what you need, and they'll save your dresses for school. . . . " This sounded quite simple and natural to her. She had been brought up in rigorous economy. Wastefulness was vulgar. It was also a sin. These were truths; she had heard them repeated many times and never once disputed.

Now the ring, shining with the serene purity of fine gold on her rather grubby thumb, turned her feelings against her overalls and sockless feet, toes sticking through the thick brown leather straps. She wanted to go back to the farmhouse, take a good cold bath, dust herself with plenty of Maria's violet talcum powder—provided Maria was not present to object, of course—put on the thinnest, most becoming dress she owned, with a big sash, and sit in a wicker chair under the trees . . . These things were not all she wanted of course; she had vague stirrings of desire for luxury and a grand way of living which could not take precise form in her imagination but were founded on family legend of past wealth and leisure. These immediate comforts were what she could have, and she wanted them at once. She lagged rather far behind Paul, and once she thought of just turning back without a word and going home. She stopped, thinking that Paul would never do that to her, and so she would have to tell him. When a rabbit leaped, she let Paul have it without dispute. He killed it with one shot.

When she came up with him, he was already kneeling, examining the wound, the rabbit trailing from his hands. "Right through the head." he said complacently, as if he had aimed for it. He took out his sharp, competent bowie knife and started to skin the body. He did it very cleanly and quickly. Uncle Jimbilly knew how to prepare the skins so that Miranda always had fur coats for her dolls, for though she never cared much for her dolls she liked seeing them in fur coats. The children knelt facing each other over the dead animal. Miranda watched admiringly while her brother stripped the skin away as if he were taking off a glove. The flayed flesh emerged dark scarlet, sleek, firm; Miranda with thumb and finger felt the long fine muscles with the silvery flat strips binding them to the joints. Brother lifted the oddly bloated belly. "Look," he said, in a low amazed voice. "It was going to have young ones."

Very carefully he slit the thin flesh from the center ribs to the flanks, and a scarlet bag appeared. He slit again and pulled the bag open, and there lay a bundle of tiny rabbits, each wrapped in a thin scarlet veil. The brother pulled these off and there they were, dark gray, their sleek wet down lying in minute even ripples, like a baby's head just washed, their unbelievably small delicate ears folded close, their little blind faces almost featureless.

Miranda said, "Oh, I want to *see,*" under her breath. She looked and looked—excited but not frightened, for she was accustomed to the sight of animals killed in hunting—filled with pity and astonishment and a kind of shocked delight in the wonderful little creatures for their own sakes, they were so pretty. She touched one of them ever so carefully. "Ah, there's blood running over them," she said and began to tremble without knowing why. Yet she wanted most deeply to see and to know. Having seen, she felt at once as if she had known all along. The very memory of her former ignorance faded, she had always known just this. No one had ever told her anything outright, she had been rather unobservant of the animal life around her because she was so accustomed to animals. They seemed simply disorderly and unaccountably rude in their habits, but altogether natural and not very interesting. Her brother had spoken as if he had known about everything all along. He may have seen all this before. He had never said a word to her, but she knew now a part at least of what he knew. She understood a little of the secret, formless intuitions in her own mind and body, which had been clearing up, taking form, so gradually and so steadily she had not realized that she was learning what she had to know. Paul said cautiously, as if he were talking about something forbidden: "They were just about ready to be born." His voice dropped on the last word. "I know," said Miranda, "like kittens. I know, like babies." She was quietly and terribly agitated, standing again with her rifle under her arm, looking down at the bloody heap. "I don't want the skin," she said, "I won't have it." Paul buried the young rabbits again in their mother's body, wrapped the skin around her, carried her to a clump of sage brushes, and hid her away. He came out again at once and said to Miranda, with an eager friendliness, a confidential tone quite unusual in him, as if he were taking her into an important secret on equal terms: "Listen now. Now you listen to me, and don't ever forget. Don't you ever tell a living soul that you saw this. Don't tell a soul. Don't tell Dad because I'll get into trouble. He'll say I'm leading you into things you ought not to do. He's always saying that. So now don't you go and forget and blab out sometime the way you're always doing . . . Now, that's a secret. Don't you tell."

Miranda never told, she did not even wish to tell anybody. She thought about the whole worrisome affair with confused unhappiness for a few days. Then it sank quietly into her mind and was heaped over by accumulated thousands of impressions, for nearly twenty years. One day she was picking her path among the puddles and crushed refuse of a market street in a strange city of a strange country, when without warning, plain and clear in its true colors as if she looked through a frame upon a scene that had not stirred nor changed since the moment it happened, the episode of that far-off day leaped from its burial place before her mind's eye. She was so reasonlessly horrified she halted suddenly staring, the scene before her eyes dimmed by the vision back of them. An Indian vendor had held up before her a tray of dyed sugar sweets, in the shapes of all kinds of small creatures: birds, baby chicks, baby rabbits, lambs, baby pigs. They were in gay colors and smelled of vanilla, maybe. . . . It was a very hot day and the smell in the market, with its piles of raw flesh and wilting flowers, was like the mingled sweetness and corruption she had smelled that other day in the empty cemetery at home: the day she had remembered always until now vaguely as the time she and her brother had found treasure in the opened graves. Instantly upon this thought the dreadful vision faded, and she saw clearly her brother, whose childhood face she had forgotten, standing again in the blazing sunshine, again twelve years old, a pleased sober smile in his eyes, turning the silver dove over and over in his hands.

William March

1893 – 1954

William Edward Campbell (who adopted the pseudonym William March as an adult) was born September 18, 1893, in Mobile, Alabama. The second of eleven children in a working-class family, March developed an early adolescent interest in creative writing and amateur theatricals, but from youth onward these artistic proclivities were necessarily linked to and enriched by the real life experiences he drew from the worlds of business, the law, and harrowing military service in World War I. From the lowly position of filing clerk in a small-town Alabama lumber company and a Mobile law firm before joining the U.S. Marines, March quickly scaled the industrial heights after the war as an employee of the Waterman Steamship Corporation during the 1920s; in 1931 he was made a vice-president of the firm and sent to Europe the following year to expand its operations in Berlin, Hamburg, and London. During the same period a steady stream of March's stories had begun appearing in "little" magazines, culminating in his first full-length work, *Company K,* published in 1933. Hailed as a classic novel of World War I, this work was quickly followed by a second novel, *Come In at the Door* (1934); a collection of short stories, *The Little Wife and Other Stories* (1935); a third novel, *The Tallons* (1936); another collection of stories, *Some Like Them Short* (1939); and a fourth novel, *The Looking Glass* (1943), which has been called his "finest literary achievement." In 1945 March published *Trial Balance,* which was primarily a retrospective grouping of the fifty-five short stories he considered his finest. His last two novels, published shortly before he died, were *October Island* (1952) and *The Bad Seed* (1954), ironically his single phenomenally popular best seller, later successfully adapted also for Broadway and as a motion picture.

Although March's novels and short stories have not been widely read during recent decades, they were well received by perceptive critics when they first appeared in the 1930s and 1940s, and were even favorably compared with those of Faulkner, Hemingway, and Fitzgerald. In 1951, for example, the British critic Alistair Cooke, boldly rating March's fiction superior to that of Faulkner—a recent Nobel Prize winner—dubbed March "the unrecognized genius of our time" and predicted that by the end of the century the precision, power, and veracity in his short fiction treatment of small-town American life would at last be suitably recognized.

Woolen Drawers

Mrs. Joe Cotton, Grand Mobilizer of the Christian Gladiators and Secretary of the Reedyville Society for the Fostering of Temperance and the Eradication of Vice, was the terror of small bootleggers and poolroom keepers, and she had tracked down and prosecuted more than one frightened prostitute who had drifted into town. She was a large, solidly built woman, with fine, black eyes and wide shoulders, and when she walked around Court House Square with her swinging stride, glancing keenly from side to side, she was a handsome woman in spite of her forty-five years.

Before her marriage she was known as Alice Ochs and she had worked at the cigar counter of a commercial hotel in Atlanta. Naturally, she had a great many friends both among traveling salesmen who came regularly to the hotel and strangers in town for a few days. These men were generally bored and lonely and many of them would come over to Alice's counter and talk to her, drawn by her black hair, pink cheeks and sparkling, jet-like eyes. (It was because of her rustic prettiness and her

"Woolen Drawers" from *Trial Balance: The Collected Short Stories of William March* by William March.

ability to attract men that she had been selected for the position she now held, a fact which Alice knew quite well.)

Alice was proud of her good looks and proud, too, of the fact that she was always dressed in the latest style. She had a contempt for dowdy women and she often told her roommate, a woman named Trix McAllister, that she didn't blame men for being untrue to their wives when she considered what most wives looked like after a few years.

It is doubtful, however, if Alice could have made such an excellent appearance on the salary the hotel paid her, but fortunately her men friends were always giving her presents of clothing, jewelry or even money after an evening spent in her company. After her brief and indiscriminate affairs, there was no sense of shame to harass her, nor was there any feeling of guilt in her mind; on the contrary, the fact that she had created powerful emotions in others and had, herself, remained entirely unaffected gave her a consciousness of superiority to her lovers. As the man lay in her arms, exhausted for the time being, Alice would kiss his lips and his eyelids in a gentle, contemptuous manner, and a feeling of power would come over her.

For awhile Alice's life moved calmly, and then one day in January, 1907, there occurred a series of trivial events which affected her entire existence. The weather, which had been mild and spring-like, changed suddenly, and Alice contracted a chest cold. The night before Trix McAllister had rubbed her with a mixture of turpentine and mutton-suet, and Alice felt considerably better the next morning. The girls arose somewhat later than usual and Alice began to dress hurriedly.

Trix watched her in surprise. "Alice Ochs!" she said. "You don't mean to tell me that you're not going to wear any more clothes than that! Why, with your cold, you'll have pneumonia before night!" Alice continued to dress. "Don't worry about me, Trix. I'll be perfectly warm. Don't worry about me at all." (Alice was fond of Trix, a woman a good deal older than herself who was always trying to mother her.)

But Trix laughed in a half-provoked way and shook her head. She went into the next room and began rummaging in her trunk. In a few minutes she returned carrying across her arm a suit of shapeless, fleece-lined underwear which had belonged to her husband during his lifetime. "You put this on, and don't be so stubborn," she said. "Nobody's going to see it. Nobody's going to know one way or the other."

Alice protested vehemently. She took a great deal of pride in her personal appearance and she was particularly proud of her beautiful, handmade underwear. She had found that men always admired elaborate underwear—her embroidered corset-covers and heavily starched petticoats—scented with violet sachet powder and decorated with cherry-colored ribbons.

Alice glanced at the grayish, rust-stained union-suit which lay across Trix's arm and contrasted it with the pair of cambric drawers she had laid out to wear that day, with their yards of cream-colored lace and insertion, through which she was running pink and blue ribbon; and the sight of the woolen underwear, its clumsy buttons, its shapeless square seat and baggy knees, made her shudder with distaste.

"No, Trix," she said firmly. "I'll be perfectly all right as I am. Don't you worry about me."

But Trix was insistent and Alice after much protesting put on the woolen drawers. Afterwards, she went to work as usual. She chatted with her customers and rolled poker-dice with them for cigars or coupons. Among Alice's friends was a man named Joseph L. Cotton who traveled for a textile house and who, when calling upon a new account, opened the conversation by saying: "My name's Cotton and I sell cotton *piece* goods!" Then he would laugh in a friendly way and show his fine teeth. Joe had blonde hair which was very curly. He liked to think that he knew a great deal about life, but in reality he was very simple.

He was in Atlanta that day, and, as usual, he came up to Alice's counter to talk to her and to joke her about being too proud to have a date with a plain drummer like himself. (He had wanted to go out with her several times in the past, but Alice had always had something better to do.) This afternoon Joe also asked for a date and finally, to his surprise, Alice gave him one. They planned having dinner together and going later to the theater.

The evening passed pleasantly enough, and after the theater was over, Joe suggested that Alice come with him to his room. Alice consented as a matter of course. When they were in his room, Joe locked the door and winked mysteriously. "We don't have to worry about the house detective," he said, "because he happens to be a personal friend of mine."

"All right, Mr. Fixer," said Alice languidly. She lighted a cigarette and inhaled deeply, her head thrown back. Joe's blue eyes became bright and excited. He took Alice in his arms, kissing her throat and her lips, and they sat for a time embracing and murmuring words of love. At last Joe moved to the bed and began unlacing his shoes. Alice picked up her cigarette, which was still burning, and drew another puff of smoke through her lungs. The smoke irritated her throat and she coughed slightly.

"I'd better let Trix rub my chest with mutton-suet again," she thought vaguely. Then she sat up straight in the chair, her languid manner gone. She had remembered just in time about the woolen union-suit which Trix had persuaded her to wear. For a moment she became panic-stricken. She knew she would die of humiliation if any man caught her wearing those baggy, woolen drawers. The very thought of such a thing filled her with shame, and she blushed. She got up quickly and put on her hat.

Joe walked to her in his stocking-feet. "What's the matter, Alice?" he asked in surprise. Alice put her hand on his arm. "I've had a very pleasant evening indeed, Mr. Croxton," she said, "but I think I'd better go on home now. Be sure and look me up again the next time you come to Atlanta."

"So that's the sort of game you play?" said Joe in a hard voice. "Well, let me tell you something, sister: you can't pull that stuff on me and get away with it!"

"I don't know what you mean, I'm sure," said Alice.

"All right, then," said Joe. "I'll show you pretty quick what I mean."

He took her by the arms and threw her roughly upon the bed, and held her there. Alice struggled to free herself. She was surprised at Joe's strength, and she had not expected him to behave in any such manner. As she struggled to free herself from his hands her brain was working with rapidity. Then, all at once, she ceased to struggle and lay beside him crying softly. After she stopped resisting him, Joe kissed her once or twice in a sullen, hangdog way and then he sat up beside her on the bed, outlining the pattern in the carpet with his toe.

"You think you're pretty wise, don't you?" he asked. "Well, by God, you can't put anything like that over on me. It may work all right with guys who haven't been around much, but it won't work with me."

Alice buried her face in her hands. "You don't understand, Mr. Croxton," she said. "I'm not the sort of girl you think I am at all." Joe made a laughing sound.

"Oh, I don't blame you for thinking those things," said Alice. "I'll admit you have a perfect right to think what you did about me."

Joe looked at her in a puzzled manner, uanble to make up his mind.

"I wanted to have a good time like other girls and I thought I could do what they do," she went on. "Other girls have always said that a man wouldn't like you until you did things like that, and I did so want *you* to like me, Mr. Croxton."

Joe looked at her uncomfortably. He wanted to say: "My name isn't Croxton; it's *Cotton,*" but he remained silent.

Alice was crying in earnest now. Slowly she raised her head and looked at Joe appealingly. She had known, of course, that he was completely defeated now, and that she could go home unmolested when she chose; but she was surprised to notice there were tears also in Joe's eyes, and that his lips were trembling like a little boy's. For a moment he regarded her simply; then he knelt before her and raised the hem of her skirt to his lips.

"I don't deserve your forgiveness, Miss Alice," he said in a choking voice. "I don't deserve it."

"Now, Mr. Croxton," said Alice nervously, "everybody makes mistakes, I guess."

When she repeated the story to Trix that night the girls laughed until they were exhausted. Trix lay on her bed and slapped at the counterpane helplessly. "I don't see how you stood it without laughing in his face, Alice! Honest to God, I don't," she gasped.

"I *had* to keep a straight face," said Alice; "but when he got down on his knees, I thought I was going to split." She raised her arms upward, put on her nightgown and yawned: "Well, I'll never see that sap again, I hope," she said.

The next day Alice received a letter from Joe by special messenger. He was leaving for Chattanooga that morning he said, and he wanted to apologize again. He went over and over the same ground for ten closely written pages, affirming and reaffirming Alice's beauty of soul and pleading that she forgive him in time for the stupid mistake he had made.

"It is hard for a girl of your innocence to understand a man of the world like me," wrote Joe; "but I've been on the road for a long time and I've met so many women of the 'other kind' that I have become hard and lost my ideals. Last night you showed me how far I had drifted. But now," he continued, "I have reached the point where I need the sweet and tender love of a good woman. Oh, Alice! Help me to renew my faith in womankind!" At first Alice didn't know what to make of the letter, but finally she showed it to Trix, and they had another good laugh at Joe's expense.

Early the next morning another letter arrived from Joe. It was much like the first one, being devoted entirely to Alice's purity and Joe's unworthiness. Alice read the letter two or three times, a thoughtful look on her face. For some reason she did not want to share this letter with Trix, from whom she had no secrets as a rule; but Trix seeing it on Alice's dressing-table, picked it up and began reading it out loud, making laughing remarks at Joe's stupidity.

Alice felt a sudden, uncalculated anger against Trix. She took the letter out of her hand and put it away without a word. After that a letter came from Joe each morning. These letters were impressing Alice against her will.

At the end of the first week she answered Joe's letters, a detail which she failed to reveal to Trix, and after that she fell naturally into the habit of writing him daily. She gave up smoking cigarettes because Joe asked her to; she began dressing more modestly because Joe liked modest women; and she gave up entirely her dates with other men. And so things went for a few months and then Alice Ochs became Mrs. Joseph L. Cotton and moved with her husband to Reedyville, where he had lived as a boy, and where he had rented a home for his bride.

Once in Reedyville, with her early life behind her, Alice Cotton drifted without effort into the church life of the town. Joe and his kinsmen were Methodists, so Alice became a member of that denomination too. At first Joe was afraid his wife would be bored in Reedyville, after the exciting life she had led, and that she would find the narrow, religious routine of the town confining, but such was far from being the case. Alice, who had never in her life received religious training, took to it instinctively, knowing that she had at length found her true vocation. As she sat in church listening to the hymns and the thundering, denunciatory sermons, she kept thinking: "This is what I really wanted. Why have I missed it in the past?" Often she was sorry that she was not a Catholic, so that she might have become a nun and dedicated her whole existence to religious worship.

During the second year of their married life, when her husband was home on one occasion, Alice locked her bedroom door against his advances and told him that that sort of relationship was over forever between them. Such a relationship was permissible only for the purpose of bringing souls into the world, she said; and it was apparent, now, that God did not see fit to bless their union with children. Joe did not agree with his wife's views, but he continued to love her patiently, hoping that her new mood would pass.

It never did, of course, and as the years went by, Joe Cotton spent more and more of his time on the road. He rarely visited Reedyville any more. During the week when he was busy he seldom thought of women, but often on a Sunday in a strange town he became lonely and picked up some girl on the street and took her to his room. At such times Joe would send out for a bottle of gin and he and the woman would drink until they were tipsy. Then he would begin to talk about his wife.

"I married an angel," he would say. "I married the best woman in the world." He would cry maudlin tears and his companion would embrace him and call him a poor boy and everything would run smoothly until they began to haggle over the amount of money he was to pay for the privilege of having his comforter spend the night with him.

Occasionally reports of Joe's goings-on got back to Reedyville and reached his wife's ears. She would sigh patiently and roll her eyes upward when people told her such things, but in reality she didn't care in the least what her husband did on the road. Gradually she took more and more interest in her church work and in time she joined Mr. Palmiller's interdenominational temperance and vice society, becoming its most efficient and belligerent member, crusading against cigarette smoking, drinking, and the sexual relationship. For the first time her life was perfect and complete. She was happy in her new work and she believed that God and His angels noticed everything she accomplished for good, and often spoke of it among themselves.

The temperance and vice society met each Monday evening, generally in the directors' room of the Palmiller State Bank. Mrs. Cotton, as secretary, always came early with her minutes and records and reports. She would seat herself at Mr. Palmiller's elbow and arrange his papers for him or fill his glass with water. Later, there would be old Miss Emmaline Maybanks sitting in a wicker chair, flanked by Mr. Baker Rice and Mrs. Daniel O'Leary.

One night after the regular business meeting had been attended to, Sister Joe Cotton began to talk about the things that went on at Mattress May's sporting house on New April Avenue, and how the night clerk at the Magnolia Hotel sent out for girls when his guests requested such attentions. There were a series of shocked exclamations and demands for more exact details. So Sister Cotton told them what they wanted to hear, omitting nothing. When she finished, Miss Eulalie Prescott banged her cane on the floor and leaned forward eagerly.

"How did you find out so much, Sister Cotton?" she asked. "How did you happen to hear about these shocking things?"

Sister Cotton smiled firmly. "It's my duty as a Christian woman to know what's going on in this town," she said. "I don't know how I do it. I just seem to be able to sit down and figure out what bad women are going to do. You might call it a kind of talent, I guess—like playing the piano by ear."

Mr. Palmiller rose and offered a prayer in which he thanked God for having given to Alice Cotton her unparalleled understanding of sin and her great power to detect and confound sinners. This virtue, according to Mr. Palmiller, was as important in its way as the power to do good, or the necessity for practicing brotherhood and love.

James Thurber

1894 – 1961

During the heyday of his career James Thurber was noted for a particularly original brand of humor, not only in the essays, fables, and stories he wrote, but also in the cartoons he drew to illustrate them. Because this humor was firmly rooted in a sensitive awareness of the lunacies of human behavior rather than a mere impulse to be the jester, Thurber won high regard as a serious critic of mankind.

Born in Columbus, Ohio, in 1894, he attended public school there and then entered Ohio State University, where he edited a humorous undergraduate magazine. In his senior year he left college for war service as a code clerk in the State Department in Washington and later (1918–1920) in the American Embassy in Paris. After the war, he made journalism his profession, working successively as a reporter on the Columbus *Dispatch,* the Paris edition of the *Chicago Tribune,* and the New York *Evening Post.* After contributing some pieces to *The New Yorker,* he joined its staff in 1927 and remained closely associated with that magazine either in an editorial capacity or as a frequent contributor until his death in 1961. His first book, *Is Sex Necessary?* (1929), a parody of sex books, was written in collaboration with E. B. White. His next two books, *The Owl in the Attic and Other Perplexities* (1931) and *The Seal in the Bedroom and Other Predicaments* (1932), both collections of nonsense essays, enhanced his reputation as a humorist. Subsequently, he maintained his position as one of America's most original and talented writers with such other volumes as *My Life and Hard Times* (1933), *The Middle Aged Man on the Flying Trapeze* (1935), *Let Your Mind Alone* (1937), *Fables for Our Time and Famous Poems Illustrated* (1946), and *The 13 Clocks* (1950). He also collaborated with Elliot Nugent on the successful play, *The Male*

Animal (1940). Primarily regarded as a humorous essayist, he also wrote a number of short stories of distinguished excellence.

With its tight plotting, neat contrasts between external situations and the defense mechanism functioning smoothly in the protagonist's mind, triumphantly to the end, "The Secret Life of Walter Mitty" would have delighted both Poe and O. Henry. The effectiveness of the story, however, depends less upon these mechanical features than on its sharply drawn characterization and its humorous tone, both of which are the result of precision, balance, and control in the use of language.

The Secret Life of Walter Mitty

"We're going through!" The Commander's voice was like thin ice breaking. He wore his full-dress uniform, with the heavily braided white cap pulled down rakishly over one cold gray eye. "We can't make it, sir. It's spoiling for a hurricane, if you ask me." "I'm not asking you, Lieutenant Berg," said the Commander. "Throw on the power lights! Rev her up to 8,500! We're going through!" The pounding of the cylinders increased: ta-pocketa-pocketa-pocketa-*pocketa-pocketa*. The Commander stared at the ice forming on the pilot window. He walked over and twisted a row of complicated dials. "Switch on No. 8 auxiliary!" he shouted. "Switch on No. 8 auxiliary!" repeated Lieutenant Berg. "Full strength in No. 3 turret!" "Full strength in No. 3 turret!" shouted the Commander. The crew, bending to their various tasks in the huge, hurtling eight-engined Navy hydroplane, looked at each other and grinned. "The Old Man'll get us through," they said to one another. "The Old Man ain't afraid of Hell!" . . .

"Not so fast! You're driving too fast!" said Mrs. Mitty. "What are you driving so fast for?"

"Hmm?" said Walter Mitty. He looked at his wife, in the seat beside him, with shocked astonishment. She seemed grossly unfamiliar, like a strange woman who had yelled at him in a crowd. "You were up to fifty-five," she said. "You know I don't like to go more than forty. You were up to fifty-five." Walter Mitty drove on toward Waterbury in silence, the roaring of the SN202 through the worst storm in twenty years of Navy flying fading in the remote, intimate airways of his mind. "You're tensed up again," said Mrs. Mitty. "It's one of your days. I wish you'd let Dr. Renshaw look you over."

Walter Mitty stopped the car in front of the building where his wife went to have her hair done. "Remember to get those overshoes while I'm having my hair done," she said. "I don't need overshoes," said Mitty. She put her mirror back into her bag. "We've been all through that," she said, getting out of the car. "You're not a young man any longer." He raced the engine a little. "Why don't you wear your gloves? Have you lost your gloves?" Walter Mitty reached in a pocket and brought out the gloves. He put them on, but after she had turned and gone into the building and he had driven on to a red light, he took them off again. "Pick it up, brother!" snapped a cop as the light changed, and Mitty hastily pulled on his gloves and lurched ahead. He drove around the streets aimlessly for a time, and then he drove past the hospital on his way to the parking lot.

. . . "It's the millionaire banker, Wellington McMillan," said the pretty nurse. "Yes?" said Walter Mitty, removing his gloves slowly. "Who has the case?" "Dr. Renshaw and Dr. Benbow, but there are two specialists here, Dr. Remington from New York and Mr. Pritchard-Mitford from London. He flew over." A door opened down a long, cool corridor and Dr. Renshaw came out. He looked distraught and haggard. "Hello, Mitty," he said. "We're having the devil's own time with McMillan, the millionaire banker and close personal friend of Roosevelt. Obstreosis of the ductal tract. Tertiary. Wish you'd take a look at him." "Glad to," said Mitty.

In the operating room there were whispered introductions: "Dr. Remington, Dr. Mitty. Mr. Pritchard-Mitford, Dr. Mitty." "I've read your book on streptothricosis," said Pritchard-Mitford, shaking hands. "A brilliant performance, sir." "Thank you," said Walter Mitty. "Didn't know you were in the States, Mitty," grumbled Remington. "Coals to Newcastle, bringing Mitford and me up here for a tertiary." "You are very kind," said Mitty. A hugh, complicated machine, connected to the operating table, with many tubes and wires, began at this moment to go pocketa-pocketa-pocketa. "The new anesthetizer is giving way!" shouted an interne. "There is no one in the East who knows how to fix it!" "Quiet, man!" said Mitty, in a low, cool voice. He sprang to the machine, which was now going pocketa-pocketa-queep-pocketa-queep. He began fingering delicately a row of glistening dials. "Give me a fountain pen!" he snapped. Someone handed him a fountain pen. He pulled a faulty piston out of the machine and inserted the pen in its place. "That will hold for ten minutes," he said. "Get on with the operation." A nurse hurried over and whispered to Renshaw, and Mitty saw the man turn pale. "Coreopsis has set in," said Renshaw nervously. "If you would take over, Mitty?" Mitty looked at him and at the craven figure of Benbow, who drank, and at the grave, uncertain faces of the two great specialists. "If you wish," he said. They slipped a white gown on him; he adjusted a mask and drew on thin gloves; nurses handed him shining . . .

"Back it up, Mac! Look out for that Buick!" Walter Mitty jammed on the brakes. "Wrong lane, Mac," said the parking-lot attendant, looking at Mitty closely. "Gee. Yeh," muttered Mitty. He began cautiously to back out of the lane marked "Exit Only." "Leave her sit there," said the attendant. "I'll put her away." Mitty got out of the car. "Hey, better leave the key." "Oh," said Mitty, handing the man the ignition key. The attendant vaulted into the car, backed it up with insolent skill, and put it where it belonged.

They're so damn cocky, thought Walter Mitty, walking along Main Street; they think they know everything. Once he had tried to take his chains off, outside New Milford, and he had got them wound around the axles. A man had had to come out in a wrecking car and unwind them, a young, grinning garageman. Since then Mrs. Mitty always made him drive to a garage to have the chains taken off. The next time, he thought, I'll wear my right arm in a sling; they won't grin at me then. I'll have my right arm in a sling and they'll see I couldn't possibly take the chains off myself. He kicked at the slush on the sidewalk. "Overshoes," he said to himself, and he began looking for a shoe store.

When he came out into the street again, with the overshoes in a box under his arm, Walter Mitty began to wonder what the other thing was his wife had told him to get. She had told him, twice, before they set out from their house for Waterbury. In a way he hated these weekly trips to town—he was always getting something wrong. Kleenex, he thought, Squibb's, razor blades? No. Toothpaste, toothbrush, bicarbonate, carborundum, initiative and referendum? He gave it up. But she would remember it. "Where's the what's-its-name?" she would ask. "Don't tell me you forgot the what's-its-name." A newsboy went by shouting something about the Waterbury trial.

. . . "Perhaps this will refresh your memory." The District Attorney suddenly thrust a heavy automatic at the quiet figure on the witness stand. "Have you ever seen this before?" Walter Mitty took the gun and examined it expertly. "This is my Webley-Vickers 50.80," he said calmly. An excited buzz ran around the courtroom. The Judge rapped for order. "You are a crack shot with any sort of firearms, I believe?" said the District Attorney, insinuatingly. "Objection!" shouted Mitty's attorney. "We have shown that the defendant could not have fired the shot. We have shown that he wore his right arm in a sling on the night of the fourteenth of July." Walter Mitty raised his hand briefly and the bickering attorneys were stilled. "With any known make of gun," he said evenly, "I could have killed Gregory Fitzhurst at three hundred feet *with my left hand.*" Pandemonium broke loose in the courtroom. A woman's scream rose above the bedlam and suddenly a lovely, dark-haired girl was in Walter Mitty's arms. The District Attorney struck at her savagely. Without rising from his chair, Mitty let the man have it on the point of the chin. "You miserable cur!" . . .

"Puppy biscuit," said Walter Mitty. He stopped walking and the buildings of Waterbury rose up out of the misty courtroom and surrounded him again. A woman who was passing laughed. "He said 'Puppy biscuit,' " she said to her companion. "That man said 'Puppy biscuit' to himself." Walter Mitty hurried on. He went into an A. & P., not the first one he came to but a smaller one farther up the street "I want some biscuit for small, young dogs," he said to the clerk. "Any special brand, sir?" The greatest pistol shot in the world thought a moment. "It says 'Puppies Bark for It' on the box," said Walter Mitty.

His wife would be through at the hairdresser's in fifteen minutes, Mitty saw in looking at his watch, unless they had trouble drying it; sometimes they had trouble drying it. She didn't like to get to the hotel first; she would want him to be there waiting for her as usual. He found a big leather chair in the lobby, facing a window, and he put the overshoes and the puppy biscuit on the floor beside it. He picked up an old copy of *Liberty* and sank down into the chair. "Can Germany Conquer the World Through the Air?" Walter Mitty looked at the pictures of bombing planes and of ruined streets.

. . . "The cannonading has got the wind up in young Raleigh, sir," said the sergeant. Captain Mitty looked up at him through touseled hair. "Get him to bed," he said wearily. "With the others. I'll fly alone." "But you can't, sir," said the sergeant anxiously. "It takes two men to handle that bomber and the Archies are pounding hell out of the air. Von Richtman's circus is between here and Saulier." "Somebody's got to get that ammunition dump," said Mitty. "I'm going over. Spot of brandy?" He poured a drink for the sergeant and one for himself. War thundered and whined around the dugout and battered at the door. There was a rending of wood and splinters flew through the room. "A bit of a near thing," said Captain Mitty carelessly. "The box barrage is closing in," said the sergeant. "We only live once, Sergeant," said Mitty, with his faint, fleeting smile. "Or do we?" He poured another brandy and tossed it off. "I never see a man could hold his brandy like you, sir," said the sergeant. "Begging your pardon, sir." Captain Mitty stood up and strapped on his huge Webley-Vickers automatic. "It's forty kilometers through hell, sir," said the sergeant. Mitty finished one last brandy. "After all," he said softly, "what isn't?" The pounding of the cannon increased; there was the rat-tat-tatting of machine guns, and from somewhere came the menacing pocketa-pocketa-pocketa of the new flame-throwers. Walter Mitty walked to the door of the dugout humming "Auprès de Ma Blonde." He turned and waved to the sergeant. "Cheerio!" he said. . . .

Something struck his shoulder. "I've been looking all over this hotel for you," said Mrs. Mitty. "Why do you have to hide in this old chair? How did you expect me to find you?" "Things close in," said Walter Mitty vaguely. "What?" Mrs. Mitty said. "Did you get the what's-its-name? The puppy biscuit? What's in that box?" "Overshoes," said Mitty. "Couldn't you have put them on in the store?" "I was thinking," said Walter Mitty. "Does it ever occur to you that I am sometimes thinking?" She looked at him. "I'm going to take your temperature when I get you home," she said.

They went out through the revolving doors that made a faintly derisive whistling sound when you pushed them. It was two blocks to the parking lot. At the drugstore on the corner she said, "Wait here for me. I forgot something. I won't be a minute." She was more than a minute. Walter Mitty lighted a cigarette. It began to rain, rain with sleet in it. He stood up against the wall of the drugstore, smoking. . . . He put his shoulders back and his heels together. "To hell with the handkerchief," said Walter Mitty scornfully. He took one last drag on his cigarette and snapped it away. Then, with that faint, fleeting smile playing about his lips, he faced the firing squad; erect and motionless, proud and disdainful, Walter Mitty the Undefeated, inscrutable to the last.

Jean Toomer

1894 – 1967

Nathan Eugene [later, Jean] Toomer, one of the most colorful figures associated with the artistic movement of the 1920s known as the Harlem Renaissance, was born in Washington, D. C., on December 26, 1894. He was named for a ne'er-do-well father who allegedly deserted his bride, Nina Pinchback, and her unborn child "as soon as he discovered that her father, Pinckney B. S. Pinchback, tightly controlled the family fortunes." As a child, young Toomer was reared in the affluent environment of his grandparents' home and thus came under the influence of both his grandfather Pinckney's powerful crusading mission for black civil rights, and his uncle Bismark's artistic and intellectual proclivities. Later in life Toomer claimed to have learned more from his uncle than from his varied exposure to formal education in high school and in several academic disciplines at leading universities in Wisconsin, Chicago, and New York. Rejected for service in both the army and the Red Cross in World War I, in 1918 Toomer began studying literature with feverish intensity in order to prepare himself for a career as a writer; and during the next few years, following a short period as a school principal in Georgia, he became totally committed to the cause of Afro-American self-expression. His book *Cane,* published in 1923, thus emerged as a concentrated, yet multifaceted stimulus to the reawakened aspirations of other black writers, artists, singers, and musicians throughout the United States. Through its poems, sketches, and stories the book struck a keynote for the yearnings of both blacks and whites at the dawn of the Jazz Age.

In "Blood-Burning Moon" Toomer's lyric voice captures both the frenzy and the horror, the beauty and the brutality of racial conflict in America.

Blood-Burning Moon

1

Up from the skeleton stone walls, up from the rotting floor boards and the solid hand-hewn beams of oak of the pre-war cotton factory, dusk came. Up from the dusk the full moon came. Glowing like a fired pine-knot, it illumined the great door and soft showered the Negro shanties aligned along the single street of factory town. The full moon in the great door was an omen. Negro women improvised songs against its spell.

Louisa sang as she came over the crest of the hill from the white folks' kitchen. Her skin was the color of oak leaves on young trees in fall. Her breasts, firm and up-pointed like ripe acorns. And her singing had the low murmur of winds in fig trees. Bob Stone, younger son of the people she worked for, loved her. By the way the world reckons things, he had won her. By measure of that warm glow which came into her mind at thought of him, he had won her. Tom Burwell, whom the whole town called Big Boy, also loved her. But working in the fields all day, and far away from her, gave him no chance to show it. Though often enough of evenings he had tried to. Somehow, he never got along. Strong as he was with hands upon the ax or plow, he found it difficult to hold her. Or so he thought. But the fact was that he held her to factory town more firmly than he thought for. His black balanced, and pulled against, the white of Stone, when she thought of them. And her mind was vaguely upon them as she came over the crest of the hill, coming from the white folks' kitchen. As she sang softly at the evil face of the full moon.

A strange stir was in her. Indolently, she tried to fix upon Bob or Tom as the cause of it. To meet Bob in the canebrake, as she was going to do an hour or so later, was nothing new. And Tom's proposal which she felt on its way to her could be indefinitely put off. Separately, there was no unusual significance to either one. But for some reason, they jumbled when her eyes gazed vacantly at the rising moon. And from the jumble came the stir that was strangely within her. Her lips trembled. The slow rhythm of her song grew agitant and restless. Rusty black and tan spotted hounds, lying in the dark corners of porches or prowling around back yards, put their noses in the air and caught its tremor. They began plaintively to yelp and howl. Chickens woke up and cackled. Intermittently, all over the countryside dogs barked and roosters crowed as if heralding a weird dawn or some ungodly awakening. The women sang lustily. Their songs were cotton-wads to stop their ears. Louisa came down into factory town and sank wearily upon the step before her home. The moon was rising towards a thick cloud-bank which soon would hide it.

Red nigger moon. Sinner!
Blood-burning moon. Sinner!
Come out that fact'ry door.

2

Up from the deep dusk of a cleared spot on the edge of the forest a mellow glow arose and spread fan-wise into the low-hanging heavens. And all around the air was heavy with scent of boiling cane. A large pile of cane-stalks lay like ribboned shadows upon the ground. A mule, harnessed to a pole, trudged lazily round and round the pivot of the grinder. Beneath a swaying oil lamp, a Negro alternately whipped out at the mule, and fed cane-stalks to the grinder. A fat boy waddled pails of fresh ground juice between the grinder and the boiling stove. Steam came from the copper boiling pan. The scent of cane came from the copper pan and drenched the forest and the hill that sloped to factory town, beneath its fragrance. It drenched the men in circle seated around the stove. Some of them chewed at the white pulp of stalks, but there was no need for them to, if all they wanted was to taste the cane. One tasted it in factory town. And from factory town one could see the soft haze thrown by the glowing stove upon the low-hanging heavens.

Old David Georgia stirred the thickening syrup with a long ladle, and ever so often drew it off. Old David Georgia tended his stove and told tales about the white folks, about moon-shining and cotton picking, and about sweet nigger gals, to the men who sat there about his stove to listen to him. Tom Burwell chewed cane-stalk and laughed with the others till someone mentioned Louisa. Till some one said something about Louisa and Bob Stone, about the silk stockings she must have gotten from him. Blood ran up Tom's neck hotter than the glow that flooded from the stove. He sprang up. Glared at the men and said, "She's my gal." Will Manning laughed. Tom strode over to him. Yanked him up and knocked him to the ground. Several of Manning's friends got up to fight for him. Tom whipped out a long knife and would have cut them to shreds if they hadnt ducked into the woods. Tom had had enough. He nodded to Old David

Georgia and swung down the path to factory town. Just then, the dogs started barking and the roosters began to crow. Tom felt funny. Away from the fight, away from the stove, chill got to him. He shivered. He shuddered when he saw the full moon rising towards the cloud-bank. He who didnt give a godam for the fears of old women. He forced his mind to fasten on Louisa. Bob Stone. Better not be. He turned into the street and saw Louisa sitting before her home. He went towards her, ambling, touched the brim of a marvelously shaped, spotted, felt hat, said he wanted to say something to her, and then found that he didnt know what he had to say, or if he did, that he couldnt say it. He shoved his big fists in his overalls, grinned, and started to move off.

"Youall want me, Tom?"

"Thats what us wants, sho, Louisa."

"Well, here I am—"

"An here I is, but that aint ahelpin none, all th same."

"You wanted to say something? . ."

"I did that, sho. But words is like th spots on dice: no matter how y fumbles em, there's times when they jes wont come. I dunno why. Seems like th love I feels fo yo done stole'm tongue. I got it now. Whee! Louisa, honey, I oughtnt tell y, I feel I oughtnt cause yo is young an goes t church an I has had other gals, but Louisa I sho do love y. Lil gal, Ise watched y from them first days when youall sat right here befo yo door befo th well an sang sometimes in a way that like t broke m heart. Ise carried y with me into th fields, day after day, an after that, an I sho can plow when yo is there, an I can pick cotton. Yassur! Come near beatin Barlo yesterday. I sho did. Yassur! And next year if ole Stone'll trust me, I'll have a farm. My own. My bales will buy yo what y gets from white folks now. Silk stockings an purple dresses—course I dont believe what some folks been whisperin as t how y gets them things now. White folks always did do for niggers what they likes. An they jes cant help alikin yo, Louisa. Bob Stone likes y. Course he does. But not th way folks is awhisperin. Does he, hon?"

"I dont know what you mean, Tom."

"Course y dont. Ise already cut two niggers. Had t hon, t tell em so. Niggers always tryin t make somethin out a nothin. An then besides, white folks aint up t them tricks so much nowadays. Godam better not be. Leastawise not with yo. Cause I wouldnt stand f it. Nassur."

"What would you do, Tom?"

"Cut him just like I cut a nigger."

"No, Tom—"

"I said I would and there aint no mo to it. But that aint th talk f now. Sing, honey Louisa, an while I'm listenin t y I'll be makin love."

Tom took her hand in his. Against the tough thickness of his own, hers felt soft and small. His huge body slipped down to the step beside her. The full moon sank upward into the deep purple of the cloud-bank.

An old woman brought a lighted lamp and hung it on the common well whose bulky shadow squatted in the middle of the road, opposite Tom and Louisa. The old woman lifted the well-lid, took hold the chain, and began drawing up the heavy bucket. As she did so, she sang. Figures shifted, restless-like, between lamp and window in the front rooms of the shanties. Shadows of the figures fought each other on the gray dust of the road. Figures raised the windows and joined the old woman in song. Louisa and Tom, the whole street, singing:

Red nigger moon. Sinner!
Blood-burning moon. Sinner!
Come out that fact'ry door.

3

Bob Stone sauntered from his veranda out into the gloom of fir trees and magnolias. The clear white of his skin paled, and the flush of his cheeks turned purple. As if to balance this outer change, his mind became consciously a white man's. He passed the house with its huge open hearth which, in the days of slavery, was the plantation cookery. He saw Louisa bent over the hearth. He went in as a master should and took her. Direct, honest, bold. None of this sneaking that he had to go through now. The contrast was repulsive to him. His family had lost ground. Hell no, his family still owned the niggers, practically. Damned if they did, or he wouldnt have to duck around so. What would they think if they knew? His mother? His sister? He shouldnt mention them, shouldnt think of them in this connection. There in the dusk he blushed at doing so. Fellows about town were all right, but how about his friends up North? He could see them incredible, repulsed. They didnt know. The thought first made him laugh. Then, with their eyes still upon him, he began to feel embarrassed. He felt the need of explaining things to them. Explain hell. They wouldnt understand, and moreover, who ever heard of a Southerner getting on his knees to any Yankee, or anyone. No sir. He was going to see Louisa to-night, and love her. She was lovely—in her way. Nigger way. What way was that? Damned if he knew. Must know. He'd known her long enough to know. Was there something about niggers that you couldnt know? Listening to them at church didnt tell you anything. Looking at them didnt tell you anything. Talking to them didnt tell you anything—unless it was gossip, unless they wanted to talk. Of course, about farming, and licker, and craps—but those werent nigger. Nigger was something more. How much more? Something to be afraid of, more?

Hell no. Who ever heard of being afraid of a nigger? Tom Burwell. Cartwell had told him that Tom went with Louisa after she reached home. No sir. No nigger had ever been with his girl. He'd like to see one try. Some position for him to be in. Him, Bob Stone, of the old Stone family, in a scrap with a nigger over a nigger girl. In the good old days. . . Ha! Those were the days. His family had lost ground. Not so much, though. Enough for him to have to cut through old Lemon's canefield by way of the woods, that he might meet her. She was worth it. Beautiful nigger gal. Why nigger? Why not, just gal? No, it was because she was nigger that he went to her. Sweet. . . The scent of boiling cane came to him. Then he saw the rich glow of the stove. He heard the voices of the men circled around it. He was about to skirt the clearing when he heard his own name mentioned. He stopped. Quivering. Leaning against a tree, he listened.

"Bad nigger. Yassur, he sho is one bad nigger when he gets started."

"Tom Burwell's been on th gang three times fo cuttin men."

"What y think he's agwine t do t Bob Stone?"

"Dunno yet. He aint found out. When he does— Baby!"

"Aint no tellin."

"Young Stone aint no quitter and I ken tell y that. Blood of th old uns in his veins."

"Thats right. He'll scrap, sho."

"Be gettin too hot f niggers round this away."

"Shut up, nigger. Y dont know what y talkin bout."

Bob Stone's ears burned as though he had been holding them over the stove. Sizzling heat welled up within him. His feet felt as if they rested on red-hot coals. They stung him to quick movement. He circled the fringe of the glowing. Not a twig cracked beneath his feet. He reached the path that led to factory town. Plunged furiously down it. Halfway along, a blindness within him veered him aside. He crashed into the bordering canebrake. Cane leaves cut his face and lips. He tasted blood. He threw himself down and dug his fingers in the ground. The earth was cool. Cane-roots took the fever from his hands. After a long while, or so it seemed to him, the thought came to him that it must be time to see Louisa. He got to his feet and walked calmly to their meeting place. No Louisa. Tom Burwell had her. Veins in his forehead bulged and distended. Saliva moistened the dried blood on his lips. He bit down on his lips. He tasted blood. Not his own blood; Tom Burwell's blood. Bob drove through the cane and out again upon the road. A hound swung down the path before him towards factory town. Bob couldnt see it. The dog loped aside to let him pass. Bob's blind rushing made him stumble over it. He fell with a thud that dazed him. The hound yelped. Answering yelps came from all over the countryside. Chickens cackled. Roosters crowed, heralding the bloodshot eyes of southern awakening. Singers in the town were silenced. They shut their windows down. Palpitant between the rooster crows, a chill hush settled upon the huddled forms of Tom and Louisa. A figure rushed from the shadow and stood before them. Tom popped to his feet.

"Whats y want?"

"I'm Bob Stone."

"Yassur—an I'm Tom Burwell. Whats y want?"

Bob lunged at him. Tom side-stepped, caught him by the shoulder, and flung him to the ground. Straddled him.

"Let me up."

"Yassur—but watch yo doins, Bob Stone."

A few dark figures, drawn by the sound of scuffle, stood about them. Bob sprang to his feet.

"Fight like a man, Tom Burwell, and I'll lick y."

Again he lunged. Tom side-stepped and flung him to the ground. Straddled him.

"Get off me, you godam nigger you."

"Yo sho has started somethin now. Get up."

Tom yanked him up and began hammering at him. Each blow sounded as if it smashed into a precious, irreplaceable soft something. Beneath them, Bob staggered back. He reached in his pocket and whipped out a knife.

"That my game, sho."

Blue flash, a steel blade slashed across Bob Stone's throat. He had a sweetish sick feeling. Blood began to flow. Then he felt a sharp twitch of pain. He let his knife drop. He slapped one hand against his neck. He pressed the other on top of his head as if to hold it down. He groaned. He turned, and staggered towards the crest of the hill in the direction of white town. Negroes who had seen the fight slunk into their homes and blew the lamps out. Louisa, dazed, hysterical, refused to go indoors. She slipped, crumbled, her body loosely propped against the woodwork of the well. Tom Burwell leaned against it. He seemed rooted there.

Bob reached Broad Street. White men rushed up to him. He collapsed in their arms.

"Tom Burwell. . . . "

White men like ants upon a forage rushed about. Except for the taut hum of their moving, all was silent. Shotguns, revolvers, rope, kerosene, torches. Two high-powered cars with glaring search-lights. They came together. The taut hum rose to a low road. Then nothing could be heard but the flop of their feet in the thick dust of the road. The moving body of their silence preceded them over the crest of the hill into factory town. It flattened the Negroes beneath it. It rolled to the wall of the factory, where it stopped. Tom knew that they were coming. He couldnt move. And then he saw the search-lights of the two cars glaring down on him. A quick shock went through him. He stiffened. He started to run. A yell went up from the mob. Tom wheeled about and faced them. They poured down on him. They swarmed. A large man with dead-white face and flabby cheeks came to him and almost jabbed a gun-barrel through his guts.

"Hands behind y, nigger."

Tom's wrist were bound. The big man shoved him to the well. Burn him over it, and when the woodwork caved in, his body would drop to the bottom. Two deaths for a godam nigger. Louisa was driven back. The mob pushed in. Its pressure, its momentum was too great. Drag him to the factory. Wood and stakes already there. Tom moved in the direction indicated. But they had to drag him. They reached the great door. Too many to get in there. The mob divided and flowed around the walls to either side. The big man shoved him through the door. The mob pressed in from the sides. Taut humming. No words. A stake was sunk into the ground. Rotting floor boards piled around it. Kerosene poured on the rotting floor boards. Tom bound to the stake. His breast was bare. Nails scratches let little lines of blood trickle down and mat into the hair. His face, his eyes were set and stony. Except for irregular breathing, one would have thought him already dead. Torches were flung onto the pile. A great flare muffled in black smoke shot upward. The mob yelled. The mob was silent. Now Tom could be seen within the flames. Only his head, erect, lean, like a blackened stone. Stench of burning flesh soaked the air. Tom's eyes popped. His head settled downward. The mob yelled. Its yell echoed against the skeleton stone walls and sounded like a hundred yells. Like a hundred mobs yelling. Its yell thudded against the thick front wall and fell back. Ghost of a yell slipped through the flames and out the great door of the factory. It fluttered like a dying thing down the single street of factory town. Louisa, upon the step before her home, did not hear it, but her eyes opened slowly. They saw the full moon glowing in the great door. The full moon, an evil thing, an omen, soft showering the homes of folks she knew. Where were they, these people? She'd sing, and perhaps they'd come out and join her. Perhaps Tom Burwell would come. At any rate, the full moon in the great door was an omen which she must sing to:

Red nigger moon. Sinner!
Blood-burning moon. Sinner!
Come out that fact'ry door.

F. Scott Fitzgerald

1896 – 1940

Closely associated in the public mind with the Jazz Age, of which he was the chief literary spokesman, F. Scott Fitzgerald suffered a decline in popularity with the passing of that era around 1930. The recent revival of interest in him reflects in part a renewed interest in the glittering, feverish life of the 1920s that he so accurately mirrored in his novels and stories, but it indicates also that the perspective of time has brought an increased appreciation of his contribution to American literature.

Fitzgerald's own life exemplifies the frenetic living of the age he recorded. He was born in St. Paul, Minnesota, in 1896, of a father who had descended from an old Maryland family and a mother who was "straight 1850 potato-famine Irish," a combination which may have contributed to his temperamental instability. After spending two years in an eastern preparatory school, he enrolled in 1913 at Princeton University. Driven by the desire to be socially prominent among his fellow students, he devoted his energies to such extracurricular activities as writing for the *Nassau Lit,* the campus literary magazine, *The Tiger,* a humorous publication, working on musical comedies for the Triangle Club, and attending the theater in New York. His course work suffered to the extent that during his junior year he was dropped from Princeton for low grades. He then served in the Army, and after the Armistice worked in a New York advertising agency. He soon quit this job to write his first novel, *This Side of Paradise,* which was immediately successful on its publication in 1920. Flushed with triumph, he married the socially prominent Zelda Sayre, whom he had met while stationed at an Army camp near her home town,

Montgomery, Alabama, and plunged into a gay whirl of New York café-society life.

As subsequent novels and stories brought additional fame and income, the Fitzgeralds continued their reckless, glittering social life in New York and Europe as members of the Paris-Riviera international set. But personal suffering and economic trouble of a sort suggestive of Fitzgerald's own stories in time disrupted this mode of living. In 1930 Zelda became mentally ill, and Fitzgerald thereafter fought a losing battle against his own irregular habits and a declining income resulting from his waning literary popularity. In his last years, however, he wrote but left unfinished at his death in 1940 a novel about Hollywood life entitled *The Last Tycoon,* which many critics regard as his most mature effort. Among his novels, *The Great Gatsby* (1925) is his masterpiece. His short story collections are *Flappers and Philosophers* (1920), *Tales of the Jazz Age* (1922), *All the Sad Young Men* (1926), and *Taps at Reveille* (1935).

As is true of many others of Fitzgerald stories, "Babylon Revisited" has autobiographical overtones in that it broadly reflects some aspects of the riotous living Scott and Zelda Fitzgerald participated in during their residence in Europe. The important fact about the story, however, is that it deals with a timeless and universal problem, that of how individuals' behavior in the past can affect their situations in the present. Artfully controlled handling of a complex emotional crisis makes it one of Fitzgerald's finest stories—despite what has been pointed out recently as "a monumental editorial error" in the "authorized" version of the story published in *Taps at Reveille.* The error, involving two successive paragraphs on p. 372 of our text, was due to the printer's failure to carry out Fitzgerald's instructions to substitute the second paragraph for the first. Instead, he printed both of them, and thus the flaw "has been preserved, unremarked, in all subsequent collections and anthologies." See Garry N. Murphy and William C. Slattery, "The Flawed Text of 'Babylon Revisited': A Challenge to Editors, A Warning to Readers," *Studies in Short Fiction,* Vol. 18: No. 3 (Summer, 1981), pp. 315–318.

Babylon Revisited

I

"And where's Mr. Campbell?" Charlie asked.

"Gone to Switzerland. Mr. Campbell's a pretty sick man, Mr. Wales."

"I'm sorry to hear that. And George Hardt?" Charlie inquired.

"Back in America, gone to work."

"And where is the Snow Bird?"

"He was in here last week. Anyway, his friend, Mr. Schaeffer, is in Paris."

Two familiar names from the long list of a year and a half ago. Charlie scribbled an address in his notebook and tore out the page.

"If you see Mr. Schaeffer, give him this," he said. "It's my brother-in-law's address. I haven't settled on a hotel yet."

He was not really disappointed to find Paris was so empty. But the stillness in the Ritz bar was strange and portentous. It was not an American bar any more—he felt polite in it, and not as if he owned it. It had gone back into France. He felt the stillness from the moment he got out of the taxi and saw the doorman, usually in a frenzy of activity at this hour, gossiping with a *chasseur* by the servants' entrance.

Passing through the corridor, he heard only a single, bored voice in the once-clamorous women's room. When he turned into the bar he travelled the twenty feet of green carpet with his eyes fixed straight ahead by old habit; and then, with his foot firmly on the rail, he turned and surveyed the room, encountering only a single pair of eyes that fluttered up from a newspaper in the corner. Charlie asked for the head barman, Paul, who in the latter days of the bull market had come to work in his own custom-built car—disembarking, however, with due nicety at the nearest corner. But Paul was at his country house today and Alix giving him information.

"No, no more," Charlie said, "I'm going slow these days."

Alix congratulated him: "You were going pretty strong a couple of years ago."

"I'll stick to it all right," Charlie assured him. "I've stuck to it for over a year and a half now."

"How do you find conditions in America?"

"I haven't been to America for months. I'm in business in Prague, representing a couple of concerns there. They don't know about me down there."

Alix smiled.

"Remember the night of George Hardt's bachelor dinner here?" said Charlie. "By the way, what's become of Claude Fessenden?"

Alix lowered his voice confidentially: "He's in Paris, but he doesn't come here any more. Paul doesn't allow it. He ran up a bill of thirty thousand francs, charging all his drinks and his lunches, and usually his dinner, for more than a year. And when Paul finally told him he had to pay, he gave him a bad check."

Alix shook his head sadly.

"I don't understand it, such a dandy fellow. Now he's all bloated up—" He made a plump apple of his hands.

Charlie watched a group of strident queens installing themselves in a corner.

"Nothing affects them," he thought. "Stocks rise and fall, people loaf or work, but they go on forever." The place oppressed him. He called for the dice and shook with Alix for the drink.

"Here for long, Mr. Wales?"

"I'm here for four or five days to see my little girl."

"Oh-h! You have a little girl?"

Outside, the fire-red, gas-blue, ghost-green signs shone smokily through the tranquil rain. It was late afternoon and the streets were in movement; the *bistros* gleamed. At the corner of the Boulevard des Capucines he took a taxi. The Place de la Concorde moved by in pink majesty; they crossed the logical Seine, and Charlie felt the sudden provincial quality of the left bank.

Charlie directed his taxi to the Avenue de l'Opera, which was out of his way. But he wanted to see the blue hour spread over the magnificent facade, and imagine that the cab horns, playing endlessly the first few bars of *Le Plus que Lent,* were the trumpets of the Second Empire. They were closing the iron grill in front of Brentano's Book-store, and people were already at dinner behind the trim little bourgeois hedge of Duval's. He had never eaten at a really cheap restaurant in Paris. Five-course dinner, four francs fifty, eighteen cents, wine included. For some odd reason he wished that he had.

As they rolled on to the Left Bank and he felt its sudden provincialism, he thought, "I spoiled this city for myself. I didn't realize it, but the days came along one after another, and then two years were gone, and everything was gone, and I was gone."

He was thirty-five, and good to look at. The Irish mobility of his face was sobered by a deep wrinkle between his eyes. As he rang his brother-in-law's bell in the Rue Palatine, the wrinkle deepened till it pulled down his brows; he felt a cramping sensation in his belly. From behind the maid who opened the door darted a lovely little girl of nine who shrieked "Daddy!" and flew up, struggling like a fish, into his arms. She pulled his head around by one ear and set her cheek against his.

"My old pie," he said.

"Oh, daddy, daddy, daddy, daddy, dads, dads, dads!"

She drew him into the salon, where the family waited, a boy and girl his daughter's age, his sister-in-law and her husband. He greeted Marion with his voice pitched carefully to avoid either feigned enthusiasm or dislike, but her response was more frankly tepid, though she minimized her expression of unalterable distrust by directing her regard toward his child. The two men clasped hands in a friendly way and Lincoln Peters rested his for a moment on Charlie's shoulder.

The room was warm and comfortably American. The three children moved intimately about, playing through the yellow oblongs that led to other rooms; the cheer of six o'clock spoke in the eager smacks of the fire and the sounds of French activity in the kitchen. But Charlie did not relax; his heart sat up rigidly in his body and he drew confidence from his daughter, who from time to time came close to him, holding in her arms the doll he had brought.

"Really extremely well," he declared in answer to Lincoln's question. "There's a lot of business there that isn't moving at all, but we're doing even better than ever. In fact, damn well. I'm bringing my sister over from America next month to keep house for me. My income last year was bigger than it was when I had money. You see, the Czechs—"

His boasting was for a specific purpose; but after a moment, seeing a faint restiveness in Lincoln's eye, he changed the subject:

"Those are fine children of yours, well brought up, good manners."

"We think Honoria's a great little girl too."

Marion Peters came back from the kitchen. She was a tall woman with worried eyes, who had once possessed a fresh American loveliness. Charlie had never been sensitive to it and was always surprised when people spoke of how pretty she had been. From the first there had been an instinctive antipathy between them.

"Well, how do you find Honoria?" she asked.

"Wonderful. I was astonished how much she's grown in ten months. All the children are looking well."

"We haven't had a doctor for a year. How do you like being back in Paris?"

"It seems very funny to see so few Americans around."

"I'm delighted," Marion said vehemently. "Now at least you can go into a store without their assuming you're a millionaire. We've suffered like everybody, but on the whole it's a good deal pleasanter."

"But it was nice while it lasted," Charlie said. "We were a sort of royalty, almost infallible, with a sort of magic around us. In the bar this afternoon"—he stumbled, seeing his mistake—"there wasn't a man I knew."

She looked at him keenly. "I should think you'd have had enough of bars."

"I only stayed a minute. I take one drink every afternoon, and no more."

"Don't you want a cocktail before dinner?" Lincoln asked.

"I take only one drink every afternoon, and I've had that."

"I hope you keep to it," said Marion.

Her dislike was evident in the coldness with which she spoke, but Charlie only smiled; he had larger plans. Her very aggressiveness gave him an advantage, and he knew enough to wait. He wanted them to initiate the discussion of what they knew had brought him to Paris.

At dinner he couldn't decide whether Honoria was most like him or her mother. Fortunate if she didn't combine the traits of both that had brought them to disaster. A great wave of protectiveness went over him. He thought he knew what to do for her. He believed in character; he wanted to jump back a whole generation and trust in character again as the eternally valuable element. Everything wore out.

He left soon after dinner, but not to go home. He was curious to see Paris by night with clearer and more judicious eyes than those of other days. He bought a *strapontin* for the Casino and watched Josephine Baker go through her chocolate arabesques.

After an hour he left and strolled toward Montmartre, up the Rue Pigalle into the Place Blanche. The rain had stopped and there were a few people in evening clothes disembarking from taxis in front of cabarets, and *cocottes* prowling singly or in pairs, and many Negroes. He passed a lighted door from which issued music, and stopped with the sense of familiarity; it was Bricktop's, where he had parted with so many hours and so much money. A few doors farther on he found another ancient rendezvous and incautiously put his head inside. Immediately an eager orchestra burst into sound, a pair of professional dancers leaped to their feet and a maître d'hôtel swooped toward him, crying, "Crowd just arriving, sir!" But he withdrew quickly.

"You have to be damn drunk," he thought.

Zelli's was closed, the bleak and sinister cheap hotels surrounding it were dark; up in the Rue Blanche there was more light and a local, colloquial French crowd. The Poet's Cave had disappeared, but the two great mouths of the Café of Heaven and the Café of Hell still yawned—even devoured, as he watched, the meagre contents of a tourist bus—a German, a Japanese, and an American couple who glanced at him with frightened eyes.

So much for the effort and ingenuity of Montmartre. All the catering to vice and waste was on an utterly childish scale, and he suddenly realized the meaning of the word "dissipate"—to dissipate into thin air; to make nothing out of something. In the little hours of the night every move from place to place was an enormous human jump, an increase of paying for the privilege of slower and slower motion.

He remembered thousand-franc notes given to an orchestra for playing a single number, hundred-franc notes tossed to a doorman for calling a cab.

But it hadn't been given for nothing.

It had been given, even the most wildly squandered sum, as an offering to destiny that he might not remember the things most worth remembering, the things that now he would always remember—his child taken from his control, his wife escaped to a grave in Vermont.

In the glare of a *brasserie* a woman spoke to him. He bought her some eggs and coffee, and then, eluding her encouraging stare, gave her a twenty-franc note and took a taxi to his hotel.

II

He woke upon a fine fall day—football weather. The depression of yesterday was gone and he liked the people on the streets. At noon he sat opposite Honoria at Le Grand Vatel, the only restaurant he could think of not reminiscent of champagne dinners and long luncheons that began at two and ended in a blurred and vague twilight.

"Now, how about vegetables? Oughtn't you to have some vegetables?"

"Well, yes."

"Here's *épinards* and *chou-fleur* and carrots and *haricots*."

"I'd like *chou-fleur*."

"Wouldn't you like to have two vegetables?"

"I usually only have one at lunch."

The waiter was pretending to be inordinately fond of children. "*Qu'elle est mignonne la petite! Elle parle exactement comme une française.*"

"How about dessert? Shall we wait and see?"

The waiter disappeared. Honoria looked at her father expectantly.

"What are we going to do?"

"First, we're going to that toy store in the Rue Saint-Honoré and buy you anything you like. And then we're going to the vaudeville at the Empire."

She hesitated. "I like it about the vaudeville, but not the toy store."

"Why not?"

"Well, you brought me this doll." She had it with her. "And I've got lots of things. And we're not rich any more, are we?"

"We never were. But today you are to have anything you want."

"All right," she agreed resignedly.

When there had been her mother and a French nurse he had been inclined to be strict; now he extended himself, reached out for a new tolerance; he must be both parents to her and not shut any of her out of communication.

"I want to get to know you," he said gravely. "First let me introduce myself. My name is Charles J. Wales, of Prague."

"Oh, daddy!" her voice cracked with laughter.

"And who are you please?" he persisted, and she accepted a rôle immediately: "Honoria Wales, Rue Palatine, Paris."

"Married or single?"

"No, not married. Single."

He indicated the doll. "But I see you have a child, madame."

Unwilling to disinherit it, she took it to her heart and thought quickly: "Yes, I've been married, but I'm not married now. My husband is dead."

He went on quickly, "And the child's name?"

"Simone. That's after my best friend at school."

"I'm very pleased that you're doing so well at school."

"I'm third this month," she boasted. "Elsie"—that was her cousin—"is only about eighteenth, and Richard is about at the bottom."

"You like Richard and Elsie, don't you?"

"Oh, yes. I like Richard quite well and I like her all right."

Cautiously and casually he asked: "And Aunt Marion and Uncle Lincoln—which do you like best?"

"Oh, Uncle Lincoln, I guess."

He was increasingly aware of her presence. As they came in, a murmur of " . . . adorable" followed them, and now the people at the next table bent all their silences upon her, staring as if she were something no more conscious than a flower.

"Why don't I live with you?" she asked suddenly. "Because mama's dead?"

"You must stay here and learn more French. It would have been hard for daddy to take care of you so well."

"I don't really need much taking care of any more. I do everything for myself."

Going out of the restaurant, a man and a woman unexpectedly hailed him!

"Well, the old Wales!"

"Hello there, Lorraine. . . . Dunc."

Sudden ghosts out of the past: Duncan Schaeffer, a friend from college. Lorraine Quarrles, a lovely, pale blond of thirty; one of a crowd who had helped them make months into days in the lavish times of three years ago.

"My husband couldn't come this year," she said, in answer to his question. "We're poor as hell. So he gave me two hundred a month and told me I could do my worst on that. . . . .This your little girl?"

"What about coming back and sitting down?" Duncan asked.

"Can't do it." He was glad for an excuse. As always, he felt Lorraine's passionate, provocative attraction, but his own rhythm was different now.

"Well, how about dinner?" she asked.

"I'm not free. Give me your address and let me call you."

"Charlie, I believe you're sober," she said judicially. "I honestly believe he's sober, Dunc. Pinch him and see if he's sober."

Charlie indicated Honoria with his head. They both laughed.

"What's your address?" said Duncan sceptically.

He hesitated, unwilling to give the name of his hotel.

"I'm not settled yet. I'd better call you. We're going to see the vaudeville at the Empire."

"There! That's what I want to do," Lorraine said. "I want to see some clowns and acrobats and jugglers. That's just what we'll do, Dunc."

"We've got to do an errand first," said Charlie. "Perhaps we'll see you there."

"All right, you snob. . . . Good-by, beautiful little girl."

"Good-by."

Honoria bobbed politely.

Somehow, an unwelcome encounter. They liked him because he was functioning, because he was serious; they wanted to see him, because he was stronger than they were now, because they wanted to draw a certain sustenance from his strength.

At the Empire, Honoria proudly refused to sit upon her father's folded coat. She was already an individual with a code of her own, and Charlie was more and more absorbed by the desire of putting a little of himself into her before she crystallized utterly. It was hopeless to try to know her in so short a time.

Between the acts they came upon Duncan and Lorraine in the lobby where the band was playing.

"Have a drink?"

"All right, but not up at the bar. We'll take a table."

"The perfect father."

Listening abstractedly to Lorraine, Charlie watched Honoria's eyes leave their table, and he followed them wistfully about the room, wondering what they saw. He met her glance and she smiled.

"I like that lemonade," she said.

What had she said? What had he expected? Going home in a taxi afterward, he pulled her over until her head rested against his chest.

"Darling, do you ever think about your mother?"

"Yes, sometimes," she answered vaguely.

"I don't want you to forget her. Have you got a picture of her?"

"Yes, I think so. Anyhow, Aunt Marion has. Why don't you want me to forget her?"

"She loved you very much."

"I loved her too."

They were silent for a moment.

"Daddy, I want to come and live with you," she said suddenly.

His heart leaped; he had wanted it to come like this.

"Aren't you perfectly happy?"

"Yes, but I love you better than anybody. And you love me better than anybody, don't you, now that mummy's dead?"

"Of course I do. But you won't always like me best, honey. You'll grow up and meet somebody your own age and go marry him and forget you ever had a daddy."

"Yes, that's true," she agreed tranquilly.

He didn't go in. He was coming back at nine o'clock and he wanted to keep himself fresh and new for the thing he must say then.

"When you're safe inside, just show yourself in that window."

"All right. Good-by, dads, dads, dads, dads."

He waited in the dark street until she appeared, all warm and glowing, in the window above and kissed her fingers out into the night.

III

They were waiting. Marion sat behind the coffee service in a dignified black dinner dress that just faintly suggested mourning. Lincoln was walking up and down with the animation of one who had already been talking. They were as anxious as he was to get into the question. He opened it almost immediately:

"I suppose you know what I want to see you about—why I really came to Paris."

Marion played with the black stars on her necklace and frowned.

"I'm awfully anxious to have a home," he continued. "And I'm awfully anxious to have Honoria in it. I appreciate your taking in Honoria for her mother's sake, but things have changed now"—he hesitated and then continued more forcibly—"changed radically with me, and I want to ask you to reconsider the matter. It would be silly for me to deny that about three years ago I was acting badly—"

Marion looked up at him with hard eyes.

"—but all that's over. As I told you, I haven't had more than a drink a day for over a year, and I take that drink deliberately, so that the idea of alcohol won't get too big in my imagination. You see the idea?"

"No," said Marion succinctly.

"It's a sort of stunt I set myself. It keeps the matter in proportion."

"I get you," said Lincoln. "You don't want to admit it's got any attraction for you."

"Something like that. Sometimes I forget and don't take it. But I try to take it. Anyhow, I couldn't afford to drink in my position. The people I represent are more than satisfied with what I've done, and I'm bringing my sister over from Burlington to keep house for me, and I want awfully to have Honoria too. You know that even when her mother and I weren't getting along well we never let anything that happened touch Honoria. I know she's fond of me and I know I'm able to take care of her and—well, there you are. How do you feel about it?"

He knew that now he would have to take a beating. It would last an hour or two hours, and it would be difficult, but if he modulated his inevitable resentment to the chastened attitude of the reformed sinner, he might win his point in the end.

Keep your temper, he told himself. You don't want to be justified. You want Honoria.

Lincoln spoke first: "We've been talking it over ever since we got your letter last month. We're happy to have Honoria here. She's a dear little thing, and we're glad to be able to help her, but of course that isn't the question—"

Marion interrupted suddenly. "How long are you going to stay sober, Charlie?" she asked.

"Permanently, I hope."

"How can anybody count on that?"

"You know I never did drink heavily until I gave up business and came over here with nothing to do. Then Helen and I began to run around with—"

"Please leave Helen out of it. I can't bear to hear you talk about her like that."

He stared at her grimly; he had never been certain how fond of each other the sisters were in life.

"My drinking only lasted about a year and a half—from the time we came over until I—collapsed."

"It was time enough."

"It was time enough," he agreed.

"My duty is entirely to Helen," she said. "I try to think what she would have wanted me to do. Frankly, from the night you did that terrible thing you haven't really existed for me. I can't help that. She was my sister."

"Yes."

"When she was dying she asked me to look out for Honoria. If you hadn't been in a sanitarium then, it might have helped matters."

He had no answer.

"I'll never in my life be able to forget the morning when Helen knocked at my door, soaked to the skin and shivering, and said you'd locked her out."

Charlie gripped the sides of the chair. This was more difficult than he expected; he wanted to launch out into a long expostulation and explanation, but he only said: "The night I locked her out—" and she interrupted, "I don't feel up to going over that again."

After a moment's silence Lincoln said: "We're getting off the subject. You want Marion to set aside her legal guardianship and give you Honoria. I think the main point for her is whether she has confidence in you or not."

"I don't blame Marion," Charlie said slowly, "but I think she can have entire confidence in me. I had a good record up to three years ago. Of course, it's within human possibilities I might go wrong any time. But if we wait much longer I'll lose Honoria's childhood and my chance for a home." He shook his head, "I'll simply lose her, don't you see?"

"Yes, I see," said Lincoln.

"Why didn't you think of all this before?" Marion asked.

"I suppose I did, from time to time, but Helen and I were getting along badly. When I consented to the guardianship, I was flat on my back in a sanitarium and the market had cleaned me out. I knew I'd acted badly, and I thought if it would bring any peace to Helen, I'd agree to anything. But now it's different. I'm functioning, I'm behaving damn well, so far as—"

"Please don't swear at me," Marion said.

He looked at her, startled. With each remark the force of her dislike became more and more apparent. She had built up all her fear of life into one wall and faced it toward him. This trivial reproof was possibly the result of some trouble with the cook several hours before. Charlie became increasingly alarmed at leaving Honoria in this atmosphere of hostility against himself; sooner or later it would come out, in a word here, a shake of the head there, and some of that distrust would be irrevocably implanted in Honoria. But he pulled his temper down out of his face and shut it up inside him; he had won a point, for Lincoln realized the absurdity of Marion's remark and asked her lightly since when she had objected to the word "damn."

"Another thing," Charlie said: "I'm able to give her certain advantages now. I'm going to take a French governess to Prague with me. I've got a lease on a new apartment—"

He stopped, realizing that he was blundering. They couldn't be expected to accept with equanimity the fact that his income was again twice as large as their own.

"I suppose you can give her more luxuries than we can," said Marion. When you were throwing away money we were living along watching every ten francs. . . . I suppose you'll start doing it again."

"Oh, no," he said. "I've learned. I worked hard for ten years, you know—until I got lucky in the market, like so many people. Terribly lucky. It didn't seem any use working any more, so I quit. It won't happen again."

There was a long silence. All of them felt their nerves straining, and for the first time in a year Charlie wanted a drink. He was sure now that Lincoln Peters wanted him to have his child.

Marion shuddered suddenly; part of her saw that Charlie's feet were planted on the earth now, and her own maternal feeling recognized the naturalness of his desire; but she had lived for a long time with a prejudice—a prejudice founded on a curious disbelief in her sister's happiness, and which, in the shock of one terrible night, had turned to hatred for him. It had all happened at a point in her life where the discouragement of ill health and adverse circumstances made it necessary for her to believe in tangible villainy and a tangible villain.

"I can't help what I think!" she cried out suddenly. "How much you were responsible for Helen's death, I don't know. It's something you'll have to square with your own conscience."

An electric current of agony surged through him; for a moment he was almost on his feet, an unuttered sound echoing in his throat. He hung on to himself for a moment, another moment.

"Hold on there," said Lincoln uncomfortably. "I never thought you were responsible for that."

"Helen died of heart trouble," Charlie said dully.

"Yes, heart trouble." Marion spoke as if the phrase had another meaning for her.

Then, in the flatness that followed her outburst, she saw him plainly and she knew he had somehow arrived at control over the situation. Glancing at her husband, she found no help from him, and as abruptly as if it were a matter of no importance, she threw up the sponge.

"Do what you like!" she cried, springing up from her chair. "She's your child. I'm not the person to stand in your way. I think if it were my child I'd rather see her—" She managed to check herself. "You two decide it. I can't stand this. I'm sick. I'm going to bed."

She hurried from the room; after a moment Lincoln said:

"This has been a hard day for her. You know how strongly she feels—" His voice was almost apologetic: "When a woman gets an idea in her head."

"Of course."

"It's going to be all right. I think she sees now that you—can provide for the child, and so we can't very well stand in your way or Honoria's way."

"Thank you, Lincoln."

"I'd better go along and see how she is."

"I'm going."

He was still trembling when he reached the street, but a walk down the Rue Bonaparte to the quais set him up, and as he crossed the Seine, fresh and new by the quai lamps, he felt exultant. But back in his room he couldn't sleep. The image of Helen haunted him. Helen whom he had loved so until they had senselessly begun to abuse each other's love, tear it into shreds. On that terrible February night that Marion remembered so vividly, a slow quarrel had gone on for hours. There was a scene at the Florida, and then he attempted to take her home, and then she kissed young Webb at a table; after that there was what she had hysterically said. When he arrived home alone he turned the key in the lock in wild anger. How could he know she would arrive an hour later alone, that there would be a snowstorm in which she wandered about in slippers, too confused to find a taxi? Then the aftermath, her escaping pneumonia by a miracle, and all the attendant horror. They were "reconciled," but that was the beginning of the end, and Marion, who had seen with her own eyes and who imagined it to be one of many scenes from her sister's martyrdom, never forgot.

Going over it again brought Helen nearer, and in the white, soft light that steals upon half sleep near morning he found himself talking to her again. She said that he was perfectly right about Honoria and she wanted Honoria to be with him. She said she was glad he was being good and doing better. She said a lot of other things—very friendly things—but she was in a swing in a white dress, and swinging faster and faster all the time, so that at the end he could not hear clearly all that she said.

IV

He woke up feeling happy. The door of the world was open again. He made plans, vistas, futures for Honoria and himself, but suddenly he grew sad, remembering all the plans he and Helen had made. She had not planned to die. The present was the thing—work to do and someone to love. But not to love too much, for he knew the injury that a father can do to a daughter or a mother to a son by attaching them too closely; afterward, out in the world, the child would seek in the marriage partner the same blind tenderness and, failing probably to find it, turn against love and life.

It was another bright, crisp day. He called Lincoln Peters at the Bank where he worked and asked if he could count on taking Honoria when he left for Prague. Lincoln agreed that there was no reason for delay. One thing—the legal guardianship. Marion wanted to retain that a while longer. She was upset by the whole matter, and it would oil things if she felt that the situation was still in her control for another year. Charlie agreed, wanted only the tangible, visible child.

Then the question of a governess. Charlie sat in a gloomy agency and talked to a cross Bernaise and to a buxom Breton peasant, neither of whom he could have endured. There were others whom he would see tomorrow.

He lunched with Lincoln Peters at Griffons, trying to keep down his exultation.

"There's nothing quite like your own child," Lincoln said. "But you understand how Marion feels too."

"She's forgotton how hard I worked for seven years there," Charlie said. "She just remembers one night."

"There's another thing." Lincoln hesitated. "While you and Helen were tearing around Europe throwing money away, we were just getting along. I didn't touch any of the prosperity because I never got ahead enough to carry anything but my insurance. I think Marion felt there was some kind of injustice in it—you not even working toward the end, and getting richer and richer."

"It went just as quick as it came," said Charlie.

"Yes, a lot of it stayed in the hands of *chasseurs* and saxophone players and maîtres d'hôtel—well, the big party's over now. I just said that to explain Marion's feeling about those crazy years. If you drop in about six o'clock tonight before Marion's too tired, we'll settle the details on the spot."

Back at his hotel, Charlie found a *pneumatique* that had been redirected from the Ritz bar where Charlie had left his address for the purpose of finding a certain man.

> *Dear Charlie: You were so strange when we saw you the other day that I wondered if I did something to offend you. If so, I'm not conscious of it. In fact, I have thought about you too much for the last year, and it's always been in the back of my mind that I might see you if I came over here. We* did *have such good times that crazy spring, like the night you and I stole the butcher's*

tricycle, and the time we tried to call on the president and you had the old derby rim and the wire cane. Everybody seems so old lately, but I don't feel old a bit. Couldn't we get together some time today for old time's sake? I've got a vile hang-over for the moment, but will be feeling better this afternoon and will look for you about five in the sweat-shop at the Ritz.

Always devotedly,
Lorraine.

His first feeling was one of awe that he had actually, in his mature years, stolen a tricycle and pedalled Lorraine all over the Étoile between the small hours and dawn. In retrospect it was a nightmare. Locking out Helen didn't fit in with any other act of his life, but the tricycle incident did—it was one of many. How many weeks or months of dissipation to arrive at that condition of utter irresponsibility?

He tried to picture how Lorraine had appeared to him then—very attractive; Helen was unhappy about it, though she said nothing. Yesterday, in the restaurant, Lorraine had seemed trite, blurred, worn away. He emphatically did not want to see her, and he was glad Alix had not given away his hotel address. It was a relief to think, instead, of Honoria, to think of Sundays spent with her and of saying good morning to her and of knowing she was there in his house at night, drawing her breath in the darkness.

At five he took a taxi and bought presents for all the Peters—a piquant cloth doll, a box of Roman soldiers, flowers for Marion, big linen handkerchiefs for Lincoln.

He saw, when he arrived in the apartment, that Marion had accepted the inevitable. She greeted him now as though he were a recalcitrant member of the family, rather than a menacing outsider. Honoria had been told she was going; Charlie was glad to see that her tact made her conceal her excessive happiness. Only on his lap did she whisper her delight and the question "When?" before she slipped away with the other children.

He and Marion were alone for a minute in the room, and on an impulse he spoke out boldly:

"Family quarrels are bitter things. They don't go according to any rules. They're not like aches or wounds; they're more like splits in the skin that won't heal because there's not enough material. I wish you and I could be on better terms."

"Some things are hard to forget," she answered. "It's a question of confidence." There was no answer to this and presently she asked, "When do you propose to take her?"

"As soon as I can get a governess. I hoped the day after tomorrow."

"That's impossible. I've got to get her things in shape. Not before Saturday."

He yielded. Coming back into the room, Lincoln offered him a drink.

"I'll take my daily whisky," he said.

It was warm here, it was a home, people together by a fire. The children felt very safe and important; the mother and father were serious, watchful. They had things to do for the children more important than his visit here. A spoonful of medicine was, after all, more important than the strained relations between Marion and himself. They were not dull people, but they were very much in the grip of life and circumstances. He wondered if he couldn't do something to get Lincoln out of his rut at the bank.

A long peal at the door-bell; the *bonne à toute faire* passed through and went down the corridor. The door opened upon another long ring, and then voices, and the three in the salon looked up expectantly; Richard moved to bring the corridor within his range of vision, and Marion rose. Then the maid came back along the corridor, closely followed by the voices, which developed under the light into Duncan Schaeffer and Lorraine Quarrles.

They were gay, they were hilarious, they were roaring with laughter. For a moment Charlie was astounded; unable to understand how they ferreted out the Peters' address.

"Ah-h-h!" Duncan wagged his finger roguishly at Charlie. "Ah-h-h!"

They both slid down another cascade of laughter. Anxious and at a loss, Charlie shook hands with them quickly and presented them to Lincoln and Marion. Marion nodded, scarcely speaking. She had drawn back a step toward the fire; her little girl stood beside her, and Marion put an arm about her shoulder.

With growing annoyance at the intrusion, Charlie waited for them to explain themselves. After some concentration Duncan said:

"We came to invite you out to dinner. Lorraine and I insist that all this shishi, cagy business 'bout your address got to stop."

Charlie came closer to them, as if to force them backward down the corridor.

"Sorry, but I can't. Tell me where you'll be and I'll phone you in half an hour."

This made no impression. Lorraine sat down suddenly on the side of a chair, and focusing her eyes on Richard, cried, "Oh, what a nice little boy! Come here, little boy." Richard glanced at his mother, but did not move. With a perceptible shrug of her shoulders, Lorraine turned back to Charlie:

"Come and dine. Sure your cousins won' mine. See you so sel'om. Or solemn."

"I can't," said Charlie sharply. "You two have dinner and I'll phone you."

Her voice became suddenly unpleasant: "All right, we'll go. But I remember once when you hammered on my door at four A.M. I was enough of a good sport to give you a drink. Come on, Dunc."

Still in slow motion, with blurred, angry faces, with uncertain feet, they retired along the corridor.

"Good night," Charlie said.

"Good night!" responded Lorraine emphatically.

When he went back into the salon Marion had not moved, only now her son was standing in the circle of her other arm. Lincoln was still swinging Honoria back and forth like a pendulum from side to side.

"What an outrage!" Charlie broke out. "What an absolute outrage!"

Neither of them answered. Charlie dropped into an armchair, picked up his drink, set it down again and said:

"People I haven't seen for two years having the colossal nerve—"

He broke off. Marion had made the sound "Oh!" in one swift, furious breath, turned her body from him with a jerk and left the room.

Lincoln set down Honoria carefully.

"You children go in and start your soup," he said, and when they obeyed, he said to Charlie:

"Marion's not well and she can't stand shocks. That kind of people make her really physically sick."

"I didn't tell them to come here. They wormed your name out of somebody. They deliberately—"

"Well, it's too bad. It doesn't help matters. Excuse me a minute."

Left alone, Charlie sat tense in his chair. In the next room he could hear the children eating, talking in monosyllables, already oblivious to the scene between their elders. He heard a murmur of conversation from a farther room and then the ticking bell of a telephone receiver picked up, and in a panic he moved to the other side of the room and out of earshot.

In a minute Lincoln came back. "Look here, Charlie. I think we'd better call off dinner for tonight. Marion's in bad shape."

"Is she angry with me?"

"Sort of," he said, almost roughly. "She's not strong and—"

"You mean she's changed her mind about Honoria?"

"She's pretty bitter right now. I don't know. You phone me at the bank tomorrow."

"I wish you'd explain to her I never dreamed these people would come here. I'm just as sore as you are."

"I couldn't explain anything to her now."

Charlie got up. He took his coat and hat and started down the corridor. Then he opened the door of the dining room and said in a strange voice, "Good night, children."

Honoria rose and ran around the table to hug him.

"Good night, sweetheart," he said vaguely, and then trying to make his voice more tender, trying to conciliate something, "Good night, dear children."

V

Charlie went directly to the Ritz bar with the furious idea of finding Lorraine and Duncan, but they were not there, and he realized that in any case there was nothing he could do. He had not touched his drink at the Peters', and now he ordered a whisky-and-soda. Paul came over to say hello.

"It's a great change," he said sadly. "We do about half the business we did. So many fellows I hear about back in the States lost everything, maybe not in the first crash, but then in the second. Your friend George Hardt lost every cent, I hear. Are you back in the States?"

"No, I'm in business in Prague."

"I hear that you lost a lot in the crash."

"I did," and he added grimly, "but I lost everything I wanted in the boom."

"Selling short."

"Something like that."

Again the memory of those days swept over him like a nightmare—the people they had met travelling; the people who couldn't add a row of figures or speak a coherent sentence. The little man Helen had consented to dance with at the ship's party, who had insulted her ten feet from the table; the women and girls carried screaming with drink or drugs out of public places—

—The men who locked their wives out in the snow, because the snow of twenty-nine wasn't real snow. If you didn't want it to be snow, you just paid some money.

He went to the phone and called the Peters' apartment; Lincoln answered.

"I called up because this thing is on my mind. Has Marion said anything definite?"

"Marion's sick," Lincoln answered shortly. "I know this thing isn't altogether your fault, but I can't have her go to pieces about it. I'm afraid we'll have to let it slide for six months; I can't take the chance of working her up to this state again."

"I see."

"I'm sorry, Charlie."

He went back to his table. His whisky glass was empty, but he shook his head when Alix looked at it questionably. There wasn't much he could do now except send Honoria some things; he would send her a lot of things tomorrow. He thought rather angrily that this was just money—he had given so many people money. . . .

"No, no more," he said to another waiter. "What do I owe you?"

He would come back some day; they couldn't make him pay forever. But he wanted his child, and nothing was much good now, beside that fact. He wasn't young any more, with a lot of nice thoughts and dreams to have by himself. He was absolutely sure Helen wouldn't have wanted him to be so alone.

William Faulkner

1897 – 1962

Since the death of William Faulkner in 1962 at the age of 64, the critical assessment of his literary achievement has continued unabated, and there seems little possibility that his ranking as one of the truly great masters of twentiety-century fiction will in the least diminish. Perhaps the single most impressive quality of his fiction is its creative range—in subject matter from hilarious comedy to violent tragedy, in technique from the straight-forward and traditional to the most complex and unconventional, and in character types from the most common and lifelike to the weirdest and most grotesque distortions. Despite the fact that his work is uneven in quality or that even his best may have its defects, the fictional world he created is one of limitless variety and richness. It is thus hardly surprising that his fiction won for him not only all the significant literary awards, including the Nobel Prize in 1950, but also an international, as well as national, audience.

Probably few writers in modern times so completely isolated themselves from metropolitan literary centers or stuck so closely to the locale of their materials as Faulkner did. He was born in 1897, in New Albany, Mississippi, but at an early age moved to the nearby university and county-seat town of Oxford, where, except for brief periods, he spent his entire life. He attended public school in Oxford but never graduated, served during World War I in the British Royal Air Force, and spent some time after his return to Oxford as a student at the University of Mississippi. After working at a succession of odd jobs in Oxford, he lived for a while in New Orleans, forming there short-lived acquaintances with Sherwood Anderson and other writers then residing in the Old French Quarter. He next worked in a New York bookstore for three months, took a long walking tour of Europe, and returned to Oxford to settle down to his writing career. As early as 1924 he published a collection of poems, *The Marble Faun,* and in 1926 his novels began to appear at regular intervals. The first five—*Soldiers' Pay* (1926), *Mosquitoes* (1927), *Sartoris* (1929), *The Sound and the Fury* (1929), and *As I Lay Dying* (1930)—brought him considerable recognition, but it was only after he published the deliberately shocking *Sanctuary* (1931) that he won fame. Other important novels include: *Light in August* (1932), *Absalom! Absalom!* (1936), *The Wild Palms* (1939), *The Hamlet* (1940), *Intruder in the Dust* (1948), *Requiem for a Nun* (1951), *A Fable* (1954), *The Town* (1957), *The Mansion* (1959), and *The Reivers* (1962). He wrote a large number of short stories, some of which were published separately and later rewoven into the fabric of his novels. Among his short story volumes are *These Thirteen* (1931), *Doctor Martino* (1934), *Go Down, Moses* (1942), and *Collected Stories* (1950).

As a contrast to the substance and style found in some of Faulkner's best known horror stories, such as "A Rose for Emily," "Barn Burning," and "That Evening Sun," his story "was" represents an admirable extension of the old Southwest humor tradition. Its looser narrative form is keyed to the character of the one who is telling it as a remembered tale "out of the old time, the old days." The point of view of the original narrator is that of a nine-year-old nephew of Uncles Buck and Buddy.

was

Isaac McCaslin, "Uncle Ike," past seventy and nearer eighty than he ever corroborated any more, a widower now and uncle to half a county and father to no one

this was not something participated in or even seen by himself, but by his elder cousin, McCaslin Edmonds, grandson of Isaac's father's sister and so descended by the distaff, yet notwithstanding the inheritor, and in his time the bequestor, of that which some had thought then and some still thought should have been Isaac's, since his was the name in which the title to the land had first been granted from the Indian patent and which some of the descendants of his father's slaves still bore in the land. But Isaac was not one of these:—a widower these twenty years, who in all his life had owned but one object more than he could wear and carry in his pockets and his hands at one time, and this was the narrow iron cot and the stained lean mattress which he used camping in the woods for deer and bear or for fishing or simply because he loved the woods; who owned no property and never desired to since the earth was no man's but all men's, as light and air and weather were; who lived still in the cheap frame bungalow in Jefferson which his wife's father gave them on their marriage and which his wife had willed to him at her death and which he had pretended to accept, acquiesce to, to humor her, ease her going but which was not his, will or not, chancery dying wishes mortmain possession or whatever, himself merely holding it for his wife's sister and her children who had lived in it with him since his wife's death, holding himself welcome to live in one room of it as he had during his wife's time or she during her time or the sister-in-law and her children during the rest of his and after

not something he had participated in or even remembered except from the hearing, the listening, come to him through and from his cousin McCaslin born in 1850 and sixteen years his senior and hence, his own father being near seventy when Isaac, an only child, was born, rather his brother than cousin and rather his father than either, out of the old time, the old days

2

When he and Uncle Buck ran back to the house from discovering that Tomey's Turl had run again, they heard Uncle Buddy cursing and bellowing in the kitchen, then the fox and the dogs came out of the kitchen and crossed the hall into the dogs' room and they heard them run through the dogs' room into his and Uncle Buck's room, then they saw them cross the hall again into Uncle Buddy's room and heard them run through Uncle Buddy's room into the kitchen again and this time it sounded like the whole kitchen chimney had come down and Uncle Buddy bellowing like a steam-boat blowing, and this time the fox and the dogs and five or six sticks of firewood all came out of the kitchen together with Uncle

Buddy in the middle of them hitting at everything in sight with another stick. It was a good race.

When Cass and Uncle Buck ran into their room to get Uncle Buck's necktie, the fox had treed behind the clock on the mantel. Uncle Buck got the necktie from the drawer and kicked the dogs off and lifted the fox down by the scruff of the neck and shoved it back into the crate under the bed and they went to the kitchen, where Uncle Buddy was picking the breakfast up out of the ashes and wiping it off with his apron. "What in damn's hell do you mean," he said, "turning that damn fox out with the dogs all loose in the house?"

"Damn the fox," Uncle Buck said. "Tomey's Turl has broke out again. Give me and Cass some breakfast quick. We might just barely catch him before he gets there."

Because they knew exactly where Tomey's Turl had gone, he went there every time he could slip off, which was about twice a year. He was heading for Mr. Hubert Beauchamp's place just over the edge of the next county, that Mr. Hubert's sister, Miss Sophonsiba (Mr. Hubert was a bachelor too, like Uncle Buck and Uncle Buddy) was still trying to make people call Warwick after the place in England that she said Mr. Hubert was probably the true earl of only he never even had enough pride, not to mention energy, to take the trouble to establish his just rights. Tomey's Turl would go there to hang around Mr. Hubert's girl Tennie, until somebody came and got him. They couldn't keep him at home by buying Tennie from Mr. Hubert because Uncle Buck said he and Uncle Buddy had so many niggers already that they could hardly walk around on their own land for them, and they couldn't sell Tomey's Turl to Mr. Hubert because Mr. Hubert said he not only wouldn't buy Tomey's Turl, he wouldn't have that damn white half-McCaslin on his place even as a free gift, not even if Uncle Buck and Uncle Buddy were to pay board and keep for him. And if somebody didn't go and get Tomey's Turl right away, Mr. Hubert would fetch him back himself, bringing Miss Sophonsiba, and they would stay for a week or longer, Miss Sophonsiba living in Uncle Buddy's room and Uncle Buddy moved clean out of the house, sleeping in one of the cabins in the quarters where the niggers used to live in his great-grandfather's time until his great-grandfather died and Uncle Buck and Uncle Buddy moved all the niggers into the big house which his great-grandfather had not had time to finish, and not even doing the cooking while they were there and not even coming to the house any more except to sit on the front gallery after supper, sitting in the darkness between Mr. Hubert and Uncle Buck until after a while even Mr. Hubert would give up telling how many more head of niggers and acres of land he would add to what he would give Miss Sophonsiba when she married, and go to bed. And one midnight last summer Uncle Buddy just happened by accident to be awake and hear Mr. Hubert drive out of the lot and by the time he waked them and they got Miss Sophonsiba up and dressed and the team put to the wagon and caught Mr. Hubert, it was almost daylight. So it was always he and Uncle Buck who went to fetch Tomey's Turl because Uncle Buddy never went anywhere, not even to town and not even to fetch Tomey's Turl from Mr. Hubert's, even though they all knew that Uncle Buddy could have risked it ten times as much as Uncle Buck could have dared.

They ate breakfast fast. Uncle Buck put on his necktie while they were running toward the lot to catch the horses. The only time he wore the necktie was on Tomey's Turl's account and he hadn't even had it out of the drawer since that night last summer when Uncle Buddy had waked them in the dark and said, "Get up out of that bed and damn quick." Uncle Buddy didn't own a necktie at all; Uncle Buck said Uncle Buddy wouldn't take that chance even in a section like theirs, where ladies were so damn seldom thank God that a man could ride for days in a straight line without having to dodge a single one. His grandmother (she was Uncle Buck's and Uncle Buddy's sister; she had raised him following his mother's death. That was where he had got his christian name: McCaslin, Carothers McCaslin Edmonds) said that Uncle Buck and Uncle Buddy both used the necktie just as another way of daring people to say they looked like twins, because even at sixty they would still fight anyone who claimed he could not tell them apart; whereupon his father had answered that any man who ever played poker once with Uncle Buddy would never mistake him again for Uncle Buck or anybody else.

Jonas had the two horses saddled and waiting. Uncle Buck didn't mount a horse like he was any sixty years old either, lean and active as a cat, with his round, close-cropped white head and his hard little gray eyes and his white-stubbled jaw, his foot in the iron and the horse already moving, already running at the open gate when Uncle Buck came into the seat. He scrabbled up too, onto the shorter pony, before Jonas could boost him up, clapping the pony with his heels into its own stiff, short-coupled canter, out the gate after Uncle Buck, when Uncle Buddy (he hadn't even noticed him) stepped out from the gate and caught the bit. "Watch him," Uncle Buddy said. "Watch Theophilus. The minute anything begins to look wrong, you ride to hell back here and get me. You hear?"

"Yes, sir," he said. "Lemme go now. I won't even ketch Uncle Buck, let alone Tomey's Turl——"

Uncle Buck was riding Black John, because if they could just catch sight of Tomey's Turl at least one mile from Mr. Hubert's gate, Black John would ride him down in two minutes. So when they came out on the long flat about three miles from Mr. Hubert's, sure enough, there was Tomey's Turl on the Jake mule about a mile ahead. Uncle Buck flung his arm out and back, reining in, crouched on the big horse, his little round head and his gnarled neck thrust forward like a cooter's. "Stole away!" he whispered. "You stay back where he won't see you and flush. I'll circle him through the woods and we will bay him at the creek ford."

He waited until Uncle Buck had vanished into the woods. Then he went on. But Tomey's Turl saw him. He closed in too fast; maybe he was afraid he wouldn't be there in time to see him when he treed. It was the best race he had ever seen. He had never seen old Jake go that fast, and nobody had ever known Tomey's Turl to go faster than his natural walk, even riding a mule. Uncle Buck whooped once from the woods, running on sight, then Black John came out of the trees, driving, soupled out flat and level as a hawk, with Uncle Buck right up behind his ears now and yelling so that they looked exactly like a big black hawk with a sparrow riding it, across the field and over the ditch and across the next field, and he was running too; the mare went out before he even knew she was ready, and he was yelling too. Because, being a nigger, Tomey's Turl should have jumped down and run for it afoot as soon as he saw them. But he didn't; maybe Tomey's Turl had been running off from Uncle Buck for so long that he had even got used to running away like a white man would do it. And it was like he and old Jake had added Tomey's Turl's natural walking speed to the best that old Jake had ever done in his life, and it was just exactly enough to beat Uncle Buck to the ford. Because when he and the pony arrived, Black John was blown and lathered and Uncle Buck was down, leading him around in a circle to slow him down, and they could already hear Mr. Hubert's dinner horn a mile away.

Only, for a while Tomey's Turl didn't seem to be at Mr. Hubert's either. The boy was still sitting on the gatepost, blowing the horn—there was no gate there; just two posts and a nigger boy about his size sitting on one of them, blowing a fox-horn; this was what Miss Sophonsiba was still reminding people was named Warwick even when they had already known for a long time that's what she aimed to have it called, until when they wouldn't call it Warwick she wouldn't even seem to know what they were talking about and it would sound as if she and Mr. Hubert owned two separate plantations covering the same area of ground, one on top of the other. Mr. Hubert was sitting in the springhouse with his boots off and his feet in the water, drinking a toddy. But nobody there had seen Tomey's Turl; for a time it looked like Mr. Hubert couldn't even place who Uncle Buck was talking about. "Oh, that nigger," he said at last. "We'll find him after dinner."

Only it didn't seem as if they were going to eat either. Mr. Hubert and Uncle Buck had a toddy, when Mr. Hubert finally sent to tell the boy on the gatepost he could quit blowing, and he and Uncle Buck had another toddy and Uncle Buck still saying, "I just want my nigger. Then we got to get on back toward home."

"After dinner," Mr. Hubert said. "If we don't start him somewhere around the kitchen, we'll put the dogs on him. They'll find him if it's in the power of mortal Walker dogs to do it."

But at last a hand began waving a handkerchief or something white through the broken place in an upstairs shutter. They went to the house, crossing the back gallery, Mr. Hubert warning them again, as he always did, to watch out for the rotted floor-board he hadn't got around to having fixed yet. Then they stood in the hall, until presently there was a jangling and swishing noise and they began to smell the perfume, and Miss Sophonsiba came down the stairs. Her hair was roached under a lace cap; she had on her Sunday dress and beads and a red ribbon around her throat and a little nigger girl carrying her fan and he stood quietly a step behind Uncle Buck, watching her lips until they opened and he could see the roan tooth. He had never known anyone before with a roan tooth and he remembered how one time his grandmother and his father were talking about Uncle Buddy and Uncle Buck and his grandmother said that Miss Sophonsiba had matured into a fine-looking woman once. Maybe she had. He didn't know. He wasn't but nine.

"Why, Mister Theophilus," she said. "And McCaslin," she said. She had never looked at him and she wasn't talking to him and he knew it, although he was prepared and balanced to drag his foot when Uncle Buck did. "Welcome to Warwick."

He and Uncle Buck dragged their feet. "I just come to get my nigger," Uncle Buck said. "Then we got to get on back home."

Then Miss Sophonsiba said something about a bumblebee, but he couldn't remember that. It was too fast and there was too much of it, the earrings and beads clashing and jingling like little trace chains on a toy mule trotting and the perfume stronger too, like the earrings and beads sprayed it out each time they moved and he watched the roan-colored tooth flick and glint between her lips; something about Uncle Buck was a bee sipping from flower to flower and not staying long anywhere and all that stored sweetness to be wasted on Uncle Buddy's desert air, calling Uncle Buddy Mister Amodeus like she called Uncle Buck Mister Theophilus, or maybe the honey was being stored up against the advent of a queen and who was the lucky queen and when? "Ma'am?" Uncle Buck said. Then Mr. Hubert said:

"Hah. A buck bee. I reckon that nigger's going to think he's a buck hornet, once he lays hands on him. But I reckon what Buck's thinking about sipping right now is some meat gravy and biscuit and a cup of coffee. And so am I."

They went into the dining room and ate and Miss Sophonsiba said how seriously now neighbors just a half day's ride apart ought not to go so long as Uncle Buck did, and Uncle Buck said Yessum, and Miss Sophonsiba said Uncle Buck was just a confirmed roving bachelor from the cradle born and this time Uncle Buck even quit chewing and looked and said, Yes, ma'am, he sure was, and born too late at it to ever change now but at least he could thank God no lady would ever have to suffer the misery of living with him and Uncle Buddy, and Miss Sophonsiba said Ah, that maybe Uncle Buck just ain't met the woman yet who would not only accept what Uncle Buck was pleased to call misery, but who would make Uncle Buck consider even his freedom a small price to pay, and Uncle Buck said, "Nome. Not yet."

Then he and Mr. Hubert and Uncle Buck went out to the front gallery and sat down. Mr. Hubert hadn't even got done taking his shoes off again and inviting Uncle Buck to take his off, when Miss Sophonsiba came out the door carrying a tray with another toddy on it. "Damnit, Sibbey," Mr. Hubert said. "He's just et. He don't want to drink that now." But Miss Sophonsiba didn't seem to hear him at all. She stood there, the roan tooth not flicking now but fixed because she wasn't talking now, handing the toddy to Uncle Buck until after a while she said how her papa always said nothing sweetened a Missippi toddy like the hand of a Missippi lady and would Uncle Buck like to see how she used to sweeten her papa's toddy for him? She lifted the toddy and took a sip of it and handed it again to Uncle Buck and this time Uncle Buck took it. He dragged his foot again and drank the toddy and said if Mr. Hubert was going to lay down, he would lay down a while too, since from the way things looked Tomey's Turl was fixing to give them a long hard race unless Mr. Hubert's dogs were a considerable better than they used to be.

Mr. Hubert and Uncle Buck went into the house. After a while he got up too and went around to the back yard to wait for them. The first thing he saw was Tomey's Turl's head slipping along above the lane fence. But when he cut across the yard to turn him, Tomey's Turl wasn't even running. He was squatting behind a bush, watching the house, peering around the bush at the back door and the upstairs windows, not whispering exactly but not talking loud either: "Whut they doing now?"

"They're taking a nap now," he said. "But never mind that; they're going to put the dogs on you when they get up."

"Hah," Tomey's Turl said. "And nem you mind that neither. I got protection now. All I needs to do is to keep Old Buck from ketching me unto I gets the word."

"What word?" he said. "Word from who? Is Mr. Hubert going to buy you from Uncle Buck?"

"Huh," Tomey's Turl said again. "I got more protection than whut Mr. Hubert got even." He rose to his feet. "I gonter tell you something to remember: anytime you wants to git something done, from hoeing out a crop to getting married, just git the womenfolks to working at it. Then all you needs to do is set down and wait. You member that."

Then Tomey's Turl was gone. And after a while he went back to the house. But there wasn't anything but the snoring coming out of the room where Uncle Buck and Mr. Hubert were, and some more light-sounding snoring coming from upstairs. He went to the springhouse and sat with his feet in the water as Mr. Hubert had been doing, because soon now it would be cool enough for a race. And sure enough, after a while Mr. Hubert and Uncle Buck came out onto the back gallery, with Miss Sophonsiba right behind them with the toddy tray only this time Uncle Buck drank his before Miss Sophonsiba had time to sweeten it, and Miss Sophonsiba told them to get back early, that all Uncle Buck knew of Warwick was just dogs and niggers and now that she had him, she wanted to show him her garden that Mr. Hubert and nobody else had any sayso in. "Yessum," Uncle Buck said. "I just want to catch my nigger. Then we got to get on back home."

Four or five niggers brought up the three horses. They could already hear the dogs waiting still coupled in the lane, and they mounted and went on down the lane, toward the quarters, with Uncle Buck already out in front of even the dogs. So he never did know just when and where they jumped Tomey's Turl, whether he flushed out of one of the cabins or not. Uncle Buck was away out in front on Black John and they hadn't even cast the dogs yet when Uncle Buck roared, "Gone away! I godfrey, he broke cover then!" and Black John's feet clapped four times like pistol shots while he was gathering to go out, then he and Uncle Buck vanished over the hill like they had run at the blank edge of the world itself. Mr. Hubert was roaring too: "Gone away! Cast them!" and they all piled over the crest of the hill just in time to see Tomey's Turl away out across the flat, almost to the woods, and the dogs streaking down the hill and out onto the flat. They just tongued once and when they came boiling up around Tomey's Turl it looked like they were trying to jump up and lick him in the face until even Tomey's Turl slowed down and he and the dogs all went into the woods together, walking, like they were going home from a rabbit hunt. And when they caught up with Uncle Buck in the woods, there was no Tomey's Turl and no dogs either, nothing but old Jake about a half an hour later, hitched in a clump of bushes with Tomey's Turl's coat tied on him for a saddle and near a half bushel of Mr. Hubert's oats scattered around on the ground that old Jake never even had enough appetite left to nuzzle up and spit back out again. It wasn't any race at all.

"We'll get him tonight though," Mr. Hubert said. "We'll bait for him. We'll throw a picquet of niggers and dogs around Tennie's house about midnight, and we'll get him."

"Tonight, hell," Uncle Buck said. "Me and Cass and that nigger all three are going to be half way home by dark. Ain't one of your niggers got a fyce or something that will trail them hounds?"

"And fool around here in the woods for half the night too?" Mr. Hubert said. "When I'll bet you five hundred dollars that all you got to do to catch that nigger is to walk up to Tennie's cabin after dark and call him?"

"Five hundred dollars?" Uncle Buck said. "Done! Because me and him neither one are going to be anywhere near Tennie's house by dark. Five hundred dollars!" He and Mr. Hubert glared at one another.

"Done!" Mr. Hubert said.

So they waited while Mr. Hubert sent one of the niggers back to the house on old Jake and in about a half an hour the nigger came back with a little bob-tailed black fyce and a new bottle of whiskey. Then he rode up to Uncle Buck and held something out to him wrapped in a piece of paper. "What?" Uncle Buck said.

"It's for you," the nigger said. Then Uncle Buck took it and unwrapped it. It was the piece of red ribbon that had been on Miss Sophonsiba's neck and Uncle Buck sat there on Black John, holding the ribbon like it was a little water moccasin only he wasn't going to let anybody see he was afraid of it, batting his eyes fast at the nigger. Then he stopped batting his eyes.

"What for?" he said.

"She just sont hit to you," the nigger said. "She say to tell you 'success.' "

"She said what?" Uncle Buck said.

"I don't know, sir," the nigger said. "She just say 'success.' "

"Oh," Uncle Buck said. And the fyce found the hounds. They heard them first, from a considerable distance. It was just before sundown and they were not trailing, they were making the noise dogs make when they want to get out of something. They found what that was too. It was a ten-foot-square cotton-house in a field about two miles from Mr. Hubert's house and all eleven of the dogs were inside it and the door wedged with a chunk of wood. They watched the dogs come boiling out when the nigger opened the door, Mr. Hubert sitting his horse and looking at the back of Uncle Buck's neck.

"Well, well," Mr. Hubert said. "That's something, anyway. You can use them again now. They don't seem to have no more trouble with your nigger than he seems to have with them."

"Not enough," Uncle Buck said. "That means both of them. I'll stick to the fyce."

"All right," Mr. Hubert said. Then he said, "Hell, 'Filus, come on. Let's go eat supper. I tell you, all you got to do to catch that nigger is—"

"Five hundred dollars," Uncle Buck said.

"What?" Mr. Hubert said. He and Uncle Buck looked at each other. They were not glaring now. They were not joking each other either. They sat there in the beginning of twilight, looking at each other, just blinking a little. "What five hundred dollars?" Mr. Hubert said. "That you won't catch that nigger in Tennie's cabin at midnight tonight?"

"That me or that nigger neither ain't going to be near nobody's house but mine at midnight tonight." Now they did glare at each other.

"Five hundred dollars," Mr. Hubert said. "Done."

"Done," Uncle Buck said.

"Done," Mr. Hubert said.

"Done," Uncle Buck said.

So Mr. Hubert took the dogs and some of the niggers and went back to the house. Then he and Uncle Buck and the nigger with the fyce went on, the nigger leading old Jake with one hand and holding the fyce's leash (it was a piece of gnawed plowline) with the other. Now Uncle Buck let the fyce smell Tomey's Turl's coat; it was like for the first time now the fyce found out what they were after and they would have let him off the leash and kept up with him on the horses, only about that time the nigger boy began blowing the fox-horn for supper at the house and they didn't dare risk it.

Then it was full dark. And then—he didn't know how much later nor where they were, how far from the house, except that it was a good piece and it had been dark for a good while and they were still going on, with Uncle Buck leaning down from time to time to let the fyce have another smell of Tomey's Turl's coat while Uncle Buck took another drink from the whiskey bottle—they found that Tomey's Turl had doubled and was making a long swing back toward the house. "I godfrey, we've got him," Uncle Buck said. "He's going to earth. We'll cut back to the house and head him before he can den." So they left the nigger to cast the fyce and follow him on old Jake, and he and Uncle Buck rode for Mr. Hubert's, stopping on the hills to blow the horses and listen to the fyce down in the creek bottom where Tomey's Turl was still making his swing.

But they never caught him. They reached the dark quarters; they could see lights still burning in Mr. Hubert's house and somebody was blowing the fox-horn again and it wasn't any boy and he had never heard a fox-horn sound mad before either, and he and Uncle Buck scattered out on the slope below Tennie's cabin. Then they heard the fyce, not trailing now but yapping, about a mile away, then the nigger whooped and they knew the fyce had faulted. It was at the creek. They hunted the banks both ways for more than an hour, but they couldn't straighten Tomey's Turl out. At last even Uncle Buck gave up and they started back toward the house, the fyce riding too now, in front of the nigger on the mule. They were just coming up the lane to the quarters; they could see on along the ridge to where Mr. Hubert's house was all dark now, when all of a sudden the fyce gave a yelp and jumped down from old Jake and hit the ground running and yelling every jump, and Uncle Buck was down too and had snatched him off the pony almost before he could clear his feet from the irons, and they ran too, on past the dark cabins toward the one where the fyce had treed. "We got him!" Uncle Buck said. "Run around to the back. Don't holler; just grab up a stick and knock on the back door, loud."

Afterward, Uncle Buck admitted that it was his own mistake, that he had forgotten when even a little child should have known: not ever to stand right in front of or right behind a nigger when you scare him; but always to stand to one side of him. Uncle Buck forgot that. He was standing facing the front door and right in front of it, with the fyce right in front of him yelling fire and murder every time it could draw a new breath; he said the first he knew was when the fyce gave a shriek and whirled and Tomey's Turl was right behind it. Uncle Buck said he never even saw the door open; that the fyce just screamed once and ran between his legs and then Tomey's Turl ran right clean over him. He never even bobbled; he knocked Uncle Buck down and then caught him before he fell without even stopping, snatched him up under one arm, still running, and carried him along for about ten feet, saying, "Look out of here, old Buck. Look out of here, old Buck," before he threw him away and went on. By that time they couldn't even hear the fyce any more at all.

Uncle Buck wasn't hurt; it was only the wind knocked out of him where Tomey's Turl had thrown him down on his back. But he had been carrying the whiskey bottle in his back pocket, saving the last drink until Tomey's Turl was captured, and he refused to move until he knew for certain if it was just whiskey and not blood. So Uncle Buck laid over on his side easy, and he knelt behind him and raked the broken glass out of his pocket. Then they went on to the house. They walked. The nigger came up with the horses, but nobody said anything to Uncle Buck about riding again. They couldn't hear the fyce at all now. "He was going fast, all right," Uncle Buck said. "But I don't believe that even he will catch that fyce, I godfrey, what a night."

"We'll catch him tomorrow," he said.

"Tomorrow, hell," Uncle Buck said. "We'll be at home tomorrow. And the first time Hubert Beauchamp or that nigger either one set foot on my land, I'm going to have them arrested for trespass and vagrancy."

The house was dark. They could hear Mr. Hubert snoring good now, as if he had settled down to roadgaiting at it. But they couldn't hear anything from upstairs, even when they were inside the dark hall, at the foot of the stairs. "Likely hers will be at the back," Uncle Buck said. "Where she can holler down to the kitchen without having to get up. Besides, an unmarried lady will sholy have her door locked with strangers in the house." So Uncle Buck eased himself down onto the bottom step, and he knelt and drew Uncle Buck's boots off. Then he removed his own and set them against the wall, and he and Uncle Buck mounted the stairs, feeling their way up and into the upper hall. It was dark too, and still there was no sound anywhere except Mr. Hubert snoring below, so they felt their way along the hall toward the front of the house, until they felt a door. They could hear nothing beyond the door, and when Uncle Buck tried the knob, it opened. "All right," Uncle Buck whispered. "Be quiet." They could see a little now, enough to see the shape of the bed and the mosquito-bar. Uncle Buck threw down his suspenders and unbuttoned his trousers and went to the bed and eased himself carefully down onto the edge of it and he knelt again and drew Uncle Buck's trousers off and he was just removing his own when Uncle Buck lifted the mosquito-bar and raised his feet and rolled into the bed. That was when Miss Sophonsiba sat up on the other side of Uncle Buck and gave the first scream.

3

When he reached home just before dinner time the next day, he was just about worn out. He was too tired to eat, even if Uncle Buddy had waited to eat dinner first; he couldn't have stayed on the pony another mile without going to sleep. In fact, he must have gone to sleep while he was telling Uncle Buddy, because the next thing he knew it was late afternoon and he was lying on some hay in the jolting wagon-bed, with Uncle Buddy sitting on the seat above him exactly the same way he sat a horse or sat in his rocking chair before the kitchen hearth while he was cooking, holding the whip exactly as he held the spoon or fork he stirred and tasted with. Uncle Buddy had some cold bread and meat and a jug of buttermilk wrapped in damp towsacks waiting when he waked up. He ate, sitting in the wagon in almost the last of the afternoon. They must have come fast, because they were not more than two miles from Mr. Hubert's. Uncle Buddy waited for him to eat. Then he said, "Tell me again," and he told it again: how he and Uncle Buck finally found a room without anybody in it, and Uncle Buck sitting on the side of the bed saying, "O godfrey, Cass. O godfrey, Cass," and then they heard Mr. Hubert's feet on the stairs and watched the light come down the hall and Mr. Hubert came in, in his nightshirt, and walked over and set the candle on the table and stood looking at Uncle Buck.

"Well, 'Filus," he said. "She's got you at last."

"It was an accident," Uncle Buck said. "I swear to godfrey——"

"Hah," Mr. Hubert said. "Don't tell me. Tell her that."

"I did," Uncle Buck said. "I did tell her. I swear to God——"

"Sholy," Mr. Hubert said. "And just listen." They listened a minute. He had been hearing her all the time. She was nowhere near as loud as at first; she was just steady. "Don't you want to go back in there and tell her again it was an accident, that you never meant nothing and to just excuse you and forget about it? All right."

"All right what?" Uncle Buck said.

"Go back in there and tell her again," Mr. Hubert said. Uncle Buck looked at Mr. Hubert for a minute. He batted his eyes fast.

"Then what will I come back and tell you?" he said.

"To me?" Mr. Hubert said. "I would call that a horse of another color. Wouldn't you?"

Uncle Buck looked at Mr. Hubert. He batted his eyes fast again. Then he stopped again. "Wait," he said. "Be reasonable. Say I did walk into a lady's bedroom, even Miss Sophonsiba's; say, just for the sake of the argument, there wasn't no other lady in the world but her and so I walked into hers and tried to get in bed with her, would I have took a nine-year-old boy with me?"

"Reasonable is just what I'm being," Mr. Hubert said. "You come into bear-country of your own free will and accord. All right; you were a grown man and you knew it was bear-country and you knew the way back out like you knew the way in and you had your chance to take it. But no. You had to crawl into the den and lay down by the bear. And whether you did or didn't know the bear was in it don't make any difference. So if you got back out of that den without even a claw-mark on you, I would not only be unreasonable, I'd be a damned fool. After all, I'd like a little peace and quiet and freedom myself, now I got a chance for it. Yes, sir. She's got you, 'Filus, and you know it. You run a hard race and you run a good one, but you skun the hen-house one time too many."

"Yes," Uncle Buck said. He drew his breath in and let it out again, slow and not loud. But you could hear it. "Well," he said. "So I reckon I'll have to take the chance then."

"You already took it," Mr. Hubert said. "You did that when you came back here." Then he stopped too. Then he batted his eyes, but only about six times. Then he stopped and looked at Uncle Buck for more than a minute. "What chance?" he said.

"That five hundred dollars," Uncle Buck said.

"What five hundred dollars?" Mr. Hubert said. He and Uncle Buck looked at one another. Now it was Mr. Hubert that batted his eyes again and then stopped again. "I thought you said you found him in Tennie's cabin."

"I did," Uncle Buck said. "What you bet me was I would catch him there. If there had been ten of me standing in front of that door, we wouldn't have caught him." Mr. Hubert blinked at Uncle Buck, slow and steady.

"So you aim to hold me to that fool bet," he said.

"You took your chance too," Uncle Buck said. Mr. Hubert blinked at Uncle Buck. Then he stopped. Then he went and took the candle from the table and went out. They sat on the edge of the bed and watched the light go down the hall and heard Mr. Hubert's feet on the stairs. After a while they began to see the light again and they heard Mr. Hubert's feet coming back up the stairs. Then Mr. Hubert entered and went to the table and set the candle down and laid a deck of cards by it.

"One hand," he said. "Draw. You shuffle, I cut, this boy deals. Five hundred dollars against Sibbey. And we'll settle this nigger business once and for all too. If you win, you buy Tennie; if I win, I buy that boy of yours. The price will be the same for each one: three hundred dollars."

"Win?" Uncle Buck said. "The one that wins buys the niggers?"

"Wins Sibbey, damn it!" Mr. Hubert said. "Wins Sibbey! What the hell else are we setting up till midnight arguing about? The lowest hand wins Sibbey and buys the niggers."

"All right," Uncle Buck said. "I'll buy the damn girl then and we'll call the rest of this foolishness off."

"Hah," Mr. Hubert said again. "This is the most serious foolishness you ever took part in in your life. No. You said you wanted your chance, and now you've got it. Here it is, right here on this table, waiting on you."

So Uncle Buck shuffled the cards and Mr. Hubert cut them. Then he took up the deck and dealt in turn until Uncle Buck and Mr. Hubert had five. And Uncle Buck looked at his hand a long time and then said two cards and he gave them to him, and Mr. Hubert looked at his hand quick and said one card and he gave it to him and Mr. Hubert flipped his discard onto the two which Uncle Buck had discarded and slid the new card into his hand and opened it out and looked at it quick again and closed it and looked at Uncle Buck and said, "Well? Did you help them threes?"

"No," Uncle Buck said.

"Well I did," Mr. Hubert said. He shot his hand across the table so that the cards fell face-up in front of Uncle Buck and they were three kings and two fives, and said, "By God, Buck McCaslin, you have met your match at last."

"And that was all?" Uncle Buddy said. It was late then, near sunset; they would be at Mr. Hubert's in another fifteen minutes.

"Yes, sir," he said, telling that too: how Uncle Buck waked him at daylight and he climbed out a window and got the pony and left, and how Uncle Buck said that if they pushed him too close in the meantime, he would climb down the gutter too and hide in the woods until Uncle Buddy arrived.

"Hah," Uncle Buddy said. "Was Tomey's Turl there?"

"Yes, sir," he said. "He was waiting in the stable when I got the pony. He said, 'Ain't they settled it yet?' "

"And what did you say?" Uncle Buddy said.

"I said, 'Uncle Buck looks like he's settled. But Uncle Buddy ain't got here yet.' "

"Hah," Uncle Buddy said.

And that was about all. They reached the house. Maybe Uncle Buck was watching them, but if he was, he never showed himself, never came out of the woods. Miss Sophonsiba was nowhere in sight either, so at least Uncle Buck hadn't quite given up; at least he hadn't asked her yet. And he and Uncle Buddy and Mr. Hubert ate supper and they came in from the kitchen and cleared the table, leaving only the lamp on it and the deck of cards.

Then it was just like it was the night before, except that Uncle Buddy had no necktie and Mr. Hubert wore clothes now instead of a nightshirt and it was a shaded lamp on the table instead of a candle, and Mr. Hubert sitting at his end of the table with the deck in his hands, riffling the edges with his thumb and looking at Uncle Buddy. Then he tapped the edges even and set the deck out in the middle of the table, under the lamp, and folded his arms on the edge of the table and leaned forward a little on the table, looking at Uncle Buddy, who was sitting at his end of the table with his hands in his lap, all one gray color, like an old gray rock or a stump with gray moss on it, that still, with his round white head like Uncle Buck's but he didn't blink like Uncle Buck and he was a little thicker than Uncle Buck, as if from sitting down so much watching food cook, as if the things he cooked had made him a little thicker than he would have been and the things he cooked with, the flour and such, had made him all one same quiet color.

"Little toddy before we start?" Mr. Hubert said.

"I don't drink," Uncle Buddy said.

"That's right," Mr. Hubert said. "I knew there was something else besides just being woman-weak that makes 'Filus seem human. But no matter." He batted his eyes twice at Uncle Buddy. "Buck McCaslin against the land and niggers you have heard me promise as Sophonsiba's dowry on the day she marries. If I beat you, 'Filus marries Sibbey without any dowry. If you beat me, you get 'Filus. But I still get the three hundred dollars 'Filus owes me for Tennie. Is that correct?"

"That's correct," Uncle Buddy said.

"Stud," Mr. Hubert said. "One hand. You to shuffle, me to cut, this boy to deal."

"No," Uncle Buddy said. "Not Cass. He's too young. I don't want him mixed up in any gambling."

"Hah," Mr. Hubert said. "It's said that a man playing cards with Amodeus McCaslin ain't gambling. But no matter." But he was still looking at Uncle Buddy; he never even turned his head when he spoke: "Go to the back door and holler. Bring the first creature that answers, animal, mule or human, that can deal ten cards."

So he went to the back door. But he didn't have to call because Tomey's Turl was squatting against the wall just outside the door, and they returned to the dining-room where Mr. Hubert still sat with his arms folded on his side of the table and Uncle Buddy sat with his hands in his lap on his side and the deck of cards face-down under the lamp between them. Neither of them even looked up when he and Tomey's Turl entered. "Shuffle," Mr. Hubert said. Uncle Buddy shuffled and set the cards back under the lamp and put his hands back into his lap and Mr. Hubert cut the deck and folded his arms back onto the table-edge. "Deal," he said. Still neither he nor Uncle Buddy looked up. They just sat there while Tomey's Turl's saddle-colored hands came into the light and took up the deck and dealt, one card face-down to Mr. Hubert and one face-down to Uncle Buddy, and one face-up to Mr. Hubert and it was a king, and one face-up to Uncle Buddy and it was a six.

"Buck McCaslin against Sibbey's dowry," Mr. Hubert said. "Deal." And the hand dealt Mr. Hubert a card and it was a three, and Uncle Buddy a card and it was a two. Mr. Hubert looked at Uncle Buddy. Uncle Buddy rapped once with his knuckles on the table.

"Deal," Mr. Hubert said. And the hand dealt Mr. Hubert a card and it was another three, and Uncle Buddy a card and it was a four. Mr. Hubert looked at Uncle Buddy's cards;. Then he looked at Uncle Buddy and Uncle Buddy rapped on the table again with his knuckles.

"Deal," Mr. Hubert said, and the hand dealt him an ace and Uncle Buddy a five and now Mr. Hubert just sat still. He didn't look at anything or move for a whole minute; he just sat there and watched Uncle Buddy put one hand onto the table for the first time since he shuffled and pinch up one corner of his face-down card and look at it and then put his hand back into his lap. "Check," Mr. Hubert said.

"I'll bet you them two niggers," Uncle Buddy said. He didn't move either. He sat there just like he sat in the wagon or on a horse or in the rocking chair he cooked from.

"Against what?" Mr. Hubert said.

"Against the three hundred dollars Theophilus owes you for Tennie, and the three hundred you and Theophilus agreed on for Tomey's Turl," Uncle Buddy said.

"Hah," Mr. Hubert said, only it wasn't loud at all this time, nor even short. Then he said "Hah. Hah. Hah," and not loud either. Then he said, "Well." Then he said, "Well, well." Then he said: "We'll check up for a minute. If I win, you take Sibbey without dowry and the two niggers, and I don't owe 'Filus anything. If you win—"

"—Theophilus is free. And you owe him the three hundred dollars for Tomey's Turl," Uncle Buddy said.

"That's just if I call you," Mr. Hubert said. "If I don't call you, 'Filus won't owe me nothing and I won't owe 'Filus nothing, unless I take that nigger which I have been trying to explain to you and him both for years that I won't have on my place. We will be right back where all this foolishness started from, except for that. So what it comes down to is, I either got to give a nigger away, or risk buying one that you done already admitted you can't keep at home." Then he stopped talking. For about a minute it was like he and Uncle Buddy had both gone to sleep. Then Mr. Hubert picked up his face-down card and turned it over. It was another three, and Mr. Hubert sat there without looking at anything at all, his fingers beating a tattoo, slow and steady and not very loud, on the table. "H'm," he said. "And you need a trey and there ain't but four of them and I already got three. And you just shuffled. And I cut afterward. And if I call you, I will have to buy that nigger. Who dealt these cards, Amodeus?" Only he didn't wait to be answered. He reached out and tilted the lamp-shade, the light moving up Tomey's Turl's arms that were supposed to be black but were not quite white, up his Sunday shirt that was supposed to be white but wasn't quite either, that he put on every time he ran away just as Uncle Buck put on the necktie each time he went to bring him back, and on to his face; and Mr. Hubert sat there, holding the lamp-shade and looking at Tomey's Turl. Then he tilted the shade back down and took up his cards and turned them face-down and pushed them toward the middle of the table. "I pass, Amodeus," he said.

4

He was still too worn out for sleep to sit on a horse, so this time he and Uncle Buddy and Tennie all three rode in the wagon, while Tomey's Turl led the pony from old Jake. And when they got home just after daylight, this time Uncle Buddy never even had time to get breakfast started and the fox never even got out of the crate, because the dogs were right there in the room. Old Moses went right into the crate with the fox, so that both of them went right on through the back end of it. That is, the fox went through, because when Uncle Buddy opened the door to come in, old Moses was still wearing most of the crate around his neck until Uncle Buddy kicked it off of him. So they just made one run, across the front gallery and around the house and they could hear the fox's claws when he went scrabbling up the lean-pole, onto the roof—a fine race while it lasted, but the tree was too quick.

"What in damn's hell do you mean," Uncle Buddy said, "casting that damn thing with all the dogs right in the same room?"

"Damn the fox," Uncle Buck said. "Go on and start breakfast. It seems to me I've been away from home a whole damn month."

Ernest Hemingway

1898 – 1961

The range of Ernest Hemingway's character types and themes is more restricted than Faulkner's. He nevertheless occupies a very high rank among twentieth-century writers because of the understated intensity of his best stories and the masterful, unadorned style in which they are written. One evidence of the considerable influence he has had on the modern short story is that the "Hemingway manner" has been widely, if rather unsuccessfully, imitated by other writers.

Hemingway's entire career matched, in muscular activity, the sinewy quality of his prose. He was born in Oak Park, Illinois, in 1898, the son of a doctor who developed in him a fondness for the out-of-doors life by taking him on frequent boating and fishing trips to northern Michigan. He attended public school in Oak Park, where he played football and boxed and worked at various odd jobs in his free time. After graduating from high school, he became a reporter for the Kansas City *Star,* but gave up this position after a few months to go to France as a volunteer ambulance driver before the United States entered World War I. He later transferred to the Italian infantry, and was wounded severely in action. After the war, he returned to newspaper work as a reporter and European correspondent for the Toronto *Star.* In Paris, he met Ezra Pound and Gertrude Stein, who offered him encouragement in his literary career. His first volume of short stories, *In Our Time* (1925), drew favorable attention, and his reputation increased as other works appeared: *The Sun Also Rises* (1926); *Men Without Women* (1927), a collection of stories; *A Farewell to Arms* (1929); *To Have and Have Not* (1937); *The Fifth Column* [a play] and the *First Forty-nine Stories* (1938); *For Whom the Bell Tolls* (1940); *Across the River and Into the Trees* (1950), and *The Old Man and the Sea* (1953). After World War II Hemingway kept on projecting his favorite image as a pugilistic literary champion by recording his activities as both spectator and participant at prize fights, bullfights, deep-sea fishing, and big-game hunting safaris. In 1961, like one of his own characters, he met death violently with a shotgun in his own hands.

A seemingly casual structure and apparent naiveté make the best of Hemingway's stories appear artless, almost childishly simple. "Hills Like White Elephants," for example, is almost barren in its simplicity. A young American and his girlfriend, seated in the shade at a railway junction in Spain, are ordering drinks while awaiting the train from Barcelona to Madrid; but her casual remark that the distant hills resemble white elephants triggers a confrontation fraught with tension, bitterness, and heartache. At issue between them are complex feelings terrifying in their implications.

Hills Like White Elephants

The hills across the valley of the Ebro were long and white. On this side there was no shade and no trees and the station was between two lines of rails in the sun. Close against the side of the station there was the warm shadow of the building and a curtain, made of strings of bamboo beads, hung across the open door into the bar, to keep out flies. The American and the girl with him sat at a table in the shade, outside the building. It was very hot and the express from Barcelona would come in forty minutes. It stopped at this junction for two minutes and went on to Madrid.

'What should we drink?' the girl asked. She had taken off her hat and put it on the table.

'It's pretty hot,' the man said.

'Let's drink beer.'

'Dos cervezas,' the man said into the curtain.

'Big ones?' a woman asked from the doorway.

'Yes. Two big ones.'

The woman brought two glasses of beer and two felt pads. She put the felt pads and the beer glasses on the table and looked at the man and the girl. The girl was looking off at the line of hills. They were white in the sun and the country was brown and dry.

'They look like white elephants,' she said.

'I've never seen one.' The man drank his beer.

'No, you wouldn't have.'

'I might have,' the man said. 'Just because you say I wouldn't have doesn't prove anything.'

The girl looked at the bead curtain. 'They've painted something on it,' she said. 'What does it say?'

'Anis del Toro. It's a drink.'

'Could we try it?'

The man called 'Listen' through the curtain.

The woman came out from the bar.

'Four reales.'

'We want two Anis del Toros.'

'With water?'

'Do you want it with water?'

'I don't know,' the girl said. 'Is it good with water?'

'It's all right.'

'You want them with water?' asked the woman.

'Yes, with water.'

'It tastes like licorice,' the girl said and put the glass down.

'That's the way with everything.'

'Yes,' said the girl. 'Everything tastes of licorice. Especially all the things you've waited so long for, like absinthe.'

'Oh, cut it out.'

'You started it,' the girl said. 'I was being amused. I was having a fine time.'

'Well, let's try and have a fine time.'

'All right. I was trying. I said the mountains looked like white elephants. Wasn't that bright?'

'That was bright.'

'I wanted to try this new drink. That's all we do, isn't it—look at things and try new drinks?'

'I guess so.'

The girl looked across at the hills.

'They're lovely hills,' she said. 'They don't really look like white elephants. I just meant the colouring of their skin through the trees.'

'Should we have another drink?'

'All right.'

The warm wind blew the bead curtain against the table.

'The beer's nice and cool,' the man said.

'It's lovely,' the girl said.

'It's really an awfully simple operation, Jig,' the man said. 'It's not really an operation at all.'

The girl looked at the ground the table legs rested on.

'I know you wouldn't mind it, Jig. It's really not anything. It's just to let the air in.'

The girl did not say anything.

'I'll go with you and I'll stay with you all the time. They just let the air in and then it's all perfectly natural.'

'Then what will we do afterwards?'

'We'll be fine afterwards. Just like we were before.'

'What makes you think so?'

'That's the only thing that bothers us. It's the only thing that's made us unhappy.'

The girl looked at the bead curtain, put her hand out and took hold of two of the strings of beads.

'And you think then we'll be all right and be happy.'

'I know we will. You don't have to be afraid. I've known lots of people that have done it.'

'So have I,' said the girl. 'And afterward they were all so happy.'

'Well,' the man said, 'if you don't want to you don't have to. I wouldn't have you do it if you didn't want to. But I know it's perfectly simple.'

'And you really want to?'

'I think it's the best thing to do. But I don't want you to do it if you don't really want to.'

'And if I do it you'll be happy and things will be like they were and you'll love me?'

'I love you now. You know I love you.'

'I know. But if I do it, then it will be nice again if I say things are like white elephants, and you'll like it?'

'I'll love it. I love it now but I just can't think about it. You know how I get when I worry.'

'If I do it you won't ever worry?'

'I won't worry about that because it's perfectly simple.'

'Then I'll do it. Because I don't care about me.'

'What do you mean?'

'I don't care about me.'

'Well, I care about you.'

'Oh, yes. But I don't care about me. And I'll do it and then everything will be fine.'

'I don't want you to do it if you feel that way.'

The girl stood up and walked to the end of the station. Across, on the other side, were fields of grain and trees along the banks of the Ebro. Far away, beyond the river, were mountains. The shadow of a cloud moved across the field of grain and she saw the river through the trees.

'And we could have all this,' she said. 'And we could have everything and every day we make it more impossible.'

'What did you say?'

'I said we could have everything.'

'We can have everything.'

'No, we can't.'

'We can have the whole world.'

'No, we can't.'

'We can go everywhere.'

'No, we can't. It isn't ours any more.'

'It's ours.'

'No, it isn't. And once they take it away, you never get it back.'

'But they haven't taken it away.'

'We'll wait and see.'

'Come on back in the shade,' he said. 'You mustn't feel that way.'

'I don't feel any way,' the girl said. 'I just know things.'

'I don't want you to do anything that you don't want to do—'

'Nor that isn't good for me,' she said. 'I know. Could we have another beer?'

'All right. But you've got to realize—'

'I realize,' the girl said. 'Can't we maybe stop talking?'

They sat down at the table and the girl looked across at the hills on the dry side of the valley and the man looked at her and at the table.

'You've got to realize,' he said, 'that I don't want you to do it if you don't want to. I'm perfectly willing to go through with it if it means anything to you.'

'Doesn't it mean anything to you? We could get along.'

'Of course it does. But I don't want anybody but you. I don't want anyone else. And I know it's perfectly simple.'

'Yes, you know it's perfectly simple.'

'It's all right for you to say that, but I do know it.'

'Would you do something for me now?'

'I'd do anything for you.'

'Would you please please please please please please please stop talking?'

He did not say anything but looked at the bags against the wall of the station. There were labels on them from all the hotels where they had spent nights.

'But I don't want you to,' he said, 'I don't care anything about it.'

'I'll scream,' the girl said.

The woman came out through the curtains with two glasses of beer and put them down on the damp felt pads. 'The train comes in five minutes,' she said.

'What did she say?' asked the girl.

'That the train is coming in five minutes.'

The girl smiled brightly at the woman, to thank her.

'I'd better take the bags over to the other side of the station,' the man said. She smiled at him.

'All right. Then come back and we'll finish the beer.'

He picked up the two heavy bags and carried them around the station to the other tracks. He looked up the tracks but could not see the train. Coming back, he walked through the bar-room, where people waiting for the train were drinking. He drank an Anis at the bar and looked at the people. They were all waiting reasonably for the train. He went out through the bead curtain. She was sitting at the table and smiled at him.

'Do you feel better?' he asked.

'I feel fine,' she said. 'There's nothing wrong with me. I feel fine.'

❧

Zora Neale Hurston

1901(3)? – 1960

Zora Neale Hurston, one of the most eloquent black writers of the 1930s, was born in Eatonville, Florida, sometime between 1901 and 1903. The only child of poor tenant farmers, shortly after her mother's death in 1904 she was placed in a nursery school in Jacksonville, where she remained until age fourteen. She then began what was to become a vibrant intellectual life, first as a maid in a traveling theatrical company, and later as a librarian, a part-time teacher, and a newspaper reporter, but primarily as a folklorist and research writer, whose chief interest centered in the cultural and anthropological characteristics of blacks in America. She entered Howard University in 1923, won a scholarship to Barnard College as the first black student admitted to Columbia University in 1926, and following her graduation two years later, became associated with that university's famed anthropologist, Franz Boas. During the following decade Hurston collected folklore through the South and pursued further research in Jamaica, Haiti, and Bermuda. From these investigations she derived abundant anthropological material for her stories of voodoo and other folkways among the blacks, published in a series of collections and novels: *Jonah's Gourd Vine* (1934), *Mules & Men* (1935), *Their Eyes Were Watching God* (1937), *Tell My Horse* (1938), *Moses, Man of the Mountain* (1939), *Dust Tracks on a Road* (1942), and *Seraph on the Sewanee* (1948).

A highly gifted writer whose effervescent style matched her mercurial personality and wandering lust, Hurston became a leading exponent of the Harlem Renaissance, capturing in many of her stories the glamor and glitter of black folkways, the attraction of her people to the large cities in the era of Cab Calloway and Louis Armstrong, but also the loneliness, impoverishment, and brutality that many of them suffered, sometimes at the hands of their own wilier fellow blacks, as in "The Gilded Six-Bits." Like Charles Chesnutt and Langston Hughes, she depicted black people as complex, many-sided individuals, not simply as innocent victims of white oppression; for this reason her reputation among dissident blacks declined sharply during the volatile protest movement of the 1950s and the ensuing years after her lonely death. More recently, however, a new generation of literary artists, such as Alice Walker and Toni Cade Bambara, have paid high tribute to Hurston's pioneering contribution to American fiction.

The Gilded Six-Bits

It was a Negro yard around a Negro house in a Negro settlement that looked to the payroll of the G. and G. Fertilizer works for its support.

But there was something happy about the place. The front yard was parted in the middle by a sidewalk from gate to doorstep, a sidewalk edged on either side by quart bottles driven neck down to the ground on a slant. A mess of homey flowers planted without a plan but blooming cheerily from their helter-skelter places. The fence and house were whitewashed. The porch and steps scrubbed white.

The front door stood open to the sunshine so that the floor of the front room could finish drying after its weekly scouring. It was Saturday. Everything clean from the front gate to the privy house. Yard raked so that the strokes of the rake would make a pattern. Fresh newspaper cut in fancy-edge on the kitchen shelves.

Missie May was bathing herself in the galvanized washtub in the bedroom. Her dark-brown skin glistened under the soapsuds that skittered down from her wash rag. Her stiff young breasts thrust forward aggressively like broad-based cones with the tips lacquered in black.

She heard men's voices in the distance and glanced at the dollar clock on the dresser.

"Humph! Ah'm way behind time t'day! Joe gointer be heah 'fore Ah git mah clothes on if Ah don't make haste."

She grabbed the clean meal sack at hand and dried herself hurriedly and began to dress. But before she could tie her slippers, there came the ring of singing metal on wood. Nine times.

Missie May grinned with delight. She had not seen the big tall man come stealing in the gate and creep up the walk grinning happily at the joyful mischief he was about to commit. But she knew that it was her husband throwing silver dollars in the door for her to pick up and pile beside her plate at dinner. It was this way every Saturday afternoon. The nine dollars hurled into the open door, he scurried to a hiding place behind the cape jasmine bush and waited.

Missie May promptly appeared at the door in mock alarm.

"Who dat chunkin' money in mah do'way?" she demanded. No answer from the yard. She leaped off the porch and began to search the shrubbery. She peeped under the porch and hung over the gate to look up and down the road. While she did this, the man behind the jasmine darted to the chinaberry tree. She spied him and gave chase.

"Nobody ain't gointer be chunkin' money at me and Ah not do 'em nothin'," she shouted in mock anger. He ran around the house with Missie May at his heels. She overtook him at the kitchen door. He ran inside but could not close it after him before she crowded in and locked with him in a rough and tumble. For several minutes the two were a furious mass of male and female energy. Shouting, laughing, twisting, turning, and Joe trying, but not too hard, to get away.

"Missie May, take yo' hand out mah pocket!" Joe shouted out between laughs.

"Ah ain't, Joe, not lessen you gwine gimme whateve' it is good you got in yo' pocket. Turn it go Joe, do Ah'll tear yo' clothes."

"Go on tear 'em. You de one dat pushes de needles round heah. Move yo' hand, Missie May."

"Lemme git dat paper sack out yo' pocket. Ah bet it's candy kisses."

"Tain't. Move yo' hand. Woman ain't got no business in a man's clothes nohow. Go 'way."

Missie May gouged way down and gave an upward jerk and triumphed.

"Unhhunh! Ah got it. It 'tis so candy kisses. Ah knowed you had somethin' for me in yo' clothes. Now Ah got to see whut's in every pocket you got."

Joe smiled indulgently and let his wife go through all of his pockets and take out the things that he had hidden there for her to find. She bore off the chewing gum, the cake of sweet soap, the pocket handkerchief as if she had wrested them from him, as if they had not been bought for the sake of this friendly battle.

"Whew! dat play-fight done got me all warmed up," Joe exclaimed. "Got me some water in de kittle?"

"Yo' water is on de fire and yo' clean things is cross de bed. Hurry up and wash yo'self and git changed so we kin eat. Ah'm hongry." As Missie said this, she bore the steaming kettle into the bedroom.

"You ain't hongry, sugar," Joe contradicted her. "Youse jes's little empty. Ah'm de one whut's hongry. Ah could eat up camp meetin,' back off'ssociation, and drink Jurdan dry. Have it on de table when Ah git out de tub."

"Don't you mess wid mah business, man. You git in yo' clothes. Ah'm a real wife, not no dress and breath. Ah might not look lak one, but if you burn me, you won't git a thing but wife ashes."

Joe splashed in the bedroom and Missie May fanned around in the kitchen. A fresh red and white checked cloth on the table. Big pitcher of buttermilk beaded with pale drops of butter from the churn. Hot fried mullet, crackling bread, ham hocks atop a mound of string beans and new potatoes, and perched on the window-sill a pone of spicy potato pudding.

Very little talk during the meal but that little consisted of banter that pretended to deny affection but in reality flaunted it. Like when Missie May reached for a second helping of the tater pone. Joe snatched it out of her reach. After Missie May had made two or three unsuccessful grabs at the pan, she begged, "Aw, Joe gimme some mo' dat tater pone."

"Nope, sweetenin' is for us men-folks. Y'all pritty li'l frail eels don't need nothin' lak dis. You too sweet already."

"Please, Joe."

"Naw, naw. Ah don't want you to git no sweeter than whut you is already. We goin' down de road a li'l piece t'night so you go put on yo' Sunday-go-to-meetin' things."

Missie May looked at her husband to see if he was playing some prank. "Sho' nuff, Joe?"

"Yeah. We goin' to de ice cream parlor."

"Where de ice cream parlor at, Joe?"

"A new man done come heah from Chicago and he done got a place and took and opened it up for a ice cream parlor, and bein' as it's real swell, Ah wants you to be one de first ladies to walk in dere and have some set down."

"Do Jesus, Ah ain't knowed nothin' 'bout it. Who de man done it?"

"Mister Otis D. Slemmons, of spots and places—Memphis, Chicago, Jacksonville, Philadephia and so on."

"Dat heavy-set man wid his mouth full of gold teethes?"

"Yeah. Where did you see 'im at?"

"Ah went down to de sto' tuh git a box of lye and Ah seen 'im standin' on de corner talkin' to some of de mens, and Ah come on back and went to scrubbin' de floor, and he passed and tipped his hat whilst Ah was scourin' de steps. Ah thought never Ah seen *him* befo'."

Joe smiled pleasantly. "Yeah, he's up to date. He got de finest clothes Ah ever seen on a colored man's back."

"Aw, he don't look no better in his clothes than you do in yourn. He got a puzzlegut on 'im and he so chuckle-headed, he got a pone behind his neck."

Joe looked down at his own abdomen and said wistfully, "Wisht Ah had a build on me lak he got. He ain't puzzle-gutted, honey. He jes' got a corperation. Dat make 'm look lak a rich white man. All rich mens is got some belly on 'em."

"Ah seen de pitchers of Henry Ford and he's a spare-built man and Rockefeller look lak he ain't got but one gut. But Ford and Rockefeller and dis Slemmons and all de rest kin be as many-gutted as dey please, Ah'm satisfied wid you jes' lak you is, baby. God took pattern after a pine tree and built you noble. Youse a pritty man, and if Ah knowed any way to make you mo' pritty still Ah'd take and do it."

Joe reached over gently and toyed with Missie May's ear. "You jes' say dat cause you love me, but Ah know Ah can't hold no light to Otis D. Slemmons. Ah ain't never been nowhere and Ah ain't got nothin' but you."

"How you know dat, Joe."

"He tole us so hisself."

"Dat don't make it so. His mouf is cut cross-ways, ain't it? Well, he kin lie jes' lak anybody els."

"Good Lawd, Missie! You womens sho' is hard to sense into things. He's got a five-dollar gold piece for a stick-pin and he got a ten-dollar gold piece on his watch chain and his mouf is jes' crammed full of gold teethes. Sho' wisht it wuz mine. And whut make it so cool, he got money 'cumulated. And womens give it all to 'im."

"Ah don't see whut de womens see on 'im. Ah wouldn't give 'im a wink if de sheriff wuz after 'im."

"Well, he tole us how de white womens in Chicago give 'im all dat gold money. So he don't 'low nobody to touch it at all. Not even put dey finger on it. Dey tole 'im not to. You kin make 'miration at it, but don't tetch it."

"Whyn't he stay up dere where dey so crazy 'bout 'im?"

"Ah reckon dey done made 'im vast-rich and he wants to travel some. He say dey wouldn't leave 'im hit a lick of work. He got mo' lady people crazy 'bout him than he kin shake a stick at."

"Joe, Ah hates to see you so dumb. Dat stray nigger jes' tell y'all anything and y'all b'lieve it."

"Go 'head on now, honey and put on yo' clothes. He talkin' 'bout his pritty womens—Ah want 'im to see *mine*."

Missie May went off to dress and Joe spent the time trying to make his stomach punch out like Slemmons' middle. He tried the rolling swagger of the stranger, but found that his tall bone-and-muscle stride fitted ill with it. He just had time to drop back into his seat before Missie May came in dressed to go.

On the way home that night Joe was exultant. "Didn't Ah say ole Otis was swell? Can't he talk Chicago talk? Wuzn't dat funny whut he said when great big fat ole Ida Armstrong come in? He asted me, 'Who is dat broad wid de forty shake?' Dat's a new word. Us always thought forty was a set of figgers but he showed us where it means a whole heap of things. Sometimes he don't say forty, he jes' say thirty-eight and two and dat mean de same thing. Know whut he tole me when Ah was payin for our ice cream? He say, 'Ah have to hand it to you, Joe. Dat wife of yours is jes' thirty-eight and two. Yessuh, she's forty!' Ain't he killin'?"

"He'll do in case of a rush. But he sho' is got uh heap uh gold on 'im. Dat's de first time Ah ever seed gold money. It lookted good on him sho' nuff, but it'd look a whole heap better on you."

"Who, me? Missie May youse crazy! Where would a po' man lak me git gold money from?"

Missie May was silent for a minute, then she said, "Us might find some goin' long de road some time. Us could."

"Who would be losin' gold money 'round heah? We ain't even seen none dese white folks wearin' no gold money on dey watch chain. You must be figgeren' Mister Packard or Mister Cadillac goin' pass through heah . . ."

"You don't know whut been lost 'round heah. Maybe somebody way back in memorial times lost they gold money and went on off and it ain't never been found. And then if we wuz to find it, you could wear some 'thout havin' no gang of womens lak dat Slemmons say he got."

Joe laughed and hugged her. "Don't be so wishful 'bout me. Ah'm satisfied de way Ah is. So long as Ah be yo' husband, Ah don't keer 'bout nothin' else. Ah'd ruther all de other womens in de world to be dead than for you to have de toothache. Less we go to bed and git our night rest."

It was Saturday night once more before Joe could parade his wife in Slemmons' ice cream parlor again. He worked the night shift and Saturday was his only night off. Every other evening around six o'clock he left home, and dying dawn saw him hustling home around the lake where the challenging sun flung a flaming sword from east to west across the trembling water.

That was the best part of life—going home to Missie May. Their whitewashed house, the mock battle on Saturday, the dinner and ice cream parlor afterwards, church on Sunday nights when Missie out-dressed any woman in town—all, everything was right.

One night around eleven the acid ran out at the G. and G. The foreman knocked off the crew and let the steam die down. As Joe rounded the lake on his way home, a lean moon rode the lake in a silver boat. If anybody had asked Joe about the moon on the lake, he would have said he hadn't paid it any attention. But he saw it with his feelings. It made him yearn painfully for Missie. Creation obsessed him. He thought about children. They had been married for more than a year now. They had money put away. They ought to be making little feet for shoes. A little boy child would be about right.

He saw a dim light in the bedroom and decided to come in through the kitchen door. He could wash the fertilizer dust off himself before presenting himself to Missie May. It would be nice for her not to know that he was there until he slipped into his place in bed and hugged her back. She always liked that.

He eased the kitchen door open slowly and silently, but when he went to set his dinner bucket on the table he bumped it into a pile of dishes, and something crashed to the floor. He heard his wife gasp in fright and hurried to reassure her.

"Iss me, honey. Don't get skeered."

There was a quick, large movement in the bedroom. A rustle, a thud, and a stealthy silence. The light went out.

What? Robbers? Murderers? Some varmint attacking his helpless wife, perhaps. He struck a match, threw himself on guard and stepped over the door-sill into the bedroom.

The great belt on the wheel of Time slipped and eternity stood still. By the match light he could see the man's legs fighting with his breeches in his frantic desire to get them on. He had both chance and time to kill the intruder in his helpless condition—half-in and half-out of his pants—but he was too weak to take action. The shapeless enemies of humanity that live in the hours of Time had waylaid Joe. He was assaulted in his weakness. Like Samson awakening after his haircut. So he just opened his mouth and laughed.

The match went out and he struck another and lit the lamp. A howling wind raced across his heart, but underneath its fury he heard his wife sobbing and Slemmons pleading for his life. Offering to buy it with all that he had. "Please, suh, don't kill me. Sixty-two dollars at de sto' gold money."

Joe just stood. Slemmons looked at the window, but it was screened. Joe stood out like a rough-backed mountain between him and the door. Barring him from escape, from sunrise, from life.

He considered a surprise attack upon the big clown that stood there laughing like a chessy cat. But before his fist could travel an inch, Joe's own rushed out to crush him like a battering ram. Then Joe stood over him.

"Git into yo' damn rags, Slemmons, and dat quick."

Slemmons scrambled to his feet and into his vest and coat. As he grabbed his hat, Joe's fury overrode his intentions and he grabbed at Slemmons with his left hand and struck at him with his right. The right landed. The left grazed the front of his vest. Slemmons was knocked a somersault into the kitchen and fled through the open door. Joe found himself alone with Missie May, with the gold watch charm clutched in his left fist. A short bit of broken chain dangled between his fingers.

Missie May was sobbing. Wails of weeping without words. Joe stood, and after awhile she found out that he had something in his hand. And then he stood and felt without thinking and without seeing with his natural eyes. Missie May kept on crying and Joe kept on feeling so much and not knowing what to do with all his feelings, he put Slemmons' watch charm in his pants pocket and took a good laugh and went to bed.

"Missie May, whut you crying for?"

"Cause Ah love you so hard and Ah know you don't love *me* no mo'."

Joe sank his face into the pillow for a spell then he said huskily, "You don't know de feelings of dat yet, Missie May."

"Oh Joe, honey, he said he wuz gointer gimme dat gold money and he jes' kept on after me—"

Joe was very still and silent for a long time. Then he said, "Well, don't cry no mo', Missie May. Ah got yo' gold piece for you."

The hours went past on their rusty ankles. Joe still and quiet on one bed-rail and Missie May wrung dry of sobs on the other. Finally the sun's tide crept upon the shore of night and drowned all its hours. Missie May with her face stiff and streaked towards the window saw the dawn come into her yard. It was day. Nothing more. Joe wouldn't be coming home as usual. No need to fling open the front door and sweep off the porch, making it nice for Joe. Never no more breakfast to cook; no more washing and starching of Joe's jumper-jackets and pants. No more nothing. So why get up?

With this strange man in her bed, she felt embarrassed to get up and dress. She decided to wait till he had dressed and gone. Then she would get up, dress quickly and be gone forever beyond the reach of Joe's looks and laughs. But he never moved. Red light turned to yellow, then white.

From beyond the no-man's land between them came a voice. A strange voice that yesterday had been Joe's.

"Missie May, ain't you gonna fix me no breakfus'?"

She sprang out of bed. "Yeah, Joe. Ah didn't reckon you wuz hongry."

No need to die today. Joe needed her for a few more minutes anyhow.

Soon there was a roaring fire in the cook stove. Water bucket full and two chickens killed. Joe loved fried chicken and rice. She didn't deserve a thing and good Joe was letting her cook him some breakfast. She rushed hot biscuits to the table as Joe took his seat.

He ate with his eyes on his plate. No laughter, no banter.

"Missie May, you ain't eatin' yo' breakfus'."

"Ah don't choose none, Ah thank yuh."

His coffee cup was empty. She sprang to refill it. When she turned from the stove and bent to set the cup beside Joe's plate, she saw the yellow coin on the table between them.

She slumped into her seat and wept into her arms.

Presently Joe said calmly, "Missie May, you cry too much. Don't look back lak Lot's wife and turn to salt."

The sun, the hero of every day, the impersonal old man that beams as brightly on death as on birth, came up every morning and raced across the blue dome and dipped into the sea of fire every evening. Water ran down hill and birds nested.

Missie knew why she didn't leave Joe. She couldn't. She loved him too much. But she couldn't understand why Joe didn't leave her. He was polite, even kind at times, but aloof.

There were no more Saturday romps. No ringing silver dollars to stack beside her plate. No pockets to rifle. In fact the yellow coin in his trousers was like a monster hiding in the cave of his pockets to destroy her.

She often wondered if he still had it, but nothing could have induced her to ask nor yet to explore his pockets to see for herself. Its shadow was in the house whether or no.

One night Joe came home around midnight and complained of pains in the back. He asked Missie to rub him down with liniment. It had been three months since Missie had touched his body and it all seemed strange. But she rubbed him. Grateful for the chance. Before morning, youth triumphed and Missie exulted. But the next day, as she joyfully made up their bed, beneath her pillow she found the piece of money with the bit of chain attached.

Alone to herself, she looked at the thing with loathing, but look she must. She took it into her hands with trembling and saw first thing that it was no gold piece. It was a gilded half-dollar. Then she knew why Slemmons had forbidden anyone to touch his gold. He trusted village eyes at a distance not to recognize his stick-pin as a gilded quarter, and his watch charm as a four-bit piece.

She was glad at first that Joe had left it there. Perhaps he was through with her punishment. They were man and wife again. Then another thought came clawing at her. He had come home to buy from her as if she were any woman in the long house. Fifty cents for her love. As if to say that he could pay as well as Slemmons. She slid the coin into his Sunday pants pocket and dressed herself and left his house.

Halfway between her house and the quarters she met her husband's mother, and after a short talk she turned and went back home. If she had not the substance of marriage, she had the outside show. Joe must leave *her*. She let him see she didn't want his old gold four-bits too.

She saw no more of the coin for some time though she knew that Joe could not help finding it in his pocket. But his health kept poor, and he came home at least every ten days to be rubbed.

The sun swept around the horizon, trailing its robes of weeks and days. One morning as Joe came in from work, he found Missie May chopping wood. Without a word he took the ax and chopped a huge pile before he stopped.

"You ain't got not business choppin' wood, and you know it."

"How come? Ah been choppin' it for de last longest."

"Ah ain't blind. You makin' feet for shoes."

"Won't you be glad to have a li'l baby chile, Joe?"

"You know dat 'thout astin' me."

"Iss gointer be a boy chile and de very spit of you."

"You reckon, Missie May?"

"Who else could it look lak?"

Joe said nothing, but he thrust his hand deep into his pocket and fingered something there.

It was almost six months later Missie May took to bed and Joe went and got his mother to come wait on the house.

Missie May delivered a fine boy. Her travail was over when Joe came in from work one morning. His mother and the old women were drinking great bowls of coffee around the fire in the kitchen.

The minute Joe came into the room his mother called him aside.

"How did Missie May make out?" he asked quickly.

"Who, dat gal? She strong as a ox. She gointer have plenty mo'. We done fixed her wid de sugar and lard to sweeten her for de nex' one."

Joe stood silent awhile.

"You ain't ast 'bout de baby, Joe. You oughter be mighty proud cause he sho' is de spittin' image of yuh, son. Dat's yourn all right, if you never git another one, dat un is yourn. And you know Ah'm mighty proud too, son, cause Ah never thought well of you marryin' Missie May cause her ma used tuh fan her foot 'round right smart and Ah been mighty skeered dat Missie May wuz gointer git misput on her road."

Joe said nothing. He fooled around the house till late in the day then just before he went to work, he went and stood at the foot of the bed and asked his wife how she felt. He did this every day during the week.

On Saturday he went to Orlando to make his market. It had been a long time since he had done that.

Meat and lard, meal and flour, soap and starch. Cans of corn and tomatoes. All the staples. He fooled around town for awhile and bought bananas and apples. Way after while he went around to the candy store.

"Hellow, Joe," the clerk greeted him. "Ain't seen you in a long time."

"Nope, Ah ain't been heah. Been 'round spots and places."

"Want some of them molasses kisses you always buy?"

"Yessuh." He threw the gilded half-dollar on the counter. "Will dat spend?"

"Whut is it, Joe? Well, I'll be doggone! A gold-plated four-bit piece. Where'd you git it, Joe?"

"Offen a stray nigger dat come through Eatonville. He had it on his watch chain for a charm—goin' 'round making out iss gold money. Ha ha! He had a quarter on his tie pin and it wuz all golded up too. Tryin' to fool people. Makin' out he so rich and everything. Ha! Ha! Tryin' to tole off folkses wives from home."

"How did you git it, Joe? Did he fool you, too?"

"Who, me? Naw suh! He ain't fooled me none. Know whut Ah done? He come 'round me wid his smart talk. Ah hauled off and knocked 'im down and took his old four-bits 'way from 'im. Gointer buy my wife some good ole 'lasses kisses wid it. Gimme fifty cents worth of dem candy kisses."

"Fifty cents buys a mightly lot of candy kisses, Joe. Why don't you split it up and take some chocolate bars, too. They eat good, too."

"Yessuh, dey do, but Ah wants all dat in kisses. Ah got a li'l boy chile home now. Tain't a week old yet, but he kin suck a sugar tit and maybe eat one them kisses hisself."

Joe got his candy and left the store. The clerk turned to the next customer. "Wisht I could be like these darkies. Laughin' all the time. Nothin' worries 'em."

Back in Eatonville, Joe reached his own front door. There was the ring of singing metal on wood. Fifteen times. Missie May couldn't run to the door, but she crept there as quickly as she could.

"Joe Banks, Ah hear you chuckin' money in mah do'way. You wait till Ah got mah strength back and Ah'm gointer fix you for dat."

John Steinbeck

1902 – 1968

Since John Steinbeck often depicted simple, rudimentary folk in his fiction, he, like Hemingway, is sometimes described as a primitivist. From another view, his involvement in sociological problems and his obvious sympathy for the underdog place him among the proletarian writers. Neither primitivism nor proletarianism, however, makes allowance for yet a third and perhaps more durable quality in his work: a concern with abstract philosophical values that often leads him into symbolism and near-mysticism. His desire that no "tag" of any kind be "pinned" on him has been realized, for his work transcends narrow classification. He was simply a thoughtful, sincere writer who saw humankind in the grip of hard and confusing battles; yet he could be strongly affirmative in his attitude toward life.

Steinbeck was born in Salinas, California, in 1902, and, during his high school years there, worked on nearby farms and in local laboratories. At Stanford University, which he attended intermittently from 1919 through 1925, he took the courses that interested him rather than those that would lead to a degree. Having already decided on writing as a career, he supported himself and enlarged his experience by working for several years at a variety of jobs: as bricklayer, ranch hand, carpenter, fruit picker, newspaper reporter in New York, and caretaker of a Lake Tahoe estate. A conscientious worker, he reputedly wrote three or four novels before his first, *Cup of Gold,* based on the life of the pirate Henry Morgan, was published in 1929; but neither this one nor his next two, *The Pastures of Heaven* (1932) and *To a God Unknown* (1933), brought him critical or financial success. *Tortilla Flat* (1935), however, was highly successful. With the publication of *In Dubious Battle* (1936), *Of Mice and Men* (1937), and especially of *The*

Grapes of Wrath (1939)—for which he was awarded the Pultizer Prize in 1940—he established himself securely in the front rank of contemporary writers. His later activities included leading a research expedition to the Galapagos Islands, serving for a period during World War II as a foreign correspondent, and taking a journey through the Soviet Union with the photographer Robert Capa. His most recent works—among which are *The Pearl* (1947), *The Wayward Bus* (1947), *Burning Bright* (1950), *Sweet Thursday* (1954), and *East of Eden* (1955)—did not add substantially to his artistic stature; yet on the strength of his literary achievement as a whole, he was awarded the Nobel Prize in 1962. He died in 1968.

Steinbeck has been praised as a superb storyteller whose "lyric prose caught the qualities of speech, the character, the legends, and the humor of his native region."* "The Chrysanthemums," one of his finest stories, vividly illustrates these virtues through its sensitive revelation of a young housewife's ambivalent feelings about herself and her role in a male-oriented society.

**Anthology of American Literature,* edited by George McMichael, et al. New York: Macmillan, 1980, Vol. 2, p. 1423.

The Chrysanthemums

The high grey-flannel fog of winter closed off the Salinas Valley from the sky and from all the rest of the world. On every side it sat like a lid on the mountains and made of the great valley a closed pot. On the broad, level land floor the gang plows bit deep and left the black earth shining like metal where the shares had cut. On the foothill ranches across the Salinas River, the yellow stubble fields seemed to be bathed in pale cold sunshine, but there was no sunshine in the valley now in December. The thick willow scrub along the river flamed with sharp and positive yellow leaves.

It was a time of quiet and of waiting. The air was cold and tender. A light wind blew up from the southwest so that the farmers were mildly hopeful of a good rain before long; but fog and rain do not go together.

Across the river, on Henry Allen's foothill ranch there was little work to be done, for the hay was cut and stored and the orchards were plowed up to receive the rain deeply when it should come. The cattle on the higher slopes were becoming shaggy and rough-coated.

Elisa Allen, working in her flower garden, looked down across the yard and saw Henry, her husband, talking to two men in business suits. The three of them stood by the tractor shed, each man with one foot on the side of the little Fordson. They smoked cigarettes and studied the machine as they talked.

Elisa watched them for a moment and then went back to her work. She was thirty-five. Her face was lean and strong and her eyes were as clear as water. Her figure looked blocked and heavy in her gardening costume, a man's black hat pulled low down over her eyes, clodhopper shoes, a figured print dress almost completely covered by a big corduroy apron with four big pockets to hold the snips, the trowel and scratcher, the seeds and the knife she worked with. She wore heavy leather gloves to protect her hands while she worked.

She was cutting down the old year's chrysanthemum stalks with a pair of short and powerful scissors. She looked down toward the men by the tractor shed now and then. Her face was eager and mature and handsome; even her work with the scissors was over-eager, over-powerful. The chrysanthemum stems seemed too small and easy for her energy.

She brushed a cloud of hair out of her eyes with the back of her glove, and left a smudge of earth on her cheek in doing it. Behind her stood the neat white farm house with red geraniums close-banked around it as high as the windows. It was a hard-swept looking little house, with hard-polished windows, and a clean mud-mat on the front steps.

Elisa cast another glance toward the tractor shed. The strangers were getting into their Ford coupe. She took off a glove and put her strong fingers down into the forest of new green chrysanthemum sprouts that were growing around the old roots. She spread the leaves and looked down among the close-growing stems. No aphids were there, no sowbugs or snails or cutworms. Her terrier fingers destroyed such pests before they could get started.

Elisa started at the sound of her husband's voice. He had come near quietly, and he leaned over the wire fence that protected her flower garden from cattle and dogs and chickens.

"At it again," he said. "You've got a strong new crop coming."

Elisa straightened her back and pulled on the gardening glove again. "Yes. They'll be strong this coming year." In her tone and on her face there was a little smugness.

"You've got a gift with things," Henry observed. "Some of those yellow chrysanthemums you had this year were ten inches across. I wish you'd work out in the orchard and raise some apples that big."

Her eyes sharpened. "Maybe I could do it, too. I've a gift with things, all right. My mother had it. She could stick anything in the ground and make it grow. She said it was having planters' hands that knew how to do it."

"Well, it sure works with flowers," he said.

"Henry, who were those men you were talking to?"

"Why, sure, that's what I came to tell you. They were from the Western Meat Company. I sold those thirty head of three-year-old steers. Got nearly my own price, too."

"Good," she said. "Good for you."

"And I thought," he continued, "I thought how it's Saturday afternoon, and we might go into Salinas for dinner at a restaurant, and then to a picture show—to celebrate, you see."

"Good," she repeated. "Oh, yes. That will be good."

Henry put on his joking tone. "There's fights tonight. How'd you like to go to the fights?"

"Oh, no," she said breathlessly. "No, I wouldn't like fights."

"Just fooling, Elisa. We'll go to a movie. Let's see. It's two now. I'm going to take Scotty and bring down those steers from the hill. It'll take us maybe two hours. We'll go in town about five and have dinner at the Cominos Hotel. Like that?"

"Of course I'll like it. It's good to eat away from home."

"All right, then, I'll go get up a couple of horses."

She said, "I'll have plenty of time to transplant some of these sets, I guess."

She heard her husband calling Scotty down by the barn. And a little later she saw the two men ride up the pale yellow hillside in search of the steers.

There was a little square sandy bed kept for rooting the chrysanthemums. With her trowel she turned the soil over and over, and smoothed it and patted it firm. Then she dug ten parallel trenches to receive the sets. Back at the chrysanthemum bed she pulled out the little crisp shoots, trimmed off the leaves of each one with her scissors and laid it on a small orderly pile.

A squeak of wheels and plod of hoofs came from the road. Elisa looked up. The country road ran along the dense bank of willows and cottonwoods that bordered the river, and up this road came a curious vehicle, curiously drawn. It was an old spring-wagon, with a round canvas top on it like the cover of a prairie schooner. It was drawn by an old bay horse and a little grey-and-white burro. A big stubble-bearded man sat between the cover flaps and drove the crawling team. Underneath the wagon, between the hind wheels, a lean and rangy mongrel dog walked sedately. Words were painted on the canvas, in clumsy, crooked letters. "Pots, pans, knives, sisors, lawn mores. Fixed." Two rows of articles, and the triumphantly definitive "Fixed" below. The black paint had run down in little sharp points beneath each letter.

Elisa, squatting on the ground, watched to see the crazy, loose-jointed wagon pass by. But it didn't pass. It turned into the farm road in front of her house, crooked old wheels skirling and squeaking. The rangy dog darted from between the wheels and ran ahead. Instantly the two ranch shepherds flew out at him. Then all three stopped, and with stiff and quivering tails, with taut straight legs, with ambassadorial dignity, they slowly circled, sniffing daintily. The caravan pulled up to Elisa's wire fence and stopped. Now the newcomer dog, feeling out-numbered, lowered his tail and retired under the wagon with raised hackles and bared teeth.

The man on the wagon seat called out, "That's a bad dog in a fight when he gets started."

Elisa laughed. "I see he is. How soon does he generally get started?"

The man caught up her laughter and echoed it heartily. "Sometimes not for weeks and weeks," he said. He climbed stiffly down, over the wheel. The horse and the donkey drooped like unwatered flowers.

Elisa saw that he was a very big man. Although his hair and beard were greying, he did not look old. His worn black suit was wrinkled and spotted with grease. The laughter had disappeared from his face and eyes the moment his laughing voice ceased. His eyes were dark, and they were full of the brooding that gets in the eyes of teamsters and of sailors. The calloused hands he rested on the wire fence were cracked, and every crack was a black line. He took off his battered hat.

"I'm off my general road, ma'am," he said. "Does this dirt road cut over across the river to the Los Angeles highway?"

Elisa stood up and shoved the thick scissors in her apron pocket. "Well, yes, it does, but it winds around and then fords the river. I don't think your team could pull through the sand."

He replied with some asperity, "It might surprise you what them beasts can pull through."

"When they get started?" she asked.

He smiled for a second. "Yes. When they get started."

"Well," said Elisa, "I think you'll save time if you go back to the Salinas road and pick up the highway there."

He drew a big finger down the chicken wire and made it sing. "I ain't in any hurry, ma'am. I go from Seattle to San Diego and back every year.

Takes all my time. About six months each way. I aim to follow nice weather."

Elisa took off her gloves and stuffed them in the apron pocket with the scissors. She touched the under edge of her man's hat, searching for fugitive hairs. "That sounds like a nice kind of a way to live," she said.

He leaned confidentially over the fence. "Maybe you noticed the writing on my wagon. I mend pots and sharpen knives and scissors. You got any of them things to do?"

"Oh, no," she said quickly. "Nothing like that." Her eyes hardened with resistance.

"Scissors is the worst thing," he explained. "Most people just ruin scissors trying to sharpen 'em, but I know how. I got a special tool. It's a little bobbit kind of thing, and patented. But it sure does the trick."

"No. My scissors are all sharp."

"All right, then. Take a pot," he continued earnestly, "a bent pot, or a pot with a hole. I can make it like new so you don't have to buy no new ones. That's a saving for you."

"No," she said shortly. "I tell you I have nothing like that for you to do."

His face fell to an exaggerated sadness. His voice took on a whining undertone. "I ain't had a thing to do today. Maybe I won't have no supper tonight. You see I'm off my regular road. I know folks on the highway clear from Seattle to San Diego. They save their things for me to sharpen up because they know I do it so good and save them money."

"I'm sorry," Elisa said irritably. "I haven't anything for you to do."

His eyes left her face and fell to searching the ground. They roamed about until they came to the chrysanthemum bed where she had been working. "What's them plants, ma'am?"

The irritation and resistance melted from Elisa's face. "Oh, those are chrysanthemums, giant whites and yellows. I raise them every year, bigger than anybody around here."

"Kind of a long-stemmed flower? Looks like a quick puff of colored smoke?" he asked.

"That's it. What a nice way to describe them."

"They smell kind of nasty till you get used to them," he said.

"It's a good bitter smell," she retorted, "not nasty at all."

He changed his tone quickly. "I like the smell myself."

"I had ten-inch blooms this year," she said.

The man leaned farther over the fence. "Look. I know a lady down the road a piece, has got the nicest garden you ever seen. Got nearly every kind of flower but no chrysantheums. Last time I was mending a copper-bottom washtub for her (that's a hard job but I do it good), she said to me, 'If you ever run acrost some nice chrysantheums I wish you'd try to get me a few seeds.' That's what she told me."

Elisa's eyes grew alert and eager. "She couldn't have known much about chrysanthemums. You *can* raise them from seed, but it's much easier to root the little sprouts you see there."

"Oh," he said. "I s'pose I can't take none to her, then."

"Why yes you can," Elisa cried. "I can put some in damp sand, and you can carry them right along with you. They'll take root in the pot if you keep them damp. And then she can transplant them."

"She'd sure like to have some, ma'am. You say they're nice ones?"

"Beautiful," she said. "Oh, beautiful." Her eyes shone. She tore off the battered hat and shook out her dark pretty hair. "I'll put them in a flower pot, and you can take them right with you. Come into the yard."

While the man came through the picket gate Elisa ran excitedly along the geranium-bordered path to the back of the house. And she returned carrying a big red flower pot. The gloves were forgotten now. She kneeled on the ground by the starting bed and dug up the sandy soil with her fingers and scooped it into the bright new flower pot. Then she picked up the little pile of shoots she had prepared. With her strong fingers she pressed them into the sand and tamped around them with her knuckles. The man stood over her. "I'll tell you what to do," she said. "You remember so you can tell the lady."

"Yes, I'll try to remember."

"Well, look. These will take root in about a month. Then she must set them out, about a foot apart in good rich earth like this, see?" She lifted a handful of dark soil for him to look at. "They'll grow fast and tall. Now remember this. In July tell her to cut them down, about eight inches from the ground."

"Before they bloom?" he asked.

"Yes, before they bloom." Her face was tight with eagerness. "They'll grow right up again. About the last of September the buds will start."

She stopped and seemed perplexed. "It's the budding that takes the most care," she said hesitantly. "I don't know how to tell you." She looked deep into his eyes, searchingly. Her mouth opened a little, and she seemed to be listening. "I'll try to tell you," she said. "Did you ever hear of planting hands?"

"Can't say I have, ma'am."

"Well, I can only tell you what it feels like. It's when you're picking off the buds you don't want. Everything goes right down into your fingertips. You watch your fingers work. They do it themselves. You can feel how it is. They pick and pick the buds. They never make a mistake. They're with the plant. Do you see? Your fingers and the plant. You can feel that, right up your arm. They know. They never make a mistake. You can feel it. When you're like that you can't do anything wrong. Do you see that? Can you understand that?"

She was kneeling on the ground looking up at him. Her breast swelled passionately.

The man's eyes narrowed. He looked away self-consciously. "Maybe I know," he said. "Sometimes in the night in the wagon there——"

Elisa's voice grew husky. She broke in on him. "I've never lived as you do, but I know what you mean. When the night is dark—why, the stars are sharp-pointed, and there's quiet. Why, you rise up and up! Every pointed star gets driven into your body. It's like that. Hot and sharp and—lovely."

Kneeling there, her hand went out toward his legs in the greasy black trousers. Her hesitant fingers almost touched the cloth. Then her hand dropped to the ground. She crouched low like a fawning dog.

He said, "It's nice, just like you say. Only when you don't have no dinner, it ain't."

She stood up then, very straight, and her face was ashamed. She held the flower pot out to him and placed it gently in his arms. "Here. Put it in your wagon, on the seat, where you can watch it. Maybe I can find something for you to do."

At the back of the house she dug in the can pile and found two old and battered aluminum saucepans. She carried them back and gave them to him. "Here, maybe you can fix these."

His manner changed. He became professional. "Good as new I can fix them." At the back of his wagon he set a little anvil, and out of an oily tool box dug a small machine hammer. Elisa came through the gate to watch him while he pounded out the dents in the kettles. His mouth grew sure and knowing. At a difficult part of the work he sucked his under-lip.

"You sleep right in the wagon?" Elisa asked.

"Right in the wagon, ma'am. Rain or shine I'm dry as a cow in there."

"It must be nice," she said. "It must be very nice. I wish women could do such things."

"It ain't the right kind of a life for a woman."

Her upper lip raised a little, showing her teeth. "How do you know? How can you tell?" she said.

"I don't know, ma'am," he protested. "Of course I don't know. Now here's your kettles, done. You don't have to buy no new ones."

"How much?"

"Oh, fifty cents'll do. I keep my prices down and my work good. That's why I have all them satisfied customers up and down the highway."

Elisa brought him a fifty-cent piece from the house and dropped it in his hand. "You might be surprised to have a rival some time. I can sharpen scissors, too. And I can beat the dents out of little pots. I could show you what a woman might do."

He put his hammer back in the oily box and shoved the little anvil out of sight. "It would be a lonely life for a woman, ma'am, and a scarey life, too, with animals creeping under the wagon all night." He climbed over the singletree, steadying himself with a hand on the burro's white rump. He settled himself in the seat, picked up the lines. "Thank you kindly, ma'am," he said. "I'll do like you told me; I'll go back and catch the Salinas road."

"Mind," she called, "if you're long in getting there, keep the sand damp."

"Sand, ma'am? . . . Sand? Oh, sure. You mean around the chrysantheums. Sure I will." He clucked his tongue. The beasts leaned luxuriously into their collars. The mongrel dog took his place between the back wheels. The wagon turned and crawled out the entrance road and back the way it had come, along the river.

Elisa stood in front of her wire fence watching the slow progress of the caravan. Her shoulders were straight, her head thrown back, her eyes half-closed, so that the scene came vaguely into them. Her lips moved silently, forming the words "Good-bye—good-bye." Then she whispered, "That's a bright direction. There's a glowing there." The sound of her whisper startled her. She shook herself free and looked about to see whether anyone had been listening. Only the dogs had heard. They lifted their heads toward her from their sleeping in the dust, and then stretched out their chins and settled asleep again. Elisa turned and ran hurriedly into the house.

In the kitchen she reached behind the stove and felt the water tank. It was full of hot water from the noonday cooking. In the bathroom she tore off her soiled clothes and flung them into the corner. And then she scrubbed herself with a little block of pumice, legs and thighs, loins and chest and arms, until her skin was scratched and red. When she had dried herself she stood in front of a mirror in her bedroom and looked at her body. She tightened her stomach and threw out her chest. She turned and looked over her shoulder at her back.

After a while she began to dress, slowly. She put on her newest underclothing and her nicest stockings and the dress which was the symbol of her prettiness. She worked carefully on her hair, penciled her eyebrows and rouged her lips.

Before she finished she heard the little thunder of hoofs and the shouts of Henry and his helper as they drove the red steers into the corral. She heard the gate bang shut and set herself for Henry's arrival.

His step sounded on the porch. He entered the house calling, "Elisa, where are you?"

"In my room, dressing. I'm not ready. There's hot water for your bath. Hurry up. It's getting late."

When she heard him splashing in the tub, Elisa laid his dark suit on the bed, and shirt and socks and tie beside it. She stood his polished shoes on the floor beside the bed. Then she went to the porch and sat primly and stiffly down. She looked toward the river road where the willow-line was still yellow with frosted leaves so that under the high grey fog they seemed a thin band of sunshine. This was the only color in the grey afternoon. She sat unmoving for a long time. Her eyes blinked rarely.

Henry came banging out of the door, shoving his tie inside his vest as he came. Elisa stiffened and her face grew tight. Henry stopped short and looked at her. "Why—why, Elisa. You look so nice!"

"Nice? You think I look nice? What do you mean by 'nice'?"

Henry blundered on. "I don't know. I mean you look different, strong and happy."

"I am strong? Yes, strong. What do you mean 'strong'?"

He looked bewildered. "You're playing some kind of a game," he said helplessly. "It's a kind of a play. You look strong enough to break a calf over your knee, happy enough to eat it like a watermelon."

For a second she lost her rigidity. "Henry! Don't talk like that. You didn't know what you said." She grew complete again. "I'm strong," she boasted. "I never knew before how strong."

Henry looked down toward the tractor shed, and when he brought his eyes back to her, they were his own again. "I'll get out the car. You can put on your coat while I'm starting."

Elisa went into the house. She heard him drive to the gate and idle down his motor, and then she took a long time to put on her hat. She pulled it here and pressed it there. When Henry turned the motor off she slipped into her coat and went out.

The little roadster bounced along on the dirt road by the river, raising the birds and driving the rabbits into the brush. Two cranes flapped heavily over the willow-line and dropped into the river-bed.

Far ahead on the road Elisa saw a dark speck. She knew.

She tried not to look as they passed it, but her eyes would not obey. She whispered to herself sadly, "He might have thrown them off the road. That wouldn't have been much trouble, not very much. But he kept the pot," she explained. "He had to keep the pot. That's why he couldn't get them off the road."

The roadster turned a bend and she saw the caravan ahead. She swung full around toward her husband so she could not see the little covered wagon and the mismatched team as the car passed them.

In a moment it was over. The thing was done. She did not look back.

She said loudly, to be heard above the motor, "It will be good, tonight, a good dinner."

"Now you're changed again," Henry complained. He took one hand from the wheel and patted her knee. "I ought to take you in to dinner oftener. It would be good for both of us. We get so heavy out on the ranch."

"Henry," she asked, "could we have wine at dinner?"

"Sure we could. Say! That will be fine."

She was silent for a while; then she said, "Henry, at those prize fights, do the men hurt each other very much?"

"Sometimes a little, not often. Why?"

"Well, I've read how they break noses, and blood runs down their chests. I've read how the fighting gloves get heavy and soggy with blood."

He looked around at her. "What's the matter, Elisa? I didn't know you read things like that." He brought the car to a stop, then turned to the right over the Salinas River bridge.

"Do any women ever go to the fights?" she asked.

"Oh, sure, some. What's the matter, Elisa? Do you want to go? I don't think you'd like it, but I'll take you if you really want to go."

She relaxed limply in the seat. "Oh, no. No. I don't want to go. I'm sure I don't." Her face was turned away from him. "It will be enough if we can have wine. It will be plenty." She turned up her coat collar so he could not see that she was crying weakly—like an old woman.

Langston Hughes

1902 – 1967

A leading figure in the Harlem Renaissance, Langston Hughes was both a prolific and versatile writer, for he published some thirty-nine volumes which encompass nearly every literary genre—poetry, fiction, drama, folk opera, biography, autobiography, the essay, and the humorous sketch. In all his work, whatever its form, he sought "to illuminate the Negro condition in America," and the important role he played in the emergence of black literature during the earlier half of the twentieth century entitles him to the high rank he has attained as Dean of black American writers.

Because Hughes's parents, James Nathaniel and Carrie Mercer Langston Hughes, separated shortly after his birth in 1902, in Joplin, Missouri, he spent part of his childhood years in Lawrence, Kansas, with his maternal grandmother and the rest with his mother, first in Lincoln, Illinois, where he attended grammar school, and later in Cleveland, Ohio, where he completed high school in 1920. After spending the following year teaching school in Mexico, he enrolled at Columbia University but left after a year to work at such odd jobs as laboring on a Staten Island truck-garden farm, serving as a mess-boy on a freighter, and dishwashing and waiting on tables in Paris night clubs. Meanwhile, following a literary bent dating from his high school career, he had begun publishing poetry and prose in black periodicals. By 1925, Hughes was back in the United States vigorously producing poems while working as a busboy in a Washington hotel, and his fledgling literary career was given a tremendous boost when Vachel Lindsay publicly praised his writing, for later that same year he also won prizes in literary contests held by *Opportunity* and *Crisis* and began publishing poems in *Vanity Fair.* Continuing to advance his writing career, Hughes resumed formal studies by enrolling at Lincoln University in Pennsylvania in 1926 and earning his B. A. degree in 1929. With two volumes of poetry already to his credit—*The Weary Blues* (1926) and *Fine Clothes to the Jew* (1927)—he turned to fiction during the 1930s, publishing a novel, *Not Without Laughter* (1930) and the first of three collections of stories, *The Ways of White Folks* (1934). During the remaining three decades of his highly productive career, as an endless variety of other works continued to pour from his pen, he earned both national and international acclaim. As the literary spokesperson for his race, he devoted considerable effort to encouraging black literary and artistic productivity. Among many other things, he founded black theatrical groups in Harlem, Los Angeles, and Chicago, and he published many works dealing with the heritage of black Americans and with the artistic achievements of blacks, such as *The Poetry of the Negro (1746–1949)* (1949), *Famous Negro Heroes of America* (1957), *Famous Negro Music Makers* (1954), *A Pictorial History of the Negro in America* (1956), and *The Best Stories by Negro Writers* (1967). Despite the incredible range of his work and his concerns with the black American's situation, he published two later collections of stories, *Laughing to Keep From Crying* (1952), and *Something in Common and Other Stories* (1963). He died in 1967.

Even though Hughes focused many of his stories on problems of racial prejudice blacks confront, others, as "Thank you Ma'm" shows, deal with the more universal theme of common people in conflict with one another and their circumstances. Two noteworthy qualities of this story, also present in his other stories, are its restrained, natural style and the amazing fidelity of its dialogue.

Thank You, Ma'm

She was a large woman with a large purse that had everything in it but hammer and nails. It had a long strap and she carried it slung across her shoulder. It was about eleven o'clock at night, and she was walking alone, when a boy ran up behind her and tried to snatch her purse. The strap broke with the single tug the boy gave it from behind. But the boy's weight, and the weight of the purse combined caused him to lose his balance so, instead of taking off full blast as he had hoped, the boy fell on his back on the sidewalk, and his legs flew up. The large woman simply turned around and kicked him right square in his blue jeaned sitter. Then she reached down, picked the boy up by his shirt front, and shook him until his teeth rattled.

After that the woman said, "Pick up my pocketbook, boy, and give it here."

She still held him. But she bent down enough to permit him to stoop and pick up her purse. Then she said, "Now ain't you ashamed of yourself?"

Firmly gripped by his shirt front, the boy said, "Yes'm."

The woman said, "What did you want to do it for?"

The boy said, "I didn't aim to."

She said, "You a lie!"

By that time two or three people passed, stopped, turned to look, and some stood watching.

"If I turn you loose, will you run?" asked the woman.

"Yes'm," said the boy.

"Then I won't turn you loose," said the woman. She did not release him.

"I'm very sorry, lady, I'm sorry," whispered the boy.

"Um-hum! And your face is dirty. I got a great mind to wash your face for you. Ain't you got nobody home to tell you to wash your face?"

"No'm," said the boy.

"Then it will get washed this evening," said the large woman starting up the street, dragging the frightened boy behind her.

He looked as if he were fourteen or fifteen, frail and willow-wild, in tennis shoes and blue jeans.

The woman said, "You ought to be my son. I would teach you right from wrong. Least I can do right now is to wash your face. Are you hungry?"

"No'm," said the being-dragged boy. "I just want you to turn me loose."

"Was I bothering *you* when I turned that corner?" asked the woman.

"No'm."

"But you put yourself in contact with *me*," said the woman. "If you think that that contact is not going to last awhile, you got another thought coming. When I get through with you, sir, you are going to remember Mrs. Luella Bates Washington Jones."

Sweat popped out on the boy's face and he began to struggle. Mrs. Jones stopped, jerked him around in front of her, put a half nelson about his neck, and continued to drag him up the street. When she got to her door, she dragged the boy inside, down a hall, and into a large kitchenette-furnished room at the rear of the house. She switched on the light and left the door open. The boy could hear other roomers laughing and talking in the large house. Some of their doors were open, too, so he knew he and the woman were not alone. The woman still had him by the neck in the middle of her room.

She said, "What is your name?"

"Roger," answered the boy.

"Then, Roger, you go to that sink and wash your face," said the woman, whereupon she turned him loose—at last. Roger looked at the door—looked at the woman—looked at the door—*and went to the sink.*

"Let the water run until it gets warm," she said. "Here's a clean towel."

"You gonna take me to jail?" asked the boy, bending over the sink.

"Not with that face, I would not take you nowhere," said the woman. "Here I am trying to get home to cook me a bite to eat and you snatch my pocketbook! Maybe you ain't been to your supper either, late as it be. Have you?"

"There's nobody home at my house," said the boy.

"Then we'll eat," said the woman. "I believe you're hungry—or been hungry—to try to snatch my pocketbook."

"I wanted a pair of blue suede shoes," said the boy.

"Well, you didn't have to snatch *my* pocketbook to get some suede shoes," said Mrs. Luella Bates Washington Jones. "You could of asked me."

"M'am?"

The water dripping from his face, the boy looked at her. There was a long pause. A very long pause. After he had dried his face and not knowing what else to do dried it again, the boy turned around, wondering what next. The door was open. He could make a dash for it down the hall. He could run, run, run, run, *run!*

The woman was sitting on the day-bed. After awhile she said, "I were young once and I wanted things I could not get."

There was another long pause. The boy's mouth opened. Then he frowned, but not knowing he frowned.

The woman said, "Um-hum! You thought I was going to say *but,* didn't you? You thought I was going to say, *but I didn't snatch people's pocketbooks.* Well, I wasn't going to say that." Pause. Silence. "I have done things, too, which I would not tell you, son—neither tell God, if he didn't already know. So you set down while I fix us something to eat. You might run that comb through your hair so you will look presentable."

In another corner of the room behind a screen was a gas plate and an icebox. Mrs. Jones got up and went behind the screen. The woman did not watch the boy to see if he was going to run now, nor did she watch her purse which she left behind her on the day-bed. But the boy took care to sit on the far side of the room where he thought she could easily see him out of the corner of her eye, if she wanted to. He did not trust the woman *not* to trust him. And he did not want to be mistrusted now.

"Do you need somebody to go to the store," asked the boy, "maybe to get some milk or something?"

"Don't believe I do," said the woman, "unless you just want sweet milk yourself. I was going to make cocoa out of this canned milk I got here."

"That will be fine," said the boy.

She heated some lima beans and ham she had in the icebox, made the cocoa, and set the table. The woman did not ask the boy anything about where he lived, or his folks, or anything else that would embarrass him. Instead, as they ate, she told him about her job in a hotel beauty-shop that stayed open late, what the work was like, and how all kinds of women came in and out, blondes, red-heads, and Spanish. Then she cut him a half of her ten-cent cake.

"Eat some more, son," she said.

When they were finished eating she got up and said, "Now, here, take this ten dollars and buy yourself some blue suede shoes. And next time, do not make the mistake of latching onto *my* pocketbook *nor nobody else's*—because shoes come by devilish like that will burn your feet. I got to get my rest now. But I wish you would behave yourself, son, from here on in."

She led him down the hall to the front door and opened it. "Good-night! Behave yourself, boy!" she said, looking out into the street.

The boy wanted to say something else other than, "Thank you, m'am," to Mrs. Luella Bates Washington Jones, but he couldn't do so as he turned at the barren stoop and looked back at the large woman in the door. He barely managed to say, "Thank you," before she shut the door. And he never saw her again.

SECTION FOUR

Tradition and Experimentation

1935 – 1975

In the generations that suffered the trauma of World War II and its aftermath, the role of the United States in world affairs and the striving of its motley citizenry at home can be viewed objectively as two sides of the same coin—an effort to achieve stability and equilibrium amid fluctuations of power and fortune. In the 1930s, as we have noted, the nation's primary domestic concern was the catastrophic economic problem spawned by the Great Depression: how to cope with industrial paralysis, massive unemployment, burgeoning homelessness and vagrancy, and a weakening of faith in the American Dream. As a counter-current to these gloomy prospects, however, the ominous growth of militaristic regimes in Europe and the Far East gradually redirected national attention toward equally grave threats of dissolution from abroad; and the onset of war in Europe in 1939 inevitably drew the United States into the conflict two years later with the Japanese bombing attack on Pearl Harbor. Once again Americans were a united community with a common goal, spiritually and materially dedicated for the next four years to their involvement in World War II.

As a result, in 1945, with Europe and the Far East devastated, America stood at the pinnacle of its power, sole possessor of the atom bomb, preparing shortly as architect of NATO and the Marshall Plan to restore and maintain order in a shattered world. But the incursion of communism into Eastern Europe and China soon gave rise to the "cold war" between East and West, leading in turn to the eruption of hostilities in Korea, the nuclear arms race, the Castro revolution in Cuba, and the nation's agonizing involvement in Vietnam and the Middle East—a series of confrontations and readjustments of policy from the 1950s on to the present. Not surprisingly, the unrest and upheaval expressed in these developments found analogous outlets within the United States during the same period. Recurring national hysteria over such events as the McCarthy trials, civil rights sit-ins and freedom rides, student demonstrations and campus bombings, ghetto riots, the drug scene, and so on, though offset in part by spectacular technological advances in medical care, nuclear physics, space explorations, moon landings, and intercontinental missiles, pointed ominously to the divisive forces at work in both the nation and the world at large.

Within the United States, these forces, erupting repeatedly over issues of public policy concerning minority rights, prison reform, voter registration, the busing of schoolchildren, and many others, reached a climax of horrors in the brutal assassinations of President John Kennedy in 1963 and, five years later, of his brother Robert, the New York Senator, and the black leader Dr. Martin Luther King, Jr. In retrospect, the cumulative effect upon the national psyche of shocking incidents like these, suffered throughout the 1960s, offers a perspective for the subsequent trauma of Watergate, the Kent State massacre of student protesters, the unprecedented dethronement of another president amid the clamor of discordant voices in the 1970s, and the attempted assassination of President Ronald Reagan in 1981. It would be strange indeed if the creative literature emerging from such an era did not also reflect—as indeed it does in its varied modes of expression—the same clamor, the same divisiveness and fragmentation, the same shocks born of violence and anxiety.

Predictably, the short stories that reflected these startling developments exhibited a more astonishing array of attitudes, philosophies, forms, and styles than ever before. Yet out of this welter of contrasting modes and methods of expression several dominant patterns have been noted, the underlying purpose of which was to dramatize a quest for positive values to replace those that had been lost in the breakdown and dispersal of old assumptions. Clearly, one of the most persistent attitudes resonant in post-war fiction was a vital concern, expressed or implied, over the apparent loss or distortion of one's personal identity in a seemingly chaotic, mechanistic world. This feeling that individuals, by becoming even more submerged in the mass than their predecessors were, lose their bearings along with their identities and importance as human beings can perhaps be blamed for much of the somberness, the fragmentation, and the disconnectedness found in modern fiction. What ideals can a man or woman hold on to—what goals realistically pursue—and still function productively in a push-button, computerized age? This has been a major problem haunting not only Faulkner and Hemingway, the pioneers in extending the range of the modern short story, but also the younger writers who have carried forward the discoveries and techniques those pioneers initiated. Thus, the serious short story of the recent past and, indeed, the present may still be regarded as a search for truth, an effort to illuminate the problems of human beings who, as one author sees them, are engaged in a constant struggle for self-fulfillment, "trying to subdue chaos outside and inside."

The many ways in which postwar writers have dealt with this problem of alienation and the individual's quest for self-fulfillment—and the results their efforts have achieved—might seem to be totally unlike those of their predecessors. For one thing, present day writers enjoy a freedom of language use that was simply unthinkable forty or fifty years ago: witness the explicit terminology applied to sexual activity even in some popular magazines. Yet it would be a mistake to assume that all serious fiction produced since the 1950s has repudiated or thrown aside traditional modes and boldly struck off in totally new directions, notwithstanding the fact that a distinct "new mode" of fiction has been developing during the past several decades. Among the works of leading younger writers there has been a readily detectable continuity of influence, a carry-over of traditional attitudes and methods inherited from such established pioneer artists as Faulkner, Hemingway, Joyce, and Katherine Anne Porter, just as there was earlier in the century among those who adapted for their own ends the pioneering artistry of James, Twain, Howells, and Crane. Many southern writers, for example, have kept their renaissance alive by reaffirming those truths of the human heart that Faulkner dramatized so vividly in the relationships he traced between men and women, whites and blacks, parents and children, the strong and the weak, the well-favored and the dispossessed.

New Southern Voices

While Faulkner's impact may be visible in the themes and characters of his disciples, their own styles and manner of presentation are seldom purely imitative but, to the contrary, are distinctly individualized, as in the stories of Eudora Welty. Since the early 1940s, Welty has been recognized as a superb artist, exhibiting in her five collections of stories (beginning with *A Curtain of Green,* 1941) a rare insight into the motives and inner conflicts of quite average and seemingly colorless individuals. In her essay "The Reading and Writing of Short Stories" (*Atlantic Monthly,* 1949) she expressed a tremendous admiration for the work of Faulkner, her fellow Mississippian, comparing the effect of his stories to that of a comet "in that they do have a wonderful course of their own: they reappear, . . . and by reiteration show a whole further story over and beyond their single significance." Yet despite the pervasive influence of Faulkner, her stories are radically different from his; they are marked by a freshness and individuality of style as well as by a surprising variety of subject matter which is nevertheless largely circumscribed by and firmly rooted in the society of rural and small-town Mississippi. A primary attribute of all her fiction, as one critic noted, is its femininity. The writing of no other fictionist, he asserts, "is so thoroughly and unmistakably feminine, and at the same time so little tainted by feminism," by which he means that she has consistently and unsentimentally explored with a vivid imagination a great range of concerns that disturb the minds of ordinary folk, including problems of solitude and alienation, sexual hang-ups, violence, perversion and criminal involvement, and most significantly, race relationships. Thus, in this critic's view, "no other modern American writer, not even Faulkner, . . . has been so intensely and responsibly alert to the significance of the Negro's presence in our society as Eudora Welty has been."[1] These are some of the reasons why so many of her stories possess that quality which she herself holds up as a *sine qua non* of good fiction: "mystery—not the puzzle kind but the mystery of allurement."

Combining comedy, pathos, satire, horror, and fantasy, these stories reveal a singleness of purpose in their varied emphasis upon the contrast between external reality and the world of dreams, between an individual's social contacts and the realm of inner life. Repeatedly, Welty's stories render the life of the subconscious with great delicacy and intensity by means of symbolic imagery, as in both "Livvie" and the much more recent "The Demonstrators," where tissues of symbols give one simultaneously a double view of life: the vivid pattern of the actual world of time and space, of field hands, cosmetic saleswomen, civil rights workers, and small town physicians, of passionate encounters and quiet deaths, inextricably tied to that other world of timeless myths and meanings embodying ancient wisdom and desires.

There is no dearth of other southern-born writers, both white and black, whose fiction along with Welty's has drawn attention in recent decades to the continuing vitality of serious literary effort dealing with varied levels of experience peculiar to their region, yet unmistakably associated with human problems anywhere. Among the more prominent whose names immediately come to mind are those of Robert Penn Warren, Carson McCullers, Peter Taylor, William Styron, Walker Percy, Richard Wright, Ralph Ellison, and Ernest Gaines. Each of them, responsive to many of the same historic forces and social relationships dramatized in Faulkner's fiction, has also produced a significant body of both short and long fiction. Nor is this list by any means exhaustive. None could be unless it included the name of still another young woman, Mary Flannery O'Connor, whose powerful stories have consistently stimulated

[1] J. E. Hardy, "The Achievement of Eudora Welty," *Southern Humanities Review*, II, 3:271, 276 (1968).

more and more diverse critical interest since her death in 1964 than during the preceding decade or so when they first appeared.

The tendency at first was to regard O'Connor's work as merely another latter-day manifestation of southern gothicism and the grotesque, to assume that the erratic, often violent behavior of her cranks, thieves, misfits, and religious fanatics simply reflected the author's ironic commentary upon the backwardness and irrationality of the social types she drew so vividly. Yet O'Connor herself plainly stated her own unwavering faith in Christian orthodoxy (" . . . for me the meaning of life is centered in our Redemption by Christ and . . . what I see in the world I see in relation to that"), implying thereby that at the basis of all her fiction there lay an intense spiritual purpose. Her stories, accordingly, can best be seen as variations on the theme of original sin; as one of her most astute fellow artists, Joyce Carol Oates, has pointed out, they are a kind of visionary art presenting a series of revelations or parables on the purification of the human heart and mind.[2] Firmly based on the theological doctrines of the Roman Catholic Church, they are concerned, as Hawthorne's are, with fundamental problems of the human soul in its quest for salvation. But unlike Hawthorne's, the souls of Miss O'Connor's characters are embodied in recognizably three-dimensional human folk, whose problems of adjusting to the violence and conflict within themselves and the world they inhabit are problems inescapably shared by all of us. There is thus a touch of Dante's inferno in all their private hells and a rugged path to tread before their attainment of the peace of mind that passes understanding. And there is more than a touch of Dante's uncompromising austerity and firm control in this author's portrayal of the human predicament. That is why we do not need to share her religious convictions precisely in order to admire her aesthetic power. But the full force of a story like "Good Country People" and the beauty of its construction may not at once strike casual readers unless they discover the close linkage between its explosive climax and the pattern of character relationships that make such a climax inevitable. For the pathetic Joy/Hulga, her fatuous mother, the diabolical Bible salesman, and the grubby Mrs. Freeman, though quite recognizable as ordinary Americans, also provide a disturbing symbolic commentary on a basic dilemma in our modern wasteland. Shared alike by the educated and the ignorant, it has to do with the lack of genuine spiritual conviction amid the artificiality of our ego-centered aims.

[2] "The Visionary Art of Flannery O'Connor," *Southern Humanities Review*, 7:3:235–246 (1973).

The Proliferation of Black Creativity

As we have seen, the deepening awareness among white writers over the plight of exploited blacks in the 1930s led to a more realistic representation, notably in the works of Faulkner and Caldwell, of the historic role of blacks in American society than had appeared in earlier writings. From the 1930s on, a similar shift of emphasis became evident in those of black writers: that is, as opposed to the formerly romanticized treatment of racial attributes, a new image of blacks began to emerge. Based upon a more critical degree of self-awareness and a more systematic exploration of the varied activities and social levels of blacks in both urban and rural settings, the literary expression of this new image, embodied in the concept of "soul" (a term reminiscent of Du Bois's early work, *The Souls of Black Folks,* and popularized by Langston Hughes in the 1920s), gathered force in all genres as many young black writers joined the chorus of voices inspired by the Harlem Renaissance.

In broadening the base of short fiction the two writers who led the way were Hughes himself and Richard Wright, whose collections *The Ways of White Folks* (1934) and *Uncle Tom's Children* (1938) presented average blacks in a wide variety of situations ranging in tone from bantering satire to bitter disillusionment. The thematic thrust in these stories was still primarily proletarian, as was characteristic of much writing in the 1930s; but their major significance lay in their mature artistry and technical finesse—in the subtle distinctions of mood, rhythm, and idiom with which they rendered black life. Probably the finest of Wright's short stories were collected in *Eight Men* (1961), a publication he oversaw just before his death. Among numerous other writers who were becoming prominent in the 1930s, however, Ralph Ellison, Arna Bontemps, Claude McKay, and Zora Neale Hurston would emerge as leading figures in the next twenty years; while still younger writers like Frank Yerby, Ann Petry, and Chester Himes quickly gained attention in the 1940s. The major outlets for the work of most of these writers throughout the 1940s were still black magazines like *Crisis, Phylon,* and *Negro Story;* but the fact that their stories were also appearing more and more frequently in established magazines like *Harper's* and *The Atlantic,* as well as winning awards and republication in Foley's *Best American Short Stories* and the annual O. Henry Memorial Award series, showed that the old double standard of judgment relegating black literary effort to an inferior status had at last broken down. As a result, the fiction produced by some of these writers became increasingly profitable as they began finding a ready market in commercial magazines. By 1946, Chester Himes, for example, had published ten stories in *Esquire* alone; while Frank Yerby, winner of an O. Henry award for his story "Health Card," published in *Harper's* in 1944, soon turned to writing the popular swashbuckling historical romances which made him a millionaire.

Since the 1950s many black writers have published short fiction, of whom possibly half a dozen or so have attained deservedly high national and international reputations. Among this select group, the stories of James Baldwin, William Melvin Kelley, Imamu Amin Baraka (LeRoi Jones), Ernest Gaines, Cyrus Colter, Alice Walker, Toni Morrison, and Toni Cade Bambara are perhaps most frequently seen in standard reprint forms such as paperback collections and textbook anthologies. The fact that, since the mid-1960s, no college textbook for studying the short story seems complete without stories by at least three or four of these writers is a significant indication of the great strides made by black writers in recent decades. Until the publication in 1966 and 1967 of the first comprehensive collections of black short stories, edited by John H. Clarke and Langston Hughes respectively, one seldom found even a single black writer represented in the average college textbook of American literature.

The task of sifting out and evaluating critically the most impressive examples of this large body of short fiction by black writers is as challenging as that of assessing the individual efforts of their white counterparts, because among them one finds an equally broad sweep of attitudes, forms, settings, and styles. Langston Hughes's stories alone, in his collection *Laughing to Keep from Crying* (1952), for instance, range widely in setting, atmosphere, and idiom, though their prevailing mood is generally one of restrained humor; while a burning intensity marks the writings of Baldwin and a harsh passion those of Wright. Both Kelley's stories and those of Baraka, on the other hand, taking full advantage of the new permissiveness regarding language usage, jauntily celebrate the black man's and woman's proud determination to be themselves, to live, act, dress, and speak in accord with the cultural patterns of their African heritage, despite the blandishments and pressures of a dominant white society to which they still feel alien.

Within the brief space available in a textbook like this, the black writers represented here offer a rich diversity of human insight and artistic skill in handling the materials of short fiction. The stories published since the 1960s deal with familiar experiences in the lives of average black folk, in their relationships with one another and their reactions to the limitations imposed upon them by the mores and conventions of their particular milieux. Yet each reveals a uniquely different approach to its subject. Toni Cade Bambara, the most provocative of the writers, shows in her portrayal of the role of black women in contemporary society a combination of strength and sensitivity that illuminates what one of her interviewers referred to as "the black female experience, specifically the double oppression of race and sex." Its effectiveness emerges clearly in her response to that interviewer's question about the egregious family reaction to the young girl's plight in "A Girl's Story." Why have they "mistaken her first menstrual period for an abortion?" Because, said Bambara, "this is a family where not much touching goes on, as is played on throughout the story. There are great distances, even though the people live close-quartered. . . . In a household like that, it stands to reason that a lot of secretiveness and isolation travel under the guise of privacy. . . . It might be true that the particular traumas and dangers of womanhood are not valued as a crucial part of our culture. . . . we did not admit, were not allowed to, could not afford to *admit* pain and suffering and hardship. You're not supposed to do that if you're a black woman."[3]

Cyrus Colter, a northern-born-and-educated public official, is the least experimental; but working with a traditional story form, he nevertheless succeeds brilliantly in "A Man in the House" in evoking a strong feeling of anticipation and dread, a product of the inescapable lure of illicit sex. There is scarcely an overt reference to racial clichés in the story; yet the principals involved are unmistakably upper middle-class blacks, and alert readers, black or white, cannot but respond sympathetically to the explosive situation in which the author places them.

In sharp contrast to the sophisticated emphasis on male dominance in Colter's story, Toni Cade Bambara shows in her portrayal of an adolescent black girl a combination of strength and sensitivity. Her response to that interviewer's question about the family reaction to the young girl's plight in "A Girl's Story" provides a formidable counterweight to the *macho* image cast by Colter's Uncle Jack Robinson.

Still, another moving portrayal of mature black female dignity emerges in Ernest Gaines's "The Sky Is Gray," which tenderly recaptures through the eyes of an eight-year-old boy the memory of pride and love sustaining the lives of an impoverished family in his native Louisiana during a critical period when the family breadwinner has been drafted into the army. The pathos of their situation, progressively intensified in a combination of descriptive and narrative detail, is heightened throughout by means of the little boy's limited vision and childish idiom. Thus, the bitterness of cold and hunger—suffered, like the pain of an aching tooth, with insufficient clothing, food, and financial resources to alleviate these ills—comes across with redoubled force as young James, trying desperately to live up to his mother's expectations, reveals the magnitude of his racial predicament in the very act of attempting to conceal his own misery. And this attempt in turn adds a further

[3]Quoted in *Sturdy Black Bridges,* edited by Roseann A. Bell, Bettye J. Parker, and Beverly Guy-Sheftall (Garden City: Doubleday, 1979), pp. 246–247.

dimension, balancing against the chill of a hostile environment a warmth of love and family solidarity which raises the story to a level of epic dignity. Holding that the artist's obligation is to use the material closest to him, Gaines has observed: "Some of the blacks I knew as a child were proud as they could be—poor as hell, but proud people. They were proud of being persons, of surviving."[4] "The Sky Is Gray" amply demonstrates his ability to dramatize more than one aspect of the black experience vividly remembered from his youth in the cane fields near Baton Rouge.

That the black experience can be both amusing and absurd, however, as well as grim and painful—even in confrontations involving deep-seated racial prejudices—is also a recurrent theme upon which leading black writers from Chesnutt and James Weldon Johnson on down to Langston Hughes, Ralph Ellison, and later writers such as Ernest Gaines and James Alan McPherson have played many delightful comic variations. Their ability to ring these changes on an old theme so successfully may be due not only to the greater freedom of movement they have fought for and won in American society, but also to the acuity of their perspective in contemplating their roles in that society. Not so long ago a perceptive black novelist observed that one advantage possessed by the black writer in the United States "is that for him the facade of the American way of life is always transparent." He may have been stretching a point in assuming that such detachment from the mainstream of society *ipso facto* enables black writers to illuminate contemporary life more effectively than their fellow artists that happen to be white or tan, but if the stories written by Colter, Gaines, and Bambara are an augury of things to come, there is no question that serious black writers in America need ever again fear that their work speaks meaningfully only to other blacks.

A New Mode: Existentialism and the Absurd

Since the 1950s the impact of existentialism has been felt in one way or another by all serious creative writers of poetry, drama, and fiction—particularly by young writers, whose response to its various implications has generally been more enthusiastic than that of their elders. To understand the nature of that response and to appreciate the many new forms in which it is expressed, one must first recognize that the philosophical concepts that stimulate and challenge it are fundamentally nihilistic. The idea that for humanity the universe as a whole has no rational meaning or purpose—that human existence makes no sense because all the religious, political, social, and moral underpinnings humanity has

[4]Quoted in *Cutting Edges*, edited by Jack Hicks (Holt, Rinehart, Winston, 1973), p. 535.

set up to create for itself the illusion of meaning and purpose have been swept away—implies that each individual is an exile, an alien adrift on a vast dark sea. Without these illusions, the individual feels lost because, as Albert Camus put it, "he is deprived of memories of a lost homeland as much as he lacks the hope of a promised land to come." Given such a bleak prospect, to maintain their equilibrium people must therefore try to make sense for themselves out of their senseless positions in a senseless world. This paradox, the corollary to the preceding concept, lies at the heart of the aesthetics of the *absurd:* the idea that whatever meaning or purpose may be attributed to human development and interaction must be a product of the individual. The self must find and determine the figure in the carpet, its own order, harmony, and design.

From the absurdist's point of view, if there is no purposeful design in the universe, the effort by writers to make sense out of senselessness can achieve either of two opposing effects. The reality they see and the forms their imaginations create out of it may arouse either satisfaction or despair. Metaphorically, the form their visions take will depend upon their approach to the well-known myth of Sisyphus, classic symbol of alienated humanity, perpetually condemned by the gods to push his heavy stone up a hill, only to have it roll back down again just as he reaches the summit. As Camus interprets the myth, although there is sheer agony in the knowledge that such effort is futile, nevertheless when Sisyphus contemplates the utter absurdity of his predicament each time he goes down to try again, "the lucidity that was to constitute his torture at the same time crowns his victory."[5] For the struggle itself, irrespective of ultimate reward or fulfillment, is his act of creation. Sisyphus can regard his predicament either in sorrow or joy, but as long as he is determined to defy the gods and to keep on pushing, he assumes a role, playing an absurd game which counteracts the overarching absurdity of his position and thereby creates of and for himself meaning out of meaninglessness.[6] Ironically, therefore, in Camus's view Sisyphus must be happy because his defiant response to the absurd is self-willed; by endlessly pushing his rock, he is "doing his own thing," making something out of nothing.

So too with the stories in this section, each of which reflects, to a greater or less degree, its author's imaginative response to a sense of the

[5]*The Myth of Sisyphus and Other Essays,* trans. Justin O'Brien (New York: Vintage, 1955), p. 90.

[6]"By creating his own meaning, Sisyphus has accomplished the supreme act of artistry; he has made something out of nothing. In terms of logic, it is ludicrous to make something out of nothing. But Sisyphus's absurd act is life-affirming as well as ludicrous. It is, then, the highest kind of joke." Richard Boyd Hauck, *A Cheerful Nihilism* (Bloomington, Indiana, 1971), p. 7.

absurd. In some of them the recognition of the individual's plight is so intense that, however comic their postures, readers cannot but feel that sorrow and despair lie in store for them. What hope can we hold out for young Connie in Joyce Carol Oates's powerful story, "Where Are You Going, Where Have You Been?" or for Bernard Malamud's pathetic rabbinical student, Leo Finkel, in "The Magic Barrel"? In their self-determined quest for identity—she in a rapist's embrace and he in a harlot's arms—both face, at best, an ambiguous if not a disastrous awakening. What substantive rewards can possibly await John Cheever's pathetic hero, Neddy Merrill, despite his absurd heroic determination to swim his way from pool to pool on his affluent Westchester neighbors' estates? The principals in these stories evoke our sympathies, however, because we recognize in their predicaments something of the alienation we too feel in confronting the absurd: their desperate need for love and understanding, the pathetic disparity between their ideals and their practices, the dilemmas they must face in adjusting to a reality they never bargained for. And yet, is there not also more than a slight touch of the comic in their several plights? Indeed, there is. Aged Aunt Munsie in Peter Taylor's story "What You Hear from 'em?" is a magnificently comic figure. Truly a modern Sisyphus if ever there was one, she will push her slop cart joyously through the streets of Thornton till she drops, defying all spurious ephemeral values in her ennobling but futile quest for the more permanent ones of the traditional family solidarity. Taylor's comic vision, like that of Malamud and Oates, captures the ambience in which his characters live and unerringly pins their actions to it. There is a degree of response to the absurd in all their stories.

To the extent that these as well as the other writers we have mentioned focus the reader's attention upon aspects of the absurd, emphasizing seemingly abnormal behavior in a chaotic, irrational, or surrealistic world, they are working in the so-called new mode of fiction, for celebration of the absurd is one of the distinguishing features of fiction's new mode. In its more extreme forms, however, fiction in the new mode celebrates the absurd in terms of its own total absurdity; that is, its structure, style, characters, settings, and action all function absurdly together in order to create a completely laughable, and only a laughable, effect. Thus, in much of the fiction that has been written by John Barth, Donald Barthelme, Philip Roth, John Cheever, Grace Paley, John Updike, and numerous others, laughter—"a cheerful nihilism"—is their creative response to the utter futility, as they see it, of any human effort to seek a rationale for living in the modern world. Endless variations can be played upon this dominant theme, but they all tend to fall into one or another of several recognizable categories, such as the parody, hoax, comic allegory, or put-on, in which oddities of style and language; elaborate puns, anagrams, jokes, and allusions; disconnected, freakish episodes; and unexplained juxtapositions of seemingly incongruous mythic elements, are more important to the writer's end than the characters themselves or what happens to them.

In Grace Paley's unpretentious little tale "Samuel," for example, the utter absurdity of the four little boys' behavior in risking their lives is ironically compounded by their impish laughter at the adult warning directed to them. It is in their view understandably ludicrous; yet the grimmer joke reverberating in the final sentence is that "never again will a boy exactly like Samuel be known." In the sort of fiction with which these writers approach reality, they may appear to be playing games with their readers, daring them to figure out its rules and their significance as the readers follow along, alternately puzzled and amused by unexpected turns of phrase. Neither the game nor its methods are altogether new, for Poe and Melville employed some of them in playing it, as did many of the old frontier humorists and, long before them, Laurence Sterne in *Tristram Shandy*. But among its leading practitioners today, both the game and its methods have become infinitely more complicated.

Since originality of style is perhaps the most noticeably distinctive element in the new mode of fiction, a comparison between the relatively simple yet precise style of James Thurber's "The Secret Life of Walter Mitty" (included in Section Three) and the progressively denser ones employed by Updike, Barth, and Barthelme may serve to illustrate why these more recent celebrations of the absurd require closer study if one expects to apprehend and savor their effects. The humor in Thurber's story becomes apparent almost from the opening lines and increases rapidly because the terms he uses to describe his central character's appearance, movements, and thoughts contrast sharply with one's normal expectations of such an innocuous person as Mitty. We can sense the discipline in Thurber's slightest details—the choice of a phrase, even single verbs and nouns, to strike off precisely the right shading of irony he is trying to achieve—and as the story unfolds we enjoy more and more his quiet mastery of recalcitrant language because the quality which makes such control all the more appreciable is the wildly comic imagination informing it. In Thurber's world there are no limits of riotous excess to which the minds of men and women may go in trying to adjust to a crazy-quilt pattern of existence; but, firmly anchored in a traditional type of plotted story, his style clearly separates Walter Mitty's world from our own. In Updike's "A & P," however, the problem of style is somewhat more acute; in fact, the style *is* the story, for instead of creating his characters and action from a detached point of view, the author assumes the mask of his narrator, entering the narrator's mind at the outset and presenting everything that happens through his eyes and voice. What happens is of relatively little moment—three young girls clad in bathing suits show up in a food store located five miles from the beach and are reprimanded by the manager for their unseemly garb—but to young Sammy, the nineteen-year-old-check-out lad who witnesses their coming and going, the experience is enormously significant. It becomes equally significant for the reader through the magic of language, imagery, syntax, speech rhythms, and voice tones issuing from Sammy's mouth as he records his observation of the girls' progress from the vantage point of his post at the cash register. Sammy's eye is sharp and discriminating, particularly as regards anatomical embellishments, and the details he notices are richly transferred in the idiom appropriate to his age and status. Yet one need not be adolescent to share his approval of the "two smoothest scoops of vanilla [he] had ever known were there" or his scorn for elderly "sheep" whose blurred vision and value judgments are so much less selective than his own.

In Barth's work style becomes even more problematic because at its best his fiction coruscates in dazzling flashes of bawdy, scholarly, and parodic wit, its satiric barbs directed simultaneously at himself and the world and even at the process of fiction writing itself. Thus, instead of assuming any single mask, like Proteus he assumes dozens, shifting roles constantly in the middle of paragraphs and sentences, keeping readers guessing as to what he is up to and what it's all about. This writer's labyrinthine style is endlessly engaged in the creation of sophisticated myths, stories within stories within stories, and absurd alternatives, as a means of transcending the absurd.

Barthelme's aim seems to point toward a similar goal, though his style and methods are much different from Barth's, if no less difficult to encompass at first. Barthelme plays another sort of game with his readers, creating in his fiction puzzles made up of scraps of information, images, ideas, reflections, intrusive afterthoughts—odd bits and pieces indiscriminately jumbled together—which nevertheless convey his sense of the chaotic world we live in. Thus, instead of the convoluted mythologizing and Scheherazade-like narratives typifying Barth's work, Barthelme's stories are built on the principle of *collage,* which he is quoted as having called "the central principle of all art in the twentieth century." In one of his best-known stories, "See the Moon," the narrator confidentially asserts: "Fragments are the only forms I trust." And though Barthelme himself scoffingly repudiated this dictum in a later interview, pointing out that all those who mistakenly assume it reflects the whole of his own aesthetic theory fail to note that one of his characters says it, not he,[7] it is nevertheless true that fragments pieced together like stones in a mosaic make up the bulk of his fiction. The point is, however, that there are patterns of meaning embedded in his mosaics; patterns, moreover, which yield different levels of meaning, as in a good poem,

[7] Joe David Bellamy, *The New Fiction* (Urbana: University of Illinois, 1975), p. 53.

each time a given story is re-read. The colloquy in "Margins," for example, between Edward, a white man, and Carl, his black friend, reveals the first time around a sizable number of the infinite, picky little differences—cultural, social, personal, historical, attitudinal—which prevent even the best-intentioned members of either race from really communicating with one another. But if re-read carefully several more times, the story reveals a good deal more of what Carl casually describes as "a kind of *merde-y* inner truth" about the chaos of human relationships in the jungle of modern civilization, and also about the extremely remote possibility of encountering in it any genuine love—except the eschatological variety which may, just possibly, exist "on the other side of Jordan."

The question of the ultimate appeal and worth of fictions like these done in the new mode is still moot. Are the stories of Barth, Barthelme, and the others, even at their best, an ephemeral fad, just a tissue of witty posturings with language for the titillation of sophisticates? Or do they lead to deeper insights, greater truths? Some critics argue that this fiction in the new mode lacks substance because it lacks characters like those of Faulkner, Welty, and Hemingway with whom readers can identify. There is possibly something valid in this argument, since it certainly seems easier to identify with Oates's young Connie or Taylor's Aunt Muncie than with Barthelme's Carl and Edward. But on the other hand, can we not respond joyfully to these "cheerful nihilists" once we catch on to what they are up to, once we discover that they are not only celebrating humanity's capacity to live—like Wallace Stevens's "Man on the Dump," surrounded by all the garbage of modern life—but even demonstrating that the garbage itself, the detritus, the *dreck,* can be aesthetically reassembled into eldless new forms through the agency of the artist's creative imagination? In any event, it is this sort of experimentalism that keeps the short story alive; for, like the drama of the absurd, it too is a living organism. Moreover, as Edward Albee has said concerning the avant-garde theatre, this mode of fiction can be fun: "it is free-swinging, bold, iconoclastic and often wildly, wildly funny. If you will approach it with childlike innocence—putting your standard responses aside, for they do not apply—if you will approach it on its own terms, I think you will be in for a liberating surprise."[8]

[8] *New York Times Magazine,* February 25, 1962, p. 66.

Richard Wright

1908 – 1960

It has been claimed that Richard Wright's *Native Son* (1940) inalterably changed the face of American literature. In this novel, Wright gave an account of being black in America that seared a shocking message on the consciousness, and conscience, of a nation. After *Native Son,* neither black nor white writers could ever approach their cultural sources or write about their own experiences in quite the same way again. In the creation of this novel's protagonist, the murderer/victim Bigger Thomas, Wright joined "the very small circle of major writers who have been able to create at least one character endowed with epic stature."[1]

Richard Wright once said that his early environment contained nothing more alien than literary self-expression. He was born on a farm near Natchez, Mississippi, in 1908. Because of his father's desertion of the family and, later, his mother's paralysis, Wright lived with various relatives in such places as Memphis, Tennessee; Elaine, Arkansas; and Jackson, Mississippi. At age fifteen, after his graduation from a "colored" high school, Wright left on his own for a menial job in Memphis, and from Memphis he migrated north to Chicago, where he worked a variety of jobs. In Chicago, he continued the ambitious reading he had begun in Memphis and began actively to pursue his goal of becoming a writer. While there he became a member of the Communist party, an affiliation he later renounced, but party publication work carried him to New York in 1937. Wright's nearly ten years in New York were his most productive and impressive as a

[1]Blyden Jackson, "Richard Wright," in *The History of Southern Literature* (Baton Rouge: Louisiana State University Press, 1985), p. 446.

writer. When he moved to Paris in 1947 he had an international reputation. Never again residing in the United States, he suffered a fatal heart attack in Paris in 1960.

Wright's later novels, such as *The Outsider* (1953), *Savage Holiday* (1954), and *The Long Dream* (1958), did not measure up to his achievement in *Native Son.* Similarly, in power and influence his later works of nonfiction, books with such titles as *Black Power* (1952) and *White Man, Listen!* (1957), fall far short of his autobiographical *Black Boy* (1945). Wright's two collections of short fiction, however, books that bracket his literary career—*Uncle Tom's Children* (1938, 1940) and *Eight Men* (1961)—provide repeated examples of his finest literary efforts. In "Big Black Good Man," from *Eight Men,* are a mature command of the short story form and a sardonic humor that is the result of understanding replacing hatred. In a number of both superficial and deeper thematic aspects, this story can be engagingly compared with Stephen Crane's "The Blue Hotel."

Big Black Good Man

Through the open window Olaf Jenson could smell the sea and hear the occasional foghorn of a freighter; outside, rain pelted down through an August night, drumming softly upon the pavements of Copenhagen, inducing drowsiness, bringing dreamy memory, relaxing the tired muscles of his work-wracked body. He sat slumped in a swivel chair with his legs outstretched and his feet propped atop an edge of his desk. An inch of white ash tipped the end of his brown cigar and now and then he inserted the end of the stogie into his mouth and drew gently upon it, letting wisps of blue smoke eddy from the corners of his wide, thin lips. The watery gray irises behind the thick lenses of his eyeglasses gave him a look of abstraction, of absentmindedness, of an almost genial idiocy.

He sighed, reached for his half-empty bottle of beer, and drained it into his glass and downed it with a long slow gulp, then licked his lips. Replacing the cigar, he slapped his right palm against his thigh and said half aloud:

"Well, I'll be sixty tomorrow. I'm not rich, but I'm not poor either . . . Really, I can't complain. Got good health. Traveled all over the world and had my share of the girls when I was young . . . And my Karen's a good wife. I own my home. Got no debts. And I love digging in my garden in the spring . . . Grew the biggest carrots of anybody last year. Ain't saved much money, but what the hell . . . Money ain't everything. Got a good job. Night portering ain't too bad." He shook his head and yawned. "Karen and I could of had some children, though. Would of been good company . . . 'Specially for Karen. And I could of taught 'em languages . . . English, French, German, Danish, Dutch, Swedish, Norwegian, and Spanish . . . " He took the cigar out of his mouth and eyed the white ash critically. "Hell of a lot of good language learning did me . . . Never got anything out of it. But those ten years in New York were fun . . . Maybe I could of got rich if I'd stayed in America . . . Maybe. But I'm satisfied. You can't have everything."

Behind him the office door opened and a young man, a medical student occupying room number nine, entered.

"Good evening," the student said.

"Good evening," Olaf said, turning.

The student went to the keyboard and took hold of the round, brown knob that anchored his key.

"Rain, rain, rain," the student said.

"That's Denmark for you," Olaf smiled at him.

"This dampness keeps me clogged up like a drainpipe," the student complained.

"That's Denmark for you," Olaf repeated with a smile.

"Good night," the student said.

"Good night, son," Olaf sighed, watching the door close.

Well, my tenants are my children, Olaf told himself. Almost all of his children were in their rooms now . . . Only seventy-two and forty-four were missing . . . Seventy-two might've gone to Sweden . . . And forty-four was maybe staying at his girl's place tonight, like he sometimes did . . . He studied the pear-shaped blobs of hard rubber, reddish brown like ripe fruit, that hung from the keyboard, then glanced at his watch. Only room thirty, eighty-one, and one hundred and one were empty . . . And it was almost midnight. In a few moments he could take a nap. Nobody hardly ever came looking for accommodations after midnight, unless a stray freighter came in, bringing thirsty, women-hungry sailors. Olaf chuckled softly. Why in hell was I ever a sailor? The whole time I was at sea I was thinking and dreaming about women. Then why didn't I stay on land where women could be had? Hunh? Sailors are crazy . . .

But he liked sailors. They reminded him of his youth, and there was something so direct, simple, and childlike about them. They always said straight out what they wanted, and what they wanted was almost always women and whisky . . . "Well, there's no harm in that . . . Nothing could be more natural," Olaf sighed, looking thirstily at his empty beer bottle. No; he'd not drink any more tonight; he'd had enough; he'd go to sleep . . .

He was bending forward and loosening his shoelaces when he heard the office door crack open. He lifted his eyes, then sucked in his breath. He did not straighten; he just stared up and around at the huge black thing that filled the doorway. His reflexes refused to function; it was not fear; it was just simple astonishment. He was staring at the biggest, strangest, and blackest man he'd ever seen in all his life.

"Good evening," the black giant said in a voice that filled the small office. "Say, you got a room?"

Olaf sat up slowly, not to answer but to look at this brooding black vision; it towered darkly some six and a half feet into the air, almost touching the ceiling, and its skin was so black that it had a bluish tint. And the sheer bulk of the man! . . . His chest bulged like a barrel; his rocklike and humped shoulders hinted of mountain ridges; the stomach ballooned like a threatening stone; and the legs were like telephone poles . . . The big black cloud of a man now lumbered into the office, bending to get its buffalolike head under the door frame, then advanced slowly upon Olaf, like a stormy sky descending.

"You got a room?" the big black man asked again in a resounding voice.

Olaf now noticed that the ebony giant was well dressed, carried a wonderful new suitcase, and wore black shoes that gleamed despite the raindrops that peppered their toes.

"You're American?" Olaf asked him.

"Yeah, man; sure," the black giant answered.

"Sailor?"

"Yeah. American Continental Lines."

Olaf had not answered the black man's question. It was not that the hotel did not admit men of color; Olaf took in all comers—blacks, yellows, whites, and browns . . . To Olaf, men were men, and in his day, he'd worked and eaten and slept and fought with all kinds of men. But this particular black man . . . Well, he didn't seem human. Too big, too black, too loud, too direct, and probably too violent to boot . . . Olaf's five feet seven inches scarcely reached the black giant's shoulder and his frail body weighed less, perhaps, than one of the man's gigantic legs . . . There was something about the man's intense blackness and ungainly bigness that frightened and insulted Olaf; he felt as though this man had come here expressly to remind him how puny, how tiny, and how weak and how white he was. Olaf knew, while registering his reactions, that he was being irrational and foolish; yet, for the first time in his life, he was emotionally determined to refuse a man a room solely on the basis of the man's size and color . . . Olaf's lips parted as he groped for the right words in which to couch his refusal, but the black giant bent forward and boomed:

"I asked you if you got a room. I got to put up somewhere tonight, man."

"Yes, we got a room," Olaf murmured.

And at once he was ashamed and confused. Sheer fear had made him yield. And he seethed against himself for his involuntary weakness. Well, he'd look over his book and pretend that he'd made a mistake; he'd tell this hunk of blackness that there was really no free room in the hotel, and that he was so sorry . . . Then, just as he took out the hotel register to make believe that he was poring over it, a thick roll of American bank notes, crisp and green, was thrust under his nose.

"Keep this for me, will you?" the black giant commanded. "Cause I'm gonna get drunk tonight and I don't wanna lose it."

Olaf stared at the roll; it was huge, in denominations of fifties and hundreds. Olaf's eyes widened.

"How much is there?" he asked.

"Two thousand six hundred," the giant said. "Just put it into an envelope and write 'Jim' on it and lock it in your safe, hunh?"

The black mass of man had spoken in a manner that indicated that it was taking it for granted that Olaf would obey. Olaf was licked. Resentment clogged the pores of his wrinkled white skin. His hands trembled as he picked up the money. No; he couldn't refuse this man . . . The impulse to deny him was strong, but each time he was about to act upon it something thwarted him, made him shy off. He clutched about desperately for an idea. Oh yes, he could say that if he planned to stay for only one night, then he could not have the room, for it was against the policy of the hotel to rent rooms for only one night . . .

'How long are you staying? Just tonight?" Olaf asked.

"Naw. I'll be here for five or six days, I reckon," the giant answered offhandedly.

"You take room number thirty," Olaf heard himself saying. "It's forty kroner a day."

"That's all right with me," the giant said.

With slow, stiff movements, Olaf put the money in the safe and then turned and stared helplessly up into the living, breathing blackness looming above him. Suddenly he became conscious of the outstretched palm of the black giant; he was silently demanding the key to the room. His eyes downcast, Olaf surrendered the key, marveling at the black man's tremendous hands . . . He could kill me with one blow, Olaf told himself in fear.

Feeling himself beaten, Olaf reached for the suitcase, but the black hand of the giant whisked it out of his grasp.

"That's too heavy for you, big boy; I'll take it," the giant said.

Olaf let him. He thinks I'm nothing . . . He led the way down the corridor, sensing the giant's lumbering presence behind him. Olaf opened the door of number thirty and stood politely to one side, allowing the black giant to enter. At once the room seemed like a doll's house, so dwarfed and filled and tiny it was with a great living blackness . . . Flinging his suitcase upon a chair, the giant turned. The two men looked directly at each other now. Olaf saw that the giant's eyes were tiny and red, buried, it seemed, in muscle and fat. Black cheeks spread, flat and broad, topping the wide and flaring nostrils. The mouth was the biggest that Olaf had ever seen on a human face; the lips were thick, pursed, parted, showing snow-white teeth. The black neck was like a bull's . . . The giant advanced upon Olaf and stood over him.

"I want a bottle of whisky and a woman," he said. "Can you fix me up?"

"Yes," Olaf whispered, wild with anger and insult.

But what was he angry about? He'd had requests like this every night from all sorts of men and he was used to fulfilling them; he was a night porter in a cheap, water-front Copenhagen hotel that catered to sailors and students. Yes, men needed women, but this man, Olaf felt, ought to have a special sort of woman. He felt a deep and strange reluctance to phone any of the women whom he habitually sent to men. Yet he had promised. Could he lie and say that none was available? No. That sounded too fishy. The black giant sat upon the bed, staring straight before him. Olaf moved about quickly, pulling down the window shades, taking the pink coverlet off the bed, nudging the giant with his elbow to make him move as he did so . . . That's the way to treat 'im . . . Show 'im I ain't scared of 'im . . . But he was still seeking for an excuse to refuse. And he could think of nothing. He felt hypnotized, mentally immobilized. He stood hesitantly at the door.

"You send the whisky and the woman quick, pal?" the black giant asked, rousing himself from a brooding stare.

"Yes," Olaf grunted, shutting the door.

Goddamn, Olaf sighed. He sat in his office at his desk before the phone. Why did *he* have to come here? . . . I'm not prejudiced . . . No, not at all . . . But . . . He couldn't think any more. God oughtn't make men as big and black as that . . . But what the hell was he worrying about? He'd sent women of all races to men of all colors . . . So why not a woman to the black giant? Oh, only if the man were small, brown, and intelligent-looking . . . Olaf felt trapped.

With a reflex movement of his hand, he picked up the phone and dialed Lena. She was big and strong and always cut him in for fifteen percent instead of the usual ten percent. Lena had four small children to feed and clothe. Lena was willing; she was, she said, coming over right now. She didn't give a good goddamn about how big and black the man was . . .

"Why you ask me that?" Lena wanted to know over the phone. "You never asked that before . . . "

"But this one is *big,*" Olaf found himself saying.

"He's just a man," Lena told him, her voice singing stridently, laughing over the wire. "You just leave that to me. You don't have to do anything. *I'll* handle 'im."

Lena had a key to the hotel door downstairs, but tonight Olaf stayed awake. He wanted to see her. Why? He didn't know. He stretched out on the sofa in his office, but sleep was far from him. When Lena arrived, he told her again how big and black the man was.

"You told me that over the phone," Lena reminded him.

Olaf said nothing. Lena flounced off on her errand of mercy. Olaf shut the office door, then opened it and left it ajar. But why? He didn't know. He lay upon the sofa and stared at the ceiling. He glanced at his watch; it was almost two o'clock . . . She's staying in there a long time . . . Ah, God, but he could do with a drink . . . Why was he so damned worked up and nervous about a nigger and a white whore? . . . He'd never been so upset in all his life. Before he knew it, he had drifted off to sleep. Then he heard the office door swinging creakingly open on its rusty hinges. Lena stood in it, grim and businesslike, her face scrubbed free of powder and rouge. Olaf scrambled to his feet, adjusting his eyeglasses, blinking.

"How was it?" he asked her in a confidential whisper.

Lena's eyes blazed.

"What the hell's that to you?" she snapped. "There's your cut," she said, flinging him his money, tossing it upon the covers of the sofa. "You're sure nosy tonight. You wanna take over my work?"

Olaf's pasty cheeks burned red.

"You go to hell," he said, slamming the door.

"I'll meet you there!" Lena's shouting voice reached him dimly.

He was being a fool; there was no doubt about it. But, try as he might, he could not shake off a primitive hate for that black mountain of energy, of muscle, of bone; he envied the easy manner in which it moved with such a creeping and powerful motion; he winced at the booming and commanding voice that came to him when the tiny little eyes were not even looking at him; he shivered at the sight of those vast and clawlike hands that seemed always to hint of death . . .

Olaf kept his counsel. He never spoke to Karen about the sordid doings at the hotel. Such things were not for women like Karen. He knew instinctively that Karen would have been amazed had he told her that he was worried sick about a nigger and a blonde whore . . . No; he couldn't talk to anybody about it, not even the hard-bitten old bitch who owned the hotel. She was concerned only about money; she didn't give a damn about how big and how black a client was as long as he paid his room rent.

Next evening, when Olaf arrived for duty, there was no sight or sound of the black giant. A little later after one o'clock in the morning he appeared, left his key, and went out wordlessly. A few moments past two the giant returned, took his key from the board, and paused.

"I want that Lena again tonight. And another bottle of whisky," he said boomingly.

"I'll call her and see if she's in," Olaf said.

"Do that," the black giant said and was gone.

He thinks he's God, Olaf fumed. He picked up the phone and ordered Lena and a bottle of whisky, and there was a taste of ashes in his mouth. On the third night came the same request: Lena and whisky. When the black giant appeared on the fifth night, Olaf was about to make a sarcastic remark to the effect that maybe he ought to marry Lena, but he checked it in time . . . after all, he could kill me with one hand, he told himself.

Olaf was nervous and angry with himself for being nervous. Other black sailors came and asked for girls and Olaf sent them, but with none of the fear and loathing that he sent Lena and a bottle of whisky to the giant . . . All right, the black giant's stay was almost up. He'd said that he was staying for five or six nights; tomorrow night was the sixth night and that ought to be the end of this nameless terror.

On the sixth night Olaf sat in his swivel chair with his bottle of beer and waited, his teeth on edge, his fingers drumming the desk. But what the hell am I fretting for? . . . The hell with 'im . . . Olaf sat and dozed. Occasionally he'd awaken and listen to the foghorns of freighters sounding as ships came and went in the misty Copenhagen harbor. He was half asleep when he felt a rough hand on his shoulder. He blinked his eyes open. The giant, black and vast and powerful, all but blotted out his vision.

"What I owe you, man?" the giant demanded. "And I want my money."

"Sure," Olaf said, relieved, but filled as always with fear of this living wall of black flesh.

With fumbling hands, he made out the bill and received payment, then gave the giant his roll of money, laying it on the desk so as not to let his hands touch the flesh of the black mountain. Well, his ordeal was over. It was past two o'clock in the morning. Olaf even managed a wry smile and muttered a gutteral "Thanks" for the generous tip that the giant tossed him.

Then a strange tension entered the office. The office door was shut and Olaf was alone with the black mass of power, yearning for it to leave. But the black mass of power stood still, immobile, looking down at Olaf. And Olaf could not, for the life of him, guess at what was transpiring in that mysterious black mind. The two of them simply stared at each other for a full two minutes, the giant's tiny little beady eyes blinking slowly as they seemed to measure and search Olaf's face. Olaf's vision dimmed for a second as terror seized him and he could feel a flush of heat overspread his body. Then Olaf sucked in his breath as the devil of blackness commanded:

"Stand up!"

Olaf was paralyzed. Sweat broke on his face. His worst premonitions about this black beast were coming true. This evil blackness was about to attack him, maybe kill him . . . Slowly Olaf shook his head, his terror permitting him to breathe:

"What're you talking about?"

"Stand up, I say!" the black giant bellowed.

As though hypnotized, Olaf tried to rise; then he felt the black paw of the beast helping him roughly to his feet.

They stood an inch apart. Olaf's pasty-white features were glued to the giant's swollen black face. The ebony ensemble of eyes and nose and mouth and cheeks looked down at Olaf, silently; then, with a slow and deliberate movement of his gorillalike arms, he lifted his mammoth hands to Olaf's throat. Olaf had long known and felt that this dreadful moment was coming; he felt trapped in a nightmare. He could not move. He wanted to scream, but could find no words. His lips refused to open; his tongue felt icy and inert. Then he knew that his end had come when the giant's black fingers slowly, softly encircled his throat while a horrible grin of delight broke out on the sooty face . . . Olaf lost control of the reflexes of his body and he felt a hot stickiness flooding his underwear . . . He stared without breathing, gazing into the grinning blackness of the face that was bent over him, feeling the black fingers caressing his throat and waiting to feel the sharp, stinging ache and pain of the bones in his neck being snapped, crushed . . . He knew all along that I hated 'im . . . Yes, and now he's going to kill me for it, Olaf told himself with despair.

The black fingers still circled Olaf's neck, not closing, but gently massaging it, as it were, moving to and fro, while the obscene face grinned into his. Olaf could feel the giant's warm breath blowing on his eyelashes and he felt like a chicken about to have its neck wrung and its body tossed to flip and flap dyingly in the dust of the barnyard . . . Then suddenly the black giant withdrew his fingers from Olaf's neck and stepped back a pace, still grinning. Olaf sighed, trembling, his body seeming to shrink; he waited. Shame sheeted him for the hot wetness that was in his trousers. Oh, God, he's teasing me . . . He's showing me how easily he can kill me . . . He swallowed, waiting, his eyes stones of gray.

The giant's barrel-like chest gave forth a low, rumbling chuckle of delight.

"You laugh?" Olaf asked whimperingly.

"Sure I laugh," the giant shouted.

"Please don't hurt me," Olaf managed to say.

"I wouldn't hurt you, boy," the giant said in a tone of mockery. "So long."

And he was gone. Olaf fell limply into the swivel chair and fought off losing consciousness. Then he wept. He was showing me how easily he could kill me . . . He made me shake with terror and then laughed and left . . . Slowly, Olaf recovered, stood, then gave vent to a string of curses:

"Goddamn 'im! My gun's right there in the desk drawer; I should of shot 'im. Jesus, I hope the ship he's on sinks . . . I hope he drowns and the sharks eat 'im . . ."

Later, he thought of going to the police, but sheer shame kept him back; and, anyway, the giant was probably on board his ship by now. And he had to get home and clean himself. Oh, Lord, what could he tell Karen? Yes, he would say that his stomach had been upset . . . He'd change clothes and return to work. He phoned the hotel owner that he was ill and wanted an hour off; the old bitch said that she was coming right over and that poor Olaf could have the evening off.

Olaf went home and lied to Karen. Then he lay awake the rest of the night dreaming of revenge. He saw that freighter on which the giant was sailing; he saw it springing a dangerous leak and saw a torrent of sea water flooding, gushing into all the compartments of the ship until it found the bunk in which the black giant slept. Ah, yes, the foamy, surging waters would surprise that sleeping black bastard of a giant and he would drown, gasping and choking like a trapped rat, his tiny eyes bulging until they glittered red, the bitter water of the sea pounding his lungs until they ached and finally burst . . . The ship would sink slowly to the bottom of the cold, black, silent depths of the sea and a shark, a *white* one, would glide aimlessly about the shut portholes until it found an open one and it would slither inside and hose about until it found that swollen, rotting, stinking carcass of the black beast and it would then begin to nibble at the decomposing mass of tarlike flesh, eating the bones clean . . . Olaf always pictured the giant's bones as being jet black and shining.

Once or twice, during these fantasies of cannibalistic revenge, Olaf felt a little guilty about all the many innocent people, women and children, all white and blonde, who would have to go down into watery graves in order that that white shark could devour the evil giant's black flesh . . . But, despite feelings of remorse, the fantasy lived persistently on, and when Olaf found himself alone, it would crowd and cloud his mind to the exclusion of all else, affording him the only revenge he knew. To make me suffer just for the pleasure of it, he fumed. Just to show me how strong he was . . . Olaf learned how to hate, and got pleasure out of it.

Summer fled on wings of rain. Autumn flooded Denmark with color. Winter made rain and snow fall on Copenhagen. Finally spring came, bringing violets and roses. Olaf kept to his job. For many months he feared the return of the black giant. But when a year had passed and the giant had not put in an appearance, Olaf allowed his revenge fantasy to peter out, indulging in it only when recalling the shame that the black monster had made him feel.

Then one rainy August night, a year later, Olaf sat drowsing at his desk, his bottle of beer before him, tilting back in his swivel chair, his feet resting atop a corner of his desk, his mind mulling over the more pleasant aspects of his life. The office door cracked open. Olaf glanced boredly up and around. His heart jumped and skipped a beat. The black nightmare of terror and shame that he had hoped that he had lost forever was again upon him . . . Resplendently dressed, suitcase in hand, the black looming mountain filled the doorway. Olaf's thin lips parted and a silent moan, half a curse, escaped them.

"Hi," the black giant boomed from the doorway.

Olaf could not reply. But a sudden resolve swept him: this time he would even the score. If this black beast came within so much as three feet of him, he would snatch his gun out of the drawer and shoot him dead, so help him God . . .

"No rooms tonight," Olaf heard himself announcing in a determined voice.

The black giant grinned; it was the same internal grimace of delight and triumph that he had had when his damnable black fingers had been around his throat . . .

"Don't want no room tonight," the giant announced.

"Then what are you doing here?" Olaf asked in a loud but tremulous voice.

The giant swept toward Olaf and stood over him; and Olaf could not move, despite his oath to kill him . . .

"What do you want then?" Olaf demanded once more, ashamed that he could not lift his voice above a whisper.

The giant still grinned, then tossed what seemed the same suitcase upon Olaf's sofa and bent over it; he zippered it open with a sweep of his clawlike hand and rummaged in it, drawing forth a flat, gleaming white object done up in a glowing cellophane. Olaf watched with lowered lids, wondering what trick was now being played on him. Then, before he could defend himself, the giant had whirled and again long, black, snakelike fingers were encircling Olaf's throat . . . Olaf stiffened, his right hand clawing blindly for the drawer where the gun was kept. But the giant was quick.

"Wait," he bellowed, pushing Olaf back from the desk.

The giant turned quickly to the sofa and, still holding his fingers in a wide circle that seemed a noose for Olaf's neck, he inserted the rounded fingers into the top of the flat, gleaming object. Olaf had the drawer open and his sweaty fingers were now touching his gun, but something made him freeze. The flat, gleaming object was a shirt and the black giant's circled fingers were fitting themselves into its neck . . .

"A perfect fit!" the giant shouted.

Olaf stared, trying to understand. His fingers loosened about the gun. A mixture of a laugh and a curse struggled in him. He watched the giant plunge his hands into the suitcase and pull out other flat, gleaming shirts.

"One, two, three, four, five, six," the black giant intoned, his voice crisp and businesslike. "Six nylon shirts. And they're all yours. One shirt for each time Lena came . . . See, Daddy-O?"

The black, cupped hands, filled with billowing nylon whiteness, were extended under Olaf's nose. Olaf eased his damp fingers from his gun and pushed the drawer closed, staring at the shirts and then at the black giant's grinning face.

"Don't you like 'em?" the giant asked.

Olaf began to laugh hysterically, then suddenly he was crying, his eyes so flooded with tears that the pile of dazzling nylon looked like snow in the dead of winter. Was this true? Could he believe it? Maybe this too was a trick? But, no. There were six shirts, all nylon, and the black giant had had Lena six nights.

"What's the matter with you, Daddy-O?" the giant asked. "You blowing your top? Laughing and crying . . . "

Olaf swallowed, dabbed his withered fists at his dimmed eyes; then he realized that he had his glasses on. He took them off and dried his eyes and sat up. He sighed, the tension and shame and fear and haunting dread of his fantasy went from him, and he leaned limply back in his chair . . .

"Try one on," the giant ordered.

Olaf fumbled with the buttons of his shirt, let down his suspenders, and pulled the shirt off. He donned a gleaming nylon one and the giant began buttoning it for him.

"Perfect, Daddy-O," the giant said.

His spectacled face framed in sparkling nylon, Olaf sat with trembling lips. So he'd not been trying to kill me after all.

"You want Lena, don't you?" he asked the giant in a soft whisper. "But I don't know where she is. She never came back here after you left—"

"I know where Lena is," the giant told him. "We been writing to each other. I'm going to her house. And, Daddy-O, I'm late." The giant zippered the suitcase shut and stood a moment gazing down at Olaf, his tiny little red eyes blinking slowly. Then Olaf realized that there was a compassion in that stare that he had never seen before.

"And I thought you wanted to kill me," Olaf told him. "I was scared of you . . . "

"Me? Kill you?" the giant blinked. "When?"

"That night when you put your fingers about my throat—"

"What?" the giant asked, then roared with laughter. "Daddy-O, you're a funny little man. I wouldn't hurt you. I like you. You a *good* man. You helped me."

Olaf smiled, clutching the pile of nylon shirts in his arms.

"You're a good man too," Olaf murmured. Then loudly: "You're a big black good man."

"Daddy-O, you're crazy," the giant said.

He swept his suitcase from the sofa, spun on his heel, and was at the door in one stride.

"Thanks!" Olaf cried after him.

The black giant paused, turned his vast black head, and flashed a grin.

"Daddy-O, drop dead," he said and was gone.

Eudora Welty
1909 –

Long established in the front rank of American story-writers and novelists, Eudora Welty uses her native state of Mississippi almost exclusively as the setting of her fiction. Her reasons for limiting her work to a restricted locale, however, are quite different from those of a "local colorist." "It is both natural and sensible," she remarked in an essay ("Place in Fiction," *South Atlantic Quarterly,* 1956), "that the place where we have our roots should become the setting, the first and primary proving ground, of our fiction." Thus, by focusing upon the life of people she knows best, she can more concretely dramatize the concerns and problems of human beings everywhere so that her work, despite its strongly localized character, transcends narrow classification as "regional."

Welty was born in Jackson, Mississippi, in 1909, and except for brief periods she has lived there throughout her career. After graduating from Central High School in Jackson, she attended Mississippi State College for Women for two years and then transferred to the University of Wisconsin, where she completed her B.A. degree in 1929. She next studied advertising at the Columbia University School of Business for a year, but returned to Jackson in 1931, working for a number of years as a copywriter for a local radio station, doing free-lance writing for Jackson newspapers, and writing a society column for the Memphis *Commercial Appeal.* Still another job, that of publicity agent for the W.P.A., required travel throughout Mississippi and resulted in her acquaintance with the prototypes of the diverse characters she would soon be depicting in her fiction. In 1936, she published her first story in *Manuscript,* and the following year her stories began appearing in the *Southern Review,* then edited by

Cleanth Brooks and Robert Penn Warren, who encouraged her in her career. Within a few years, she was reaching a wider audience through such periodicals as *Harper's Bazaar, Scholastic,* and the *Atlantic Monthly.* Her first collection of stories, *A Curtain of Green,* appeared in 1941. It was followed by The *Wide Net and Other Stories* (1943), *The Golden Apples* (1949)—a book of connected stories—and *The Bride of Innisfallen* (1955). In the meantime, she also published three novels: *The Robber Bridegroom* (1942), *Delta Wedding* (1946), and *The Ponder Heart* (1954). Later, she was primarily engaged in writing novels rather than short stories and published two highly successful ones, *Losing Battles* (1970) and *The Optimist's Daughter* (1972), which won the Pulitzer Prize in 1973. Her most recent books are *The Eye of the Story* (1978), *Collected Stories of Eudora Welty* (1980), and the autobiographical *One Writer's Beginnings* (1984). Among the other awards Welty's fiction has brought her are four O. Henry Memorial Prize Awards, two Guggenheim Fellowships, and two awards from the American Academy of Arts and Letters.

In an essay, "How I Write," Welty remarked that stories have their origin in the "lyrical impulse of the mind—the impulse to praise, to love, to call up, to prophesy," and in another essay, "The Reading and Writing of Stories," she defined form in the short story as "beauty of organization," one of its prominent manifestations being the "sensory impressions" the story contains. "Livvie" is remarkable both for its lyricism and its sensory impressions, which consist of images of angularity, balance, and rest contrasted with ones of roundness, circularity, and action. These images support the polarities of age-youth, winter-spring, death-life, restraint-freedom, and so on, which stand at the thematic center of the story and govern its basic structure.

Livvie

Solomon carried Livvie twenty-one miles away from her home when he married her. He carried her away up on the Old Natchez Trace into the deep country to live in his house. She was sixteen—an only girl, then. Once people said he thought nobody would ever come along there. He told her himself that it had been a long time, and a day she did not know about, since that road was a traveled road with *people* coming and going. He was good to her, but he kept her in the house. She had not thought that she could not get back. Where she came from, people said an old man did not want anybody in the world to ever find his wife, for fear they would steal her back from him. Solomon asked her before he took her, "Would she be happy?"—very dignified, for he was a colored man that owned his land and had it written down in the courthouse; and she said, "Yes, sir," since he was an old man and she was young and just listened and answered. He asked her, if she was choosing winter, would she pine for spring, and she said, "No indeed." Whatever she said, always, was because he was an old man . . . while nine years went by. All the time, he got old, and he got so old he gave out. At least he slept the whole day in bed, and she was young still.

It was a nice house, inside and outside both. In the first place, it had three rooms. The front room was papered in holly paper, with green palmettos from the swamp spaced at careful intervals over the walls. There was fresh newspaper cut with fancy borders on the mantel-shelf, on which were propped photographs of old or very young men printed in faint yellow—Solomon's people. Solomon had a houseful of furniture. There was a double settee, a tall scrolled rocker and an organ in the front room, all around a three-legged table with a pink marble top, on which was set a lamp with three gold feet, besides a jelly glass with pretty hen feathers in it. Behind the front room, the other room had the bright iron bed with the polished knobs like a throne, in which Solomon slept all day. There were snow-white curtains of wiry lace at the window, and a lace bed-spread belonged on the bed. But what old Solomon slept so sound under was a big feather-stitched piece-quilt in the pattern "Trip Around the World," which had twenty-one different colors, four hundred and forty pieces, and a thousand yards of thread, and that was what

Solomon's mother made in her life and old age. There was a table holding the Bible, and a trunk with a key. On the wall were two calendars, and a diploma from somewhere in Solomon's family, and under that Livvie's one possession was nailed, a picture of the little white baby of the family she worked for, back in Natchez before she was married. Going through that room and on to the kitchen, there was a big wood stove and a big round table always with a wet top and with the knives and forks in one jelly glass and the spoons in another, and a cut-glass vinegar bottle between, and going out from those, many shallow dishes of pickled peaches, fig preserves, watermelon pickles and blackberry jam always sitting there. The churn sat in the sun, the doors of the safe were always both shut, and there were four baited mouse-traps in the kitchen, one in every corner.

The outside of Solomon's house looked nice. It was not painted, but across the porch was an even balance. On one side there was one easy chair with high springs, looking out, and a fern basket hanging over it from the ceiling, and a dishpan of zinnia seedlings growing at its foot on the floor. By the door was a plow-wheel, just a pretty iron circle, nailed up on one wall and a square mirror on the other, a turquoise-blue comb stuck up in the frame, with the wash stand beneath it. On the door was a wooden knob with a pearl in the end, and Solomon's black hat hung on that, if he was in the house.

Out front was a clean dirt yard with every vestige of grass patiently uprooted and the ground scarred in deep whorls from the strike of Livvie's broom. Rose bushes with tiny blood-red roses blooming every month grew in threes on either side of the steps. On one side was a peach tree, on the other a pomegranate. Then coming around up the path from the deep cut of the Natchez Trace below was a line of bare crape-myrtle trees with every branch of them ending in a colored bottle, green or blue. There was no word that fell from Solomon's lips to say what they were for, but Livvie knew that there could be a spell put in trees, and she was familiar from the time she was born with the way bottle trees kept evil spirits from coming into the house—by luring them inside the colored bottles, where they cannot get out again. Solomon had made the bottle trees with his own hands over the nine years, in labor amounting to about a tree a year, and without a sign that he had any uneasiness in his heart, for he took as much pride in his precautions against spirits coming in the house as he took in the house, and sometimes in the sun the bottle trees looked prettier than the house did.

It was a nice house. It was in a place where the days would go by and surprise anyone that they were over. The lamplight and the firelight would shine out the door after dark, over the still and breathing country, lighting the roses and the bottle trees, and all was quiet there.

But there was nobody, nobody at all, not even a white person. And if there had been anybody, Solomon would not have let Livvie look at them, just as he would not let her look at a field hand, or a field hand look at her. There was no house near, except for the cabins of the tenants that were forbidden to her, and there was no house as far as she had been, stealing away down the still, deep Trace. She felt as if she waded a river when she went, for the dead leaves on the ground reached as high as her knees, and when she was all scratched and bleeding she said it was not a road that went anywhere. One day, climbing up the high bank, she had found a graveyard without a church, with ribbon-grass growing about the foot of an angel (she had climbed up because she thought she saw angel wings), and in the sun, trees shining like burning flames through the great caterpillar nets which enclosed them. Scarey thistles stood looking like the prophets in the Bible in Solomon's house. Indian paint brushes grew over her head, and the mourning dove made the only sound in the world. Oh for a stirring of the leaves, and a breaking of the nets! But not by a ghost, prayed Livvie, jumping down the bank. After Solomon took to his bed, she never went out, except one more time.

Livvie knew she made a nice girl to wait on anybody. She fixed things to eat on a tray like a surprise. She could keep from singing when she ironed, and to sit by a bed and fan away the flies, she could be so still she could not hear herself breathe. She could clean up the house and never drop a thing, and wash the dishes without a sound, and she would step outside to churn, for churning sounded too sad to her, like sobbing, and if it made her home-sick and not Solomon, she did not think of that.

But Solomon scarcely opened his eyes to see her, and scarcely tasted his food. He was not sick or paralyzed or in any pain that he mentioned, but he was surely wearing out in the body, and no matter what nice hot thing Livvie would bring him to taste, he would only look at it now, as if he were past seeing how he could add anything more to himself. Before she could beg him, he would go fast asleep. She could not surprise him any more, if he would not taste, and she was afraid that he was never in the world going to taste another thing she brought him—and so how could he last?

But one morning it was breakfast time and she cooked his eggs and grits, carried them in on a tray, and called his name. He was sound asleep. He lay in a dignified way with his watch beside him, on his back in the middle of the bed. One hand drew the quilt up high, though it was the first day of spring. Through the wide lace curtains a little puffy wind was blowing as if it came from round cheeks. All night the frogs had sung out in the swamp, like a commotion in the room, and he had not stirred, though she lay wide awake and saying "Shh, frogs!" for fear he would mind them.

He looked as if he would like to sleep a little longer, and so she put back the tray and waited a little. When she tiptoed and stayed so quiet, she surrounded herself with a little reverie, and sometimes it seemed to her when she was so stealthy that the quiet she kept was for a sleeping baby, and that she had a baby and was its mother. When she stood at Solomon's bed and looked down at him, she would be thinking, "He sleeps so well," and she would hate to wake him up. And in some other way, too, she was afraid to wake him up because even in his sleep he seemed to be such a strict man.

Of course, nailed to the wall over the bed—only she would forget who it was—there was a picture of him when he was young. Then he had a fan of hair over his forehead like a king's crown. Now his hair lay down on his head, the spring had gone out of it. Solomon had a lightish face, with eyebrows scattered but rugged, the way privet grows, strong eyes, with second sight, a strict mouth, and a little gold smile. This was the way he looked in his clothes, but in bed in the daytime he looked like a different and smaller man, even when he was wide awake, and holding the Bible. He looked like somebody kin to himself. And then sometimes when he lay in sleep and she stood fanning the flies away, and the light came in, his face was like new, so smooth and clear that it was like a glass of jelly held to the window, and she could almost look through his forehead and see what he thought.

She fanned him and at length he opened his eyes and spoke her name, but he would not taste the nice eggs she had kept warm under a pan.

Back in the kitchen she ate heartily, his breakfast and hers, and looked out the open door at what went on. The whole day, and the whole night before, she had felt the stir of spring close to her. It was as present in the house as a young man would be. The moon was in the last quarter and outside they were turning the sod and planting peas and beans. Up and down the red fields, over which smoke from the brush-burning hung showing like a little skirt of sky, a white horse and a white mule pulled the plow. At intervals hoarse shouts came through the air and roused her as if she dozed neglectfully in the shade, and they were telling her, "Jump up!" She could see how over each ribbon of field were moving men and girls, on foot and mounted on mules, with hats set on their heads and bright with tall hoes and forks as if they carried streamers on them and were going to some place on a journey—and how as if at a signal now and then they would all start at once shouting, hollering, cajoling, calling and answering back, running, being leaped on and breaking away, flinging to earth with a shout and lying motionless in the trance of twelve o'clock. The old women came out of the cabins and brought them the food they had ready for them, and then all worked together, spread evenly out. The little children came too, like a bouncing stream overflowing the fields, and set upon the men, the women, the dogs, the rushing birds, and the wave-like rows of earth, their little voices almost too high to be heard. In the middle distance like some white and gold towers were the haystacks, with black cows coming around to eat their edges. High above everything, the wheel of fields, house, and cabins, and the deep road surrounding like a moat to keep them in, was the turning sky, blue with long, far-flung white mare's-tail clouds, serene and still as high flames. And sound asleep while all this went around him that was his, Solomon was like a little still spot in the middle.

Even in the house the earth was sweet to breathe. Solomon had never let Livvie go any farther than the chicken house and the well. But what if she would walk now into the heart of the fields and take a hoe and work until she fell stretched out and drained with her efforts, like other girls, and laid her cheek against the laid-open earth, and shamed the old man with her humbleness and delight? To shame him! A cruel wish could come in uninvited and so fast while she looked out the back door. She washed the dishes and scrubbed the table. She could hear the cries of the little lambs. Her mother, that she had not seen since her wedding day, had said one time, "I rather a man be anything, than a woman be mean."

So all morning she kept tasting the chicken broth on the stove, and when it was right she poured off a nice cup-ful. She carried it in to Solomon, and there he lay having a dream. Now what did he dream about? For she saw him sigh gently as if not to disturb some whole thing he held round in his mind, like a fresh egg. So even an old man dreamed about something pretty. Did he dream of her, while his eyes were shut and sunken, and his small hand with the wedding ring curled close in sleep around the quilt? He might be dreaming of what time it was, for even through his sleep he kept track of it like a clock, and knew how much of it went by, and waked up knowing where the hands were even before he consulted the silver watch that he never let go. He would sleep with the watch in his palm, and even holding it to his cheek like a child that loves a plaything. Or he might dream of journeys and travels on a steamboat to Natchez. Yet she thought he dreamed of her; but even while she scrutinized him, the rods of the foot of the bed seemed to rise up like a rail fence between them, and she could see that people never could be sure of anything as long as one of them was asleep and the other awake. To look at him dreaming of her when he might be going to die frightened her a little, as if he might carry her with him that way, and she wanted to run out of the room. She took hold of the bed and held on, and Solomon opened his eyes and called her name, but he did not want anything. He would not taste the good broth.

Just a little after that, as she was taking up the ashes in the front room for the last time in the year, she heard a sound. It was somebody coming. She pulled the curtains together and looked through the slit.

Coming up the path under the bottle trees was a white lady. At first she looked young, but then she looked old. Marvelous to see, a little car stood steaming like a kettle out in the field-track—it had come without a road.

Livvie stood listening to the long, repeated knockings at the door, and after a while she opened it just a little. The lady came in through the crack, though she was more than middle-sized and wore a big hat.

"My name is Miss Baby Marie," she said.

Livvie gazed respectfully at the lady and at the little suitcase she was holding close to her by the handle until the proper moment. The lady's eyes were running over the room, from palmetto to palmetto, but she was saying, "I live at home . . . out from Natchez . . . and get out and show these pretty cosmetic things to the white people and the colored people both . . . all around . . . years and years . . . Both shades of powder and rouge . . . It's the kind of work a girl can do and not go clear 'way from home . . ." And the harder she looked, the more she talked. Suddenly she turned up her nose and said, "It is not Christian or sanitary to put feathers in a vase," and then she took a gold key out of the front of her dress and began unlocking the locks on her suitcase. Her face drew the light, the way it was covered with intense white and red, with a little patty-cake of white between the wrinkles by her upper lip. Little red tassels of hair bobbed under the rusty wires of her picture-hat, as with an air of triumph and secrecy she now drew open her little suitcase and brought out bottle after bottle and jar after jar, which she put down on the table, the mantel-piece, the settee, and the organ.

"Did you ever see so many cosmetics in your life?" cried Miss Baby Marie.

"No'm," Livvie tried to say, but the cat had her tongue.

"Have you ever applied cosmetics?" asked Miss Baby Marie next.

"No'm," Livvie tried to say.

"Then look!" she said, and pulling out the last thing of all, "Try this!" she said. And in her hand was unclenched a golden lipstick which popped open like magic. A fragrance came out of it like incense, and Livvie cried out suddenly, "Chinaberry flowers!"

Her hand took the lipstick, and in an instant she was carried away in the air through the spring, and looking down with a half-drowsy smile from a purple cloud she saw from above a chinaberry tree, dark and smooth and neatly leaved, neat as a guinea hen in the doorway, and there was her home that she had left. On one side of the tree was her mama holding up her heavy apron, and she could see it was loaded with ripe figs, and on the other side was her papa holding a fish-pole over the pond, and she could see it transparently, the little clear fishes swimming up to the brim.

"Oh, no, not chinaberry flowers—secret ingredients," said Miss Baby Marie. "My cosmetics have secret ingredients—not chinaberry flowers."

"It's purple," Livvie breathed, and Miss Baby Marie said, "Use it freely. Rub it on."

Livvie tiptoed out to the wash stand on the front porch and before the mirror put the paint on her mouth. In the wavery surface her face danced before her like a flame. Miss Baby Marie followed her out, took a look at what she had done and said, "That's it."

Livvie tried to say "Thank you" without moving her parted lips where the paint lay so new.

By now Miss Baby Marie stood behind Livvie and looked in the mirror over her shoulder, twisting up the tassels of her hair. "The lipstick I can let you have for only two dollars," she said, close to her neck.

"Lady, but I don't have no money, never did have," said Livvie.

"Oh, but you don't pay the first time. I make another trip, that's the way I do. I come back again—later."

"Oh," said Livvie, pretending she understood everything so as to please the lady.

"But if you don't take it now, this may be the last time I'll call at your house," said Miss Baby Marie sharply. "It's far away from anywhere, I'll tell you that. You don't live close to anywhere."

"Yes'm. My husband, he keep the *money,*" said Livvie, trembling. "He is strict as he can be. He don't know *you* walk in here—Miss Baby Marie!"

"Where is he?"

"Right now, he in yonder sound asleep, an old man. I wouldn't ever ask him for anything."

Miss Baby Marie took back the lipstick and packed it up. She gathered up the jars for both black and white and got them all inside the suitcase, with the same little fuss of triumph with which she had brought them out. She started away.

"Goodbye," she said, making herself look grand from the back, but at the last minute she turned around in the door. Her old hat wobbled as she whispered, "Let me see your husband."

Livvie obediently went on tiptoe and opened the door to the other room. Miss Baby Marie came behind her and rose on her toes and looked in.

"My, what a little tiny old, old man!" she whispered, clasping her hands and shaking her head over them. "What a beautiful quilt! What a tiny old, old man!"

"He can sleep like that all day," whispered Livvie proudly.

They looked at him awhile so fast asleep, and then all at once they looked at each other. Somehow that was as if they had a secret, for he had never stirred. Livvie then politely, but all at once, closed the door.

"Well! I'd certainly like to leave you with a lipstick!" said Miss Baby Marie vivaciously. She smiled in the door.

"Lady, but I told you I don't have no money, and never did have."

"And never will?" In the air and all around, like a bright halo around the white lady's nodding head, it was a true spring day.

"Would you take eggs, lady?" asked Livvie softly.

"No, I have plenty of eggs—plenty," said Miss Baby Marie.

"I still don't have no money," said Livvie, and Miss Baby Marie took her suitcase and went on somewhere else.

Livvie stood watching her go and all the time she felt her heart beating in her left side. She touched the place with her hand. It seemed as if her heart beat and her whole face flamed from the pulsing color of her lips. She went to sit by Solomon and when he opened his eyes he could not see a change in her. "He's fixin' to die," she said inside. That was the secret. That was when she went out of the house for a little breath of air.

She went down the path and down the Natchez Trace a way, and she did not know how far she had gone, but it was not far, when she saw a sight. It was a man, looking like a vision—she standing on one side of the Old Natchez Trace and he standing on the other.

As soon as this man caught sight of her, he began to look himself over. Starting at the bottom with his pointed shoes, he began to look up, lifting his peg-top pants the higher to see fully his bright socks. His coat long and wide and leaf-green he opened like doors to see his high-up tawny pants and his pants he smoothed downward from the points of his collar, and he wore a luminous baby-pink satin shirt. At the end, he reached gently above his wide platter-shaped round hat, the color of a plum, and one finger touched at the feather, emerald green, blowing in the spring winds.

No matter how she looked, she could never look so fine as he did, and she was not sorry for that, she was pleased.

He took three jumps, one down and two up, and was by her side.

"My name is Cash," he said.

He had a guinea pig in his pocket. They began to walk along. She stared on and on at him, as if he were doing some daring spectacular thing, instead of just walking beside her. It was not simply the city way he was dressed that made her look at him and see hope in its insolence looking back. It was not only the way he moved along kicking the flowers as if he could break through everything in the way and destroy anything in the world, that made her eyes grow bright. It might be, if he had not appeared the way he did appear that day she would never have looked so closely at him, but the time people come makes a difference.

They walked through the still leaves of the Natchez Trace, the light and the shade falling through trees about them, the white irises shining like candles on the banks and the new ferns shining like green stars up in the oak branches. They came out at Solomon's house bottle trees and all. Livvie stopped and hung her head.

Cash began whistling a little tune. She did not know what it was, but she had heard it before from a distance, and she had a revelation. Cash was a field hand. He was a transformed field hand. Cash belonged to Solomon. But he had stepped out of his overalls into this. There in front of Solomon's house he laughed. He had a round head, a round face, all of him was young, and he flung his head up, rolled it against the mare's tail sky in his round hat, and he could laugh just to see Solomon's house sitting there. Livvie looked at it, and there was Solomon's black hat hanging on the peg on the front door, the blackest thing in the world.

"I been to Natchez," Cash said, wagging his head around against the sky "*I* taken a trip, *I* ready for Easter!"

How was it possible to look so fine before the harvest? Cash must have stolen the money, stolen it from Solomon. He stood in the path and lifted his spread hand high and brought it down again and again in his laughter. He kicked up his heels. A little chill went through her. It was as if Cash was bringing that strong hand down to beat a drum or to rain blows upon a man, such an abandon and menace were in his laugh. Frowning, she went closer to him and his swinging arm drew her in at once and the fright was crushed from her body, as a little match-flame might be smothered out by what it lighted. She gathered the folds of his coat behind him and fastened her red lips to his mouth, and she was dazzled by herself then, the way he had been dazzled at himself to begin with.

In that instant she felt something that could not be told—that Solomon's death was at hand, that he was the same to her as if he were dead now. She cried out, and uttering little cries turned and ran for the house.

At once Cash was coming, following after, he was running behind her. He came close, and halfway up the path he laughed and passed her. He even picked up a stone and sailed it into the bottle trees. She put her hands over her head, and sounds clattered through the bottle trees like cries of outrage. Cash stamped and plunged zigzag up the front steps and in at the door.

When she got there, he had stuck his hands in his pockets and was turning slowly about in the front room. The little guinea pig peeped out. Around Cash, the pinned-up palmettos looked as if a lazy green monkey had walked up and down and around the walls leaving green prints of his hands and feet.

She got through the room and his hands were still in his pockets, and she fell upon the closed door to the other room and pushed it open. She ran to Solomon's bed, calling "Solomon! Solomon!" The little shape of the old man never moved at all, wrapped under the quilt as if it were winter still.

"Solomon!" she pulled the quilt away, but there was another one under that, and she fell on her knees beside him. He made no sound except a sigh, and then she could hear in the silence the light springy steps of Cash walking in the front room, and the ticking of Solomon's silver watch, which came from the bed. Old Solomon was far away in his sleep, his face looked small, relentless, and devout, as if he were walking somewhere where she could imagine the snow falling.

Then there was a noise like a hoof pawing the floor, and the door gave a creak, and Cash appeared beside her. When she looked up, Cash's face was so black it was bright, and so bright and bare of pity that it looked sweet to her. She stood up and held up her head. Cash was so powerful that his presence gave her strength even when she did not need any.

Under their eyes Solomon slept. People's faces tell of things and places not known to the one who looks at them while they sleep, and while Solomon slept under the eyes of Livvie and Cash his face told them like a mythical story that all his life he had built, little scrap by little scrap, respect. A beetle could not have been more laborious or more ingenious in the task of its destiny. When Solomon was young, as he was in his picture overhead, it was the infinite thing with him, and he could see no end to the respect he would contrive and keep in a house. He had built a lonely house, the way he would make a cage, but it grew to be the same with him as a great monumental pyramid and sometimes in his absorption of getting it erected he was like the builder-slaves of Egypt who forgot or never knew the origin and meaning of the thing to which they gave all the strength of their bodies and used up all their days. Livvie and Cash could see that as a man might rest from a life-labor he lay in his bed, and they could hear how, wrapped in his quilt, he sighed to himself comfortably in sleep, while in his dreams he might have been an ant, a beetle, a bird, an Egyptian, assembling and carrying on his back and building with his hands, or he might have been an old man of India or a swaddled baby, about to smile and brush all away.

Then without warning old Solomon's eyes flew wide open under the hedge-like brows. He was wide awake.

And instantly Cash raised his quick arm. A radiant sweat stood on his temples. But he did not bring his arm down—it stayed in the air, as if something might have taken hold.

It was not Livvie—she did not move. As if something said "Wait," she stood waiting. Even while her eyes burned under motionless lids, her lips parted in a stiff grimace, and with her arms stiff at her sides she stood above the prone old man and the panting young one, erect and apart.

Movement when it came came in Solomon's face. It was an old and strict face, a frail face, but behind it, like a covered light, came an animation that could play hide and seek, that would dart and escape, had always escaped. The mystery flickered in him, and invited from his eyes. It was that very mystery that Cash with his quick arm would have to strike, and that Livvie could not weep for. But Cash only stood holding his arm in the air, when the gentlest flick of his great strength, almost a puff of his breath, would have been enough, if he had known how to give it, to send the old man over the obstruction that kept him away from death.

If it could not be that the tiny illumination in the fragile and ancient face caused a crisis, a mystery in the room that would not permit a blow to fall, at least it was certain that Cash, throbbing in his Easter clothes, felt a pang of shame that the vigor of a man would come to such an end that he could not be struck without warning. He took down his hand and stepped back behind Livvie, like a round-eyed schoolboy on whose unsuspecting head the dunce cap has been set.

"Young ones can't wait," said Solomon.

Livvie shuddered violently, and then in a gush of tears she stooped for a glass of water and handed it to him, but he did not see her.

"So here come the young man Livvie wait for. Was no prevention. No prevention. Now I lay eyes on young man and it come to be somebody I know all the time, and been knowing since he were born in a cotton patch, and watched grow up year to year, Cash McCord, growed to size, growed up to come in my house in the end—ragged and barefoot."

Solomon gave a cough of distaste. Then he shut his eyes vigorously, and his lips began to move like a chanter's.

"When Livvie married, her husband were already somebody. He had paid great cost for his land. He spread sycamore leaves over the ground from wagon to door, day he brought her home, so her foot would not have to touch ground. He carried her through his door. Then he growed old and could not lift her, and she were still young."

Livvie's sobs followed his words like a soft melody repeating each thing as he stated it. His lips moved for a little without sound, or she cried too fervently, and unheard he might have been telling his whole life, and then he said, "God forgive Solomon for sins great and small. God forgive Solomon for carrying away too young girl for wife and keeping her away from her people and from all the young people would clamor for her back."

Then he lifted up his right hand toward Livvie where she stood by the bed and offered her his silver watch. He dangled it before her eyes, and she hushed crying; her tears stopped. For a moment the watch could be heard ticking as it always did, precisely in his proud hand. She lifted it away. Then he took hold of the quilt; then he was dead.

Livvie left Solomon dead and went out of the room. Stealthily, nearly without noise, Cash went beside her. He was like a shadow, but his shiny shoes moved over the floor in spangles, and the green downy feather shone like a light in his hat. As they reached the front room, he seized her deftly as a long black cat and dragged her hanging by the waist round and round him, while he turned in a circle, his face bent down to hers. The first moment, she kept one arm and its hand stiff and still, the one that held Solomon's watch. Then the fingers softly let go, all of her was limp, and the watch fell somewhere on the floor. It ticked away in the still room, and all at once there began outside the full song of a bird.

They moved around and around the room and into the brightness of the open door, then he stopped and shook her once. She rested in silence in his trembling arms, unprotesting as a bird on a nest. Outside the redbirds were flying and crisscrossing, the sun was in all the bottles on the prisoned trees, and the young peach was shining in the middle of them with the bursting light of spring.

Cyrus Colter
1910 –

Some contemporary story-writers are convinced that traditional methods of writing stories have become exhausted and that radically different ones must be sought if the complex realities of modern life are to be adequately expressed. Other writers, of whom Cyrus Colter is an example, demonstrate that older forms and methods continue to be adaptable to contemporary subject matter and still enable story-tellers to make powerful statements about life if, in the first place, they have anything significant to say about it, as Colter does.

Born in 1910, in Noblesville, Indiana, Colter received his educational training at Youngstown (Ohio) University, Ohio State University, and the Chicago-Kent College of Law, where he earned the LL.B. degree in 1940. After serving as a United States deputy collector of Internal Revenue from 1940 to 1942, he entered military service during World War II and served as an officer in the field artillery, experiencing combat in Italy. In 1946, following his army duty, he entered into the practice of law in Chicago. In 1950, he was appointed to the Illinois Commerce Commission. Appointed to the faculty of Northwestern University in 1973 and serving for two terms as chair of the Department of Afro-American Studies there, he is now an emeritus professor of humanities and still resides in Chicago. Presenting the unusual case of a person who turned to writing as a weekend hobby when he was fifty years of age, Colter first began publishing stories during the 1960s; in 1970 he won the first Iowa School of Letters Award for Short Fiction for his collection, *The Beach Umbrella.* Since then, he has published four novels, *The Rivers of Eros* (1972), *The Hippodrome* (1973), *Night Studies* (1979), and *A Chocolate Soldier* (1988).

Despite differences in time, race, and locality, "A Man in the House" bears a thematic similarity to Kate Chopin's "The Storm" in that it depicts a young woman whose aroused sexuality places her in a painful, highly emotional conflict with traditional moral codes, a conflict wherein her reason and conventional upbringing urge her in one direction while her natural impulses aroused by the attraction of virile maleness urge her in another. The struggle in "A Man in the House" is intensified by the fact that the main character is a girl growing from adolescence into maturity.

A Man in the House

Verna bent over the old-fashioned bath tub—the kind with legs, and the white enamel worn thin in places—to turn the faucet and start the hot water running. But the motions she was going through were mechanical, for her vivid, purposeful mind ranged elsewhere: it had just occurred to her she was beginning to like Chicago. Her unconscious psyche had toyed with the idea for days; now *she* was adopting it. But the reasons were not at all clear to her, and she was aware of faint misgivings about probing them too far. She was seventeen now, and spent most of her time in a ritualistic reverie about herself, her current projects, and the small, but earnest world she moved in—and she considered herself the center of that world. But this self-love—actually, unrecognized by her—was almost always hidden behind a tender-maiden exterior. That was her uniqueness; except, possibly, for an odd, brown, virginal beauty—a source of great anxiety to her widowed mother.

Steam was billowing up out of the tub now, and she started a jet of cold water into the hot. It was almost eight weeks since she had left her mother and sister, Cindy, for the summer, and, although at first she had been homesick, she seldom ever missed them now; and whenever she did, it was with the slightest tincture of guilt—she did not know why. She knew her mother had fretted about every boy she dated down in Memphis, and she thought this silly, for she had never been attracted to any of them, and, as far as she knew, had never acted like it. Yet after June graduation, her mother had poorly concealed her eagerness for the present visit. But, so far, the visit hadn't been a bit dull—with the boys, and dates, and all. And her Aunt Ruby (her mother's sister) and Uncle Jack Robinson were extremely nice to her—she felt sometimes it was because they had no children of their own.

Now Verna took pains to keep her mother comfortable with long, frank letters about her activities—especially her dates; but somehow she had never mentioned her strange initial fear—fear, not of the boys, or of the big city, although Chicago was at first bewildering, but of herself. She had experienced a brand-new feeling in this very different house, stirrings inside her that were at once confusing and sometimes faintly frightening. But that had been in the beginning. Since then, vague, imperceptible changes had taken place, each defying a neat label; but there was no change in the intensity of her involvement. The fear returned occasionally, but never with its old alarm, and what finally remained was—well, to Verna, it was bliss; still something akin to dread; ecstatically satisfying, yet itself unsatisfied.

The tub was two-thirds full now, and, after turning off the water, she went back into her tidy bedroom. She took her blue dress from the closet and laid it out across the bed. The style of the dress and its shade of blue, an ultramarine, always pleased her, as did the perfect way it fit her, giving her the quiet, worldly air she craved. She turned to look at herself in the dresser mirror, and raised the palms of both hands to her freshly-done hair and ruffled it into a more casual shape. But it was always well-groomed because she cared for it with one of those harsh little passions she directed at certain special things in her life. The velvety brown of her skin, with its peach fuzz, the almond eyes, the curved, ample mouth, all combined to convey the tender, fondled look that drove her handsome Uncle Jack Robinson to refer to her as "quail." He would put his burly arm around her shoulders and squeeze her hard against his heaving ribs, and tease, "You little quail, you!" This had terrified her at first, but now no more—although she was still flustered if her Aunt Ruby happened to be looking. Aunt Ruby would give her high, fluttering, nervous laugh, and say, but not too boldly, "You let that child alone, Jack Robinson!"

Verna heard the telephone ring downstairs, as she picked up the dress off the bed and held it out in front of her. She had decided to wear it that evening because Stanley, her date, had seen it once before and said he liked it; but he was probably jiving, she thought—all these Chicago boys were so full of jive, and so grown up! What would her mother ever say about *them!*—even the real young ones; they were certainly different from the boys in Memphis. But Stanley wasn't too bad—he just thought he was such a man; it really made him funny, if he only knew it. Yet he was a merry, off-beat date—you never knew exactly what was going to happen, but you always had a good time. And he liked her. They were both going away to college in September—or rather, she was supposed to go, if her mother could raise a few more dollars. But Stanley wasn't as nice as Curtis down in Memphis; Curtis was more of a gentleman, certainly; he always helped her off the bus, and made sure she was walking on the inside of the sidewalk. And he'd never tried to force her mouth open when he kissed her—nor had he ever told her how "fine" he bet she was, like Stanley had once.

"*Verna,* baby!" It was Aunt Ruby's jumpy, soprano voice from the living room downstairs.

" . . . Yes?" Verna's voice was soft like a child's. She liked her Aunt Ruby, but with a trace of condescension.

"What time's your date, honey? That was your Uncle Jack Robinson on the phone—he wants to take us to the ball game tonight. I told him you had a date, but he said for you to bring your date along."

"Oh . . . Gee." Verna stepped to the head of the stairs. "I don't know . . . Stanley said we were going over to a friend of his to listen to records."

"Well, you know how your uncle is. He wants to run everything and everybody." Ruby emitted the fluttering laugh.

"We can ask Stanley, Aunt Ruby—when he comes. It'll be around eight."

"That may be too late for your Uncle Jack Robinson," Ruby said, in thoughtful apprehension.

Verna was thoughtful too. Her mother had warned her to be nice to her uncle, who had hinted at helping out with her college tuition—he operated two big taverns. "Well . . . "—she hesitated—"maybe we'd better wait, then; and ask him, when he gets home. . . . " She felt exhilarating jitters.

"All right then, honey," Ruby said from the foot of the stairs—she was a light-skinned, flabby-fat woman of thirty-nine who looked easily ten years older from the cruel lines in her already-sagging face; she ate insatiably, feared God and her husband, and kept a clean house. When she was a thin, rather slow-witted quadroon of nineteen, she ran away from home in Memphis to marry Jack Robinson Brown, and ever since had thought herself extremely happy, despite her inevitable stomach-writhings whenever he was around. "It's four-thirty now," she called up to Verna. "He'll be home around six, I guess."

" . . . Okay." Verna, on her way back to the bedroom, had already started undressing for her bath. She felt strange—and eager—now. She was naked when she began looking around the room for her robe.

Suddenly she paused in front of the mirror. She cautiously viewed herself. Her nut-brown breasts were small and firm, and the nipples were almost black; the fertile curvature of her hips and thighs expressed the ripened child-woman, and she was pleased with herself.

Ruby and Verna were in the kitchen when, about six-fifteen, Jack Robinson let himself in at the front door. He was tall, medium-brown, and weighed a muscular two hundred pounds in his business suit. His rather sharp, severe jaw jutted forward prominently, and was swathed in a smooth beard-shadow; and he clenched a wet cigar butt between his teeth.

"Hey!" he greeted them, tossing his soft straw hat onto the rack before coming into the kitchen. Verna looked wide-eyed at his strong hands. "What're you two up to *now*?" he asked with a raffish grin, his prankster's eyes roving the room.

"We're up to fixing you a nice dinner, honey!" Ruby beamed. "That's what we're up to!"

Verna, wearing a tiny white apron around her waist over the blue dress, stood behind her Aunt Ruby and smiled out shyly at him—but somehow she felt exposed. She couldn't help wondering what he'd been like when he was Stanley's or Curtis's age, for instance. Had he always been so rash, so dare-devilish?—he was forty-eight now, she knew. She had never seen any man like him—not even in the movies; and, apprehensively watching him, she shuddered from the primeval hurt in her loins—a dulcet, gossamer hurt, that cringed in the face of half-wished-for cruelties. She was helplessly confused, and longed to run and hide.

"A nice dinner, eh!" hectored Jack Robinson. "Well, that's mighty white of you—as the white folks say." With his long arm reaching high over his head, he pulled open a top door of the cabinet and took down a fifth of Gordon's gin. "And what've you been doing with *yourself* all day, gingerbread?" he asked without looking at Verna—he was taking down a glass now.

Near panic, she said nothing, until he turned to her. "Oh . . . not much . . . have we?"—she looked at Aunt Ruby.

"Not much," affirmed Ruby. "We did go to the supermarket, around noon."

Jack Robinson now opened the freezer compartment of the refrigerator and lifted out a small bucket of ice cubes, and then, for a mixer, took out a cold bottle of Squirt from the section below. "Will anybody join me?" he asked—his grin was a leer. He stepped to the kitchen table, half-singing, half-reciting, " 'Whiskey for the head; rum for the feet; and gin for in between!' "

"Jack Robinson! You *stop* that!" cried Ruby, giggling. "That child's not used to talk like that! Her mother'd die! Now you stop it!"

Jack Robinson's shoulders shook a little as he chortled, and poured a half glass of gin over frosted ice, before adding Squirt. As he stirred the drink with his forefinger, he gazed at Verna with the tenderest, most gentle smile.

She felt needles on her face and neck; yet she wanted to laugh; the man could be so funny at times!—but crafty and wicked too, she sensed. She looked at him, and gave a little laugh.

"Look at her!" scolded Ruby, but still giggling. "She's embarrassed!"

"Hummph!" grunted Jack Robinson after drinking off half the glass at one sally. "If she keeps on runnin' around with these little purse-snatchers here in Chicago, she won't be getting embarrassed long—I'll guarantee you that!" He backed up and took a seat on the tall kitchen stool.

"Now, honey! Those're nice boys Verna goes out with—and you know it!"

"Nice my eye! Nice, till they get her cornered! You'll see how nice they are *then*! And that's when you'll have to come out to Cook County jail to see *me*!" Jack Robinson hit himself on the chest twice with the protruding thumb of his clenched fist—and his voice was rising now as the gin hit home.

"Now, *honeeeey*!" Ruby whinnied.

Verna, her mind now clear and alert, wished her Aunt Ruby would hurry up and ask about the ball game. She knew—deep in her clever heart—she wanted to go; the heck with Stanley. Then Jack Robinson, perched on the tall stool, looked across the kitchen at her. "Come over here, sugar," he beckoned with his noisy glass, "and tell Uncle Jack Robinson if any of those boys're trying to take advantage of you."

Verna crossed the kitchen and stood submissively at his side—she thought he smelled deliciously of strong tobacco. She reflected for an instant how she might have been different if only she could have grown up in a house with a man in it—she'd had no father since the age of five. "No . . . the boys are all nice," she said. He put his arm around her waist and gazed in her eyes, his grim face shadowed with tenderness. "Little quail," he said, "you know you've always got your Uncle Jack Robinson to look after you, don't you?—y'know that."

"Yes," Verna said, trembling at his touch—she had never in her brief life's experience felt the way she felt now. Wildfire sensations climbed her spine, and the young flesh on her face and neck went ablaze; she stood numbly rigid, afraid of falling.

Ruby was putting the rolls in the oven now, and, after closing the oven door, turned and beamed at her husband and Verna. "That's right, honey," she said to Verna. "Your uncle means that." She did not see her husband's face cloud up at the intrusion. He released Verna, and she quickly sat down in a kitchen chair. No one spoke. Then he vengefully tossed off the rest of his drink, and set the glass down hard.

"Why don't you go wash up, honey?" Ruby coaxed him. "As soon as the rolls are brown, we'll be ready."

He looked at her coldly. "Don't rush me," he said. "I'm gonna have another drink." He began mixing a second strong gin-and-Squirt. But soon he took it with him upstairs.

Ruby leaned over the table and whispered to Verna, "Don't pay him any mind, honey; he'll be all right afterwhile—something's on his mind . . . something's bothering him."

Verna looked at her aunt, and was inwardly annoyed with her.

When Jack Robinson came down to the kitchen again, the glass in his hand was empty; yet he seemed more composed. He did not look at Verna. "Did the newspaper come yet, Babe?" he asked Ruby.

"Yes, honey—but dinner's ready now," Ruby said.

They sat down to dinner. And Ruby and Verna bowed their heads, as Ruby, in wheedling tones, began saying grace. When she got to: " . . . please bless this food, dear Lord, and sanctify it for its intended purpose . . . ," she opened her eyes wide, and seemed to stare up at the pink kitchen curtains, her high voice rising and falling. When they began to eat, Jack Robinson suddenly seemed cheerful. There was chuck roast and potatoes, and Ruby stealthily waited until the other plates were served before she helped her own, diverting attention from the heaping portions she gave herself.

Soon, with a trace of eagerness, Jack Robinson said, "Let's all go out to that game tonight—and watch the Yankees lynch the White Sox! They do it every time they come here—it'll be the same again tonight!" His laugh was a scoff.

Verna's heart vaulted.

"Honey," Ruby said, this time directing the wheedling tone at her husband, "I told you on the phone—Verna's got a date. *She* can't come."

"Yeah, *I* know," Jack Robinson scowled. He turned on Verna. "Date with who?"

"With Stanley."

"Where you going?"

"Over to a friend of his—to listen to records."

"Who is this '*friend*'?" Jack Robinson's voice was getting high and hoarse.

"I've never met him—at least, I don't remember him. Stanley says I met him once at a dance, though—when I first came. His name is Julius."

"Where's Julius's *place*?" He spat the words.

"*I* don't know." Verna's voice broke—and soon tears were wetting her long lashes.

"*Honey*!" Ruby pleaded with Jack Robinson, "don't be so rough! Look—you've spoiled her dinner! . . . Stanley's a nice boy—you know that!"

"I don't know any such a *damn thing*!" Jack Robinson exploded. "To *me*, all them little reefer-smokers are alike!"

Verna looked on in awe through the glaze of her tears at his fury. And she felt guilty to find no zeal in her heart for defending Stanley. She said nothing.

The three ate in silence. The electric clock over the refrigerator made a faint whirring sound as the long second hand made its slow trek around the dial. Verna's tears dried readily; she was not hurt. She felt a disheveled relief—as at the violent settling, once and for all, of a burning question. She ate well, and relished her food. Suddenly, Jack Robinson, ignoring her, said to Ruby, "All right then—get your things on. *We'll* go." He finished his meal in a sullen silence.

Stanley arrived shortly before eight. When he rang the doorbell, Jack Robinson, who had been pretending to read the newspaper, got up and stalked off upstairs. Verna, all ready to go, realized he was willing to be late for the ball game rather than leave her to greet Stanley alone. She was nervous, and very glad Stanley was on time; and got him out of the house quickly—before he could sit down. Walking to the bus stop, she was silent, preoccupied.

When the bus finally came, and they had boarded and taken seats, Stanley, with a quizzical little frown, turned to her and said, "What's eating you?"

"Nothing's eating me," she quietly lied.

"All you do is look out the window." He watched her. He was a tall, gangling, brown-skinned boy, and wore an Ivy League summer suit and a pair of big black-rimmed glasses he did not need. He was doing most of the talking.

Verna sat inert; re-living dinner and its revelation; and once more she was afraid—afraid of herself. In her *mind* she had ceased to be chaste already. Aunt Ruby was right—but for the wrong reason—Verna's mother *would* die, if she knew. A feeling of doom came over her, and she saw all too clearly what she must do—but this thought of leaving Chicago plunged her into despair, and made the past eight weeks seem a nostalgic Shangri-La.

By the time the bus reached Eighty-second Street, where they were to get off, glib Stanley, now thoroughly dejected, had stopped talking; but as they left the bus, Verna, sorry for him, resolved to be more cheerful. It was almost dark as they started walking the two blocks to Julius's.

People were out sprinkling their lawns, and the children were whooping and romping on the wet sidewalks.

"Who's going to be there?"—Verna was smiling now, and seemed lighthearted.

"Slick Fambro and Gwen Smith," Stanley said, still glum. "And Julius, of course—and Dotty, his girl. You've heard of Slick—he's the prep basketball star."

"I hope Julius has got some good records." She was making conversation.

"Don't worry about a thing. He's *got* 'em." Stanley was so positive—she was amused.

Julius lived with his mother and father in a small, one-story brick with a trim little lawn. When he opened the door to them, Verna did remember him—as Stanley said. The music was going and everybody was there already, in the attractive living room that seemed large for the house. Both Dotty and Gwen were young like Verna, but they viewed her with anxious interest when Julius introduced her around. Slick stood up when introduced, and then grinned over at Stanley, giving him a low whistle of congratulations. The music was cool, progressive jazz, coming out of the stereo speakers in the far corner, and Gwen was busily searching through a stack of albums on the floor for the next record. When Julius had finished serving everyone rum and coke, he went and brought his mother—a tiny woman—for Verna to meet.

They were all gay—sometimes hilarious—and even Verna, at times, sipping her drink, was drawn away from the fever of the earlier evening. She danced with all the boys, and smiled when Slick furtively told her how beautiful she was. But as the evening wore on, her mood began to change—to darken. She was thinking of herself again: of how poised she was among these kids; how experienced; how bored. *They* hadn't lived—they just thought they had. She kept a set smile on her face, and felt detached. It did not occur to her now that only two months before, fresh up from Memphis, she would not have felt so secure among these same "kids" now the object of her mild hauteur.

After an hour they were still dancing, and when Julius put a very modern version of "Stella by Starlight" on the turntable, Stanley avidly claimed Verna, and they danced. He was possessive, and held her tightly. "I'm overboard about you," he said. "Real gone. You know that. I just can't get you out of my head . . . you're all I think about—morning, noon, and night." He put his cheek down against her hair and held her even tighter. She tried to keep her breathing in, and say nothing—as her mind shot away. Stanley was offensive to her now, and she longed to wriggle free.

When the record finished playing, everyone sat down. "Now, how about some *listening* music?" Julius said, kneeling on the floor to go through the stack of records.

"Oh, play something by the Soft Sounds Trio, Julius!" Dotty cried, bounding over to him and looking over his shoulder at each record.

Verna sat on the sofa, with Stanley, his drink in his hand, sprawled on the floor at her feet.

When Julius and Dotty finally found the record, and Julius was putting it on, Stanley yelled at him, "Hey, man, d'you need all this light?—you said *listening* music!" Everybody laughed, and Julius reached over and turned off one of the table lamps, transforming the room into a soft gloaming.

When the first pensive notes of the piano came out of the stereo speakers, Gwen squealed. "Oh, it's 'The Party's Over'! I *love* this!" The music played by the smooth combo echoed the break-up of a love affair. It was bittersweet and haunting, and no one spoke. Its mood somehow caught them up in the spell of their own fantasies and dreams of love—yet to be lived—with all the filmy visions of romance with the ideal boy or girl, broken up for a time by some dazzling intruder, but ultimately and rapturously restored in a blaze of passion, tears and remorse. But not Verna. She felt *her* dreams were in the past already. Then the aching deep in her returned, and she felt flawed and contemptible. She reflected bitterly *she* didn't feel moon-struck by the music. She felt cursed. Her mind had returned to early evening in the kitchen, when she had stood beside the tall stool—to the ecstacy, the near swooning, the ravish-wish. She was convinced now she must return to her mother—and at once.

Stanley brought her home in a taxi around midnight. She was moody and would not let him kiss her. As she quietly let herself in the house, she hoped nobody was still up. As usual, the squat little lamp on the kitchen table had been left lighted for her. She went into the kitchen, opened the refrigerator, and stared in absently—she knew she wasn't hungry. But maybe milk would hasten sleep. She took down a glass from the cupboard and poured herself a glass of milk, and sat down at the kitchen table to sip it. Her mind was listless now—she had thought too much for one day. Yet the images of her mother and Cindy came to her clearly, and would not go away. How the weeks did fly! Cindy would be fifteen in October. What would she say when Verna came home so unexpectedly—Cindy could be so nosey! But her mother would *never* understand—and she could never tell her. And college was probably out of the question now—wouldn't her mother be furious! Curtis, though, would be glad she'd come back. But she didn't care about any of these things, really. They were nothing to the sickening feeling in her heart at leaving. There had never been an iron will in her house, since she could remember—and what a difference that made; otherwise maybe she wouldn't be so mesmerized now. And *he* had never had a daughter—maybe he'd be different, too. It was all so everlastingly mixed up—she wanted to cry, but she knew her stony heart wouldn't let her.

She finished the glass of milk and turned out the light. And as she slowly climbed the dimly-lit stairs, she thought of the ball game, and how she had yearned to go—there'd never be another.

She entered her room and switched on the light; and was startled by the white sheet of paper lying in the center of the bed. She picked it up, and recognized her Aunt Ruby's pencilled handwriting:

Verna, honey,
Your Uncle Jack Robinson asked me to write you this. He's so sorry the way he acted at dinner. He says he's been upset lately about some things. He never tells me much, so I don't know what things. But he don't want you to feel upset and mad at him, because he said to tell you he loves you. He's a wonderful guy, honey, a wonderful guy, when you get to know him. This note is all his idea—so you see?
The Yankees won! Just like he said!

Nighty night,
Aunt Ruby

Verna slowly sank down on the edge of the bed, clutching the note in her hand, her fingernails digging into the flesh of her palms. The old beautiful, dulcet feeling had returned, creeping and glowing over her like a meadow haze; and it hurt, too—terribly. But she accepted it—with its portent—gladly, eagerly, her decision forgotten. She knew now she would never go home—*never.* Instinctively she went into the bathroom to brush her teeth, and when she returned she fancied herself no longer alone in the room, and started undressing feverishly, heaping all her clothes on a chair, and then flicked out the light and, naked, leapt into bed.

John Cheever

1912 – 1982

John Cheever's literary works have won such favor and renown that he now ranks among America's foremost creative writers. His novels and short stories are chiefly concerned with the values of middle-class urban and suburban society, but there is great diversity in his themes, settings, and characterizations. He is particularly adept at revealing both the interactions among his characters and the effect of outer events upon their inner lives.

Cheever was born in Quincy, Massachusetts, in 1912. His brief formal schooling at the Thayer Academy of South Braintree ended abruptly upon his expulsion from there in 1929. Having already determined to become a writer, he used that event as the basis of his first story, "Expelled," written when he was only seventeen and published in the *New Republic* in 1930. For a while he lived in Boston with his brother Frederick, but presently he moved to New York City to write book synopses for MGM. After service in the United States Army from 1941 to 1945, Cheever wrote television scripts for several years; but he had already begun publishing stories in the *New Yorker* in 1940 and before long became one of its most frequent contributors.[1] His first collection of stories, *The Way Some People Live,* appeared in 1943; his second, *The Enormous Radio and Other Stories,* in 1953. Later collections were published at fairly regular intervals: *The Housebreaker of Shady Hill and Other Stories* (1958), *Some People, Places and Things That Will Not Appear in My Next Novel* (1961), *The Brigadier and the Golf Widow* (1964), *The World of Apples* (1973), and *The Stories of John Cheever* (1978). Besides his short story collections,

[1]See Lynn Waldeland, *John Cheever* (Boston: Twayne Publishers, 1979), p. 26.

Cheever published four novels: *The Wapshot Chronicle* (1957), *The Wapshot Scandal* (1964), *Bullet Park* (1969), and *The Falconer* (1978). His fiction brought him many awards and he served as Writer-in-Residence at the University of Iowa (1974) and at Boston University.

The abrupt ending of "The Swimmer" may come as a surprise—even a shock—unless the reader has noted Cheever's careful preparation leading up to it through Neddy Merrill's visit to the Welchers' deserted house and pool, his conversations with the Hallorans and the Sachses, and the snide comments that Grace Biswanger makes behind his back. The heroic journey Merrill undertakes through the swimming pools of his hard-drinking suburbanite friends and neighbors has an ironic resonance of symbolic overtones hinting at a journey through life, from mid-summer into fall, from bright cheerfulness and forgetfulness into the darkening realization of a harsh predicament.

The Swimmer

It was one of those midsummer Sundays when everyone sits around saying: "I *drank* too much last night." You might have heard it whispered by the parishioners leaving church, heard it from the lips of the priest himself, struggling with his cassock in the *vestiarium,* heard it from the golf links and the tennis courts, heard it from the wildlife preserve where the leader of the Audubon group was suffering from a terrible hangover. "I *drank* too much," said Donald Westerhazy. "We all *drank* too much," said Lucinda Merrill. "It must have been the wine," said Helen Westerhazy. "I *drank* too much of that claret."

This was at the edge of the Westerhazy's pool. The pool, fed by an artesian well with a high iron content, was a pale shade of green. It was a fine day. In the west there was a massive stand of cumulus cloud so like a city seen from a distance—from the bow of an approaching ship—that it might have had a name. Lisbon. Hackensack. The sun was hot. Neddy Merrill sat by the green water, one hand in it, one around a glass of gin. He was a slender man—he seemed to have the especial slenderness of youth—and while he was far from young he had slid down his banister that morning and given the bronze backside of Aphrodite on the hall table a smack, as he jogged down toward the smell of coffee in his dining room. He might have been compared to a summer's day, particularly the last hours of one, and while he lacked a tennis racket or a sail bag the impression was definitely one of youth, sport, and clement weather. He had been swimming and now he was breathing deeply, stertorously as if he could gulp into his lungs the components of that moment, the heat of the sun, the intenseness of his pleasure. It all seemed to flow into his chest. His own house stood in Bullet Park, eight miles to the south, where his four beautiful daughters would have had their lunch and might be playing tennis. Then it occurred to him that by taking a dogleg to the southwest he could reach his home by water.

His life was not confining and the delight he took in this observation could not be explained by its suggestion of escape. He seemed to see, with a cartographer's eye, that string of swimming pools, that quasi-subterranean stream that curved across the country. He had made a discovery, a contribution to modern geography; he would name the stream Lucinda after his wife. He was not a practical joker nor was he a fool but he was determinedly original and had a vague and modest idea of himself as a legendary figure. The day was beautiful and it seemed to him that a long swim might enlarge and celebrate its beauty.

He took off a sweater that was hung over his shoulders and dove in. He had an inexplicable contempt for men who did not hurl themselves into pools. He swam a choppy crawl, breathing either with every stroke or every fourth stroke and counting somewhere well in the back of his mind the one-two one-two of a flutter kick. It was not a serviceable stroke for long distances but the domestication of swimming had saddled the sport with some customs and in his part of the world a crawl was customary. To be embraced and sustained by the light green water was less a pleasure, it seemed, than the resumption of a natural condition, and he would have liked to swim without trunks, but this was not possible, considering his project. He hoisted himself up on the far curb—he never used the ladder—and started across the lawn. When Lucinda asked where he was going he said he was going to swim home.

The only maps and charts he had to go by were remembered or imaginary but these were clear enough. First there were the Grahams, the Hammers, the Lears, the Howlands, and the Crosscups. He would cross Ditmar Street to the Bunkers and come, after a short portage, to the Levys, the Welchers, and the public pool in Lancaster. Then there were the Hallorans, the Sachses, the Biswangers, Shirley Adams, the Gilmartins, and the Clydes. The day was lovely, and that he lived in a world so generously supplied with water seemed like a clemency, a beneficence. His heart was high and he ran across the grass. Making his way home by an uncommon route gave him the feeling that he was a pilgrim, an explorer, a man with a destiny, and he knew that he would find friends all along the way; friends would line the banks of the Lucinda River.

He went through a hedge that separated the Westerhazys' land from the Grahams', walked under some flowering apple trees, passed the shed that housed their pump and filter, and came out at the Grahams' pool. "Why, Neddy," Mrs. Graham said, "what a marvelous surprise. I've been trying to get you on the phone all morning. Here, let me get you a drink." He saw then, like any explorer, that the hospitable customs and traditions of the natives would have to be handled with diplomacy if he was ever going to reach his destination. He did not want to mystify or seem rude to the Grahams nor did he have the time to linger there. He swam the length of their pool and joined them in the sun and was rescued, a few minutes later, by the arrival of two carloads of friends from Connecticut. During the uproarious reunions he was able to slip away. He went down by the front of the Grahams' house, stepped over a thorny hedge, and crossed a vacant lot to the Hammers'. Mrs. Hammer, looking up from her roses, saw him swim by although she wasn't quite sure who it was. The Lears heard him splashing past the open windows of their living room. The Howlands and the Crosscups were away. After leaving the Howlands' he crossed Ditmar Street and started for the Bunkers', where he could hear, even at that distance, the noise of a party.

The water refracted the sound of voices and laughter and seemed to suspend it in midair. The Bunkers' pool was on a rise and he climbed some stairs to a terrace where twenty-five or thirty men and women were drinking. The only person in the water was Rusty Towers, who floated there on a rubber raft. Oh how bonny and lush were the banks of the Lucinda River! Prosperous men and women gathered by the sapphire-colored waters while caterer's men in white coats passed them cold gin. Overhead a red de Haviland trainer was circling around and around and around in the sky with something like the glee of a child in a swing. Ned felt a passing affection for the scene, a tenderness for the gathering, as if it was something he might touch. In the distance he heard thunder. As soon as Enid Bunker saw him she began to scream: "Oh look who's here! What a marvelous surprise! When Lucinda said that you wouldn't come I thought I'd *die*." She made her way to him through the crowd, and when they had finished kissing she led him to the bar, a progress that was slowed by the fact that he stopped to kiss eight or ten other women and shake the hands of as many men. A smiling bartender he had seen at a hundred parties gave him a gin and tonic and he stood by the bar for a moment, anxious not to get stuck in any conversation that would delay his voyage. When he seemed about to be surrounded he dove in and swam close to the side to avoid colliding with Rusty's raft. At the far end of the pool he bypassed the Tomlinsons with a broad smile and jogged up the garden path. The gravel cut his feet but this was the only unpleasantness. The party was confined to the pool, and as he went toward the house he heard the brilliant, watery sound of voices fade, heard the noise of a radio from the Bunkers' kitchen, where someone was listening to a ballgame. Sunday afternoon. He made his way through the parked cars and down the grassy border of their driveway to Alewives' Lane. He did not want to be seen on the road in his bathing trunks but there was no traffic and he made the short distance to the Levys' driveway, marked with a private property sign and a green tube for the *New York Times*. All the doors and windows of the big house were open but there were no signs of life; not even a dog barked. He went around the side of the house to the pool and saw that the Levys had only recently left. Glasses and bottles and dishes of nuts were on a table at the deep end, where there was a bathhouse or gazebo, hung with Japanese lanterns. After swimming the pool he got himself a glass and poured a drink. It was his fourth or fifth drink and he had swum nearly half the length of the Lucinda River. He felt tired, clean, and pleased at that moment to be alone; pleased with everything.

It would storm. The stand of cumulus cloud—that city—had risen and darkened, and while he sat there he heard the percussiveness of thunder again. The de Haviland trainer was still circling overhead and it seemed to Ned that he could almost hear the pilot laugh with pleasure in the afternoon; but when there was another peal of thunder he took off for home. A train whistle blew and he wondered what time it had gotten to be. Four? Five? He thought of the provincial station at that hour, where a waiter, his tuxedo concealed by a raincoat, a dwarf with some flowers wrapped in newspaper, and a woman who had been crying would be waiting for the local. It was suddenly growing dark; it was that moment when the pin-headed birds seem to organize their song into some acute and knowledgeable recognition of the storm's approach. Then there was a fine noise of rushing water from the crown of an oak at his back, as if a spigot there had been turned. Then the noise of fountains came from the crowns of all the tall trees. Why did he love storms, what was the meaning of his excitement when the door sprang open and the rain wind fled rudely up the stairs, why had the simple task of shutting the windows of an old house seemed fitting and urgent, why did the first watery notes of a storm wind have for him the unmistakable sound of good news, cheer, glad tidings? Then there was an explosion, a smell of cordite, and rain lashed the Japanese lanterns that Mrs. Levy had bought in Kyoto the year before last, or was it the year before that?

He stayed in the Levys' gazebo until the storm had passed. The rain had cooled the air and he shivered. The force of the wind had stripped a maple of its red and yellow leaves and scattered them over the grass and the water. Since it was midsummer the tree must be blighted, and yet he felt a peculiar sadness at this sign of autumn. He braced his shoulders, emptied his glass, and started for the Welchers' pool. This meant crossing the Lindleys' riding ring and he was surprised to find it overgrown with grass and all the jumps dismantled. He wondered if the Lindleys had sold their horses or gone away for the summer and put them out to board. He seemed to remember having heard something about the Lindleys and their horses but the memory was unclear. On he went, barefoot through the wet grass, to the Welchers', where he found their pool was dry.

This breach in his chain of water disappointed him absurdly, and he felt like some explorer who seeks a torrential headwater and finds a dead stream. He was disappointed and mystified. It was common enough to go away for the summer but no one ever drained his pool. The Welchers had definitely gone away. The pool furniture was folded, stacked, and covered with a tarpaulin. The bathhouse was locked. All the windows of the house were shut, and when he went around to the driveway in front he saw a for-sale sign nailed to a tree. When had he last heard from the Welchers—when, that is, had he and Lucinda last regretted an invitation to dine with them? It seemed only a week or so ago. Was his memory failing or had he so disciplined it in the repression of unpleasant facts that he had damaged his sense of the truth? Then in the distance he heard the sound of a tennis game. This cheered him, cleared away all his apprehensions and let him regard the overcast sky and the cold air with indifference. This was the day that Neddy Merrill swam across the country. That was the day! He started off then for his most difficult portage.

Had you gone for a Sunday afternoon ride that day you might have seen him, close to naked, standing on the shoulder of route 424, waiting for a chance to cross. You might have wondered if he was the victim of foul play, had his car broken down, or was he merely a fool. Standing barefoot in the deposits of the highway—beer cans, rags, and blowout patches—exposed to all kinds of ridicule, he seemed pitiful. He had known when he started that this was a part of his journey—it had been on his maps—but confronted with the lines of traffic, worming through the summery light, he found himself unprepared. He was laughed at, jeered at, a beer can was thrown at him, and he had no dignity or humor to bring to the situation. He could have gone back, back to the Westerhazys', where Lucinda would still be sitting in the sun. He had signed nothing, vowed nothing, pledged nothing not even to himself. Why, believing as he did, that all human obduracy was susceptible to common sense, was he unable to turn back? Why was he determined to complete his journey even if it meant putting his life in danger? At what point had this prank, this joke, this piece of horseplay become serious? He could not go back, he could not even recall with any clearness the green water at the Westerhazys', the sense of inhaling the day's components, the friendly and relaxed voices saying that they had *drunk* too much. In the space of an hour, more or less, he had covered a distance that made his return impossible.

An old man, tooling down the highway at fifteen miles an hour, let him get to the middle of the road, where there was a grass divider. Here he was exposed to the ridicule of the northbound traffic, but after ten or fifteen minutes he was able to cross. From here he had only a short walk to the Recreation Center at the edge of the Village of Lancaster, where there were some handball courts and a public pool.

The effect of the water on voices, the illusion of brilliance and suspense, was the same here as it had been at the Bunkers' but the sounds here were louder, harsher and more shrill, and as soon as he entered the crowded enclosure he was confronted with regimentation. "ALL SWIMMERS MUST TAKE A SHOWER BEFORE USING THE POOL. ALL SWIMMERS MUST USE THE FOOTBATH. ALL SWIMMERS MUST WEAR THEIR IDENTIFICATION DISKS." He took a shower, washed his feet in a cloudy bitter solution and made his way to the edge of the water. It stank of chlorine and looked to him like a sink. A pair of lifeguards in a pair of towers blew police whistles at what seemed to be regular intervals and abused the swimmers through a public address system. Neddy remembered the sapphire water at the Bunkers' with longing and thought that he might contaminate himself—damage his own prosperousness and charm—by swimming in this murk, but he reminded himself that he was an explorer, a pilgrim, and that this was merely a stagnant bend in the Lucinda River. He dove, scowling with distaste, into the chlorine and had to swim with his head above water to avoid collisions, but even so he was bumped into, splashed and jostled. When he got to the shallow end both lifeguards were shouting at him: "Hey, you, you without the identification disk, get outa the water." He did, but they had no way of pursuing him and he went through the reek of suntan oil and chlorine out through the hurricane fence and passed the handball courts. By crossing the road he entered the wooded part of the Halloran estate. The woods were not cleared and the footing was treacherous and difficult until he reached the lawn and the clipped beech hedge that encircled their pool.

The Hallorans were friends, an elderly couple of enormous wealth who seemed to bask in the suspicion that they might be Communists. They were zealous reformers but they were not Communists, and yet when they were accused, as they sometimes were, of subversion, it seemed to gratify and excite them. Their beech hedge was yellow and he guessed this had been blighted like the Levys' maple. He called hullo, hullo, to warn the Hallorans of his approach, to palliate his invasion of their privacy. The Hallorans, for reasons that had never been explained to him, did not wear bathing suits. No explanations were in order, really. Their nakedness was a detail in their uncompromising zeal for reform and he stepped politely out of his trunks before he went through the opening in the hedge.

Mrs. Halloran, a stout woman with white hair and a serene face, was reading the *Times*. Mr. Halloran was taking beech leaves out of the water with a scoop. They seemed not surprised or displeased to see him. Their pool was perhaps the oldest in the county, a fieldstone rectangle, fed by a brook. It had no filter or pump and its waters were the opaque gold of the stream.

"I'm swimming across the county," Ned said.

"Why, I didn't know one could," exclaimed Mrs. Halloran.

"Well, I've made it from the Westerhazys'." Ned said. "That must be about four miles."

He left his trunks at the deep end, walked to the shallow end, and swam this stretch. As he was pulling himself out of the water he heard Mrs. Halloran say: "We've been *terribly* sorry to hear about all your misfortunes, Neddy."

"My misfortunes?" Ned asked. "I don't know what you mean."

"Why, we heard that you'd sold the house and that your poor children . . . "

"I don't recall having sold the house," Ned said, "and the girls are at home."

"Yes," Mrs. Halloran sighed. "Yes . . . " Her voice filled the air with an unseasonable melancholy and Ned spoke briskly. "Thank you for the swim."

"Well, have a nice trip," said Mrs. Halloran.

Beyond the hedge he pulled on his trunks and fastened them. They were loose and he wondered if, during the space of an afternoon, he could have lost some weight. He was cold and he was tired and the naked Hallorans and their dark water had depressed him. The swim was too much for his strength but how could he have guessed this, sliding down the banister that morning and sitting in the Westerhazys' sun? His arms were lame. His legs felt rubbery and ached at the joints. The worst of it was the cold in his bones and the feeling that he might never be warm again. Leaves were falling down around him and he smelled woodsmoke on the wind. Who would be burning wood at this time of year?

He needed a drink. Whiskey would warm him, pick him up, carry him through the last of his journey, refresh his feeling that it was original and valorous to swim across the county. Channel swimmers took brandy.

He needed a stimulant. He crossed the lawn in front of the Hallorans' house and went down a little path to where they had built a house for their only daughter Helen and her husband Eric Sachs. The Sachses' pool was small and he found Helen and her husband there.

"Oh, *Neddy,*" Helen said. "Did you lunch at Mother's?"

"Not *really,*" Ned said. "I *did* stop to see your parents." This seemed to be explanation enough. "I'm terribly sorry to break in on you like this but I've taken a chill and I wondered if you'd give me a drink."

"Why, I'd *love* to," Helen said, "but there hasn't been anything in this house to drink since Eric's operation. That was three years ago."

Was he losing his memory, had his gift for concealing painful facts let him forget that he had sold his house, that his children were in trouble, and that his friend had been ill? His eyes slipped from Eric's face to his abdomen, where he saw three pale, sutured scars, two of them at least a foot long. Gone was his navel, and what, Neddy thought, would the roving hand, bed-checking one's gifts at 3 A.M. make of a belly with no navel, no link to birth, this breach in the succession?

"I'm sure you can get a drink at the Biswangers'," Helen said. "They're having an enormous do. You can hear it from here. Listen!"

She raised her head and from across the road, the lawns, the gardens, the woods, the fields, he heard again the brilliant noise of voices over water. "Well, I'll get wet," he said, still feeling that he had no freedom of choice about his means of travel. He dove into the Sachses' cold water and, gasping, close to drowning, made his way from one end of the pool to the other. "Lucinda and I want *terribly* to see you," he said over his shoulder, his face set toward the Biswangers'. "We're sorry it's been so long and we'll call you *very* soon."

He crossed some fields to the Biswangers' and the sounds of revelry there. They would be honored to give him a drink, they would be happy to give him a drink, they would in fact be lucky to give him a drink. The Biswangers invited him and Lucinda for dinner four times a year, six weeks in advance. They were always rebuffed and yet they continued to send out their invitations, unwilling to comprehend the rigid and undemocratic realities of their society. They were the sort of people who discussed the price of things at cocktails, exchanged market tips during dinner, and after dinner told dirty stories to mixed company. They did not belong to Neddy's set—they were not even on Lucinda's Christmas card list. He went toward their pool with feelings of indifference, charity, and some unease, since it seemed to be getting dark and these were the longest days of the year. The party when he joined it was noisy and large. Grace Biswanger was the kind of hostess who asked the optometrist, the veterinarian, the real-estate dealer and the dentist. No one was swimming and the twilight, reflected on the water of the pool, had a wintry gleam. There was a bar and he started for this. When Grace Biswanger saw him she came toward him, not affectionately as he had every right to expect, but bellicosely.

"Why, this party has everything," she said loudly, "including a gate crasher."

She could not deal him a social blow—there was no question about this and he did not flinch. "As a gate crasher," he asked politely, "do I rate a drink?"

"Suit yourself," she said. "You don't seem to pay much attention to invitations."

She turned her back on him and joined some guests, and he went to the bar and ordered a whiskey. The bartender served him but he served him rudely. His was a world in which the caterer's men kept the social score, and to be rebuffed by a part-time barkeep meant that he had suffered some loss of social esteem. Or perhaps the man was new and uninformed. Then he heard Grace at his back say: "They went for broke overnight—nothing but income—and he showed up drunk one Sunday and asked us to loan him five thousand dollars. . . . " She was always talking about money. It was worse than eating your peas off a knife. He dove into the pool, swam its length and went away.

The next pool on his list, the last but two, belonged to his old mistress, Shirley Adams. If he had suffered any injuries at the Biswangers' they would be cured here. Love—sexual roughhouse in fact—was the supreme elixir, the painkiller, the brightly colored pill that would put the spring back into his step, the joy of life in his heart. They had had an affair last week, last month, last year. He couldn't remember. It was he who had broken it off, his was the upper hand, and he stepped through the gate of the wall that surrounded her pool with nothing so considered as self-confidence. It seemed in a way to be his pool as the lover, particularly the illicit lover, enjoys the possessions of his mistress with an authority unknown to holy matrimony. She was there, her hair the color of brass, but her figure, at the edge of the lighted, cerulean water, excited in him no profound memories. It had been, he thought, a lighthearted affair, although she had wept when he broke it off. She seemed confused to see him and he wondered if she was still wounded. Would she, God forbid, weep again?

"What do you want?" she asked.

"I'm swimming across the county."

"Good Christ. Will you ever grow up?"

"What's the matter?"

"If you've come here for money," she said, "I won't give you another cent."

"You could give me a drink."

"I could but I won't. I'm not alone."

"Well, I'm on my way."

He dove in and swam the pool, but when he tried to haul himself up onto the curb he found that the strength in his arms and shoulders had gone, and he paddled to the ladder and climbed out. Looking over his shoulder he saw, in the lighted bathhouse, a young man. Going out onto the dark lawn he smelled chrysanthemums or marigolds—some stubborn autumnal fragrance—on the night air, strong as gas. Looking overhead he saw that the stars had come out, but why should he seem to see Andromeda, Cepheus, and Casiopeia? What had become of the constellations of midsummer? He began to cry.

It was probably the first time in his adult life that he had ever cried, certainly the first time in his life that he had ever felt so miserable, cold, tired, and bewildered. He could not understand the rudeness of the caterer's barkeep or the rudeness of the mistress who had come to him on her knees and showered his trousers with tears. He had swum too long, he had been immersed too long, and his nose and his throat were sore from the water. What he needed then was a drink, some company, and some clean dry clothes, and while he could have cut directly across the road to his home he went on to the Gilmartins' pool. Here, for the first time in his life, he did not dive but went down the steps into the icy water and swam a hobbled side stroke that he might have learned as a youth. He staggered with fatigue on his way to the Clydes' and paddled the length of their pool, stopping again and again with his hand on the curb to rest. He climbed up the ladder and wondered if he had the strength to get home. He had done what he wanted, he had swum the county, but he was so stupified with exhaustion that his triumph seemed vague. Stooped, holding onto the gateposts for support, he turned up the driveway of his own house.

The place was dark. Was it so late that they had all gone to bed? Had Lucinda stayed at the Westerhazys' for supper? Had the girls joined her there or gone someplace else? Hadn't they agreed, as they usually did on Sunday, to regret all their invitations and stay at home? He tried the garage doors to see what cars were in but the doors were locked and rust came off the handles onto his hands. Going toward the house, he saw that the force of the thunderstorm had knocked one of the rain gutters loose. It hung down over the front door like an umbrella rib, but it could be fixed in the morning. The house was locked, and he thought that the stupid cook or the stupid maid must have locked the place up until he remembered that it had been some time since they had employed a maid or a cook. He shouted, pounded on the door, tried to force it with his shoulder, and then, looking in at the windows, saw that the place was empty.

Bernard Malamud

1914 – 1986

Although Bernard Malamud believed the fiction writer should "tell the truth about life," he rejected "pure, dead, documentary realism" for more imaginative approaches to the "truth" and wrote in a manner he himself described as the "realistic, expressionistic mode." Often mingling fantasy with reality and comedy with tragedy, he produced an important body of strikingly fresh and emotionally powerful fiction, both stories and novels.

Born in Brooklyn in 1914, Malamud attended Erasmus High School, where he served on the staff of the school paper, *The Erasmian,* and contributed his early fiction to its columns. Continuing his education in the metropolitan area, he received the B.A. degree from the City College of New York in 1936 and the M.A. in English from Columbia University in 1942. He had held various jobs—as a factory hand and as a clerk in the Census Bureau in Washington—before he began teaching night classes at Erasmus High School in 1941. In 1949 he joined the faculty of Oregon State College, where he taught composition and literature for the next twelve years, with the exception of 1956, which he spent in Italy on a writing grant awarded him by the *Partisan Review* from funds supplied by the Rockefeller Foundation. In 1961, he became a member of the English faculty of Bennington College. His published fiction includes four collections of short stories, *The Magic Barrel* (1958), *Idiots First* (1963), *Rembrant's Hat* (1973), and *The Stories of Bernard Malamud* (1983), and seven novels, *The Natural* (1952), *The Assistant* (1957), *A New Life* (1961), *The Fixer* (1963) as well as *Pictures of Fidelman* (1969), which may be classified either as a loosely structured novel or as a group of interconnected stories, *The Tenants* (1971), *Dubin's Lives* (1978), and

God's Grace (1982). *The Magic Barrel* won the National Book Award for 1959.

"The Magic Barrel," one of Malamud's finest stories, treats a theme basic to much of his fiction: the quest for personal redemption. In this story, a rabbinical student, awaking to the painful self-knowledge that he has never really loved God or humanity, seeks as a bride a sinful woman, hoping "to convert her to goodness, himself to God." Even though the story leaves it to the reader to determine whether or not the rabbinical student thereby does indeed achieve redemption, it nevertheless clearly embodies Malamud's affirmative conviction that suffering can lead to enlightenment and spiritual growth.

The Magic Barrel

Not long ago there lived in uptown New York, in a small, almost meager room, though crowded with books, Leo Finkle, a rabbinical student in the Yeshivah University. Finkle, after six years of study, was to be ordained in June and had been advised by an acquaintance that he might find it easier to win himself a congregation if he were married. Since he had no present prospects of marriage, after two tormented days of turning it over in his mind, he called in Pinye Salzman, a marriage broker whose two-line advertisement he had read in the *Forward*.

The matchmaker appeared one night out of the dark, fourth-floor hallway of the graystone rooming house where Finkle lived, grasping a black, strapped portfolio that had been worn thin with use. Salzman, who had been long in the business, was of slight but dignified build, wearing an old hat, and an overcoat too short and tight for him. He smelled frankly of fish, which he loved to eat, and although he was missing a few teeth, his presence was not displeasing, because of an amiable manner curiously contrasted with mournful eyes. His voice, his lips, his wisp of beard, his bony fingers were animated, but give him a moment of repose and his mild blue eyes revealed a depth of sadness, a characteristic that put Leo a little at ease although the situation, for him, was inherently tense.

He at once informed Salzman why he had asked him to come, explaining that his home was in Cleveland, and that but for his parents, who had married comparatively late in life, he was alone in the world. He had for six years devoted himself almost entirely to his studies, as a result of which, understandably, he had found himself without time for a social life and the company of young women. Therefore he thought it the better part of trial and error—of embarrassing fumbling—to call in an experienced person to advise him on these matters. He remarked in passing that the function of the marriage broker was ancient and honorable, highly approved in the Jewish community, because it made practical the necessary without hindering joy. Moreover, his own parents had been brought together by a matchmaker. They had made, if not a financially profitable marriage—since neither had possessed any worldly goods to speak of—at least a successful one in the sense of their everlasting devotion to each other. Salzman listened in embarrassed surprise, sensing a sort of apology. Later, however, he experienced a glow of pride in his work, an emotion that had left him years ago, and he heartily approved of Finkle.

The two went to their business. Leo had led Salzman to the only clear place in the room, a table near a window that overlooked the lamp-lit city. He seated himself at the matchmaker's side but facing him, attempting by an act of will to suppress the unpleasant tickle in his throat. Salzman eagerly unstrapped his portfolio and removed a loose rubber band from a thin packet of much-handled cards. As he flipped through them, a gesture and sound that physically hurt Leo, the student pretended not to see and gazed steadfastly out the window. Although it was still February, winter was on its last legs, signs of which he had for the first time in years begun to notice. He now observed the round white moon, moving high in the sky through a cloud menagerie, and watched with half-open mouth as it penetrated a huge hen, and dropped out of her like an egg laying itself. Salzman, though pretending through eyeglasses he had just slipped on to be engaged in scanning the writing on the cards, stole occasional glances at the young man's distinguished face, noting with pleasure the long, severe scholar's nose, brown eyes heavy with learning, sensitive yet ascetic lips, and a certain, almost hollow quality of the dark cheeks. He gazed around at shelves upon shelves of books and let out a soft, contented sigh.

When Leo's eyes fell upon the cards, he counted six spread out in Salzman's hand.

"So few?" he asked in disappointment.

"You wouldn't believe me how much cards I got in my office," Salzman replied. "The drawers are already filled to the top, so I keep them now in a barrel, but is every girl good for a new rabbi?"

Leo blushed at this, regretting all he had revealed of himself in a curriculum vitae he had sent to Salzman. He had thought it best to acquaint him with his strict standards and specifications, but in having done so, felt he had told the marriage broker more than was absolutely necessary.

He hesitantly inquired, "Do you keep photographs of your clients on file?"

"First comes family, amount of dowry also what kind promises," Salzman replied, unbuttoning his tight coat and settling himself in the chair. "After comes pictures, rabbi."

"Call me Mr. Finkle. I'm not yet a rabbi."

Salzman said he would, but instead called him doctor, which he changed to rabbi when Leo was not listening too attentively.

Salzman adjusted his horn-rimmed spectacles, gently cleared his throat and read in an eager voice the contents of the top card:

"Sophie P. Twenty four year. Widow one year. No children. Educated high school and two years college. Father promises eight thousand dollars. Has wonderful wholesale business. Also real estate. On the mother's side comes teachers, also one actor. Well known on Second Avenue."

Leo gazed up in surprise. "Did you say a widow?"

"A widow don't mean spoiled, rabbi. She lived with her husband maybe four months. He was a sick boy she made a mistake to marry him."

"Marrying a widow has never entered my mind."

"This is because you have no experience. A widow, especially if she is young and healthy like this girl, is a wonderful person to marry. She will be thankful to you the rest of her life. Believe me, if I was looking now for a bride, I would marry a widow."

Leo reflected, then shook his head.

Salzman hunched his shoulders in an almost imperceptible gesture of disappointment. He placed the card down on the wooden table and began to read another:

"Lily H. High school teacher. Regular. Not a substitute. Has savings and new Dodge car. Lived in Paris one year. Father is successful dentist thirty-five years. Interested in professional man. Well Americanized family. Wonderful opportunity.

"I knew her personally," said Salzman. "I wish you could see this girl. She is a doll. Also very intelligent. All day you could talk to her about books and theater and what not. She also knows current events."

"I don't believe you mentioned her age?"

"Her age?" Salzman said, raising his brows. "Her age is thirty-two years."

Leo said after awhile, "I'm afraid that seems a little too old."

Salzman let out a laugh. "So how old are you, rabbi?"

"Twenty-seven."

"So what is the difference, tell me, between twenty-seven and thirty-two? My own wife is seven years older than me. So what did I suffer?—Nothing. If Rothschild's a daughter wants to marry you, would you say on account her age, no?"

"Yes," Leo said dryly.

Salzman shook off the no in the yes. "Five years don't mean a thing. I give you my word that when you will live with her for one week you will forget her age. What does it mean five years—that she lived more and knows more than somebody who is younger? On this girl, God bless her, years are not wasted. Each one that it comes makes better the bargain."

"What subject does she teach in high school?"

"Languages. If you heard the way she speaks French, you will think it is music. I am in the business twenty-five years, and I recommend her with my whole heart. Believe me, I know what I'm talking, rabbi."

"What's on the next card?" Leo said abruptly.

Saltzman reluctantly turned up the third card:

"Ruth K. Nineteen years. Honor student. Father offers thirteen thousand cash to the right bridegroom. He is a medical doctor. Stomach specialist with marvelous practice. Brother in law owns own garment business. Particular people."

Salzman looked as if he had read his trump card.

"Did you say nineteen?" Leo asked with interest.

"On the dot."

"Is she attractive?" He blushed. "Pretty?"

Salzman kissed his finger tips. "A little doll. On this I give you my word. Let me call the father tonight and you will see what means pretty."

But Leo was troubled. "You're sure she's that young?"

"This I am positive. The father will show you the birth certificate."

"Are you positive there isn't something wrong with her?" Leo insisted.

"Who says there is wrong?"

"I don't understand why an American girl her age should go to a marriage broker."

A smile spread over Salzman's face.

"So for the same reason you went, she comes."

Leo flushed. "I am pressed for time."

Salzman, realizing he had been tactless, quickly explained. "The father came, not her. He wants she should have the best, so he looks around himself. When we will locate the right boy he will introduce him and encourage. This makes a better marriage than if a young girl without experience takes for herself. I don't have to tell you this."

"But don't you think this young girl believes in love?" Leo spoke uneasily.

Salzman was about to guffaw but caught himself and said soberly, "Love comes with the right person, not before."

Leo parted dry lips but did not speak. Noticing that Salzman had snatched a glance at the next card, he cleverly asked, "How is her health?"

"Perfect," Salzman said, breathing with difficulty. "Of course, she is a little lame on her right foot from an auto accident that it happened to her when she was twelve years, but nobody notices on account she is so brilliant and also beautiful."

Leo got up heavily and went to the window. He felt curiously bitter and upbraided himself for having called in the marriage broker. Finally, he shook his head.

"Why not?" Salzman persisted, the pitch of his voice rising.

"Because I detest stomach specialists."

"So what do you care what is his business? After you marry her do you need him? Who says he must come every Friday night in your house?"

Ashamed of the way the talk was going, Leo dismissed Salzman, who went home with heavy, melancholy eyes.

Though he had felt only relief at the marriage broker's departure, Leo was in low spirits the next day. He explained it as arising from Salzman's failure to produce a suitable bride for him. He did not care for his type of clientele. But when Leo found himself hesitating whether to seek out another matchmaker, one more polished than Pinye, he wondered if it could be—his protestations to the contrary, and although he honored his father and mother—that he did not, in essence, care for the matchmaking institution? This thought he quickly put out of mind yet found himself still upset. All day he ran around in the woods—missed an important appointment, forgot to give out his laundry, walked out of a Broadway cafeteria without paying and had to run back with the ticket in his hand; had even not recognized his landlady in the street when she passed with a friend and courteously called out, "A good evening to you, Doctor Finkle." By nightfall, however, he had regained sufficient calm to sink his nose into a book and there found peace from his thoughts.

Almost at once there came a knock on the door. Before Leo could say enter, Salzman, commercial cupid, was standing in the room. His face was gray and meager, his expression hungry, and he looked as if he would expire on his feet. Yet the marriage broker managed, by some trick of the muscles, to display a broad smile.

"So good evening. I am invited?"

Leo nodded, disturbed to see him again, yet unwilling to ask the man to leave.

Beaming still, Salzman laid his portfolio on the table. "Rabbi, I got for you tonight good news."

"I've asked you not to call me rabbi. I'm still a student."

"Your worries are finished. I have for you a first-class bride."

"Leave me in peace concerning this subject." Leo pretended lack of interest.

"The world will dance at your wedding."

"Please, Mr. Salzman, no more."

"But first must come back my strength," Salzman said weakly. He funbled with the portfolio straps and took out of the leather case an oily paper bag, from which he extracted a hard, seeded roll and a small, smoked white fish. With a quick motion of his hand he stripped the fish out of its skin and began ravenously to chew. "All day in a rush," he muttered.

Leo watched him eat.

"A sliced tomato you have maybe?" Salzman hesitantly inquired.

"No."

The marriage broker shut his eyes and ate. When he had finished he carefully cleaned up the crumbs and rolled up the remains of the fish, in the paper bag. His spectacled eyes roamed the room until he discovered, amid some piles of books, a one-burner gas stove. Lifting his hat he humbly asked, "A glass tea you got, rabbi?"

Conscience-stricken, Leo rose and brewed the tea. He served it with a chunk of lemon and two cubes of lump sugar, delighting Salzman.

After he had drunk his tea, Salzman's strength and good spirits were restored.

"So tell me, rabbi," he said amiably, "you considered some more the three clients I mentioned yesterday?"

"There was no need to consider."

"Why not?"

"None of them suits me."

"What then suits you?"

Leo let it pass because he could give only a confused answer.

Without waiting for a reply, Salzman asked, "You remember this girl I talked to you—the high school teacher?"

"Age thirty-two?"

But, surprisingly, Salzman's face lit in a smile. "Age twenty-nine."

Leo shot him a look. "Reduced from thirty-two?"

"A mistake," Salzman avowed. "I talked today with the dentist. He took me to his safety deposit box and showed me the birth certificate. She was twenty-nine years last August. They made her a party in the mountains where she went for her vacation. When her father spoke to me the first time I forgot to write the age and I told you thirty-two, and now I remember this was a different client, a widow."

"The same one you told me about? I thought she was twenty-four?"

"A different. Am I responsible that the world is filled with widows?"

"No, but I'm not interested in them, nor for that matter, in school teachers."

Salzman pulled his clasped hands to his breast. Looking at the ceiling he devoutly exclaimed, "Yiddishe kinder, what can I say to somebody that he is not interested in high school teachers? So what then you are interested?"

Leo flushed but controlled himself.

"In what else will you be interested," Salzman went on, "if you not interested in this fine girl that she speaks four languages and has personally in the bank ten thousand dollars? Also her father guarantees further twelve thousand. Also she has a new car, wonderful clothes, talks on all subjects, and she will give you a first-class home and children. How near do we come in our life to paradise?"

"If she's so wonderful, why wasn't she married ten years ago?"

"Why?" said Salzman with a heavy laugh. "—Why? Because she is *partikiler*. This is why. She wants the *best*."

Leo was silent, amused at how he had entangled himself. But Salzman had aroused his interest in Lily H., and he began seriously to consider calling on her. When the marriage broker observed how intently Leo's mind was at work on the facts he had supplied, he felt certain they would soon come to an agreement.

Late Saturday afternoon, conscious of Salzman, Leo Finkle walked with Lily Hirschorn along Riverside Drive. He walked briskly and erectly, wearing with distinction the black fedora he had that morning taken with trepidation out of the dusty hat box on his closet shelf, and the heavy black Saturday coat he had thoroughly whisked clean. Leo also owned a walking stick, a present from a distant relative, but quickly put temptation aside and did not use it. Lily, petite and not unpretty, had on something signifying the approach of spring. She was au courant, animatedly, with all sorts of subjects, and he weighed her words and found her surprisingly sound—score another for Salzman, whom he uneasily sensed to be somewhere around, hiding perhaps high in a tree along the street, flashing the lady signals with a pocket mirror; or perhaps a cloven-hoofed Pan, piping nuptial ditties as he danced his invisible way before them, strewing wild buds on the walk and purple grapes in their paths, symbolizing fruit of a union, though there was of course still none.

Lily startled Leo by remarking, "I was thinking of Mr. Salzman, a curious figure, wouldn't you say?"

Not certain what to answer, he nodded.

She bravely went on, blushing, "I for one am grateful for his introducing us. Aren't you?"

He courteously replied, "I am."

"I mean," she said with a little laugh—and it was all in good taste, or at least gave the effect of being not in bad—"do you mind that we came together so?"

He was not displeased with her honesty, recognizing that she meant to set the relationship aright, and understanding that it took a certain amount of experience in life, and courage, to want to do it quite that way. One had to have some sort of past to make that kind of beginning.

He said that he did not mind. Salzman's function was traditional and honorable—valuable for what it might achieve, which, he pointed out, was frequently nothing.

Lily agreed with a sigh. They walked on for a while and she said after a long silence, again with a nervous laugh, "Would you mind if I asked you something a little bit personal? Frankly, I find the subject fascinating." Although Leo shrugged, she went on half embarrassedly, "How was it that you came to your calling? I mean was it a sudden passionate inspiration?"

Leo, after a time, slowly replied, "I was always interested in the Law."

"You saw revealed in it the presence of the Highest?"

He nodded and changed the subject. "I understand that you spent a little time in Paris, Miss Hirschorn?"

"Oh, did Mr. Salzman tell you, Rabbi Finkle?" Leo winced but she went on, "It was ages ago and almost forgotten. I remember I had to return for my sister's wedding."

And Lily would not be put off. "When," she asked in a trembly voice, "did you become enamored of God?"

He stared at her. Then it came to him that she was talking not about Leo Finkle, but of a total stranger, some mystical figure, perhaps even passionate prophet that Salzman had dreamed up for her—no relation to the living or dead. Leo trembled with rage and weakness. The trickster had obviously sold her a bill of goods, just as he had him, who'd expected to become acquainted with a young lady of twenty-nine, only to behold, the moment he laid eyes upon her strained and anxious face, a woman past thirty-five and aging rapidly. Only his self control had kept him this long in her presence.

"I am not," he said gravely, "a talented religious person," and in seeking words to go on found himself possessed by shame and fear. "I think," he said in a strained manner, "that I came to God not because I loved Him, but because I did not."

This confession he spoke harshly because its unexpectedness shook him.

Lily wilted. Leo saw a profusion of loaves of bread go flying like ducks high over his head, not unlike the winged loaves by which he had counted himself to sleep last night. Mercifully, then, it snowed, which he would not put past Salzman's machinations.

He was infuriated with the marriage broker and swore he would throw him out of the room the minute he reappeared. But Salzman did not come that night, and when Leo's anger had subsided, an unaccountable despair grew in its place. At first he thought this was caused by his disappointment in Lily, but before long it became evident that he had involved himself with Salzman without a true knowledge of his own intent. He gradually realized—with an emptiness that seized him with six hands—that he had called in the broker to find him a bride because he was incapable of doing it himself. This terrifying insight he had derived as a result of his meeting and conversation with Lily Hirschorn. Her probing questions had somehow irritated him into revealing—to himself more than her—the true nature of his relationship to God, and from that it had come upon him, with shocking force, that apart from his parents, he had never loved anyone. Or perhaps it went the other way, that he did not love God so well as he might, because he had not loved man. It seemed to Leo that his whole life stood starkly revealed and he saw himself for the first time as he truly was—unloved and loveless. This bitter but somehow not fully unexpected revelation brought him to a point of panic, controlled only by extraordinary effort. He covered his face with his hands and cried.

The week that followed was the worst of his life. He did not eat and lost weight. His beard darkened and grew ragged. He stopped attending seminars and almost never opened a book. He seriously considered leaving Yeshivah, although he was deeply troubled at the thought of the loss of all his years of study—saw them like pages torn from a book, strewn over the city—and at the devastating effect of this decision upon his parents. But he had lived without knowledge of himself, and never in the Five Books and all the Commentaries—mea culpa—had the truth been revealed to him. He did not know where to turn, and in all this desolating loneliness there was no *to whom,* although he often thought of Lily but not once could bring himself to go downstairs and make the call. He became touchy and irritable, especially with his landlady who asked him all manner of personal questions; on the other hand, sensing his own disagreeableness, he waylaid her on the stairs and apologized abjectly, until mortified, she ran from him. Out of this, however, he drew the consolation that he was a Jew and that a Jew suffered. But gradually, as the long and terrible week drew to a close, he regained his composure and some idea of purpose in life: to go on as planned. Although he was imperfect, the ideal was not. As for his quest of a bride, the thought of continuing afflicted him with anxiety and heartburn, yet perhaps with this new knowledge of himself he would be more successful than in the past. Perhaps love would now come to him and a bride to that love. And for this sanctified seeking who needed a Salzman?

The marriage broker, a skeleton with haunted eyes, returned that very night. He looked, withal, the picture of frustrated expectancy—as if he had steadfastly waited the week at Miss Lily Hirschorn's side for a telephone call that never came.

Casually coughing, Salzman came immediately to the point: "So how did you like her?"

Leo's anger rose and he could not refrain from chiding the matchmaker: "Why did you lie to me, Salzman?"

Salzman's pale face went dead white, the world had snowed on him.

"Did you not state that she was twenty-nine?" Leo insisted.

"I give you my word—"

"She was thirty-five, if a day. *At least* thirty-five."

"Of this don't be too sure. Her father told me—"

"Never mind. The worst of it was that you lied to her."

"How did I lie to her, tell me?"

"You told her things about me that weren't true. You made me out to be more, consequently less than I am. She had in mind a totally different person, a sort of semi-mystical Wonder Rabbi."

"All I said, you was a religious man."

"I can imagine."

Salzman sighed. "This is my weakness that I have," he confessed. "My wife says to me I shouldn't be a salesman, but when I have two fine people that they would be wonderful to be married, I am so happy that I talk too much." He smiled wanly. "This is why Salzman is a poor man."

Leo's anger left him. "Well, Salzman, I'm afraid that's all."

The marriage broker fastened hungry eyes on him.

"You don't want any more a bride?"

"I do," said Leo, "but I have decided to seek her in a different way. I am no longer interested in an arranged marriage. To be frank, I now admit the necessity of premarital love. That is, I want to be in love with the one I marry."

"Love?" said Salzman, astounded. After a moment he remarked, "For us, our love is our life, not for the ladies. In the ghetto they—"

"I know, I know," said Leo. "I've thought of it often. Love, I have said to myself, should be a by-product of living and worship rather than its own end. Yet for myself I find it necessary to establish the level of my need and fulfill it."

Salzman shrugged but answered, "Listen, rabbi, if you want love, this I can find for you also. I have such beautiful clients that you will love them the minute your eyes will see them."

Leo smiled unhappily. "I'm afraid you don't understand."

But Salzman hastily unstrapped his portfolio and withdrew a manila packet from it.

"Pictures," he said quickly laying the envelope on the table.

Leo called after him to take the pictures away, but as if on the wings of the wind, Salzman had disappeared.

March came. Leo had returned to his regular routine. Although he felt not quite himself yet—lacked energy—he was making plans for a more active social life. Of course it would cost something, but he was an expert in cutting corners; and when there were no corners left he would make circles rounder. All the while Salzman's pictures had lain on the table, gathering dust. Occasionally as Leo sat studying, or enjoying a cup of tea, his eyes fell on the manila envelope, but he never opened it.

The days went by and no social life to speak of developed with a member of the opposite sex—it was difficult, given the circumstances of his situation. One morning Leo toiled up the stairs to his room and stared out the window at the city. Although the day was bright his view of it was dark. For some time he watched the people in the street below hurrying along and then turned with a heavy heart to his little room. On the table was the packet. With a sudden relentless gesture he tore it open. For a half-hour he stood by the table in a state of excitement, examining the photographs of the ladies Salzman had included. Finally, with a deep sigh he put them down. There were six, of varying degrees of attractiveness, but look at them long enough and they all became Lily Hirschorn: all past their prime, all starved behind bright smiles, not a true personality in the lot. Life, despite their frantic yoohooings, had passed them by; they were pictures in a briefcase that stank of fish. After a while, however, as Leo attempted to return the photographs into the envelope, he found in it another, a snapshot of the type taken by a machine for a quarter. He gazed at it a moment and let out a cry.

Her face deeply moved him. Why, he could at first not say. It gave him the impression of youth—spring flowers, yet age—a sense of having been used to the bone, wasted; this came from the eyes, which were hauntingly familiar, yet absolutely strange. He had a vivid impression that he had met her before, but try as he might he could not place her although he could almost recall her name, as if he had read it in her own handwriting. No, this couldn't be; he would have remembered her. It was not, he affirmed, that she had an extraordinary beauty—no, though her face was attractive enough; it was that *something* about her moved him. Feature for feature, even some of the ladies of the photographs could do better; but she leaped forth to his heart—had *lived,* or wanted to—more than just wanted, perhaps regretted how she had lived—had somehow deeply suffered: it could be seen in the depths of those reluctant eyes, and from the way the light enclosed and shone from her, and within her, opening realms of possibility: this was her own. Her he desired. His head ached and eyes narrowed with the intensity of his gazing, then as if an obscure fog had blown up in the mind, he experienced fear of her and was aware that he had received an impression, somehow, of evil. He shuddered, saying softly, it is thus with us all. Leo brewed some tea in a small pot and sat sipping it without sugar, to calm himself. But before he had finished drinking, again with excitement he examined the face and found it good: good for Leo Finkle. Only such a one could understand him and help him seek whatever he was seeking. She might, perhaps, love him. How she had happened to be among the discards in Salzman's barrel he could never guess, but he knew he must urgently go find her.

Leo rushed downstairs, grabbed up the Bronx telephone book, and searched for Salzman's home address. He was not listed, nor was his office. Neither was he in the Manhattan book. But Leo remembered having written down the address on a slip of paper after he had read Salzman's advertisement in the "personals" column of the *Forward.* He ran up to his room and tore through his papers, without luck. It was exasperating. Just when he needed the matchmaker he was nowhere to be found. Fortunately Leo remembered to look in his wallet. There on a card he found his name written and a Bronx address. No phone number was listed, the reason—Leo now recalled—he had originally communicated with Salzman by letter. He got on his coat, put a hat over his skull cap and hurried to the subway station. All the way to the far end of the Bronx he sat on the edge of his seat. He was more than once tempted to take out the picture and see if the girl's face was as he remembered it, but he refrained, allowing the snapshot to remain in his inside coat pocket, content to have her so close. When the train pulled into the station he was waiting at the door and bolted out. He quickly located the street Salzman had advertised.

The building he sought was less than a block from the subway, but it was not an office building, nor even a loft, nor a store in which one could rent office space. It was a very old tenement house. Leo found Salzman's name in pencil on a soiled tag under the bell and climbed three dark flights to his apartment. When he knocked, the door was opened by a thin, asthmatic, gray-haired woman, in felt slippers.

"Yes?" she said, expecting nothing. She listened without listening. He could have sworn he had seen her, too, before but knew it was an illusion.

"Salzman—does he live here? Pinye Salzman," he said, "the matchmaker?"

She stared at him a long minute. "Of course."

He felt embarrassed. "Is he in?"

"No." Her mouth, though left open, offered nothing more.

"The matter is urgent. Can you tell me where his office is?"

"In the air." She pointed upward.

"You mean he has no office?" Leo asked.

"In his socks."

He peered into the apartment. It was sunless and dingy, one large room divided by a half-open curtain, beyond which he could see a sagging metal bed. The near side of the room was crowded with rickety chairs, old bureaus, a three-legged table, racks of cooking utensils, and all the apparatus of a kitchen. But there was no sign of Salzman or his magic barrel, probably also a figment of the imagination. An odor of frying fish made Leo weak to the knees.

"Where is he?" he insisted. "I've got to see your husband."

At length she answered, "So who knows where he is? Every time he thinks a new thought he runs to a different place. Go home, he will find you."

"Tell him Leo Finkle."

She gave no sign she had heard.

He walked downstairs, depressed.

But Salzman, breathless, stood waiting at his door.

Leo was astounded and overjoyed. "How did you get here before me?"

"I rushed."

"Come inside."

They entered. Leo fixed tea, and a sardine sandwich for Salzman. As they were drinking he reached behind him for the packet of pictures and handed them to the marriage broker.

Salzman put down his glass and said expectantly, "You found somebody you like?"

"Not among these."

The marriage broker turned away.

"Here is the one I want." Leo held forth the snapshot.

Salzman slipped on his glasses and took the picture into his trembling hand. He turned ghastly and let out a groan.

"What's the matter?" cried Leo.

"Excuse me. Was an accident this picture. She isn't for you."

Salzman frantically shoved the manila packet into his portfolio. He thrust the snapshot into his pocket and fled down the stairs.

Leo, after momentary paralysis, gave chase and cornered the marriage broker in the vestibule. The landlady made hysterical outcries but neither of them listened.

"Give me back the picture, Salzman."

"No." The pain in his eyes was terrible.

"Tell me who she is then."

"This I can't tell you. Excuse me."

He made to depart, but Leo, forgetting himself, seized the matchmaker by his tight coat and shook him frenziedly.

"Please," sighed Salzman. "*Please.*"

Leo ashamedly let him go. "Tell me who she is," he begged. "It's very important for me to know."

"She is not for you. She is a wild one—wild, without shame. This is not a bride for a rabbi."

"What do you mean wild?"

"Like an animal. Like a dog. For her to be poor was a sin. This is why to me she is dead now."

"In God's name, what do you mean?"

"Her I can't introduce to you," Salzman cried.

"Why are you so excited?"

"Why, he asks," Salzman said, bursting into tears. "This is my baby, my Stella, she should burn in hell."

Leo hurried up to bed and hid under the covers. Under the covers he thought his life through. Although he soon fell asleep he could not sleep her out of his mind. He woke, beating his breast. Though he prayed to be rid of her, his prayers went unanswered. Through days of torment he endlessly struggled not to love her; fearing success, he escaped it. He then concluded to convert her to goodness, himself to God. The idea alternately nauseated and exalted him.

He perhaps did not know that he had come to a final decision until he encountered Salzman in a Broadway cafeteria. He was sitting alone at a rear table, sucking the bony remains of a fish. The marriage broker appeared haggard, and transparent to the point of vanishing.

Salzman looked up at first without recognizing him. Leo had grown a pointed beard and his eyes were weighted with wisdom.

"Salzman," he said, "love has at last come to my heart."

"Who can love from a picture?" mocked the marriage broker.

"It is not impossible."

"If you can love her, then you can love anybody. Let me show you some new clients that they just sent me their photographs. One is a little doll."

"Just her I want," Leo murmured.

"Don't be a fool, doctor. Don't bother with her."

"Put me in touch with her, Salzman," Leo said humbly. "Perhaps I can be of service."

Salzman had stopped eating and Leo understood with emotion that it was now arranged.

Leaving the cafeteria, he was, however, afflicted by a tormenting suspicion that Salzman had planned it all to happen this way.

Leo was informed by letter that she would meet him on a certain corner, and she was there one spring night, waiting under a street lamp. He appeared, carrying a small bouquet of violets and rosebuds. Stella stood by the lamp post, smoking. She wore white with red shoes, which fitted his expectations, although in a troubled moment he had imagined the dress red, and only the shoes white. She waited uneasily and shyly. From afar he saw that her eyes—clearly her father's—were filled with desperate innocence. He pictured, in her, his own redemption. Violins and lit candles revolved in the sky. Leo ran forward with flowers outthrust.

Around the corner, Salzman, leaning against a wall, chanted prayers for the dead.

Peter Taylor

1919 –

Peter Taylor has made middle-class life of the urban South his special fictional province, the locale of his stories typically being such cities as Nashville, Memphis, and Chattanooga. Unlike some of his Southern as well as Northern contemporaries, he shuns violence and grotesquerie in his fiction and finds his subjects instead in the quieter, if none the less painful, dramas of domestic relationships and family affairs. Taylor's vivid character portrayal, flawless style, and subtle command of form place him among the foremost masters of the contemporary short story.

Born in Trenton, Tennessee, in 1919, Taylor received his early educational training at schools in Nashville, St. Louis, and Memphis. He continued his studies at Southwestern University in Memphis, Vanderbilt University, and Kenyon College, receiving his bachelor's degree from the last named school in 1940. In 1946, after spending two years in England during World War II as a sergeant in the Rail Transportation Corps, he joined the faculty of the University of North Carolina at Greensboro. In 1967, he became a professor at the University of Virginia. At various times he has also taught at Indiana University, Ohio State University, University of Chicago, Harvard University, and Kenyon College; and in 1955 he was a lecturer in The American Studies Institute of the University College, Oxford. Among the honors and awards his fiction have brought him are a Guggenheim Fellowship in 1950–1951, a $1000 grant from the National Institute of Arts and Letters in 1952, and the first prize in the 1959 O. Henry Memorial awards. He has published two novels, *A Woman of Means* (1950) and the Pulitzer Prize-winning *A Summons to Memphis* (1986); two plays, *Tennessee Day in St. Louis* (1957) and *A Stand in the*

Mountains (1985); and seven collections of short stories, *A Long Fourth and Other Stories* (1948), *The Widows of Thornton* (1954), *Happy Families Are All Alike* (1959), *Miss Leonora When Last Seen and 15 Other Stories* (1963), *Collected Stories* (1969), *In the Miro District and Other Stories* (1977), and *The Old Forest and Other Stories* (1985).

A recurring theme in Taylor's stories is the impact changing social and economic patterns make on southern life and character not only in the larger cities but also, and particularly, in smaller cities and towns, such as Thornton in "What You Hear from 'em?" These changes disrupt traditional values and the intertwined strong sense of family and place many of his characters have, a sense often fully shared by and even most prominently displayed in the black servant of an old, established white family of the kind Aunt Munsie in this story represents. Aunt Munsie, who is monumentally portrayed, heroically resists the changing order of life as long as she can, and her ultimate defeat is a dramatic commentary on the timeless clash between traditional values and concepts and new ones.

What You Hear from 'em?

Whenever someone misunderstood Aunt Munsie's question, she didn't bother to clarify it. She might repeat it two or three times, in order to drown out some fool answer she was getting from some fool white woman, or man, either. "What you hear from 'em?" she'd ask. "What you hear from 'em? *What you hear from 'em?*" She was so deaf that anyone whom she thoroughly drowned out only laughed and said Aunt Munsie had got so deaf she couldn't hear it thunder. It was, of course, only the most utterly fool answers that ever received the drowning-out treatment. For a number of years, Aunt Munsie was willing to listen to those who mistook her "'em" to mean any and all of the Dr. Tolliver children. And for more years than that she would listen to those who thought she wanted just *any* news of her two favorites among the Tolliver children—Thad and Will. But later on she stopped putting the question to all insensitive and frivolous souls who didn't understand that what she was interested in hearing—and *all* she was interested in hearing—was when Mr. Thad and Mr. Will Tolliver were going to pack up their families and come back to Thornton for good.

They had always promised her to come back—to come back sure enough, that is. On separate occasions, both Thad and Will had promised her. For ten years, she hadn't seen them together, but each of them had made visits to Thornton now and then with his own family. She would see a big car stopping in front of her house on a Sunday afternoon and see either Will or Thad with his wife and children piling out into the dusty street—it was nearly always summer when they came—and then see them filing across the street, jumping the ditch, and unlatching the gate to her yard. She always met them in that pen of a yard, but long before they had jumped the ditch she was clapping her hands and calling out, "Hai-ee! Hai-ee, now! Look-a-here! Whee! Whee! Look-a-here!"She had got so blind that she was never sure whether it was Mr. Thad or Mr. Will until she had her arms about his waist. They had always looked a great deal alike, and their city clothes made them look even more alike nowadays. Aunt Munsie's eyes were so bad, besides being so full of moisture on those occasions, that she really recognized them by their girth. Will had grown a regular washpot of a stomach and Thad was still thin as a rail. They would sit on her porch for twenty or thirty minutes—whichever one it was and his family—and then they would be gone again.

Aunt Munsie wouldn't try to detain them—not seriously. Those short little old visits didn't mean a thing to her. He—Thad or Will—would lean against the banister rail and tell her how well his children were doing in school or college, and she would make each child in turn come and sit beside her on the swing for a minute and receive a hug about the waist or shoulders. They were timid with her, not seeing her any more than they did, but she could tell from their big Tolliver smiles that they liked her to hug them and make over them. Usually, she would lead them all out to her back yard and show them her pigs and dogs and chickens. (She always had at least one frizzly chicken to show the children.) They would traipse through her house to the back yard and then traipse through again to the front porch. It would be time for them to go when they came back, and Aunt Munsie wold look up at *him*—Mr. Thad or Mr. Will (she had begun calling them "Mr." the day they married—and say, "Now, look here. When you comin' back?"

Both Thad and Will knew what she meant, of course, and whichever it was would tell her he was making definite plans to wind up his business and that he was going to buy a certain piece of property, "a mile north of town" or "on the old River Road," and build a jim-dandy house there. He would say, too, how good Aunt Munsie's own house was looking, and his wife would say how grand the zinnias and cannas looked in the yard. (The yard was all flowers—not a blade of grass.) The visit was almost over then. There remained only the exchange of presents. One of the children would hand Aunt Munsie a paper bag containing a pint of whiskey or a carton of cigarettes. Aunt Munsie would go to her back porch or to the pit in the yard and get a fern or a wandering Jew, potted in a rusty lard bucket, and make Mrs. Thad or Mrs. Will take it along. Then the visit was over, and they would leave. From the porch, Aunt Munsie would wave good-bye with one hand and lay the other hand, trembling slightly, on the banister rail. (The banisters had come off a porch of the house where Thad and Will had grown up. Dr. Tolliver had been one of the first to widen his porches and remove the gingerbread from his house.) The children and their mother would wave to Aunt Munsie from the street. Their father would close the gate, resting his hand a moment on its familiar wrought-iron frame, and wave to her before he jumped the ditch. (The iron fence, with its iron gate, had been around the yard at Dr. Tolliver's till he took it down and set out a hedge, just a few weeks before he died.)

Such paltry little visits meant nothing to Aunt Munsie. No more did the letters that came with "her things" at Christmas. She was supposed to get her daughter, Lucrecie, who lived next door, to read the letters, but in late years she had taken to putting them away unopened, and some of the presents, too. All she wanted to hear from *them* was when they were coming back for good, and she had learned that the Christmas letters never told her that. On her daily route with her slop wagon through the Square, up Jackson Street, and down Jefferson, there were only four or five houses left where she asked her question. These were houses where the amount of pig slop was not worth stopping for, houses where one old maid, or maybe two, lived, or a widow with one old bachelor son who had never amounted to anything and ate no more than a woman. And so—in the summertime, anyway—she took to calling out at the top of her lungs, when she approached the house of one of the elect, "What you hear from 'em?" Sometimes a Miss Patty or a Miss Lucille or a Mr. Ralph would get up out of a porch chair and come down the brick walk to converse with Aunt Munsie. Or sometimes one of them would just lean out over the shrubbery planted around the porch and call, "Not a thing, Munsie. Not a thing lately."

She would shake her head and call back, "Naw. Naw. Not a thing. Nobody don't hear from 'em. Too busy, they be!"

Aunt Munsie's skin was the color of a faded tow sack. She was hardly four feet tall. She was generally believed to be totally bald, and on her head she always wore a white dust cap with an elastic band. She wore an apron, too, while making her rounds with her slop wagon. Even when the weather got bad and she tied a wool scarf about her head and wore an overcoat, she put on an apron over the coat. Her hands and feet were delicately small, which made the old-timers sure she was of Guinea stock that had come to Tennessee out of South Carolina. What most touched the hearts of old ladies on Jackson and Jefferson Streets was her little feet. The sight of her feet "took them back to the old days," they said, because Aunt Munsie still wore flat-heeled, high-button shoes. Where ever did Munsie find such shoes any more?

She walked down the street, the very center of the street, with a spry step and was continually turning her head from side to side, as though looking at the old houses and trees for the first time. If her sight was as bad as she sometimes let on it was, she probably recognized the houses only by their roof lines against the Thornton sky. Since this was nearly thirty years ago, most of the big Victorian and ante-bellum houses were still standing, though with their yard fences already gone and their lovely gingerbread work beginning to go. (It went first from houses where there was someone, like Dr. Tolliver, with a special eye for style and for keeping up with the times.) The streets hadn't yet been broadened—or only Nashville Street had—and the maples and elms met above the streets. In the autumn, their leaves covered the high banks and filled the deep ditches on either side. The dark macadam surfacing itself was barely wide enough for two automobiles to pass. Aunt Munsie, pulling her slop wagon, which was a long, low, four-wheeled vehicle about the size and shape of a coffin, paraded down the center of the street without any regard for, if with any awareness of, the traffic problems she sometimes made. Grasping the wagon's decidedly sawed-off-looking tongue, she pulled it after her with a series of impatient jerks, as though that tongue were the arm of some very stubborn, overgrown white child she had to nurse in her old age. Strangers in town or trifling high-school boys would blow their horns at her, but she was never known to so much as glance over her shoulder at the sound of the horn. Now and then, a pedestrian on the sidewalk would call out to the driver of an automobile, "She's so deaf she can't hear it thunder."

It wouldn't have occurred to anyone in Thornton—not in those days—that something ought to be done about Aunt Munsie and her wagon for the sake of the public good. In those days, everyone had equal rights on the streets of Thornton. A vehicle was a vehicle, and a person was a person, each with the right to move as slowly as he pleased and to stop where and as often as he pleased. In the Thornton mind, there was no imaginary line down the middle of the street, and, indeed, no one there at that time had heard of drawing a real line on *any* street. It was merely out of politeness that you made room for others to pass. Nobody would have blown a horn at an old colored woman with her slop wagon—nobody but some Yankee stranger or a trifling high-school boy or maybe old Mr. Ralph Hadley in a special fit of temper. When citizens of Thornton were in a real hurry and got caught behind Aunt Munsie, they leaned out their car windows and shouted, "Aunt Munsie, can you make a little room?" And Aunt Munsie didn't fail to hear *them*. She would holler "Hai-ee, now! Whee! Look-a-here!" and jerk her wagon to one side. As they passed her, she would wave her little hand and grin a toothless, pink-gummed grin.

Yet, without any concern for the public good, Aunt Munsie's friends among the white women began to worry more and more about the danger of her being run down by an automobile. They talked among themselves and they talked to her about it. They wanted her to give up collecting slop, now she had got so blind and deaf. "Pshaw," said Aunt Munsie, closing her eyes contemptuously. "Not me." She meant by that that no one would dare run into her or her wagon. Sometimes when she crossed the Square on a busy Saturday morning or on a first Monday, she would hold up one hand with the palm turned outward and stop all traffic until she was safely across and in the alley beside the hotel.

Thornton wasn't even then what it had been before the Great World War. In every other house, there was a stranger or a mill hand who had moved up from Factory Town. Some of the biggest old places stood empty, the way Dr. Tolliver's had until it burned. They stood empty not because nobody wanted to rent them or buy them but because the heirs who had gone off somewhere making money could never be got to part with "the home place." The story was that Thad Tolliver nearly went crazy when he heard their old house had burned, and wanted to sue the town, and even said he was going to help get the Republicans into office. Yet Thad had hardly put foot in the house since the day his daddy died. It was said the Tolliver house had caught fire from the Major Pettigru house, which had burned two nights before, and no doubt it had. Sparks could have smoldered in that roof of rotten shingles for a long time before bursting into flame. Some even said the Pettigru house might have caught from the Johnston house, which had burned earlier that same fall. But Thad knew and Will knew and everybody knew the town wasn't to blame, and knew there was no firebug. Why, those old houses stood there empty year after year, and in the fall the leaves fell from the trees and settled around the porches and stoops, and who was there to rake the leaves? Maybe it was a good thing those houses burned, and maybe it would have been as well if some of the houses that still had people in them burned, too. There were houses in Thornton the heirs had never left that looked far worse than the Tolliver or the Pettigru or the Johnston house ever had. The people who lived in them were the ones who gave Aunt

Munsie the biggest fool answers to her question, the people whom she soon quit asking her question of or even passing the time of day with, except when she couldn't help it, out of politeness. For, truly, to Aunt Munsie there were things under the sun worse than going off and getting rich in Nashville and Memphis and even in Washington, D.C. This was a subject she and her daughter Lucrecie mouthed at each other about across their back fence sometimes. Lucrecie was shiftless, and she liked shiftless white people like the ones who didn't have the ambition to leave Thornton. She thought their shiftlessness showed they were *quality*. "Quality?" Aunt Munsie would echo, her voice full of sarcasm. "Whee! Hai-ee! You talk like *you* was *my* mammy, Crecie. Well, if there be quality, there be quality *and* quality. There's quality and there's *has-been* quality, Crecie." There was no end to that argument Aunt Munsie had with Crecie, and it wasn't at all important to Aunt Munsie. The people who still lived in these houses—the ones she called has-been quality—meant little more to her than the mill hands, and the strangers from up North who ran the Piggly Wiggly, the five-and-ten-cent store, and the roller-skating rink.

There was this to be said, though, for the has-been quality: They knew *who* Aunt Munsie was, and in a limited literal way they understood what she said. But those *others*—why, they thought Aunt Munsie a beggar, and she knew they did. They spoke of her as Old What You Have For Mom, because that's what they thought she was saying when she called out, "What you hear from 'em?" Their ears were not attuned to that soft "r" she put in "from" or the elision that made "from 'em" sound to them like "for Mom." Many's the time Aunt Munsie had seen, or sensed the presence of, one of those *other* people, watching from next door, when Miss Leonora Lovell, say, came down her front walk and handed her a little parcel of scraps across the ditch. Aunt Munsie knew what they thought of her—how they laughed at her and felt sorry for her and despised her all at once. But, like the has-been quality, they didn't matter, never had, never would.

Oh, they mattered in a way to Lucrecie. Lucrecie thought about them and talked about them a lot. She called them "white trash" and even "radical Republicans." It made Aunt Munsie grin to hear Crecie go on, because she knew Crecie got all her notions from her own has-been-quality people. And so it didn't matter, except that Aunt Munsie knew Crecie truly had all sorts of good sense and had only been carried away and spoiled by such folks as she had worked for, such folks as had really raised Crecie from the time she was big enough to run errands for them, fifty years back. In her heart, Aunt Munsie knew that even Lucrecie didn't matter to her the way a daughter might. It was because while Aunt Munsie had been raising a family of white children, a different sort of white people from hers had been raising her own child, Crecie. Sometimes, if Aunt Munsie was in her chicken yard or out in her little patch of cotton when Mr. Thad or Mr. Will arrived, Crecie would come out to the fence and say, "Mama, some of your chillun's out front."

Miss Leonora Lovell and Miss Patty Bean, and especially Miss Lucille Satterfield, were all the time after Aunt Munsie to give up collecting slop. "You're going to get run over by one of those crazy drivers, Munsie," they said. Miss Lucille was the widow of old Judge Satterfield. "If the Judge were alive, Munsie," she said, "I'd make him find a way to stop you. But the men down at the courthouse don't listen to the women in this town any more. And I think they'd be 'most too scared of you to do what I want them to do." Aunt Munsie wouldn't listen to any of that. She knew that if Miss Lucille had come out there to her gate, she must have *something* she was going to say about Mr. Thad or Mr. Will. Miss Lucille had two brothers and a son of her own who were lawyers in Memphis, and who lived in style down there and kept Miss Lucille in style here in Thornton. Memphis was where Thad Tolliver had his Ford-and-Lincoln agency, and so Miss Lucille always had news about Thad, and, indirectly, about Will, too.

"Is they doin' any good? What you hear from 'em?" Aunt Munsie asked Miss Lucille one afternoon in early spring. She had come along just when Miss Lucille was out picking some of the jonquils that grew in profusion on the steep bank between the sidewalk and the ditch in front of her house.

"Mr. Thad and his folks will be up one day in April, Munsie," Miss Lucille said in her pleasantly hoarse voice. "I understand Mr. Will and his crowd may come for Easter Sunday."

"One day, and gone again!" said Aunt Munsie.

"We always try to get them to stay at least one night, but they're busy folks, Munsie."

"When they comin' back sure enough, Miss Lucille?"

"Goodness knows, Munsie. Goodness knows. Goodness knows when any of them are coming back to stay." Miss Lucille took three quick little steps down the bank and hopped lightly across the ditch. "They're prospering so, Munsie," she said throwing her chin up and smiling proudly. This fragile lady, this daughter, wife, sister, mother of lawyers (and, of course, the darling of all their hearts), stood there in the street with her pretty little feet and shapely ankles close together, and holding a handful of jonquils before her as if it were her bridal bouquet. "They're *all* prospering so, Munsie. Mine *and* yours. You ought to go down to Memphis to see them now and then, the way I do. Or go up to Nashville to see Mr. Will. I understand he's got an even finer establishment than Thad. They've done well, Munsie—yours *and* mine—and we can be proud of them. You owe it to yourself to go and see how well they're fixed. They're rich men by our standards in Thornton, and they're going farther—*all* of them."

Aunt Munsie dropped the tongue of her wagon noisily on the pavement. "What I want go see 'em for?" she said angrily and with a lowering brow. Then she stooped and, picking up the wagon tongue again, she wheeled her vehicle toward the center of the street, to get by Miss Lucille, and started off toward the Square. As she turned out into the street, the brakes of a car, as so often, screeched behind her. Presently everyone in the neighborhood could hear Mr. Ralph Hadley tooting the insignificant little horn on his mama's coupé and shouting at Aunt Munsie in his own tooty voice, above the sound of the horn. Aunt Munsie pulled over, making just enough room to let poor old Mr. Ralph get by but without once looking back at him. Suddenly, before Mr. Ralph could get his car started again, Miss Lucille was running along beside Aunt Munsie, saying, "Munsie, you be careful! You're going to meet your death on the streets of Thornton, Tennessee!"

"Let 'em," said Aunt Munsie. Miss Lucille didn't know whether Munsie meant "Let 'em run over me; I don't care" or meant "Let 'em just dare!" Miss Lucille soon turned back, without Aunt Munsie's ever looking at her. And when Mr. Ralph Hadley did get his motor started, and sailed past in his mama's coupé, Aunt Munsie didn't give him a look, either. Nor did Mr. Ralph turn his face to look at Aunt Munsie. He was on his way to the drugstore, to pick up his mama's prescriptions, and he was too entirely put out, peeved, and upset to endure even the briefest exchange with that ugly, uppity old Munsie of the Tollivers'.

Aunt Munsie continued pulling her slop wagon toward the Square. There was a more animated expression on her face than usual, and every so often her lips would move rapidly and emphatically over a phrase or sentence. Why should she go to Memphis and Nashville and see how rich they were? No matter how rich they were, what difference did it make, if they didn't own any land, or none in Cameron County. She had heard the old Doctor tell them—tell both his boys and his girls, and the old lady, too, in her day—that nobody was rich who didn't own land, and nobody stayed rich who didn't see after his land first-hand. But, of course, Aunt Munsie had herself mocked the old Doctor to his face for going on about land so much. She used to tell him she hadn't ever seen *him* behind a plow. And was anybody ever more scared of a mule than Dr. Tolliver was? Mules or horses, either? Aunt Munsie had heard him say that the happiest day of his life was the day he first learned that the horseless carriage was a reality.

No, it wasn't really to own land that Thad and Will ought to come back to Thornton. It was more that if they were going to be rich, they ought to come home where their money counted for something. How could Will or Thad ever be rich anywhere else? They could just have a lot of money in the bank, that was all—like that mill manager from Chi. The mill manager could have a yard full of big cars and a stucco house as big as you like, but who would ever take him for rich? Aunt Munsie would sometimes say all these things to Crecie, or something as nearly like them as she could find words for. Crecie might nod her head in agreement or she might be in a mood to say being rich wasn't any good for anybody and didn't matter, and that you could live on just being quality better than on being rich in Thornton. "Quality's better than land or better than money in the bank here," Crecie would say.

Aunt Munsie would sneer at her and say, "It never were."

Lucrecie could talk all she wanted about the old times! Aunt Munsie knew too much about what they were like, for both the richest white folks and the blackest field hands. Nothing about the old times was as good as these days, and there were going to better times yet when Mr. Thad and Mr. Will came back. Everybody lived easier now than they used to, and were better off. She could never be got to reminisce about her childhood in slavery, or her life with her husband, or even about those halcyon days after the old Mizziz had died and Aunt Munsie's word had become law in the Tolliver household. Without being able to book-read or even to make numbers, she had finished raising the whole pack of towheaded Tollivers just as the Mizziz would have wanted it done. The Doctor told her she *had* to—he didn't ever once think about getting another wife, or taking in some cousin, not after his "Molly darling"—and Aunt Munsie *did*. But, as Crecie said, when a time was past in her mama's life, it seemed to be gone and done with in her head, too.

Lucrecie would say frankly she thought her mama was "hard about people and things in the world." She talked about her mama not only to the Blalocks, for whom she had worked all her life, but to anybody else who gave her an opening. It wasn't just about her mama, though, that she would talk to anybody. She liked to talk, and she talked about Aunt Munsie not in an ugly, resentful way but as she would about the rainy season or where the fire was last night. (Crecie was twice the size of her mama, and black the way her old daddy had been, and loud and good-natured the way he was—or at least the way Aunt Munsie wasn't. You wouldn't have known they were mother and daughter, and not many of the young people in town did realize it. Only by accident did they live next door to each other; Mr. Thad and Mr. Will had bought Munsie her house, and Crecie had heired hers from her second husband.) *That* was how she talked about her mama—as she would have about any lonely, eccentric, harmless neighbor. "I may be dead wrong, but I think Mama's kind of hardhearted," she would say. "She's a good old soul, I reckon, but when something's past, it's gone and done with for Mama. She don't think about day before yestiddy—or yestiddy, either. I don't know, maybe that's the way to be. Maybe that's why the old soul's gonna outlive us all." Then, obviously thinking about what a picture of health she herself was at sixty, Crecie would throw back her head and laugh so loud you might hear her out at the fairgrounds.

Crecie, however, knew her mama wasn't honest-to-God mean and hadn't ever been mean to the Tolliver children, the way the Blalocks liked to make out she had. All the Tolliver children but Mr. Thad and Mr. Will had quarrelled with her for good by the time they were grown, but they had quarrelled with the old Doctor, too (and as if they were the only ones who shook off their old folks this day and time). When Crecie talked about her mama, she didn't spare her anything, but she was fair to her, too. And it was in no hateful or disloyal spirit that she took part in the conspiracy that finally got Aunt Munsie and her slop wagon off the streets of Thornton. Crecie would have done the same for any neighbor. She had small part enough, actually, in that conspiracy. Her part was merely to break the news to Aunt Munsie that there was now a law against keeping pigs within the city limits. It was a small part but one that no one else quite dared to take.

"They ain't no such law!" Aunt Munsie roared back at Crecie. She was slopping her pigs when Crecie came to the fence and told her about the law. It had seemed the most appropriate time to Lucrecie. "They ain't never been such a law, Crecie," Aunt Munsie said. "Every house on Jackson and Jefferson used to keep pigs."

"It's a brand-new law, Mama."

Aunt Munsie finished bailing out the last of the slop from her wagon. It was just before twilight. The last, weak rays of the sun colored the clouds behind the mock-orange tree in Crecie's yard. When Aunt Munsie turned around from the sty, she pretended that the little bit of light in the clouds hurt her eyes, and turned away her head. And when Lucrecie said that everybody had until the first of the year to get rid of their pigs, Aunt Munsie was in a spell of deafness. She headed out toward the crib to get some corn for the chickens. She was trying to think whether anybody else inside the town still kept pigs. Herb Mallory did—two doors beyond Crecie. Then Aunt Munsie remembered Herb didn't pay city taxes. The town line ran between him and Shad Willis.

That was sometime in June, and before July came, Aunt Munsie knew all there was worth knowing about the conspiracy. Mr. Thad and Mr. Will had each been in town for a day during the spring. They and their families had been to her house and sat on the porch; the children had gone back to look at her half-grown collie dog and the two hounds, at the old sow and her farrow of new pigs, and at the frizzliest frizzly chicken Aunt Munsie had ever had. And on those visits to Thornton, Mr. Thad and Mr. Will had also made their usual round among their distant kin and close friends. Everywhere they went, they had heard of the near-accidents Aunt Munsie was causing with her slop wagon and the real danger there was of her being run over. Miss Lucille Satterfield and Miss Patty Bean had both been to the Mayor's office and also to see Judge Lawrence to try to get Aunt Munsie "ruled" off the streets, but the men in the courthouse and in the Mayor's office didn't listen to the women in Thornton any more. And so either Mr. Thad or Mr. Will—how would which one of them it was matter to Munsie?—had been prevailed upon to stop by Mayor Lunt's office, and in a few seconds' time had set the wheels of conspiracy in motion. Soon a general inquiry had been made in the town as to how many citizens still kept pigs. Only two property owners besides Aunt Munsie had been found to have pigs on their premises, and they, being men, had been docile and reasonable enough to sell what they had on hand to Mr. Will or Mr. Thad Tolliver. Immediately afterward—within a matter of weeks, that is—a city ordinance had been passed forbidding the possession of swine within the corporate limits of Thornton. Aunt Munsie had got the story bit by bit from Miss Leonora and Miss Patty and Miss Lucille and others, including the constable himself, whom she didn't hesitate to stop right in the middle of the Square on a Saturday noon. Whether it was Mr. Thad or Mr. Will who had been prevailed upon by the ladies she never ferreted out, but that was only because she did not wish to do so.

The constable's word was the last word for her. The constable said yes, it was a law, and he admitted yes, he had sold his own pig—for the constable was one of those two reasonable souls—to Mr. Thad or Mr. Will. He didn't say which of them it was, or if he did, Aunt Munsie couldn't remember it. After her interview with the constable, Aunt Munsie never again exchanged words with any human being about the ordinance against pigs. That afternoon, she took a fishing pole from under her house and drove the old sow and the nine shoats down to Herb Mallory's, on the outside of town. They were his, she said, if he wanted them, and he could pay her at killing time.

It was literally true that Aunt Munsie never again exchanged words with anyone about the ordinance against pigs or about the conspiracy she had discovered against herself. But her daughter Lucrecie had a tale to tell about what Aunt Munsie did that afternoon after she had seen the constable and before she drove the pigs over to Herb Mallory's. It was mostly a tale of what Aunt Munsie said to her pigs and to her dogs and her chickens.

Crecie was in her own back yard washing her hair when her mama came down the rickety porch steps and into the yard next door. Crecie had her head in the pot of suds, and so she couldn't look up, but she knew by the way Mama flew down the steps that there was trouble. "She came down them steps like she was wasp-nest bit, or like some youngon who's got hisself wasp-nest bit—and her all of eighty, I reckon!" Then, as Crecie told it, her mama scurried around in the yard for a minute or so like she thought Judgment was about to catch up with her, and pretty soon she commenced slamming at something. Crecie wrapped a towel about her soapy head, squatted low, and edged over to the plank fence. She peered between the planks and saw what her mama was up to. Since there never had been a gate to the fence around the pigsty, Mama had taken the wood axe and was knocking a hole in it. But directly, just after Crecie had taken her place by the plank fence, her mama had left off her slamming at the sty and turned about so quickly and so exactly toward Crecie that Crecie thought the poor, blind old soul had managed to spy her squatting there. Right away, though, Crecie realized it was not *her* that Mama was staring at. She saw that all Aunt Munsie's chickens and those three dogs of hers had come up behind her, and were clucking and whining to know why she didn't stop that infernal racket and put out some feed for them.

Crecie's mama set one hand on her hip and rested the axe on the ground. "Just look at yuh!" she said, and then she let the chickens and the dogs—and the pigs, too—have it. She told them what a miserable bunch of creatures they were, and asked them what right they had to always be looking for handouts from her. She sounded like the boss-man who's caught all his pickers laying off before sundown, and she sounded, too, like the preacher giving his sinners Hail Columbia at camp meeting. Finally, shouting explosively, "Now, g'wine! G'wine! G'wine! G'wine widja!," and swinging the axe wide and broad above their heads, she sent the dogs howling under the house and the chickens scattering in every direction. Only the collie pup, of the three dogs, didn't scamper to the farthest corner underneath the house. He stopped under the steps, and not two seconds later he was poking his long head out again and showing the whites of his doleful brown eyes. Crecie's mama took a step toward him and then she halted. "You want to know what's the commotion about? I reckoned you would," she said with profound contempt, as though the collie were a more reasonable soul than the other animals, and as though there were nothing she held in such thorough disrespect as reason. "I tell you what the commotion's about," she said. "They *ain't* comin' back." She turned her head to one side, and the only explanation Crecie could find for her mama's next words was that that collie pup did look so much like Miss Lucille Satterfield.

"Why don't I go down to Memphis or up to Nashville and see 'em sometime, like *you* does?" Aunt Munsie asked the collie. "I tell you why. Becaze I ain't nothin' to 'em in Memphis, and they ain't nothin' to me in Nashville. *You* can go!" she said, advancing and shaking the big axe at the dog. "A collie dog's a collie dog anywhar. But Aunt Munsie, she's just their Aunt Munsie here in Thornton. I got sense enough to see *that*." The collie slowly pulled his head back under the steps, and Aunt Munsie watched for a minute to see if he would show himself again. When he didn't, she went and jerked the fishing pole out from under the house and headed toward the pigsty. Crecie remained squatting beside the fence until her mama and the pigs were out in the street and on their way to Herb Mallory's.

That was the end of Aunt Munsie's keeping pigs and the end of her daily rounds with her slop wagon, but it wasn't the end of Aunt Munsie. She lived on for nearly twenty years after that, till long after Lucrecie had been put away, in fine style, by the Blalocks. Ever afterward, though, Aunt Munsie seemed different to people. They said she softened, and everybody said it was a change for the better. She would take paper money from under her carpet, or out of the chinks in her walls, and buy things for up at the church, or buy her own whiskey when she got sick, instead of making somebody bring her a nip. On the Square, she would laugh and holler with the white folks the way Crecie and all the other old-timers did, and she even took to tying a bandanna about her head—took to talking old-nigger foolishness, too, about the Bell Witch, and claiming she remembered the day General N. B. Forrest rode into town and saved all the cotton from the Yankees at the depot. When Mr. Will and Mr. Thad came to see her with their families, she got so she would reminisce with them about their daddy and tease them about all the silly things they had done when they were growing up. "Mr. Thad—him still in kilts, too—he say, 'Aunt Munsie, reach down in yo' stockin' and git me a copper cent. I want some store candy.' " She told them how Miss Yola Ewing, the sewing woman, heard her threatening to bust Will's back wide open when he broke the lamp chimney, and how Miss Yola went to the Doctor and told him he ought to run Aunt Munsie off. Aunt Munsie and the Doctor had had a big laugh about it in the kitchen, and Miss Yola must have eavesdropped on them, because she left without finishing the girls' Easter dresses.

The visits from Mr. Thad and Mr. Will continued as long as Aunt Munsie lived, but she never asked them any more about when they were sure enough coming back. And the children, though she hugged them more than ever—and, toward the last, there were the children's children to be hugged—never set foot in her back yard again. Aunt Munsie lived on for nearly twenty years, and when they finally buried her, they put on her tombstone that she was aged one hundred years, though nobody knew how old she was. There was no record of when she was born. All anyone knew was that in her last years she had said she was a girl helping about the big house when freedom came. That would have made her probably about twelve years old in 1865, according to her statements and depictions. But all agreed that in her old age Aunt Munsie, like other old darkies, was not very reliable about such things. Her spirit softened, and she became not very reliable about facts.

Elizabeth Spencer
1921 –

Born in Carrollton, Mississippi, in 1921, Elizabeth Spencer developed an early passion for literature as a student at Belhaven College, where she also enjoyed the rare bounty of her neighbor Eudora Welty's friendship and literary advice. After her graduation from Belhaven in 1942, Spencer earned a master's degree at Vanderbilt University the following year and then served for a while as a reporter for the Nashville *Tennessean.* To give full time to her own writing, however, she quit that job in 1946 and two years later published her first of eight novels, *Fire in the Morning,* a complex narrative of tangled past and present family relationships reminiscent of the works of William Faulkner and Robert Penn Warren. This and her next two novels—*This Crooked Way* (1952) and *The Voice at the Back Door* (1956)—all received lavish praise for the clarity with which she could weave an intricate plot within a richly detailed pattern of Southern town life. Having won a Guggenheim Fellowship, by 1956 Spencer had been living in Italy for several years and had shifted her creative attention to another locale; that year she married John Rusher, an Englishman, and for the next two years Italy provided the major setting for three more of her longer works of fiction: *The Light in the Piazza* (1960), a novella, *Knights & Dragons* (1965), and *No Place for an Angel* (1967). These and her last two novels, *The Snare* (1972) and *The Salt Line* (1984), were all published after she and her husband left Europe in 1958 for their present residence in Montreal, Canada.

By 1956, Spencer's short stories had also begun appearing fairly regularly in *The New Yorker* and other leading national magazines. Ten of them were reissued in a collection dedicated to Eudora Welty, *Ship Island and Other Stories* (1968); and these ten, plus twenty-three more previously uncollected stories and the novella *Knights & Dragons,* were republished in a definitive collection, *The Stories of Elizabeth Spencer* (1981), together with her luminous author's Preface and a Foreword by Eudora Welty. Spencer's short stories, like her longer works, have received deservedly high praise for their combined power and sensitivity, for displaying, in Welty's words, her "finely shaded perceptions" and "her cool deliberateness to pull no punches."

First Dark

When Tom Beavers started coming back to Richton, Mississippi, on weekends, after the war was over, everybody in town was surprised and pleased. They had never noticed him much before he paid them this compliment; now they could not say enough nice things. There was not much left in Richton for him to call family—just his aunt who had raised him, Miss Rita Beavers, old as God, ugly as sin, deaf as a post. So he must be fond of the town, they reasoned; certainly it was a pretty old place. Far too many young men had left it and never come back at all.

He would drive in every Friday night from Jackson, where he worked. All weekend, his Ford, dusty of flank, like a hard-ridden horse, would sit parked down the hill near Miss Rita's old wire front gate, which sagged from the top hinge and had worn a span in the ground. On Saturday morning, he would head for the drugstore, then the post office; then he would be observed walking here and there around the streets under the shade trees. It was as though he were looking for something.

He wore steel taps on his heels, and in the still the click of them on the sidewalks would sound across the big front lawns and all the way up to the porches of the houses, where two ladies might be sitting behind a row of ferns. They would identify him to one another, murmuring in their fine little voices, and say it was just too bad there was nothing here for young people. It was just a shame they didn't have one or two more old houses, here, for a Pilgrimage—look how Natchez had waked up.

One Saturday morning in early October, Tom Beavers sat at the counter in the drugstore and reminded Totsie Poteet, the drugstore clerk, of a ghost story. Did he remember the strange old man who used to appear to people who were coming into Richton along the Jackson road at twilight—what they called "first dark"?

"Sure I remember," said Totsie. "Old Cud'n Jimmy Wiltshire used to tell us about him every time we went 'possum hunting. I could see him plain as I can see you, the way he used to tell it. Tall, with a top hat on, yeah, and waiting in the weeds alongside the road ditch, so'n you couldn't tell if he wasn't taller than any mortal man could be, because you couldn't tell if he was standing down in the ditch or not. It would look like he just grew up out of the weeds. Then he'd signal to you."

"Them that stopped never saw anybody," said Tom Beavers, stirring his coffee. "There were lots of folks besides Mr. Jimmy that saw him."

"There was, let me see . . . " Totsie enumerated others—some men, some women, some known to drink, others who never touched a drop. There was no way to explain it. "There was that story the road gang told. Do you remember, or were you off at school? It was while they were straightening the road out to the highway—taking the curves out and building a new bridge. Anyway, they said that one night at quitting time, along in the winter and just about dark, this old guy signaled to some of 'em. They said they went over and he asked them to move a bulldozer they had left across the road, because he had a wagon back behind on a little dirt road, with a sick nigger girl in it. Had to get to the doctor and this was the only way. They claimed they knew didn't nobody live back there on that little old road, but niggers can come from anywhere. So they moved the bulldozer and cleared back a whole lot of other stuff, and waited and waited. Not only didn't no wagon ever come, but the man that had stopped them, he was gone, too. They was right shook up over it. You never heard that one?"

"No, I never did." Tom Beavers said this with his eyes looking up over his coffee cup, as though he sat behind a hand of cards. His lashes and brows were heavier than was ordinary, and worked as a veil might, to keep you away from knowing exactly what he was thinking.

"They said he was tall and had a hat on." The screen door flapped to announce a customer, but Totsie kept on talking. "But whether he was a white man or a real light-colored nigger they couldn't say. Some said one and some said another. I figured they'd been pulling on the jug a little earlier than usual. You know why? I never heard of *our* ghost *saying* nothing. Did you, Tom?"

He moved away on the last words, the way a clerk will, talking back over his shoulder and ahead of him to his new customer at the same time, as though he had two voices and two heads. "And what'll it be today, Miss Frances?"

The young woman standing at the counter had a prescription already out of her bag. She stood with it poised between her fingers, but her attention was drawn toward Tom Beavers, his coffee cup, and the conversation she had interrupted. She was a girl whom no ordinary description would fit. One would have to know first of all who she was: Frances Harvey. After that, it was all right for her to be a little odd-looking, with her reddish hair that curled back from her brow, her light eyes, and her high, pale temples. This is not the material for being pretty, but in Frances Harvey it was what could sometimes be beauty. Her family home was laden with history that nobody but the Harveys could remember. It would have been on a Pilgrimage if Richton had had one. Frances still lived in it, looking after an invalid mother.

"What were you-all talking about?" she wanted to know.

"About that ghost they used to tell about," said Totsie, holding out his hand for the prescription. "The one people used to see just outside of town, on the Jackson road."

"But why?" she demanded. "Why were you talking about him?"

"Tom, here—" the clerk began, but Tom Beavers interrupted him.

"I was asking because I was curious," he said. He had been studying her from the corner of his eye. Her face was beginning to show the wear of her mother's long illness, but that couldn't be called change. Changing was something she didn't seem to have done, her own style being the only one natural to her.

"I was asking," he went on, "because I saw him." He turned away from her somewhat too direct gaze and said to Totsie Poteet, whose mouth had fallen open, "It was where the new road runs close to the old road, and as far as I could tell he was right on the part of the old road where people always used to see him."

"But when?" Frances Harvey demanded.

"Last night," he told her. "Just around first dark. Driving home."

A wealth of quick feeling came up in her face. "So did I! Driving home from Jackson! I saw him, too!"

For some people, a liking for the same phonograph record or for Mayan archaeology is enough of an excuse to get together. Possibly, seeing the same ghost was no more than that. Anyway, a week later, on Saturday at first dark, Frances Harvey and Tom Beavers were sitting together in a car parked just off the highway, near the spot where they agreed the ghost had appeared. The season was that long, peculiar one between summer and fall, and there were so many crickets and tree frogs going full tilt in their periphery that their voices could hardly be distinguished from the background noises, though they both would have heard a single footfall in the grass. An edge of autumn was in the air at night, and Frances had put on a tweed jacket at the last minute, so the smell of moth balls was in the car, brisk and most unghostlike.

But Tom Beavers was not going to forget the value of the ghost, whether it put in an appearance or not. His questions led Frances into reminiscence.

"No, I never saw him before the other night," she admitted. "The Negroes used to talk in the kitchen, and Regina and I—you know my sister Regina—would sit there listening, scared to go and scared to stay. Then finally going to bed upstairs was no relief, either, because sometimes Aunt Henrietta was visiting us, and *she'd* seen it. Or if she wasn't visiting us, the front room next to us, where she stayed, would be empty, which was worse. There was no way to lock ourselves in, and besides, what was there to lock out? We'd lie all night like two sticks in bed, and shiver. Papa finally had to take a hand. He called us in and sat us down and said that the whole thing was easy to explain—it was all automobiles. What their headlights did with the dust and shadows out on the Jackson road. 'Oh, but Sammie and Jerry!' we said, with great big eyes, sitting side by side on the sofa, with our tennis shoes flat on the floor."

"Who were Sammie and Jerry?" asked Tom Beavers.

"Sammie was our cook. Jerry was her son, or husband, or something. Anyway, they certainly didn't have cars. Papa called them in. They were standing side by side by the bookcase, and Regina and I were on the sofa—four pairs of big eyes, and Papa pointing his finger. Papa said, 'Now, you made up these stories about ghosts, didn't you?' 'Yes, sir,' said Sammie. 'We made them up.' 'Yes, sir,' said Jerry. 'We sho did.' Well, then, you can just stop it;' Papa said. 'See how peaked these children look?' Sammie and Jerry were terribly polite to us for a week, and we got in the car and rode up and down the Jackson road at first dark to see if the headlights really did it. But we never saw anything. We didn't tell Papa, but headlights had nothing whatever to do with it."

"You had your own *car* then?" He couldn't believe it.

"Oh no!" She was emphatic. "We were too young for that. Too young to drive, really, but we did anyway."

She leaned over to let him give her cigarette a light, and saw his hand tremble. Was he afraid of the ghost or of her? She would have to stay away from talking family.

Frances remembered Tommy Beavers from her childhood—a small boy going home from school down a muddy side road alone, walking right down the middle of the road. His old aunt's house was at the bottom of a hill. It was damp there, and the yard was always muddy, with big fat chicken tracks all over it, like Egyptian writing. How did Frances know? She could not remember going there, ever. Miss Rita Beavers was said to order cold ham, mustard, bread, and condensed milk from the grocery store. "I doubt if that child ever has anything hot," Frances's mother had said once. He was always neatly dressed in the same knee pants, high socks, and checked shirt, and sat several rows ahead of Frances in study hall, right in the middle of his seat. He was three grades behind her; in those days, that much younger seemed very young indeed. What had happened to his parents? There was some story, but it was not terribly interesting, and, his people being of no importance, she had forgotten.

"I think it's past time for our ghost," she said. "He's never out so late at night."

"He gets hungry, like me," said Tom Beavers. "Are you hungry, Frances?"

They agreed on a highway restaurant where an orchestra played on weekends. Everyone went there now.

From the moment they drew up on the graveled entrance, cheerful lights and a blare of music chased the spooks from their heads. Tom Beavers ordered well and danced well, as it turned out. Wasn't there something she had heard about his being "smart"? By "smart," Southerners mean intellectual, and they say it in an almost condescending way, smart being what you are when you can't be anything else, but it is better, at least, than being nothing. Frances Harvey had been away enough not to look at things from a completely Southern point of view, and she was encouraged to discover that she and Tom had other things in common besides a ghost, though all stemming, perhaps, from the imagination it took to see one.

They agreed about books and favorite movies and longing to see more plays. She sighed that life in Richton was so confining, but he assured her that Jackson could be just as bad; *it* was getting to be like any Middle Western city, he said, while Richton at least had a sense of the past. This was the main reason, he went on, gaining confidence in the jumble of commonplace noises—dishes, music, and a couple of drinkers chattering behind them—that he had started coming back to Richton so often. He wanted to keep a connection with the past. He lived in a modern apartment, worked in a soundproof office—he could be in any city. But Richton was where he had been born and raised, and nothing could be more old-fashioned. Too many people seemed to have their lives cut in two. He was earnest in desiring that this should not happen to him.

"You'd better be careful," Frances said lightly. Her mood did not incline her to profound conversation. "There's more than one ghost in Richton. You may turn into one yourself, like the rest of us."

"It's the last thing I'd think of you," he was quick to assure her.

Had Tommy Beavers really said such a thing, in such a natural, charming way? Was Frances Harvey really so pleased? Not only was she pleased but, feeling warmly alive amid the music and small lights, she agreed with him. She could not have agreed with him more.

"I hear that Thomas Beavers has gotten to be a very attractive man," Frances Harvey's mother said unexpectedly one afternoon.

Frances had been reading aloud—Jane Austen this time. Theirs was one house where the leather-bound sets were actually read. In Jane Austen, men and women seesawed back and forth for two or three hundred pages until they struck a point of balance; then they got married. She had just put aside the book, at the end of a chapter, and risen to lower the shade against the slant of afternoon sun. "Or so Cud'n Jennie and Mrs. Giles Antley and Miss Fannie Stapleton have been coming and telling you," she said.

"People talk, of course, but the consensus is favorable," Mrs. Harvey said. "Wonders never cease; his mother ran away with a brush salesman. But nobody can make out what he's up to, coming back to Richton."

"Does he have to be 'up to' anything?" Frances asked.

"Men are always up to something," said the old lady at once. She added, more slowly, "In Thomas's case, maybe it isn't anything it oughtn't to be. They say he reads a lot. He may just have taken up with some sort of idea."

Frances stole a long glance at her mother's face on the pillow. Age and illness had reduced the image of Mrs. Harvey to a kind of caricature, centered on a mouth that Frances could not help comparing to that of a fish. There was a tension around its rim, as though it were outlined in bone, and the underlip even stuck out a little. The mouth ate, it took medicine, it asked for things, it gasped when breath was short, it commented. But when it commented, it ceased to be just a mouth and became part of Mrs. Harvey, that witty tyrant with the infallible memory for the right detail, who was at her terrible best about men.

"And what could he be thinking of?" she was wont to inquire when some man had acted foolishly. No one could ever defend accurately the man in question, and the only conclusion was Mrs. Harvey's; namely, that he wasn't thinking, if, indeed, he could. Although she had never been a belle, never a flirt, her popularity with men was always formidable. She would be observed talking marathons with one in a corner, and could you ever be sure, when they both burst into laughter, that they had not just exchanged the most shocking stories? "Of course, *he*—" she would begin later, back with the family, and the masculinity that had just been encouraged to strut and preen a little was quickly shown up as idiotic. Perhaps Mrs. Harvey hoped by this method to train her daughters away from a lot of sentimental nonsense that was their birthright as pretty Southern girls in a house with a lawn that moonlight fell on and that was often lit also by Japanese lanterns hung for parties. "Oh, he's not like that, Mama!" the little girls would cry. They were already alert for heroes who would ride up and cart them off. "Well, then, you watch," she would say. Sure enough, if you watched, she would be right.

Mrs. Harvey's younger daughter, Regina, was a credit to her mother's long campaign; she married well. The old lady, however, never tired of pointing out behind her son-in-law's back that his fondness for money was ill-concealed, that he had the longest feet she'd ever seen, and that he sometimes made grammatical errors.

Her elder daughter, Frances, on a trip to Europe, fell in love, alas! The gentleman was of French extraction but Swiss citizenship, and Frances did not marry him, because he was already married—that much filtered back to Richton. In response to a cable, she had returned home one hot July in time to witness her father's wasted face and last weeks of life. That same September, the war began. When peace came, Richton wanted to know if Frances Harvey would go back to Europe. Certain subtly complicated European matters, little understood in Richton, seemed to be obstructing Romance; one of them was probably named Money. Meanwhile, Frances's mother took to bed, in what was generally known to be her last illness.

So no one crossed the ocean, but eventually Tom Beavers came up to Mrs. Harvey's room one afternoon, to tea.

Though almost all her other faculties were seriously impaired, in ear and tongue Mrs. Harvey was as sound as a young beagle, and she could still weave a more interesting conversation than most people who go about every day and look at the world. She was of the old school of Southern lady talkers; she vexed you with no ideas, she tried to protect you from even a moment of silence. In the old days, when a bright company filled the downstairs rooms, she could keep the ball rolling amongst a crowd. Everyone—all the men especially—got their word in, but the flow of things came back to her. If one of those twenty-minutes-to-or-after silences fell—and even with her they did occur—people would turn and look at her daughter Frances. "And what do you think?" some kind-eyed gentleman would ask. Frances did not credit that she had the sort of face people would turn to, and so did not know how to take advantage of it. What did she think? Well, to answer that honestly took a moment of reflection—a fatal moment, it always turned out. Her mother would be up instructing the maid, offering someone an ashtray or another goody, or remarking outright, "Frances is so timid. She never says a word."

Tom Beavers stayed not only past teatime that day but for a drink as well. Mrs. Harvey was induced to take a glass of sherry, and now her bed became her enormous throne. Her keenest suffering as an invalid was occasioned by the absence of men. "What is a house without a man in it?" she would often cry. From her eagerness to be charming to Frances's guest that afternoon, it seemed that she would have married Tom Beavers herself if he had asked her. The amber liquid set in her small four-sided glass glowed like a jewel, and her diamond flashed; she had put on her best ring for the company. What a pity no longer to show her ankle, that delicious bone, so remarkably slender for so ample a frame.

Since the time had flown so, they all agreed enthusiastically that Tom should wait downstairs while Frances got ready to go out to dinner with him. He was hardly past the stair landing before the old lady was seized by such a fit of coughing that she could hardly speak. "It's been—it's been too much—too *much* for me!" she gasped out.

But after Frances had found the proper sedative for her, she was calmed, and insisted on having her say.

"Thomas Beavers has a good job with an insurance company in Jackson," she informed her daughter, as though Frances were incapable of finding out anything for herself. "He makes a good appearance. He is the kind of man"—she paused—"who would value a wife of good family." She stopped, panting for breath. It was this complimenting a man behind his back that was too much for her—as much out of character, and hence as much of a strain, as if she had got out of bed and tried to tap-dance.

"Heavens, Mama," Frances said, and almost giggled.

At this, the old lady, thinking the girl had made light of her suitor, half screamed at her, "Don't be so critical, Frances! You can't be so critical of men!" and fell into an even more terrible spasm of coughing. Frances had to lift her from the pillow and hold her straight until the fit passed and her breath returned. Then Mrs. Harvey's old, dry, crooked, ineradicably feminine hand was laid on her daughter's arm, and when she spoke again she shook the arm to emphasize her words.

"When your father knew he didn't have long to live," she whispered, "we discussed whether to send for you or not. You know you were his favorite, Frances. 'Suppose our girl is happy over there,' he said. 'I wouldn't want to bring her back on my account.' I said you had to have the right to choose whether to come back or not. You'd never forgive us, I said, if you didn't have the right to choose."

Frances could visualize this very conversation taking place between her parents; she could see them, decorous and serious, talking over the fact of his approaching death as though it were a piece of property for agreeable disposition in the family. She could never remember him without thinking, with a smile, how he used to come home on Sunday from church (he being the only one of them who went) and how, immediately after hanging his hat and cane in the hall, he would say, "Let all things proceed in orderly progression to their final confusion. How long before dinner?" No, she had had to come home. Some humor had always existed between them—her father and her—and humor, of all things, cannot be betrayed.

"I meant to go back," said Frances now. "But there was the war. At first I kept waiting for it to be over. I still wake up at night sometimes thinking, I wonder how much longer before the war will be over. And then—" She stopped short. For the fact was that her lover had been married to somebody else, and her mother was the very person capable of pointing that out to her. Even in the old lady's present silence she heard the unspoken thought, and got up nervously from the bed, loosing herself from the hand on her arm, smoothing her reddish hair where it was inclined to straggle. "And then he wrote me that he had gone back to his wife. Her family and his had always been close, and the war brought them back together. This was in Switzerland—naturally, he couldn't stay on in Paris during the war. There were the children, too—all of them were Catholic. Oh, I do understand how it happened."

Mrs. Harvey turned her head impatiently on the pillow. She dabbed at her moist upper lip with a crumpled linen handkershief; her diamond flashed once in motion. "War, religion, wife, children—yes. But men do what they want to."

Could anyone make Frances as angry as her mother could? "Believe what you like then! You always know so much better than I do. *You* would have managed things somehow. Oh, you would have had your way!"

"Frances," said Mrs. Harvey, "I'm an old woman." The hand holding the handkerchief fell wearily, and her eyelids dropped shut. "If you should want to marry Thomas Beavers and bring him here, I will accept it. There will be no distinctions. Next, I suppose, we will be having his old deaf aunt for tea. I hope she has a hearing aid. I haven't got the strength to holler at her."

"I don't think any of these plans are necessary, Mama."

The eyelids slowly lifted. "None?"

"None."

Mrs. Harvey's breathing was as audible as a voice. She spoke, at last, without scorn, honestly. "I cannot bear the thought of leaving you alone. You, nor the house, nor your place in it—alone. I foresaw Tom Beavers here! What has he got that's better than you and this place? I knew he would come!"

Terrible as her mother's meanness was, it was not half so terrible as her love. Answering nothing, explaining nothing, Frances stood without giving in. She trembled, and tears ran down her cheeks. The two women looked at each other helplessly across the darkening room.

In the car, later that night, Tom Beavers asked, "Is your mother trying to get rid of me?" They had passed an unsatisfactory evening, and he was not going away without knowing why.

"No, it's just the other way around," said Frances, in her candid way. "She wants you so much she'd like to eat you up. She wants you in the house, Couldn't you tell?"

"She once chased me out of the yard," he recalled.

"Not really!"

They turned into Harvey Street (that was actually the name of it), and when he had drawn the car up before the dark front steps, he related the incident. He told her that Mrs. Harvey had been standing just there in the yard, talking to some visitor who was leaving by inches, the way ladies used to—ten minutes' more talk for every forward step. He, a boy not more than nine, had been crossing a corner of the lawn where a faint path had already been worn; he had had nothing to do with wearing the path and had taken it quite innocently and openly. "You, boy!" Mrs. Harvey's fan was an enormous painted thing. She had furled it with a clack so loud he could still hear it. "You don't cut through my yard again! Now, you stop where you are and you go all the way back around by the walk, and don't you ever do that again." He went back and all the way around. She was fanning comfortably as he passed. "Old Miss Rita Beavers' nephew," he heard her say, and though he did not speak of it now to Frances, Mrs. Harvey's rich tone had been as stuffed with wickedness as a fruitcake with goodies. In it you could have found so many things: that, of course, he didn't know any better, that he was poor, that she knew his first name but would not deign to mention it, that she meant him to understand all this and more. Her fan was probably still somewhere in the house, he reflected. If he ever opened the wrong door, it might fall from above and brain him. It seemed impossible that nowadays he could even have the chance to open the wrong door in the Harvey house. With its graceful rooms and big lawn, its camellias and magnolia trees, the house had been one of the enchanted castles of his childhood, and Frances and Regina Harvey had been two princesses running about the lawn one Saturday morning drying their hair with big white towels and not noticing when he passed.

There was a strong wind that evening. On the way home, Frances and Tom had noticed how the night was streaming, but whether with mist or dust or the smoke from some far-off fire in the dry winter woods they could not tell. As they stood on the sidewalk, the clouds raced over them, and moonlight now and again came through. A limb rubbed against a high cornice. Inside the screen area of the porch, the swing jangled in its iron chains. Frances's coat blew about her, and her hair blew. She felt herself to be no different from anything there that the wind was blowing on, her happiness of no relevance in the dark torrent of nature.

"I can't leave her, Tom. But I can't ask you to live with her, either. Of all the horrible ideas! She'd make demands, take all my time, laugh at you behind your back—she has to run everything. You'd hate me in a week."

He did not try to pretty up the picture, because he had a feeling that it was all too accurate. Now, obviously, was the time she should go on to say there was no good his waiting around through the years for her. But hearts are not noted for practicality, and Frances stood with her hair blowing, her hands stuck in her coat pockets, and did not go on to say anything. Tom pulled her close to him—in, as it were, out of the wind.

"I'll be coming by next weekend, just like I've been doing. And the next one, too," he said. "We'll just leave it that way, if it's O.K. with you."

"Oh yes, it is, Tom!" Never so satisfied to be weak, she kissed him and ran inside.

He stood watching on the walk until her light flashed on. Well, he had got what he was looking for; a connection with the past, he had said. It was right upstairs, a splendid old mass of dictatorial female flesh, thinking about him. Well, they could go on, he and Frances, sitting on either side of a sickbed, drinking tea and sipping sherry with streaks of gray broadening on their brows, while the familiar seasons came and went. So he thought. Like Frances, he believed that the old lady had a stranglehold on life.

Suddenly, in March, Mrs. Harvey died.

A heavy spring funeral, with lots of roses and other scented flowers in the house, is the worst kind of all. There is something so recklessly fecund about a south Mississippi spring that death becomes just another word in the dictionary, along with swarms of others, and even so pure and white a thing as a gardenia has too heavy a scent and may suggest decay. Mrs. Harvey, amid such odors, sank to rest with a determined pomp, surrounded by admiring eyes.

While Tom Beavers did not "sit with the family" at this time, he was often observed with the Harveys, and there was whispered speculation among those who were at the church and the cemetery that the Harvey house might soon come into new hands, "after a decent interval." No one would undertake to judge for a Harvey how long an interval was decent.

Frances suffered from insomnia in the weeks that followed, and at night she wandered about the spring-swollen air of the old house, smelling now spring and now death. "Let all things proceed in orderly progression to their final confusion." She had always thought that the final confusion referred to death, but now she began to think that it could happen any time; that final confusion, having found the door ajar, could come into a house and show no inclination to leave. The worrisome thing, the thing it all came back to, was her mother's clothes. They were numerous, expensive, and famous, and Mrs. Harvey had never discarded any of them. If you opened a closet door, hatboxes as big as crates towered above your head. The shiny black trim of a great shawl stuck out of a wardrobe door just below the lock. Beneath the lid of a cedar chest, the bright eyes of a tippet were ready to twinkle at you. And the jewels! Frances's sister had restrained her from burying them all on their mother, and had even gone off with a wad of them tangled up like fishing tackle in an envelope, on the ground of promises made now and again in the course of the years.

("Regina," said Frances, "what else were you two talking about besides jewelry?" "I don't remember," said Regina, getting mad.

"Frances makes me so mad," said Regina to her husband as they were driving home. "I guess I can love Mama and jewelry, too. Mama certainly loved *us* and jewelry, too.")

One afternoon, Frances went out to the cemetery to take two wreaths sent by somebody who had "just heard." She drove out along the winding cemetery road, stopping the car a good distance before she reached the gate, in order to walk through the woods. The dogwood was beautiful that year. She saw a field where a house used to stand but had burned down; its cedar trees remained, and two bushes of bridal wreath marked where the front gate had swung. She stopped to admire the clusters of white bloom massing up through the young, feathery leaf and stronger now than the leaf itself. In the woods, the redbud was a smoke along shadowy ridges, and the dogwood drifted in layers, like snow suspended to give you all the time you needed to wonder at it. But why, she wondered, do they call it bridal *wreath?* It's not a wreath but a little bouquet. Wreaths are for funerals, anyway. As if to prove it, she looked down at the two she held, one in each hand. She walked on, and such complete desolation came over her that it was more of a wonder than anything in the woods—more, even, than death.

As she returned to the car from the two parallel graves, she met a thin, elderly, very light-skinned Negro man in the road. He inquired if she would mind moving her car so that he could pass. He said that there was a sick colored girl in his wagon, whom he was driving in to the doctor. He pointed out politely that she had left her car right in the middle of the road. "Oh, I'm terribly sorry," said Frances, and hurried off toward the car.

That night, reading late in bed, she thought, I could have given her a ride into town. No wonder they talk about us up North. A mile into town in a wagon! She might have been having a baby. She became conscience-stricken about it—foolishly so, she realized, but if you start worrying about something in a house like the one Frances Harvey lived in, in the dead of night, alone, you will go on worrying about it until dawn. She was out of sleeping pills.

She remembered having brought a fresh box of sedatives for her mother the day before she died. She got up and went into her mother's closed room, where the bed had been dismantled for airing, its wooden parts propped along the walls. On the closet shelf she found the shoe box into which she had packed away the familiar articles of the bedside table. Inside she found the small enameled-cardboard box, with the date and prescription inked on the cover in Totsie Poteet's somewhat prissy handwriting, but the box was empty. She was surprised, for she realized that her mother could have used only one or two of the pills. Frances was so determined to get some sleep that she searched the entire little store of things in the shoe box quite heartlessly, but there were no pills. She returned to her room and tried to read, but could not, and so smoked instead and stared out at the dawn-blackening sky. The house sighed. She could not take her mind off the Negro girl. If she died . . . When it was light, she dressed and got into the car.

In town, the postman was unlocking the post office to sort the early mail. "I declare," he said to the rural mail carrier who arrived a few minutes later, "Miss Frances Harvey is driving herself crazy. Going back out yonder to the cemetery, and it not seven o'clock in the morning."

"Aw," said the rural deliveryman skeptically, looking at the empty road.

"That's right. I was here and seen her. You wait there, you'll see her come back. She'll drive herself nuts. Them old maids like that, left in them old houses—crazy and sweet, or crazy and mean, or just plain crazy. They just ain't locked up like them that's down in the asylum. That's the only difference."

"Miss Frances Harvey ain't no more than thirty-two, -three years old."

"Then she's just got more time to get crazier in. You'll see."

That day was Friday, and Tom Beavers, back from Jackson, came up Frances Harvey's sidewalk, as usual, at exactly a quarter past seven in the evening. Frances was not "going out" yet, and Regina had telephoned her long distance to say that "in all probability" she should not be receiving gentlemen "in." "What would Mama say?" Regina asked. Frances said she didn't know, which was not true, and went right on cooking dinners for Tom every weekend.

In the dining room that night, she sat across one corner of the long table from Tom. The useless length of polished cherry stretched away from them into the shadows as sadly as a road. Her plate pushed back, her chin resting on one palm, Frances stirred her coffee and said, "I don't know what on earth to do with all of Mama's clothes. I can't give them away, I can't sell them, I can't burn them, and the attic is full already. What can I do?"

"You look better tonight," said Tom.

"I slept," said Frances. "I slept and slept. From early this morning until just 'while ago. I never slept so well."

Then she told him about the Negro near the cemetery the previous afternoon, and how she had driven back out there as soon as dawn came, and found him again. He had been walking across the open field near the remains of the house that had burned down. There was no path to him from her, and she had hurried across ground uneven from old plowing and covered with the kind of small, tender grass it takes a very skillful mule to crop. "Wait!" she had cried. "Please wait!" The Negro had stopped and waited for her to reach him. "Your daughter?" she asked, out of breath.

"Daughter?" he repeated.

"The colored girl that was in the wagon yesterday. She was sick, you said, so I wondered. I could have taken her to town in the car, but I just didn't think. I wanted to know, how is she? Is she very sick?"

He had removed his old felt nigger hat as she approached him. "She a whole lot better, Miss Frances. She going to be all right now." Then he smiled at her. He did not say thank you, or anything more. Frances turned and walked back to the road and the car. And exactly as though the recovery of the negro girl in the wagon had been her own recovery, she felt the return of a quiet breath and a steady pulse, and sensed the blessed stirring of a morning breeze. Up in her room, she had barely time to draw an old quilt over her before she fell asleep.

"When I woke, I knew about Mama," she said now to Tom. By the deepened intensity of her voice and eyes, it was plain that this was the important part. "It isn't right to say I *knew,*" she went on, "because I had known all the time—ever since last night. I just realized it, that's all. I realized she had killed herself. It had to be that."

He listened soberly through the story about the box of sedatives. "But why?" he asked her. "It maybe looks that way, but what would be her reason for doing it?"

"Well, you see—" Frances said, and stopped.

Tom Beavers talked quietly on. "She didn't suffer. With what she had, she could have lived five, ten, who knows how many years. She was well cared for. Not hard up, I wouldn't say. Why?"

The pressure of his questioning could be insistent, and her trust in him, even if he was nobody but old Miss Rita Beavers' nephew, was well-nigh complete. "Because of you and me," she said, finally. "I'm certain of it, Tom. She didn't want to stand in our way. She never knew how to express love, you see." Frances controlled herself with an effort.

He did not reply, but sat industriously balancing a match folder on the tines of an unused serving fork. Anyone who has passed a lonely childhood in the company of an old deaf aunt is not inclined to doubt things hastily, and Tom Beavers would not have said he disbelieved anything Frances had told him. In fact, it seemed only too real to him. Almost before his eyes, that imperial, practical old hand went fumbling for the pills in the dark. But there had been much more to it than just love, he reflected. Bitterness, too, and pride, and control. And humor, perhaps, and the memory of a frightened little boy chased out of the yard by a twitch of her fan. Being invited to tea was one thing; suicide was quite another. Times had certainly changed, he thought.

But, of course, he could not say that he believed it, either. There was only Frances to go by. The match folder came to balance and rested on the tines. He glanced up at her, and a chill walked up his spine, for she was too serene. Cheek on palm, a lock of reddish hair fallen forward, she was staring at nothing with the absorbed silence of a child, or of a sweet, silver-haired old lady engaged in memory. Soon he might find that more and more of her was vanishing beneath this placid surface.

He himself did not know what he had seen that Friday evening so many months ago—what the figure had been that stood forward from the roadside at the tilt of the curve and urgently waved an arm to him. By the time he had braked and backed, the man had disappeared. Maybe it had been somebody drunk (for Richton had plenty of those to offer), walking it off in the cool of the woods at first dark. No such doubts had occurred to Frances. And what if he told her now the story Totsie had related of the road gang and the sick Negro girl in the wagon? Another labyrinth would open before her; she would never get out.

In Richton, the door to the past was always wide open, and what came in through it and went out of it had made people "different." But it scarcely ever happens, even in Richton, that one is able to see the precise moment when fact becomes faith, when life turns into legend, and people start to bend their finest loyalties to make themselves bemused custodians of the grave. Tom Beavers saw that moment now, in the profile of this dreaming girl, and he knew there was no time to lose.

He dropped the match folder into his coat pocket. "I think we should be leaving, Frances."

"Oh well, I don't know about going out yet," she said. "People criticize you so. Regina even had the nerve to telephone. Word had got all the way to her that you came here to have supper with me and we were alone in the house. When I tell the maid I want biscuits made up for two people, she looks like 'What would yo' mama say?' "

"I mean," he said, "I think it's time we left for good."

"And never came back?" It was exactly like Frances to balk at going to a movie but seriously consider an elopement.

"Well, never is a long time. I like to see about Aunt Rita every once in a great while. She can't remember from one time to the next whether it's two days or two years since I last came."

She glanced about the walls and at the furniture, the pictures, and the silver. "But I thought you would want to live here, Tom. It never occurred to me. I know it never occurred to Mama . . . This house . . . It can't be just left."

"It's a fine old house, he agreed. "But what would you do with all your mother's clothes?"

Her freckled hand remained beside the porcelain cup for what seemed a long time. He waited and made no move toward her; he felt her uncertainty keenly, but he believed that some people should not be startled out of a spell.

"It's just as you said," he went on, finally. "You can't give them away, you can't sell them, you can't burn them, and you can't put them in the attic, because the attic is full already. So what are you going to do?"

Between them, the single candle flame achieved a silent altitude. Then, politely, as on any other night, though shaking back her hair in a decided way, she said, "Just let me get my coat, Tom."

She locked the door when they left, and put the key under the mat—a last obsequy to the house. Their hearts were bounding ahead faster than they could walk down the sidewalk or drive off in the car, and, mindful, perhaps, of what happened to people who did, they did not look back.

Had they done so, they would have seen that the Harvey house was more beautiful than ever. All unconscious of its rejection by so mere a person as Tom Beavers, it seemed, instead, to have got rid of what did not suit it, to be free, at last, to enter with abandon the land of mourning and shadows and memory.

Grace Paley

1922 –

Grace Paley writes primarily about little or insignificant people—often Jewish women and children—who live and struggle in the Big City. She has an excellent ear for the idiom of "street people" and ethnic groups. Though some critics have complained that her stories are often too brief to allow for full plot development, they have also been highly praised for their presentation of character.

Born in 1922, Paley was educated at Hunter College (1935–39) and at New York University. During the early 1960s she taught at Columbia and Syracuse Universities, and she is now on the faculty of Sarah Lawrence and City College. She received a Guggenheim Fellowship in 1961 and a grant from the National Institute of Arts and Letters in 1970 for short story writing. She has published three collections of short stories, *The Little Disturbances of Man* (1959), *Enormous Changes At the Last Minute* (1974), and *Later the Same Day* (1985). A volume of poems, *Leaning Forward,* also appeared in 1985.

If some of Paley's stories have been criticized for their lack of plot and their abrupt endings, "Samuel," brief as it is, disproves that charge. It is an exceptionally well-constructed story, resonant with mingled overtones.

Samuel

Some boys are very tough. They're afraid of nothing. They are the ones who climb a wall and take a bow at the top. Not only are they brave on the roof, but they make a lot of noise in the darkest part of the cellar where even the super hates to go. They also jiggle and hop on the platform between the locked doors of the subway cars.

Four boys are jiggling on the swaying platform. Their names are Alfred, Calvin, Samuel, and Tom. The men and the women in the cars on either side watch them. They don't like them to jiggle or jump but don't want to interfere. Of course some of the men in the cars were once brave boys like these. One of them had ridden the tail of a speeding truck from New York to Rockaway Beach without getting off, without his sore fingers losing hold. Nothing happened to him then or later. He had made a compact with other boys who preferred to watch: Starting at Eighth Avenue and Fifteenth Street, he would get to some specified place, maybe Twenty-third and the river, by hopping the tops of the moving trucks. This was hard to do when one truck turned a corner in the wrong direction and the nearest truck was a couple of feet too high. He made three or four starts before succeeding. He had gotten this idea from a film at school called *The Romance of Logging*. He had finished high school, married a good friend, was in a responsible job and going to night school.

These two men and others looked at the four boys jumping and jiggling on the platform and thought, It must be fun to ride that way, especially now the weather is nice and we're out of the tunnel and way high over the Bronx. Then they thought, These kids do seem to be acting sort of stupid. They *are* little. Then they thought of some of the brave things they had done when they were boys and jiggling didn't seem so risky.

The ladies in the car became very angry when they looked at the four boys. Most of them brought their brows together and hoped the boys could see their extreme disapproval. One of the ladies wanted to get up and say, Be careful you dumb kids, get off that platform or I'll call a cop. But three of the boys were Negroes and the fourth was something else she couldn't tell for sure. She was afraid they'd be fresh and laugh at her and embarrass her. She wasn't afraid they'd hit her, but she was afraid of embarrassment. Another lady thought, Their mothers never know where they are. It wasn't true in this particular case. Their mothers all knew that they had gone to see the missile exhibit on Fourteenth Street.

Out on the platform, whenever the train accelerated, the boys would raise their hands and point them up to the sky to act like rockets going off, then they rat-tat-tatted the shatterproof glass pane like machine guns, although no machine guns had been exhibited.

For some reason known only to the motorman, the train began a sudden slowdown. The lady who was afraid of embarrassment saw the boys jerk forward and backward and grab the swinging guard chains. She had her own boy at home. She stood up with determination and went to the door. She slid it open and said, "You boys will be hurt. You'll be killed. I'm going to call the conductor if you don't just go into the next car and sit down and be quiet."

Two of the boys said, "Yes'm," and acted as though they were about to go. Two of them blinked their eyes a couple of times and pressed their lips together. The train resumed its speed. The door slid shut, parting the lady and the boys. She leaned against the side door because she had to get off at the next stop.

The boys opened their eyes wide at each other and laughed. The lady blushed. The boys looked at her and laughed harder. They began to pound each other's back. Samuel laughed the hardest and pounded Alfred's back until Alfred coughed and the tears came. Alfred held tight to the chain hook. Samuel pounded him even harder when he saw the tears. He said, "Why you bawling? You a baby, huh?" and laughed. One of the men whose boyhood had been more watchful than brave became angry. He stood up straight and looked at the boys for a couple of seconds. Then he walked in a citizenly way to the end of the car, where he pulled the emergency cord. Almost at once, with a terrible hiss, the pressure of air abandoned the brakes and the wheels were caught and held.

People standing in the most secure places fell forward, then backward. Samuel had let go of his hold on the chain so he could pound Tom as well as Alfred. All the passengers in the card whipped back and forth, but he pitched only forward and fell head first to be crushed and killed between the cars.

The train had stopped hard, halfway into the station, and the conductor called at once for the trainmen who knew about this kind of death and how to take the body from the wheels and brakes. There was silence except for passengers from other cars who asked, What happened! What happened! The ladies waited around wondering if he might be an only child. The men recalled other afternoons with very bad endings. The little boys stayed close to each other, leaning and touching shoulders and arms and legs.

When the policeman knocked at the door and told her about it, Samuel's mother began to scream. She screamed all day and moaned all night, though the doctors tried to quiet her with pills.

Oh, oh, she hopelessly cried. She did not know how she could ever find another boy like that one. However, she was a young woman and she became pregnant. Then for a few months she was hopeful. The child born to her was a boy. They brought him to be seen and nursed. She smiled. But immediately she saw that this baby wasn't Samuel. She and her husband together have had other children, but never again will a boy exactly like Samuel be known.

Truman Capote

1924 – 1984

Truman Capote was named Truman Streckfus Persons at the time of his birth in New Orleans in 1924, and renamed at the age of ten after his mother's second marriage. Capote spent little time with any of his parents during his growing up; stays with relatives in Monroeville, Alabama, where he and Harper Lee were childhood friends, proved in his later writings to be particularly affecting and memory-rich. At seventeen Capote was hired as a copyboy at *The New Yorker.* Although he left the magazine in 1944, this employment gave him intimate introduction to the world of national publishing, and New York City was to become his permanent "home" base. During the mid-forties his short stories secured important magazine publication and prestigious prizes, and his first two books, the autobiographical novel *Other Voices, Other Rooms* (1948) and *A Tree of Night and Other Stories* (1949), firmly established his reputation by the time he was twenty-five. The decade of the fifties was a productive one for Capote, the sixties less so, and the seventies much less so. A self-confessed homosexual, drug addict, and alcoholic, he died in California in 1984. Although it was put into print after his death, Capote never finished *Answered Prayers,* a novel for which he had signed a contract almost twenty years earlier and which, he maintained, was to be his masterpiece.

Richly talented and personally tormented, Truman Capote was a spectacular artistic presence in mid-twentieth- century America. His eccentric, indulgent life-style amidst the rich and famous brought him extensive publicity and not always popular approval. His literature, however, aided by movie and television versions of his work, gained him wide positive public recognition and status. *Breakfast at Tiffany's*

(1956) and the "nonfiction novel" *In Cold Blood* (1965) helped make his name a household word, and "A Christmas Memory" has today become part of the mythology and ritual of the American celebration of the holiday. At his lyrical best, Capote's graceful, evocative prose style is scarcely matched by any other American writer.

"Children on Their Birthdays" comes close to revealing both the essential Capote and much of the essence of human life, whether in the small-town South or not. It describes vividly a particular place and time, but it also captures the general, wider perspective of adolescent childhood and the bittersweet process of youthful education. Neither pure comedy nor pure tragedy, this story is guaranteed to linger in the reader's memory: the extraordinary Miss Bobbit cannot soon be forgotten, nor the meaning of her life quickly and comfortably fathomed.

Children on Their Birthdays

Yesterday afternoon the six-o'clock bus ran over Miss Bobbit. I'm not sure what there is to be said about it; after all, she was only ten years old, still I know no one of us in this town will forget her. For one thing, nothing she ever did was ordinary, not from the first time that we saw her, and that was a year ago. Miss Bobbit and her mother, they arrived on that same six-o'clock bus, the one that comes through from Mobile. It happened to be my cousin Billy Bob's birthday, and so most of the children in town were here at our house. We were sprawled on the front porch having tutti-frutti and devil cake when the bus stormed around Deadman's Curve. It was the summer that never rained; rusted dryness coated everything; sometimes when a car passed on the road, raised dust would hang in the still air an hour or more. Aunt El said if they didn't pave the highway soon, she was going to move down to the seacoast; but she'd said that for such a long time. Anyway, we were sitting on the porch, tutti-frutti melting on our plates, when suddenly, just as we were wishing that something would happen, something did; for out of the red road dust appeared Miss Bobbit. A wiry little girl in a starched lemon-colored party dress, she sassed along with a grown-up mince, one hand on her hip, the other supporting a spinsterish umbrella. Her mother, lugging two cardboard valises and a wind-up victrola, trailed in the background. She was a gaunt shaggy woman with silent eyes and a hungry smile.

All the children on the porch had grown so still that when a cone of wasps started humming, the girls did not set up their usual holler. Their attention was too fixed upon the approach of Miss Bobbit and her mother, who had by now reached the gate. "Begging your pardon," called Miss Bobbit in a voice that was at once silky and childlike, like a pretty piece of ribbon, and immaculately exact, like a movie star or a schoolmarm, "but might we speak with the grown-up persons of the house?" This, of course, meant Aunt El; and, at least to some degree, myself. But Billy Bob and all the other boys, no one of whom was over thirteen, followed down to the gate after us. From their faces you would have thought they'd never seen a girl before. Certainly not like Miss Bobbit. As Aunt El said, whoever heard tell of a child wearing make-up? Tangee gave her lips an orange glow, her hair, rather like a costume wig, was a mass of rosy curls, and her eyes had a knowing, penciled tilt; even so, she had a skinny dignity, she was a lady, and, what is more, she looked you in the eye with manlike directness. "I'm Miss Lily Jane Bobbit, Miss Bobbit from Memphis, Tennessee," she said solemnly. The boys looked down at their toes, and, on the porch, Cora McCall, whom Billy Bob was courting at the time, led the girls into a fanfare of giggles. "*Country* children," said Miss Bobbit with an understanding smile, and gave her parasol a saucy whirl. "My mother"—and this homely woman allowed an abrupt nod to acknowledge herself—"my mother and I have taken rooms here. Would you be so kind as to point out the house? It belongs to a Mrs. Sawyer." Why, sure, said Aunt El, that's Mrs. Sawyer's, right there across the street. The only boardinghouse around here, it is an old tall dark place with about two dozen lightning rods scattered on the roof: Mrs. Sawyer is scared to death in a thunderstorm.

Coloring like an apple, Billy Bob said, please, ma'am, it being such a hot day and all, wouldn't they rest a spell and have some tutti-frutti? and Aunt El said yes, by all means, but Miss Bobbit shook her head. "Very fattening, tutti-frutti; but *merci* you kindly," and they started across the road, the mother half-dragging her parcels in the dust. Then, and with an earnest expression, Miss Bobbit turned back; the sunflower yellow of her eyes darkened, and she rolled them slightly sideways, as if trying to remember a poem. "My mother has a disorder of the tongue, so it is necessary that I speak for her," she announced rapidly and heaved a sigh. "My mother is a very fine seamstress; she has made dresses for the society of many cities and towns, including Memphis and Tallahassee. No doubt you have noticed and admired the dress I am wearing. Every stitch of it was hand-sewn by my mother. My mother can copy any pattern, and just recently she won a twenty-five-dollar prize from the *Ladies' Home Journal.* My mother can also crochet, knit and embroider. If you want any kind of sewing done, please come to my mother. Please advise your friends and family. Thank you." And then, with a rustle and a swish, she was gone.

Cora McCall and the girls pulled their hair-ribbons nervously, suspiciously, and looked very put out and prune-faced. I'm *Miss* Bobbit, said Cora, twisting her face into an evil imitation, and I'm Princess Elizabeth, that's who I am, ha, ha, ha. Furthermore, said Cora, that dress was just as tacky as could be; personally, Cora said, all my clothes come from Atlanta; plus a pair of shoes from New York, which is not even to mention my silver turquoise ring all the way from Mexico City, Mexico. Aunt El said they ought not to behave that way about a fellow child, a stranger in the town, but the girls went on like a huddle of witches, and certain boys, the sillier ones that liked to be with the girls, joined in and said things that made Aunt El go red and declare she was going to send them all home and tell their daddies, to boot. But before she could carry forward this threat Miss Bobbit herself intervened by traipsing across the Sawyer porch, costumed in a new and startling manner.

The older boys, like Billy Bob and Preacher Star, who had sat quiet while the girls razzed Miss Bobbit, and who had watched the house into which she'd disappeared with misty, ambitious faces, they now straightened up and ambled down to the gate. Cora McCall sniffed and poked out her lower lip, but the rest of us went and sat on the steps. Miss Bobbit paid us no mind whatever. The Sawyer yard is dark with mulberry trees and it is planted with grass and sweet shrub. Sometimes after a rain you can smell the sweet shrub all the way into our house; and in the center of this yard there is a sundial which Mrs. Sawyer installed in 1912 as a memorial to her Boston bull, Sunny, who died after having lapped up a bucket of paint. Miss Bobbit pranced into the yard toting the victrola, which she put on the sundial; she wound it up, and started a record playing, and it played the Court of Luxemborg. By now it was almost nightfall, a firefly hour, blue as milkglass; and birds like arrows swooped together and swept into the folds of trees. Before storms, leaves and flowers appear to burn with a private light, color, and Miss Bobbit, got up in a little white skirt like a powerpuff and with strips of gold-glittering tinsel ribboning her hair, seemed, set against the darkening all around, to contain this illuminated quality. She held her arms arched over her head, her hands lily-limp, and stood straight up on the tips of her toes. She stood that way for a good long while, and Aunt El said it was right smart of her. Then she began to waltz around and around, and around and around she went until Aunt El said, why, she was plain dizzy from the sight. She stopped only when it was time to rewind the victrola; and when the moon came rolling down the ridge, and the last supper bell had sounded, and all the children had gone home, and the night iris was beginning to bloom, Miss Bobbit was still there in the dark turning like a top.

We did not see her again for some time. Preacher Star came every morning to our house and stayed straight through to supper. Preacher is a rail-thin boy with a butchy shock of red hair; he has eleven brothers and sisters, and even they are afraid of him, for he has a terrible temper, and is famous in these parts for his green-eyed meanness: last Fourth of July he whipped Ollie Overton so bad that Ollie's family had to send him to the hospital in Pensacola; and there was another time he bit off half a mule's ear, chewed it and spit it on the ground. Before Billy Bob got his growth, Preacher played the devil with him, too. He used to drop cockleburrs down his collar, and rub pepper in his eyes, and tear up his homework. But now they are the biggest friends in town: talk alike, walk alike; and occasionally they disappear together for whole days, Lord knows where to. But during these days when Miss Bobbit did not appear they stayed close to the house. They would stand around in the yard trying to slingshot sparrows off telephone poles; or sometimes Billy Bob would play his ukulele, and they would sing so loud Uncle Billy Bob, who is Judge for this county, claimed he could hear them all the way to the courthouse: *send me a letter, send it by mail, send it in care of the Birming-ham jail.* Miss Bobbit did not hear them; at least she never poked her head out the door. Then one day Mrs. Sawyer, coming over to borrow a cup of sugar, rattled on a good deal about her new boarders. You know, she said, squinting her chicken-bright eyes, the husband was a crook, uh huh, the child told me herself. Hasn't an ounce of shame, not a mite. Said her daddy was the dearest daddy and the sweetest singing man in the whole of Tennessee. . . . And I said, honey, where is he? and just as offhand as you please she says, Oh, he's in the penitentiary and we don't hear from him no more. Say, now, does that make your blood run cold? Uh huh, and I been thinking, her mama, I been thinking she's some kinda foreigner: never says a word, and sometimes it looks like she don't understand what nobody says to her. And you know, they eat everything *raw. Raw* eggs, *raw* turnips, carrots—no meat whatsoever. For reasons of health, the child says, but ho! she's been straight out on the bed running a fever since last Tuesday.

That same afternoon, Aunt El went out to water her roses, only to discover them gone. These were special roses, ones she'd planned to send to the flower show in Mobile, and so naturally she got a little hysterical. She rang up the Sheriff, and said, listen here, Sheriff, you come over here right fast. I mean somebody's got off with all my Lady Anne's that I've devoted myself to heart and soul since early spring. When the Sheriff's car pulled up outside our house, all the neighbors along the street came out on their porches, and Mrs. Sawyer, layers of cold cream whitening her face, trotted across the road. Oh shoot, she said, very disappointed to find no one had been murdered, oh shoot, she said, nobody's stole them roses. Your Billy Bob brought them roses over and left them for little Bobbit. Aunt El did not say one word. She just marched over to the peach tree, and cut herself a switch. Ohhh, Billy Bob, she stalked along the street calling his name, and then she found him down at Speedy's garage, where he and Preacher were watching Speedy take a motor apart. She simply lifted him by the hair and, switching blueblazes, towed him home. But she couldn't make him say he was sorry and she couldn't make him cry. And when she was finished with him he ran into the backyard and climbed high into the tower of a pecan tree and swore he wasn't ever going to come down. Then his daddy stood at the window and called to him: Son, we aren't mad with you, so come down and eat your supper. But Billy Bob wouldn't budge. Aunt El went and leaned against the tree. She spoke in a voice soft as the gathering light. I'm sorry, son, she said, I didn't mean whipping you so hard like that. I've fixed a nice supper, son, potato salad and boiled ham and deviled eggs. Go away, said Billy Bob, I don't want no supper, and I hate you like all-fire. His daddy said he ought not to talk like that to his mother, and she began to cry. She stood there under the tree and cried, raising the hem of her skirt to dab at her eyes. I don't hate you, son. . . . If I didn't love you, I wouldn't whip you. The pecan leaves began to rattle; Billy Bob slid slowly to the ground, and Aunt El, rushing her fingers through his hair, pulled him against her. Aw, Ma, he said, Aw, Ma.

After supper Billy Bob came and flung himself on the foot of my bed. He smelled all sour and sweet, the way boys do, and I felt very sorry for him, especially because he looked so worried. His eyes were almost shut with worry. You're s'posed to send sick folks flowers, he said righteously. About this time we heard the victrola, a lilting faraway sound, and a night moth flew through the window, drifting in the air delicate as the music. But it was dark now, and we couldn't tell if Miss Bobbit was dancing. Billy Bob, as though he were in pain, doubled up on the bed like a jackknife; but his face was suddenly clear, his grubby boy-eyes twitching like candles. She's so cute, he whispered, she's the cutest dickens I ever saw, gee, to hell with it, I don't care, I'd pick all the roses in China.

Preacher would have picked all the roses in China, too. He was as crazy about her as Billy Bob. But Miss Bobbit did not notice them. The sole communication we had with her was a note to Aunt El thanking her for the flowers. Day after day she sat on her porch, always dressed to beat the band, and doing a piece of embroidery, or combing curls in her hair, or reading a Webster's dictionary—formal, but friendly enough; if you said good-day to her, she said good-day to you. Even so, the boys never could seem to get up the nerve to go over and talk with her, and most of the time she simply looked through them, even when they tomcatted up and down the street trying to get her eye. They wrestled, played Tarzan, did fool-headed bicycle tricks. It was a sorry business. A great many girls in town strolled by the Sawyer house two and three times within an hour just on the chance of getting a look. Some of the girls who did this were: Cora McCall, Mary Murphy Jones, Janice Ackerman. Miss Bobbit did not show any interest in them either. Cora would not speak to Billy Bob anymore. The same was true with Janice and Preacher. As a matter of fact, Janice wrote Preacher a letter in red ink on lace-trimmed paper in which she told him he was vile beyond all human beings and words, that she considered their engagement broken, that he could have back the stuffed squirrel he'd given her. Preacher, saying he wanted to act nice, stopped her the next time she passed our house, and said, well, hell, she could keep that old squirrel if she wanted to. Afterward, he couldn't understand why Janice ran away bawling the way she did.

Then one day the boys were being crazier than usual; Billy Bob was sagging around in his daddy's World War khakis, and Preacher, stripped to the waist, had a naked woman drawn on his chest with one of Aunt El's old lipsticks. They looked like perfect fools, but Miss Bobbit, reclining in a swing, merely yawned. It was noon, and there was no one passing in the street, except a colored girl, baby-fat and sugarplum-shaped, who hummed along carrying a pail of blackberries. But the boys, teasing at her like gnats, joined hands and wouldn't let her go by, not until she paid a tariff. I ain't studyin' no tariff, she said, what kinda tariff you talkin' about, mister? A party in the barn, said Preacher, between clenched teeth, mighty nice party in the barn. And she, with a sulky shrug, said, huh, she intended studyin' no barn parties. Whereupon Billy Bob capsized her berry pail, and when she, with despairing, piglike shrieks, bent down in futile gestures of rescue, Preacher, who can be mean as the devil, gave her behind a kick which sent her sprawling jellylike among the blackberries and the dust. Miss Bobbit came tearing across the road, her finger wagging like a metronome; like a schoolteacher she clapped her hands, stamped her foot, said: "It is a well-known fact that gentlemen are put on the face of this earth for the protection of ladies. Do you suppose boys behave this way in towns like Memphis, New York, London, Hollywood or Paris?" The boys hung back and shoved their hands in their pockets. Miss Bobbit helped the colored girl to her feet; she dusted her off, dried her eyes, held out a handkerchief and told her to blow. "A pretty pass," she said, "a fine situation when a lady can't walk safely in the public daylight."

Then the two of them went back and sat on Mrs. Sawyer's porch; and for the next year they were never far apart, Miss Bobbit and this baby elephant, whose name was Rosalba Cat. At first, Mrs. Sawyer raised a fuss about Rosalba being so much at her house. She told Aunt El that it went against the grain to have a nigger lolling smack there in plain sight on her front porch. But Miss Bobbit had a certain magic, whatever she did she did it with completeness, and so directly, so solemnly, that there was nothing to do but accept it. For instance, the tradespeople in town used to snicker when they called her *Miss* Bobbit; but by and by she was Miss Bobbit, and they gave her stiff little bows as she whirled by spinning her parasol. Miss Bobbit told everyone that Rosalba was her sister, which caused a good many jokes; but like most of her ideas, it gradually seemed natural, and when we would overhear them calling each other Sister Rosalba and Sister Bobbit, none of us cracked a smile. But Sister Rosalba and Sister Bobbit did some queer things. There was the business about the dogs. Now there are a great many dogs in this town, rat terriers, bird dogs, bloodhounds; they trail along the forlorn noon-hot streets in sleepy herds of six to a dozen, all waiting only for dark and the moon, when straight through the lonesome hours you can hear them howling: someone is dying, someone is dead. Miss Bobbit complained to the Sheriff; she said that certain of the dogs always planted themselves under her window, and that she was a light sleeper to begin with; what is more, and as Sister Rosalba said, she did not believe they were dogs at all, but some kind of devil. Naturally the Sheriff did nothing; and so she took the matter into her own hands. One morning after an especially loud night, she was seen stalking through the town with Rosalba at her side, Rosalba carrying a flower basket filled with rocks; whenever they saw a dog they paused while Miss Bobbit scrutinized them. Sometimes she would shake her head, but more often she said, "Yes, that's one of them, Sister Rosalba," and Sister Rosalba, with ferocious aim, would take a rock from her basket and crack the dog between the eyes.

Another thing that happened concerns Mr. Henderson. Mr. Henderson has a back room in the Sawyer house; a tough runt of a man who formerly was a wildcat oil prospector in Oklahoma, he is about seventy years old and, like a lot of old men, obsessed by functions of the body. Also, he is a terrible drunk. One time he had been drunk for two weeks; whenever he heard Miss Bobbit and Sister Rosalba moving around the house, he would charge to the top of the stairs and bellow down to Mrs. Sawyer that there were midgets in the walls trying to get at his supply of toilet paper. They've already stolen fifteen cents' worth, he said. One evening, when the two girls were sitting under a tree in the yard, Mr. Henderson, sporting nothing more than a nightshirt, stamped out after them. Steal all my toilet paper, will you? he hollered, I'll show you midgets. . . . Somebody come help me, else these midget bitches are liable to make off with every sheet in town. It was Billy Bob and Preacher who caught Mr. Henderson and held him until some grown men arrived and began to tie him up. Miss Bobbit, who had behaved with admirable calm, told the men they did not know how to tie a proper knot, and undertook to do so herself. She did such a good job that all the circulation stopped in Mr. Henderson's hands and feet and it was a month before he could walk again.

It was shortly afterward that Miss Bobbit paid us a call. She came on Sunday and I was there alone, the family having gone to church. "The odors of a church are so offensive," she said, leaning forward and with her hands folded primly before her. "I don't want you to think I'm a heathen, Mr. C.; I've had enough experience to know that there is a God and that there is a Devil. But the way to tame the Devil is not to go down there to church and listen to what a sinful mean fool he is. No, love the Devil like you love Jesus: because he is a powerful man, and will do you a good turn if he knows you trust him. He has frequently done me good turns, like at dancing school in Memphis. . . . I always called in the Devil to help me get the biggest part in our annual show. That is common sense; you see, I knew Jesus wouldn't have any truck with dancing. Now, as a matter of fact, I have called in the Devil just recently. He is the only one who can help me get out of this town. Not that I live here, not exactly. I think always about somewhere else, somewhere else where everything is dancing, like people dancing in the streets, and everything is pretty, like children on their birthdays. My precious papa said I live in the sky, but if he'd lived more in the sky, he'd be rich like he wanted to be. The trouble with my papa was he did not love the Devil, he let the Devil love him. But I am very smart in that respect; I know the next best thing is very often the best. It was the next best thing for us to move to this town; and since I can't pursue my career here, the next best thing for me is to start a little business on the side. Which is what I have done. I am sole subscription agent in this county for an impressive list of magazines, including *Reader's Digest, Popular Mechanics, Dime Detective* and *Child's Life.* To be sure, Mr. C., I'm not here to sell you anything. But I have a thought in mind. I was thinking those two boys that are always hanging around here, it occurred to me that they are men, after all. Do you suppose they would make a pair of likely assistants?"

Billy Bob and Preacher worked hard for Miss Bobbit, and for Sister Rosalba, too. Sister Rosalba carried a line of cosmetics called Dewdrop, and it was part of the boys' job to deliver purchases to her customers. Billy Bob used to be so tired in the evening he could hardly chew his supper. Aunt El said it was a shame and a pity, and finally one day when Billy Bob came down with a touch of sunstroke she said, all right, that settled it, Billy Bob would just have to quit Miss Bobbit. But Billy Bob cussed her out until his daddy had to lock him in his room; whereupon he said he was going to kill himself. Some cook we'd had told him once that if you ate a mess of collards all slopped over with molasses, it would kill you sure as shooting; and so that is what he did. I'm dying, he said, rolling back and forth in his bed, I'm dying and nobody cares.

Miss Bobbit came over and told him to hush up. "There's nothing wrong with you, boy," she said. "All you've got is a stomachache." Then she did something that shocked Aunt El very much: she stripped the covers off Billy Bob and rubbed him down with alcohol from head to toe. When Aunt El told her she did not think that was a nice thing for a little girl to do, Miss Bobbit replied: "I don't know whether it's nice or not, but it's certainly very refreshing." After which Aunt El did all she could to keep Billy Bob from going back to work for her, but his daddy said to leave him alone, they would have to let the boy lead his own life.

Miss Bobbit was very honest about money. She paid Billy Bob and Preacher their exact commission, and she would never let them treat her, as they often tried to do, at the drugstore or to the picture show. "You'd better save your money," she told them. "That is, if you want to go to college. Because neither one of you has got the brains to win a scholarship, not even a football scholarship." But it was over money that Billy Bob and Preacher had a big falling-out; that was not the real reason, of course: the real reason was that they had grown cross-eyed jealous over Miss Bobbit. So one day, and he had the gall to do this right in front of Billy Bob, Preacher said to Miss Bobbit that she'd better check her accounts carefully because he had more than a suspicion that Billy Bob wasn't turning over to her *all* the money he collected. That's a damned lie, said Billy Bob, and with a clean left hook he knocked Preacher off the Sawyer porch and jumped after him into a bed of nasturtiums. But once Preacher got a hold on him, Billy Bob didn't stand a chance. Preacher even rubbed dirt in his eyes. During all this, Mrs. Sawyer, leaning out an upper-story window, screamed like an eagle, and Sister Rosalba, fatly cheerful, ambiguously shouted, Kill him! Kill him! Kill him! Only Miss Bobbit seemed to know what she was doing. She plugged in the lawn hose, and gave the boys a close-up, blinding bath. Gasping, Preacher staggered to his feet. Oh, honey, he said, shaking himself like a wet dog, honey, you've got to decide. "Decide *what?*" said Miss Bobbit, right away in a huff. Oh, honey, wheezed Preacher, you don't want us boys killing each other. You got to decide who is your real true sweetheart. "Sweetheart, my eye," said Miss Bobbit. "I should've known better than to get myself involved with a lot of country children. What sort of businessman are you going to make? Now, you listen here, Preacher Star: I don't want a sweetheart, and if I did, it wouldn't be you. As a matter of fact, you don't even get up when a lady enters the room."

Preacher spit on the ground and swaggered over to Billy Bob. Come on, he said, just as though nothing had happened, she's a hard one, she is, she don't want nothing but to make trouble between two good friends. For a moment it looked as if Billy Bob was going to join him in a peaceful togetherness; but suddenly, coming to his senses, he drew back and made a gesture. The boys regarded each other a full minute, all the closeness between them turning an ugly color: you can't hate so much unless you love, too. And Preacher's face showed all of this. But there was nothing for him to do except go away. Oh, yes, Preacher, you looked so lost that day that for the first time I really liked you, so skinny and mean and lost going down the road all by yourself.

They did not make it up, Preacher and Billy Bob; and it was not because they didn't want to, it was only that there did not seem to be any straight way for their friendship to happen again. But they couldn't get rid of this friendship: each was always aware of what the other was up to; and when Preacher found himself a new buddy, Billy Bob moped around for days, picking things up, dropping them again, or doing sudden wild things, like purposely poking his finger in the electric fan. Sometimes in the evenings Preacher would pause by the gate and talk with Aunt El. It was only to torment Billy Bob, I suppose, but he stayed friendly with all of us, and at Christmastime he gave us a huge box of shelled peanuts. He left a present for Billy Bob, too. It turned out to be a book of Sherlock Holmes; and on the flyleaf there was scribbled, "Friends Like Ivy On the Wall Must Fall." That's the corniest thing I ever saw, Billy Bob said. Jesus, what a dope he is! But then, and though it was a cold winter day, he went in the backyard and climbed up into the pecan tree, crouching there all afternoon in the blue December branches.

But most of the time he was happy, because Miss Bobbit was there, and she was always sweet to him now. She and Sister Rosalba treated him like a man; that is to say, they allowed him to do everything for them. On the other hand, they let him win at three-handed bridge, they never questioned his lies, nor discouraged his ambitions. It was a happy while. However, trouble started again when school began. Miss Bobbit refused to go. "It's ridiculous," she said, when one day the principal, Mr. Copland, came around to investigate, "really ridiculous; I can read and write and there are *some* people in this town who have every reason to know that I can count money. No, Mr. Copland, consider for a moment and you will see neither of us has the time nor energy. After all, it would only be a matter of whose spirit broke first, yours or mine. And besides, what is there for you to teach me? Now, if you knew anything about dancing, that would be another matter; but under the circumstances, yes, Mr. Copland, under the circumstances, I suggest we forget the whole thing." Mr. Copland was perfectly willing to. But the rest of the town thought she ought to be whipped. Horace Deasley wrote a piece in the paper which was titled "A Tragic Situation." It was, in his opinion, a tragic situation when a small girl could defy what he, for some reason, termed the Constitution of the United States. The article ended with a question: *Can she get away with it?* She did; and so did Sister Rosalba. Only she was colored, so no one cared. Billy Bob was not as lucky. It was school for him, all right; but he might as well have stayed home for the good it did him. On his first report card he got three F's, a record of some sort. But he is a smart boy. I guess he just couldn't live through those hours without Miss Bobbit; away from her he always seemed half-asleep. He was always in a fight, too; either his eye was black or his lip was split or his walk had a limp. He never talked about these fights, but Miss Bobbit was shrewd enough to guess the reason why. "You are a dear, I know, I know. And I appreciate you, Billy Bob. Only don't fight with people because of me. Of course they say mean things about me. But do you know why that is, Billy Bob? It's a compliment, kind of. Because deep down they think I'm absolutely wonderful."

And she was right: if you are not admired, no one will take the trouble to disapprove. But actually we had no idea of how wonderful she was until there appeared the man known as Manny Fox. This happened late in February. The first news we had of Manny Fox was a series of jovial placards posted up in the stores around town: Manny Fox Presents the Fan Dancer Without the Fan; then, in smaller print: Also, Sensational Amateur Program Featuring Your Own Neighbors—First Prize, A Genuine Hollywood Screen Test. All this was to take place the following Thursday. The tickets were priced at one dollar each, which around here is a lot of money; but it is not often that we get any kind of flesh entertainment, so everybody shelled out their money and made a great to-do over the whole thing. The drugstore cowboys talked dirty all week, mostly about the fan dancer without the fan, who turned out to be Mrs. Manny Fox. They stayed down the highway at the Chucklewood Tourist Camp; but they were in town all day, driving around in an old Packard which had Manny Fox's full name stenciled on all four doors. His wife was a deadpan pimento-tongued redhead with wet lips and moist eyelids; she was quite large actually, but compared to Manny Fox she seemed rather frail, for he was a fat cigar of a man.

They made the pool hall their headquarters, and every afternoon you could find them there, drinking beer and joking with the town loafs. As it developed, Manny Fox's business affairs were not restricted to theatrics. He also ran a kind of employment bureau: slowly he let it be known that for a fee of $150 he could get for any adventurous boys in the county high-class jobs working on fruit ships sailing from New Orleans to South America. The chance of a lifetime, he called it. There are not two boys around here who readily lay their hands on so much as five dollars; nevertheless, a good dozen managed to raise the money. Ada Willingham took all she'd saved to buy an angel tombstone for her husband and gave it to her son, and Acey Trump's papa sold an option on his cotton crop.

But the night of the show! That was a night when all was forgotten: mortgages, and the dishes in the kitchen sink. Aunt El said you'd think we were going to the opera, everybody so dressed up, so pink and sweet-smelling. The Odeon had not been so full since the night they gave away the matched set of sterling silver. Practically everybody had a relative in the show, so there was a lot of nervousness to contend with. Miss Bobbit was the only contestant we knew real well. Billy Bob couldn't sit still; he kept telling us over and over that we mustn't applaud for anybody but Miss Bobbit; Aunt El said that would be very rude, which sent Billy Bob off into a state again; and when his father bought us all bags of popcorn he wouldn't touch his because it would make his hands greasy, and please, another thing, we mustn't be noisy and eat ours while Miss Bobbit was performing. That she was to be a contestant had come as a last-minute surprise. It was logical enough, and there were signs that should've told us; the fact, for instance, that she had not set foot outside the Sawyer house in how many days? And the victrola going half the night, her shadow whirling on the window shade, and the secret, stuffed look on Sister Rosalba's face whenever asked after Sister Bobbit's health. So there was her name on the program, listed second, in fact, though she did not appear for a long while. First came Manny Fox, greased and leering, who told a lot of peculiar jokes, clapping his hands, ha, ha. Aunt El said if he told another joke like that, she was going to walk straight out: he did, and she didn't. Before Miss Bobbit came on, there were eleven contestants, including Eustacia Bernstein, who imitated movie stars so that they all sounded like Eustacia, and there was an extraordinary Mr. Buster Riley, a jug-eared old wool-hat from way in the back country who played "Waltzing Matilda" on a saw. Up to that point, he was the hit of the show; not that there was any marked difference in the various receptions, for everybody applauded generously, everybody, that is, except Preacher Star. He was sitting two rows ahead of us, greeting each act with a donkey-loud boo. Aunt El said she was never going to speak to him again. The only person he ever applauded was Miss Bobbit. No doubt the Devil was on her side, but she deserved it. Out she came, tossing her hips, her curls, rolling her eyes. You could tell right away it wasn't going to be one of her classical numbers. She tapped across the stage, daintily holding up the sides of a cloud-blue skirt. That's the cutest thing I ever saw, said Billy Bob, smacking his thigh, and Aunt El had to agree that Miss Bobbit looked real sweet. When she started to twirl the whole audience broke into spontaneous applause; so she did it all over again, hissing, "Faster, faster," at poor Miss Adelaide, who was at the piano doing her Sunday-school best. "I was born in China, and raised in Jay-pan . . ." We had never heard her sing before, and she had a rowdy sandpaper voice. " . . . if you don't like my peaches, stay away from my can, o-ho o-ho!" Aunt El gasped; she gasped again when Miss Bobbit, with a bump, up-ended her skirt to display blue-lace underwear, thereby collecting most of the whistles the boys had been saving for the fan dancer without the fan, which was just as well, as it later turned out, for that lady, to the tune of "An Apple for the Teacher" and cries of gyp gyp, did her routine attired in a bathing suit. But showing off her bottom was not Miss Bobbit's final triumph. Miss Adelaide commenced an ominous thundering in the darker keys, at which point Sister Rosalba, carrying a lighted Roman candle, rushed onstage and handed it to Miss Bobbit, who was in the midst of a full split; she made it, too, and just as she did the Roman candle burst into fiery balls of red, white and blue, and we all had to stand up because she was singing "The Star-Spangled Banner" at the top of her lungs. Aunt El said afterward that it was one of the most gorgeous things she'd ever seen on the American stage.

Well, she surely did deserve a Hollywood screen test and, inasmuch as she won the contest, it looked as though she were going to get it. Manny Fox said she was: honey, he said, you're real star stuff. Only he skipped town the next day, leaving nothing but hearty promises. Watch the mails, my friends, you'll all be hearing from me. That is what he said to the boys whose money he'd taken, and that is what he said to Miss Bobbit. There are three deliveries daily, and this sizable group gathered at the post office for all of them, a jolly crowd growing gradually joyless. How their hands trembled when a letter slid into their mailbox. A terrible hush came over them as the days passed. They all knew what the other was thinking, but no one could bring himself to say it, not even Miss Bobbit. Postmistress Patterson said it plainly, however: the man's a crook, she said, I knew he was a crook to begin with, and if I have to look at your faces one more day I'll shoot myself.

Finally, at the end of two weeks, it was Miss Bobbit who broke the spell. Her eyes had grown more vacant than anyone had ever supposed they might, but one day, after the last mail was up, all her old sizzle came back. "Okay, boys, it's lynch law now," she said, and proceeded to herd the whole troupe home with her. This was the first meeting of the Manny Fox Hangman's Club, an organization which, in a more social form, endures to this day, though Manny Fox has long since been caught and, so to say, hung. Credit for this went quite properly to Miss Bobbit. Within a week she'd written over three hundred descriptions of Manny Fox and dispatched them to Sheriffs throughout the South; she also wrote letters to papers in the larger cities, and these attracted wide attention. As a result, four of the robbed boys were offered good-paying jobs by the United Fruit Company, and late this spring, when Manny Fox was arrested in Uphigh, Arkansas, where he was pulling the same old dodge, Miss Bobbit was presented with a Good Deed Merit award from the Sunbeam Girls of America. For some reason, she made a point of letting the world know that this did not exactly thrill her. "I do not approve of the organization," she said. "All that rowdy bugle blowing. It's neither good-hearted nor truly feminine. And anyway, what is a good deed? Don't let anybody fool you, a good deed is something you do because you want something in return." It would be reassuring to report she was wrong, and that her just reward, when at last it came, was given out of kindness and love. However, this is not the case. About a week ago the boys involved in the swindle all received from Manny Fox checks covering their losses, and Miss Bobbit, with clodhopping determination, stalked into a meeting of the Hangman's Club, which is now an excuse for drinking beer and playing poker every Thursday night. "Look, boys," she said, laying it on the line, "none of you ever thought to see that money again, but now that you have, you ought to invest it in something practical—like me." The proposition was that they should pool their money and finance her trip to Hollywood; in return, they would get ten percent of her life's earnings which, after she was a star, and that would not be very long, would make them all rich men. "At least," as she said, "in this part of the country." Not one of the boys wanted to do it: but when Miss Bobbit looked at you, what was there to say?

Since Monday, it has been raining buoyant summer rain shot through with sun, but dark at night and full of sound, full of dripping leaves, watery chimings, sleepless scuttlings. Billy Bob is wide-awake, dry-eyed, though everything he does is a little frozen and his tongue is as stiff as a bell tongue. It has not been easy for him, Miss Bobbit's going. Because she'd meant more than that. Than what? Than being thirteen years old and crazy in love. She was the queer things in him, like the pecan tree and liking books and caring enough about people to let them hurt him. She was the things he was afraid to show anyone else. And in the dark the music trickled through the rain: won't there be nights when we will hear it just as though it were really there? And afternoons when the shadows will be all at once confused, and she will pass before us, unfurling across the lawn like a pretty piece of ribbon? She laughed to Billy Bob; she held his hand, she even kissed him. "I'm not going to die," she said. "You'll come out there, and we'll climb a mountain, and we'll all live there together, you and me and Sister Rosalba." But Billy Bob knew it would never happen that way, and so when the music came through the dark he would stuff the pillow over his head.

Only there was a strange smile about yesterday, and that was the day she was leaving. Around noon the sun came out, bringing with it into the air all the sweetness of wisteria. Aunt El's yellow Lady Anne's were blooming again, and she did something wonderful, she told Billy Bob he could pick them and give them to Miss Bobbit for good-bye. All afternoon Miss Bobbit sat on the porch surrounded by people who stopped by to wish her well. She looked as though she were going to Communion, dressed in white and with a white parasol. Sister Rosalba had given her a handkerchief, but she had to borrow it back because she couldn't stop blubbering. Another little girl brought a baked chicken, presumably to be eaten on the bus; the only trouble was she'd forgotten to take out the insides before cooking it. Miss Bobbit's mother said that was all right by her, chicken was chicken; which is memorable because it is the single opinion she ever voiced. There was only one sour note. For hours Preacher Star had been hanging around down at the corner, sometimes standing at the curb tossing a coin, sometimes hiding behind a tree, as if he didn't want anyone to see him. It made everybody nervous. About twenty mintues before bus time he sauntered up and leaned against our gate. Billy Bob was still in the garden picking roses; by now he had enough for a bonfire, and their smell was as heavy as wind. Preacher stared at him until he lifted his head. As they looked at each other the rain began again, falling fine as sea spray and colored by a rainbow. Without a word, Preacher went over and started helping Billy Bob separate the roses into two giant bouquets: together they carried them to the curb. Across the street there were bumblebees of talk, but when Miss Bobbit saw them, two boys whose flower-masked faces were like yellow moons, she rushed down the steps, her arms outstretched. You could see what was going to happen; and we called out, our voices like lightning in the rain, but Miss Bobbit, running toward those moons of roses, did not seem to hear. That is when the six-o'clock bus ran over her.

Flannery O'Connor

1925 – 1964

During her brief life, Flannery O'Connor wrote enough stories to fill only two volumes of modest size, but the superior merit of her work, as small in quantity as it is, entitles her to a rank among the foremost American masters of the short story. Her stories frequently depict violence, horror, and grotesqueries of the most shocking kind, but not as an end in themselves, as she made clear in an essay, "The Fiction Writer and His Country." There she noted that "writers who see by the light of their Christian faith will have . . . the sharpest eyes for the grotesque, for the perverse, and for the unacceptable." The problem that writers with "Christian concerns" have, however, is making "these distortions appear as distortions to an audience which is used to seeing them as natural." What this circumstance compels the writer to do is to make "his vision apparent by shock—to the hard of hearing you shout, and for the almost blind you draw large and startling pictures." The sheer, brutal power of her stories is nearly unmatched in the annals of the short story.

O'Connor was born in 1925 in Savannah, Georgia, but at an early age moved with her family to Milledgeville, Georgia. She attended Peabody High School in Milledgeville, earned her bachelor's degree at Georgia State College for Women in 1945, and then continued her education at the State University of Iowa, where she studied creative writing in Paul Engle's writers' workshop for two years, earning an MFA degree in 1947. She then lived in New York City and Connecticut for a period before returning to Milledgeville in 1950, where she continued to reside until her death in 1964. Her fiction began appearing in 1946, first in *Accent* and then in the *Sewanee, Partisan,* and *Kenyon* reviews, as well as in various other periodicals such as *Harper's Bazaar,*

Mademoiselle, and *New World Writing.* Her first collection of stories, *A Good Man Is Hard to Find and Other Stories* appeared in 1955, and her second collection, *Everything That Rises Must Converge,* appeared posthumously in 1965. In addition she published two novels, *Wise Blood* (1952) and *The Violent Bear It Away* (1960). A collection of her "occasional prose," *Mystery and Manners,* edited by Sally and Robert Fitzgerald, was published in 1969 and won The National Catholic Book Award. During her lifetime, her fiction brought her many important awards, including grants from The National Institute of Arts and Letters and from the Ford Foundation.

"Good Country People" is a noteworthy example of O'Connor's art. Thematically, it reflects her deep concern with the "heart condition" or spiritual barrenness which afflicts members of modern society and is more territying than mere physical illness. Structurally, it illustrates her characteristic method of writing wherein a seemingly casual flow of events culminates suddenly in an explosive and—in this case—bizarre climax.

Good Country People

Besides the neutral expression that she wore when she was alone, Mrs. Freeman had two others, forward and reverse, that she used for all her human dealings. Her forward expression was steady and driving like the advance of a heavy truck. Her eyes never swerved to left or right but turned as the story turned as if they followed a yellow line down the center of it. She seldom used the other expression because it was not often necessary for her to retract a statement, but when she did, her face came to a complete stop, there was an almost imperceptible movement of her black eyes, during which they seemed to be receding, and then the observer would see that Mrs. Freeman, though she might stand there as real as several grain sacks thrown on top of each other, was no longer there in spirit. As for getting anything across to her when this was the case, Mrs. Hopewell had given it up. She might talk her head off. Mrs. Freeman could never be brought to admit herself wrong on any point. She would stand there and if she could be brought to say anything, it was something like, "Well, I wouldn't of said it was and I wouldn't of said it wasn't," or letting her gaze range over the top kitchen shelf where there was an assortment of dusty bottles, she might remark, "I see you ain't ate many of them figs you put up last summer."

They carried on their most important business in the kitchen at breakfast. Every morning Mrs. Hopewell got up at seven o'clock and lit her gas heater and Joy's. Joy was her daughter, a large blonde girl who had an artificial leg. Mrs. Hopewell thought of her as a child though she was thirty-two years old and highly educated. Joy would get up while her mother was eating and lumber into the bathroom and slam the door, and before long, Mrs. Freeman would arrive at the back door. Joy would hear her mother call, "Come on in," and then they would talk for a while in low voices that were indistinguishable in the bathroom. By the time Joy came in, they had usually finished the weather report and were on one or the other of Mrs. Freeman's daughters, Glynese or Carramae. Joy called them Glycerin and Caramel. Glynese, a redhead, was eighteen and had many admirers; Carramae, a blonde was only fifteen but already married and pregnant. She could not keep anything on her stomach. Every morning Mrs. Freeman told Mrs. Hopewell how many times she had vomited since the last report.

Mrs. Hopewell liked to tell people that Glynese and Carramae were two of the finest girls she knew and that Mrs. Freeman was a *lady* and that she was never ashamed to take her anywhere or introduce her to anybody they might meet. Then she would tell how she had happened to hire the Freemans in the first place and how they were a godsend to her and how she had had them four years. The reason for her keeping them so long was that they were not trash. They were good country people. She had telephoned the man whose name they had given as a reference and he had told her that Mr. Freeman was a good farmer but that his wife was the nosiest woman ever to walk the earth. "She's got to be into everything," the man said. "If she don't get there before the dust settles, you can bet she's dead, that's all. She'll want to know all your business. I can stand him real good," he had said, "but me nor my wife neither could have stood that woman one more minute on this place." That had put Mrs. Hopewell off for a few days.

She had hired them in the end because there were no other applicants but she had made up her mind beforehand exactly how she would handle the woman. Since she was the type who had to be into everything, then, Mrs. Hopewell had decided, she would not only let her be into everything, she would *see to it* that she was into everything—she would give her the responsibility of everything, she would put her in charge. Mrs. Hopewell had no bad qualities of her own but she was able to use other people's in such a constructive way that she never felt the lack. She had hired the Freemans and she had kept them four years.

Nothing is perfect. This was one of Mrs. Hopewell's favorite sayings. Another was: that is life! And still another, the most important, was: well, other people have their opinions too. She would make these statements, usually at the table, in a tone of gentle insistence as if no one held them but her, and the large hulking Joy, whose constant outrage had obliterated every expression from her face, would stare just a little to the side of her, her eyes icy blue, with the look of someone who has achieved blindness by an act of will and means to keep it.

When Mrs. Hopewell said to Mrs. Freeman that life was like that, Mrs. Freeman would say, "I always said so myself." Nothing had been arrived at by anyone that had not first been arrived at by her. She was quicker than Mr. Freeman. When Mrs. Hopewell said to her after they had been on the place a while, "You know, you're the wheel behind the wheel," and winked, Mrs. Freeman had said, "I know it. I've always been quick. It's some that are quicker than others."

"Everybody is different," Mrs. Hopewell said.

"Yes, most people is," Mrs. Freeman said.

"It takes all kinds to make the world."

"I always said it did myself."

The girl was used to this kind of dialogue for breakfast and more of it for dinner; sometimes they had it for supper too. When they had no guest they ate in the kitchen because that was easier. Mrs. Freeman always managed to arrive at some point during the meal and to watch them finish it. She would stand in the doorway if it were summer but in the winter she would stand with one elbow on top of the refrigerator and look down on them, or she would stand by the gas heater, lifting the back of her skirt slightly. Occasionally she would stand against the wall and roll her head from side to side. At no time was she in any hurry to leave. All this was very trying on Mrs. Hopewell but she was a woman of great patience. She realized that nothing is perfect and that in the Freemans she had good country people and that if, in this day and age, you get good country people, you had better hang onto them.

She had had plenty of experience with trash. Before the Freemans she had averaged one tenant family a year. The wives of these farmers were not the kind you would want to be around you for very long. Mrs. Hopewell, who had divorced her husband long ago, needed someone to walk over the fields with her; and when Joy had to be impressed for these services, her remarks were usually so ugly and her face so glum that Mrs. Hopewell would say, "If you can't come pleasantly, I don't want you at all," to which the girl, standing square and rigid-shouldered with her neck thrust slightly forward, would reply, "If you want me, here I am—LIKE I AM."

Mrs. Hopewell excused this attitude because of the leg (which had been shot off in a hunting accident when Joy was ten). It was hard for Mrs. Hopewell to realize that her child was thirty-two now and that for more than twenty years she had had only one leg. She thought of her still as a child because it tore her heart to think instead of the poor stout girl in her thirties who had never danced a step or had any *normal* good times. Her name was really Joy but as soon as she was twenty-one and away from home, she had had it legally changed. Mrs. Hopewell was certain that she had thought and thought until she had hit upon the ugliest name in any language. Then she had gone and had the beautiful name, Joy, changed without telling her mother until after she had done it. Her legal name was Hulga.

When Mrs. Hopewell thought the name, Hulga, she thought of the broad blank hull of a battleship. She would not use it. She continued to call her Joy to which the girl responded but in a purely mechanical way.

Hulga had learned to tolerate Mrs. Freeman who saved her from taking walks with her mother. Even Glynese and Carramae were useful when they occupied attention that might otherwise have been directed at her. At first she had thought she could not stand Mrs. Freeman for she had found that it was not possible to be rude to her. Mrs. Freeman would take on strange resentments and for days together she would be sullen but the source of her displeasure was always obscure; a direct attack, a positive leer, blatant ugliness to her face—these never touched her. And without warning one day, she began calling her Hulga.

She did not call her that in front of Mrs. Hopewell who would have been incensed but when she and the girl happened to be out of the house together, she would say something and add the name Hulga to the end of it, and the big spectacled Joy-Hulga would scowl and redden as if her privacy had been intruded upon. She considered the name her personal affair. She had arrived at it first purely on the basis of its ugly sound and then the full genius of its fitness had struck her. She had a vision of the name working like the ugly sweating Vulcan who stayed in the furnace and to whom, presumably, the goddess had to come when called. She saw it as the name of her highest creative act. One of her major triumphs was that her mother had not been able to turn her dust into Joy, but the greater one was that she had been able to turn it herself into Hulga. However, Mrs. Freeman's relish for using the name only irritated her. It was as if Mrs. Freeman's beady steel-pointed eyes had penetrated far enough behind her face to reach some secret fact. Something about her seemed to fascinate Mrs. Freeman and then one day Hulga realized that it was the artificial leg. Mrs. Freeman had a special fondness for the details of secret infections, hidden deformities, assaults upon children. Of diseases, she preferred the lingering or incurable. Hulga had heard Mrs. Hopewell give her the details of the hunting accident, how the leg had been literally blasted off, how she had never lost consciousness. Mrs. Freeman could listen to it any time as if it had happened an hour ago.

When Hulga stumped into the kitchen in the morning (she could walk without making the awful noise but she made it—Mrs. Hopewell was certain—because it was ugly-sounding), she glanced at them and did not speak. Mrs. Hopewell would be in her red kimono with her hair tied around her head in rags. She would be sitting at the table, finishing her breakfast and Mrs. Freeman would be hanging by her elbow outward from the refrigerator, looking down at the table. Hulga always put her eggs on the stove to boil and then stood over them with her arms folded, and Mrs. Hopewell would look at her—a kind of indirect gaze divided between her and Mrs. Freeman—and would think that if she would only keep herself up a little, she wouldn't be so bad looking. There was nothing wrong with her face that a pleasant expression wouldn't help. Mrs. Hopewell said that people who looked on the bright side of things would be beautiful even if they were not.

Whenever she looked at Joy this way, she could not help but feel that it would have been better if the child had not taken the Ph.D. It had certainly not brought her out any and now that she had it, there was no more excuse for her to go to school again. Mrs. Hopewell thought it was nice for girls to go to school to have a good time but Joy had "gone through." Anyhow, she would not have been strong enough to go again. The doctors had told Mrs. Hopewell that with the best of care, Joy might see forty-five. She had a weak heart. Joy had made it plain that if it had not been for this condition, she would be far from these red hills and good country people. She would be in a university lecturing to people who knew what she was talking about. And Mrs. Hopewell could very well picture her there, looking like a scarecrow and lecturing to more of the same. Here she went about all day in a six-year-old skirt and a yellow sweat shirt with a faded cowboy on a horse embossed on it. She thought this was funny; Mrs. Hopewell thought it was idiotic and showed simply that she was still a child. She was brilliant but she didn't have a grain of sense. It seemed to Mrs. Hopewell that every year she grew less like other people and more like herself—bloated, rude, and squint-eyed. And she said such strange things! To her own mother she had said—without warning, without excuse, standing up in the middle of a meal with her face purple and her mouth half full—"Woman! do you ever look inside? Do you ever look inside and see what you are *not?* God!" she had cried sinking down again and staring at her plate, "Malebranche was right: we are not our own light. We are not our own light!" Mrs. Hopewell had no idea to this day what brought that on. She had only made the remark, hoping Joy would take it in, that a smile never hurt anyone. The girl had taken the Ph.D. in philosophy and this left Mrs. Hopewell at a complete loss. You could say, "My daughter is a nurse," or "My daughter is a school teacher," or even, "My daughter is a chemical engineer." You could not say, "My daughter is a philosopher." That was something that had ended with the Greeks and Romans. All day Joy sat on her neck in a deep chair, reading. Sometimes she went for walks but she didn't like dogs or cats or birds or flowers or nature or nice young men. She looked at nice young men as if she could smell their stupidity.

One day Mrs. Hopewell had picked up one of the books the girl had just put down and opening it at random, she read, "Science, on the other hand, has to assert its soberness and seriousness afresh and declare that it is concerned solely with what-is. Nothing—how can it be for science anything but a horror and a phantasm? If science is right, then one thing stands firm: science wishes to know nothing of nothing. Such is after all the strictly scientific approach to Nothing. We know it by wishing to know nothing of Nothing." These words had been underlined with a blue pencil and they worked on Mrs. Hopewell like some evil incantation in gibberish. She shut the book quickly and went out of the room as if she were having a chill.

This morning when the girl came in, Mrs. Freeman was on Carramae. "She thrown up four times after supper," she said, "and was up twict in the night after three o'clock. Yesterday she didn't do nothing but ramble in the bureau drawer. All she did. Stand up there and see what she could run up on."

"She's got to eat," Mrs. Hopewell muttered, sipping her coffee, while she watched Joy's back at the stove. She was wondering what the child had said to the Bible salesman. She could not imagine what kind of a conversation she could possibly have had with him.

He was a tall gaunt hatless youth who had called yesterday to sell them a Bible. He had appeared at the door, carrying a large black suitcase that weighted him so heavily on one side that he had to brace himself against the door facing. He seemed on the point of collapse but he said in a cheerful voice, "Good morning, Mrs. Cedars!" and set the suitcase down on the mat. He was not a bad-looking young man though he had on a bright blue suit and yellow socks that were not pulled up far enough. He had prominent face bones and a streak of sticky-looking brown hair falling across his forehead.

"I'm Mrs. Hopewell," she said.

"Oh!" he said, pretending to look puzzled but with his eyes sparkling. I saw it said 'The Cedars,' on the mailbox so I thought you was Mrs. Cedars!" and he burst out in a pleasant laugh. He picked up the satchel and under cover of a pant, he fell forward into her hall. It was rather as if the suitcase had moved first, jerking him after it. "Mrs. Hopewell!" he said and grabbed her hand. "I hope you are well!" and he laughed again and then all at once his face sobered completely. He paused and gave her a straight earnest look and said, "Lady, I've come to speak of serious things."

"Well, come in," she muttered, none too pleased because her dinner was almost ready. He came into the parlor and sat down on the edge of a straight chair and put the suitcase between his feet and glanced around the room as if he were sizing her up by it. Her silver gleamed on the two sideboards; she decided he had never been in a room as elegant as this.

"Mrs. Hopewell," he began, using her name in a way that sounded almost intimate, "I know you believe in Chrustian service."

"Well, yes," she murmured.

"I know," he said and paused, looking very wise with his head cocked on one side, "that you're a good woman. Friends have told me."

Mrs. Hopewell never liked to be taken for a fool. "What are you selling?" she asked.

"Bibles," the young man said and his eye raced around the room before he added, "I see you have no family Bible in your parlor, I see that is the one lack you got!"

Mrs. Hopewell could not say, "My daughter is an atheist and won't let me keep the Bible in the parlor." She said, stiffening slightly, "I keep my Bible by my bedside." This was not the truth. It was in the attic somewhere.

"Lady," he said, "the word of God ought to be in the parlor."

"Well, I think that's a matter of taste," she began. "I think . . ."

"Lady," he said, "for a Chrustian, the word of God ought to be in every room in the house besides in his heart. I know you're a Chrustian because I see it in every line of your face."

She stood up and said, "Well, young man, I don't want to buy a Bible and I smell my dinner burning."

He didn't get up. He began to twist his hands and looking down at them, he said softly, "Well lady, I'll tell you the truth—not many people want to buy one nowadays and besides, I know I'm real simple. I don't know how to say a thing but to say it. I'm just a country boy." He glanced up into her unfriendly face. "People like you don't like to fool with country people like me!"

"Why!" she cried, "good country people are the salt of the earth! Besides, we all have different ways of doing, it takes all kinds to make the world go 'round. That's life!"

"You said a mouthful," he said.

"Why, I think there aren't enough good country people in the world!" she said, stirred. "I think that's what wrong with it!"

His face had brightened. "I didn't inraduce myself," he said. "I'm Manley Pointer from out in the country around Willohobie, not even from a place, just from near a place."

"You wait a minute," she said. "I have to see about my dinner." She went out to the kitchen and found Joy standing near the door where she had been listening.

"Get rid of the salt of the earth," she said, "and let's eat."

Mrs. Hopewell gave her a pained look and turned the heat down under the vegetables. "*I* can't be rude to anybody," she murmured and went back into the parlor.

He had opened the suitcase and was sitting with a Bible on each knee.

"You might as well put those up," she told him. "I don't want one."

"I appreciate your honesty," he said. "You don't see any more real honest people unless you go way out in the country."

"I know," she said, "real genuine folks!" Through the crack in the door she heard a groan.

"I guess a lot of boys come telling you they're working their way through college," he said, "but I'm not going to tell you that. Somehow," he said, "I don't want to go to college. I want to devote my life to Chrustian service. See," he said, lowering his voice, "I got this heart condition. I may not live long. When you know it's something wrong with you and you may not live long, well then, lady . . . " He paused, with his mouth open, and stared at her.

He and Joy had the same condition! She knew that her eyes were filling with tears but she collected herself quickly and murmured, "Won't you stay for dinner? We'd love to have you!" and was sorry the instant she heard herself say it.

"Yes mam," he said in an abashed voice, "I would sher love to do that!"

Joy had given him one look on being introduced to him and then throughout the meal had not glanced at him again. He had addressed several remarks to her, which she had pretended not to hear. Mrs. Hopewell could not understand deliberate rudeness, although she lived with it, and she felt she had always to overflow with hospitality to make up for Joy's lack of courtesy. She urged him to talk about himself and he did. He said he was the seventh child of twelve and that his father had been crushed under a tree when he himself was eight year old. He had been crushed very badly, in fact, almost cut in two and was practically not recognizable. His mother had got along the best she could by hard working and she had always seen that her children went to Sunday School and that they read the Bible every evening. He was now nineteen year old and he had been selling Bibles for four months. In that time he had sold seventy-seven Bibles and had the promise of two more sales. He wanted to become a missionary because he thought that was the way you could do most for people. "He who losest his life shall find it," he said simply and he was so sincere, so genuine and earnest that Mrs. Hopewell would not for the world have smiled. He prevented his peas from sliding onto the table by blocking them with a piece of bread which he later cleaned his plate with. She could see Joy observing sidewise how he handled his knife and fork and she saw too that every few minutes, the boy would dart a keen appraising glance at the girl as if he were trying to attract her attention.

After dinner Joy cleared the dishes off the table and disappeared and Mrs. Hopewell was left to talk with him. He told her again about his childhood and his father's accident and about various things that had happened to him. Every five minutes or so she would stifle a yawn. He sat for two hours until finally she told him she must go because she had an appointment in town. He packed his Bibles and thanked her and prepared to leave, but in the doorway he stopped and wrung her hand and said that not on any of his trips had he met a lady as nice as her and he asked if he could come again. She had said she would always be happy to see him.

Joy had been standing in the road, apparently looking at something in the distance, when he came down the steps toward her, bent to the side with his heavy valise. He stopped where she was standing and confronted her directly. Mrs. Hopewell could not hear what he said but she trembled to think what Joy would say to him. She could see that after a minute Joy said something and that then the boy began to speak again, making an excited gesture with his free hand. After a minute Joy said something else at which the boy began to speak once more. Then to her amazement, Mrs. Hopewell saw the two of them walk off together, toward the gate. Joy had walked all the way to the gate with him and Mrs. Hopewell could not imagine what they had said to each other, and she had not yet dared to ask.

Mrs. Freeman was insisting upon her attention. She had moved from the refrigerator to the heater so that Mrs. Hopewell had to turn and face her in order to seem to be listening. "Glynese gone out with Harvey Hill again last night," she said. "She had this sty."

"Hill," Mrs. Hopewell said absently, "is that the one who works in the garage?"

"Nome, he's the one that goes to chiropracter school," Mrs. Freeman said. "She had this sty. Been had it two days. So she says when he brought her in the other night he says, 'Lemme get rid of that sty for you,' and she says, 'How?' and he says, 'You just lay yourself down acrost the seat of that car and I'll show you.' So she done it and he popped her neck. Kept on a-popping it several times until she made him quit. This morning," Mrs. Freeman said, "she ain't got no sty. She ain't got no traces of a sty."

"I never heard of that before," Mrs. Hopewell said.

"He ast her to marry him before the Ordinary." Mrs. Freeman went on, "and she told him she wasn't going to be married in no *office.*"

"Well, Glynese is a fine girl," Mrs. Hopewell said, "Glynese and Carramae are both fine girls."

"Carramae said when her and Lyman was married Lyman said it sure felt sacred to him. She said he said he wouldn't take five hundred dollars for being married by a preacher."

"How much would he take?" the girl asked from the stove.

"He said he wouldn't take five hundred dollars," Mrs. Freeman repeated.

"Well we all have work to do," Mrs. Hopewell said.

"Lyman said it just felt more sacred to him," Mrs. Freeman said. "The doctor wants Carramae to eat prunes. Says instead of medicine. Says them cramps is coming from pressure. You know where I think it is?"

"She'll be better in a few weeks," Mrs. Hopewell said.

"In the tube," Mrs. Freeman said. "Else she wouldn't be as sick as she is."

Hulga had cracked her two eggs into a saucer and was bringing them to the table along with a cup of coffee that she had filled too full. She sat down carefully and began to eat, meaning to keep Mrs. Freeman there by questions if for any reason she showed an inclination to leave. She could perceive her mother's eye on her. The first roundabout question would be about the Bible salesman and she did not wish to bring it on. "How did he pop her neck?" she asked.

Mrs. Freeman went into a description of how he had popped her neck. She said he owned a '55 Mercury but that Glynese said she would rather marry a man with only a '36 Plymouth who would be married by a preacher. The girl asked what if he had a '32 Plymouth and Mrs. Freeman said what Glynese had said was a '36 Plymouth.

Mrs. Hopewell said there were not many girls with Glynese's common sense. She said what she admired in those girls was their common sense. She said that reminded her that they had had a nice visitor yesterday, a young man selling Bibles. "Lord," she said, "he bored me to death but he was so sincere and genuine I couldn't be rude to him. He was just good country people, you know," she said, "—just the salt of the earth."

"I seen him walk up," Mrs. Freeman said, "and then later—I seen him walk off," and Hulga could feel the slight shift in her voice, the slight insinuation, that he had not walked off alone, had he? Her face remained expressionless but the color rose into her neck and she seemed to swallow it down with the next spoonful of egg. Mrs. Freeman was looking at her as if they had a secret together.

"Well it takes all kinds of people to make the world go 'round," Mrs. Hopewell said. "It's very good we aren't all alike."

"Some people are more alike than others," Mrs. Freeman said.

Hulga got up and stumped, with about twice the noise that was necessary, into her room and locked the door. She was to meet the Bible salesman at ten o'clock at the gate. She had thought about it half the night. She had started thinking of it as a great joke and then she had begun to see profound implications in it. She had lain in bed imagining dialogues for them that were insane on the surface but that reached below to depths that no Bible salesman would be aware of. Their conversation yesterday had been of this kind.

He had stopped in front of her and had simply stood there. His face was bony and sweaty and bright, with a little pointed nose in the center of it, and his look was different from what it had been at the dinner table. He was gazing at her with open curiosity, with fascination, like a child watching a new fantastic animal at the zoo, and he was breathing as if he had run a great distance to reach her. His gaze seemed somehow familiar but she could not think where she had been regarded with it before. For almost a minute he didn't say anything. Then on what seemed an insuck of breath, he whispered, "You ever ate a chicken that was two days old?"

The girl looked at him stonily. He might have just put this question up for consideration at the meeting of a philosophical association. "Yes," she presently replied as if she had considered it from all angles.

"It must have been mighty small!" he said triumphantly and shook all over with little nervous giggles, getting very red in the face, and subsiding finally into his gaze of complete admiration, while the girl's expression remained exactly the same.

"How old are you?" he asked softly.

She waited some time before she answered. Then in a flat voice she said, "Seventeen."

His smiles came in succession like waves breaking on the surface of a little lake. "I see you got a wooden leg," he said. "I think you're real brave. I think you're real sweet."

The girl stood blank and solid and silent.

"Walk to the gate with me," he said. "You're a brave sweet little thing and I liked you the minute I seen you walk in the door."

Hulga began to move forward.

"What's your name?" he asked, smiling down on the top of her head.

"Hulga," she said.

"Hulga," he murmured, "Hulga. Hulga. I never heard of anybody name Hulga before. You're shy, aren't you, Hulga?" he asked.

She nodded, watching his large red hand on the handle of the giant valise.

"I like girls that wear glasses," he said. "I think a lot. I'm not like these people that a serious thought don't ever enter their heads. It's because I may die."

"I may die too," she said suddenly and looked up at him. His eyes were very small and brown, glittering feverishly.

"Listen," he said, "don't you think some people was meant to meet on account of what all they got in common and all? Like they both think serious thoughts and all?" He shifted the valise to his other hand so that the hand nearest her was free. He caught hold of her elbow and shook it a little. "I don't work on Saturday," he said. "I like to walk in the woods and see what Mother Nature is wearing. O'er the hills and far away. Picnics and things. Couldn't we go on a pic-nic tomorrow? Say yes, Hulga," he said and gave her a dying look as if he felt his insides about to drop out of him. He had even seemed to sway slightly toward her.

During the night she had imagined that she seduced him. She imagined that the two of them walked on the place until they came to the storage barn beyond the two back fields and there, she imagined, that things came to such a pass that she very easily seduced him and that then, of course, she had to reckon with his remorse. True genius can get an idea across even to an inferior mind. She imagined that she took his remorse in hand and changed it into a deeper understanding of life. She took all his shame away and turned it into something useful.

She set off for the gate at exactly ten o'clock, escaping without drawing Mrs. Hopewell's attention. She didn't take anything to eat, forgetting that food is usually taken on a picnic. She wore a pair of slacks and a dirty white shirt, and as an afterthought, she had put some Vapex on the collar of it since she did not own any perfume. When she reached the gate no one was there.

She looked up and down the empty highway and had the furious feeling that she had been tricked, that he had only meant to make her walk to the gate after the idea of him. Then suddenly he stood up, very tall, from behind a bush on the opposite embankment. Smiling, he lifted his hat which was new and wide-brimmed. He had not worn it yesterday and she wondered if he had bought it for the occasion. It was toast-colored with a red and white band around it and was slightly too large for him. He stepped from behind the bush still carrying the black valise. He had on the same suit and the same yellow socks sucked down in his shoes from walking. He crossed the highway and said, "I knew you'd come!"

The girl wondered acidly how he had known this. She pointed to the valise and asked, "Why did you bring your Bibles?"

He took her elbow, smiling down on her as if he could not stop. "You can never tell when you'll need the word of God, Hulga," he said. She had a moment in which she doubted that this was actually happening and then they began to climb the embankment. They went down into the pasture toward the woods. The boy walked lightly by her side, bouncing on his toes. The valise did not seem to be heavy today; he even swung it. They crossed half the pasture without saying anything and then, putting his hand easily on the small of her back, he asked softly, "Where does your wooden leg join on?"

She turned an ugly red and glared at him and for an instant the boy looked abashed. "I didn't mean you no harm," he said. "I only meant you're so brave and all. I guess God takes care of you."

"No," she said, looking forward and walking fast, "I don't even believe in God."

At this he stopped and whistled. "No!" he exclaimed as if he were too astonished to say anything else.

She walked on and in a second he was bouncing at her side, fanning with his hat. "That's very unusual for a girl," he remarked, watching her out of the corner of his eye. When they reached the edge of the wood, he put his hand on her back again and drew her against him without a word and kissed her heavily.

The kiss, which had more pressure than feeling behind it, produced that extra surge of adrenalin in the girl that enables one to carry a packed trunk out of a burning house, but in her, the power went at once to the brain. Even before he released her, her mind, clear and detached and ironic anyway, was regarding him from a great distance, with amusement but with pity. She had never been kissed before and she was pleased to discover that it was an unexceptional experience and all a matter of the mind's control. Some people might enjoy drain water if they were told it was vodka. When the boy, looking expectant but uncertain, pushed her gently away, she turned and walked on, saying nothing as if such business, for her, were common enough.

He came along panting at her side, trying to help her when he saw a root that she might trip over. He caught and held back the long swaying blades of thorn vine until she had passed beyond them. She led the way and he came breathing heavily behind her. Then they came out on a sunlit hillside, sloping softly into another one a little smaller. Beyond, they could see the rusted top of the old barn where the extra hay was stored.

The hill was sprinkled with small pink weeds. "Then you ain't saved?" he asked suddenly, stopping.

The girl smiled. It was the first time she had smiled at him at all. "In my economy," she said, "I'm saved and you are damned but I told you I didn't believe in God."

Nothing seemed to destory the boy's look of admiration. He gazed at her now as if the fantastic animal at the zoo had put its paw through the bars and given him a loving poke. She thought he looked as if he wanted to kiss her again and she walked on before he had the chance.

"Ain't there somewheres we can sit down sometime?" he murmured, his voice softening toward the end of the sentence.

"In that barn," she said.

They made for it rapidly as if it might slide away like a train. It was a large two-story barn, cool and dark inside. The boy pointed up the ladder that led into the loft and said, "It's too bad we can't go up there."

"Why can't we?" she asked.

"Yer leg," he said reverently.

The girl gave him a contemptuous look and putting both hands on the ladder, she climbed it while he stood below, apparently awestruck. She pulled herself expertly through the opening and then looked down at him and said, "Well come on if you're coming." and he began to climb the ladder, awkwardly bringing the suitcase with him.

"We won't need the Bible." she observed.

"You can never tell," he said, panting. After he had got into the loft, he was a few seconds catching his breath. She had sat down in a pile of straw. A wide sheath of sunlight, filled with dust particles, slanted over her. She lay back against a bale, her face turned away, looking out the front opening of the barn where hay was thrown from a wagon into the loft. The two pink-speckled hillsides lay back against a dark ridge of woods. The sky was cloudless and cold blue. The boy dropped down by her side and put one arm under her and the other over her and began methodically kissing her face, making little noises like a fish. He did not remove his hat but it was pushed far enough back not to interfere. When her glasses got in his way, he took them off of her and slipped them into his pocket.

The girl at first did not return any of the kisses but presently she began to and after she had put several on his check, she reached his lips and remained there, kissing him again and again as if she were trying to draw all the breath out of him. His breath was clear and sweet like a child's and the kisses were sticky like a child's. He mumbled about loving her and about knowing when he first seen her that he loved her, but the mumbling was like the sleepy fretting of a child being put to sleep by his mother. Her mind, throughout this, never stopped or lost itself for a second to her feelings. "You ain't said you loved me none," he whispered finally, pulling back from her. "You got to say that."

She looked away from him off into the hollow sky and then down at a black ridge and then down farther into what appeared to be two green swelling lakes. She didn't realize he had taken her glasses but this landscape could not seem exceptional to her for she seldom paid any close attention to her surroundings.

"You got to say it," he repeated. "You got to say you love me."

She was always careful how she committed herself. "In a sense," she began, "if you use the word loosely, you might say that. But it's not a word I use. I don't have illusions. I'm one of those people who see *through* to nothing."

The boy was frowning. "You got to say it. I said it and you got to say it," he said.

The girl looked at him almost tenderly. "You poor baby," she murmured. "It's just as well you don't understand," and she pulled him by the neck, face-down, against her. "We are all damned," she said, "but some of us have taken off our blindfolds and see that there's nothing to see. It's a kind of salvation."

The boy's astonished eyes looked blankly through the ends of her hair. "Okay," he almost whispered, "but do you love me or don'tcher?"

"Yes," she said and added, "in a sense. But I must tell you something. There mustn't be anything dishonest between us." She lifted his head and looked him in the eye. "I am thirty years old," she said. "I have a number of degrees."

The boy's look was irritated but dogged. "I don't care," he said. "I don't care a thing about what all you done. I just want to know if you love me or don'tcher?" and he caught her to him and wildly planted her face with kisses until she said, "Yes, yes."

"Okay then," he said, letting her go. "Prove it."

She smiled, looking dreamily out on the shifty landscape. She had seduced him without even making up her mind to try. "How?" she asked, feeling that he should be delayed a little.

He leaned over and put his lips to her ear. "Show me where your wooden leg joins on," he whispered.

The girl uttered a sharp little cry and her face instantly drained of color. The obscenity of the suggestion was not what shocked her. As a child she had sometimes been subject to feelings of shame but education had removed the last traces of that as a good surgeon scrapes for cancer; she would no more have felt it over what he was asking than she would have believed in his Bible. But she was as sensitive about the artificial leg as a peacock about his tail. No one ever touched it but her. She took care of it as someone else would his soul, in private and almost with her own eyes turned away. "No," she said.

"I known it," he muttered, sitting up. "You're just playing me for a sucker."

"Oh no no!" she cried. "It joins on at the knee. Only at the knee. Why do you want to see it?"

The boy gave her a long penetrating look. "Because," he said, "it's what makes you different. You ain't like anybody else."

She sat staring at him. There was nothing about her face or her round freezing-blue eyes to indicate that this had moved her; but she felt as if her heart had stopped and left her mind to pump her blood. She decided that for the first time in her life she was face to face with real innocence. This boy, with an instinct that came from beyond wisdom, had touched the truth about her. When after a minute, she said in a hoarse high voice, "All right," it was like surrendering to him completely. It was like losing her own life and finding it again, miraculously, in his.

Very gently he began to roll the slack leg up. The artificial limb, in a white sock and brown flat shoe, was bound in a heavy material like canvas and ended in an ugly jointure where it was attached to the stump. The boy's face and his voice were entirely reverent as he uncovered it and said, "Now show me how to take it off and on."

She took it off for him and put it back on again and then he took it off himself, handling it as tenderly as if it were a real one. "See!" he said with a delighted child's face. "Now I can do it myself!"

"Put it back on," she said. She was thinking that she would run away with him and that every night he would take the leg off and every morning put it back on again. "Put it back on," she said.

"Not yet," he murmured, setting it on its foot out of her reach. "Leave it off for a while. You got me instead."

She gave a little cry of alarm but he pushed her down and began to kiss her again. Without the leg she felt entirely dependent on him. Her brain seemed to have stopped thinking altogether and to be about some other function that it was not very good at. Different expressions raced back and forth over her face. Every now and then the boy, his eyes like two steel spikes, would glance behind him where the leg stood. Finally she pushed him off and said, "Put it back on me now."

"Wait," he said. He leaned the other way and pulled the valise toward him and opened it. It had a pale blue spotted lining and there were only two Bibles in it. He took one of these out and opened the cover of it. It was hollow and contained a pocket flask of whiskey, a pack of cards, and a small blue box with printing on it. He laid these out in front of her one at a time in an evenly-spaced row, like presenting offerings at the shrine of a goddess. He put the blue box in her hand. THIS PRODUCT TO

BE USED ONLY FOR THE PREVENTION OF DISEASE, she read, and dropped it. The boy was unscrewing the top of the flask. He stopped and pointed, with a smile, to the deck of cards. It was not an ordinary deck but one with an obscene picture on the back of each card. "Take a swig," he said, offering her the bottle first. He held it in front of her, but like one mesmerized, she did not move.

Her voice when she spoke had an almost appealing sound. "Aren't you," she murmured, "aren't you just good country people?"

The boy cocked his head. He looked as if he were just beginning to understand that she might be trying to insult him. "Yeah," he said, curling his lip slightly, "but it ain't held me back none. I'm as good as you any day in the week."

"Give me my leg," she said.

He pushed it farther away with his foot. "Come on now, let's begin to have us a good time," he said coaxingly. "We ain't got to know one another good yet."

"Give me my leg!" she screamed and tried to lunge for it but he pushed her down easily.

"What's the matter with you all of a sudden?" he asked, frowning as he screwed the top on the flask and put it quickly back inside the Bible. "You just a while ago said you didn't believe in nothing. I thought you was some girl!"

Her face was almost purple. "You're a Christian!" she hissed. "You're a fine Christian! You're just like them all—say one thing and do another. You're a perfect Christian, you're . . . "

The boy's mouth was set angrily. "I hope you don't think," he said in a lofty indignant tone, "that I believe in that crap! I may sell Bibles but I know which end is up and I wasn't born yesterday and I know where I'm going!"

"Give me my leg!" she screeched. He jumped up so quickly that she barely saw him sweep the cards and the blue box back into the Bible and throw the Bible into the valise. She saw him grab the leg and then she saw it for an instant slanted forlornly across the inside of the suitcase with a Bible at either side of its opposite ends. He slammed the lid shut and snatched up the valise and swung it down the hole and then stepped through himself.

When all of him had passed but his head, he turned and regarded her with a look that no longer had any admiration in it. "I've gotten a lot of interesting things," he said. "One time I got a woman's glass eye this way. And you needn't to think you'll catch me because Pointer ain't really my name. I use a different name at every house I call at and don't stay nowhere long. And I'll tell you another thing, Hulga," he said, using the name as if he didn't think much of it, "you ain't so smart. I been believing in nothing ever since I was born!" and then the toast-colored hat disappeared down the hole and the girl was left, sitting on the straw in the dusty sunlight. When she turned her churning face toward the opening, she saw his blue figure struggling successfully over the green speckled lake.

Mrs. Hopewell and Mrs. Freeman, who were in the back pasture, digging up onions, saw him emerge a little later from the woods and head across the meadow toward the highway. "Why, that looks like that nice dull young man that tried to sell me a Bible yesterday," Mrs. Hopewell said, squinting. "He must have been selling them to the Negroes back in there. He was so simple," she said, "but I guess the world would be better off if we were all that simple."

Mrs. Freeman's gaze drove forward and just touched him before he disappeared under the hill. Then she returned her attention to the evil-smelling onion shoot she was lifting from the ground. "Some can't be that simple," she said. "I know I never could."

Donald Barthelme

1931 –

Donald Barthelme's work provides an interesting example of the new fiction that became prominent in the sixties and is particularly noteworthy for the radically new methods its creators use in seeking to give fresh "versions of reality." As is true of other new fiction writers, Barthelme composes his stories in a manner peculiarly his own, both in their style and in their structure, creating startlingly original effects by employing fantastic and incongruous imagery and by mixing the real and the unreal, the factual and the imaginary. As he himself has implied, his stylistic and structural method resembles collage, the principle of which "is that unlike things are stuck together to make, in the best case, a new reality," one which "may be also a comment on the other reality from which it came, and may be also much else. It's an *itself,* if it's successful. . . ."[1] Despite the problems of understanding which his fiction poses for the reader, it is nevertheless clearly a serious commentary on the "sludge" and "trash" he sees as afflicting the intellectual, moral, and aesthetic values of modern life as well as the environment in which this life flourishes.

Born in 1931, in Philadelphia, Barthelme grew up in Texas. After attending the University of Houston, he worked as a newspaper reporter, as the editor of *Location* (an art and literature review), and as a museum director. Now devoting most of his time to writing, he was associated with the City College of New York as a teacher of creative writing in 1974–75. His stories have appeared in such periodicals as *The New Yorker*, the *Paris Review*, and *Harper's Bazaar*. His

[1] Joe D. Bellamy, *The New Fiction: Interviews with Innovative American Writers* (Urbana: The University of Illinois Press, 1975), pp. 51–52.

publications include three novels, *Snow White* (1967), *The Dead Father* (1975), and *Paradise* (1986), and ten collections of stories, *Come Back, Dr. Caligari* (1964), *Unspeakable Practices, Unnatural Acts* (1968), *City Life* (1970), *Sadness* (1973), *Guilty Pleasures* (1974), *Amateurs* (1976), *Great Days* (1979), *Sixty Stories* (1981), *Overnight to Many Distant Cities* (1983), and *Forty Stories* (1987). He has won a number of awards—a Guggenheim Fellowship (1966), the National Book Award for Children's Literature (1972) (for his *The Slightly Irregular Fire Engine or The Hithering Thithering Djinn*), and a National Institute of Arts and Letters Award (1972).

Constructed in a more conventional form that most Barthelme stories, "Margins" simply presents a sidewalk conversation between a black man and a white man. "I'm communicating with you . . . across a vast gulf of ignorance and darkness," the white man tells the black; but as their dialogue touches lightly and amusingly on such diverse topics as what one's handwriting reveals about one's character, the racial situation, reading, stealing books, and the "inner reality," it becomes apparent that the only meaningful communication between the two occurs in the exchange of slaps at the end of the story, an action suggesting the seriousness of attitudes underlying their seemingly casual banter.

Margins

Edward was explaining to Carl about margins. "The *width* of the margin shows culture, aestheticism and a sense of values or the lack of them," he said. "A very wide left margin shows an impractical person of culture and refinement with a deep appreciation for the best in art and music. Whereas," Edward said, quoting his handwriting analysis book, "whereas, narrow left margins show the opposite. No left margin at all shows a practical nature, a wholesome economy and a general lack of good taste in the arts. A very wide *right* margin shows a person afraid to face reality, oversensitive to the future and generally a poor mixer."

"I don't believe in it," Carl said.

"Now," Edward continued, "with reference to your sign here, you have an *all-around wide margin* which shows a person of extremely delicate sensibilities with love of color and form, one who holds aloof from the multitude and lives in his own dream world of beauty and good taste."

"Are you sure you got that right?"

"I'm communicating with you," Edward said, "across a vast gulf of ignorance and darkness."

"*I* brought the darkness, is that the idea?" Carl asked.

"You brought the darkness, you black mother," Edward said. "Funky, man."

"Edward," Carl said, "for God's sake."

"Why did you write all that jazz on your sign, Carl? Why? It's not true, is it? Is it?"

"It's kind of true," Carl said. He looked down at his brown sandwich boards, which said: *I Was Put In Jail in Selby County Alabama For Five Years For Stealing A Dollar and A Half Which I Did Not Do. While I Was In Jail My Brother was Killed & My Mother Ran Away When I Was Little. In Jail I Began Preaching & I Preach to People Wherever I Can Bearing the Witness of Eschatological Love. I Have Filled Out Papers for Jobs But Nobody Will Give Me a Job Because I Have Been In Jail & The Whole Scene Is Very Dreary, Pepsi Cola. I Need Your Offerings to Get Food. Patent Applied For & Deliver Us From Evil.* "It's true," Carl said, "with a kind of *merde-y* inner truth which shines forth as the objective correlative of what actually did happen, back home."

"Now, look at the way you made that 'm' and that 'n' there," Edward said. "The tops are pointed rather than rounded. That indicates aggressiveness and energy. The fact that they're also pointed rather than rounded at the bottom indicates a sarcastic, stubborn and irritable nature. See what I mean?"

"If you say so," Carl said.

"Your capitals are very small," Edward said, "indicating humility."

"My mother would be pleased," Carl said, "if she knew."

"On the other hand, the excessive size of the loops in your 'y' and your 'g' display exaggeration and egoism."

"That's always been one of my problems," Carl answered.

"What's your whole name?" Edward asked, leaning against a building. They were on Fourteenth Street, near Broadway.

"Carl Maria von Weber," Carl said.

"Are you a drug addict?"

"Edward," Carl said, "you *are* a swinger."

"Are you a Muslim?"

Carl felt his long hair. "Have you read *The Mystery of Being*, by Gabriel Marcel? I really liked that one. I thought that one was fine."

"No, c'mon Carl, answer the question," Edward insisted. "There's got to be frankness and honesty between the races. Are you one?"

"I think an accommodation can be reached and the government is doing all it can at the moment," Carl said. "I think there's something to be said on all sides of the question. This is not such a good place to hustle, you know that? I haven't got but two offerings all morning."

"People like people who look neat," Edward said. "You look kind of crummy, if you don't mind my saying so."

"You really think it's too long?" Carl asked, feeling his hair again.

"Do you think I'm a pretty color?" Edward asked. "Are you envious?"

"No," Carl said. "Not envious."

"See? Exaggeration and egoism. Just like I said."

"You're kind of boring, Edward. To tell the truth."

Edward thought about this for a moment. Then he said: "But I'm white."

"It's the color of choice," Carl said. "I'm tired of talking about color, though. Let's talk about values or something."

"Carl, I'm a fool," Edward said suddenly.

"Yes," Carl said.

"But I'm a *white* fool," Edward said. "That's what's so lovely about me."

"You *are* lovely, Edward," Carl said. "It's true. You have a nice look. Your aspect is good."

"Oh, hell," Edward said despondently. "You're very well-spoken," he said. "I noticed that."

"The reason for that is," Carl said, "I read. Did you read *The Cannibal* by John Hawkes? I thought that was a hell of a book."

"Get a haircut, Carl," Edward said. "Get a new suit. Maybe one of those new Italian suits with the tight coats. You could be upwardly mobile, you know, if you just put your back into it."

"Why are you worried, Edward? Why does my situation distress you? Why don't you just walk away and talk to somebody else?"

"You bother me," Edward confessed. "I keep trying to penetrate your inner reality, to find out what it is. Isn't that curious?"

"John Hawkes also wrote *The Beetle Leg* and a couple of other books whose titles escape me at the moment," Carl said. "I think he's one of the best of our younger American writers."

"Carl," Edward said, "*what is* your inner reality? Blurt it out, baby."

"It's mine," Carl said quietly. He gazed down at his shoes, which resembled a pair of large dead brownish birds.

"Are you sure you didn't steal that dollar and a half mentioned on your sign?"

"Edward, I *told* you I didn't steal that dollar and a half." Carl stamped up and down in his sandwich boards. "It sure is *cold* here on Fourteenth Street."

"That's your imagination, Carl," Edward said. "This street isn't any colder than Fifth, or Lex. Your feeling that it's colder here probably just arises from your marginal status as a despised person in our society."

"Probably," Carl said. There was a look on his face. "You know I went to the government, and asked them to give me a job in the Marine Band, and they wouldn't do it?"

"Do you blow good, man? Where's your axe?"

"They wouldn't *give* me that cotton-pickin' job," Carl said. "What do you think of that?"

"This eschatological love," Edward said, "what kind of love is that?"

"That is later love," Carl said. "That's what I call it, anyhow. That's love on the other side of the Jordan. The term refers to a set of conditions which . . . It's kind of a story we black people tell to ourselves to make ourselves happy."

"Oh me," Edward said. "Ignorance and darkness."

"Edward," Carl said, "you don't *like* me."

"I do too like you, Carl," Edward said. "Where do you steal your books, mostly?"

"Mostly in drugstores," Carl said. "I find them good because mostly they're long and narrow and the clerks tend to stay near the prescription counters at the back of the store, whereas the books are usually in those revolving racks near the front of the store. It's normally pretty easy to slip a couple in your overcoat pocket, if you're wearing an overcoat."

"But . . . "

"Yes," Carl said, "I know what you're thinking. If I'll steal books I'll steal other things. But stealing books is metaphysically different from stealing money. Villon has something pretty good to say on the subject I believe."

"Is that in 'If I Were King'?"

"Besides," Carl added, "haven't *you* ever stolen anything? At some point in your life?"

"My life," Edward said. "Why do you remind me of it?"

"Edward, you're not satisfied with your life! I thought white lives were *nice!*" Carl said, surprised. "I love that word 'nice.' It makes me so happy."

"Listen Carl," Edward said, "why don't you just concentrate on improving your handwriting."

"My character, you mean."

"No," Edward said, "don't bother improving your character. Just improve your handwriting. Make larger capitals. Make smaller loops in your 'y' and 'g'. Watch your word-spacing so as not to display disorientation. Watch your margins."

"It's an idea. But isn't that kind of a superficial approach to the problem?"

"Be careful about the spaces between the lines," Edward went on. "Spacing of lines shows clearness of thought. Pay attention to your finals. There are twenty-two different kinds of finals and each one tells a lot about a person. I'll lend you the book. Good handwriting is the key to advancement, or if not *the* key, at least *a* key. You could be the first man of your race to be Vice-President."

"That's something to shoot for, all right."

"Would you like me to go get the book?"

"I don't think so," Carl said, "no thanks. It's not that I don't have any faith in your solution. What I *would* like is to take a leak. Would you mind holding my sandwich boards for a minute?"

"Not at all," Edward said, and in a moment had slipped Carl's sandwich boards over his own slight shoulders. "Boy, they're kind of heavy, aren't they?"

"They cut you a bit," Carl said with a malicious smile. "I'll just go into this men's store here."

When Carl returned the two men slapped each other sharply in the face with the back of the hand, that beautiful part of the hand where the knuckles grow.

John Updike
1932 –

John Updike has firmly established a reputation as a gifted and versatile writer. Preferring, as Peter Taylor does, to concentrate on the quieter, more ordinary phases of life, Updike places less emphasis on plot and dramatic physical conflicts in his fiction than on the tensions, dilemmas, and frustrations members of the human family experience in their daily involvements with one another. He is the master of a facile style which is characterized by a graphic clarity of imagery and diction and, at its best, by a brilliant intensity and terseness.

Updike was born in Shillington, Pennsylvania, in 1932. After attending public school in Shillington, he entered Harvard University, where he majored in English and became president of the Harvard *Lampoon.* Graduating *summa cum laude* in 1954, he spent a year studying art at the Ruskin School of Drawing and Fine Art in Oxford, England. Returning to the United States, he worked from 1955 to 1957 for *The New Yorker* magazine, to which he contributed stories, parodies, essays, and verse. His first published volume, *The Carpentered Hen and Other Tame Creatures* (1958) was a collection of verse.

Subsequently, in addition to other volumes of poetry and non-fiction, he has published fourteen novels, among the most recent of which are *Rabbit Redux* (1971), *A Month of Sundays* (1975), *The Coup* (1978), *Rabbit Is Rich* (1981), *The Witches of Eastwick* (1984), *Roger's Version* (1986), and *S.* (1988), and nine collections of stories, *Pigeon Feathers and Other Stories* (1959), *The Same Door* (1959), *The Music School* (1962), *Olinger Stories* (1964), *Museums and Women* (1972), *Problems and Other Stories* (1979), *Too Far To Go,* (1979), *Bech Is Back* (1982), and *Trust Me* (1987).

In his stories, Updike demonstrates an impressive ability to fabricate compellingly interesting and dramatic narratives from commonplace characters and events, as "A & P" illustrates. Typically, as in "A & P," his story situations unfold quickly in one place during a brief time interval and focus on central characters who experience a sudden revelation about themselves or someone else. In thus giving the reader vivid glimpses into life, his stories suggest the countless minor and major dramas which occur continuously everywhere in daily life as human beings interact with one another in a countless variety of situations.

A & P

In walks these three girls in nothing but bathing suits. I'm in the third checkout slot, with my back to the door, so I don't see them until they're over by the bread. The one that caught my eye first was the one in the plaid green two-piece. She was a chunky kid, with a good tan and a sweet broad soft-looking can with those two crescents of white just under it, where the sun never seems to hit, at the top of the backs of her legs. I stood there with my hand on a box of HiHo crackers trying to remember if I rang it up or not. I ring it up again and the customer starts giving me hell. She's one of these cash-register-watchers, a witch about fifty with rouge on her cheekbones and no eyebrows, and I know it made her day to trip me up. She'd been watching cash registers for fifty years and probably never seen a mistake before.

By the time I got her feathers smoothed and her goodies into a bag—she gives me a little snort in passing, if she'd been born at the right time they would have burned her over in Salem—by the time I get her on her way the girls had circled around the bread and were coming back, without a pushcart, back my way along the counters, in the aisle between the checkouts and the Special bins. They didn't even have shoes on. There was this chunky one, with two-piece—it was bright green and the seams on the bra were still sharp and her belly was still pretty pale so I guessed she just got it (the suit)—there was this one, with one of those chubby berry-faces, the lips all bunched together under her nose, this one, and a tall one, with black hair that hadn't quite frizzed right, and one of these sunburns right across the eyes, and a chin that was too long—you know, the kind of girl other girls think is very "striking" and "attractive" but never quite makes it, as they very well know, which is why they like her so much—and then the third one, that wasn't quite so tall. She was the queen. She kind of led them, the other two peeking around and making their shoulders round. She didn't look around, not this queen, she just walked straight on slowly, on these long white prima-donna legs. She came down a little hard on her heels, as if she didn't walk in her bare feet that much, putting down her heels and then letting the weight move along to her toes as if she was testing the floor with every step, putting a little deliberate extra action into it. You never know for sure how girls' minds work (do you really think it's a mind in there or just a little buzz like a bee in a glass jar?) but you got the idea she had talked the other two into coming in here with her, and now she was showing them how to do it, walk slow and hold yourself straight.

She had on a kind of dirty-pink—beige maybe, I don't know—bathing suit with a little nubble all over it and, what got me, the straps were down. They were off her shoulders looped loose around the cool tops of her arms, and I guess as a result the suit had slipped a little on her, so all around the top of the cloth there was this shining rim. If it hadn't been there you wouldn't have known there could have been anything whiter than those shoulders. With the straps pushed off, there was nothing between the top of the suit and the top of her head except just *her,* this clean bare plane of the top of her chest down from the shoulder bones like a dented sheet of metal tilted in the light. I mean, it was more than pretty.

She had sort of oaky hair that the sun and salt had bleached, done up in a bun that was unravelling, and a kind of prim face. Walking into the A & P with your straps down, I suppose it's the only kind of face you *can* have. She held her head so high her neck, coming up out of those white shoulders, looked kind of stretched, but I didn't mind. The longer her neck was, the more of her there was.

She must have felt in the corner of her eye me and over my shoulder Stokesie in the second slot watching, but she didn't tip. Not this queen. She kept her eyes moving across the racks, and stopped, and turned so slow it made my stomach rub the inside of my apron, and buzzed to the other two, who kind of huddled against her for relief, and then they all three of them went up the cat-and-dog-food-breakfast-cereal-macaroni-rice-raisins-seasonings-spreads- spaghetti-soft-drinks-crackers-and-cookies aisle. From the third slot I look straight up this aisle to the meat counter, and I watched them all the way. The fat one with the tan sort of fumbled with the cookies, but on second thought she put the packages back. The sheep pushing their carts down the aisle—the girls were walking against the usual traffic (not that we have one-way signs or anything)—were pretty hilarious. You could see them, when Queenie's white shoulders dawned on them, kind of jerk, or hop, or hiccup, but their eyes snapped back to their own baskets and on they pushed. I bet you could set off dynamite in an A & P and the people would by and large keep reaching and checking oatmeal off their lists and muttering "Let me see, there was a third thing, began with A, asparagus, no, ah, yes applesauce!" or whatever it is they do mutter. But there was no doubt, this jiggled them. A few houseslaves in pin curlers even looked around after pushing their carts past to make sure what they had seen was correct.

You know, it's one thing to have a girl in a bathing suit down on the beach, where what with the glare nobody can look at each other much anyway, and another thing in the cool of the A & P, under the fluorescent lights, against all those stacked packages, with her feet paddling along naked over our checkerboard green-and-cream rubber-tile floor.

"Oh Daddy," Stokesie said beside me. "I feel so faint."

"Darling," I said. "Hold me tight." Stokesie's married, with two babies chalked up on his fuselage already, but as far as I can tell that's the only difference. He's twenty-two, and I was nineteen this April.

"Is it done?" he asks, the responsible married man finding his voice. I forgot to say he thinks he's going to be manager some sunny day, maybe in 1990 when it's called the Great Alexandrov and Petrooshki Tea Company or something.

What he meant was, our town is five miles from a beach, with a big summer colony out on the Point, but we're right in the middle of town, and the women generally put on a shirt or shorts or something before the get out of the car into the street. And anyway these are usually women with six children and varicose veins mapping their legs and nobody, including them, could care less. As I say, we're right in the middle of town, and if you stand at our front doors you can see two banks and the Congregational church and the newspaper store and three real-estate offices and about twenty-seven old freeloaders tearing up Central Street because the sewer broke again. It's not as if we're on the Cape; we're north of Boston and there's people in this town haven't seen the ocean for twenty years.

The girls had reached the meat counter and were asking McMahon something. He pointed, they pointed, and they shuffled out of sight behind a pyramid of Diet Delight peaches. All that was left for us to see was old McMahon patting his mouth and looking after them sizing up their joints. Poor kids, I began to feel sorry for them, they couldn't help it.

• • •

Now here comes the sad part of the story, at least my family says it's sad, but I don't think it's sad myself. The store's pretty empty, it being Thursday afternoon, so there was nothing much to do except lean on the register and wait for the girls to show up again. The whole store was like a pinball machine and I didn't know which tunnel they'd come out of. After a while they come around out of the far aisle, around the light bulbs, records at discount of the Caribbean Six or Tony Martin Sings or some such gunk you wonder they waste the wax on, sixpacks of candy bars, and plastic toys done up in cellophane that fall apart when a kid looks at them anyway. Around they come, Queenie still leading the way, and holding a little gray jar in her hand. Slots Three through Seven are unmanned and I could see her wondering between Stokes and me, but Stokesie with his usual luck draws an old party in baggy gray pants who stumbles up with four giant cans of pineapple juice (what do these bums *do* with all that pineapple juice? I've often asked myself) so the girls come to me. Queenie puts down the jar and I take it into my fingers icy cold. Kingfish Fancy Herring Snacks in Pure Sour Cream: 49¢. Now her hands are empty, not a ring or a bracelet, bare as God made them, and I wonder where the money's coming from. Still with that prim look she lifts a folded dollar bill out of the hollow at the center of her nubbled pink top. The jar went heavy in my hand. Really, I thought that was so cute.

Then everybody's luck begins to run out. Lengel comes in from haggling with a truck full of cabbages on the lot and is about to scuttle into that door marked MANAGER behind which he hides all day when the girls touch his eye. Lengel's pretty dreary, teaches Sunday school and the rest, but he doesn't miss that much. He comes over and says, "Girls, this isn't the beach."

Queenie blushes, though maybe it's just a brush of sunburn I was noticing for the first time, now that she was so close. "My mother asked me to pick up a jar of herring snacks." Her voice kind of startled me, the way voices do when you see the people first, coming out so flat and dumb yet kind of tony, too, the way it ticked over "pick up" and "snacks." All of a sudden I slid right down her voice into her living room. Her father and the other men were standing around in ice-cream coats and bow ties and the women were in sandals picking up herring snacks on toothpicks off a big glass plate and they were all holding drinks the color of water with olives and sprigs of mint in them. When my parents have somebody over they get lemonade and if it's a real racy affair Schlitz in tall glasses with "They'll Do It Every Time" cartoons stencilled on.

"That's all right," Lengel said. "But this isn't the beach." His repeating this struck me as funny, as if it had just occurred to him, and he had been thinking all these years the A & P was a great big dune and he was the head lifeguard. He didn't like my smiling—as I say he doesn't miss much—but he concentrates on giving the girls that sad Sunday-school-superintendent stare.

Queenie's blush is no sunburn now, and the plump one in plaid, that I liked better from the back—a really sweet can—pipes up. "We weren't doing any shopping. We just came in for the one thing."

"That makes no difference," Lengel tells her, and I could see from the way his eyes went that he hadn't noticed she was wearing a two-piece before. "We want you decently dressed when you come in here."

"We *are* decent," Queenie says suddenly, her lower lip pushing, getting sore now that she remembers her place, a place from which the crowd that runs the A & P must look pretty crummy. Fancy Herring Snacks flashed in her very blue eyes.

"Girls, I don't want to argue with you. After this come in here with your shoulders covered. It's our policy." He turns back. That's policy for you. Policy is what the kingpins want. What the others want is juvenile delinquency.

All this while, the customers had been showing up with their carts but, you know, sheep, seeing a scene, they had all bunched up on Stokesie, who shook open a paper bag as gently as peeling a peach, not wanting to miss a word. I could feel in the silence everybody getting nervous, most of all Lengel, who asks me, "Sammy, have you rung up their purchase?"

I thought and said "No" but it wasn't about that I was thinking. I go through the punches, 4, 9, GROC, TOT—it's more complicated than you think, and after you do it often enough, it begins to make a little song, that you hear words to, in my case "Hello *(bing)* there, you *(gung)* hap-py pee-pul *(splat)*!"—the *splat* being the drawer flying out. I uncrease the bill, tenderly as you may imagine, it just having come from between the two smoothest scoops of vanilla I had ever known were there, and pass a half and a penny into her narrow pink palm, and nestle the herrings in a bag and twist its neck and hand it over, all the time thinking.

The girls, and who'd blame them, are in a hurry to get out, so I say "I quit" to Lengel quick enough for them to hear, hoping they'll stop and watch me, their unsuspected hero. They keep right on going, into the electric eye; the door flies open and they flicker across the lot to their car. Queenie and Plaid and Big Tall Goony-Goony (not that as raw material she was so bad), leaving me with Lengel and a kink in his eyebrow.

"Did you say something, Sammy?"

"I said I quit."

"I thought you did."

"You didn't have to embarrass them."

"It was they who were embarrassing us."

I started to say something that came out "Fiddle-de-doo." It's a saying of my grandmother's, and I know she would have been pleased.

"I don't think you know what you're saying," Lengel said.

"I know you don't," I said. "But I do." I pull the bow at the back of my apron and start shrugging it off my shoulders. A couple customers that had been heading for my slot begin to knock against each other, like scared pigs in a chute.

Lengel sighs and begins to look very patient and old and gray. He's been a friend of my parents for years. "Sammy, you don't want to do this to your Mom and Dad," he tells me. It's true. I don't. But it seems to me that once you begin a gesture it's fatal not to go through with it. I fold my apron, "Sammy" stitched in red on the pocket, and put it on the counter, and drop the bow tie on top of it. The bow tie is theirs, if you've ever wondered. "You'll feel this for the rest of your life," Lengel says, and I know that's true, too, but remembering how he made that pretty girl blush makes me so scrunchy inside I punch the No Sale tab and the machine whirs "pee-pul" and the drawer splats out. One advantage to this scene taking place in summer, I can follow this up with a clean exit, there's no fumbling around getting your coat and galoshes, I just saunter into the electric eye in my white shirt that my mother ironed the night before, and the door heaves itself open, and outside the sunshine is skating around on the asphalt.

I look around for my girls, but they're gone, of course. There wasn't anybody but some young married screaming with her children about some candy they didn't get by the door of a powder-blue Falcon station wagon. Looking back in the big windows, over the bags of peat moss and aluminum lawn furniture stacked on the pavement, I could see Lengel in my place in the slot, checking the sheep through. His face was dark gray and his back stiff, as if he'd just had an injection of iron, and my stomach kind of fell as I felt how hard the world was going to be to me hereafter.

Ernest J. Gaines

1933 –

Ernest J. Gaines, according to one critic, "may just be the best black writer in America." Regardless of whether one agrees with this evaluation, Gaines's work provides solid evidence that the tradition of American black writing is flourishing more vigorously today than ever before. It is, of course, less important that Gaines is a black writer than that he is a very stimulating one. His work in the short story is particularly impressive.

Born in 1933 on a plantation near Oscar, Louisiana—the state which provides the setting for most of his stories—Gaines moved to Valleja, California, with his family when he was fifteen years of age. After serving in the Army for two years (1953–55), he attended San Francisco State College, graduating in 1957. The following year he won a Wallace Stegner Fellowship in creative writing which enabled him to spend a year studying and writing at Stanford University, and in 1959 he received the Joseph Henry Jackson Literary Award for Creative Writing. The stories he began publishing during the late 1950s appeared in his major collection, *Bloodline,* in 1968. He has also thus far published five novels, including *Catherine Carmier* (1964), *Of Love and Dust* (1967), and the *Autobiography of Miss Jane Pittman* (1971). This last novel, a re-creation of the career of an aged woman who began life as a slave and lived to lead a protest march in the 1960s when she was over one hundred years old, has been made into one of the most effective motion pictures of recent years. His fourth novel, *In My Father's House,* appeared in 1978; his fifth, *A Gathering of Old Men,* in 1983.

As shown in "The Sky is Gray," Gaines achieves powerful effects, not through flashy technique or showy plot manipulations, but through the straightforward, organic development of the basic situation. A salient feature of his method is the use of exact detail, what Henry James described as "solidity of specification," to give a lifelike reality and immediacy to his characters and their actions. The detail used in this story forces the reader to sense fully both the young boy's suffering from his toothache, his hunger, and the cold—and the mother's courage, dignity, and pride. Further, the story also shows that Gaines has a remarkable mastery of both the idioms and the rhythms of black speech.

The Sky Is Gray

1

Go'n be coming in a few minutes. Coming round that bend down there full speed. And I'm go'n get out my handkerchief and wave it down, and we go'n get on it and go.

I keep looking for it, but Mama don't look that way no more. She's looking down the road where we just come from. It's a long old road, and far 's you can see you don't see nothing but gravel. You got dry weeds on both sides, and you got trees on both sides, and fences on both sides, too. And you got cows in the pastures and they standing close together. And when we was coming out here to catch the bus I seen the smoke coming out of the cows's noses.

I look at my mama and I know what she's thinking. I been with Mama so much, just me and her, I know what she's thinking all the time. Right now it's home—Auntie and them. She's thinking if they got enough wood—if she left enough there to keep them warm till we get back. She's thinking if it go'n rain and if any of them go'n have to go out in the rain. She's thinking 'bout the hog—if he go'n get out, and if Ty and Val be able to get him back in. She always worry like that when she leaves the house.

She don't worry too much if she leave me there with the smaller ones, 'cause she know I'm go'n look after them and look after Auntie and everything else. I'm the oldest and she say I'm the man.

I look at my mama and I love my mama. She's wearing that black coat and that black hat and she's looking sad. I love my mama and I want put my arm round her and tell her. But I'm not supposed to do that. She say that's weakness and that's crybaby stuff, and she don't want no crybaby round her. She don't want you to be scared, either. 'Cause Ty's scared of ghosts and she's always whipping him. I'm scared of the dark, too, but I make 'tend I ain't. I make 'tend I ain't 'cause I'm the oldest, and I got to set a good sample for the rest. I can't ever be scared and I can't ever cry. And that's why I never said nothing 'bout my teeth. It's been hurting me and hurting me close to a month now, but I never said it. I didn't say it 'cause I didn't want act like a crybaby, and 'cause I know we didn't have enough money to go have it pulled. But, Lord, it been hurting me. And look like it wouldn't start till at night when you was trying to get yourself little sleep. Then soon 's you shut your eyes—ummm-ummm, Lord, look like it go right down to your heartstring.

"Hurting, hanh?" Ty'd say.

I'd shake my head, but I wouldn't open my mouth for nothing. You open your mouth and let that wind in, and it almost kill you.

I'd just lay there and listen to them snore. Ty there, right 'side me, and Auntie and Val over by the fireplace. Val younger than me and Ty, and he sleeps with Auntie. Mama sleeps round the other side with Louis and Walker.

I'd just lay there and listen to them, and listen to that wind out there, and listen to that fire in the fireplace. Sometimes it'd stop long enough to let me get little rest. Sometimes it just hurt, hurt, hurt. Lord, have mercy.

2

Auntie knowed it was hurting me. I didn't tell anybody but Ty, 'cause we buddies and he ain't go'n tell nobody. But some kind of way Auntie found out. When she asked me, I told her no, nothing was wrong. But she knowed it all the time. She told me to mash up a piece of aspirin and wrap it in some cotton and jugg it down in that hole. I did it, but it didn't do no good. It stopped for a little while, and started right back again. Auntie wanted to tell Mama, but I told her, "Uh-uh." 'Cause I knowed we didn't have any money, and it just was go'n make her mad again. So Auntie told

Monsieur Bayonne, and Monsieur Bayonne came over to the house and told me to kneel down 'side him on the fireplace. He put his finger in his mouth and made the Sign of the Cross on my jaw. The tip of Monsieur Bayonne's finger is some hard, 'cause he's always playing on that guitar. If we sit outside at night we can always hear Monsieur Bayonne playing on his guitar. Sometimes we leave him out there playing on the guitar.

Monsieur Bayonne made the Sign of the Cross over and over on my jaw, but that didn't do no good. Even when he prayed and told me to pray some, too, that tooth still hurt me.

"How you feeling?" he say.

"Same," I say.

He kept on praying and making the Sign of the Cross and I kept on praying, too.

"Still hurting?" he say.

"Yes, sir."

Monsieur Bayonne mashed harder and harder on my jaw. He mashed so hard he almost pushed me over on Ty. But then he stopped.

"What kind of prayers you praying, boy?" he say.

"Baptist," I say.

"Well, I'll be—no wonder that tooth killing him. I'm going one way and he pulling the other. Boy, don't you know any Catholic prayers?"

"I know 'Hail Mary,' " I say.

"Then you better start saying it."

"Yes, sir."

He started mashing on my jaw again, and I could hear him praying at the same time. And, sure enough, after while it stopped hurting me.

Me and Ty went outside where Monsieur Bayonne's two hounds was and we started playing with them. "Let's go hunting," Ty say. "All right," I say; and we went on back in the pasture. Soon the hounds got on a trail, and me and Ty followed them all 'cross the pasture and then back in the woods, too. And then they cornered this little old rabbit and killed him, and me and Ty made them get back, and we picked up the rabbit and started back home. But my tooth had started hurting me again. It was hurting me plenty now, but I wouldn't tell Monsieur Bayonne. That night I didn't sleep a bit, and first thing in the morning Auntie told me to go back and let Monsieur Bayonne pray over me some more. Monsieur Bayonne was in his kitchen making coffee when I got there. Soon 's he seen me he knowed what was wrong.

"All right, kneel down there 'side that stove," he say. "And this time make sure you pray Catholic. I don't know nothing 'bout that Baptist, and I don't want know nothing 'bout him."

3

Last night Mama say, "Tomorrow we going to town."

"It ain't hurting me no more," I say. "I can eat anything on it."

"Tomorrow we going to town," she say.

And after she finished eating, she got up and went to bed. She always go to bed early now. 'Fore Daddy went in the Army, she used to stay up late. All of us sitting out on the gallery or round the fire. But now, look like soon 's she finish eating she go to bed.

This morning when I woke up, her and Auntie was standing 'fore the fireplace. She say: "Enough to get there and get back. Dollar and a half to have it pulled. Twenty-five for me to go, twenty-five for him. Twenty-five for me to come back, twenty-five for him. Fifty cents left. Guess I get little piece of salt meat with that."

"Sure can use it," Auntie say. "White beans and no salt meat ain't white beans."

"I do the best I can," Mama say.

They was quiet after that, and I made 'tend I was still sleep.

"James, hit the floor," Auntie say.

I still made 'tend I was asleep. I didn't want them to know I was listening.

"All right," Auntie say, shaking me by the shoulder. "Come on. Today's the day."

I pushed the cover down to get out, and Ty grabbed it and pulled it back.

"You, too, Ty," Auntie say.

"I ain't getting no teef pulled," Ty say.

"Don't mean it ain't time to get up." Auntie say. "Hit it, Ty."

Ty got up grumbling.

"James, you hurry up and get in your clothes and eat your food," Auntie say. "What time y'all coming back?" she said to Mama.

"That 'leven o'clock bus," Mama say. "Got to get back in that field this evening."

"Get a move on you, James," Auntie say.

I went in the kitchen and washed my face, then I ate my breakfast. I was having bread and syrup. The bread was warm and hard and tasted good. And I tried to make it last a long time.

Ty came back there grumbling and mad at me.

"Got to get up," he say. "I ain't having no teefes pulled. What I got to be getting up for?"

Ty poured some syrup in his pan and got a piece of bread. He didn't wash his hands, neither his face, and I could see that white stuff in his eyes.

"You the one getting your teef pulled," he say. "What I got to get up for. I bet if I was getting a teef pulled, you wouldn't be getting up. Shucks; syrup again. I'm getting tired of this old syrup. Syrup, syrup, syrup. I'm go'n take with the sugar diabetes. I want me some bacon sometime."

"Go out in the field and work and you can have your bacon," Auntie say. She stood in the middle door looking at Ty. "You better be glad you got syrup. Some people ain't got that—hard 's time is."

"Shucks," Ty say. "How can I be strong."

"I don't know too much 'bout your strength," Auntie say; "but I know where you go'n be hot at, you keep that grumbling up. James, get a move on you; your mama waiting."

I ate my last piece of bread and went in the front room. Mama was standing 'fore the fireplace warming her hands. I put on my coat and my cap, and we left the house.

4

I look down there again, but it still ain't coming. I almost say, "It ain't coming yet," but I keep my mouth shut. 'Cause that's something else she don't like. She don't like for you to say something just for nothing. She can see it ain't coming, I can see it ain't coming, so why say it ain't coming. I don't say it, I turn and look at the river that's back of us. It's so cold the smoke's just raising up from the water. I see a bunch of pool-doos not too far out—just on the other side the lilies. I'm wondering if you can eat pool-doos. I ain't too sure, 'cause I ain't never ate none. But I done ate owls and blackbirds, and I done ate redbirds, too. I didn't want kill the redbirds, but she made me kill them. They had two of them back there. One in my trap, one in Ty's trap. Me and Ty was go'n play with them and let them go, but she made me kill them 'cause we needed the food.

"I can't," I say. "I can't."

"Here," she say. "Take it."

"I can't," I say. "I can't. I can't kill him, Mama, please."

"Here," she say. "Take this fork, James."

"Please, Mama, I can't kill him," I say.

I could tell she was go'n hit me. I jerked back, but I didn't jerk back soon enough.

"Take it," she say.

I took it and reached in for him, but he kept on hopping to the back.

"I can't, Mama," I say. The water just kept on running down my face. "I can't," I say.

"Get him out of there," she say.

I reached in for him and he kept on hopping to the back. Then I reached in farther, and he pecked me on the hand.

"I can't, Mama," I say.

She slapped me again.

I reached in again, but he kept on hopping out my way. Then he hopped to one side and I reached there. The fork got him on the leg and I heard his leg pop. I pulled my hand out 'cause I had hurt him.

"Give it here," she say, and jerked the fork out my hand.

She reached in and got the little bird right in the neck. I heard the fork go in his neck, and I heard it go in the ground. She brought him out and helt him right in front of me.

"That's one," she say. She shook him off and gived me the fork. "Get the other one."

"I can't, Mama," I say. "I'll do anything, but don't make me do that."

She went to the corner of the fence and broke the biggest switch over there she could find. I knelt 'side the trap, crying.

"Get him out of there," she say.

"I can't, Mama."

She started hitting me 'cross the back. I went down on the ground, crying.

"Get him," she say.

"Octavia?" Auntie say.

'Cause she had come out of the house and she was standing by the tree looking at us.

"Get him out of there," Mama say.

"Octavia," Auntie say, "explain to him. Explain to him. Just don't beat him. Explain to him."

But she hit me and hit me and hit me.

I'm still young—I ain't no more than eight; but I know now; I know why I had to do it. (They was so little, though. They was so little. I 'member how I picked the feathers off them and cleaned them and helt them over the fire. Then we all ate them. Ain't had but a little bitty piece each, but we all had a little bitty piece, and everybody just looked at me 'cause they was so proud.) Suppose she had to go away? That's why I had to do it. Suppose she had to go away like Daddy went away? Then who was go'n look after us? They had to be somebody left to carry on. I didn't know it then, but I know it now. Auntie and Monsieur Bayonne talked to me and made me see.

5

Time I see it I get out my handkerchief and start waving. It's still 'way down there, but I keep waving anyhow. Then it come up and stop and me and Mama get on. Mama tell me go sit in the back while she pay. I do like she say, and the people look at me. When I pass the little sign that say "White" and "Colored," I start looking for a seat. I just see one of them back there, but I don't take it, 'cause I want my mama to sit down herself. She comes in the back and sit down, and I lean on the seat. They got seats in the front, but I know I can't sit there, 'cause I have to sit back of the sign. Anyhow, I don't want sit there if my mama go'n sit back here.

They got a lady sitting 'side my mama and she looks at me and smiles little bit. I smile back, but I don't open my mouth, 'cause the wind'll get in and make that tooth ache. The lady take out a pack of gum and reach me a slice, but I shake my head. The lady just can't understand why a little boy'll turn down gum, and she reach me a slice again. This time I point to my jaw. The lady understands and smiles little bit, and I smile little bit, but I don't open my mouth, though.

They got a girl sitting 'cross from me. She got on a red overcoat and her hair's plaited in one big plait. First, I make 'tend I don't see her over there, but then I start looking at her little bit. She make 'tend she don't see me, either, but I catch her looking that way. She got a cold, and every now and then she h'ist that little handkerchief to her nose. She ought to blow it, but she don't. Must think she's too much a lady or something.

Every time she h'ist that little handkerchief, the lady side her say something in her ear. She shakes her head and lays her hands in her lap again. Then I catch her kind of looking where I'm at. I smile at her little bit. But think she'll smile back? Uh-uh. She just turn up her little old nose and turn her head. Well, I show her both of us can turn us head. I turn mine too and look out at the river.

The river is gray. The sky is gray. They have pool-doos on the water. The water is wavy, and the pool-doos go up and down. The bus go round a turn, and you got plenty trees hiding the river. Then the bus go round another turn, and I can see the river again.

I look toward the front where all the white people sitting. Then I look at that little old gal again. I don't look right at her, 'cause I don't want all them people to know I love her. I just look at her little bit, like I'm looking out that window over there. But she knows I'm looking that way, and she kind of look at me, too. The lady sitting 'side her catch her this time, and she leans over and says something in her ear.

"I don't love him nothing," that little old gal says out loud.

Everybody back there hear her mouth, and all of them look at us and laugh.

"I don't love you, either," I say. "So you don't have to turn up your nose, Miss."

"You the one looking," she say.

"I wasn't looking at you," I say. "I was looking out that window, there."

"Out that window my foot," she say. "I seen you. Everytime I turned round you was looking at me."

"You must of been looking yourself if you seen me all them times," I say.

"Shucks," she say, "I got me all kind of boyfriends."

"I got girlfriends, too," I say.

"Well, I just don't want you getting your hopes up," she say.

I don't say no more to that little old gal 'cause I don't want have to bust her in the mouth. I lean on the seat where Mama sitting, and I don't even look that way no more. When we get to Bayonne, she jugg her little old tongue out at me. I make 'tend I'm go'n hit her, and she duck down 'side her mama. And all the people laugh at us again.

6

Me and Mama get off and start walking in town. Bayonne is a little bitty town. Baton Rouge is a hundred times bigger than Bayonne. I went to Baton Rouge once—me, Ty, Mama, and Daddy. But that was 'way back yonder, 'fore Daddy went in the Army. I wonder when we go'n see him again. I wonder when. Look like he ain't ever coming back home. . . . Even the pavement all cracked in Bayonne. Got grass shooting right out in the sidewalk. Got weeds in the ditch, too; just like they got at home.

It's some cold in Bayonne. Look like it's colder than it is home. The wind blows in my face, and I feel that stuff running down my nose. I sniff. Mama says use that handkerchief. I blow my nose and put it back.

We pass a school and I see them white children playing in the yard. Big old red school, and them children just running and playing. Then we pass a café, and I see a bunch of people in there eating. I wish I was in there 'cause I'm cold. Mama tells me keep my eyes in front where they belong.

We pass stores that's got dummies, and we pass another café, and then we pass a shoe shop, and that bald-head man in there fixing on a shoe. I look at him and I butt into that white lady, and Mama jerks me in front and tells me stay there.

We come up to the courthouse, and I see the flag waving there. This flag ain't like the one we got at school. This one here ain't got but a handful of stars. One at school got a big pile of stars—one for every state. We pass it and we turn and there it is—the dentist office. Me and Mama go in, and they got people sitting everywhere you look. They even got a little boy in there younger than me.

Me and Mama sit on that bench, and a white lady come in there and ask me what my name is. Mama tells her and the white lady goes on back. Then I hear somebody hollering in there. Soon 's that little boy hear him hollering, he starts hollering, too. His mama pats him and pats him, trying to make him hush up, but he ain't thinking 'bout his mama.

The man that was hollering in there comes out holding his jaw. He is a big old man and he's wearing overalls and a jumper.

"Got it, hanh?" another man asks him.

The man shakes his head—don't want to open his mouth.

"Man, I thought they was killing you in there," the other man says. "Hollering like a pig under a gate."

The man don't say nothing. He just heads for the door, and the other man follows him.

"John Lee," the white lady says. "John Lee Williams."

The little boy juggs his head down in his mama's lap and holler more now. His mama tells him go with the nurse, but he ain't thinking 'bout his mama. His mama tells him again, but he don't even hear her. His mama picks him up and takes him in there, and even when the white lady shuts the door I can still hear little old John Lee.

"I often wonder why the Lord let a child like that suffer," a lady says to my mama. The lady's sitting right in front of us on another bench. She's got on a white dress and a black sweater. She must be a nurse or something herself, I reckon.

"Not us to question," a man says.

"Sometimes I don't know if we shouldn't," the lady says.

"I know definitely we shouldn't," the man says. The man looks like a preacher. He's big and fat and he's got on a black suit. He's got a gold chain, too.

"Why?" the lady said.

"Why anything?" the preacher says.

"Yes," the lady says. "Why anything?'

"Not us to question," the preacher says.

The lady looks at the preacher a little while and looks at Mama again.

"And look like it's the poor who suffers the most," she says. "I don't understand it."

"Best not to even try," the preacher says. "He works in mysterious ways—wonders to perform."

Right then little John Lee bust out hollering, and everybody turn their head to listen.

"He's not a good dentist," the lady says. "Dr. Robillard is much better. But more expensive. That's why most of the colored people come here. The white people go to Dr. Robillard. Y'all from Bayonne?"

"Down the river," my mama says. And that's all she go'n say, 'cause she don't talk much. But the lady keeps on looking at her, and so she says, "Near Morgan."

"I see," the lady says.

7

"That's the trouble with the black people in this country today," somebody else says. This one here's sitting on the same side me and Mama's sitting, and he is kind of sitting in front of that preacher. He looks like a teacher or somebody that goes to college. He's got on a suit, and he's got a book that he's been reading. "We don't question is exactly our problem," he says. "We should question and question and question—question everything."

The preacher just looks at him a long time. He done put a toothpick or something in his mouth, and he just keeps on turning it and turning it. You can see he don't like that boy with that book.

"Maybe you can explain what you mean," he says.

"I said what I meant," the boy says. "Question everything. Every stripe, every star, every word spoken. Everything."

"It 'pears to me that this young lady and I was talking 'bout God, young man," the preacher says.

"Question Him, too," the boy says.

"Wait," the preacher says. "Wait now."

"You heard me right," the boy says. "His existence as well as everything else. Everything."

The preacher just looks across the room at the boy. You can see he's getting madder and madder. But mad or no mad, the boy ain't thinking 'bout him. He looks at that preacher just 's hard 's the preacher looks at him.

"Is this what they coming to?" the preacher says. "Is this what we educating them for?"

"You're not educating me," the boy says. "I wash dishes at night so that I can go to school in the day. So even the words you spoke need questioning."

The preacher just looks at him and shakes his head.

"When I come in this room and seen you there with your book, I said to myself, 'There's an intelligent man.' How wrong a person can be."

"Show me one reason to believe in the existence of a God," the boy says.

"My heart tells me," the preacher says.

" 'My heart tells me,' " the boy says. " 'My heart tells me.' Sure. 'My heart tells me.' And as long as you listen to what your heart tells you, you will have only what the white man gives you and nothing more. Me, I don't listen to my heart. The purpose of the heart is to pump blood throughout the body, and nothing else."

"Who's your paw, boy?" the preacher says.

"Why?"

"Who is he?"

"He's dead."

"And your mom?"

"She's in Charity Hospital with pneumonia. Half killed herself, working for nothing."

"And 'cause he's dead and she's sick, you mad at the world?"

"I'm not mad at the world. I'm questioning it with cold logic, sir. What do words like Freedom, Liberty, God, White, Colored mean? I want to know. That's why *you* are sending us to school, to read and to ask questions. And because we ask these questions, you call us mad. No sir, it is not us who are mad."

"You keep saying 'us'?"

" 'Us.' Yes—us. I'm not alone."

The preacher just shakes his head. Then he looks at everybody in the room—everybody. Some of the people look down at the floor, keep from looking at him. I think of look 'way myself, but soon 's I know he done turn his head, I look that way again.

"I'm sorry for you," he says to the boy.

"Why?" the boy says. "Why not be sorry for yourself? Why are you so much better off than I am? Why aren't you sorry for these other people in here? Why not be sorry for the lady who had to drag her child into the dentist office? Why not be sorry for the lady sitting on that bench over there? Be sorry for them. Not for me. Some way or the other I'm going to make it."

"No, I'm sorry for you," the preacher says.

"Of course, of course," the boy says, nodding his head. "You're sorry for me because I rock that pillar you're leaning on."

"You can't ever rock the pillar I'm leaning on, young man. It's stronger than anything man can ever do."

"You believe in God because a man told you to believe in God," the boy says. "A white man told you to believe in God. And why? To keep you ignorant so he can keep his feet on your neck."

"So now we the ignorant?" the preacher says.

"Yes," the boy says. "Yes." And he opens his book again.

The preacher just looks at him sitting there. The boy done forgot all about him. Everybody else make 'tend they done forgot the squabble, too.

Then I see that preacher getting up real slow. Preacher's a great big old man and he got to brace himself to get up. He comes over where the boy is sitting. He just stands there a little while looking down at him, but the boy don't raise his head.

"Get up, boy," preacher says.

The boy looks up at him, then he shuts his book real slow and stands up. Preacher just hauls back and hit him in the face. The boy falls back 'gainst the wall, but he straightens himself up and looks right back at that preacher.

"You forgot the other cheek," he says.

The preacher hauls back and hit him again on the other side. But this time the boy braces himself and don't fall.

"That hasn't changed a thing," he says.

The preacher just looks at the boy. The preacher's breathing real hard like he just run up a big hill. The boy sits down and opens his book again.

"I feel sorry for you," the preacher says. "I never felt so sorry for a man before."

The boy makes 'tend he don't even hear that preacher. He keeps on reading his book. The preacher goes back and gets his hat off the chair.

"Excuse me," he says to us. "I'll come back some other time. Y'all, please excuse me."

And he looks at the boy and goes out the room. The boy h'ist his hand up to his mouth one time to wipe 'way some blood. All the rest of the time he keeps on reading. And nobody else in there say a word.

8

Little John Lee and his mama come out the dentist office, and the nurse calls somebody else in. Then little bit later they come out, and the nurse calls another name. But fast 's she calls somebody in there, somebody else comes in the place where we sitting, and the room stays full.

The people coming in now, all of them wearing big coats. One of them says something 'bout sleeting, another one says he hope not. Another one says he think it ain't nothing but rain. 'Cause, he says, rain can get awful cold this time of year.

All round the room they talking. Some of them talking to people right by them, some of them talking to people clear 'cross the room, some of them talking to anybody'll listen. It's a little bitty room, no bigger than us kitchen, and I can see everybody in there. The little old room's full of smoke, 'cause you got two old men smoking pipes over by that side door. I think I feel my tooth thumping me some, and I hold my breath and wait. I wait and wait, but it don't thump me no more. Thank God for that.

I feel like going to sleep, and I lean back 'gainst the wall. But I'm scared to go to sleep. Scared 'cause the nurse might call my name and I won't hear her. And Mama might go to sleep, too, and she'll be mad if neither one of us heard the nurse.

I look up at Mama. I love my mama. And when cotton come I'm go'n get her a new coat. And I ain't go'n get a black one, either. I think I'm go'n get her a red one.

"They got some books over there," I say. "Want read one of them?"

Mama looks at the books, but she don't answer me.

"You got yourself a little man there," the lady says.

Mama don't say nothing to the lady, but she must've smiled, 'cause I seen the lady smiling back. The lady looks at me a little while, like she's feeling sorry for me.

"You sure got that preacher out here in a hurry," she says to that boy.

The boy looks up at her and looks in his book again. When I grow up I want be just like him. I want clothes like that and I want keep a book with me, too.

"You really don't believe in God?" the lady says.

"No," he says.

"But why?" the lady says.

"Because the wind is pink," he says.

"What?" the lady says.

The boy don't answer her no more. He just reads in his book.

"Talking 'bout the wind is pink," that old lady says. She's sitting on the same bench with the boy and she's trying to look in his face. The boy makes 'tend the old lady ain't even there. He just keeps on reading. "Wind is pink," she says again. "Eh, Lord, what children go'n be saying next?"

The lady 'cross from us bust out laughing.

"That's a good one," she says. "The wind is pink. Yes sir, that's a good one."

"Don't you believe the wind is pink?" the boy says. He keeps his head down in the book.

"Course I believe it, honey," the lady says. "Course I do." She looks at us and winks her eye. "And what color is grass, honey?"

"Grass? Grass is black."

She bust out laughing again. The boy looks at her.

"Don't you believe grass is black?" he says.

The lady quits her laughing and looks at him. Everybody else looking at him, too. The place quiet, quiet.

"Grass is green, honey," the lady says. "It was green yesterday, it's green today, and it's go'n be green tomorrow."

"How do you know it's green?"

"I know because I know."

"You don't know it's green," the boy says. "You believe it's green because someone told you it was green. If someone had told you it was black you'd believe it was black."

"It's green," the lady says. "I know green when I see green."

"Prove it's green," the boy says.

"Sure, now," the lady says. "Don't tell me it's coming to that."

"It's coming to just that," the boy says. "Words mean nothing. One means no more than the other."

"That's what it all coming to?" the old lady says. That old lady got on a turban and she got on two sweaters. She got a green sweater under a black sweater. I can see the green sweater 'cause some of the buttons on the the other sweater's missing.

"Yes ma'am," the boy says. "Words mean nothing. Action is the only thing. Doing. That's the only thing."

"Other words, you want the Lord to come down here and show Hisself to you?" she says.

"Exactly, ma'am," he says.

"You don't mean that, I'm sure?" she says.

"I do, ma'am," he says.

"Done, Jesus," the lady says, shaking her head.

"I didn't go 'long with that preacher at first," the other lady says; "but now—I don't know. When a person says the grass is black, he's either a lunatic or something's wrong."

"Prove to me that it's green," the boy says.

"It's green because the people say it's green."

"Those same people say we're citizens of these United States," the boy says.

"I think I'm a citizen," the lady says.

"Citizens have certain rights," the boy says. "Name me one right that you have. One right, granted by the Constitution, that you can exercise in Bayonne."

The lady don't answer him. She just looks at him like she don't know what he's talking 'bout. I know I don't.

"Things changing," she says.

"Things are changing because some black men have begun to think with their brains and not their hearts," the boy says.

"You trying to say these people don't believe in God?"

"I'm sure some of them do. Maybe most of them do. But they don't believe that God is going to touch these white people's hearts and change things tomorrow. Things change through action. By no other way."

Everybody sit quiet and look at the boy. Nobody says a thing. Then the lady 'cross the room from me and Mama just shakes her head.

"Let's hope that not all your generation feel the same way you do," she says.

"Think what you please, it doesn't matter," the boy says. "But it will be men who listen to their heads and not their hearts who will see that your children have a better chance than you had."

"Let's hope they ain't all like you, though," the old lady says. "Done forgot the heart absolutely."

"Yes ma'am, I hope they aren't all like me," the boy says. "Unfortunately, I was born too late to believe in your God. Let's hope that the ones who come after will have your faith—if not in your God, then in something else, something definitely that they can lean on. I haven't anything. For me, the wind is pink, the grass is black."

9

The nurse comes in the room where we are all sitting and waiting and says the doctor won't take no more patients till one o'clock this evening. My mama jumps up off the bench and goes up to the white lady.

"Nurse, I have to go back in the field this evening," she says.

"The doctor is treating his last patient now," the nurse says. "One o'clock this evening."

"Can I at least speak to the doctor?" my mama asks.

"I'm his nurse," the lady says.

"My little boy's sick," my mama says. "Right now his tooth almost killing him."

The nurse looks at me. She's trying to make up her mind if to let me come in. I look at her real pitiful. The tooth ain't hurting me at all, but Mama say it is, so I make 'tend for her sake.

"This evening," the nurse says, and goes on back in the office.

"Don't feel 'jected, honey," the lady says to Mama. "I been round them a long time—they take you when they want to. If you was white, that's something else; but we the wrong color."

Mama don't say nothing to the lady, and me and her go outside and stand 'gainst the wall. It's cold out there. I can feel that wind going through my coat. Some of the other people come out of the room and go up the street. Me and Mama stand there a little while and we start walking. I don't know where we going. When we come to the other street we just stand there.

"You don't have to make water, do you?" Mama says. "No, ma'am," I say.

We go on up the street. Walking real slow. I can tell Mama don't know where she's going. When we come to a store we stand there and look at the dummies. I look at a little boy wearing a brown overcoat. He's got on brown shoes, too. I look at my old shoes and look at his'n again. You wait till summer, I say.

Me and Mama walk away. We come up to another store and we stop and look at them dummies, too. Then we go on again. We pass a café where the white people in there eating. Mama tells me keep my eyes in front where they belong, but I can't help from seeing them people eat. My stomach starts to growling 'cause I'm hungry. When I see people eating, I get hungry; when I see a coat, I get cold.

A man whistles at my mama when we go by a filling station. She makes 'tend she don't even see him. I look back and I feel like hitting him in the mouth. If I was bigger, I say; if I was bigger, you'd see.

We keep on going. I'm getting colder and colder, but I don't say nothing. I feel that stuff running down my nose and I sniff.

"That rag," Mama says.

I get it out and wipe my nose. I'm getting cold all over now—my face, my hands, my feet, everything. We pass another little café, but this'n for white people, too, and we can't go in there, either. So we just walk. I'm so cold now I'm 'bout ready to say it. If I knowed where we was going I wouldn't be so cold, but I don't know where we going. We go, we go, we go. We walk clean out of Bayonne. Then we cross the street and we come back. Same thing I seen when I got off the bus this morning. Same old trees, same old walks, same old weeds, same old cracked pave—same old everything.

I sniff again.

"That rag," Mama says.

I wipe my nose real fast and jugg that handkerchief back in my pocket 'fore my hand gets too cold. I raise my head and I can see David's hardware store. When we come up to it, we go in. I don't know why, but I'm glad.

It's warm in there. It's so warm in there you don't ever want to leave. I look for the heater, and I see it over by them barrels. Three white men standing round the heater talking in Creole. One of them comes over to see what my mama want.

"Got any axe handles?" she says.

Me, Mama and the white man start to the back, but Mama stops me when we come up to the heater. She and the white man go on. I hold my hands over the heater and look at them. They go all the way to the back, and I see the white man pointing to the axe handles 'gainst the wall.

Mama takes one of them and shakes it like she's trying to figure how much it weighs. The she rubs her hand over it from one end to the other end. She turns it over and looks at the other side, then she shakes it again, and shakes her head and puts it back. She gets another one and she does it just like she did the first one, then she shakes her head. Then she gets a brown one and do it that, too. But she don't like this one, either. Then she gets another one, but 'fore she shakes it or anything, she looks at me. Look like she's trying to say something to me, but I don't know what it is. All I know is I done got warm now and I'm feeling right smart better. Mama shakes this axe handle just like she did the others, and shakes her head and says something to the white man. The white man just looks at his pile of axe handles, and when Mama pass him to come to the front, the white man just scratch his head and follows her. She tells me to come on and we go on out and start walking again.

We walk and walk, and no time at all I'm cold again. Look like I'm colder now 'cause I can still remember how good it was back there. My stomach growls and I suck it in to keep Mama from hearing it. She's walking right 'side me, and it growls so loud you can hear it a mile. But Mama don't say a word.

10

When we come up to the courthouse, I look at the clock. It's got quarter to twelve. Mean we got another hour and a quarter to be out here in the cold. We go and stand 'side a building. Something hits my cap and I look up at the sky. Sleet's falling.

I look at Mama standing there. I want stand close 'side her, but she don't like that. She say that's crybaby stuff. She say you got to stand for yourself, by yourself.

"Let's go back to that office," she says.

We cross the street. When we get to the dentist office I try to open the door, but I can't. I twist and twist, but I can't. Mama pushes me to the side and she twist the knob, but she can't open the door, either. She turns 'way from the door. I look at her, but I don't move and I don't say nothing. I done seen her like this before and I'm scared of her.

"You hungry?" she says. She says it like she's mad at me, like I'm the cause of everything.

"No, ma'am," I say.

"You want eat and walk back, or you rather don't eat and ride?"

"I ain't hungry," I say.

I ain't just hungry, but I'm cold, too. I'm so hungry and cold I want to cry. And look like I'm getting colder and colder. My feet done got numb. I try to work my toes, but I don't even feel them. Look like I'm go'n die. Look like I'm go'n stand right here and freeze to death. I think 'bout home. I think 'bout Val and Auntie and Ty and Louis and Walker. It's 'bout twelve o'clock and I know they eating dinner now. I can hear Ty making jokes. He done forgot 'bout getting up early this morning and right now he's probably making jokes. Always trying to make somebody laugh. I wish I was right there listening to him. Give anything in the world if I was home round the fire.

"Come on," Mama says.

We start walking again. My feet so numb I can't hardly feel them. We turn the corner and go on back up the street. The clock in the courthouse starting hitting for twelve.

The sleet's coming down plenty now. They hit the pave and bounce like rice. Oh, Lord; oh, Lord, I pray. Don't let me die, don't let me die, don't let me die, Lord.

11

Now I know where we going. We going back of town where the colored people eat. I don't care if I don't eat. I been hungry before. I can stand it. But I can't stand the cold.

I can see we go'n have a long walk. It's 'bout a mile down there. But I don't mind. I know when I get there I'm go'n warm myself. I think I can hold out. My hands numb in my pockets and my feet numb, too, but if I keep moving I can hold out. Just don't stop no more, that's all.

The sky's gray. The sleet keeps on falling. Falling like rain now—plenty, plenty. You can hear it hitting the pave. You can see it bouncing. Sometimes it bounces two times 'fore it settles.

We keep on going. We don't say nothing. We just keep on going, keep on going.

I wonder what Mama's thinking. I hope she ain't mad at me. When summer come I'm go'n pick plenty cotton and get her a coat. I'm go'n get her a red one.

I hope they'd make it summer all the time. I'd be glad if it was summer all the time—but it ain't. We got to have winter, too. Lord, I hate the winter. I guess everybody hate the winter.

I don't sniff this time, I get out my handkerchief and wipe my nose. My hands's so cold I can hardly hold the handkerchief.

I think we getting close, but we ain't there yet. I wonder where everybody is. Can't see a soul but us. Look like we the only two people moving round today. Must be too cold for the rest of the people to move round in.

I can hear my teeth. I hope they don't knock together too hard and make that bad one hurt. Lord, that's all I need, for that bad one to start off.

I hear a church bell somewhere. But today ain't Sunday. They must be ringing for a funeral or something.

I wonder what they doing at home. They must be eating. Monsieur Bayonne might be there with his guitar. One day Ty played with Monsieur Bayonne's guitar and broke one of the strings. Monsieur Bayonne was some mad with Ty. He say Ty wasn't go'n ever 'mount to nothing. Ty can go just like Monsieur Bayonne when he ain't there. Ty can make everybody laugh when he starts to mocking Monsieur Bayonne.

I used to like to be with Mama and Daddy. We used to be happy. But they took him in the Army. Now, nobody happy no more. . . . I be glad when Daddy comes home.

Monsieur Bayonne say it wasn't fair for them to take Daddy and give Mama nothing and give us nothing. Auntie say, "Shhh, Etienne. Don't let them hear you talk like that." Monsieur Bayonne say, "It's God truth. What they giving his children? They have to walk three and a half miles to school hot or cold. That's anything to give for a paw? She's got to work in the field rain or shine just to make ends meet. That's anything to give for a husband?" Auntie say, "Shhh, Etienne, shhh." "Yes, you right," Monsieur Bayonne say. "Best don't say it in front of them now. But one day they go'n find out. One day." "Yes, I suppose so." Auntie say. "Then what, Rose Mary?" Monsieur Bayonne say. "I don't know, Etienne," Auntie say. "All we can do is us job, and leave everything else in His hand . . . "

We getting closer, now. We getting closer. I can even see the railroad tracks.

We cross the tracks, and now I see the café. Just to get in there, I say. Just to get in there. Already I'm starting to feel little better.

12

We go in. Ahh, it's good. I look for the heater; there 'gainst the wall. One of them little brown ones. I just stand there and hold my hands over it. I can't open my hands too wide 'cause they almost froze.

Mama's standing right 'side me. She done unbuttoned her coat. Smoke rises out of the coat, and the coat smells like a wet dog.

I move to the side so Mama can have more room. She opens out her hands and rubs them together. I rub mine together, too, 'cause this keep them from hurting. If you let them warm too fast, they hurt you sure. But if you let them warm just little bit at a time, and you keep rubbing them, they be all right every time.

They got just two more people in the café. A lady back of the counter, and a man on this side of the counter. They been watching us ever since we come in.

Mama gets out the handkerchief and count up the money. Both of us know how much money she's got there. Three dollars. No, she ain't got three dollars, 'cause she had to pay us way up here. She ain't got but two dollars and a half left. Dollar and half to get my tooth pulled, and fifty cents for us to go back on, and fifty cents worth of salt meat.

She stirs the money round with her finger. Most of the money is change 'cause I can hear it rubbing together. She stirs it and stirs it. Then she looks at the door. It's still sleeting. I can hear it hitting 'gainst the wall like rice.

"I ain't hungry, Mama," I say.

"Got to pay them something for they heat," she says.

She takes a quarter out the handkerchief and ties the handkerchief up again. She looks over her shoulder at the people, but she still don't move. I hope she don't spend the money. I don't want her spending it on me. I'm hungry, I'm almost starving I'm so hungry, but I don't want her spending the money on me.

She flips the quarter over like she's thinking. She's must be thinking 'bout us walking back home. Lord, I sure don't want walk home. If I thought it'd do any good to say something, I'd say it. But Mama makes up her own mind 'bout things.

She turns 'way from the heater right fast, like she better hurry up and spend the quarter 'fore she change her mind. I watch her go toward the counter. The man and the lady look at her, too. She tells the lady something and the lady walks away. The man keeps on looking at her. Her back's turned to the man, and she don't even know he's standing there.

The lady puts some cakes and a glass of milk on the counter. Then she pours up a cup of coffee and set it 'side the other stuff. She's looking real sad. I say to myself, I'm go'n make all this up one day. You see, one day, I'm go'n make all this up. I want say it now; I want tell her how I feel right now; but Mama don't like to us to talk like that.

"I can't eat all this," I say.

They ain't got but just three little old cakes there. I'm so hungry right now, the Lord knows I can eat a hundred times three, but I want my mama to have one.

Mama don't even look my way. She knows I'm hungry, she knows I want it. I let it stay there a little while, then I get it and eat it. I eat just on my front teeth, though 'cause if cake touch that back tooth I know what'll happen. Thank God it ain't hurt me at all today.

After I finish eating I see the man go to the juke box. He drops a nickel in it, then he just stand there a little while looking at the record. Mama tells me keep my eyes in front where they belong. I turn my head like she say, but then I hear the man coming toward us.

"Dance, pretty?" he says.

Mama gets up to dance with him. But 'fore you know it, she done grabbed the little man in the collar and done heaved him 'side the wall. He hit the wall so hard he stop the juke box from playing.

"Some pimp," the lady back of the counter says. "Some pimp."

The little man jumps up off the floor and starts toward my mama. 'Fore you know it, Mama done sprung open her knife and she's waiting for him.

"Come on." she says. "Come on. I'll gut you from your neighbo to your throat. Come on."

I go up to the little man to hit him, but Mama makes me come and stand 'side her. The little man looks at me and Mama and goes on back to the counter.

"Some pimp," the lady back of the counter says. "Some pimp." She starts laughing and pointing at the little man. "Yes sir, you a pimp, all right. Yes sir-ree."

13

"Fasten that coat, let's go," Mama says.

"You don't have to leave," the lady says.

Mama don't answer the lady, and we right out in the cold again. I'm warm right now—my hands, my ears, my feet—but I know this ain't go'n last too long. It done sleet so much now you got ice everywhere you look.

We cross the railroad tracks, and soon's we do, I get cold. That wind goes through this little old coat like it ain't even there. I got on a shirt and a sweater under the coat, but that wind don't pay them no mind. I look up and I can see we got a long way to go. I wonder if we go'n make it 'fore I get too cold.

We cross over to walk on the sidewalk. They got just one sidewalk back here, and it's over there.

After we go just a little piece, I smell bread cooking. I look, then I see a baker shop. When we get closer, I can smell it more better, I shut my eyes and make 'tend I'm eating. But I keep them shut too long and I butt up 'gainst a telephone post. Mama grabs me and see if I'm hurt. I ain't bleeding or nothing and she turns me loose.

I can feel I'm getting colder and colder, and I look up to see how far we still got to go. Uptown is 'way up yonder. A half mile more, I reckon. I try to think of something. They say think and you won't get cold. I think of that poem, "Annabel Lee." I ain't been to school in so long—this bad weather—I reckon they done passed "Annabel Lee" by now. But passed it or not, I'm sure Miss Walker go'n make me recite it when I get there. That woman don't never forget nothing. I ain't never seen nobody like that in my life.

I'm still getting cold. "Annabel Lee" or no "Annabel Lee," I'm still getting cold. But I can see we getting closer. We getting there gradually.

Soon's we turn the corner, I see a little old white lady up in front of us. She's the only lady on the street. She's all in black and she's got a long black rag over her head.

"Stop," she says.

Me and Mama stop and look at her. She must be crazy to be out in all this bad weather. Ain't got but a few other people out there, and all of them's men.

"Y'all done ate?" she says.

"Just finish," Mama says.

"Y'all must be cold then?" she says.

"We headed for the dentist," Mama says. "We'll warm up when we get there."

"What dentist?" the old lady says. "Mr. Bassett?"

"Yes, Ma'am," Mama says.

"Come on in," the old lady says. "I'll telephone him and tell him y'all coming."

Me and Mama follow the old lady in the store. It's a little bitty store, and it don't have much in there. The old lady takes off her head rag and folds it up.

"Helena?" somebody calls from the back.

"Yes, Alnest?" the old lady says.

"Did you see them?"

"They're here. Standing beside me."

"Good. Now you can stay inside."

The old lady looks at Mama. Mama's waiting to hear what she brought us in here for. I'm waiting for that, too.

"I saw y'all each time you went by," she says. "I came out to catch you, but you were gone."

"We went back of town," Mama says.

"Did you eat?"

"Yes, ma'am."

The old lady looks at Mama a long time, like she's thinking Mama might be just saying that. Mama looks right back at her. The old lady looks at me to see what I have to say. I don't say nothing. I sure ain't going 'gainst my mama.

"There's food in the kitchen," she says to Mama. "I've been keeping it warm."

Mama turns right around and starts for the door.

"Just a minute," the old lady says. Mama stops. "The boy'll have to work for it. It isn't free."

"We don't take no handout," Mama says.

"I'm not handing out anything," the old lady says. "I need my garbage moved to the front. Ernest has a bad cold and can't go out there."

"James'll move it for you," Mama says.

"Not unless you eat," the old lady says. "I'm old, but I have my pride, too, you know."

Mama can see she ain't go'n beat this old lady down, so she just shakes her head.

"All right," the old lady says. "Come into the kitchen."

She leads the way with that rag in her hand. The kitchen is a little bitty little old thing, too. The table and the stove just 'bout fill it up. They got a little room to the side. Somebody in there laying 'cross the bed—'cause I can see one of his feet. Must be the person she was talking to: Ernest or Alnest—something like that.

"Sit down," the old lady says to Mama. "Not you," she says to me. "You have to move the cans."

"Helena?" the man says in the other room.

"Yes, Alnest?" the old lady says.

"Are you going out there again?"

"I must show the boy where the garbage is, Alnest," the old lady says.

"Keep that shawl over your head," the old man says.

"You don't have to remind me, Alnest. Come, boy," the old lady says.

We go out in the yard. Little old back yard ain't no bigger than the store or the kitchen. But it can sleet here just like it can sleet in any big back yard. And 'fore you know it, I'm trembling.

"There," the old lady says, pointing to the cans. I pick up one of the cans and set it right back down. The can's so light, I'm go'n see what's inside of it.

"Here," the old lady says. "Leave that can alone."

I look back at her standing there in the door. She's got that black rag wrapped around her shoulders, and she's pointing one of her little old fingers at me.

"Pick it up and carry it to the front," she says. I go by her with the can, and she's looking at me all the time. I'm sure the can's empty. I'm sure she could've carried it herself—maybe both of them at the same time. "Set it on the sidewalk by the door and come back for the other one," she says.

I go and come back, and Mama looks at me when I pass her. I get the other can and take it to the front. It don't feel a bit heavier than that first one. I tell myself I ain't go'n be nobody's fool, and I'm go'n look inside this can to see just what I been hauling. First, I look up the street, then down the street. Nobody coming. Then I look over my shoulder toward the door. That little old lady done slipped up there quiet's mouse, watching me again. Look like she knowed what I was go'n do.

"Ehh, Lord," she says. "Children, children. Come in here, boy, and go wash your hands."

I follow her in the kitchen. She point toward the bathroom, and I go in there and wash up. Little bitty old bathroom, but it's clean, clean. I don't use any of her towels; I wipe my hands on my pants legs.

When I come back in the kitchen, the old lady done dished up the food. Rice, gravy, meat—and she even got some lettuce and tomato in a saucer. She even got a glass of milk and a piece of cake there, too. It looks so good, I almost start eating 'fore I say my blessing.

"Helena?" the old man says.

"Yes, Alnest?"

"Are they eating?"

"Yes," she says.

"Good," he says. "Now you'll stay inside."

The old lady goes in there where he is and I can hear them talking. I look at Mama. She's eating slow like she's thinking. I wonder what's the matter now. I reckon she's thinking 'bout home.

The old lady comes back in the kitchen.

"I talked to Dr. Bassett's nurse," she says. "Dr. Bassett will take you as soon as you get there."

"Thank you, ma'am," Mama says.

"Perfectly all right," the old lady says. "Which one is it?"

Mama nods toward me. The old lady looks at me real sad. I look sad, too.

"You're not afraid, are you?" she says.

"No, ma'am," I say.

"That's a good boy," the old lady says. "Nothing to be afraid of. Dr. Bassett will not hurt you."

When me and Mama get through eating, we thank the old lady again.

"Helena, are they leaving?" the old man says.

"Yes, Alnest."

"Tell them I say good-bye."

"They can hear you, Alnest."

"Good-bye both mother and son," the old man says. "And may God be with you."

Me and Mama tell the old man good-bye, and we follow the old lady in the front room. Mama opens the door to go out, but she stops and comes back in the store.

"You sell salt meat?" she says.

"Yes."

"Give me two bits worth."

"That isn't very much salt meat," the old lady says.

"That's all I have," Mama says.

The old lady goes back of the counter and cuts a big piece off the chunk. Then she wraps it up and put it in a paper bag.

"Two bits," she says.

"That looks like awful lot of meat for a quarter," Mama says.

"Two bits," the old lady says. "I've been selling salt meat behind this counter twenty-five years. I think I know what I'm doing."

"You got a scale there," Mama says.

"What?" the old lady says.

"Weigh it," Mama says.

"What?" the old lady says. "Are you telling me how to run my business?"

"Thanks very much for the food," Mama says.

"Just a minute," the old lady says.

"James," Mama says to me. I move toward the door.

"Just one minute, I said," the old lady says.

Me and Mama stop again and look at her. The old lady takes the meat out the bag and unwraps it and cuts 'bout half of it off. Then she wraps it up again and juggs it back in the bag and gives the bag to Mama. Mama lays the quarter on the counter.

"Your kindness will never be forgotten," she says. "James," she says to me.

We go out, and the old lady comes to the door to look at us. After we go a little piece I look back, and she's still there watching us.

The sleet's coming down heavy, heavy now, and I turn up my coat collar to keep my neck warm. My Mama tells me turn it right back down.

"You not a bum," she says. "You a man."

Joyce Carol Oates

1938 –

Joyce Carol Oates began her literary career in 1963, when she published her first collection of stories; since then, she has established herself as one of our most brilliant and gifted writers. Her thematic concern with violence, brutality, and emotional disturbance has led critics to compare her work with that of such predecessors as Dreiser, Faulkner, and O'Connor; what kinship there may be between her work and theirs, however, is less a matter of similar styles and methods than of their similar concern with human beings "trying to subdue chaos outside and inside" in their "constant battle with nature. . . . " If her stories are often grim enough to warrant calling her "the dark lady of American letters," as one critic does, it is because they are firmly anchored in the reality of a troubled modern society.

Born in 1938, in Lockport, New York, Oates earned her B.A. degree from Syracuse University in 1960, and her M.A. degree in English from the University of Wisconsin in 1961. From 1961 to 1967, she taught English at the University of Detroit, and then for nearly twenty years she was on the faculty of the University of Windsor (Ontario, Canada) where her husband, Raymond Smith, a specialist in Eighteenth-Century English Literature, also taught. She now teaches creative writing at Princeton University. Oates began publishing stories when she was twenty-one, and brought out her first collection, *By the North Gate,* in 1963. Subsequently, she has authored, co-authored, or edited almost sixty other books, including twenty novels and fourteen collections of her stores. *American Appetites* (1989) is her latest novel, *Raven's Wing* (1986) her most recent collection of short stories.

Her work has received wide critical attention and won her many awards, including a Guggenheim Fellowship in 1967, The Rosenthal Award of the National Institute of Arts and Letters in 1968, The National Book Award in 1970, and several special awards for continuing achievement in the short story.

It would be unsound to regard "Where Are You Going, Where Have You Been?" as a "typical" Joyce Carol Oates story, for, believing that each story "has a form and style that is best suited for it," she displays an amazing diversity of techniques, methods, and structures in her stories so that no two of them are alike. Regardless of what approach she takes in a particular story, however, Oates creates powerful, emotion-charged situations, as is illustrated by "Where Are You Going, Where Have You Been?" which develops step by step from commonplace events to an ominous, even eerie conclusion.

Where Are You Going, Where Have You Been?

For Bob Dylan

Her name was Connie. She was fifteen and she had a quick nervous giggling habit of craning her neck to glance into mirrors, or checking other people's faces to make sure her own was all right. Her mother, who noticed everything and knew everything and who hadn't much reason any longer to look at her own face, always scolded Connie about it. "Stop gawking at yourself, who are you? You think you're so pretty?" she would say. Connie would raise her eyebrows at these familiar complaints and look right through her mother, into a shadowy vision of herself as she was right at that moment: she knew she was pretty and that was everything.

Her mother had been pretty once too, if you could believe those old snapshots in the album, but now her looks were gone and that was why she was always after Connie.

"Why don't you keep your room clean like your sister? How've you got your hair fixed—what the hell stinks? Hair spray? You don't see your sister using that junk."

Her sister June was twenty-four and still lived at home. She was a secretary in the high school Connie attended, and if that wasn't bad enough—with her in the same building—she was so plain and chunky and steady that Connie had to hear her praised all the time by her mother and her mother's sisters. June did this, June did that, she saved money and helped clean the house and cooked and Connie couldn't do a thing, her mind was all filled with trashy daydreams. Their father was away at work most of the time and when he came home he wanted supper and he read the newspaper at supper and after supper he went to bed. He didn't bother talking much to them, but around his bent head Connie's mother kept picking at her until Connie wished her mother was dead and she herself was dead and it was all over. "She makes me want to throw up sometimes," she complained to her friends. She had a high, breathless, amused voice which made everything she said sound a little forced, whether it was sincere or not.

There was one good thing: June went places with girl friends of hers, girls who were just as plain and steady as she, and so when Connie wanted to do that her mother had no objections. The father of Connie's best girl friend drove the girls the three miles to town and left them off at a shopping plaza, so that they could walk through the stores or go to a movie, and when he came to pick them up again at eleven he never bothered to ask what they had done.

They must have been familiar sights, walking around that shopping plaza in their shorts and flat ballerina slippers that always scuffed the sidewalk, with charm bracelets jingling on their thin wrists; they would lean together to whisper and laugh secretly if someone passed by who amused or interested them. Connie had long dark blond hair that drew anyone's eye to it, and she wore part of it pulled up on her head and puffed out and the rest of it she let fall down her back. She wore a pullover jersey blouse that looked one way when she was home and another way when she was away from home. Everything about her had two sides to it, one for home and one for anywhere that was not home: her walk that could be childlike and bobbing, or languid enough to make anyone think she was hearing music in her head, her mouth which was pale and smirking most of the time, but bright and pink on these evenings out, her laugh which was cynical and drawling at home—"Ha ha, very funny"—but high-pitched and nervous anywhere else, like the jingling of the charms on her bracelet.

Sometimes they did go shopping or to a movie, but sometimes they went across the highway, ducking fast across the busy road, to a drive-in restaurant where older kids hung out. The restaurant was shaped like a big bottle, though squatter than a real bottle, and on its cap was a revolving figure of a grinning boy who held a hamburger aloft. One night in mid-summer they ran across, breathless with daring, and right away someone leaned out a car window and invited them over, but it was just a boy from high school they didn't like. It made them feel good to be able to ignore him. They went up through the maze of parked and cruising cars to the bright-lit, fly-infested restaurant, their faces pleased and expectant as if they were entering a sacred building that loomed out of the night to give them what haven and what blessing they yearned for. They sat at the counter and crossed their legs at the ankles, their thin shoulders rigid with excitement and listened to the music that made everything so good: the music was always in the background like music at a church service, it was something to depend upon.

A boy named Eddie came in to talk with them. He sat backwards on his stool, turning himself jerkily around in semi-circles and then stopping and turning again, and after a while he asked Connie if she would like something to eat. She said she did and so she tapped her friend's arm on her way out—her friend pulled her face up into a brave droll look—and Connie said she would meet her at eleven, across the way. "I just hate to leave her like that," Connie said earnestly, but the boy said that she wouldn't be alone for long. So they went out to his car and on the way Connie couldn't help but let her eyes wander over the windshields and faces all around her, her face gleaming with the joy that had nothing to do with Eddie or even this place; it might have been the music. She drew her shoulders up and sucked in her breath with the pure pleasure of being alive, and just at that moment she happened to glance at a face just a few feet from hers. It was a boy with shaggy black hair, in a convertible jalopy painted gold. He stared at her and then his lips widened into a grin. Connie slit her eyes at him and turned away, but she couldn't help glancing back and there he was still watching her. He wagged a finger and laughed and said, "Gonna get you, baby," and Connie turned away again without Eddie noticing anything.

She spent three hours with him, at the restaurant where they ate hamburgers and drank Cokes in wax cups that were always sweating, and then down an alley a mile or so away, and when he left her off at five to eleven only the movie house was still open at the plaza. Her girl friend was there, talking with a boy. When Connie came up the two girls smiled at each other and Connie said, "How was the movie?" and the girl said, "*You* should know." They rode off with the girl's father, sleepy and pleased, and Connie couldn't help but look at the darkened shopping plaza with its big empty parking lot and its signs that were faded and ghostly now, and over at the drive-in restaurant where cars were still circling tirelessly. She couldn't hear the music at this distance.

Next morning June asked her how the movie was and Connie said, "So-so."

She and that girl and occasionally another girl went out several times a week that way, and the rest of the time Connie spent around the house—it was summer vacation—getting in her mother's way and thinking, dreaming, about the boys she met. But all the boys fell back and dissolved into a single face that was not even a face, but an idea, a feeling, mixed up with the urgent insistent pounding of the music and the humid night air of July. Connie's mother kept dragging her back to the daylight by finding things for her to do or saying suddenly, "What's this about the Pettinger girl?"

And Connie would say nervously, "Oh, her. That dope." She always drew thick clear lines between herself and such girls, and her mother was simple and kindly enough to believe her. Her mother was so simple, Connie thought, that it was maybe cruel to fool her so much. Her mother went scuffling around the house in old bedroom slippers and complained over the telephone to one sister about the other, then the other called up and the two of them complained about the third one. If June's name was mentioned her mother's tone was approving, and if Connie's name was mentioned it was disapproving. This did not really mean she disliked Connie and actually Connie thought that her mother preferred her to June because she was prettier, but the two of them kept up a pretense of exasperation, a sense that they were tugging and struggling over something of little value to either of them. Sometimes, over coffee, they were almost friends, but something would come up—some vexation that was like a fly buzzing suddenly around their heads—and their faces went hard with contempt.

One Sunday Connie got up at eleven—none of them bothered with church—and washed her hair so that it could dry all day long, in the sun. Her parents and sister were going to a barbecue at an aunt's house and Connie said no, she wasn't interested, rolling her eyes, to let mother know just what she thought of it. "Stay home alone then," her mother said sharply. Connie sat out back in a lawn chair and watched them drive away, her father quiet and bald, hunched around so that he could back the car out, her mother with a look that was still angry and not at all softened through the windshield, and in the back seat poor old June all dressed up as if she didn't know what a barbecue was, with all the running yelling kids and the flies. Connie sat with her eyes closed in the sun, dreaming and dazed with the warmth about her as if this were a kind of love, the caresses of love, and her mind slipped over onto thoughts of the boy she had been with the night before and how nice he had been, how sweet it always was, not the way someone like June would suppose but sweet, gentle, the way it was in movies and promised in songs; and when she opened her eyes she hardly knew where she was, the back yard ran off into weeds and a fence-line of trees and behind it the sky was perfectly blue and still. The asbestos "ranch house" that was now three years old startled her—it looked small. She shook her head as if to get awake.

It was too hot. She went inside the house and turned on the radio to drown out the quiet. She sat on the edge of her bed, barefoot, and listened for an hour and a half to a program called XYZ Sunday Jamboree, record after record of hard, fast, shrieking songs she sang along with, interspersed by exclamations from "Bobby King": "An' look here you girls at Napoleon's—Son and Charley want you to pay real close attention to this song coming up!"

And Connie paid close attention herself, bathed in a glow of slow-pulsed joy that seemed to rise mysteriously out of the music itself and lay languidly about the airless little room, breathed in and breathed out with each gentle rise and fall of her chest.

After a while she heard a car coming up the drive. She sat up at once, startled, because it couldn't be her father so soon. The gravel kept crunching all the way in from the road—the driveway was long—and Connie ran to the window. It was a car she didn't know. It was an open jalopy, painted a bright gold that caught the sun opaquely. Her heart began to pound and her fingers snatched at her hair, checking it, and she whispered "Christ. Christ," wondering how bad she looked. The car came to a stop at the side door and the horn sounded four short taps as if this were a signal Connie knew.

She went into the kitchen and approached the door slowly, then hung out the screen door, her bare toes curling down off the step. There were two boys in the car and now she recognized the driver: he had shaggy, shabby black hair that looked crazy as a wig and he was grinning at her.

"I ain't late, am I?" he said.

"Who the hell do you think you are?" Connie said.

"Toldja I'd be out, didn't I?"

"I don't even know who you are."

She spoke sullenly, careful to show no interest or pleasure, and he spoke in a fast bright monotone. Connie looked past him to the other boy, taking her time. He had fair brown hair, with a lock that fell onto his forehead. His sideburns gave him a fierce, embarrassed look, but so far he hadn't even bothered to glance at her. Both boys wore sunglasses. The driver's glasses were metallic and mirrored everything in miniature.

"You wanta come for a ride?" he said.

Connie smirked and let her hair fall loose over one shoulder.

"Don'tcha like my car? New paint job," he said. "Hey."

"What?"

"You're cute."

She pretended to fidget, chasing flies away from the door.

"Don'tcha believe me, or what?" he said.

"Look, I don't even know who you are," Connie said in disgust.

"Hey, Ellie's got a radio, see. Mine's broke down." He lifted his friend's arm and showed her the little transistor the boy was holding, and now Connie began to hear the music. It was the same program that was playing inside the house.

"Bobby King?" she said.

"I listen to him all the time. I think he's great."

"He's kind of great," Connie said reluctantly.

"Listen, that guy's *great*. He knows where the action is."

Connie blushed a little, because the glasses made it impossible for her to see just what this boy was looking at. She couldn't decide if she liked him or if he was just a jerk, and so she dawdled in the doorway and wouldn't come down or go back inside. She said, 'What's all that stuff painted on your car?"

"Can'tcha read it?" He opened the door very carefully, as if he was afraid it might fall off. He slid out just as carefully, planting his feet firmly on the ground, the tiny metallic world in his glasses slowing down like gelatine hardening and in the midst of it Connie's bright green blouse. "This here is my name, to begin with," he said. ARNOLD FRIEND was written in tar-like black letters on the side, with a drawing of a round grinning face that reminded Connie of a pumpkin, except it wore sunglasses. "I wanta introduce myself I'm Arnold Friend and that's my real name and I'm gonna be your friend, honey, and inside the car's Ellie Oscar, he's kinda shy." Ellie brought his transistor up to his shoulder and balanced it there. "Now these numbers are a secret code, honey." Arnold Friend explained. He read off the numbers, 33, 19, 17 and raised his eyebrows at her to see what she thought of that, but she didn't think much of it. The left rear fender had been smashed and around it was written, on the gleaming gold background: DONE BY CRAZY WOMAN DRIVER. Connie had to laugh at that. Arnold Friend was pleased at her laughter and looked up at her. "Around the other side's a lot more—you wanta come and see them?"

"No."

"Why not?"

"Why should I?"

"Don'tcha wanta see what's on the car? Don'tcha wanta go for a ride?"

"I don't know."

"Why not?"

"I got things to do."

"Like what?"

"Things."

He laughed as if she had said something funny. He slapped his thighs. He was standing in a strange way, leaning back against the car as if he were balancing himself. He wasn't tall, only an inch or so taller than she would be if she came down to him. Connie liked the way he was dressed, which was the way all of them dressed: tight faded jeans stuffed into black, scuffed boots, a belt that pulled his waist in and showed how lean he was, and a white pull-over shirt that was a little soiled and showed the hard small muscles of his arms and shoulders. He looked as if he probably did hard work, lifting and carrying things. Even his neck looked muscular. And his face was a familiar face, somehow: the jaw and chin and cheeks slightly darkened, because he hadn't shaved for a day or two, and the nose long and hawk-like, sniffing as if she were a treat he was going to gobble up and it was all a joke.

"Connie, you ain't telling the truth. This is your day set aside for a ride with me and you know it," he said, still laughing. The way he straightened and recovered from his fit of laughing showed that it had been all fake.

"How do you know what my name is?" she said suspiciously.

"It's Connie."

"Maybe and maybe not."

"I know my Connie," he said, wagging his finger. Now she remembered him even better, back at the restaurant, and her cheeks warmed at the thought of how she sucked in her breath just at the moment she passed him—how she must have looked to him. And he had remembered her. "Ellie and I come out here especially for you," he said. "Ellie can sit in back. How about it?"

"Where?"

"Where what?"

"Where're we going?"

He looked at her. He took off the sunglasses and she saw how pale the skin around his eyes was, like holes that were not in shadow but instead in light. His eyes were like chips of broken glass that catch the light in an amiable way. He smiled. It was as if the idea of going for a ride somewhere, to some place, was a new idea to him.

"Just for a ride, Connie sweetheart."

"I never said my name was Connie," she said.

"But I know what it is. I know your name and all about you, lots of things," Arnold Friend said. He had not moved yet but stood still leaning back against the side of his jalopy. "I took a special interest in you, such a pretty girl, and found out all about you like I know your parents and sister are gone somewheres and I know where and how long they're going to be gone, and I know who you were with last night, and your best girl friend's name is Betty. Right?"

He spoke in a simple lilting voice, exactly as if he were reciting the words to a song. His smile assured her that everything was fine. In the car Ellie turned up the volume on his radio and did not bother to look around at them.

"Ellie can sit in the back seat," Arnold Friend said. He indicated his friend with a casual jerk of his chin, as if Ellie did not count and she should not bother with him.

"How'd you find out all that stuff?" Connie said.

"Listen: Betty Schultz and Tony Fitch and Jimmy Pettinger and Nancy Pettinger," he said, in a chant. "Raymond Stanley and Bob Hutter—"

"Do you know all those kids?"

"I know everybody."

"Look, you're kidding. You're not from around here."

"Sure."

"But—how come we never saw you before?"

"Sure you saw me before," he said. He looked down at his boots, as if he were a little offended. "You just don't remember."

"I guess I'd remember you," Connie said.

"Yeah?" He looked up at this, beaming. He was pleased. He began to mark time with the music from Ellie's radio, tapping his fists lightly together. Connie looked away from his smile to the car, which was painted so bright it almost hurt her eyes to look at it. She looked at that name, ARNOLD FRIEND. And up at the front fender was an expression that was familiar—MAN THE FLYING SAUCERS. It was an expression kids had used the year before, but didn't use this year. She looked at it for a while as if the words meant something to her that she did not yet know.

"What're you thinking about? Huh?" Arnold Friend demanded. "Not worried about your hair blowing around in the car, are you?"

"No."

"Think I maybe can't drive good?"

"How do I know?"

"You're a hard girl to handle. How come?" he said. "Don't you know I'm your friend? Didn't you see me put my sign in the air when you walked by?"

"What sign?"

"My sign." And he drew an X in the air, leaning out toward her. They were maybe ten feet apart. After his hand fell back to his side the X was still in the air, almost visible. Connie let the screen door close and stood perfectly still inside it, listening to the music from her radio and the boy's blend together. She stared at Arnold Friend. He stood there so stiffly relaxed, pretending to be relaxed, with one hand idly on the door handle as if he were keeping himself up that way and had no intention of ever moving again. She recognized most things about him, the tight jeans that showed his thighs and buttocks and the greasy leather boots and the tight shirt, and even that slippery friendly smile of his, that sleepy dreamy smile that all the boys used to get across ideas they didn't want to put into words. She recognized all this and also the singsong way he talked, slightly mocking, kidding, but serious and a little melancholy, and she recognized the way he tapped one fist against the other in homage to the perpetual music behind him. But all these things did not come together.

She said suddenly, "Hey, how old are you?"

His smile faded. She could see then that he wasn't a kid, he was much older—thirty, maybe more. At this knowledge her heart began to pound faster.

"That's a crazy thing to ask. Can'tcha see I'm your own age?"

"Like hell you are."

"Or maybe a coupla years older, I'm eighteen."

"Eighteen?" she said doubtfully.

He grinned to reassure her and lines appeared at the corners of his mouth. His teeth were big and white. He grinned so broadly his eyes became slits and she saw how thick the lashes were, thick and black as if painted with a black tar-like material. Then he seemed to become embarrassed, abruptly, and looked over his shoulder at Ellie. "*Him,* he's crazy," he said. "Ain't he a riot, he's a nut, a real character." Ellie was still listening to the music. His sunglasses told nothing about what he was thinking. He wore a bright orange shirt unbuttoned halfway to show his chest, which was a pale, bluish chest and not muscular like Arnold Friend's. His shirt collar was turned up all around and the very tips of the collar pointed out past his chin as if they were protecting him. He was pressing the transistor radio up against his ear and sat there in a kind of daze, right in the sun.

"He's kinda strange," Connie said.

"Hey, she says you're kinda strange! Kinda strange!" Arnold Friend cried. He pounded on the car to get Ellie's attention. Ellie turned for the first time and Connie saw with shock that he wasn't a kid either—he had a fair, hairless face, cheeks reddened slightly as if the veins grew too close to the surface of his skin, the face of a forty-year-old baby. Connie felt a wave of dizziness rise in her at this sight and she stared at him as if waiting for something to change the shock of the moment, make it all right again. Ellie's lips kept shaping words, mumbling along with the words blasting his ear.

"Maybe you two better go away," Connie said faintly.

"What? How come?" Arnold Friend cried. "We come out here to take you for a ride. It's Sunday." He had the voice of the man on the radio now. It was the same voice, Connie thought. "Don'tcha know it's Sunday all day and honey, no matter who you were with last night today you're with Arnold Friend and don't you forget it!—Maybe you better step out here," he said, and this last was in a different voice. It was a little flatter, as if the heat was finally getting to him.

"No. I got things to do."

"Hey."

"You two better leave."

"We ain't leaving until you come with us."

"Like hell I am—"

"Connie, don't fool around with me. I mean, I mean, don't fool *around,*" he said, shaking his head. He laughed incredulously. He placed his sunglasses on top of his head, carefully, as if he were indeed wearing a wig, and brought the stems down behind his ears. Connie stared at him, another wave of dizziness and fear rising in her so that for a moment he wasn't even in focus but was just a blur, standing there against his gold car, and she had the idea that he had driven up the driveway all right but had come from nowhere before that and belonged nowhere and that everything about him and even the music that was so familiar to her was only half real.

"If my father comes and sees you—"

"He ain't coming. He's at a barbecue."

"How do you know that?"

"Aunt Tillie's. Right now they're—uh—they're drinking. Sitting around," he said vaguely, squinting as if he were staring all the way to town and over to Aunt Tillie's back yard. Then the vision seemed to clear and he nodded energetically. "Yeah. Sitting around. There's your sister in a blue dress, huh? And high heels, the poor sad bitch—nothing like you, sweetheart! And your mother's helping some fat woman with the corn, they're cleaning the corn—husking the corn—"

"What fat woman?" Connie cried.

"How do I know what fat woman. I don't know every goddam fat woman in the world!" Arnold Friend laughed.

"Oh, that's Mrs. Hornby. . . . Who invited her?" Connie said. She felt a little light-headed. Her breath was coming quickly.

"She's too fat. I don't like them fat. I like them the way you are, honey," he said, smiling sleepily at her. They stared at each other for a while, through the screen door. He said softly, "Now what you're going to do is this: you're going to come out that door. You're going to sit up front with me and Ellie's going to sit in the back, the hell with Ellie, right? This isn't Ellie's date. You're my date. I'm your lover, honey."

"What? You're crazy—"

"Yes, I'm your lover. You don't know what that is but you will," he said. "I know that too. I know all about you. But look: it's real nice and you couldn't ask for nobody better than me, or more polite. I always keep my word. I'll tell you how it is, I'm always nice at first, the first time. I'll hold you so tight you won't think you have to try to get away or pretend anything because you'll know you can't. And I'll come inside you where it's all secret and you'll give in to me and you'll love me—"

"Shut up! You're crazy!" Connie said. She backed away from the door. She put her hands against her ears as if she'd heard something terrible, something not meant for her. "People don't talk like that, you're crazy," she muttered. Her heart was almost too big now for her chest and its pumping made sweat break out all over her. She looked out to see Arnold Friend pause and then take a step toward the porch lurching. He almost fell. But, like a clever drunken man, he managed to catch his balance. He wobbled in his high boots and grabbed hold of one of the porch posts.

"Honey?" he said. "You still listening?"

"Get the hell out of here!"

"Be nice, honey. Listen."

"I'm going to call the police—"

He wobbled again and out of the side of his mouth came a fast spat curse, an aside not meant for her to hear. But even this "Christ!" sounded forced. Then he began to smile again. She watched this smile come, awkward as if he were smiling from inside a mask. His whole face was a mask, she thought wildly, tanned down onto his throat but then running out as if he had plastered make-up on his face but had forgotten about his throat.

"Honey—? Listen, here's how it is. I always tell the truth and I promise you this: I ain't coming in that house after you."

"You better not! I'm going to call the police if you—if you don't—"

"Honey," he said, talking right through her voice, "honey, I'm not coming in there but you are coming out here. You know why?"

She was panting. The kitchen looked like a place she had never seen before, some room she had run inside but which wasn't good enough, wasn't going to help her. The kitchen window had never had a curtain, after three years, and there were dishes in the sink for her to do—probably—and if you ran your hand across the table you'd probably feel something sticky there.

"You listening, honey? Hey?"

"—going to call the police—"

"Soon as you touch the phone I don't need to keep my promise and can come inside. You won't want that."

She rushed forward and tried to lock the door. Her fingers were shaking. "But why lock it," Arnold Friend said gently, talking right into her face. "It's just a screen door. It's just nothing." One of his boots was at a strange angle, as if his foot wasn't in it. It pointed out to the left, bent at the ankle. "I mean, anybody can break through a screen door and glass and wood and iron or anything else if he needs to, anybody at all and specially Arnold Friend. If the place got lit up with a fire honey you'd come running out into my arms, right into my arms and safe at home—like you knew I was your lover and'd stopped fooling around. I don't mind a nice shy girl but I don't like no fooling around." Part of those words were spoken with a slight rhythmic lilt, and Connie somehow recognized them—the echo of a song from last year, about a girl rushing into her boy friend's arms and coming home again—

Connie stood barefoot on the linoleum floor, staring at him. "What do you want?" she whispered.

"I want you," he said.

"What?"

"Seen you that night and thought, that's the one, yes sir. I never needed to look any more."

"But my father's coming back. He's coming to get me. I had to wash my hair first—" She spoke in a dry, rapid voice, hardly raising it for him to hear.

"No, your daddy is not coming and yes, you had to wash your hair and you washed it for me. It's nice and shining and all for me, I thank you, sweetheart," he said, with a mock bow, but again he almost lost his balance. He had to bend and adjust his boots. Evidently his feet did not go all the way down; the boots must have been stuffed with something so that he would seem taller. Connie stared out at him and behind him Ellie in the car, who seemed to be looking off toward Connie's right, into nothing. This Ellie said, pulling the words out of the air one after another as if he were just discovering them, "You want me to pull out the phone?"

"Shut your mouth and keep it shut," Arnold Friend said, his face red from bending over or maybe from embarrassment because Connie had seen his boots. "This ain't none of your business."

"What—what are you doing? What do you want?" Connie said. "If I call the police they'll get you, they'll arrest you—"

"Promise was not to come in unless you touch that phone, and I'll keep that promise," he said. He resumed his erect position and tried to force his shoulders back. He sounded like a hero in a movie, declaring something important. He spoke too loudly and it was as if he were speaking to someone behind Connie. "I ain't made plans for coming in that house where I don't belong but just for you to come out to me, the way you should. Don't you know who I am?"

"You're crazy," she whispered. She backed away from the door but did not want to go into another part of the house, as if this would give him permission to come through the door. "What do you. . . . You're crazy, you . . ."

"Huh? What're you saying, honey?"

Her eyes darted everywhere in the kitchen. She could not remember what it was, this room.

"This is how it is, honey: you come out and we'll drive away, have a nice ride. But if you don't come out we're gonna wait till your people come home and then they're all going to get it."

"You want that telephone pulled out?" Ellie said. He held the radio away from his ear and grimaced, as if without the radio the air was too much for him.

"I toldja shut up, Ellie," Arnold Friend said, "you're deaf, get a hearing aid, right? Fix yourself up. This little girl's no trouble and's gonna be nice to me, so Ellie keep to yourself, this ain't your date—right? Don't hem in on me. Don't hog. Don't crush. Don't bird dog. Don't trail me," he said in a rapid meaningless voice, as if he were running through all the expressions he'd learned but was no longer sure which one of them was in style, then rushing on to new ones, making them up with his eyes closed, "Don't crawl under my fence, don't squeeze in my chipmunk hole, don't sniff my glue, suck my popsicle, keep your own greasy fingers on yourself!" He shaded his eyes and peered in at Connie, who was backed against the kitchen table. "Don't mind him honey he's just a creep. He's a dope. Right? I'm the boy for you and like I said you come out here nice like a lady and give me your hand, and nobody else gets hurt, I mean, your nice old bald-headed daddy and your mummy and your sister in her high heels. Because listen: why bring them in this?"

"Leave me alone," Connie whispered.

"Hey, you know that old woman down the road, the one with the chickens and stuff—you know her?"

"She's dead!"

"Dead? What? You know her?" Arnold Friend said.

"She's dead—"

"Don't you like her?"

"She's dead—she's—she isn't here any more—"

"But don't you like her, I mean, you got something against her? Some grudge or something?" Then his voice dipped as if he were conscious of rudeness. He touched the sunglasses on top of his head as if to make sure they were still there. "Now you be a good girl."

"What are you going to do?"

"Just two things, or maybe three," Arnold Friend said. "But I promise it won't last long and you'll like me that way you get to like people you're close to. You will. It's all over for you here, so come on out. You don't want your people in any trouble, do you?"

She turned and bumped against a chair or something, hurting her leg, but she ran into the back room and picked up the telephone. Something roared in her ear, a tiny roaring, and she was so sick with fear that she could do nothing but listen to it—the telephone was clammy and very heavy and her fingers groped down to the dial but were too weak to touch it. She began to scream into the phone, into the roaring. She cried out, she cried for her mother, she felt her breath start jerking back and forth in her lungs as if it were something Arnold Friend were stabbing her with again and again with no tenderness. A noisy sorrowful wailing rose all about her and she was locked inside it the way she was locked inside this house.

After a while she could hear again. She was sitting on the floor with her wet back against the wall.

Arnold Friend was saying from the door, "That's a good girl. Put the phone back."

She kicked the phone away from her.

"No, honey. Pick it up. Put it back right."

She picked it up and put it back. The dial tone stopped.

"That's a good girl. Now you come outside."

She was hollow with what had been fear, but what was now just an emptiness. All that screaming had blasted it out of her. She sat, one leg cramped under her, and deep inside her brain was something like a pin-point of light that kept going and would not let her relax. She thought, I'm not going to see my mother again. She thought, I'm not going to sleep in my bed again. Her bright green blouse was all wet.

Arnold Friend said, in a gentle-loud voice that was like a stage voice, "The place where you came from ain't there any more, and where you had in mind to go is cancelled out. This place you are now—inside your daddy's house—is nothing but a cardboard box I can knock down any time. You know that and always did know it. You hear me?"

She thought, I have got to think. I have to know what to do.

"We'll go out to a nice field, out in the country here where it smells so nice and it's sunny," Arnold Friend said. "I'll have my arms tight around you so you won't need to try to get away and I'll show you what love is like, what it does. The hell with this house! It looks solid all right," he said. He ran a fingernail down the screen and the noise did not make Connie shiver, as it would have the day before. "Now put your hand on your heart, honey. Feel that? That feels solid too but we know better, be nice to me, be sweet like you can because what else is there for a girl like you but to be sweet and pretty and give in?—and get away before her people come back?"

She felt her pounding heart. Her hands seemed to enclose it. She thought for the first time in her life that it was nothing that was hers, that belonged to her, but just a pounding, living thing inside this body that wasn't hers either.

"You don't want them to get hurt," Arnold Friend went on. "Now get up, honey. Get up all by youself."

She stood.

"Now turn this way. That's right. Come over here to me—Ellie, put that away, didn't I tell you? You dope. You miserable creepy dope," Arnold Friend said. His words were not angry but only part of an incantation. The incantation was kindly. "Now come out through the kitchen to me honey and let's see a smile, try it, you're a brave sweet little girl and now they're eating corn and hotdogs cooked to bursting over an outdoor fire, and they don't know one thing about you and never did and honey you're better than them because not a one of them would have done this for you."

Connie felt the linoleum under her feet; it was cool. She brushed her hair back out of her eyes. Arnold Friend let go of the post tentatively and opened his arms for her, his elbows pointing up toward each other and his wrists limp, to show that this was an embarrassed embrace and a little mocking, he didn't want to make her self-conscious.

She put out her hand against the screen. She watched herself push the door slowly open as if she were safe back somewhere in the other doorway, watching this body and this head of long hair moving out into the sunlight where Arnold Friend waited.

"My sweet little blue-eyed girl," he said, in a half-sung sigh that had nothing to do with her brown eyes but was taken up just the same by the vast sunlit reaches of the land behind him and on all sides of him, so much land that Connie had never seen before and did not recognize except to know that she was going to it.

Toni Cade Bambara

1939 –

In an interview, Toni Cade Bambara remarked that she preferred "the short story genre because it's quick, it makes a modest appeal for your attention, it can creep up on your blind side"; and, she added, "the short story deals with economy, gets it said, and gets out of the way." Her fiction is concerned with blacks—more specifically with the black woman, "with the caring that lies beneath the antagonisms between black men and black women."[1]

Bambara was born in New York City in 1939 and was reared there and in nearby New Jersey. She received her B. A. degree from Queens College in 1959, attended the University of Florence, Italy (Commedia dell'Arte) in 1961, studied at the Ecole de Mime Etienne Decroux in Paris during the same year and in New York in 1963. She received her M. A. degree from the City University of New York in 1964 and carried on further postgraduate study in linguistics at New York University and at the New School for Social Research. She has also studied dance, drama, and film.

Thus far Bambara's career has been as varied as her educational training. From 1959 to 1961 she was a social investigator for the New York Department of Welfare; the next year she worked at the Venice Ministry of Museums in Italy and as a free-lance writer; then she served as the director of recreation in the psychiatry department of the New York Metropolitan Hospital, 1962–64; as the program director of the New York Colony House Community Center, 1964–65; as an

[1]"Commitment: Toni Cade Bambara Speaks," *Sturdy Black Bridges: Visions of Black Women in Literature,* ed. by Roseann A. Bell, Bettye J. Parker, and Beverly Guy-Sheftall (Garden City: Doubleday, 1979), pp. 241–242.

English instructor in the SEEK program of City College, New York, 1965–69; in the New Careers Program of Newark, New Jersey, 1969; as director of the preschool summer program at Livingston College, Rutgers University, New Brunswick, New Jersey, 1969; and as Assistant Professor of English there from 1969 to 1974. She has also taught at Stephens College, Spelman College, and Atlanta University.

Besides her two volumes of short stories—*Gorilla, My Love and Other Stories* (1972) and *The Sea Birds Are Still Alive* (1977)—Bambara has edited *Tales and Stories for Black Folks* (1971), *The Black Woman* (1970), and written poetry and educational television scripts. Her two novels are *The Salt Eaters* (1980) and *If Blessing Comes* (1987).

The theme of initiation or rites of passage of the adolescent boy into young manhood has often been treated in the short story; but the initiation of the young girl—which Bambara says can be "mysterious and frightening"—has been treated less frequently and rarely with the graphic power of "A Girl's Story." Interested readers may find fuller comments on this story in the interview mentioned in the footnotes.

A Girl's Story

She was afraid to look at herself just yet. By the time I count to twenty, she decided, if the bleeding hasn't stopped . . . she went blank. She hoisted her hips higher toward the wall. Already her footprints were visible. Sweat prints on the wall, though she was shivering. She swung her feet away from the map she'd made with Dada Bibi, the map of Africa done in clay and acrylics. The bright colors of Mozambique distracted her for a moment. She pictured herself in one of the wraps Dada Bibi had made for them to dance in. Pictured herself in Africa talking another language in that warm rich way Dada Bibi and the brother who tutored the little kids did. Peaceful, friendly, sharing.

Rae Ann swept through her head again for other possible remedies to her situation. For a nosebleed, you put your head way back and stuffed tissue up your nostrils. Once she'd seen her brother Horace plaster his whole set of keys on the back of the neck. The time he had the fight with Joe Lee and his nose bled. Well, she'd tried ice cubes on the neck, on the stomach, on the thighs. Had stuffed herself with tissue. Had put her hips atop a pile of sofa cushions. And still she was bleeding. And what was she going to do about M'Dear's towels? No one would miss the panties and skirt she'd bundled up in the bottom of the garbage. But she couldn't just disappear a towel, certainly not two. M'Dear always counted up the stacks of laundry before the Saturday put-away.

Rae Ann thought about Dada Bibi over at the Center. If the shiny-faced woman were here now with her, it wouldn't be so bad. She'd know exactly what to do. She would sit in the chair and examine Rae Ann's schoolbooks. Would talk calmly. Would help her. Would tell her there was nothing to worry about, that she was a good girl and was not being punished. Would give an explanation and make things right. But between the house and the Center she could bleed to death.

Between her bed and the toilet she'd already left many a trail. Had already ragged the green sponge a piece, scrubbing up after herself. If Horace came home, she could maybe ask him to run over to the Center. Cept he'd want to know what for. Besides, he didn't go round the Center any more since they jumped on his case so bad about joining the army. He didn't want to hear no more shit about the Vietnamese were his brothers and sisters, were fighting the same enemy as Black folks and was he crazy, stupid or what. And he surely wouldn't want to have to walk all the long way back alone with Dada Bibi in her long skirt and turban, trying to make conversation and getting all tongue-tied sliding around the cussin he always did, and everybody checking them out walking as they were toward his house and all. But maybe if she told him it was an emergency and cried hard, he wouldn't ask her nothing, would just go.

Yesterday Dada Bibi had hugged her hello and didn't even fuss where you been little sister and why ain't you been coming round, don't you want to know about your heritage, ain't you got no pride? Dada Bibi never said none of them things ever. She just hugged you and helped you do whatever it was you thought you came to do at the Center. Rae Ann had come to cut a dress for graduation. She'd be going to intermediate in the fall, and that was a big thing. And maybe she had come to hear about the African queens. Yesterday as they sewed, Dada Bibi told them about some African queen in the old days who kept putting off marriage cause she had to be a soldier and get the Europeans out the land and stop the slaving.

She liked the part where Dada Bibi would have the dude come over to propose umpteen times. Rae Ann could just see him knocking real polite on the screen door and everything. Not like Horace do, or like Pee Wee neither, the boy she was halfway liking but really couldn't say she respected any. They just stood on the corner and hollered for their women, who had better show up quick or later for their ass.

Dada Bibi would have the dude say, "Well, darling, another harvest has past and I now have twenty acres to work and have started building on the new house and the cattle have multiplied. When can we marry?" And then Dada Bibi would have the sister say, "My husband-to-be, there are enemies in the land, crushing our people, our traditions underfoot. We must raise an army and throw them out." And then the dude would go sell a cow or something and help organize the folks on the block to get guns and all. And the sister would get the blacksmith to make her this bad armor stuff. Course Gretchen got to interrupt the story to say the sister chumping the dude, taking his money to have her some boss jewelry made and what a fool he was. But the girls tell her to hush so they can hear the rest. Dada Bibi maintaining it's important to deal with how Gretchen seeing things go down. But no one really wants to give Gretchen's view a play.

Anyway, after many knocks on the screen door and raising of armies and battles, the two of them are old-timers. Then the sister finally says, "My husband-to-be, there is peace in the land now. The children are learning, the folks are working, the elders are happy, our people prosper. Let us get married on the new moon." Gretchen got to spoil it all saying what old folks like that need to get married for, too old to get down anyway. And Dada Bibi try to get the girls to talk that over. But they just tell Gretchen to shut her big mouth and stop hogging all the straight pins. Rae Ann liked to retell the stories to the kids on the block. She always included Gretchen's remarks and everybody's response, since they seemed, in her mind, so much a part of the story.

Rae Ann's legs were tiring. Her left foot was stinging, going to sleep. Her back hurt. And her throat was sore with tension. She looked up at the map and wondered if Dada Bibi had seen the whole trouble coming. When Rae Ann had stayed behind to clean up the sewing scraps, the woman had asked her if there way anything she wanted to talk about now she was getting to be such a young woman. And Rae Ann had hugged her arms across her chest and said, "No, ma'am," cause she figured she might have to hear one of them oneway talks like M'Dear do about not letting boys feel on your tits. But when she got ready to leave, Dada Bibi hugged her like she always did, even to the girls who squirmed out of her reach and would rather not even wave hello and goodbye, just come in and split at their leisure.

"My sister," she had said into her ear, gently releasing her with none of the embarrassed shove her relatives seemed to always punctuate their embraces with. "You're becoming a woman and that's no private thing. It concerns us all who love you. Let's talk sometimes?"

Rae Ann liked the way she always made it a question. Not like the teachers, who just flat-out told you you were going to talk, or rather they were going to talk at you. And not like M'Dear or Aunt Candy, who always just jumped right in talking without even a let's this or could we that.

Maybe Dada Bibi had seen something in her face, in her eyes. Or maybe there had been a telltale spot on the back of her jeans as early as yesterday. Rae Ann twisted her head around toward the pile of clothes on the back of her chair. Upside down her jeans were spotless. Well, then, she reasoned methodically, how did Dada Bibi know? But then who said she had known anything? "That ole plain-face bitch don't know nuthin" was Horace's word to the wise. But just the same, he hung around the bus stop on Tuesday nights, acting blasé like he didn't know Dada Bibi had Tuesday night classes at the college. Not that anybody would speak on this. Joe Lee had cracked and had his ass whipped for his trouble.

Rae Ann was smelling herself and not liking it. She'd already counted three sets of twenties, which meant it was time to move. She rejected the notion of a bath. The last bath had only made it worse. Fore she could even get one foot good out the water, red spots were sliding off the side of the tub onto the tile. She exhaled deeply and tried to make a list in her head. New tissue, tight pants to hold it all in place, the last of the ice tray still in the sink on her twat. She closed her eyes and moaned. Her list was all out of order. She tried again. Check floors and tub. Put towels in bottom of garbage. Put garbage out. Scrape carrots and make salad. Secrete a roll of tissue in her closet for later. Get to the Center. She opened her eyes. What would she say?

Rae Ann pulled her legs down and swung off the bed. She checked to see that the newspaper was still in place before drawing the covers up. She stood and parted the flaps of her bathrobe. Last time she had moved too quickly and the oozing had started, a blob of syrupy brown slipping down the inside of her leg and she afraid to touch it, to stop it, just stood there like a simpleton till it reached her ankle, and then she fled into the bathroom too late. She was looking into the toilet as the water swirled away the first wad of tissue. What if the toilet stuffed up, backed up on the next flush? She could imagine M'Dear bellowing the roof down as the river of red overran the rim and spilled over onto the tiles, flooding the bathroom, splashing past the threshold and onto the hall linoleum.

"Get out the bathroom, willya damn it!"

She jumped and banged an elbow on the sink. She hadn't heard Horace come into the house. He usually announced his arrivals by singing, stamping, and doing a bump-de-bump against the furniture. Had thought she was all alone with her terror. Hadn't even locked the door and here she was with her pants down and the last clump of tissue shredding, sticky red.

"Come on now. I gotta shower fore M'Dear get home."

She was trapped. If she unhooked the roll of toilet paper to take into her room, he'd see that. And M'Dear would be in any minute and would come into her room to set her bags down and get her slippers. If she hid in the closet and squatted down behind the bundles of mothballed blankets . . .

"Hey," Horace was bamming on the door. "You okay?"

Something in her brother's voice startled her. Before she could stop herself she was brimming over and shivering hard.

"Rae Ann?" he called through the door. "Rachel?"

"Don't come in!" she screamed. "Don't come in."

The door knob was being held in position, she could see that. It had stopped turning. And it seemed to her that he was holding his breath on his side of the door just like she was holding hers on hers.

"Hey," he whispered, "you okay?" When she didn't answer, he let go of the knob. She watched it move back into place and then heard him walk away. She sat there hugging herself, trying to ease the chattering of her teeth. She leaned over to yank her washcloth off the hook. And then the smell gripped her. That smell was in everything. In her bed, her clothes, her breath. The smell of death. A dry, rank graveyard smell. The smell of her mother's sickroom years ago, so long ago all the memory that had survived was the smell of the off-yellow color from the lamp, a color she'd never ever seen again anywhere. A brown stain was smack in the middle of the washcloth. She flung it into the basin and ran the water.

"She in there crying."

Rae Ann's heart stopped. M'Dear was in the kitchen. Just behind the medicine cabinet, just behind the wall, they were talking about her. She jumped up and ran to the door.

"Don't be locking that door," the voice boomed through the wall. "We hear you in there."

"And we know what you been doin too," her brother's voice rang out. She wondered what happened to that something that was in his voice just minutes ago. Where had that brother gone to so quick? Maybe cause he was scared he sounded so nice. That time when Furman and his gang were after Pee Wee he had sounded like that. Up on the roof, scrunched between the pigeon coop and the chimney, Pee Wee revealed a voice Rae Ann had never known he had. Told her she was a nice girl and shouldn't mess around with guys like him, would have to be careful. Not at all the voice bragging on the handball court, Pee Wee mounting his motorbike, Pee Wee in the schoolyard smoking. Why did it take scarifying to bring out the voice?

"Horace just scared I may die in here and he won't be able to take his damn shower," she mumbled into the washcloth, gagging on the smell. She was too afraid to think anything else.

"You best get in here, Madame." The voice came at her through the mirror. Madame. She was freezing again. Madame never meant anything good. Madame, you best cut a switch. Madame, there's a letter here from school. Madame, where's the receipt from the telephone bill. Madame, do you think you too grown to mind.

Rae Ann swished around some mouthwash and rewrapped her bathrobe tight. She knew she was waddling, the minute she saw the way they looked at her, but she couldn't get herself together. Horace turned back to a plate in the icebox he was eating from. M'Dear was leaning up against the sink, her hat still on her head, the shopping bags leaning against her legs, her shoes not even unlaced.

"You had somebody in here?"

"No, ma'am."

"Ask her how come she in her bathrobe."

"You hush," the old woman warned, and Horace disappeared behind the icebox door.

"What you been doin?"

"Nothin."

"Don't tell me nothin when I'm trying to find out somethin. Miz Gladys run all the way up to the bus stop to tell me she seen you comin home from school way before three o'clock."

Rae Ann heard the pause, felt the pause on top of her head, weighing it down into her shoulders. She shrugged. She didn't know how to fill it and lift it.

"You play hookey from school today? Went somewhere with somebody?"

"No, ma'am."

M'Dear breathing in and out, the huffin-puffin getting wheezy. It was clear Rae Ann had better say something, cause there wouldn't be too many more questions, just a heavier pausing swelling, swelling to crush her.

"You cold or somethin?" A question that came out finally and lifted her from her knees. She didn't know why she was so grateful to hear it. She hadn't expected it. Was nodding yes while her mouth said no and smiling and fixing to cry all at the same time.

"Tears don't tell me a damn thing, Rachel Ann."

"Tears say a whole lot to me," Horace was telling the toaster, singing it lest the woman get on him again for butting in.

"I sure wish you'd go somewhere," Rae Ann said over her shoulder. It might be easier to talk with just her grandmother. Though she was still a blank as to what she could possibly say to take the hardness out of her grandmother's face. M'Dear's eyes shot from the boy to the girl to the boy then back again, her head swiveling, her eyes flashing, like she was on the trail of something and there was danger sure for somebody.

"M'Dear, I'm bleeding," she heard herself say, huddling smaller into her bathrobe, feeling an oozing on the inside of her leg.

The old woman's face looked red-hot and strangled, and for a minute the girl thought she was going to be slapped.

"Whatcha been doin?" she hissed through clenched teeth. Rae Ann backed up as a whole bunch of questions and accusations tumbled out of the woman's mouth ramming into her. "You been to the barbershop, haven't you? Let that filthy man go up inside you with a clothes hanger. You going to be your mama all over again. Why didn't you come to me? Who's the boy? Tell me his name quick. And you better not lie."

M'Dear had snatched up her pocketbook, not waiting on an answer in the meantime, and was heading out the door, waving Horace to come on. He burned his fingers pulling out the toast, eager for the adventure.

"I didn't do anything," Rae Ann screamed, racing to the door before it closed against the back of her brother. "I didn't do anything, I swear to God," her throat raspy, failing her, the words barely pushed out and audible.

"Oooooh," she heard echoing in the tiled hallway, the word hollow and cool, bouncing off the walls as the old woman shoved past the boy back into the kitchen. "Oh, my goodness," she said through her hands. And then Rae Ann felt the hands on her shoulders moist from the mouth coming right through the terry cloth. The hands giving slight pull, pat, tug but not a clear embrace. "Oh, Rachel Ann," the woman whispered, steering her gently down the hall. "Girl, why didn't you say so?" she said, helping her into bed.

Rae Ann bent her knees and eased herself down onto the newspapers. She watched the woman back out of the room, her hands smoothing her waistband, as though she were leaving the dishes to make a call or leaning up from the dough on the breadboard to shout across the air shaft to Miz Gladys. Smoothing the bulk that bunched up over the waistband, nervous.

"Be right back, sugar," still backing out the room. And Rae Ann glad she'd moved her sneakers out the doorway. That'd be all she needed, M'Dear falling over some sneakers.

"Hush your ugly mouth, cause you don't know what you talkin about," she heard in the kitchen just before the front door slammed. Was she going to get a doctor? Maybe she'd gone for Dada Bibi? That wasn't likely. I ain't studyin them folks over there, M'Dear and Miz Gladys like to say, sucking their teeth at the letters, flyers, posters, numerous papers that came into the block, the building, the house, explaining what the Center was about.

"I ain't nobody's African," Miz Gladys had said. "One hundred percent American and proud of it." And M'Dear had jerked her head in agreement, trashing the latest flyer Rae Ann had slipped onto the table.

Rae Ann had tried to push all they said up against other things in her head. Being American and being proud and they weren't the same in her head. When Dada Bibi talked about Harriet Tubman and them, she felt proud. She felt it in her neck and in her spine. When the brother who ran the program for the little kids talked about powerful white Americans robbing Africa and bombing Vietnam and doing ugly all over the world, causing hard times for Black folks and other colored people, she was glad not to be American. And when she watched films about Africans fighting white folks so that hospitals and schools could be built for the kids, and the books about Fanny Lew somebody and Malcolm fighting for freedom, and the posters about the kids, kids littler than her even, studying and growing vegetables and all and the print saying how even kids were freedom fighters—she was proud not to be American. What she heard in school she pushed up against what was in her head. Then she started looking, just looking in the teacher's bloodshot eyes, looking at M'Dear's fat, looking at Dada Bibi's shiny skin, to decide just how she was going to arrange things in her head. It was simpler to watch than to listen.

"Ma Dear gone for the ambulance?" Horace in the doorway grinning, biting at the toast. "Old Freeny botch up the job? Next time I can take you to this nurse who—"

"Go to hell, nigger."

"Okay, okay," he said, closing his eyes and raising his hands like he wouldn't dream of pressing the magic number on nobody, would gladly take his pot of gold elsewhere. "But when that dead baby drops down and rips you open, don't yell for me to save ya. You'll bleed to death first."

Her sneaker missed his head by a fraction of an inch. And she sang real loud the Guinea-Bissau marching song the brother at the Center had taught her, to drown out his laughing. Her song ended as the door slammed. She eased into the mattress, not realizing she'd been tensed up and inches off the newspaper. Her body was sore with the clutching. She wanted to sleep, her eyes dry and stinging. She'd been afraid that if she blinked too long, she'd never open them again in life.

"To die for the people." Somebody in one of the films had said that. It had seemed okay to her at first. She tried to picture Pee Wee willing to die for the people. But all the pictures that came into her head about Pee Wee dying were mostly about Pee Wee and not the people. She tried to picture Horace standing up against the cops in the name of the kids, protecting Pee Wee maybe, or the other boys the pigs liked to beat up on.

But it didn't exactly fit. She dreamed up another dude altogether. He looked a little like the brother in the film, only he was different cause he was hers. And he was blowing up police stations and running through the alleyways back of the projects, and she hiding him in her closet, sneaking him food from the kitchen. Was helping him load his guns to shoot the big businessmen with. And she was seeing him dragging through the streets, one leg shot off. And the President's special cops bending in the street to squeeze off the final bullet in his back. And she'd be holding his head in her lap, the blood trickling out of the side of his mouth, just like in the movies. But the pictures were no fun after a while.

So when Dada Bibi was rewinding, just looking at them, one at a time, but not pressing any discussion, Rae Ann'd said, "I want to live for the people." And Gretchen had said, "Right on." Wasn't nothin hip about dying. Then they started talking about what they could do with their lives to help Black people, to free Black people. And Gretchen said she didn't know if she'd feel like going to school long enough to teach, and she knew for sure she didn't like going back to the country so she couldn't see herself feeding nobody directly.

"Shit. I'm just here and ain't nobody gonna run no lame shit on me. Specially them teachers up at the school. Shit. That's the best I can do for the people, give them teachers hell. Shit," she added again, just to make clear no one had better ask her anything else about what she was prepared to do for her people.

"That's cool," said Dada Bibi, surprising them all. "Giving the teachers some static means you gotta hit them books, eat well, get plenty rest to keep the mind alert. Can't hit them with no lame shit, right?" She nodding to Gretchen.

"That's right," Gretchen said, her ass off her shoulders and her whole self trapped.

Rae Ann sniffled back a tear. She wasn't convinced she was really dying, but there was something righteous in the pain that came with thinking it. Something was wrong. She was being punished, that she knew. But she probably wasn't going to really die. She looked hard at the posters by the window, the wood carving she'd make for Kwanza on her desk, the map on the wall, the picture of Jesus on the closet she shared with her grandmother. She wasn't sure just who to make the promise to. So she simply addressed it to them all. If I can get through this time, she promised, I'm going to do something good. It left her dissatisfied, cold. To die for the people left her scared, mad, it wasn't fair. To live for the people left her confused, faintly inadequate. Was she up to it? And what?

"Here you go," M'Dear was saying, pitching the bag onto her bed. "Dinner be on in a minute."

What's wrong with me, she thought. M'Dear fraid to come in the room and get her slippers, fraid to come near me. What have I done? She up-ended the bag and set everything out neatly. A plan. She had do think methodically and stop all this crying and confusion. I will read everything two times. Then I'll know what to do. She allowed herself a moist blink. She would find out what she had done and take her whipping. Then everything would be like before. M'Dear would come into the room again and set awhile talking while she changed her shoes. Dada Bibi would hug her again. But then Dada Bibi would hug her no matter what. She even hugged the dirty kids from Mason Street. And drank behind them too without even rinsing the cup. Either Dada Bibi had a powerful health to combat germs, she thought, ripping open the packages, or the woman was crazy.

SECTION FIVE

Contemporary Flowering
1975 –

A recent literary critic has said that the "dying literary form" of the short story experienced a significant "reviving" in the United States in the 1970s and 1980s. Although in fact the form was never really moribund, its current reinvigoration is unquestionable. If not a full-blown "Renaissance" or "Golden Age," as is frequently asserted, the present period, claimed *Newsweek,* is at least a new "Silver Age" for short stories in America.

Today an unprecedented number of short story collections by an extraordinary number of talented writers are appearing from both large and small commercial publishers and university presses. Publication of individual stories in periodicals remains the usual antecedent if not prerequisite for "collected" book publication, but historic changes have occurred in magazine or journal outlets for short fiction. Many new, small-circulation periodicals are now based at colleges and universities. Flourishing creative writing programs help to augment the large number of short fiction writers presently at work across the nation. At the same time, certain mainstream influences have continued to aid the proliferation of short fiction: for instance, certain national commercial magazines whose role, if anything, has grown more dominant; the expanding corps of women writers; and the thrust of regional influences, particularly in the South. Finally, although there are new, impelling cultural motives, the basic human reasons for attempting literary art in the short story form remain constant.

Noting an increase in the numbers of writers and published collections while confronting the seemingly contradictory conclusion that the audience of the American short story is constricting, the historian of today's literary scene has to deal all along with the most surprising constant of all: in its variety and artistic allure the contemporary American short story is dazzling. If the death of the form were ever close, at present it seems far, far away.

Big and Little Magazines

In the introductions to both the 1983 and 1984 annual volumes of *Prize Stories: The O. Henry Awards,* William Abrahams called attention to the difference between earlier and more recent publication outlets for the twentieth-century American short story. Predominant among the places of publication for the prize short stories of 1984, he says, are the "little magazines" and literary quarterlies "that address themselves to a small audience of discriminating readers whose taste is away from gossip . . . and the short read . . . and who accepts without protest writing that is intelligent, free of stereotype, and even at times difficult."[1] Little magazines, which were once where new young writers got their start, are now serving "established writers, in the full mastery of their art" just as the populist large-circulation magazines regularly used to do.

This state of affairs is partly the result of the sheer number of writers, as both Abrahams and John Updike have recognized, but the many new little magazines do not offer the same financial rewards that successful writers earned in the past. Since the mid-thirties, Updike noted, there has been a revolutionary reduction in the number of general magazines that publish fiction: "The field of weekly national magazines that print fiction" has shrunk to precisely one. "Twelve at most" is the number of magazines that now pay well—four figures—for short fiction; and of these twelve, Updike says, only four are open to "artistic experimentation."[2] Only two of these four are famous "old-line" periodicals, the *Atlantic* and *The New Yorker,* and both appeal to highbrow, sophisticated readers. (The other two, according to Updike, are *Esquire* and *Playboy.)*

Has television become the medium of story for the masses? One thing is clear: American magazines are no longer the same kinds of magazines nor the same means of information and entertainment they once were for a broad general audience, an audience that is not reading what it once did, nor as much as it once did. Yet, the short story is thriving. And because of that thriving, somewhat ironically, there are signs that soon there may be yet another change, a turn back again to at least one kind of periodical of the past. A telling test will be *Story* magazine (1931–1967), whose attempted resurrection began in the late 1980s.

[1]"Introduction," xi.
[2]"Introduction," *The Year's Best American Short Stories 1985* (London: Severn House, 1985), xiv.

New Academic Influences

Comparing the lists of magazines publishing potentially prize-winning American stories in 1943 and 1983 reveals a numerical increase as well as exotic new journal names. Another striking difference is the addresses of these periodicals. Time after time, from Oregon to Connecticut, from Minnesota to Alabama, the address in the later list is that of a university. Short-story publication appears to have become one of the missions of American higher education: during the last fifteen years there has been a virtual explosion in "creative writing" programs around the country. Not just at national universities with long histories and glorious reputations in such endeavors—like Stanford and Iowa—or with shorter histories and growing reputations—Johns Hopkins and Arkansas—but at nearly every regional or sub-regional university or college today there seem to be writers-in-residence and creative writing degrees. In the course of a single quarter or semester, the short story is the form of fiction that can be most attentively produced for the scrutiny of classmates and teacher.

Thus, a heavy academic flavor has become more and more noticeable in the short-story "renaissance" of the 1970s and 1980s. In its pervasiveness, this "academicization" has been decried by some critics as a pernicious new species of elitism that is drying up and debilitating the traditional, vigorous life of the short story. Like other Americans, more and more of our short story writers are becoming professionally trained holders of college degrees; hence the result of an increasing number of professional writers along with an increasingly career-only educated public may well be more stories for a smaller general audience. This need not, however, bring about progressive diminishing of the art of fiction. In fact, the emotional power of these contemporary stories on the one hand and, on the other, the dissatisfaction that a growing number of Americans are likely to experience in excessively specialized, dehumanizing jobs hold promise of a literary impact unrivalled in the depth of its individual penetration and the extent of its public breadth.

Developing Forms and Expanding Recognition

As carryovers, or carryons, from earlier twentieth-century literary expression in the United States, three groups of short fiction artists in particular have attained noticeably increased prominence and prestige on the contemporary scene: black writers, Southern writers, and women writers. Though these groups are obviously not mutually exclusive, each emerged historically as a result of changing social and political mores, and the leading members of each group served as role models for younger writers. Thus, as distinctive, talented Southern writers emerged, and as their emphases and styles altered without diminishment of their "Southernness" or of their art, a second and now a third "generation" of Southern masters of fiction have gained favorable recognition. Just as Richard Wright, Zora Neale Hurston, Eudora Welty, and Katherine Anne Porter provide supreme first-generation illustration of the central roles of black and women writers in the achievements of the Southern short story, so do Flannery O'Connor and Ernest J. Gaines for the second generation, and Alice Walker, James Alan McPherson, Arthenia J. Bates Millican, Ellen Gilchrist, and Bobbie Ann Mason for the third.

The contemporary period is rich from the perspective of any of these classifications of writers—regional, ethnic, or gender-based. At this time, however, most striking is the output of women writers, whose significant present achievement seems to promise future imaginative treasure of great proportion. Whichever region of the country they come from or from whatever collective past they draw their inspiration, a universally important human consciousness is presently being explored in the short story by such artists as Mary Hood, Mary Ward Brown, Mary Robison, Ann Beattie, Joy Williams, Jayne Anne Phillips, Louise Erdrich, and Nancy Huddleston Packer. The list could, and will, go on.

In this anthology it might well be assumed that the authors of "Cheers," "Kindred Spirits," and "Fleur" (Jayne Anne Phillips, Alice Walker, and Louise Erdrich respectively) are women, so finely is female experience directly rendered in these stories. This kind of deep understanding is present also in Bobbie Ann Mason's "Shiloh," but it is an understanding that extends to Leroy as well as to Norma Jean Moffitt. And the unnamed title-character/protagonist of Joy Williams's "The Yard Boy," plumbed passionately in her dispassionate style, is clearly not female. A young girl is the protagonist of "Doe Season," a story that in its moving essence is a gender piece; the surprise that its creator is not a woman is tribute to the expansive, insightful sympathy of David Michael Kaplan. This story, however, is also testimony to the value of long ignored aspects of human experience that women writers had to struggle to open up for an American reading public that was, ironically, largely female.

An indirect effect of increased critical attention to the work of black and female writers in America has been new recognition of what could be called non-highbrow/non-literary-establishment kinds of writing. The general labels most frequently applied to such writing include "popular literature," "formula fiction," and "genre fiction." Although different schemes of sub-division and sub-categorization are possible, the genres or types most commonly seen as comprising this general type are the western, the thriller (including the detective story and spy fiction), the romance (may include historical or gothic), horror fiction, fantasy fiction, and science fiction. Of these, none has flourished more impressively in twentieth-century America than science fiction has.

Once it became the subject of scholarly interest and inquiry, science fiction, like the other types, could be shown to have an impressive literary genealogy. Modern science fiction, which had its birth in cheaply-produced, specialized all-fiction magazines, dates from the mid-1920s in the United States. In the following twenty years, there developed a hard-core group of "sci-fi fans," a close and essentially closed community of writers, editors, and readers. However, in 1946, with the appearance of two major anthologies, *Adventures in Time and Space* and *The Best of Science Fiction,* by two major national publishers, Crown and Random House, science fiction can be said to have "suddenly emerged from the pulp-magazine underground into the brilliant light of publishing respectability."[3] During the 1950s, the genre enjoyed an unprecedented public popularity, which led in the next decade to a new kind of writer and a new kind of literary product. "New Wave" writers, according to one historian of science fiction, began during this time to make greater use of mythology, to turn to new internal rather than external techniques.[4] Although its "commercial style," which had historically eschewed plot intricacy, subtle characterization, and sophisticated style, continued in evidence, and even though it remained more a literature of ideas than of aesthetics, science fiction had come to be viewed by the 1970s, by the popular press at least, "as a legitimate, if somewhat exotic, genre of literature, capable of contributing useful insights into the human condition in a quickly changing world."[5]

If in the 1970s and 1980s the emphasis in science fiction has continued to be on *what* a work means, increased attention has been given also to *how* it means. More aesthetic and artistically traditional principles came into play for both writer and critic of the genre, and more and more writers could play both sides of the net between science fiction and so-called mainstream literature. Kurt Vonnegut, Jr. and Ursula K. LeGuin are two such players. Isaac Asimov, Ray Bradbury, Arthur C. Clarke, Harlan Ellison, Philip K. Dick, and LeGuin are now among the most prominent science fiction writers in the United States—with, for example, Bradbury's "There Will Come Soft Rains," Clarke's "The Star," Ellison's " 'Repent, Harlequin!' Said the Ticktockman," and LeGuin's "The Ones Who Walk Away from Omelas" and "Nine Lives" being regarded as classic short stories of this kind. Classic science fiction literature has been defined as "a branch of fantasy" that utilizes "an

[3]"Introduction," *The Arbor House Treasury of Science Fiction* (New York: Arbor House, 1980), x.
[4]Frederick Andrew Lerner, *Modern Science Fiction and the American Literary Community* (Methuen, N.J.: Scarecrow, 1985), 61.
[5]Lerner, 77.

atmosphere of scientific credibility for its imaginative speculations in physical science, space, time, social science and philosophy."[6] These stories and numerous others not only do this sort of thing extremely well but in so doing call our admiring attention to how it has been done. Although some members of the sci-fi clan may regard the process as a "descent into respectability,"[7] certainly science fiction stories have moved dramatically in the last sixty years from contempt and condescension to toleration and respect from the traditional literary establishment.

Along with science fiction, the "short short" story is another old fictional type recently raised to prominence in the United States. Or is the contemporary short short, in artistic terms, a new literary genre? The abbreviated tale, the anecdote, the fable, the parable, the joke are its clear ancestors, but as yet there is neither a common definition nor even a name for this new literary phenomenon. "Sudden fiction" it has been called, as well as "quick fiction," "mini-," "micro-," or "flash fiction," "skinny fiction," "auto-rich fiction," the "four-minute story," and the "short short story." No established word limits exist to designate its briefness: whatever "short" may mean in defining a short story, then this creation is short*er* than that characteristic length.

In 1948, William March had great fun in producing, and titling, the "shortest story ever written." The full text of "History of the Credulous Widow, Who Met an Admiring Stranger in a Cocktail Lounge, and Who After Turning her Liquid Assets Over to Him, Was Never Seen Again by Her Friends" was not much longer than its title:

On Monday she was in his thoughts.
On Tuesday she was in his automobile.
On Wednesday she was in his hotel room.
On Thursday she was in his arms.
On Friday she was in his big wardrobe trunk,
checked through to Los Angeles.

In the 1960s, however, such writers as Russel Edson and Enrique Anderson Imbert began quite seriously to experiment formally with the very short story. By the early 1980s, with production of the type by other contemporary writers, which both proceeded from and compelled historical interest in earlier producers of short fiction, anthologies of short shorts began to appear—notably, Jack David and Jon Redfern's *Short Short Stories* (1981) and Irving and Ilana Weiner Howe's *Short Shorts: An Anthology of the Shortest Stories* (1982). That the stories were tighter, uniformly shorter in Robert Shapard and James Thomas's *Sudden Fic-*

[6]Quoted in Dick Allen, "Introduction," *Science Fiction: The Future,* 2nd ed. (New York: Harcourt Brace Jovanovich, 1983), 1.
[7]Lerner, 151.

tion: American Short Short Stories (1986) seems to reflect an advancing definition and refinement of the form. Such a process continues in the *North American Review*'s regular publication of the "four-minute story" and the World's Best Short Short Story Contest sponsored annually at Florida State University, a contest that places a strict 250-word limit on submissions and draws thousands of entries from writers all over the world.

Michael Martone and Jayne Anne Phillips are only two of the many noteworthy contemporary American fiction writers who have worked impressively in this demanding form. Martone in particular emphasizes shortness and concentration in virtually all of his fiction, so that his comparatively *very* short stories are especially impressive. "The short short has to be more perfect than any other piece of fiction," says Janet Burroway from the perspective of the writer, "because, as with a poem, you're trying to make every word matter."[8] For the reader of a short short, because the focus is so small and the situation so foreshortened and circumscribed, the result may be a destructive irresistible feeling that one needs to know more, to have a larger context. But it may also be a depth and intensity of penetration into human life that is a luminous difference in kind, and not just degree, from "long" short fiction.

New Categories, New Achievements

If the style necessary to produce the short short story can be described as "minimalist," the resultant art is better described as "miniaturist." "Minimalistic," however, has become a key descriptive term and "minimalism" the generally accepted label for a kind of short story writing that has become increasingly prominent since the early 1970s. To the literary historian, this "movement" appears to follow the pattern of the inevitable pendulum swing away from a kind of writing that had just previously dominated. In this case, that previous style was writing that turned in upon the self, often the writer as self, and that was "maximalist" in its outpourings of words and images. Now, the increasing negative reactions to the minimalists as the decade of the 1990s begins may or may not indicate the fading of this new distinctive style, or approach, or literary product. But it does clearly indicate that in a relatively short time, minimalism came to dominate the American short story scene.

A recent critic of the minimalists asserts that these writers see themselves as "trenchant impassive observers" of the world's "universal

[8]Quoted in Steve Watkins, "A Man Was Born, He Died, The End," *Florida State University Bulletin "Research in Review"* 81 (Spring 1987): 12.

offensiveness"; that they see it as their task to "document the pathos and idiocy of those unintelligent enough not to have been offended, or chronicle the lives of the offended and unenlightened, who seem to live mainly in diners and trailers"; that they have "taken their stylistic cue from the haiku" and "worship spare strokes."[9] Another nonadmirer describes in hopeful past tense what he calls the rules of current literary fashion: "the characters were flat, the prose dry and passionless, the plots jejeune; the stories were occupied with surfaces, crowded with banal domestic detail."[10]

In less judgmental terms, minimalism is the label literary history has given to a clear "movement from something resembling an 'experimental', 'disruptive', or 'self-reflexive' Postmodernism to something different from that." More specifically and descriptively the term is often applied to short stories "loosely characterized by equanimity of surface, 'ordinary' subjects, recalcitrant narrators and deadpan narratives, slightness of story, and characters who don't think out loud."[11] Minimalism, simply put, is a resurgence of historical literary realism, but, as Kim A. Herzingen has noted, with a significant difference: "Where the traditional 'realists' had a world and used a complex of ideas and emotions—done up in language—to describe it, the 'minimalists' have a complex of ideas and emotions—done up in language—which they use the world to describe."[12]

Whether they themselves would agree or not, most of the best-known contemporary short story writers in the country have been put, by someone, into the minimalist camp: Raymond Carver, Ann Beattie, Mary Robison, Alice Adams, Bobbie Ann Mason, Andre Dubus, Richard Ford, Tobias Wolff, Elizabeth Tallent, David Leavitt, Jayne Anne Phillips. Heading every list, surely, is Raymond Carver. And surely Carver's late brilliant short story, "Errand," about the death of Anton Chekhov, testifies to a key Carver (and minimalist) influence while evidencing the literary artistry of the master of contemporary "minimalism."

A recognition of only one, even if the predominant, categorical achievement falls far short of describing the full contemporary activity and accomplishment of the American short story. The genre, says Gordon Weaver, remains dynamic, "as vital and viable a form of literary expression as it has ever been."[13]

[9]Mark Helprin, "Introduction: The Canon Under Siege," *The Best American Short Stories 1988* (Boston: Houghton Mifflin, 1988), xx.
[10]Bruce Bawer, *Diminishing Fictions* (St. Paul: Graywolf Press, 1988), 298.
[11]Kim Herzingen, "Introduction: On the New Fiction," *Mississippi Review,* No. 40/41 (Winter 1985): 7.
[12]Herzingen, 20.
[13]"Introduction," *The American Short Story 1945–1980* (Boston: G. K. Hall, 1983), n. p.

An anthology such as this one makes it easy to show "connectedness," a word that a number of short story writers, including Eudora Welty, have used in talking about the characters and human themes of their work. It is instructive, for instance, to pair stories in the first section of this book with those in the last section, a difference now of two hundred years of the American short story. Clearly, a concern with male-female relationships, with all of their attendant consequences, continues: from "The Story of the Captain's Wife . . . ," "The Child of Snow," and "Young Goodman Brown," to "Shiloh," "Kindred Spirits," and "Fleur." Murder, and motive, and mystery occupy us in the stories of Erdrich, Wolff, and O'Brien as they did in those of Poe and Simms. We continue to read about hunts and hunting—so that we may wonder if these are not in some way centrally mythic for America. We continue to be confronted with the supernatural, to be made to wonder about what happened or didn't happen, to have to make judgments about appearance versus reality, to witness and experience the conclusions that individual human beings make in and for their lives.

Whatever groupings or categories scholars may make, whatever approaches critics may take, "in fiction that matters," said Raymond Carver, "the significance of the action inside the story translates to the lives of people outside the story." John Updike once feared that such translation was beginning not to occur, that the short story in America was becoming a narrowly "fine" art and ceasing to be a popular art. But Updike himself can be seen to provide an answer to his fears, to let us all know that the short story can and must be both kinds of art. "Our information about each other remains, in the midst of a sophistication glut, wonderfully faulty," he wrote, "and for this reason we need short stories." "Each," he went on, "is a glimpse into another country: an occasion for surprise, an excuse for wisdom, and an argument for charity."[14] Today America's democratic *and* artistic short story tradition is impressively alive and flourishing.

[14]"Introduction," *The Year's Best American Short Stories 1985*, xxii.

Ursula K. LeGuin

1929 –

Ursula LeGuin was born in Berkeley, California, in 1929. She received a B.A. degree from Radcliffe in 1951 and an M.A. degree from Columbia University in 1952. She has taught creative writing at Mercer University, the University of Idaho, and the University of California at San Diego, among others. Having won a Fulbright Fellowship in 1953, LeGuin became active in TV broadcasting and the writing of science fiction. During the past three decades, she has had more than a dozen novels, novellas, and short story collections, published chiefly in the areas of fantasy and science fiction. Her novel trilogy—*A Wizard of Earthsea* (1968), *The Tombs of Atuan* (1971), and *The Farthest Shore* (1972)—captured several prestigious prizes, including the National Book Award; and her more recent short story collections such as *The Wind's Twelve Quarters* (1975), *Orsinian Tales* (1976), *Interfaces* (1980), and *The Compass Rose* (1982) have been equally well received.

LeGuin's works in fantasy and science fiction are indeed highly regarded, not only among specialists in these popular contemporary genres, but also among serious literary critics generally. Calling attention repeatedly to her sensitivity to language and to her symbols and imagery, for example, J. D. Olander and M. H. Greenberg assert that "while LeGuin's fiction may be filled with wizards, aliens, and clones . . . the vision contained in her novels and stories is, above all, concerned with what is most permanent about the human condition. When one enters the world of her fiction, one encounters a distinctive universe of discourse." "Nine Lives" exhibits many of the qualities that make LeGuin's fiction so popular.

Nine Lives

She was alive inside but dead outside, her face a black and dun net of wrinkles, tumors, cracks. She was bald and blind. The tremors that crossed Libra's face were mere quiverings of corruption. Underneath, in the black corridors, the halls beneath the skin, there were crepitations in darkness, ferments, chemical nightmares that went on for centuries. "O the damned flatulent planet," Pugh murmured as the dome shook and a boil burst a kilometer to the southwest, spraying silver pus across the sunset. The sun had been setting for the last two days. "I'll be glad to see a human face."

"Thanks," said Martin.

"Yours is human to be sure," said Pugh, "but I've seen it so long I can't see it."

Radvid signals cluttered the communicator which Martin was operating, faded, returned as face and voice. The face filled the screen, the nose of an Assyrian king, the eyes of a samurai, skin bronze, eyes the color of iron: young, magnificent. "Is that what human beings look like?" said Pugh with awe. "I'd forgotten."

"Shut up, Owen, we're on."

"Libra Exploratory Mission Base, come in please, this is *Passerine* launch."

"Libra here. Beam fixed. Come on down, launch."

"Expulsion in seven E-seconds. Hold on." The screen blanked and sparkled.

"Do they all look like that? Martin, you and I are uglier men than I thought."

"Shut up, Owen. . . . "

For twenty-two minutes Martin followed the landing craft down by signal and then through the cleared dome they saw it, small star in the blood-colored east, sinking. It came down neat and quiet, Libra's thin atmosphere carrying little sound. Pugh and Martin closed the headpieces of their imsuits, zipped out of the dome airlocks, and ran with soaring strides, Nijinsky and Nureyev, toward the boat. Three equipment modules came floating down at four-minute intervals from each other and hundred-meter intervals east of the boat. "Come on out," Martin said on his suit radio, "we're waiting at the door."

"Come on in, the methane's fine," said Pugh.

The hatch opened. The young man they had seen on the screen came out with one athletic twist and leaped down onto the shaky dust and clinkers of Libra. Martin shook his hand, but Pugh was staring at the hatch, from which another young man emerged with the same neat twist and jump, followed by a young woman who emerged with the same neat twist, ornamented by a wriggle, and the jump. They were all tall, with bronze skin, black hair, high-bridged noses, epicanthic fold, the same face. They all had the same face. The fourth was emerging from the hatch with a neat twist and jump. "Martin bach," said Pugh, "we've got a clone."

"Right," said one of them, "we're a tenclone. John Chow's the name. You're Lieutenant Martin?"

"I'm Owen Pugh."

"Alvaro Guillen Martin," said Martin, formal, bowing slightly. Another girl was out, the same beautiful face; Martin stared at her and his eye rolled like a nervous pony's. Evidently he had never given any thought to cloning and was suffering technological shock. "Steady," Pugh said in the Argentine dialect, "it's only excess twins." He stood close by Martin's elbow. He was glad himself of the contact.

It is hard to meet a stranger. Even the greatest extravert meeting even the meekest stranger knows a certain dread, though he may not know he knows it. Will he make a fool of me wreck my image of myself invade me destroy me change me? Will he be different from me? Yes, that he will. There's the terrible thing: the strangeness of the stranger.

After two years on a dead planet, and the last half year isolated as a team of two, oneself and one other, after that it's even harder to meet a stranger, however welcome he may be. You're out of the habit of difference, you've lost the touch; and so the fear revives, the primitive anxiety, the old dread.

The clone, five males and five females, had got done in a couple of minutes what a man might have got done in twenty: greeted Pugh and Martin, had a glance at Libra, unloaded the boat, made ready to go. They went, and the dome filled with them, a hive of golden bees. They hummed and buzzed quietly, filled up all silences, all spaces with a honey-brown swarm of human presence. Martin looked bewildered at the long-limbed girls, and they smiled at him, three at once. Their smile was gentler than that of the boys, but no less radiantly self-possessed.

"Self-possessed," Owen Pugh murmured to his friend, "that's it. Think of it, to be oneself ten times over. Nine seconds for every motion, nine ayes on every vote. It would be glorious." But Martin was asleep. And the John Chows had all gone to sleep at once. The dome was filled with their quiet breathing. They were young, they didn't snore. Martin sighed and snored, his Hershey-bar-colored face relaxed in the dim afterglow of Libra's primary, set at last. Pugh had cleared the dome and stars looked in, Sol among them, a great company of lights, a clone of splendors. Pugh slept and dreamed of a one-eyed giant who chased him through the shaking halls of Hell.

From his sleeping bag Pugh watched the clone's awakening. They all got up within one minute except for one pair, a boy and a girl, who lay snugly tangled and still sleeping in one bag. As Pugh saw this there was a shock like one of Libra's earthquakes inside him, a very deep tremor. He was not aware of this and in fact thought he was pleased at the sight; there was no other such comfort on this dead hollow world. More power to them, who made love. One of the others stepped on the pair. They woke and the girl sat up flushed and sleepy, with bare golden breasts. One of her sisters murmured something to her; she shot a glance at Pugh and disappeared in the sleeping bag; from another direction came a fierce stare, from still another direction a voice: "Christ, we're used to having a room to ourselves. Hope you don't mind, Captain Pugh."

"It's a pleasure," Pugh said half truthfully. He had to stand up then wearing only the shorts he slept in, and he felt like a plucked rooster, all white scrawn and pimples. He had seldom envied Martin's compact brownness so much. The United Kingdom had come through the Great Famines well, losing less than half its population: a record achieved by rigorous food control. Black marketeers and hoarders had been executed. Crumbs had been shared. Where in richer lands most had died and a few had thriven, in Britain fewer died and none throve. They all got lean. Their sons were lean, their grandsons lean, small, brittle-boned, easily infected. When civilization became a matter of standing in lines, the British had kept queue, and so had replaced the survival of the fittest with the survival of the fair-minded. Owen Pugh was a scrawny little man. All the same, he was there.

At the moment he wished he wasn't.

At breakfast a John said, "Now if you'll brief us, Captain Pugh—"

"Owen, then."

"Owen, we can work out our schedule. Anything new on the mine since your last report to your Mission? We saw your reports when *Passerine* was orbiting Planet V, where they are now."

Martin did not answer, though the mine was his discovery and project, and Pugh had to do his best. It was hard to talk to them. The same faces, each with the same expression of intelligent interest, all leaned toward him across the table at almost the same angle. They all nodded together.

Over the Exploitation Corps insigne on their tunics each had a nameband, first name John and last name Chow of course, but the middle names different. The men were Aleph, Kaph, Yod, Gimel, and Samedh; the women Sadhe, Daleth, Zayin, Beth, and Resh. Pugh tried to use the names but gave it up at once; he could not even tell sometimes which one had spoken, for all the voices were alike.

Martin buttered and chewed his toast, and finally interrupted: "You're a team. Is that it?"

"Right," said two Johns.

"God, what a team! I hadn't seen the point. How much do you each know what the others are thinking?"

"Not at all, properly speaking," replied one of the girls, Zayin. The others watched her with the proprietary, approving look they had. "No ESP, nothing fancy. But we think alike. We have exactly the same equipment. Given the same stimulus, the same problem, we're likely to be coming up with the same reactions and solutions at the same time. Explanations are easy—don't even have to make them, usually. We seldom misunderstand each other. It does facilitate our working as a team."

"Christ yes," said Martin. "Pugh and I have spent seven hours out of ten for six months misunderstanding each other. Like most people. What about emergencies, are you as good at meeting the unexpected problem as a nor . . . an unrelated team?"

"Statistics so far indicate that we are," Zayin answered readily. Clones must be trained, Pugh thought, to meet questions, to reassure and reason. All they said had the slightly bland and stilted quality of answers furnished to the Public. "We can't brainstorm as singletons can, we as a team don't profit from the interplay of varied minds; but we have a compensatory advantage. Clones are drawn from the best human material, individuals of IQ ninety-ninth percentile, Genetic Constitution alpha double A, and so on. We have more to draw on than most individuals do."

"And it's multiplied by a factor of ten. Who is—who was John Chow?"

"A genius surely," Pugh said politely. His interest in cloning was not so new and avid as Martin's.

"Leonardo Complex type," said Yod. "Biomath, also a cellist and an undersea hunter, and interested in structural engineering problems and so on. Died before he'd worked out his major theories."

"Then you each represent a different facet of his mind, his talents?"

"No," said Zayin, shaking her head in time with several others. "We share the basic equipment and tendencies, of course, but we're all engineers in Planetary Exploitation. A later clone can be trained to develop other aspects of the basic equipment. It's all training; the genetic substance is identical. We *are* John Chow. But we are differently trained."

Martin looked shell-shocked. "How old are you?"

"Twenty-three."

"You say he died young—had they taken germ cells from him beforehand or something?"

Gimel took over: "He died at twenty-four in an air car crash. They couldn't save the brain, so they took some intestinal cells and cultured them for cloning. Reproductive cells aren't used for cloning, since they have only half the chromosomes. Intestinal cells happen to be easy to despecialize and reprogram for total growth."

"All chips off the old block," Martin said valiantly. "But how can . . . some of you be women . . . ?"

Beth took over: "It's easy to program half the clonal mass back to the female. Just delete the male gene from half the cells and they revert to the basic, that is, the female. It's trickier to go the other way, have to hook in artificial Y chromosomes. So they mostly clone from males, since clones function best bisexually."

Gimel again: "They've worked these matters of technique and function out carefully. The taxpayer wants the best for his money, and of course clones are expensive. With the cell manipulations, and the incubation in Ngama Placentae, and the maintenance and training of the foster-parent groups, we end up costing about three million apiece."

"For your next generation," Martin said, still struggling, "I suppose you . . . you breed?"

"We females are sterile," said Beth with perfect equanimity. "You remember that the Y chromosome was deleted from our original cell. The males can interbreed with approved singletons, if they want to. But to get John Chow again as often as they want, they just reclone a cell from this clone."

Martin gave up the struggle. He nodded and chewed cold toast. "Well," said one of the Johns, and all changed mood, like a flock of starlings that change course in one wingflick, following a leader so fast that no eye can see which leads. They were ready to go. "How about a look at the mine? Then we'll unload the equipment. Some nice new models in the roboats; you'll want to see them. Right?" Had Pugh or Martin not agreed they might have found it hard to say so. The Johns were polite but unanimous; their decisions carried. Pugh, Commander of Libra Base 2, felt a qualm. Could he boss around this super-man/woman-entity-of-ten? and a genius at that? He stuck close to Martin as they suited for outside. Neither said anything.

Four apiece in the three large airjets, they slipped off north from the dome, over Libra's dun rugose skin, in starlight.

"Desolate," one said.

It was a boy and girl with Pugh and Martin. Pugh wondered if these were the two that had shared a sleeping bag last night. No doubt they wouldn't mind if he asked them. Sex must be as handy as breathing to them. Did you two breathe last night?

"Yes," he said, "it is desolate."

"This is our first time off, except training on Luna." The girl's voice was definitely a bit higher and softer.

"How did you take the big hop?"

"They doped us. I wanted to experience it." That was the boy; he sounded wistful. They seemed to have more personality, only two at a time. Did repetition of the individual negate individuality?

"Don't worry," said Martin, steering the sled, "you can't experience no-time because it isn't there."

"I'd just like to once," one of them said. "So we'd know."

The Mountains of Merioneth showed leprotic in starlight to the east, a plume of freezing gas trailed silvery from a vent-hole to the west, and the sled tilted groundward. The twins braced for the stop at one moment, each with a slight protective gesture to the other. Your skin is my skin, Pugh thought, but literally, no metaphor. What would it be like, then, to have someone as close to you as that? Always to be answered when you spoke; never to be in pain alone. Love your neighbor as you love yourself .... That hard old problem was solved. The neighbor was the self: the love was perfect.

And here was Hellmouth, the mine.

Pugh was the Exploratory Mission's E.T. geologist, and Martin his technician and cartographer; but when in the course of a local survey Martin had discovered the U-mine, Pugh had given him full credit, as well as the onus of prospecting the lode and planning the Exploitation Team's job. These kids had been sent out from Earth years before Martin's reports got there and had not known what their job would be until they got here. The Exploitation Corps simply sent out teams regularly and blindly as a dandelion sends out its seed, knowing there would be a job for them on Libra or the next planet out or one they hadn't even heard about yet. The government wanted uranium too urgently to wait while reports drifted home across the lightyears. The stuff was like gold, old-fashioned but essential, worth mining extraterrestrially and shipping interstellar. Worth its weight in people, Pugh thought sourly, watching the tall young men and women go one by one, glimmering in starlight, into the black hole Martin had named Hellmouth.

As they went in their homeostatic forehead-lamps brightened. Twelve nodding gleams ran along the moist, wrinkled walls. Pugh heard Martin's radiation counter peeping twenty to the dozen up ahead. "Here's the drop-off," said Martin's voice in the suit intercom, drowning out the peeping and the dead silence that was around them. "We're in a side-fissure, this is the main vertical vent in front of us." The black void gaped, its far side not visible in the headlamp beams. "Last vulcanism seems to have been a couple of thousand years ago. Nearest fault is twenty-eight kilos east, in the Trench. This area seems to be as safe seismically as anything in the area. The big basalt-flow overhead stabilizes all these substructures, so long as it remains stable itself. Your central lode is thirty-six meters down and runs in a series of five bubble caverns northeast. It is a lode, a pipe of very high-grade ore. You saw the percentage figures, right? Extraction's going to be no problem. All you've got to do is get the bubbles topside."

"Take off the lid and let 'em float up." A chuckle. Voices began to talk, but they were all the same voice and the suit radio gave them no location in space. "Open the thing right up. —Safer that way. —But it's a solid basalt roof, how thick, ten meters here? —Three to twenty, the report said. —Blow good ore all over the lot. —Use this access we're in, straighten it a bit and run slider rails for the robos. —Import burros. —Have we got enough propping material? —What's your estimate of total payload mass, Martin?"

"Say over five million kilos and under eight."

"Transport will be here in ten E-months. —It'll have to go pure. —No, they'll have the mass problem in NAFAL shipping licked by now, remember it's been sixteen years since we left Earth last Tuesday. —Right, they'll send the whole lot back and purify it in Earth orbit. —Shall we go down, Martin?"

"Go on. I've been down."

The first one—Aleph? (Heb., the ox, the leader)—swung onto the ladder and down; the rest followed. Pugh and Martin stood at the chasm's edge. Pugh set his intercom to exchange only with Martin's suit, and noticed Martin doing the same. It was a bit wearing, this listening to one person think aloud in ten voices, or was it one voice speaking the thoughts of ten minds?

"A great gut," Pugh said, looking down into the black pit, its veined and warted walls catching stray gleams of headlamps far below. "A cow's bowel. A bloody great constipated intestine."

Martin's counter peeped like a lost chicken. They stood inside the dead but epileptic planet, breathing oxygen from tanks, wearing suits impermeable to corrosives and harmful radiations, resistant to a 200-degree range of temperatures, tear-proof, and as shock-resistant as possible given the soft vulnerable stuff inside.

"Next hop," Martin said, "I'd like to find a planet that has nothing whatever to exploit."

"You found this."

"Keep me home next time."

Pugh was pleased. He had hoped Martin would want to go on working with him, but neither of them was used to talking much about their feelings, and he had hesitated to ask. "I'll try that," he said.

"I hate this place. I like caves, you know. It's why I came in here. Just spelunking. But this one's a bitch. Mean. You can't ever let down in here. I guess this lot can handle it, though. They know their stuff."

"Wave of the future, whatever," said Pugh.

The wave of the future came swarming up the ladder, swept Martin to the entrance, gabbled at and around him: "Have we got enough material for supports? —If we convert one of the extractor servos to anneal, yes. —Sufficient if we miniblast? —Kaph can calculate stress." Pugh had switched his intercom back to receive them; he looked at them, so many thoughts jabbering in an eager mind, and at Martin standing silent among them, and at Hellmouth and the wrinkled plain. "Settled! How does that strike you as a preliminary schedule, Martin?"

"It's your baby," Martin said.

Within five E-days the Johns had all their material and equipment unloaded and operating and were starting to open up the mine. They worked with total efficiency. Pugh was fascinated and frightened by their effectiveness, their confidence, their independence. He was no use to them at all. A clone, he thought, might indeed be the first truly stable, self-reliant human being. Once adult it would need nobody's help. It would be sufficient to itself physically, sexually, emotionally, intellectually. Whatever he did, any member of it would always receive the support and approval of his peers, his other selves. Nobody else was needed.

Two of the clone stayed in the dome doing calculations and paperwork, with frequent sled trips to the mine for measurements and tests. They were the mathematicians of the clone, Zayin and Kaph. That is, as Zayin explained, all ten had had thorough mathematical training from age three to twenty-one, but from twenty-one to twenty-three she and Kaph had gone on with math while the others intensified study in other specialties, geology, mining, engineering, electronic engineering, equipment robotics, applied atomics, and so on. "Kaph and I feel," she said, "that we're the element of the clone closest to what John Chow was in his singleton lifetime. But of course he was principally in biomath, and they didn't take us far in that."

"They needed us most in this field," Kaph said, with the patriotic priggishness they sometimes evinced.

Pugh and Martin soon could distinguish this pair from the others, Zayin by gestalt, Kaph only by a discolored left fourth fingernail, got from an ill-aimed hammer at the age of six. No doubt there were many such differences, physical and psychological, among them; nature might be identical, nurture could not be. But the differences were hard to find. And part of the difficulty was that they never really talked to Pugh and Martin. They joked with them, were polite, got along fine. They gave nothing. It was nothing one could complain about; they were very pleasant, they had the standardized American friendliness. "Do you come from Ireland, Owen?"

"Nobody comes from Ireland, Zayin."

"There are lots of Irish-Americans."

"To be sure, but no more Irish. A couple of thousand in all the island, the last I knew. They didn't go in for birth control, you know, so the food ran out. By the Third Famine there were no Irish left at all but the priesthood, and they all celibate, or nearly all."

Zayin and Kaph smiled stiffly. They had no experience of either bigotry or irony. "What are you then, ethnically?" Kaph asked, and Pugh replied, "A Welshman."

"Is it Welsh that you and Martin speak together?"

None of your business, Pugh thought, but said, "No, it's his dialect, not mine: Argentinean. A descendant of Spanish."

"You learned it for private communication?"

"Whom had we here to be private from? It's just that sometimes a man likes to speak his native language."

"Ours is English," Kaph said unsympathetically. Why should they have sympathy? That's one of the things you give because you need it back.

"Is Wells quaint?" asked Zayin.

"Wells? Oh, Wales, it's called. Yes, Wales is quaint." Pugh switched on his rock-cutter, which prevented further conversation by a synapse-destroying whine, and while it whined he turned his back and said a profane word in Welsh.

That night he used the Argentine dialect for private communication. "Do they pair off in the same couples or change every night?"

Martin looked surprised. A prudish expression, unsuited to his features, appeared for a moment. It faded. He too was curious. "I think it's random."

"Don't whisper, man, it sounds dirty. I think they rotate."

"On a schedule?"

"So nobody gets omitted."

Martin gave a vulgar laugh and smothered it. "What about us? Aren't we omitted?"

"That doesn't occur to them."

"What if I proposition one of the girls?"

"She'd tell the others and they'd decide as a group."

"I am not a bull," Martin said, his dark, heavy face heating up. "I will not be judged—"

"Down, down, *machismo,*" said Pugh. "Do you mean to proposition one?"

Martin shrugged, sullen. "Let 'em have their incest."

"Incest is it, or masturbation?"

"I don't care, if they'd do it out of earshot!"

The clone's early attempts at modesty had soon worn off, unmotivated by any deep defensiveness of self or awareness of others. Pugh and Martin were daily deeper swamped under the intimacies of its constant emotional-sexual-mental interchange: swamped yet excluded.

"Two months to go," Martin said one evening.

"To what?" snapped Pugh. He was edgy lately, and Martin's sullenness got on his nerves.

"To relief."

In sixty days the full crew of their Exploratory Mission were due back from their survey of the other planets of the system. Pugh was aware of this.

"Crossing off the days on your calendar?" he jeered.

"Pull yourself together, Owen."

"What do you mean?"

"What I say."

They parted in contempt and resentment.

Pugh came in after a day alone on the Pampas, a vast lava plain the nearest edge of which was two hours south by jet. He was tired but refreshed by solitude. They were not supposed to take long trips alone but lately had often done so. Martin stooped under bright lights, drawing one of his elegant masterly charts. This one was of the whole face of Libra, the cancerous face. The dome was otherwise empty, seeming dim and large as it had before the clone came. "Where's the golden horde?"

Martin grunted ignorance, cross-hatching. He straightened his back to glance round at the sun, which squatted feebly like a great red toad on the eastern plain, and at the clock, which said 18:45. "Some big quakes today," he said, returning to his map. "Feel them down there? Lots of crates were falling around. Take a look at the seismo."

The needle jigged and wavered on the roll. It never stopped dancing here. The roll had recorded five quakes of major intensity back in midafternoon; twice the needle had hopped off the roll. The attached computer had been activated to emit a slip reading, "Epicenter 61′ N by 42′ 4″ E."

"Not in the Trench this time."

"I thought it felt a bit different from usual. Sharper."

"In Base One I used to lie awake all night feeling the ground jump. Queer how you get used to things."

"Go spla if you didn't. What's for dinner?"

"I thought you'd have cooked it."

"Waiting for the clone."

Feeling put upon, Pugh got out a dozen dinnerboxes, stuck two in the Instobake, pulled them out. "All right, here's dinner."

"Been thinking," Martin said, coming to table. "What if some clone cloned itself? Illegally. Made a thousand duplicates—ten thousand. Whole army. They could make a tidy power grab, couldn't they?"

"But how many millions did this lot cost to rear? Artificial placentae and all that. It would be hard to keep secret, unless they had a planet to themselves. . . . Back before the Famines when Earth had national governments, they talked about that: clone your best soldiers, have whole regiments of them. But the food ran out before they could play that game."

They talked amicably, as they used to do.

"Funny," Martin said, chewing. "They left early this morning, didn't they?"

"All but Kaph and Zayin. They thought they'd get the first pay-load above ground today. What's up?"

"They weren't back for lunch."

"They won't starve, to be sure."

"They left at seven."

"So they did." Then Pugh saw it. The air tanks held eight hours' supply.

"Kaph and Zayin carried out spare cans when they left. Or they've got a heap out here."

"They did, but they brought the whole lot in to recharge." Martin stood up, pointing to one of the stacks of stuff that cut the dome into rooms and alleys.

"There's an alarm signal on every imsuit."

"It's not automatic."

Pugh was tired and still hungry. "Sit down and eat, man. That lot can look after themselves."

Martin sat down but did not eat. "There was a big quake, Owen. The first one. Big enough it scared me."

After a pause Pugh sighed and said, "All right."

Unenthusiastically, they got out the two-man sled that was always left for them and headed it north. The long sunrise covered everything in poisonous red jello. The horizontal light and shadow made it hard to see, raised walls of fake iron ahead of them which they slid through, turned the convex plain beyond Hellmouth into a great dimple full of bloody water. Around the tunnel entrance a wilderness of machinery stood, cranes and cables and servos and wheels and diggers and robocarts and sliders and control huts, all slanting and bulking incoherently in the red light. Martin jumped from the sled, ran into the mine. He came out again, to Pugh. "Oh God, Owen, it's down," he said. Pugh went in and saw, five meters from the entrance, the shiny moist, black wall that ended the tunnel. Newly exposed to air, it looked organic, like visceral tissue. The tunnel entrance, enlarged by blasting and double-tracked for robocards, seemed unchanged until he noticed thousands of tiny spiderweb cracks in the walls. The floor was wet with some sluggish fluid.

"They were inside," Martin said.

"They may be still. They surely had extra air cans—"

"Look, Owen, look at the basalt flow, at the roof, don't you see what the quake did, look at it."

The low hump of land that roofed the caves still had the unreal look of an optical illusion. It had reversed itself, sunk down, leaving a vast dimple or pit. When Pugh walked on it he saw that it too was cracked with many tiny fissures. From some a whitish gas was seeping, so that the sunlight on the surface of the gas pool was shafted as if by the waters of a dim red lake.

"Mine's not on the fault. There's no fault here!"

Pugh came back to him quickly. "No, there's no fault, Martin—Look, they surely weren't all inside together."

Martin followed him and searched among the wrecked machines dully, then actively. He spotted the airsled. It had come down heading south, and stuck at an angle in a pothole of colloidal dust. It had carried two riders. One was half sunk in the dust, but his suit meters registered normal functioning; the other hung strapped onto the tilted sled. Her imsuit had burst open on the broken legs, and the body was frozen hard as any rock. That was all they found. As both regulation and custom demanded, they cremated the dead at once with the laser guns they carried by regulation and had never used before. Pugh, knowing he was going to be sick, wrestled the survivor onto the two-man sled and sent Martin off to the dome with him. Then he vomited and flushed the waste out of his suit, and finding one four-man sled undamaged, followed after Martin, shaking as if the cold of Libra had got through to him.

The survivor was Kaph. He was in deep shock. They found a swelling on the occiput that might mean concussion, but no fracture was visible.

Pugh brought two glasses of food concentrate and two chasers of aquavit. "Come on," he said. Martin obeyed, drinking off the tonic. They sat down on crates near the cot and sipped the aquavit.

Kaph lay immobile, face like beeswax, hair bright black to the shoulders, lips stiffly parted for faintly gasping breaths.

"It must have been the first shock, the big one," Martin said. "It must have slid the whole structure sideways. Till it fell in on itself. There must be gas layers in the lateral rocks, like those formations in the Thirty-first Quadrant. But there wasn't any sign—" As he spoke the world slid out from under them. Things leaped and clattered, hopped and jigged, shouted Ha! Ha! Ha! "It was like this at fourteen hours," said Reason shakily in Martin's voice, amidst the unfastening and ruin of the world. But Unreason sat up, as the tumult lessened and things ceased dancing, and screamed aloud.

Pugh leaped across his split aquavit and held Kaph down. The muscular body flailed him off. Martin pinned the shoulders down. Kaph screamed, struggled, choked; his face blackened. "Oxy," Pugh said, and his hand found the right needle in the medical kit as if by homing instinct; while Martin held the mask he struck the needle home to the vagus nerve, restoring Kaph to life.

"Didn't know you knew that stunt," Martin said, breathing hard.

"The Lazarus Jab, my father was a doctor. It doesn't often work," Pugh said. "I want that drink I spilled. Is the quake over? I can't tell."

"Aftershocks. It's not just you shivering."

"Why did he suffocate?"

"I don't know, Owen. Look in the book."

Kaph was breathing normally and his color was restored; only the lips were still darkened. They poured a new shot of courage and sat down by him again with their medical guide. "Nothing about cyanosis or asphyxiation under 'Shock' or 'Concussion.' He can't have breathed in anything with his suit on. I don't know. We'd get as much good out of *Mother Mog's Home Herbalist*. . . . 'Anal Hemorrhoids,' fy!" Pugh pitched the book to a crate table. It fell short, because either Pugh or the table was still unsteady.

"Why didn't he signal?"

"Sorry?"

"The eight inside the mine never had time. But he and the girl must have been outside. Maybe she was in the entrance and got hit by the first slide. He must have been outside, in the control hut maybe. He ran in, pulled her out, strapped her onto the sled, started for the dome. And all that time never pushed the panic button in his imsuit. Why not?"

"Well, he'd had that whack on his head. I doubt he ever realized the girl was dead. He wasn't in his senses. But if he had been I don't know if he'd have thought to signal us. They looked to one another for help."

Martin's face was like an Indian mask, grooves at the mouth corners, eyes of dull coal. "That's so. What must he have felt, then, when the quake came and he was outside, alone—"

In answer Kaph screamed.

He came off the cot in the heaving convulsions of one suffocating, knocked Pugh right down with his flailing arm, staggered into a stack of crates and fell to the floor, lips blue, eyes white. Martin dragged him back onto the cot and gave him a whiff of oxygen, then knelt by Pugh, who was sitting up, and wiped at his cut cheekbone. "Owen, are you all right, are you going to be all right, Owen?"

"I think I am," Pugh said. "Why are you rubbing that on my face?"

It was a short length of computer tape, now spotted with Pugh's blood. Martin dropped it. "Thought it was a towel. You clipped your cheek on that box there."

"Is he out of it?"

"Seems to be."

They stared down at Kaph lying stiff, his teeth a white line inside dark parted lips.

"Like epilepsy. Brain damage maybe?"

"What about shooting him full of meprobamate?"

Pugh shook his head. "I don't know what's in that shot I already gave him for shock. Don't want to overdose him."

"Maybe he'll sleep it off now."

"I'd like to myself. Between him and the earthquake I can't seem to keep on my feet."

"You got a nasty crack there. Go on, I'll sit up a while."

Pugh cleaned his cut cheek and pulled off his shirt, then paused.

"Is there anything we ought to have done—have tried to do—"

"They're all dead," Martin said heavily, gently.

Pugh lay down on top of his sleeping bag and one instant later was wakened by a hideous, sucking, struggling noise. He staggered up, found the needle, tried three times to jab it in correctly and failed, began to massage over Kaph's heart. "Mouth-to-mouth," he said, and Martin obeyed. Presently Kaph drew a harsh breath, his heartbeat steadied, his rigid muscles began to relax.

"How long did I sleep?"

"Half an hour."

They stood up sweating. The ground shuddered, the fabric of the dome sagged and swayed. Libra was dancing her awful polka again, her *Totentanz*. The sun, though rising, seemed to have grown larger and redder; gas and dust must have been stirred up in the feeble atmosphere.

"What's wrong with him, Owen?"

"I think he's dying with them."

"Them— But they're all dead, I tell you."

"Nine of them. They're all dead, they were crushed or suffocated. They were all him, he is all of them. They died, and now he's dying their deaths one by one."

"Oh, pity of God," said Martin.

The next time was much the same. The fifth time was worse, for Kaph fought and raved, trying to speak but getting no words out, as if his mouth were stopped with rocks or clay. After that the attacks grew weaker, but so did he. The eighth seizure came at about four-thirty; Pugh and Martin worked till five-thirty doing all they could to keep life in the body that slid without protest into death. They kept him, but Martin said, "The next will finish him." And it did; but Pugh breathed his own breath into the inert lungs, until he himself passed out.

He woke. The dome was opaqued and no light on. He listened and heard the breathing of two sleeping men. He slept, and nothing woke him till hunger did.

The sun was well up over the dark plains, and the planet had stopped dancing. Kaph lay asleep. Pugh and Martin drank tea and looked at him with proprietary triumph.

When he woke Martin went to him: "How do you feel, old man?" There was no answer. Pugh took Martin's place and looked into the brown, dull eyes that gazed toward but not into his own. Like Martin he quickly turned away. He heated food concentrate and brought it to Kaph. "Come on, drink."

He could see the muscles in Kaph's throat tighten. "Let me die," the young man said.

"You're not dying."

Kaph spoke with clarity and precision: "I am nine-tenths dead. There is not enough of me left alive."

That precision convinced Pugh, and he fought the conviction. "No," he said, peremptory. "They are dead. The others. Your brothers and sisters. You're not them, you're alive. You are John Chow. Your life is in your own hands."

The young man lay still, looking into a darkness that was not there.

Martin and Pugh took turns taking the Exploitation hauler and a spare set of robos over to Hellmouth to salvage equipment and protect it from Libra's sinister atmosphere, for the value of the stuff was, literally, astronomical. It was slow work for one man at a time, but they were unwilling to leave Kaph by himself. The one left in the dome did paperwork, while Kaph sat or lay and stared into his darkness and never spoke. The days went by, silent.

The radio spat and spoke: the Mission calling from the ship. "We'll be down on Libra in five weeks, Owen. Thirty-four E-days nine hours I make it as of now. How's tricks in the old dome?"

"Not good, chief. The Exploit team were killed, all but one of them, in the mine. Earthquake. Six days ago."

The radio crackled and sang starsong. Sixteen seconds' lag each way; the ship was out around Planet II now. "Killed, all but one? You and Martin were unhurt?"

"We're all right, chief."

Thirty-two seconds.

"*Passerine* left an Exploit team out here with us. I may put them on the Hellmouth project then, instead of the Quadrant Seven project. We'll settle that when we come down. In any case you and Martin will be relieved at Dome Two. Hold tight. Anything else?"

"Nothing else."

Thirty-two seconds.

"Right then. So long, Owen."

Kaph had heard all this, and later on Pugh said to him, "The chief may ask you to stay here with the other Exploit team. You know the ropes here." Knowing the exigencies of Far Out life, he wanted to warn the young man. Kaph made no answer. Since he had said, "There is not enough of me left alive," he had not spoken a word.

"Owen," Martin said on suit intercom, "he's spla. Insane. Psycho."

"He's doing very well for a man who's died nine times."

"Well? Like a turned-off android is well? The only emotion he has left is hate. Look at his eyes."

"That's not hate, Martin. Listen, it's true that he has, in a sense, been dead. I cannot imagine what he feels. But it's not hatred. He can't even see us. It's too dark."

"Throats have been cut in the dark. He hates us because we're not Aleph and Yod and Zayin."

"Maybe. But I think he's alone. He doesn't see us or hear us, that's the truth. He never had to see anyone else before. He never was alone before. He had himself to see, talk with, live with, nine other selves all his life. He doesn't know how you go it alone. He must learn. Give him time."

Martin shook his heavy head. "Spla," he said. "Just remember when you're alone with him that he could break your neck one-handed."

"He could do that," said Pugh, a short, soft-voiced man with a scarred cheekbone; he smiled. They were just outside the dome airlock, programming one of the servos to repair a damaged hauler. They could see Kaph sitting inside the great half-egg of the dome like a fly in amber.

"Hand me the insert pack there. What makes you think he'll get any better?"

"He has a strong personality, to be sure."

"Strong? Crippled. Nine-tenths dead, as he put it."

"But he's not dead. He's a live man: John Kaph Chow. He had a jolly queer upbringing, but after all every boy has got to break free of his family. He will do it."

"I can't see it."

"Think a bit, Martin bach. What's this cloning for? To repair the human race. We're in a bad way. Look at me. My IIQ and GC are half this John Chow's. Yet they wanted me so badly for the Far Out Service that when I volunteered they took me and fitted me out with an artificial lung and corrected my myopia. Now if there were enough good sound lads about would they be taking one-lunged short-sighted Welshmen?"

"Didn't know you had an artificial lung."

"I do then. Not tin, you know. Human, grown in a tank from a bit of somebody; cloned, if you like. That's how they make replacement organs, the same general idea as cloning, but bits and pieces instead of whole people. It's my own lung now, whatever. But what I am saying is this, there are too many like me these days and not enough like John Chow. They're trying to raise the level of the human genetic pool, which is a mucky little puddle since the population crash. So then if a man is cloned, he's a strong and clever man. It's only logic, to be sure."

Martin grunted; the servo began to hum.

Kaph had been eating little; he had trouble swallowing his food, choking on it, so that he would give up trying after a few bites. He had lost eight or ten kilos. After three weeks or so, however, his appetite began to pick up, and one day he began to look through the clone's possessions, the sleeping bags, kits, papers which Pugh had stacked neatly in a far angle of a packing-crate alley. He sorted, destroyed a heap of papers and oddments, made a small packet of what remained, then relapsed into his walking coma.

Two days later he spoke. Pugh was trying to correct a flutter in the tape-player and failing; Martin had the jet out, checking their maps of the Pampas. "Hell and damnation!" Pugh said, and Kaph said in a toneless voice, "Do you want me to do that?"

Pugh jumped, controlled himself, and gave the machine to Kaph. The young man took it apart, put it back together, and left it on the table.

"Put on a tape," Pugh said with careful casualness, busy at another table.

Kaph put on the topmost tape, a chorale. He lay down on his cot. The sound of a hundred human voices singing together filled the dome. He lay still, his face blank.

In the next days he took over several routine jobs, unasked. He undertook nothing that wanted initiative, and if asked to do anything he made no response at all.

"He's doing well," Pugh said in the dialect of Argentina.

"He's not. He's turning himself into a machine. Does what he's programmed to do, no reaction to anything else. He's worse off than when he didn't function at all. He's not human any more."

Pugh sighed. "Well, good night," he said in English. "Good night, Kaph."

"Good night," Martin said; Kaph did not.

Next morning at breakfast Kaph reached across Martin's plate for the toast. "Why don't you ask for it?" Martin said with the geniality of repressed exaspertion. "I can pass it."

"I can reach it," Kaph said in his flat voice.

"Yes, but look. Asking to pass things, saying good night or hello, they're not important, but all the same when somebody says something a person ought to answer. . . ."

The young man looked indifferently in Martin's direction; his eyes still did not seem to see clear through to the person he looked toward. "Why should I answer?"

"Because somebody has said something to you."

"Why?"

Martin shrugged and laughed. Pugh jumped up and turned on the rock-cutter.

Later on he said, "Lay off that, please, Martin."

"Manners are essential in small isolated crews, some kind of manners, whatever you work out together. He's been taught that, everybody in Far Out knows it. Why does he deliberately flout it?"

"Do you tell yourself good night?"

"So?"

"Don't you see Kaph's never known anyone but himself?"

Martin brooded and then broke out. "Then by God this cloning business is all wrong. It won't do. What are a lot of duplicate geniuses going to do for us when they don't even know we exist?" Pugh nodded. "It might be wiser to separate the clones and bring them up with others. But they make such a grand team this way."

"Do they? I don't know. If this lot had been ten average inefficient E. T. engineers, would they all have got killed? What if, when the quake came and things started caving in, what if all those kids ran the same way, farther into the mine, maybe, to save the one who was farthest in? Even Kaph was outside and went in. . . . It's hypothetical. But I keep thinking, out of ten ordinary confused guys, more might have got out."

"I don't know. It's true that identical twins tend to die at about the same time, even when they have never seen each other. Identity and death, it is very strange. . . ."

The days went on, the red sun crawled across the dark sky, Kaph did not speak when spoken to, Pugh and Martin snapped at each other more frequently each day. Pugh complained of Martin's snoring. Offended, Martin moved his cot clear across the dome and also ceased speaking to Pugh for some while. Pugh whistled Welsh dirges until Martin complained, and then Pugh stopped speaking for a while.

The day before the Mission ship was due, Martin announced he was going over to Merioneth.

"I thought at least you'd be giving me a hand with the computer to finish the rock analyses," Pugh said, aggrieved.

"Kaph can do that. I want one more look at the Trench. Have fun," Martin added in dialect, and laughed, and left.

"What is that language?"

"Argentinean. I told you that once, didn't I?"

"I don't know." After a while the young man added, "I have forgotten a lot of things, I think."

"It wasn't important, to be sure," Pugh said gently, realizing all at once how important this conversation was. "Will you give me a hand runing the computer, Kaph?"

He nodded.

Pugh had left a lot of loose ends, and the job took them all day. Kaph was a good co-worker, quick and systematic, much more so than Pugh himself. His flat voice, now that he was talking again, got on the nerves; but it didn't matter, there was only this one day left to get through and then the ship would come, the old crew, comrades and friends.

During tea break Kaph said, "What will happen if the Explore ship crashes?"

"They'd be killed."

"To you, I mean."

"To us? We'd radio SOS signals and live on half rations till the rescue cruiser from Area Three Base came. Four and a half E-years away it is. We have life support here for three men for, let's see, maybe between four and five years. A bit tight, it would be."

"Would they send a cruiser for three men?"

"They would."

Kaph said no more.

"Enough cheerful speculations," Pugh said cheerfully, rising to get back to work. He slipped sideways and the chair avoided his hand; he did a sort of half-pirouette and fetched up hard against the dome hide. "My goodness," he said, reverting to his native idiom, "what is it?"

"Quake," said Kaph.

The teacups bounced on the table with a plastic crackle, a litter of papers slid off a box, the skin of the dome swelled and sagged. Underfoot there was a huge noise, half sound, half shaking, a subsonic boom.

Kaph sat unmoved. An earthquake does not frighten a man who died in an earthquake.

Pugh, white-faced, wiry black hair sticking out, a frightened man, said, "Martin is in the Trench."

"What trench?"

"The big fault line. The epicenter for the local quakes. Look at the seismograph." Pugh struggled with the stuck door of a still-jittering locker.

"Where are you going?"

"After him."

"Martin took the jet. Sleds aren't safe to use during quakes. They go out of control."

"For God's sake man, shut up."

Kaph stood up, speaking in a flat voice as usual. "It's unnecessary to go out after him now. It's taking an unnecessary risk."

"If his alarm goes off, radio me," Pugh said, shut the head-piece of his suit, and ran to the lock. As he went out Libra picked up her ragged skirts and danced a belly dance from under his feet clear to the red horizon.

Inside the dome, Kaph saw the sled go up, tremble like a meteor in the dull red daylight, and vanish to the northeast. The hide of the dome quivered, the earth coughed. A vent south of the dome belched up a slow-flowing bile of black gas.

A bell shrilled and a red light flashed on the central control board. The sign under the light read Suit 2 and scribbled under that, A. G. M. Kaph did not turn the signal off. He tried to radio Martin, then Pugh, but got no reply from either.

When the aftershocks decreased he went back to work and finished up Pugh's job. It took him about two hours. Every half hour he tried to contact Suit 1 and got no reply, then Suit 2 and got no reply. The red light had stopped flashing after an hour.

It was dinnertime. Kaph cooked dinner for one and ate it. He lay down on his cot.

The aftershocks had ceased except for faint rolling tremors at long intervals. The sun hung in the west, oblate, pale red, immense. It did not sink visibly. There was no sound at all.

Kaph got up and began to walk about the messy, half-packed-up, overcrowded, empty dome. The silence continued. He went to the player and put on the first tape that came to hand. It was pure music, electronic, without harmonies, without voices. It ended. The silence continued.

Pugh's uniform tunic, one button missing, hung over a stack of rock samples. Kaph stared at it a while.

The silence continued.

The child's dream: There is no one else alive in the world but me. In all the world.

Low, north of the dome, a meteor flickered.

Kaph's mouth opened as if he were trying to say something, but no sound came. He went hastily to the north wall and peered out into the gelatinous red light.

The little star came in and sank. Two figures blurred the airlock. Kaph stood close beside the lock as they came in. Martin's imsuit was covered with some kind of dust so that he looked raddled and warty like the surface of Libra. Pugh had him by the arm.

"Is he hurt?"

Pugh shucked his suit, helped Martin peel off his. "Shaken up," he said, curt.

"A piece of cliff fell onto the jet," Martin said, sitting down at the table and waving his arms. "Not while I was in it though. I was parked, see, and poking about that carbon-dust area when I felt things humping. So I went out onto a nice bit of early igneous I'd noticed from above, good footing and out from under the cliffs. Then I saw this bit of the planet fall off onto the flyer, quite a sight it was, and after a while it occurred to me the spare aircans were in the flyer, so I leaned on the panic button. But I didn't get any radio reception, that's always happening here during quakes, so I didn't know if the signal was getting through either. And things went on jumping around and pieces of the cliff coming off. Little rocks flying around, and so dusty you couldn't see a meter ahead. I was really beginning to wonder what I'd do for breathing in the small hours, you know, when I saw old Owen buzzing up the Trench in all that dust and junk like a big ugly bat—"

"Want to eat?" said Pugh.

"Of course I want to eat. How'd you come through the quake here, Kaph? No damage? It wasn't a big one actually, was it, what's the seismo say? My trouble was I was in the middle of it. Old Epicenter Alvaro. Felt like Richter fifteen there—total destruction of planet—"

"Sit down," Pugh said. "Eat."

After Martin had eaten a little his spate of talk ran dry. He very soon went off to his cot, still in the remote angle where he had removed it when Pugh complained of his snoring. "Good night, you one-lunged Welshman," he said across the dome.

"Good night."

There was no more out of Martin. Pugh opaqued the dome, turned the lamp down to a yellow glow less than a candle's light, and sat doing nothing, saying nothing, withdrawn.

The silence continued.

"I finished the computations."

Pugh nodded thanks.

"The signal from Martin came through, but I couldn't contact you or him."

Pugh said with effort, "I should not have gone. He had two hours of air left even with only one can. He might have been heading home when I left. This way we were all out of touch with one another. I was scared."

The silence came back, punctuated now by Martin's long, soft snores.

"Do you love Martin?"

Pugh looked up with angry eyes: "Martin is my friend. We've worked togther, he's a good man." He stopped. After a while he said, "Yes, I love him. Why did you ask that?"

Kaph said nothing, but he looked at the other man. His face was changed, as if he were glimpsing something he had not seen before; his voice too was changed. "How can you . . . How do you . . ."

But Pugh could not tell him. "I don't know," he said, "it's practice, partly. I don't know. We're each of us alone, to be sure. What can you do but hold your hand out in the dark?"

Kaph's strange gaze dropped, burned out by its own intensity.

"I'm tired," Pugh said. "That was ugly, looking for him in all that black dust and muck, and mouths opening and shutting in the ground . . . . I'm going to bed. The ship will be transmitting to us by six or so." He stood up and stretched.

"It's a clone," Kaph said. "The other Exploit Team they're bringing with them."

"Is it then?"

"A twelveclone. They came out with us on the *Passerine.*"

Kaph sat in the small yellow aura of the lamp seeming to look past it at what he feared: the new clone, the multiple self of which he was not part. A lost piece of a broken set, a fragment, inexpert at solitude, not knowing even how you go about giving love to another individual, now he must face the absolute, closed self-sufficiency of the clone of twelve; that was a lot to ask of the poor fellow, to be sure. Pugh put a hand on his shoulder in passing. "The chief won't ask you to stay here with a clone. You can go home. Or since you're Far Out maybe you'll come on farther out with us. We could use you. No hurry deciding. You'll make out all right."

Pugh's quiet voice trailed off. He stood unbuttoning his coat, stooped a little with fatigue. Kaph looked at him and saw the thing he had never seen before, saw him: Owen Pugh, the other, the stranger who held his hand out in the dark.

"Good night," Pugh mumbled, crawling into his sleeping bag and half asleep already, so that he did not hear Kaph reply after a pause, repeating, across darkness, benediction.

Raymond Carver

1938 – 1988

By both critics and fellow practitioners, Raymond Carver has been accorded a place of singular preeminence among his generation of American short story writers. Such recognition, which credits him with a major role in the resurgence of short fiction in the United States, was slow and difficult in coming. Born in Clatskanie, Oregon, in 1938, Carver was a husband and father before he was twenty. Working at a long series of low-paying jobs, he completed a bachelor's degree at Humbolt State College in California in 1963, and went on for brief additional study at the Writers' Workshop of the University of Iowa. His first college enrollment was at California's Chico State College, where he took an influential creative writing course under John Gardner. Because of the circumstances of his life, Carver began writing poems and short stories that he could draft in a single sitting, and these forms became the ones he finally *chose* to work in. Among his books of poetry are *Near Klamath* (1968), *Winter Insomnia* (1970), *Where Water Comes Together with Other Water* (1985), and *Ultramarine* (1986). His highly-regarded short story collections include *Will You Please Be Quiet, Please?* (1976), *What We Talk About When We Talk About Love* (1981), *Cathedral* (1984), and *Where I'm Calling From: New and Collected Stories* (1988). Carver died of cancer shortly after his fiftieth birthday.

Called by Laurie Stone "the bard of menace in ordinary life" and by Michael Koepf "the consummate master of Now," Carver became famous for his distinctive depiction of the difficulties and desperations of a working-class America that he knew firsthand. Such characters and his "pared-down, blunt," "willfully simple" style became the hallmarks of "minimalism."

In later work, Carver deliberately began to move away from the minimalist qualities that had been seen to characterize his literary vision and execution. At first glance, "Errand" seems far removed from the usual setting, narrative mode, and characters of Carver's best-known fiction. If one focuses on the bellboy, however, a basic continuity in these respects is clear, and this story's clear-eyed celebration of death and life, of work and art, becomes profoundly prophetic as well as elegiac. In several deep senses, none of his other stories illustrates so well one of Carver's most often quoted assertions. "Good fiction," he said, "is partly a bringing of the news from one world to another."

Errand

Chekhov. On the evening of March 22, 1897, he went to dinner in Moscow with his friend and confidant Alexei Suvorin. This Suvorin was a very rich newspaper and book publisher, a reactionary, a self-made man whose father was a private at the battle of Borodino. Like Chekhov, he was the grandson of a serf. They had that in common: each had peasant's blood in his veins. Otherwise, politically and temperamentally, they were miles apart. Nevertheless, Suvorin was one of Chekhov's few intimates, and Chekhov enjoyed his company.

Naturally, they went to the best restaurant in the city, a former town house called the Hermitage—a place where it could take hours, half the night even, to get through a ten-course meal that would, of course, include several wines, liqueurs, and coffee. Chekhov was impeccably dressed, as always—a dark suit and waistcoat, his usual pince-nez. He looked that night very much as he looks in the photographs taken of him during this period. He was relaxed, jovial. He shook hands with the maître d', and with a glance took in the large dining room. It was brilliantly illuminated by ornate chandeliers, the tables occupied by elegantly dressed men and women. Waiters came and went ceaselessly. He had just been seated across the table from Suvorin when suddenly, without warning, blood began gushing from his mouth. Suvorin and two waiters helped him to the gentlemen's room and tried to stanch the flow of blood with ice packs. Suvorin saw him back to his own hotel and had a bed prepared for Chekhov in one of the rooms of the suite. Later, after another hemorrhage, Chekhov allowed himself to be moved to a clinic that specialized in the treatment of tuberculosis and related respiratory infections. When Suvorin visited him there, Chekhov apologized for the "scandal" at the restaurant three nights earlier but continued to insist there was nothing seriously wrong. "He laughed and jested as usual," Suvorin noted in his diary, "while spitting blood into a large vessel."

Maria Chekhov, his younger sister, visited Chekhov in the clinic during the last days of March. The weather was miserable; a sleet storm was in progress, and frozen heaps of snow lay everywhere. It was hard for her to wave down a carriage to take her to the hospital. By the time she arrived she was filled with dread and anxiety.

"Anton Pavlovich lay on his back," Maria wrote in her *Memoirs.* "He was not allowed to speak. After greeting him, I went over to the table to hide my emotions." There, among bottles of champagne, jars of caviar, bouquets of flowers from well-wishers, she saw something that terrified her: a freehand drawing, obviously done by a specialist in these matters, of Chekhov's lungs. It was the kind of sketch a doctor often makes in order to show his patient what he thinks is taking place. The lungs were outlined in blue, but the upper parts were filled with red. "I realized they were diseased," Maria wrote.

Leo Tolstoy was another visitor. The hospital staff were awed to find themselves in the presence of the country's greatest writer. The most famous man in Russia? Of course they had to let him in to see Chekhov, even though "nonessential" visitors were forbidden. With much obsequiousness on the part of the nurses and resident doctors, the bearded, fierce-looking old man was shown into Chekhov's room. Despite his low opinion of Chekhov's abilities as a playwright (Tolstoy felt the plays were static and lacking in any moral vision. "Where do your characters take you?" he once demanded of Chekhov. "From the sofa to the junk room and back"), Tolstoy liked Chekhov's short stories. Furthermore, and quite simply, he loved the man. He told Gorky, "What a beautiful, magnificent man: modest and quiet, like a girl. He even walks like a girl. He's simply wonderful." And Tolstoy wrote in his journal (everyone kept a journal or a diary in those days), "I am glad I love . . . Chekhov."

Tolstoy removed his woolen scarf and bearskin coat, then lowered himself into a chair next to Chekhov's bed. Never mind that Chekhov was taking medication and not permitted to talk, much less carry on a conversation. He had to listen, amazedly, as the Count began to discourse on his theories of the immortality of the soul. Concerning that visit, Chekhov later wrote, "Tolstoy assumes that all of us (humans and animals alike) will live on in a principle (such as reason or love) the essence and goals of which are a mystery to us. . . . I have no use for that kind of immortality. I don't understand it, and Lev Nikolayevich was astonished I didn't."

Nevertheless, Chekhov was impressed with the solicitude shown by Tolstoy's visit. But, unlike Tolstoy, Chekhov didn't believe in an afterlife and never had. He didn't believe in anything that couldn't be apprehended by one or more of his five senses. And as far as his outlook on life and writing went, he once told someone that he lacked "a political, religious, and philosophical world view. I change it every month, so I'll have to limit myself to the description of how my heroes love, marry, give birth, die, and how they speak."

Earlier, before his t.b. was diagnosed, Chekhov had remarked, "When a peasant has consumption, he says, 'There's nothing I can do. I'll go off in the spring with the melting of the snows.' " (Chekhov himself died in the summer, during a heat wave.) But once Chekhov's own tuberculosis was discovered he continually tried to minimize the seriousness of his condition. To all appearances, it was as if he felt, right up to the end, that he might be able to throw off the disease as he would a lingering catarrh. Well into his final days, he spoke with seeming conviction of the possibility of an improvement. In fact, in a letter written shortly before his end, he went so far as to tell his sister that he was "getting fat" and felt much better now that he was in Badenweiler.

Badenweiler is a spa and resort city in the western area of the Black Forest, not far from Basel. The Vosges are visible from nearly anywhere in the city, and in those days the air was pure and invigorating. Russians had been going there for years to soak in the hot mineral baths and promenade on the boulevards. In June, 1904, Chekhov went there to die.

Earlier that month, he'd made a difficult journey by train from Moscow to Berlin. He traveled with his wife, the actress Olga Knipper, a woman he'd met in 1898 during rehearsals for "The Seagull." Her contemporaries describe her as an excellent actress. She was talented, pretty, and almost ten years younger than the playwright. Chekhov had been immediately attracted to her, but was slow to act on his feelings. As always, he preferred a flirtation to marriage. Finally, after a three-year courtship involving many separations, letters, and the inevitable misunderstandings, they were at last married, in a private ceremony in Moscow, on May 25, 1901. Chekhov was enormously happy. He called

Olga his "pony," and sometimes "dog" or "puppy." He was also fond of addressing her as "little turkey" or simply as "my joy."

In Berlin, Chekhov consulted with a renowned specialist in pulmonary disorders, a Dr. Karl Ewald. But, according to an eyewitness, after the doctor examined Chekhov he threw up his hands and left the room without a word. Chekhov was too far gone for help: this Dr. Ewald was furious with himself for not being able to work miracles, and with Chekhov for being so ill.

A Russian journalist happened to visit the Chekhovs at their hotel and sent back this dispatch to his editor: "Chekhov's days are numbered. He seems mortally ill, is terribly thin, coughs all the time, gasps for breath at the slightest movement, and is running a high temperature." This same journalist saw the Chekhovs off at Potsdam Station when they boarded their train for Badenweiler. According to his account, "Chekhov had trouble making his way up the small staircase at the station. He had to sit down for several minutes to catch his breath." In fact, it was painful for Chekhov to move: his legs ached continually and his insides hurt. The disease had attacked his intestines and spinal cord. At this point he had less than a month to live. When Chekhov spoke of his condition now, it was, according to Olga, "with an almost reckless indifference."

Dr. Schwöhrer was one of the many Badenweiler physicians who earned a good living by treating the well-to-do who came to the spa seeking relief from various maladies. Some of his patients were ill and infirm, others simply old and hypochondriacal. But Chekhov's was a special case: he was clearly beyond help and in his last days. He was also very famous. Even Dr. Schwöhrer knew his name: he'd read some of Chekhov's stories in a German magazine. When he examined the writer early in June, he voiced his appreciation of Chekhov's art but kept his medical opinions to himself. Instead, he prescribed a diet of cocoa, oatmeal drenched in butter, and strawberry tea. This last was supposed to help Chekhov sleep at night.

On June 13, less than three weeks before he died, Chekhov wrote a letter to his mother in which he told her his health was on the mend. In it he said, "It's likely that I'll be completely cured in a week." Who knows why he said this? What could he have been thinking? He was a doctor himself, and he knew better. He was dying, it was as simple and as unavoidable as that. Nevertheless, he sat out on the balcony of his hotel room and read railway timetables. He asked for information on sailings of boats bound for Odessa from Marseilles. But he *knew.* At this stage he had to have known. Yet in one of the last letters he ever wrote he told his sister he was growing stronger by the day.

He no longer had any appetite for literary work, and hadn't for a long time. In fact, he had very nearly failed to complete *The Cherry Orchard* the year before. Writing that play was the hardest thing he'd ever done in his life. Toward the end, he was able to manage only six or seven lines a day. "I've started losing heart," he wrote Olga. "I feel I'm finished as a writer, and every sentence strikes me as worthless and of no use whatever." But he didn't stop. He finished his play in October, 1903. It was the last thing he ever wrote, except for letters and a few entries in his notebook.

A little after midnight on July 2, 1904, Olga sent someone to fetch Dr. Schwöhrer. It was an emergency: Chekhov was delirious. Two young Russians on holiday happened to have the adjacent room, and Olga hurried next door to explain what was happening. One of the youths was in his bed asleep, but the other was still awake, smoking and reading. He left the hotel at a run to find Dr. Schwöhrer. "I can still hear the sound of the gravel under his shoes in the silence of that stifling July night," Olga wrote later on in her memoirs. Chekhov was hallucinating, talking about sailors, and there were snatches of something about the Japanese. "You don't put ice on an empty stomach," he said when she tried to place an ice pack on his chest.

Dr. Schwöhrer arrived and unpacked his bag, all the while keeping his gaze fastened on Chekhov, who lay gasping in the bed. The sick man's pupils were dilated and his temples glistened with sweat. Dr. Schwöhrer's face didn't register anything. He was not an emotional man, but he knew Chekhov's end was near. Still, he was a doctor, sworn to do his utmost, and Chekhov held on to life, however tenuously. Dr Schwöhrer prepared a hypodermic and administered an injection of camphor, something that was supposed to speed up the heart. But the injection didn't help—nothing, of course, could have helped. Nevertheless, the doctor made known to Olga his intention of sending for oxygen. Suddenly, Chekhov roused himself, became lucid, and said quietly, "What's the use? Before it arrives I'll be a corpse."

Dr. Schwöhrer pulled on his big moustache and stared at Chekhov. The writer's cheeks were sunken and gray, his complexion waxen; his breath was raspy. Dr. Schwöhrer knew the time could be reckoned in minutes. Without a word, without conferring with Olga, he went over to an alcove where there was a telephone on the wall. He read the instructions for using the device. If he activated it by holding his finger on a button and turning a handle on the side of the phone, he could reach the lower regions of the hotel—the kitchen. He picked up the receiver, held it to his ear, and did as the instructions told him. When someone finally answered, Dr. Schwöhrer ordered a bottle of the hotel's best champagne. "How many glasses?" he was asked. "Three glasses!" the doctor shouted into the mouthpiece. "And hurry, do you hear?" It was one of those rare moments of inspiration that can easily enough be overlooked later on, because the action is so entirely appropriate it seems inevitable.

The champagne was brought to the door by a tired-looking young man whose blond hair was standing up. The trousers of his uniform were wrinkled, the creases gone, and in his haste he'd missed a loop while buttoning his jacket. His appearance was that of someone who'd been resting (slumped in a chair, say, dozing a little), when off in the distance the phone had clamored in the early-morning hours—great God in Heaven!—and the next thing he knew he was being shaken awake by a superior and told to deliver a bottle of Moët to Room 211. "And hurry, do you hear?"

The young man entered the room carrying a silver ice bucket with the champagne in it and a silver tray with three cut-crystal glasses. He found a place on the table for the bucket and glasses, all the while craning his neck, trying to see into the other room, where someone panted ferociously for breath. It was a dreadful, harrowing sound, and the young man lowered his chin into his collar and turned away as the ratchety breathing worsened. Forgetting himself, he stared out the open window toward the darkened city. Then this big imposing man with a thick moustache pressed some coins into his hand—a large tip, by the feel of it—and suddenly the young man saw the door open. He took some steps and found himself on the landing, where he opened his hand and looked at the coins in amazement.

Methodically, the way he did everything, the doctor went about the business of working the cork out of the bottle. He did it in such a way as to minimize, as much as possible, the festive explosion. He poured three glasses and, out of habit, pushed the cork back into the neck of the bottle. He then took the glasses of champagne over to the bed. Olga momentarily released her grip on Chekhov's hand—a hand, she said later, that burned her fingers. She arranged another pillow behind his head. Then she put the cool glass of champagne against Chekhov's palm and made sure his fingers closed around the stem. They exchanged looks—Chekhov, Olga, Dr. Schwöhrer. They didn't touch glasses. There was no toast. What on earth was there to drink to? To death? Chekhov summoned his remaining strength and said, "It's been so long since I've had champagne." He brought the glass to his lips and drank. In a minute or two Olga took the empty glass from his hand and set it on the nightstand. Then Chekhov turned onto his side. He closed his eyes and sighed. A minute later, his breathing stopped.

Dr. Schwöhrer picked up Chekhov's hand from the bedsheet. He held his fingers to Chekhov's wrist and drew a gold watch from his vest pocket, opening the lid of the watch as he did so. The second hand on the watch moved slowly, very slowly. He let it move around the face of the watch three times while he waited for signs of a pulse. It was three o'clock in the morning and still sultry in the room. Badenweiler was in the grip of its worst heat wave in years. All the windows in both rooms stood open, but there was no sign of a breeze. A large, black-winged moth flew through a window and banged wildly against the electric lamp. Dr. Schwöhrer let go of Chekhov's wrist. "It's over," he said. He closed the lid of his watch and returned it to his vest pocket.

At once Olga dried her eyes and set about composing herself. She thanked the doctor for coming. He asked if she wanted some medication—laudanum, perhaps, or a few drops of valerian. She shook her head. She did have one request, though: before the authorities were notified and the newspapers found out, before the time came when Chekhov was no longer in her keeping, she wanted to be alone with him for a while. Could the doctor help with this? Could he withhold, for a while anyway, the news of what had just occurred?

Dr. Schwöhrer stroked his moustache with the back of a finger. Why not? After all, what difference would it make to anyone whether this matter became known now or a few hours from now? The only detail that remained was to fill out a death certificate, and this could be done at his office later on in the morning, after he'd slept a few hours. Dr. Schwöhrer nodded his agreement and prepared to leave. He murmured a few words of condolence. Olga inclined her head. "An honor," Dr. Schwöhrer said. He picked up his bag and left the room and, for that matter, history.

It was at this moment that the cork popped out of the champagne bottle; foam spilled down onto the table. Olga went back to Chekhov's bedside. She sat on a footstool, holding his hand, from time to time stroking his face. "There were no human voices, no everyday sounds," she wrote. "There was only beauty, peace, and the grandeur of death."

She stayed with Chekhov until day-break, when thrushes began to call from the garden below. Then came the sound of tables and chairs being moved about down there. Before long, voices carried up to her. It was then a knock sounded at the door. Of course she thought it must be an official of some sort—the medical examiner, say, or someone from the police who had questions to ask and forms for her to fill out, or maybe, just maybe, it could be Dr. Schwöhrer returning with a mortician to render assistance in embalming and transporting Chekhov's remains back to Russia.

But, instead, it was the same blond young man who'd brought the champagne a few hours earlier. This time, however, his uniform trousers were neatly pressed, with stiff creases in front, and every button on his snug green jacket was fastened. He seemed quite another person. Not only was he wide awake but his plump cheeks were smooth-shaven, his hair was in place, and he appeared anxious to please. He was holding a porcelain vase with three long-stemmed yellow roses. He presented these to Olga with a smart click of his heels. She stepped back and let him into the room. He was there, he said, to collect the glasses, ice bucket, and tray, yes. But he also wanted to say that, because of the extreme heat, breakfast would be served in the garden this morning. He hoped this weather wasn't too bothersome; he apologized for it.

The woman seemed distracted. While he talked, she turned her eyes away and looked down at something in the carpet. She crossed her arms and held her elbows. Meanwhile, still holding his vase, waiting for a sign, the young man took in the details of the room. Bright sunlight flooded through the open windows. The room was tidy and seemed undisturbed, almost untouched. No garments were flung over chairs, no shoes, stockings, braces, or stays were in evidence, no open suitcases. In short, there was no clutter, nothing but the usual heavy pieces of hotel-room furniture. Then, because the woman was still looking down, he looked down, too, and at once spied a cork near the toe of his shoe. The woman did not see it—she was looking somewhere else. The young man wanted to bend over and pick up the cork, but he was still holding the roses and was afraid of seeming to intrude even more by drawing any further attention to himself. Reluctantly, he left the cork where it was and raised his eyes. Everything was in order except for the uncorked, half-empty bottle of champagne that stood alongside two crystal glasses over on the little table. He cast his gaze about once more. Through an open door he saw that the third glass was in the bedroom, on the nightstand. But someone still occupied the bed! He couldn't see a face, but the figure under the covers lay perfectly motionless and quiet. He noted the figure and looked elsewhere. Then, for a reason he couldn't understand, a feeling of uneasiness took hold of him. He cleared his throat and moved his weight to the other leg. The woman still didn't look up or break her silence. The young man felt his cheeks grow warm. It occurred to him, quite without his having thought it through, that he should perhaps suggest an alternative to breakfast in the garden. He coughed, hoping to focus the woman's attention, but she didn't look at him. The distinguished foreign guests could, he said, take breakfast in their rooms this morning if they wished. The young man (his name hasn't survived, and it's likely he perished in the Great War) said he would be happy to bring up a tray. Two trays, he added, glancing uncertainly once again in the direction of the bedroom.

He fell silent and ran a finger around the inside of his collar. He didn't understand. He wasn't even sure the woman had been listening. He didn't know what else to do now; he was still holding the vase. The sweet odor of the roses filled his nostrils and inexplicably caused a pang of regret. The entire time he'd been waiting, the woman had apparently been lost in thought. It was as if all the while he'd been standing there, talking, shifting his weight, holding his flowers, she had been someplace else, somewhere far from Badenweiler. But now she came back to herself, and her face assumed another expression. She raised her eyes, looked at him, and then shook her head. She seemed to be struggling to understand what on earth this young man could be doing there in the room holding a vase with three yellow roses. Flowers? She hadn't ordered flowers.

The moment passed. She went over to her handbag and scooped up some coins. She drew out a number of banknotes as well. The young man touched his lips with his tongue; another large tip was forthcoming, but for what? What did she want him to do? He'd never before waited on such guests. He cleared his throat once more.

No breakfast, the woman said. Not yet, at any rate. Breakfast wasn't the important thing this morning. She required something else. She needed him to go out and bring back a mortician. Did he understand her? Herr Chekhov was dead, you see. *Comprenez-vous?* Young man? Anton Chekhov was dead. Now listen carefully to me, she said. She wanted him to go downstairs and ask someone at the front desk where he could go to find the most respected mortician in the city. Someone reliable, who took great pains in his work and whose manner was appropriately reserved. A mortician, in short, worthy of a great artist. Here, she said, and pressed the money on him. Tell them downstairs that I have specifically requested you to perform this duty for me. Are you listening? Do you understand what I'm saying to you?

The young man grappled to take in what she was saying. He chose not to look again in the direction of the other room. He had sensed that something was not right. He became aware of his heart beating rapidly under his jacket, and he felt perspiration break out on his forehead. He didn't know where he should turn his eyes. He wanted to put the vase down.

Please do this for me, the woman said. I'll remember you with gratitude. Tell them downstairs that I insist. Say that. But don't call any unnecessary attention to yourself or to the situation. Just say that this is necessary, that I request it—and that's all. Do you hear me? Nod if you understand. Above all, don't raise an alarm. Everything else, all the rest, the commotion—that'll come soon enough. The worst is over. Do we understand each other?

The young man's face had grown pale. He stood rigid, clasping the vase. He managed to nod his head.

After securing permission to leave the hotel he was to proceed quietly and resolutely, though without any unbecoming haste, to the mortician's. He was to behave exactly as if he were engaged on a very important errand, nothing more. He *was* engaged on an important errand, she said. And if it would help keep his movements purposeful he should imagine himself as someone moving down the busy sidewalk carrying in his arms a porcelain vase of roses that he had to deliver to an important man. (She spoke quietly, almost confidentially, as if to a relative or a friend.) He could even tell himself that the man he was going to see was expecting him, was perhaps impatient for him to arrive with his flowers. Nevertheless, the young man was not to become excited and run, or otherwise break his stride. Remember the vase he was carrying! He was to walk briskly, comporting himself at all times in as dignified a manner as possible. He should keep walking until he came to the mortician's house and stood before the door. He would then raise the brass knocker and let it fall, once, twice, three times. In a minute the mortician himself would answer.

This mortician would be in his forties, no doubt, or maybe early fifties—bald, solidly built, wearing steel-frame spectacles set very low on his nose. He would be modest, unassuming, a man who would ask only the most direct and necessary questions. An apron. Probably he would be wearing an apron. He might even be wiping his hands on a dark towel while he listened to what was being said. There'd be a faint whiff of formaldehyde on his clothes. But it was all right, and the young man shouldn't worry. He was nearly a grown-up now and shouldn't be frightened or repelled by any of this. The mortician would hear him out. He was a man of restraint and bearing, this mortician, someone who could help allay people's fears in this situation, not increase them. Long ago he'd acquainted himself with death in all its various guises and forms; death held no surprises for him any longer, no hidden secrets. It was this man whose services were required this morning.

The mortician takes the vase of roses. Only once while the young man is speaking does the mortician betray the least flicker of interest, or indicate that he's heard anything out of the ordinary. But the one time the young man mentions the name of the deceased, the mortician's eyebrows rise just a little. Chekhov, you say? Just a minute, and I'll be with you.

Do you understand what I'm saying, Olga said to the young man. Leave the glasses. Don't worry about them. Forget about crystal wineglasses and such. Leave the room as it is. Everything is ready now. We're ready. Will you go?

But at that moment the young man was thinking of the cork still resting near the toe of his shoe. To retrieve it he would have to bend over, still gripping the vase. He would do this. He leaned over. Without looking down, he reached out and closed it into his hand.

Bobbie Ann Mason

1940 –

Born in Mayfield, Kentucky, in 1940, Bobbie Ann Mason was educated at the University of Kentucky, where she received her B.A. degree in 1962, the State University of New York at Binghamton, where she received an M.A. degree in 1966, and the University of Connecticut, where she earned a Ph.D. in 1972. She served as an Assistant Professor of English at Mansfield State College of Pennsylvania from 1972 to 1979. Since the early 1980s, she has been writing short stories and winning prizes for them, among others the National Book Critics Circle Award for her first collection, *Shiloh and Other Stories* (1982). Since then she has contributed stories regularly to *The New Yorker, Atlantic,* and *Redbook,* as well as to the *Best American Short Stories* volumes.

With her first collection, Mason established a firm reputation as a rising young voice in Southern literature and was rated highly by Anne Tyler and other critics for her treatment of working class people in both rural and urban settings. Her ability to evoke strong feelings for such folk as they cope with the mutual frustrations and routine problems of everyday life is due, say the critics, to the fact that she neither sentimentalizes them, nor makes caricatures of them. "Shiloh" explores many of the themes that occur regularly in Mason's stories.

Shiloh

Leroy Moffitt's wife, Norma Jean, is working on her pectorals. She lifts three-pound dumbbells to warm up, then progresses to a twenty-pound barbell. Standing with her legs apart, she reminds Leroy of Wonder Woman.

"I'd give anything if I could just get these muscles to where they're real hard," says Norma Jean. "Feel this arm. It's not as hard as the other one."

"That's 'cause you're right-handed," says Leroy, dodging as she swings the barbell in an arc.

"Do you think so?"

"Sure."

Leroy is a truckdriver. He injured his leg in a highway accident four months ago, and his physical therapy, which involves weights and a pulley, prompted Norma Jean to try building herself up. Now she is attending a body-building class. Leroy has been collecting temporary disability since his tractor-trailer jackknifed in Missouri, badly twisting his left leg in its socket. He has a steel pin in his hip. He will probably not be able to drive his rig again. It sits in the backyard, like a gigantic bird that has flown home to roost. Leroy has been home in Kentucky for three months, and his leg is almost healed, but the accident frightened him and he does not want to drive any more long hauls. He is not sure what to do next. In the meantime, he makes things from craft kits. He started by building a miniature log cabin from notched Popsicle sticks. He varnished it and placed it on the TV set, where it remains. It reminds him of a rustic Nativity scene. Then he tried string art (sailing ships on black velvet), a macramé owl kit, a snap-together B-17 Flying Fortress, and a lamp made out of a model truck, with a light fixture screwed in the top of the cab. At first the kits were diversions, something to kill time, but now he is thinking about building a full-scale log house from a kit. It would be considerably cheaper than building a regular house, and besides, Leroy has grown to appreciate how things are put together. He has begun to realize that in all the years he was on the road he never took time to examine anything. He was always flying past scenery.

"They won't let you build a log cabin in any of the new subdivisions," Norma Jean tells him.

"They will if I tell them it's for you," he says, teasing her. Ever since they were married, he has promised Norma Jean he would build her a new home one day. They have always rented and the house they live in is small and nondescript. It does not even feel like a home, Leroy realizes now.

Norma Jean works at the Rexall drugstore, and she has acquired an amazing amount of information about cosmetics. When she explains to Leroy the three stages of complexion care, involving creams, toners, and moisturizers, he thinks happily of other petroleum products—axle grease, diesel fuel. This is a connection between him and Norma Jean. Since he has been home, he has felt unusually tender about his wife and guilty over his long absences. But he can't tell what she feels about him. Norma Jean has never complained about his traveling; she has never made hurt remarks, like calling his truck a "widow-maker." He is reasonably certain she has been faithful to him, but he wishes she would celebrate his permanent homecoming more happily. Norma Jean is often startled to find Leroy at home, and he thinks she seems a little disappointed about it. Perhaps he reminds her too much of the early days of their marriage, before he went on the road. They had a child who died as an infant, years ago. They never speak about their memories of Randy, which have almost faded, but now that Leroy is home all the time, they sometimes feel awkward around each other, and Leroy wonders if one of them should mention the child. He has the feeling that they are waking up out of a dream together—that they must create a new marriage, start afresh. They are lucky they are still married. Leroy has read that for most people losing a child destroys the marriage—or else he heard this on *Donahue*. He can't always remember where he learns things anymore.

At Christmas, Leroy bought an electric organ for Norma Jean. She used to play the piano when she was in high school. "It don't leave you," she told him once. "It's like riding a bicycle."

The new instrument had so many keys and buttons that she was bewildered by it at first. She touched the keys tentatively, pushed some buttons, then pecked out "Chopsticks." It came out in an amplified fox-trot rhythm, with marimba sounds.

"It's an orchestra!" she cried.

The organ had a pecan-look finish and eighteen preset chords, with optional flute, violin, trumpet, clarinet, and banjo accompaniments. Norma Jean mastered the organ almost immediately. At first she played Christmas songs. Then she bought *The Sixties Songbook* and learned every tune in it, adding variations to each with the rows of brightly colored buttons.

"I didn't like these old songs back then," she said. "But I have this crazy feeling I missed something."

"You didn't miss a thing," said Leroy.

Leroy likes to lie on the couch and smoke a joint and listen to Norma Jean play "Can't Take My Eyes Off You" and "I'll Be Back." He is back again. After fifteen years on the road, he is finally settling down with the woman he loves. She is still pretty. Her skin is flawless. Her frosted curls resemble pencil trimmings.

Now that Leroy has come home to stay, he notices how much the town has changed. Subdivisions are spreading across western Kentucky like an oil slick. The sign at the edge of town says "Pop: 11,500"—only seven hundred more than it said twenty years before. Leroy can't figure out who is living in all the new houses. The farmers who used to gather around the courthouse square on Saturday afternoons to play checkers and spit tobacco juice have gone. It has been years since Leroy has thought about the farmers, and they have disappeared without his noticing.

Leroy meets a kid named Stevie Hamilton in the parking lot at the new shopping center. While they pretend to be strangers meeting over a stalled car, Stevie tosses an ounce of marijuana under the front seat of Leroy's car. Stevie is wearing orange jogging shoes and a T-shirt that says CHATTAHOOCHEE SUPER-RAT. His father is a prominent doctor who lives in one of the expensive subdivisions in a new white-columned brick house that looks like a funeral parlor. In the phone book under his name there is a separate number, with the listing "Teenagers."

"Where do you get this stuff?" asks Leroy. "From your pappy?"

"That's for me to know and you to find out," Stevie says. He is slit-eyed and skinny.

"What else you got?"

"What you interested in?"

"Nothing special. Just wondered."

Leroy used to take speed on the road. Now he has to go slowly. He needs to be mellow. He leans back against the car and says, "I'm aiming to build me a log house, soon as I get time. My wife, though, I don't think she likes the idea."

"Well, let me know when you want me again," Stevie says. He has a cigarette in his cupped palm, as though sheltering it from the wind. He takes a long drag, then stomps it on the asphalt and slouches away.

Stevie's father was two years ahead of Leroy in high school. Leroy is thirty-four. He married Norma Jean when they were both eighteen, and their child Randy was born a few months later, but he died at the age of four months and three days. He would be about Stevie's age now. Norma Jean and Leroy were at the drive-in watching a double feature *(Dr.*

Strangelove and *Lover Come Back),* and the baby was sleeping in the back seat. When the first movie ended, the baby was dead. It was the sudden infant death syndrome. Leroy remembers handing Randy to a nurse at the emergency room, as though he were offering her a large doll as a present. A dead baby feels like a sack of flour. "It just happens sometimes," said the doctor, in what Leroy always recalls as a nonchalant tone. Leroy can hardly remember the child anymore, but he still sees vividly a scene from *Dr. Strangelove* in which the President of the United States was talking in a folksy voice on the hot line to the Soviet Premier about the bomber accidentally headed toward Russia. He was in the War Room, and the world map was lit up. Leroy remembers Norma Jean standing catatonically beside him in the hospital and himself thinking: Who is this strange girl? He had forgotten who she was. Now scientists are saying that crib death is caused by a virus. Nobody knows anything, Leroy thinks. The answers are always changing.

When Leroy gets home from the shopping center, Norma Jean's mother, Mabel Beasley, is there. Until this year, Leroy has not realized how much time she spends with Norma Jean. When she visits, she inspects the closets and then the plants, informing Norma Jean when a plant is droopy or yellow. Mabel calls the plants "flowers," although there are never any blooms. She always notices if Norma Jean's laundry is piling up. Mabel is a short, overweight woman whose tight, brown-dyed curls look more like a wig than the actual wig she sometimes wears. Today she has brought Norma Jean an off-white dust ruffle she made for the bed; Mabel works in a custom-upholstery shop.

"This is the tenth one I made this year," Mabel says. "I got started and couldn't stop."

"It's real pretty," says Norma Jean.

"Now we can hide things under the bed," says Leroy, who gets along with his mother-in-law primarily by joking with her. Mabel has never really forgiven him for disgracing her by getting Norma Jean pregnant. When the baby died, she said that fate was mocking her.

"What's that thing?" Mabel says to Leroy in a loud voice, pointing to a tangle of yarn on a piece of canvas.

Leroy holds it up for Mabel to see. "It's my needlepoint," he explains. "This is a *Star Trek* pillow cover."

"That's what a woman would do," says Mabel. "Great day in the morning!"

"All the big football players on TV do it," he says.

"Why, Leroy, you're always trying to fool me. I don't believe you for one minute. You don't know what to do with yourself—that's the whole trouble. Sewing!"

"I'm aiming to build us a log house," says Leroy. "Soon as my plans come."

"Like *heck* you are," says Norma Jean. She takes Leroy's needlepoint and shoves it into a drawer. "You have to find a job first. Nobody can afford to build now anyway."

Mabel straightens her girdle and says, "I still think before you get tied down y'all ought to take a little run to Shiloh."

"One of these days, Mama," Norma Jean says impatiently.

Mabel is talking about Shiloh, Tennessee. For the past few years, she has been urging Leroy and Norma Jean to visit the Civil War battleground there. Mabel went there on her honeymoon—the only real trip she ever took. Her husband died of a perforated ulcer when Norma Jean was ten, but Mabel, who was accepted into the United Daughters of the Confederacy in 1975, is still preoccupied with going back to Shiloh.

"I've been to kingdom come and back in that truck out yonder," Leroy says to Mabel, "but we never yet set foot in that battleground. Ain't that something? How did I miss it?"

"It's not even that far," Mabel says.

After Mabel leaves, Norma Jean reads to Leroy from a list she has made. "Things you could do," she announces. "You could get a job as a guard at Union Carbide, where they'd let you set on a stool. You could get on at the lumberyard. You could do a little carpenter work, if you want to build so bad. You could—"

"I can't do something where I'd have to stand up all day."

"You ought to try standing up all day behind a cosmetics counter. It's amazing that I have strong feet, coming from two parents that never had strong feet at all." At the moment Norma Jean is holding on to the kitchen counter, raising her knees one at a time as she talks. She is wearing two-pound ankle weights.

"Don't worry," says Leroy. "I'll do something."

"You could truck calves to slaughter for somebody. You wouldn't have to drive any big old truck for that."

"I'm going to build you this house," says Leroy. "I want to make you a real home."

"I don't want to live in any log cabin."

"It's not a cabin. It's a house."

"I don't care. It looks like a cabin."

"You and me together could lift those logs. It's just like lifting weights."

Norma Jean doesn't answer. Under her breath, she is counting. Now she is marching through the kitchen. She is doing goose steps.

Before his accident, when Leroy came home he used to stay in the house with Norma Jean, watching TV in bed and playing cards. She would cook fried chicken, picnic ham, chocolate pie—all his favorites. Now he is home alone much of the time. In the mornings, Norma Jean disappears, leaving a cooling place in the bed. She eats a cereal called Body Buddies, and she leaves the bowl on the table, with the soggy tan balls floating in a milk puddle. He sees things about Norma Jean that he never realized before. When she chops onions, she stares off into a corner, as if she can't bear to look. She puts on her house slippers almost precisely at nine o'clock every evening and nudges her jogging shoes under the couch. She saves bread heels for the birds. Leroy watches the birds at the feeder. He notices the peculiar way goldfinches fly past the window. They close their wings, then fall, then spread their wings to catch and lift themselves. He wonders if they close their eyes when they fall. Norma Jean closes her eyes when they are in bed. She wants the lights turned out. Even then, he is sure she closes her eyes.

He goes for long drives around town. He tends to drive a car rather carelessly. Power steering and an automatic shift make a car feel so small and inconsequential that his body is hardly involved in the driving process. His injured leg stretches out comfortably. Once or twice he has almost hit something, but even the prospect of an accident seems minor in a car. He cruises the new subdivisions, feeling like a criminal rehearsing for a robbery. Norma Jean is probably right about a log house being inappropriate here in the new subdivisions. All the houses look grand and complicated. They depress him.

One day when Leroy comes home from a drive he finds Norma Jean in tears. She is in the kitchen making a potato and mushroom-soup casserole, with grated-cheese topping. She is crying because her mother caught her smoking.

"I didn't hear her coming. I was standing here puffing away pretty as you please," Norma Jean says, wiping her eyes.

"I knew it would happen sooner or later," says Leroy, putting his arm around her.

"She don't know the meaning of the word 'knock,' " says Norma Jean. "It's a wonder she hadn't caught me years ago."

"Think of it this way," Leroy says. "What if she caught me with a joint?"

"You better not let her!" Norma Jean shrieks. "I'm warning you, Leroy Moffitt!"

"I'm just kidding. Here, play me a tune. That'll help you relax."

Norma Jean puts the casserole in the oven and sets the timer. Then she plays a ragtime tune, with horns and banjo, as Leroy lights up a joint and lies on the couch, laughing to himself about Mabel's catching him at it. He thinks of Stevie Hamilton—a doctor's son pushing grass. Everything is funny. The whole town seems crazy and small. He is reminded of Virgil Mathis, a boastful policeman Leroy used to shoot pool with. Virgil recently led a drug bust in a back room at a bowling alley, where he seized ten thousand dollars' worth of marijuana. The newspaper had a picture of him holding up the bags of grass and grinning widely. Right now, Leroy can imagine Virgil breaking down the door and arresting him with a lungful of smoke. Virgil would probably have been alerted to the scene because of all the racket Norma Jean is making. Now she sounds like a hard-rock band. Norma Jean is terrific. When she switches to a Latin-rhythm version of "Sunshine Superman," Leroy hums along. Norma Jean's foot goes up and down, up and down.

"Well, what do you think?" Leroy says, when Norma Jean pauses to search through her music.

"What do I think about what?"

His mind has gone blank. Then he says, "I'll sell my rig and build us a house." That wasn't what he wanted to say. He wanted to know what she thought—what she *really* thought—about them.

"Don't start in on that again," says Norma Jean. She begins playing "Who'll Be the Next in Line?"

Leroy used to tell hitchhikers his whole life story—about his travels, his hometown, the baby. He would end with a question: "Well, what do you think?" It was just a rhetorical question. In time, he had the feeling that he'd been telling the same story over and over to the same hitchhikers. He quit talking to hitchhikers when he realized how his voice sounded—whining and self-pitying, like some teenage-tragedy song. Now Leroy has the sudden impulse to tell Norma Jean about himself, as if he had just met her. They have known each other so long they have forgotten a lot about each other. They could become reacquainted. But when the oven timer goes off and she runs to the kitchen, he forgets why he wants to do this.

The next day, Mabel drops by. It is Saturday and Norma Jean is cleaning. Leroy is studying the plans of his log house, which have finally come in the mail. He has them spread out on the table—big sheets of stiff blue paper, with diagrams and numbers printed in white. While Norma Jean runs the vacuum, Mabel drinks coffee. She sets her coffee cup on a blueprint.

"I'm just waiting for time to pass," she says to Leroy, drumming her fingers on the table.

As soon as Norma Jean switches off the vacuum, Mabel says in a loud voice, "Did you hear about the datsun dog that killed the baby?"

Norma Jean says, "The word is 'dachshund.' "

"They put the dog on trial. It chewed the baby's legs off. The mother was in the next room all the time." She raises her voice. "They thought it was neglect."

Norma Jean is holding her ears. Leroy manages to open the refrigerator and get some Diet Pepsi to offer Mabel. Mabel still has some coffee and she waves away the Pepsi.

"Datsuns are like that," Mabel says. "They're jealous dogs. They'll tear a place to pieces if you don't keep an eye on them."

"You better watch out what you're saying, Mabel," says Leroy.

"Well, facts is facts."

Leroy looks out the window at his rig. It is like a huge piece of furniture gathering dust in the backyard. Pretty soon it will be an antique. He hears the vacuum cleaner. Norma Jean seems to be cleaning the living room rug again.

Later, she says to Leroy, "She just said that about the baby because she caught me smoking. She's trying to pay me back."

"What are you talking about?" Leroy says, nervously shuffling blueprints.

"You know good and well," Norma Jean says. She is sitting in a kitchen chair with her feet up and her arms wrapped around her knees. She looks small and helpless. She says, "The very idea, her bringing up a subject like that! Saying it was neglect."

"She didn't mean that," Leroy says.

"She might not have *thought* she meant it. She always says things like that. You don't know how she goes on."

"But she didn't really mean it. She was just talking."

Leroy opens a king-sized bottle of beer and pours it into two glasses, dividing it carefully. He hands a glass to Norma Jean and she takes it from him mechanically. For a long time, they sit by the kitchen window watching the birds at the feeder.

Something is happening. Norma Jean is going to night school. She has graduated from her six-week body-building course and now she is taking an adult-education course in composition at Paducah Community College. She spends her evenings outlining paragraphs.

"First you have a topic sentence," she explains to Leroy. "Then you divide it up. Your secondary topic has to be connected to your primary topic."

To Leroy, this sounds intimidating. "I never was any good in English," he says.

"It makes a lot of sense."

"What are you doing this for, anyhow?"

She shrugs. "It's something to do." She stands up and lifts her dumbbells a few times.

"Driving a rig, nobody cared about my English."

"I'm not criticizing your English."

Norma Jean used to say, "If I lose ten minutes' sleep, I just drag all day." Now she stays up late, writing compositions. She got a B on her first paper—a how-to theme on soup-based casseroles. Recently Norma Jean has been cooking unusual foods—tacos, lasagna, Bombay chicken.

She doesn't play the organ anymore, though her second paper was called "Why Music Is Important to Me." She sits at the kitchen table, concentrating on her outlines, while Leroy plays with his log house plans, practicing with a set of Lincoln Logs. The thought of getting a truckload of notched, numbered logs scares him, and he wants to be prepared. As he and Norma Jean work together at the kitchen table, Leroy has the hopeful thought that they are sharing something, but he knows he is a fool to think this. Norma Jean is miles away. He knows he is going to lose her. Like Mabel, he is just waiting for time to pass.

One day, Mabel is there before Norma Jean gets home from work, and Leroy finds himself confiding in her. Mabel, he realizes, must know Norma Jean better than he does.

"I don't know what's got into that girl," Mabel says. "She used to go to bed with the chickens. Now you say she's up all hours. Plus her a-smoking. I like to died."

"I want to make her this beautiful home," Leroy says, indicating the Lincoln Logs. "I don't think she even wants it. Maybe she was happier with me gone."

"She don't know what to make of you, coming home like this."

"Is that it?"

Mabel takes the roof off his Lincoln Log cabin. "You couldn't get *me* a log cabin," she says. "I was raised in one. It's no picnic, let me tell you."

"They're different now," says Leroy.

"I tell you what," Mabel says, smiling oddly at Leroy.

"What?"

"Take her on down to Shiloh. Y'all need to get out together, stir a little. Her brain's all balled up over them books."

Leroy can see traces of Norma Jean's features in her mother's face. Mabel's worn face has the texture of crinkled cotton, but suddenly she looks pretty. It occurs to Leroy that Mabel has been hinting all along that she wants them to take her with them to Shiloh.

"Let's all go to Shiloh," he says. "You and me and her. Come Sunday."

Mabel throws up her hands in protest. "Oh, no, not me. Young folks want to be by theirselves."

When Norma Jean comes in with groceries, Leroy says excitedly, "Your mama here's been dying to go to Shiloh for thirty-five years. It's about time we went, don't you think?"

"I'm not going to butt in on anybody's second honeymoon," Mabel says.

"Who's going on a honeymoon, for Christ's sake?" Norma Jean says loudly.

"I never raised no daughter of mine to talk that-a-way," Mabel says.

"You ain't seen nothing yet," says Norma Jean. She starts putting away boxes and cans, slamming cabinet doors.

"There's a log cabin at Shiloh," Mabel says. "It was there during the battle. There's bullet holes in it."

"When are you going to *shut up* about Shiloh, Mama?" asks Norma Jean.

"I always thought Shiloh was the prettiest place, so full of history," Mabel goes on. "I just hoped y'all could see it once before I die, so you could tell me about it." Later, she whispers to Leroy, "You do what I said. A little change is what she needs."

"Your name means 'the king,'" Norma Jean says to Leroy that evening. He is trying to get her to go to Shiloh, and she is reading a book about another century.

"Well, I reckon I ought to be right proud."

"I guess so."

"Am I still king around here?"

Norma Jean flexes her biceps and feels them for hardness. "I'm not fooling around with anybody, if that's what you mean," she says.

"Would you tell me if you were?"

"I don't know."

"What does *your* name mean?"

"It was Marilyn Monroe's real name."

"No kidding!"

"Norma comes from the Normans. They were invaders," she says. She closes her book and looks hard at Leroy. "I'll go to Shiloh with you if you'll stop staring at me."

On Sunday, Norma Jean packs a picnic and they go to Shiloh. To Leroy's relief, Mabel says she does not want to come with them. Norma Jean drives, and Leroy, sitting beside her, feels like some boring hitchhiker she has picked up. He tries some conversation, but she answers him in monosyllables. At Shiloh, she drives aimlessly through the park, past bluffs and trails and steep ravines. Shiloh is an immense place, and Leroy cannot see it as a battleground. It is not what he expected. He thought it would look like a golf course. Monuments are everywhere, showing through the thick clusters of trees. Norma Jean passes the log cabin Mabel mentioned. It is surrounded by tourists looking for bullet holes.

"That's not the kind of log house I've got in mind," says Leroy apologetically.

"I know *that*."

"This is a pretty place. Your mama was right."

"It's O.K," says Norma Jean. "Well, we've seen it. I hope she's satisfied."

They burst out laughing together.

At the park museum, a movie on Shiloh is shown every half hour, but they decide that they don't want to see it. They buy a souvenir Confederate flag for Mabel, and then they find a picnic spot near the cemetery. Norma Jean has brought a picnic cooler, with pimiento sandwiches, soft drinks, and Yodels. Leroy eats a sandwich and then smokes a joint, hiding it behind the picnic cooler. Norma Jean has quit smoking altogether. She is picking cake crumbs from the cellophane wrapper, like a fussy bird.

Leroy says, "So the boys in gray ended up in Corinth. The Union soldiers zapped 'em finally. April 7, 1862."

They both know that he doesn't know any history. He is just talking about some of the historical plaques they have read. He feels awkward, like a boy on a date with an older girl. They are still just making conversation.

"Corinth is where Mama eloped to," says Norma Jean.

They sit in silence and stare at the cemetery for the Union dead and, beyond, at a tall cluster of trees. Campers are parked nearby, bumper to bumper, and small children in bright clothing are cavorting and squealing. Norma Jean wads up the cake wrapper and squeezes it tightly in her hand. Without looking at Leroy, she says, "I want to leave you."

Leroy takes a bottle of Coke out of the cooler and flips off the cap. He holds the bottle poised near his mouth but cannot remember to take a drink. Finally he says, "No, you don't."

"Yes, I do."

"I won't let you."

"You can't stop me."

"Don't do me that way."

Leroy knows Norma Jean will have her own way. "Didn't I promise to be home from now on?" he says.

"In some ways, a woman prefers a man who wanders," says Norma Jean. "That sounds crazy, I know."

"You're not crazy."

Leroy remembers to drink from his Coke. Then he says, "Yes, you *are* crazy. You and me could start all over again. Right back at the beginning."

"We *have* started all over again," says Norma Jean. "And this is how it turned out."

"What did I do wrong?"

"Nothing."

"Is this one of those women's lib things?" Leroy asks.

"Don't be funny."

The cemetery, a green slope dotted with white markers, looks like a subdivision site. Leroy is trying to comprehend that his marriage is breaking up, but for some reason he is wondering about white slabs in a graveyard.

"Everything was fine till Mama caught me smoking," says Norma Jean standing up. "That set something off."

"What are you talking about?"

"She won't leave me alone—*you* won't leave me alone." Norma Jean seems to be crying, but she is looking away from him. "I feel eighteen again. I can't face that all over again." She starts walking away. "No, it *wasn't* fine. I don't know what I'm saying. Forget it."

Leroy takes a lungful of smoke and closes his eyes as Norma Jean's words sink in. He tries to focus on the fact that thirty-five hundred soldiers died on the grounds around him. He can only think of that war as a board game with plastic soldiers. Leroy almost smiles, as he compares the Confederates' daring attack on the Union camps and Virgil Mathis's raid on the bowling alley. General Grant, drunk and furious, shoved the Southerners back to Corinth, where Mabel and Jet Beasley were married years later, when Mabel was still thin and good-looking. The next day, Mabel and Jet visited the battleground, and then Norma Jean was born, and then she married Leroy and they had a baby, which they lost, and now Leroy and Norma Jean are here at the same battleground. Leroy knows he is leaving out a lot. He is leaving out the insides of history. History was always just names and dates to him. It occurs to him that building a house out of logs is similarly empty—too simple. And the real inner workings of a marriage, like most of history, have escaped him. Now he sees that building a log house is the dumbest idea he could have had. It was clumsy of him to think Norma Jean would want a log house. It was a crazy idea. He'll have to think of something else, quickly. He will wad the blueprints into tight balls and fling them into the lake. Then he'll get moving again. He opens his eyes. Norma Jean has moved away and is walking through the cemetery, following a serpentine brick path.

Leroy gets up to follow his wife, but his good leg is asleep and his bad leg still hurts him. Norma Jean is far away, walking rapidly toward the bluff by the river, and he tries to hobble toward her. Some children run past him, screaming noisily. Norma Jean has reached the bluff, and she is looking out over the Tennessee River. Now she turns toward Leroy and waves her arms. Is she beckoning to him? She seems to be doing an exercise for her chest muscles. The sky is unusually pale—the color of the dust ruffle Mabel made for their bed.

Alice Walker

1944 –

Though probably best known for her novel *The Color Purple* (1982), Alice Walker is also a prolific short story writer, poet, and essayist. Her other novels include *Meridian* (1975), *The Third Life of Grange Copeland* (1976) and *The Temple of My Familiar* (1989). Her collections of poems include *Once: Poems* (1975), *Good Night, Willie Lee, I'll See You in the Morning* (1983), and *Horses Make a Landscape Look More Beautiful* (1984). Her essays have been collected in *In Search of Our Mothers' Gardens: Womanist Prose* (1983) and *Living by the Word: Selected Writings, 1973–1987* (1988). To date, Walker has published two collections of short stories: *In Love and Trouble: Stories of Black Women* (1973) and *You Can't Keep a Good Woman Down* (1981).

Born in Eatonton, Georgia, Walker was educated at Spelman College and Sarah Lawrence College, from which she received a B.A. degree in 1965. She has been a writer-in-residence or a lecturer at a number of universities, including Jackson State College, the University of Massachusetts, and the University of California at Berkeley. She currently lives in the San Francisco area.

In addition to winning both the Pulitzer Prize and the American Book Award, *The Color Purple* was widely hailed for its depiction of the effects of racism and sexism on the lives of black women. The emotional, physical, and spiritual strength that are common in Walker's female characters are evident in "Kindred Spirits."

Kindred Spirits

Rosa could not tell her sister how scared she was or how glad she was that she had consented to come with her. Instead they made small talk on the plane, and Rosa looked out of the window at the clouds.

It was a kind of sentimental journey for Rosa, months too late, going to visit the aunt in whose house their grandfather had died. She did not even know why she must do it: she had spent the earlier part of the summer in such far-flung places as Cyprus and Greece. Jamaica. She was at a place in her life where she seemed to have no place. She'd left the brownstone in Park Slope, given up the car and cat. Her child was at camp. She was in pain. That, at least, she knew. She hardly slept. If she did sleep, her dreams were cold, desolate, and full of static. She ate spaghetti, mostly, with shrimp, from a recipe cut out from the *Times*. She listened to the jazz radio station all the time, her heart in her mouth.

"So how is Ivan?" her sister, Barbara, asked.

Barbara was still fond of her brother-in-law, and hurt that after his divorce from Rosa he'd sunk back into the white world so completely that even a Christmas card was too much trouble to send people who had come to love him.

"Oh, fine," Rosa said. "Living with a nice Jewish girl, at last." Which might have explained the absence of a Christmas card, Rosa thought, but she knew it really didn't.

"Really? What's she like?"

"Warm. Attractive. Loves him."

This was mostly guesswork on Rosa's part; she'd met Sheila only once. She hoped she had these attributes, for his sake. A week after she'd moved out of the brownstone, Sheila had moved in, and all her in-laws, especially Ivan's mother, seemed very happy. Once Rosa had "borrowed" the car (her own, which she'd left with him), and when she returned it, mother and girlfriend met her at her own front gate, barring her way into her own house, their faces flushed with the victory of finally seeing her outside where she belonged. Music and laughter of many guests came from inside.

But did she care? No. She was free. She took to the sidewalk, the heels of her burgundy suede boots clicking, free. Her heart making itself still by force. *Ah,* but then at night when she slept, it awoke, and the clicking of her heels was nothing to the rattling and crackling of her heart.

"Mama misses him," said Barbara.

Rosa knew she did. How could she even begin to understand that this son-in-law she doted on was incapable, after divorcing her daughter, of even calling on the phone to ask how she felt, as she suffered stroke after frightening and debilitating stroke? It must have seemed totally unnatural to her, a woman who had rushed to comfort the sick and shut-in all her life. It seemed unnatural even to Rosa, who about most other things was able to take a somewhat more modern view.

At last they were in sight of the Miami airport. Before they could be prevented by the stewardess, Barbara and Rosa managed to exchange seats. Barbara sat by the window because she flew very rarely and it was a treat for her to "see herself" landing. Rosa no longer cared to look down. She had traveled so much that summer. The trip to Cyprus in particular had been so long it had made her want to scream. And then, in Nicosia, the weather was abominable. One hundred twenty degrees. It hurt to breathe. And there had been days of visiting Greeks in refugee camps and listening to socialists and visiting the home of a family in which an only son—standing next to a socialist leader at a rally—was assassinated by mistake. Though it had happened over a year earlier his father still wept as he told of it, and looked with great regret at his surviving daughter and *her* small daughter. "A man must have many sons," he said over and over, never seeming to realize that under conditions of war even a dozen sons could be killed. And not under war alone.

And then Rosa had flown to Greece, and Athens had been like New York City in late July and the Parthenon tiny. . . .

When they arrived at the Miami airport they looked about with the slightly anxious interest of travelers who still remembered segregated travel facilities. If a white person had materialized beside them and pointed out a colored section they would have attacked him or her on principle, but have been only somewhat surprised. Their formative years had been lived under racist restrictions so pervasive that wherever they traveled in the world they expected, on some level, in themselves and in whatever physical circumstances they found themselves, to encounter some, if only symbolic, racial barrier.

And there it was now: on a poster across from them a blond white woman and her dark-haired male partner danced under the stars while a black band played and a black waiter waited and a black chef beamed from the kitchen.

A striking woman, black as midnight, in a blue pastel cotton dress, tall, straight of bearing, with a firm bun of silver-white hair, bore down upon them.

It's me, thought Rosa. My old self.

"Aunt Lily!" said Barbara, smiling and throwing her arms around her.

When it was her turn to be hugged, Rosa gave herself up to it, enjoying the smells of baby shampoo, Jergens lotion, and Evening in Paris remembered from childhood embraces, which, on second sniff, she decided was all Charlie. That was this aunt, full of change and contradictions, as she had known her.

Not that she ever had, really. Aunt Lily had come to visit summers, when Rosa was a child. She had been straight and black and as vibrant as fire. She was always with her husband, whose tan face seemed weak next to hers. He drove the car, but she steered it; the same seemed true of their lives.

They had moved to Florida years ago, looking for a better life "somewhere else in the South that wasn't so full of southerners." Looking at her aunt now—with her imperial bearing, directness of speech, and a great height—Rosa could not imagine anyone having the nerve to condescend to her, or worse, attempt to cheat her. Once again Rosa was amazed at the white man's arrogance and racist laws. Ten years earlier this sweet-smelling, squeaky-clean aunt of hers would not have been permitted to try on a dress in local department stores. She could not have drunk at certain fountains. The main restaurants of the city would have been closed to her. The public library. The vast majority of the city's toilets.

Aunt Lily had an enormous brown station wagon, into which Rosa and Barbara flung their light travel bags. Barbara, older than Rosa and closer to Aunt Lily, sat beside her on the front seat. Rosa sat behind them, looking out the window at the passing scenery, admiring the numerous canals—she was passionately fond of water—and yet wondering about the city's sewerage problems, of which she had heard.

How like them, really, she thought, to build canals around their pretty segregated houses—canals so polluted that to fall into one was to risk disease.

When they arrived at Aunt Lily's squat, green house, with its orange and lemon trees in the yard, far from canals and even streetlights, they were met in the narrow hall by five of her aunt's seven foster children and a young woman who had been a foster child herself but was now sharing the house and helping to look after the children with Aunt Lily. Her name was Raymyna Ann.

Aunt Lily had, a long time ago, a baby son who died. For years she had not seemed to care for children. Rosa had never felt particularly valued by her whenever Aunt Lily had come to visit. Aunt Lily acknowledged her brother's children by bringing them oranges and grapefruit packed in orange net bags, but she rarely hugged or kissed them. Well, she rarely touched these foster children, either, Rosa noticed. There were so many of them, so dark (all as black, precisely, as her aunt) and so woundedly silent. But at dinner the table was piled high with food, the little ones were encouraged to have seconds, and when they all trooped off to bed they did so in a cloud of soapy smells and dazzling linen.

Rosa lay in the tiny guest room, which had been her grandfather's room, and smoked a cigarette. Aunt Lily's face appeared at the door.

"Now, Rosa, I don't allow smoking or drinking in my house."

Rosa rose from the bed to put her cigarette out, her aunt watching her as if she were a child.

"*You* used to smoke and drink," Rosa said, piqued at her aunt's self-righteous tone.

"Your mama told you that lie," said Aunt Lily, unsmiling. "She was always trying to say I was fast. But I never did drink. I tried to, and it made me sick. Every time she said she didn't want me laying on her freshly made-up bed drunk, I wasn't drunk, I was sick."

"Oh," said Rosa. She had the unfortunate tendency of studying people very closely when they spoke. It occurred to her for the first time that Aunt Lily didn't like her mother.

But *why* didn't Aunt Lily like her mother? The question nagged at her that night as she tried to sleep, then became lost in the many other questions that presented themselves well into the dawn.

Why, for instance, did Ivan no longer like her? And how could you live with someone for over a decade and "love" them, and then, as soon as you were no longer married, you didn't even like them?

Her marriage had been wonderful, she felt. Only the divorce was horrible.

The most horrible thing of all was losing Ivan's friendship and comradely support, which he yanked out of her reach with a vengeance that sent her reeling. Two weeks after the divorce became final, when she was in the hospital for surgery that only after the fact proved to have been minor, he neither called nor sent a note. Sheila, now his wife, wouldn't have liked it, he later (years later) explained.

The next day all the children were in school, and Barbara stood behind Aunt Lily's chair combing and braiding her long silver hair. Rosa sat on the couch looking at them. Raymyna busily vacuumed the bedroom floors, popping in occasionally to bring the mail or a glass of water. She was getting married in a couple of weeks and would be moving out to start her own family. Rosa had of course not said anything when she heard this, but her inner response was surprise. She could not easily comprehend anyone getting married, now that she no longer was, but it was impossible for her to feel happy at the prospect of yet another poor black woman marrying God knows who and starting a family. She would have thought Raymyna would have already had enough.

But who was she to talk. Miss Cynical. She had married. And enjoyed it. She had had a child, and adored it.

In the afternoon her aunt and Raymyna took them sight-seeing. As she understood matters from the local newspapers, all the water she saw—whether canal, river, or ocean—was polluted beyond recall, so that it was hard even to look at it, much less to look at it admiringly. She could only gaze at it in sympathy. The beach she also found pitiable. In their attempt to hog it away from the poor, the black, and the local in general, the beachfront "developers" had erected massive box-like hotels that blocked the view of the water for all except those rich enough to pay for rooms on the beach side of the hotels. Through the cracks between hotels Rosa saw the mostly elderly sun worshipers walking along what seemed to be a pebbly, eroded beach, stretching out their poor white necks to the sun.

Of course they cruised through Little Havana, which stretched for miles. Rosa looked at the new Cuban immigrants with interest. *Gusanos,* Fidel called them, "worms." She was startled to see that already they seemed as a group to live better and to have more material goods than the black people. Like many Americans who supported the Cuban revolution, she found the Cubans who left Cuba somewhat less noble than the ones who stayed. Clearly the ones who left were the ones with money. Hardly anyone in Cuba could afford the houses, the cars, the clothes, the television sets, and the lawn mowers she saw.

At dinner she tried to explain why and how she had missed her grandfather's funeral. The telegram had come the evening before she left for Cyprus. As she had left her stoop the next morning she had felt herself heading in the wrong direction. But she could not stop herself. It had taken all her meager energy to plan the trip to Cyprus, with a friend who claimed it was beautiful, and she simply could not think to change her plans. Nor could she, still bearing the wounds of her separation from Ivan, face her family.

Barbara and Aunt Lily listened to her patiently. It didn't surprise her that neither knew where Cyprus was, or what its politics and history were. She told them about the man whose son was killed and how he seemed to hate his "worthless" daughter for being alive.

"Women are not valued in their culture," she explained. "In fact, the Greeks, the Turks, and the Cypriots have this one thing in common, though they fight over everything else. The father kept saying, 'A man should have many sons.' His wife flinched guiltily when he said it."

After Ma died, I went and got my father," Aunt Lily was saying. "And I told him, 'No smoking and drinking in my house.' "

But her grandfather had always smoked. He smoked a pipe. Rosa had liked the smell of it.

"And no card playing and no noise and no complaining, because I don't want to hear it."

Others of Rosa's brothers and sister had come to see him. She had been afraid to. In the pictures she saw, he always looked happy. When he was not dead-tired or drunk, happy was how he'd looked. A deeply silent man, with those odd peaceful eyes. She did not know, and she was confident her aunt didn't, what he really thought about anything. So he had stopped smoking, her aunt thought, but Rosa's brothers had always slipped him tobacco. He had stopped drinking. That was possible. Even before his wife, Rosa's grandmother, had died, he had given up liquor. Or, as he said, it had given him up. So, no noise. Little company. No complaining. But he wasn't the complaining type, was he? He liked best of all, Rosa thought, to be left alone. And he liked baseball. She felt he had liked her too. She hoped he did. But never did he say so. And he was so stingy! In her whole life he'd only given her fifteen cents. On the other hand, he financed her sister Barbara's trade-school education, which her father, his son, had refused to do.

Was that what she had held against him on the flight toward the Middle East? There was no excuse, she'd known it all the time. She needed to be back there, to say goodbye to the spiritcase. For wasn't she beginning to understand the appearance of his spiritcase as her own spirit struggled and suffered?

That night, massaging Barbara's thin shoulders before turning in, she looked into her own face reflected in the bureau mirror. She was beginning to have the look her grandfather had when he was very, very tired. The look he got just before something broke in him and he went on a mind-killing drunk. It was there in her eyes. So clearly. The look of abandonment. Of having no support. Of loneliness so severe every minute was a chant against self-destruction.

She massaged Barbara, but she knew her touch was that of a stranger. At what point, she wondered, did you lose connection with the people you loved? And she remembered going to visit Barbara when she was in college and Barbara lived a short bus ride away. And she was present when Barbara's husband beat her and called her names and once he had locked both of them out of the house overnight. And her sister called the police and they seemed nice to Rosa, so recently up from the South, but in fact they were bored and cynical as they listened to Barbara's familiar complaint. Rosa was embarrassed and couldn't believe anything so sordid could be happening to them, so respected was their family in the small town they were from. But, in any event, Barbara continued to live with her husband many more years. Rosa was so hurt and angry she wanted to kill, but most of all, she was disappointed in

Barbara, who threw herself into the inevitable weekend battles with passionately vulgar language Rosa had never heard any woman, not to mention her gentle sister, use before. Her sister's spirit seemed polluted to her, so much so that the sister she had known as a child seemed gone altogether.

Was disappointment, then, the hardest thing to bear? Or was it the consciousness of being powerless to change things, to help? And certainly she had been very conscious of that. As her brother-in-law punched out her sister, Rosa had almost felt the blows on her body. But she had not flung herself between them wielding a butcher knife, as she had done once when Barbara was being attacked by their father, another raving madman.

Barbara had wanted to go to their brother's grammar-school graduation. Their father had insisted that she go to the funeral of an elderly church mother instead. Barbara had tried to refuse. But *crack,* he had slapped her across the face. She was sixteen, plump, and lovely. Rosa adored her. She ran immediately to get the knife, but she was so small no one seemed to notice her, wedging herself between them. But had she been larger and stronger she might have killed him, for even as a child she was serious in all she did—and then what would her life, the life of a murderer, have been like?

Thinking of that day now, she wept. At her love, at her sister's anguish.

Barbara had been forced to go to the funeral, the print of her father's fingers hidden by powder and rouge. Rosa had been little and weak, and she did not understand what was going on anyway between her father and her sister. To her, her father acted like he was jealous. And in college later, after such a long struggle to get there, how could she stab her brother-in-law to death without killing her future, herself? And so she had lain on her narrow foldaway cot in the tiny kitchen in the stuffy apartment over the Laundromat and had listened to the cries and whispers, the pummelings, the screams and pleas. And then, still awake, she listened to the sibilant sounds of "making up," harder to bear and to understand than the fights.

She had not killed for her sister. (And one would have had to kill the mindless drunken brutalizing husband; a blow to the head might only have made him more angry.) Her guilt had soon clouded over the love, and around Barbara she retreated into a silence that she now realized was very like her grandfather's. The sign in him of disappointment hinged to powerlessness. A thoughtful black man in the racist early-twentieth-century South, he probably could have told her a thing or two about the squeaking of the hinge. But had he? No. He'd only complained about his wife, and so convincingly that for a time Rosa, like everyone else in the family, lost respect for her grandmother. It seemed her problem was that she was not mentally quick; and because she stayed with him even as he said this, Rosa and her relatives were quick to agree. Yet there was nowhere else she could have gone. Perhaps her grandfather had found the house in which they lived, but she, her grandmother, had made it a home. Once the grandmother died, the house seemed empty, though he remained behind until Aunt Lily had moved him into her house in Miami.

The day before Rosa and Barbara were to fly back north, Aunt Lily was handing out the remaining odds and ends of their grandfather's things. Barbara got the trunk, that magic repository of tobacco and candy when they were children. Rosa received a small shaving mirror with a gilt lion on its back. There were several of the large, white "twenty-five-cent hanskers" her grandfather had used. The granddaughters received half a dozen each. That left only her grandfather's hats. One brown and one gray: old, worn, none-too-clean fedoras. Rosa knew Barbara was far too fastidious to want them. She placed one on her head. She loved how she looked—she looked like him—in it.

It was killing her, how much she loved him. And he'd been so mean to her grandmother, and so stingy too. Once he had locked her grandmother out of the house because she had bought herself a penny stick of candy from the grocery money. But this was a story her parents told her, from a time before Rosa was born.

By the time she knew him he was mostly beautiful. Peaceful, mystical almost, in his silences and calm, and she realized he was imprinted on her heart just that way. It really did not seem fair.

To check her tears, she turned to Aunt Lily.

"Tell me what my father was like as a boy," she said.

Her aunt looked at her, she felt, with hatred.

"You should have asked him when he was alive."

Rosa looked about for Barbara, who had disappeared into the bathroom. By now she was weeping openly. Her aunt looking at her impassively.

"I don't want to find myself in anything you write. And you can just leave your daddy alone, too."

She could not remember whether she'd ever asked her father about his life. But surely she had, since she knew quite a lot. She turned and walked into the bathroom, forgetful that she was thirty-five, her sister forty-one, and that you can only walk in on your sister in the toilet if you are both children. But it didn't matter. Barbara had always been accessible, always protective. Rosa remembered one afternoon when she was five or six, she and Barbara and a cousin of theirs about Barbara's age set out on an errand. They were walking silently down the dusty road when a large car driven by a white man nearly ran them down. His car sent up billows of dust from the dirt road that stung their eyes and stained their clothes. Instinctively Rosa had picked up a fistful of sand from the road and thrown it after him. He stopped the car, backed it up furiously, and slammed on the brakes, getting out next to them, three black, barefoot girls who looked at him as only they could. Was he a human being? Or a devil? At any rate, he had seen Rosa throw the sand, he said, and he wanted the older girls to warn her against doing such things, "for the little nigger's own good."

Rosa would have admitted throwing the sand. After all, the man had seen her.

But "she didn't throw no sand," said Barbara, quietly, striking a heavy, womanish pose with both hands on her hips.

"She did so," said the man, his face red from heat and anger.

"She didn't," said Barbara.

The cousin simply stared at the man. After all, what was a small handful of sand compared to the billows of sand with which he'd covered them?

Cursing, the man stomped into his car, and drove off.

For a long time it had seemed to Rosa that only black people were always in danger. But there was also the sense that her big sister would know how to help them out of it.

But now, as her sister sat on the commode, Rosa saw a look on her face that she had never seen before, and she realized her sister had heard what Aunt Lily said. It was a look that said she'd got the reply she deserved. For wasn't she always snooping about the family's business and turning things about in her writing in ways that made the family shudder? There was no talking to her as you talked to regular people. The minute you opened your mouth a meter went on. Rosa could read all this on her sister's face. She didn't need to speak. And it was a lonely feeling that she had. For Barbara was right. Aunt Lily, too. And she could no more stop the meter running than she could stop her breath. An odd look across the room fifteen years ago still held the power to make her wonder about it, try to "decipher" or at least understand it. This was her curse: never to be able to forget, truly, but only to appear to forget. And then to record what she could not forget.

Suddenly, in her loneliness, she laughed.

"He was a recorder with his eyes," she said, under her breath. For it seemed to her she'd penetrated her grandfather's serenity, his frequent silences. The meter had ticked in him, too; he, too, was all attentiveness. But for him that had had to be enough. She'd rarely seen him with a pencil in his hand; she thought he'd only had one or two years of school. She imagined him "writing" stories during his long silences merely by thinking them, not embarrassing other people with them, as she did.

She had been obsessed by this old man whom she so definitely resembled. And now, perhaps, she knew why.

We were kindred spirits, she thought, as she sat, one old dusty fedora on her head, the other in her lap, on the plane home. But in a lot of ways, before I knew him, he was a jerk.

She thought of Ivan. For it was something both of them had said often about their relationship: that though he was white and she was black, they were in fact kindred spirits. And she had thought so, until the divorce, after which his spirit became as unfathomable to her as her grandfather's would have been before she knew him. But perhaps Ivan, too, was simply acting like a jerk?

She felt, as she munched the dry crackers and cheese the pert stewardess brought, in the very wreckage of her life. She had not really looked at Barbara since that moment in the toilet, when it became clear to her how her sister really perceived her. She knew she would not see Aunt Lily again and that if Aunt Lily died before she herself did, she would not go to her funeral. Nor would she ever, ever write about her. She took a huge swallow of ginger ale and tried to drown out the incessant ticking of the meter.

She stroked the soft felt of her grandfather's hat, thought of how peculiarly the human brain grows, from an almost invisible seed, and how, in this respect, it was rather similar to understanding, a process it engendered. She looked into her grandfather's shaving mirror and her eyes told her she could bear very little more. She felt herself begin to slide into the long silence in which such thoughts would be her sole companions. Maybe she would even find happiness there.

But then, just when she was almost gone, Barbara put on her grandfather's other hat and reached for her hand.

Joy Williams

1944 –

Joy Williams was born in Chelmsford, Massachusetts, in 1944. She graduated from Marietta College and also earned an M.F.A. degree at the University of Iowa. Williams served as a researcher and data analyst at the U. S. Navy Marine Laboratory in Siesta Key, Florida, from 1967 to 1969; later she served as a visiting instructor at the University of Houston, the University of Florida, the University of California at Irvine, the University of Iowa, and the University of Arizona. In 1973 and 1974, she won grants for literary work from the New England Arts and the Guggenheim Foundations, and in 1980 she received the National Magazine Award for Fiction for her story "The Farm." Her published writings to date include three novels (*State of Grace,* 1973, *The Changeling,* 1978, and *Breaking and Entering,* 1988) and one collection of short stories, *Taking Care* (1982).

Williams's stories have drawn highly favorable response from the critics, especially for the intensity of feeling displayed in them; a reviewer in the *Chicago Tribune Book World,* for example, said: "they're finely made and perfectly matched [and] hold love up to us like a dark, fractured bauble that we should see, reflected and to our astonishment, what moments in our familiar lives it dominates." Others associate her stories with those of Flannery O'Connor and Joyce Carol Oates because in them "madness, murder, and surrender of hope become commonplace rather than extreme behaviors, and even those characters who sustain the ability to love seem perplexed, even encumbered, by their triumph." Singly, say these critics, each story becomes "a gem of despair," while collectively, the pure feeling in them is "like fine music . . . circumvent[ing] the intellect." "The Yard Boy" is a prime example of her style and themes.

The Yard Boy

The yard boy was a spiritual materialist. He lived in the Now. He was free from the karmic chain. Being enlightened wasn't easy. It was very hard work. It was manual labor actually.

The enlightened being is free. He feels the sorrows and sadness of those around him but does not necessarily feel his own. The yard boy felt that he had been enlightened for about two months, at the most.

The yard boy had two possessions. One was a pickup truck. The other was a plover he had stuffed and mounted when he thought he wanted to be an ornithologist, in the days before he had become a spiritual materialist. The bird was in the room he rented. The only other thing in the room was a bed. The landlady provided sheets and towels. Sometimes when he came back from work hot and sweaty with little bits of leaves and stuff caught in his hair, the landlady would give him a piece of key lime pie on a blue plate.

The yard boy was content. He had hard muscular arms and a tanned back. He had compassion. He had a girl friend. When he thought about it, he supposed that having a girl friend was a cop-out to the security which he had eschewed. This was a preconception however and a preconception was the worst form of all the forms of security. The yard boy believed he was in balance on this point. He tried to see things the way they were from the midst of nowhere, and he felt that he had worked out this difficulty about the girl friend satisfactorily. The important thing was to be able to see through the veils of preconception.

The yard boy was a handsome fellow. He seldom spoke. He was appealing. Once he had run over an old lady and had broken her leg, but no one had gotten mad at him about it. Now that he was a yard boy his hands smelled of 6-6-6. His jeans smelled of tangelos. He was honest and truthful, a straightforward person who did not distinguish between this and that. For the girl friend he always had a terrific silky business which was always at the ready.

The yard boy worked for several very wealthy people. In the morning of every day he got into his pickup and drove over the causeways to the Keys where he mowed and clipped and cut and hauled. He talked to the plants. He always told them what he was going to do before he did it so that they would have a chance to prepare themselves. Plants have lived in the Now for a long time but they still have to have some things explained to them.

At the Wilsons' house the yard boy clips a sucker from an orange tree. It is February. Even so, the orange tree doesn't like it much. Mrs. Wilson comes out and watches the yard boy while he works. She has her son with her. He is about three. He doesn't talk yet. His name is Tao. Mrs. Wilson is wealthy and can afford to be wacky. What was she supposed to do after all, she asked the yard boy once, call her kid George? Fred? For Godssakes.

Her obstetrician had told her at the time that he had never seen a more perfectly shaped head.

The Wilsons' surroundings are splendid. Mrs. Wilson has splendid clothes, a splendid figure. She has a wonderful Cuban cook. The house is worth three quarters of a million dollars. The plantings are worth a hundred thousand dollars. Everything has a price. It is fantastic. A precise worth has been ascribed to everything. Every worm and aphid can be counted upon. It costs a certain amount of money to eradicate them. The sod is laid down fresh every year. For weeks after the lawn is installed, the seams are visible and then the squares of grass gather together and it becomes, everywhere, in sun or shade, a smooth, witty and improbable green like the color of a parrot.

Mrs. Wilson follows the yard boy around as he tends to the hibiscus, the bougainvillea, the poinciana, the horse cassia, the Java flower, the flame vine. They stand beneath the mango, looking up.

"Isn't it pagan," Mrs. Wilson says.

Close the mouth, shut the doors, untie the tangles, soften the light, the yard boy thinks.

Mrs. Wilson says, "It's a waste this place, don't you think? I've never understood nature, all this effort. All this will . . . " She flaps her slender arms at the reeking of odors, the rioting colors. Still, she looks up at the mangoes, hanging. Uuuuuh, she thinks.

Tao is standing between the yard boy and Mrs. Wilson with an oleander flower in his mouth. It is pink. Tao's hair is golden. His eyes are blue.

The yard boy removes the flower from the little boy's mouth. "Toxic," the yard boy says.

"What is it!" Mrs. Wilson cries.

"Oleander," the yard boy says.

"Cut it down, dig it out, get rid of it," Mrs. Wilson cries. "My precious child!" She imagines Tao being kidnapped, held for an astronomical ransom by men with acne.

Mrs. Wilson goes into the house and makes herself a drink. The yard boy walks over to the oleander. The oleander shakes a little in the breeze.

The yard boy stands in front of it for a few minutes, his clippers by his side.

Mrs. Wilson watches him from the house. She swallows her drink and rubs the glass over her hot nipples. The ice clinks. The yard boy raises the clippers and spreads them wide. The bolt connecting the two shears breaks. The yard boy walks over to the house, over to where Mrs. Wilson stands behind glass doors. The house weighs a ton with the glass. The house's architect was the South's most important architect, Mrs. Wilson once told the yard boy. Everything he made was designed to give a sense of freedom and space. Everything was designed to give the occupants the impression of being outside. His object was to break down definitions, the consciousness of boundaries. Mrs. Wilson told the yard boy the architect was an asshole.

Behind the glass, Mrs. Wilson understands the difficulty. Behind Mrs. Wilson's teeth is a tongue that tastes of bourbon.

"I'll drive you downtown and we can get a new whatever," she says. She is determined.

She and he and Tao get into Mrs. Wilson's Mercedes 350 SL. Mrs. Wilson is a splendid driver. She has taken the Mercedes up to 130, she tells the yard boy. It is 130 that the engine is capable of, nothing more. The engine stroked beautifully at 130, no sound of strain at all.

She drives past the beaches, over the causeways. She darts in and out of traffic with a fine sense of timing. Behind them, occasionally, old men in Gremlins jump the curb in fright. Mrs. Wilson glances at them in the rear-view mirror seeming neither satisfied nor dissatisfied. She puts her hand on the yard boy's knee. She rubs his leg.

Tao scrambles from the back into the front seat. He gets on the other side of the yard boy. He bites him.

I am living in a spiritual junkyard, thinks the yard boy. I must make it into a simple room with one beautiful object.

Sweat runs down the yard boy's spine. Tao is gobbling at his arm as though it is junket.

"What is going on!" yells Mrs. Wilson. She turns the Mercedes around in the middle of the highway. A Good Humor truck scatters a tinkle of music and a carton of Fudgesicles as it grinds to a stop. Mrs. Wilson is cuffing Tao as she speeds back home. She is embarrassed at his rudeness. Her shaven armpit rises and falls before the yard boy's eyes.

"Save the oleander!" she yells at both of them. "What do I care!"

In the driveway she runs around to Tao's side of the car and pinches the child's nose. He opens his mouth. She grabs him by the hair and carries him suspended into the house.

The yard boy walks to his truck, gets in and drives off. The world is neither nest nor playground, the yard boy thinks.

The yard boy lies in his room thinking about his girl friend.

Open up, give in, allow some space, sprinkle and pour, he thinks.

Outside, the garbage men are picking up the trash. They whistle and bang the cans about. The trash from the house where the yard boy lives contains the discards of the righteous. Tea bags, lime rinds, Charmin tubes, wilted flowers. The garbage men whoop to the truck that carries them off as though it were a horse. Sometimes the yard boy has bad dreams in this room. Sometimes he dreams of demons with eyes as big as saucepans and bodies the size of thumbs. But mostly he has good thoughts about his girl friend. He believes that her mind has the same energy, speed and pattern of his mind even though she isn't a spiritual materialist.

The yard boy is mowing the grass around Johnny Dakota's swimming pool. Dakota is into heroin and intangible property. As he is working, the yard boy hears a big splash behind him. He looks into the swimming pool and sees a rock on the bottom of it. He finishes mowing the grass and then he gets a net and fishes the rock out. It is as big as his hand. It is grey with bubbly streaks of iron and metal running through it. The yard boy thinks it is a meteorite. It would probably still be smoldering with heat had it not landed in the swimming pool.

It is interesting but not all that interesting. The possibility of its surviving the earth's atmosphere is one tenth of one percent. Other things are more interesting than this. Nevertheless, the yard boy shows it to Johnny Dakota. Johnny Dakota might want to place it in a taped-up box in his house to prevent the air from corroding it.

Johnny Dakota looks up at the sky, then at the piece of space junk and then at the yard boy. He is a sleek, fit man. Only his eyes and his hands look old. His hands have deep ridges in them and smashed nails. He once told the yard boy that his mother, whom he loved, had died from plucking a wild hair from her nose while vacationing in Calabria. His father had choked on a bread stick in a Chicago restaurant. Life is ruthless, he had told the yard boy. The darkness is always near.

Johnny Dakota usually takes his swim at this time of the morning. He is wearing his swim trunks and flip-flops. If he had been in the pool he could have been brained. Once his mother had dreamed of losing a tooth and two days later her cousin dropped dead.

Johnny Dakota is angry. Anyone could tell. His face is dark. His mouth is a thin line. He gives the yard boy two twenties and tells him to bury the rock in the back yard. He tells him not to mention this to anyone.

The yard boy takes the rock and buries it beneath a fiddleleaf fig at the north end of the house. The fig tree is distressed. It's magnetic, that's the only thing known about this rock. The fig tree is almost as upset as Johnny Dakota.

The yard boy lies in his room. His girl friend is giving him a hard time. She used to visit him in his room several nights a week but now she doesn't. He will take her out to dinner. He will spend the two twenties on a fantastic dinner.

The yard boy is disgusted with himself. The spider's web is woven in the wanting, he thinks. He has desire for his girl friend. His mind is shuttling between thoughts of the future and thoughts of the past. He is dissatisfied. He is out of touch with the sharp simplicity and wonderfulness of the moment. He looks around him. He opens his eyes wide. The yard boy's jeans are filthy. A green insect crawls in and out of the scapular feathers of the plover.

The yard boy goes downstairs. He gives the plover to his landlady. She seems delighted. She puts it on a shelf in the pantry, just above the pie plates. The landlady has white hair, a wen, and old legs that end in sneakers. She wants the yard boy to look at a plant she has just bought. It is in a big green plastic pot in the sunshine of her kitchen. Nothing is more obvious than the hidden, the yard boy thinks.

"This plant is insane," the yard boy says.

The landlady is shocked. She backs off a little from the plant which is a rabbit's-foot fern.

"It has seen something terrible," the yard boy says.

"I bought it on sale," the landlady says. "At that place where I always go."

The yard boy shakes his head. The plant waves a wrinkly leaf and drops it.

"Insane?" the landlady asks. She would like to cry. She has no family, no one.

"Mad as a hatter," the yard boy says.

The restaurant that the yard boy's girl friend chooses is not expensive. It is a fish restaurant. The plates are plastic. There is a bottle of tabasco sauce on each table. The girl friend doesn't at all like fancy food, although she doesn't mind accepting a bowl of chowder and a few glasses of wine.

A few booths over, a middle-aged couple are having an argument. They both have sunburns and wear white skirts and Haitian shirts. The argument seems to be about monograms. They are both yelling and one woman picks up a handful of oyster crackers and flings it into the other woman's face. The oyster crackers stick all over the woman's damp, sunburned face. The yard boy knows he should be satisfied with whatever situation arises but he is having a little difficulty with his enlightenment.

The yard boy's girl friend is not talking to him. She has not been talking to him for days actually.

The woman that has been hit with the handful of oyster crackers walks past, an oyster cracker bobbing on her widow's peak.

The yard boy miserably eats his pompano. When they are finished, his girl friend goes to the cashier for some toothpicks. While she is gone, another girl comes up with a baby.

"Would you watch my baby for me while I go to the ladies'?" she asks.

The yard boy holds the baby. The girl leaves. The yard boy's girl friend returns. They don't talk about the baby or anything. The girl friend sighs and crosses her legs. An hour passes. The restaurant is about to close. The yard boy and his girl friend and the baby are the last patrons. There is no one in the ladies'. The yard boy calls the manager and the manager calls the police. The baby chortles and spits up a little, not much. The police let the girl friend go first, and a few hours later they let the yard boy go.

The yard boy gets into his truck and drives off.

Life and the world are merely the dance of illusion, the yard boy thinks. He smells baby on his sweater.

The yard boy's landlady has put her rabbit's-foot fern out by the garbage cans. The yard boy picks it up and puts it in the cab of his truck. It goes wherever he goes now.

The yard boy gets a note from his girl friend. It says:

My ego is too healthy for real involvement with you. I don't like you. Good-by.

Alyce

The yard boy works for Mr. Crown who is an illustrator. Mr. Crown lives in a fine house on the bay. Across the street, someone is building an even finer house on the Gulf. Mr. Crown was once the most renowned illustrator of Western art in the country. In his studio he has George Custer's jacket. Sometimes the yard boy poses for Mr. Crown. The year before, a gentleman in Cody, Wyoming, bought Mr. Crown's painting of an Indian who was the yard boy for fifty thousand dollars. This year, however, Mr. Crown is not doing so well. He has been reduced to illustrating children's books. His star is falling. Also, the construction across the street infuriates him. The new house will block off his view of the sun as the sun slides daily into the water.

Mr. Crown's publishers have told him that they are not interested in cowboys. There have been too many cowboys for too long.

The yard boy is spraying against scale and sooty mold.

"I don't need the money but I am insulted," Mr. Crown tells the yard boy.

Mr. Crown goes back into the house. The yard boy seeds some rye on the lawn's bare spots and then takes a break to get a drink of water. He sits in the cab of his truck and drinks from a plastic jug. He sprinkles some water on the rabbit's-foot fern. The fern sits there on the seat, dribbling a little vermiculite, crazy as hell.

The fern and the yard boy sit.

It is not a peaceful spot to sit. The racket of the construction on the Gulf is considerable. Nonetheless, the yard boy swallows his water and attempts to dwell upon the dignity and simplicity of the moment.

Then there is a sound of gunfire. The yard boy cranes his neck out of the window of his pickup truck and sees Mr. Crown firing from his studio at the workers across the street. It takes the workers several moments to realize that they are being shot at. The bullets make big mealy holes in the concrete. The bullets whine through the windows that will exhibit the sunset. The workers all give a howl and try to find cover. The yard boy curls up behind the wheel of his truck. The little rushy brown hairs on the fern's stalks stick straight out.

A few minutes later the firing stops. Mr. Crown goes back to the drawing board. No one is hurt. Mr. Crown is arrested and posts twenty-five thousand dollars bond. Charges are later dropped. The house across the street is built. Still, Mr. Crown seems calmer now. He gives up illustrating. When he wants to look at something, he looks at the bay. He tells the yard boy he is putting sunsets behind him.

The yard boy and the rabbit's-foot fern drive from lawn to lawn in the course of their days, the fern tipping forward a little in its green pot, the wind folding back its leaves. In the wind, its leaves curl back like the lips of a Doberman pinscher.

The yard boy sees things in the course of his work that he wouldn't dream of telling the fern even though the fern is his only confidant. The fern has a lot of space around it in which anything can happen but it doesn't have much of an emotional life because it is insane. Therefore, it makes a good confidant.

The yard boy has always been open. He has always let be and disowned. Nevertheless, he has lost the spontaneity of his awakened state. He is sad. He can feel it. The fern can feel it too which makes it gloomier than ever. Even so, the fern has grown quite fond of the yard boy. It wants to help him any way it can.

The yard boy doesn't rent a room any more. He lives in his truck. Then he sells his truck. He and the rabbit's-foot fern sit on the beach. The fern lives in the shade of the yard boy. The yard boy doesn't live in the

Now at all any more. He lives in the past. He thinks of his childhood. As a child he had a comic-book-collection high of three hundred and seventy-four with perfect covers. His parents had loved him. His parents had another son whom they loved too. One morning this son had fallen out of a tree onto the driveway and played with nothing but a spoon and saucepan for the next twenty-five years. When the yard boy has lived in the past as much as is reliable, he lives in the future. It is while he is living in the future that his girl friend walks by on the beach. She is walking by in a long wet T-shirt that says I'M NOT A TOURIST I LIVE HERE. The rabbit's-foot fern alerts the yard boy and they both stare at her as she walks by.

It is a beautiful day. The water is a smooth green, broken occasionally by porpoises rising. Between the yard boy and his girl friend is sand a little less white than the clouds. Behind the yard boy are plantings of cabbage palms and succulents and Spanish bayonets. The bayonets are harsh and green with spikes that end in black tips like stilettos.

Act but do not rely upon one's own abilities, thinks the yard boy. He chews upon his nails. The moon can shine in one hundred different bowls, he thinks. What a lot of junk the yard boy thinks. He is as lost in the darkness of his solid thoughts as a yard boy can be. He watches his girl friend angrily as she boogies by.

The rabbit's-foot fern brightens at the yard boy's true annoyance. Its fuzzy long-haired rhizomes clutch its pot tightly. The space around it simmers, it bubbles. Each cell mobilizes its intent of skillful and creative action. It turns its leaves toward the Spanish bayonet. It straightens and sways. Straightens and sways. A moment passes. The message of retribution is received along the heated air. The yard boy sees the Spanish bayonet uproot itself and move out.

Tobias Wolff

1945 –

Born in Birmingham, Alabama, Tobias Wolff grew up in the Pacific Northwest. His *This Boy's Life: A Memoir* (1989) is an autobiographical account of the writer's youth. After four years in the army, including duty in Vietnam, he went on to receive degrees from Oxford University and Stanford University. He has been a faculty member at Stanford, Goddard College, Arizona State University, and Syracuse University, where he is presently on appointment. Wolff is the author of two books of short stories, *In the Garden of the North American Martyrs* (1981) and *Back in the World* (1985), and the editor of an anthology, *Matters of Life and Death: New American Stories* (1983). His 1984 novella *The Barracks Thief,* which was rooted in his army experience, won the P.E.N./Faulkner Award.

Wolff has been called a natural storyteller, and his work has enjoyed high critical praise. Readers "care" for the people in his stories because of the understanding and sympathy he seems to have for them. As "Hunters in the Snow" exhibits, however, if Wolff's view of his characters is generous, it is not necessarily admiring. It is not without humor, but it is without illusion. It is a hard and truthful view, won and rendered with difficulty. Wolff says that he has to discover who his characters are through "many, many drafts" of each of his stories: "that is why I rewrite, to try to find ways of getting closer and closer to my characters."

Hunters In The Snow

Tub had been waiting for an hour in the falling snow. He paced the sidewalk to keep warm and stuck his head out over the curb whenever he saw lights approaching. One driver stopped for him but before Tub could wave the man on he saw the rifle on Tub's back and hit the gas. The tires spun on the ice.

The fall of snow thickened. Tub stood below the overhang of a building. Across the road the clouds whitened just above the rooftops, and the street lights went out. He shifted the rifle strap to his other shoulder. The whiteness seeped up the sky.

A truck slid around the corner, horn blaring, rear end sashaying. Tub moved to the sidewalk and held up his hand. The truck jumped the curb and kept coming, half on the street and half on the sidewalk. It wasn't slowing down at all. Tub stood for a moment, still holding up his hand, then jumped back. His rifle slipped off his shoulder and clattered on the ice, a sandwich fell out of his pocket. He ran for the steps of the building. Another sandwich and a package of cookies tumbled onto the new snow. He made the steps and looked back.

The truck had stopped several feet beyond where Tub had been standing. He picked up his sandwiches and his cookies and slung the rifle and went up to the driver's window. The driver was bent against the steering wheel, slapping his knees and drumming his feet on the floorboards. He looked like a cartoon of a person laughing, except that his eyes watched the man on the seat beside him. "You ought to see yourself," the driver said. "He looks just like a beach ball with a hat on, doesn't he? Doesn't he, Frank?"

The man beside him smiled and looked off.

"You almost ran me down," Tub said. "You could've killed me."

"Come on, Tub," said the man beside the driver. "Be mellow. Kenny was just messing around." He opened the door and slid over to the middle of the seat.

Tub took the bolt out of his rifle and climbed in beside him. "I waited an hour," he said. "If you meant ten o'clock why didn't you say ten o'clock?"

"Tub, you haven't done anything but complain since we got here," said the man in the middle. "If you want to piss and moan all day you might as well go home and bitch at your kids. Take your pick." When Tub didn't say anything he turned to the driver. "Okay, Kenny, let's hit the road."

Some juvenile delinquents had heaved a brick through the windshield on the driver's side, so the cold and snow tunneled right into the cab. The heater didn't work. They covered themselves with a couple of blankets Kenny had brought along and pulled down the muffs on their caps. Tub tried to keep his hands warm by rubbing them under the blanket but Frank made him stop.

They left Spokane and drove deep into the country, running along black lines of fences. The snow let up, but still there was no edge to the land where it met the sky. Nothing moved in the chalky fields. The cold bleached their faces and made the stubble stand out on their cheeks and along their upper lips. They stopped twice for coffee before they got to the woods where Kenny wanted to hunt.

Tub was for trying someplace different; two years in a row they'd been up and down this land and hadn't seen a thing. Frank didn't care one way or the other, he just wanted to get out of the goddamned truck. "Feel that," Frank said, slamming the door. He spread his feet and closed his eyes and leaned his head way back and breathed deeply. "Tune in on that energy."

"Another thing," Kenny said. "This is open land. Most of the land around here is posted."

"I'm cold," Tub said.

Frank breathed out. "Stop bitching, Tub. Get centered."

"I wasn't bitching."

"Centered," Kenny said. "Next thing you'll be wearing a nightgown, Frank. Selling flowers out at the airport."

"Kenny," Frank said, "you talk too much."

"Okay," Kenny said. "I won't say a word. Like I won't say anything about a certain babysitter."

"What babysitter?" Tub asked.

"That's between us," Frank said, looking at Kenny. "That's confidential. You keep your mouth shut."

Kenny laughed.

"You're asking for it," Frank said.

"Asking for what?"

"You'll see."

"Hey," Tub said, "are we hunting or what?"

They started off across the field. Tub had trouble getting through the fences. Frank and Kenny could have helped him; they could have lifted up on the top wire and stepped on the bottom wire, but they didn't. They stood and watched him. There were a lot of fences and Tub was puffing when they reached the woods.

They hunted for over two hours and saw no deer, no tracks, no sign. Finally they stopped by the creek to eat. Kenny had several slices of pizza and a couple of candy bars: Frank had a sandwich, an apple, two carrots, and a square of chocolate; Tub ate one hard-boiled egg and a stick of celery.

"You ask me how I want to die today," Kenny said, "I'll tell you burn me at the stake." He turned to Tub. "You still on that diet?" He winked at Frank.

"What do you think? You think I like hard-boiled eggs?"

"All I can say is, it's the first diet I ever heard of where you gained weight from it."

"Who said I gained weight?"

"Oh, pardon me. I take it back. You're just wasting away before my very eyes. Isn't he, Frank?"

Frank had his fingers fanned out, tips against the bark of the stump where he'd laid his food. His knuckles were hairy. He wore a heavy wedding band and on his right pinky another gold ring with a flat face and an "F" in what looked like diamonds. He turned the ring this way and that. "Tub," he said, "you haven't seen your own balls in ten years."

Kenny doubled over laughing. He took off his hat and slapped his leg with it.

"What am I supposed to do?" Tub said. "It's my glands."

They left the woods and hunted along the creek. Frank and Kenny worked one bank and Tub worked the other, moving upstream. The snow was light but the drifts were deep and hard to move through. Wherever Tub looked the surface was smooth, undisturbed, and after a time he lost interest. He stopped looking for tracks and just tried to keep up with Frank and Kenny on the other side. A moment came when he realized he hadn't seen them in a long time. The breeze was moving from him to them; when it stilled he could sometimes hear Kenny laughing but that was all. He quickened his pace, breasting hard into the drifts, fighting away the snow with his knees and elbows. He heard his heart and felt the flush on his face but he never once stopped.

Tub caught up with Frank and Kenny at a bend of the creek. They were standing on a log that stretched from their bank to his. Ice had backed up behind the log. Frozen reeds stuck out, barely nodding when the air moved.

"See anything?" Frank asked.

Tub shook his head.

There wasn't much daylight left and they decided to head back toward the road. Frank and Kenny crossed the log and they started downstream, using the trail Tub had broken. Before they had gone very far Kenny stopped. "Look at that," he said, and pointed to some tracks going from the creek back into the woods. Tub's footprints crossed right over them. There on the bank, plain as day, were several mounds of deer sign. "What do you think that is, Tub?" Kenny kicked at it. "Walnuts on vanilla icing?"

"I guess I didn't notice."

Kenny looked at Frank.

"I was lost."

"You were lost. Big deal."

They followed the tracks into the woods. The deer had gone over a fence half buried in drifting snow. A no hunting sign was nailed to the top of one of the posts. Frank laughed and said the son of a bitch could read. Kenny wanted to go after him but Frank said no way, the people out here didn't mess around. He thought maybe the farmer who owned the land would let them use it if they asked. Kenny wasn't so sure. Anyway, he figured that by the time they walked to the truck and drove up the road and doubled back it would be almost dark.

"Relax," Frank said. "You can't hurry nature. If we're meant to get that deer, we'll get it. If we're not, we won't."

They started back toward the truck. This part of the woods was mainly pine. The snow was shaded and had a glaze on it. It held up Kenny and Frank but Tub kept falling through. As he kicked forward, the edge of the crust bruised his shins. Kenny and Frank pulled ahead of him, to where he couldn't even hear their voices any more. He sat down on a stump and wiped his face. He ate both the sandwiches and half the cookies, taking his own sweet time. It was dead quiet.

When Tub crossed the last fence into the road the truck started moving. Tub had to run for it and just managed to grab hold of the tailgate and hoist himself into the bed. He lay there, panting. Kenny looked out the rear window and grinned. Tub crawled into the lee of the cab to get out of the freezing wind. He pulled his earflaps low and pushed his chin into the collar of his coat. Someone rapped on the window but Tub would not turn around.

He and Frank waited outside while Kenny went into the farmhouse to ask permission. The house was old and paint was curling off the sides. The smoke streamed westward off the top of the chimney, fanning away into a thin gray plume. Above the ridge of the hills another ridge of blue clouds was rising.

"You've got a short memory," Tub said.

"What?" Frank said. He had been staring off.

"I used to stick up for you."

"Okay, so you used to stick up for me. What's eating you?"

"You shouldn't have just left me back there like that."

"You're a grown-up, Tub. You can take care of yourself. Anyway, if you think you're the only person with problems I can tell you that you're not."

"Is something bothering you, Frank?"

Frank kicked at the branch poking out of the snow. "Never mind," he said.

"What did Kenny mean about the babysitter?"

"Kenny talks too much," Frank said. "You just mind your own business."

Kenny came out of the farmhouse and gave the thumbs-up and they began walking back toward the woods. As they passed the barn a large black hound with a grizzled snout ran out and barked at them. Every time he barked he slid backwards a bit, like a cannon recoiling. Kenny got down on all fours and snarled and barked back at him, and the dog slunk away into the barn, looking over his shoulder and peeing a little as he went.

"That's an old-timer," Frank said. "A real graybeard. Fifteen years if he's a day."

"Too old," Kenny said.

Past the barn they cut off through the fields. The land was unfenced and the crust was freezing up thick and they made good time. They kept to the edge of the field until they picked up the tracks again and followed them into the woods, farther and farther back toward the hills. The trees started to blur with the shadows and the wind rose and needled their faces with the crystals it swept off the glaze. Finally they lost the tracks.

Kenny swore and threw down his hat. "This is the worst day of hunting I ever had, bar none." He picked up his hat and brushed off the snow. "This will be the first season since I was fifteen I haven't got my deer."

"It isn't the deer," Frank said. "It's the hunting. There are all these forces out here and you just have to go with them."

"You go with them," Kenny said. "I came out here to get me a deer, not listen to a bunch of hippie bullshit. And if it hadn't been for dimples here I would have, too."

"That's enough," Frank said.

"And you—you're so busy thinking about that little jailbait of yours you wouldn't know a deer if you saw one."

"Drop dead," Frank said, and turned away.

Kenny and Tub followed him back across the fields. When they were coming up to the barn Kenny stopped and pointed. "I hate that post," he said. He raised his rifle and fired. It sounded like a dry branch cracking. The post splintered along its right side, up towards the top. "There," Kenny said. "It's dead."

"Knock it off," Frank said, walking ahead.

Kenny looked at Tub. He smiled. "I hate that tree," he said, and fired again. Tub hurried to catch up with Frank. He started to speak but just then the dog ran out of the barn and barked at them. "Easy, boy," Frank said.

"I hate that dog." Kenny was behind them.

"That's enough," Frank said. "You put that gun down."

Kenny fired. The bullet went in between the dog's eyes. He sank right down into the snow, his legs splayed out on each side, his yellow eyes open and staring. Except for the blood he looked like a small bearskin rug. The blood ran down the dog's muzzle into the snow.

They all looked at the dog lying there.

"What did he ever do to you?" Tub asked. "He was just barking."

Kenny turned to Tub. "I hate you."

Tub shot from the waist. Kenny jerked backward against the fence and buckled to his knees. He folded his hands across his stomach. "Look," he said. His hands were covered with blood. In the dusk his blood was more blue than red. It seemed to belong to the shadows. It didn't seem out of place. Kenny eased himself onto his back. He sighed several times, deeply. "You shot me," he said.

"I had to," Tub said. He knelt beside Kenny. "Oh God," he said. "Frank. Frank."

Frank hadn't moved since Kenny killed the dog.

"Frank!" Tub shouted.

"I was just kidding around," Kenny said. "It was a joke. Oh!" he said, and arched his back suddenly. "Oh!" he said again, and dug his heels into the snow and pushed himself along on his head for several feet. Then he stopped and lay there, rocking back and forth on his heels and head like a wrestler doing warm-up exercises.

Frank roused himself. "Kenny," he said. He bent down and put his gloved hand on Kenny's brow. "You shot him," he said to Tub.

"He made me," Tub said.

"No no no," Kenny said.

Tub was weeping from the eyes and nostrils. His whole face was wet. Frank closed his eyes, then looked down at Kenny again. "Where does it hurt?"

"Everywhere," Kenny said, "just everywhere."

"Oh God," Tub said.

"I mean where did it go in?" Frank said.

"Here." Kenny pointed at the wound in his stomach. It was welling slowly with blood.

"You're lucky," Frank said. "It's on the left side. It missed your appendix. If it had hit your appendix you'd really be in the soup." He turned and threw up onto the snow, holding his sides as if to keep warm.

"Are you all right?" Tub said.

"There's some aspirin in the truck," Kenny said.

"I'm all right," Frank said.

"We'd better call an ambulance," Tub said.

"Jesus," Frank said. "What are we going to say?"

"Exactly what happened," Tub said. "He was going to shoot me but I shot him first."

"No sir!" Kenny said. "I wasn't either!"

Frank patted Kenny on the arm. "Easy does it, partner." He stood. "Let's go."

Tub picked up Kenny's rifle as they walked down toward the farmhouse. "No sense leaving this around," he said. "Kenny might get ideas."

"I can tell you one thing," Frank said. "You've really done it this time. This definitely takes the cake."

They had to knock on the door twice before it was opened by a thin man with lank hair. The room behind him was filled with smoke. He squinted at them. "You get anything?" he asked.

"No," Frank said.

"I knew you wouldn't. That's what I told the other fellow."

"We've had an accident."

The man looked past Frank and Tub into the gloom. "Shoot your friend, did you?"

Frank nodded.

"I did," Tub said.

"I suppose you want to use the phone."

"If it's okay."

The man in the door looked behind him, then stepped back. Frank and Tub followed him into the house. There was a woman sitting by the stove in the middle of the room. The stove was smoking badly. She looked up and then down again at the child asleep in her lap. Her face was white and damp; strands of hair were pasted across her forehead. Tub warmed his hands over the stove while Frank went into the kitchen to call. The man who had let them in stood at the window, his hands in his pockets.

"My friend shot your dog," Tub said.

The man nodded without turning around. "I should have done it myself. I just couldn't."

"He loved that dog so much," the woman said. The child squirmed and she rocked it.

"You asked him to?" Tub said. "You asked him to shoot your dog?"

"He was old and sick. Couldn't chew his food any more. I would have done it myself but I don't have a gun."

"You couldn't have anyway," the woman said. "Never in a million years."

The man shrugged.

Frank came out of the kitchen. "We'll have to take him ourselves. The nearest hospital is fifty miles from here and all their ambulances are out anyway."

The woman knew a shortcut but the directions were complicated and Tub had to write them down. The man told them where they could find some boards to carry Kenny on. He didn't have a flashlight but he said he would leave the porch light on.

It was dark outside. The clouds were low and heavy-looking and the wind blew in shrill gusts. There was a screen loose on the house and it banged slowly and then quickly as the wind rose again. They could hear it all the way to the barn. Frank went for the boards while Tub looked for Kenny, who was not where they had left him. Tub found him farther up the drive, lying on his stomach. "You okay?" Tub said.

"It hurts."

"Frank says it missed your appendix."

"I already had my appendix out."

"All right," Frank said, coming up to them. "We'll have you in a nice warm bed before you can say Jack Robinson." He put the two boards on Kenny's right side.

"Just as long as I don't have one of those male nurses," Kenny said.

"Ha ha," Frank said. "That's the spirit. Get ready, set, *over you go,*" and he rolled Kenny onto the boards. Kenny screamed and kicked his legs in the air. When he quieted down Frank and Tub lifted the boards and carried him down the drive. Tub had the back end, and with the snow blowing into his face he had trouble with his footing. Also he was tired and the man inside had forgotten to turn the porch light on. Just past the house Tub slipped and threw out his hands to catch himself. The boards fell and Kenny tumbled out and rolled to the bottom of the drive, yelling all the way. He came to rest against the right front wheel of the truck.

"You fat moron," Frank said. "You aren't good for diddly."

Tub grabbed Frank by the collar and backed him hard up against the fence. Frank tried to pull his hands away but Tub shook him and snapped his head back and forth and finally Frank gave up.

"What do you know about fat," Tub said. "What do you know about glands." As he spoke he kept shaking Frank. "What do you know about me."

"All right," Frank said.

"No more," Tub said.

"All right."

"No more talking to me like that. No more watching. No more laughing."

"Okay, Tub. I promise."

Tub let go of Frank and leaned his forehead against the fence. His arms hung straight at his sides.

"I'm sorry, Tub." Frank touched him on the shoulder. "I'll be down at the truck."

Tub stood by the fence for a while and then got the rifles off the porch. Frank had rolled Kenny back onto the boards and they lifted him into the bed of the truck. Frank spread the seat blankets over him. "Warm enough?" he asked.

Kenny nodded.

"Okay. Now how does reverse work on this thing?"

"All the way to the left and up." Kenny sat up as Frank started forward to the cab. "Frank!"

"What?"

"If it sticks don't force it."

The truck started right away. "One thing," Frank said, "you've got to hand it to the Japanese. A very ancient, very spiritual culture and they can still make a hell out of a truck." He glanced over at Tub. "Look, I'm sorry. I didn't know you felt that way, honest to God I didn't. You should have said something."

"I did."

"When? Name one time."

"A couple of hours ago."

"I guess I wasn't paying attention."

"That's true, Frank," Tub said. "You don't pay attention very much."

"Tub," Frank said, "what happened back there, I should have been more sympathetic. I realize that. You were going through a lot. I just want you to know it wasn't your fault. He was asking for it."

"You think so?"

"Absolutely. It was him or you. I would have done the same thing in your shoes, no question."

The wind was blowing into their faces. The snow was a moving white wall in front of their lights; it swirled into the cab through the hole in the windshield and settled on them. Tub clapped his hands and shifted around to stay warm, but it didn't work.

"I'm going to have to stop," Frank said. "I can't feel my fingers."

Up ahead they saw some lights off the road. It was a tavern. Outside in the parking lot there were several jeeps and trucks. A couple of them had deer strapped across their hoods. Frank parked and they went back to Kenny. "How you doing, partner," Frank said.

"I'm cold."

"Well, don't feel like the Lone Ranger. It's worse inside, take my word for it. You should get that windshield fixed."

"Look," Tub said, "he threw the blankets off." They were lying in a heap against the tailgate.

"Now look, Kenny," Frank said, "it's no use whining about being cold if you're not going to try and keep warm. You've got to do your share." He spread the blankets over Kenny and tucked them in at the corners.

"They blew off."

"Hold on to them then."

"Why are we stopping, Frank?"

"Because if me and Tub don't get warmed up we're going to freeze solid and then where will you be?" He punched Kenny lightly in the arm. "So just hold your horses."

The bar was full of men in colored jackets, mostly orange. The waitress brought coffee. "Just what the doctor ordered," Frank said, cradling the steaming cup in his hand. His skin was bone white. "Tub, I've been thinking. What you said about me not paying attention, that's true."

"It's okay."

"No. I really had that coming. I guess I've just been a little too interested in old number one. I've had a lot on my mind. Not that that's any excuse."

"Forget it, Frank. I sort of lost my temper back there. I guess we're all a little on edge."

Frank shook his head. "It isn't just that."

"You want to talk about it?"

"Just between us, Tub?"

"Sure, Frank. Just between us."

"Tub, I think I'm going to be leaving Nancy."

"Oh, Frank. Oh, Frank." Tub sat back and shook his head.

Frank reached out and laid his hand on Tub's arm. "Tub, have you ever been really in love?"

"Well—"

"I mean *really* in love." He squeezed Tub's wrist. "With your whole being."

"I don't know. When you put it like that, I don't know."

"You haven't then. Nothing against you, but you'd know if you had." Frank let go of Tub's arm. "This isn't just some bit of fluff I'm talking about."

Frank paused. He looked into his empty cup. "Roxanne Brewer."

"Cliff Brewer's kid? The babysitter?"

"You can't just put people into categories like that, Tub. That's why the whole system is wrong. And that's why this country is going to hell in a rowboat."

"But she can't be more than—" Tub shook his head.

"Fifteen. She'll be sixteen in May." Frank smiled. "May fourth, three twenty-seven P.M. Hell, Tub, a hundred years ago she'd have been an old maid by that age. Juliet was only thirteen."

"Juliet? Juliet Miller? Jesus, Frank, she doesn't even have breasts. She doesn't even wear a top to her bathing suit. She's still collecting frogs."

"Not Juliet Miller. The real Juliet. Tub, don't you see how you're dividing people up into categories? He's an executive, she's a secretary, he's a truck driver, she's fifteen years old. Tub, this so-called babysitter, this so-called fifteen-year-old has more in her little finger than most of us have in our entire bodies. I can tell you this little lady is something special."

Tub nodded. "I know the kids like her."

"She's opened up whole worlds to me that I never knew were there."

"What does Nancy think about all of this?"

"She doesn't know."

"You haven't told her?"

"Not yet. It's not so easy. She's been damned good to me all these years. Then there's the kids to consider." The brightness in Frank's eyes trembled and he wiped quickly at them with the back of his hand. "I guess you think I'm a complete bastard."

"No, Frank. I don't think that."

"Well, you *ought* to."

"Frank, when you've got a friend it means you've always got someone on your side, no matter what. That's the way I feel about it, anyway."

"You mean that, Tub?"

"Sure I do."

Frank smiled. "You don't know how good it feels to hear you say that."

Kenny had tried to get out of the truck but he hadn't made it. He was jackknifed over the tailgate, his head hanging above the bumper. They lifted him back into the bed and covered him again. He was sweating and his teeth chattered. "It hurts, Frank.'"

"It wouldn't hurt so much if you just stayed put. Now we're going to the hospital. Got that? Say it—I'm going to the hospital."

"I'm going to the hospital."

"Again."

"I'm going to the hospital."

"Now just keep saying that to yourself and before you know it we'll be there."

After they had gone a few miles Tub turned to Frank. "I just pulled a real boner," he said.

"What's that?"

"I left the directions on the table back there."

"That's okay. I remember them pretty well."

The snowfall lightened and the clouds began to roll back off the fields, but it was no warmer and after a time both Frank and Tub were bitten through and shaking. Frank almost didn't make it around a curve, and they decided to stop at the next roadhouse.

There was an automatic hand-dryer in the bathroom and they took turns standing in front of it, opening their jackets and shirts and letting the jet of hot air breathe across their faces and chests.

"You know," Tub said, "what you told me back there, I appreciate it. Trusting me."

Frank opened and closed his fingers in front of the nozzle. "The way I look at it, Tub, no man is an island. You've got to trust someone."

"Frank—"

Frank waited.

"When I said that about my glands, that wasn't true. The truth is I just shovel it in."

"Well, Tub—"

"Day and night, Frank. In the shower. On the freeway." He turned and let the air play over his back. "I've even got stuff in the paper towel machine at work."

"There's nothing wrong with your glands at all?" Frank had taken his boots and socks off. He held first his right, then his left foot up to the nozzle.

"No. There never was."

"Does Alice know?" The machine went off and Frank started lacing up his boots.

"Nobody knows. That's the worst of it, Frank. Not the being fat, I never got any big kick out of being thin, but the lying. Having to lead a double life like a spy or a hit man. This sounds strange but I feel sorry for those guys, I really do. I know what they go through. Always having to think about what you say and do. Always feeling like people are watching you, trying to catch you at something. Never able to just be yourself. Like when I make a big deal about only having an orange for breakfast and then scarf all the way to work. Oreos, Mars Bars, Twinkies. Sugar Babies. Snickers." Tub glanced at Frank and looked quickly away. "Pretty disgusting, isn't it?"

"Tub. Tub." Frank shook his head. "Come on." He took Tub's arm and led him into the restaurant half of the bar. "My friend is hungry," he told the waitress. "Bring four orders of pancakes, plenty of butter and syrup."

"Frank—"

"Sit down."

When the dishes came Frank carved out slabs of butter and just laid them on the pancakes. Then he emptied the bottle of syrup, moving it back and forth over the plates. He leaned forward on his elbows and rested his chin in one hand. "Go on, Tub."

Tub ate several mouthfuls, then started to wipe his lips. Frank took the napkin away from him. "No wiping," he said. Tub kept at it. The syrup covered his chin; it dripped to a point like a goatee. "Weigh in, Tub," Frank said, pushing another fork across the table. "Get down to business." Tub took the fork in his left hand and lowered his head and started really chowing down. "Clean your plate," Frank said when the pancakes were gone, and Tub lifted each of the four plates and licked it clean. He sat back, trying to catch his breath.

"Beautiful," Frank said. "Are you full?"

"I'm full," Tub said. "I've never been so full."

Kenny's blankets were bunched up against the tailgate again.

"They must have blown off," Tub said.

"They're not doing him any good," Frank said. "We might as well get some use out of them."

Kenny mumbled. Tub bent over him. "What? Speak up."

"I'm going to the hospital," Kenny said.

"Attaboy," Frank said.

The blankets helped. The wind still got their faces and Frank's hands but it was much better. The fresh snow on the road and the trees sparkled under the beam of the headlight. Squares of light from farmhouse windows fell onto the blue snow in the fields.

"Frank," Tub said after a time, "you know that farmer? He told Kenny to kill the dog."

"You're kidding!" Frank leaned forward, considering. "That Kenny. What a card." He laughed and so did Tub. Tub smiled out the back window. Kenny lay with his arms folded over his stomach, moving his lips at the stars. Right overhead was the Big Dipper, and behind, hanging between Kenny's toes in the direction of the hospital, was the North Star, Pole Star, Help to Sailors. As the truck twisted through the gentle hills the star went back and forth between Kenny's boots, staying always in his sight. "I'm going to the hospital," Kenny said. But he was wrong. They had taken a different turn a long way back.

Tim O'Brien

1946 –

William Timothy O'Brien was born in Austin, Minnesota, and educated at Macalester College and Harvard University. Drafted in 1968, he spent two years in the U.S. Army, years that included service as an infantryman in Vietnam. O'Brien's combat experience became a central stimulus for his writing. His first book, a war memoir, *If I Die in a Combat Zone, Box Me Up and Ship Me Home* (1973) was followed by *Northern Lights* (1974), *Going After Cacciato* (1978), and *The Nuclear Age* (1985), novels in which war, directly or indirectly, figures prominently. Portions of *Northern Lights* and *Going After Cacciato* (winner of the National Book Award) were originally published as short stories.

Because of his subject matter, style, and outlook, O'Brien's fiction is frequently compared to that of Ernest Hemingway and Joseph Heller. "The Things They Carried" invites comparison with the stories of Ambrose Bierce, another combat veteran. Revealing the nature of war, both Bierce and O'Brien are at pains to provide readers with the full ironies of truth, but O'Brien does so with a "lyrical melancholy" not usually discovered in Bierce.

The Things They Carried

First Lieutenant Jimmy Cross carried letters from a girl named Martha, a junior at Mount Sebastian College in New Jersey. They were not love letters, but Lieutenant Cross was hoping, so he kept them folded in plastic at the bottom of his rucksack. In the late afternoon, after a day's march, he would dig his foxhole, wash his hands under a canteen, unwrap the letters, hold them with the tips of his fingers, and spend the last hour of light pretending. He would imagine romantic camping trips into the White Mountains in New Hampshire. He would sometimes taste the envelope flaps, knowing her tongue had been there. More than anything, he wanted Martha to love him as he loved her, but the letters were mostly chatty, elusive on the matter of love. She was a virgin, he was almost sure. She was an English major at Mount Sebastian, and she wrote beautifully about her professors and roommates and midterm exams, about her respect for Chaucer and her great affection for Virginia Woolf. She often quoted lines of poetry; she never mentioned the war, except to say, Jimmy, take care of yourself. The letters weighed ten ounces. They were signed "Love, Martha," but Lieutenant Cross understood that Love was only a way of signing and did not mean what he sometimes pretended it meant. At dusk, he would carefully return the letters to his rucksack. Slowly, a bit distracted, he would get up and move among his men, checking the perimeter, then at full dark he would return to his hole and watch the night and wonder if Martha was a virgin.

The things they carried were largely determined by necessity. Among the necessities or near-necessities were P-38 can openers, pocket knives, heat tabs, wristwatches, dog tags, mosquito repellent, chewing gum, candy, cigarettes, salt tablets, packets of Kool-Aid, lighters, matches, sewing kits, Military Payment Certificates, C rations, and two or three canteens of water. Together, these items weighed between fifteen and twenty pounds, depending upon a man's habits or rate of metabolism. Henry Dobbins, who was a big man, carried extra rations; he was especially fond of canned peaches in heavy syrup over pound cake. Dave Jensen, who practiced field hygiene, carried a toothbrush, dental floss, and several hotel-size bars of soap he'd stolen on R&R in Sydney,

Australia. Ted Lavender, who was scared, carried tranquilizers until he was shot in the head outside the village of Than Khe in mid-April. By necessity, and because it was SOP, they all carried steel helmets that weighed five pounds including the liner and camouflage cover. They carried the standard fatigue jackets and trousers. Very few carried underwear. On their feet they carried jungle boots—2.1 pounds—and Dave Jensen carried three pairs of socks and a can of Dr. Scholl's foot powder as a precaution against trench foot. Until he was shot, Ted Lavender carried six or seven ounces of premium dope, which for him was a necessity. Mitchell Sanders, the RTO, carried condoms. Norman Bowker carried a diary. Rat Kiley carried comic books. Kiowa, a devout Baptist, carried an illustrated New Testament that had been presented to him by his father, who taught Sunday school in Oklahoma City, Oklahoma. As a hedge against bad times, however, Kiowa also carried his grandmother's distrust of the white man, his grandfather's old hunting hatchet. Necessity dictated. Because the land was mined and booby-trapped, it was SOP for each man to carry a steel-centered, nylon-covered flak jacket, which weighed 6.7 pounds, but which on hot days seemed much heavier. Because you could die so quickly, each man carried at least one large compressed bandage, usually in the helmet band for easy access. Because the nights were cold, and because the monsoons were wet, each carried a green plastic poncho that could be used as a raincoat or groundsheet or makeshift tent. With its quilted liner, the poncho weighed almost two pounds, but it was worth every ounce. In April, for instance, when Ted Lavender was shot, they used his poncho to wrap him up, then to carry him across the paddy, then to lift him into the chopper that took him away.

They were called legs or grunts.

To carry something was to "hump" it, as when Lieutenant Jimmy Cross humped his love for Martha up the hills and through the swamps. In its intransitive form, "to hump" meant "to walk," or "to march," but it implied burdens far beyond the intransitive.

Almost everyone humped photographs. In his wallet, Lieutenant Cross carried two photographs of Martha. The first was a Kodachrome snapshop signed "Love," though he knew better. She stood against a brick wall. Her eyes were gray and neutral, her lips slightly open as she stared straight-on at the camera. At night, sometimes, Lieutenant Cross wondered who had taken the picture, because he knew she had boyfriends, because he loved her so much, and because he could see the shadow of the picture taker spreading out against the brick wall. The second photograph had been clipped from the 1968 Mount Sebastian yearbook. It was an action shot—women's volleyball—and Martha was bent horizontal to the floor, reaching, the palms of her hands in sharp focus, the tongue taut, the expression frank and competitive. There was no visible sweat. She wore white gym shorts. Her legs, he thought, were almost certainly the legs of a virgin, dry and without hair, the left knee cocked and carrying her entire weight, which was just over one-hundred pounds. Lieutenant Cross remembered touching that left knee. A dark theater, he remembered, and the movie was *Bonnie and Clyde,* and Martha wore a tweed skirt, and during the final scene, when he touched her knee, she turned and looked at him in a sad, sober way that made him pull his hand back, but he would always remember the feel of the tweed skirt and the knee beneath it and the sound of the gunfire that killed Bonnie and Clyde, how embarrassing it was, how slow and oppressive. He remembered kissing her goodnight at the dorm door. Right then, he thought, he should've done something brave. He should've carried her up the stairs to her room and tied her to the bed and touched that left knee all night long. He should've risked it. Whenever he looked at the photographs, he thought of new things he should've done.

What they carried was partly a function of rank, partly of field specialty.

As a first lieutenant and platoon leader, Jimmy Cross carried a compass, maps, code books, binoculars, and a .45-caliber pistol that weighed 2.9 pounds fully loaded. He carried a strobe light and the responsibility for the lives of his men.

As an RTO, Mitchell Sanders carried the PRC-25 radio, a killer, twenty-six pounds with its battery.

As a medic, Rat Kiley carried a canvas satchel filled with morphine and plasma and malaria tablets and surgical tape and comic books and all the things a medic must carry, including M&M's for especially bad wounds, for a total weight of nearly twenty pounds.

As a big man, therefore a machine gunner, Henry Dobbins carried the M-60, which weighed twenty-three pounds unloaded, but which was almost always loaded. In addition, Dobbins carried between ten and fifteen pounds of ammunition draped in belts across his chest and shoulders.

As PFCs or Spec 4s, most of them were common grunts and carried the standard M-16 gas-operated assault rifle. The weapon weighed 7.5 pounds unloaded, 8.2 pounds with its full twenty-round magazine. Depending on numerous factors, such as topography and psychology, the riflemen carried anywhere from twelve to twenty magazines, usually in cloth bandoliers, adding on another 8.4 pounds at minimum, fourteen pounds at maximum. When it was available, they also carried M-16 maintenance gear—rods and steel brushes and swabs and tubes of LSA oil—all of which weighed about a pound. Among the grunts, some carried the M-79 grenade launcher, 5.9 pounds unloaded, a reasonably light weapon except for the ammunition, which was heavy. A single round weighed ten ounces. The typical load was twenty-five rounds. But Ted Lavender, who was scared, carried thirty-four rounds when he was shot and killed outside Than Khe, and he went down under an exceptional burden, more than twenty pounds of ammunition, plus the flak jacket and helmet and rations and water and toilet paper and tranquilizers and all the rest, plus the unweighed fear. He was dead weight. There was no twitching or flopping. Kiowa, who saw it happen, said it was like watching a rock fall, or a big sandbag or something—just boom, then down—not like the movies where the dead guy rolls around and does fancy spins and goes ass over teakettle—not like that, Kiowa said, the poor bastard just flat-fuck fell. Boom. Down. Nothing else. It was a bright morning in mid-April. Lieutenant Cross felt the pain. He blamed himself. They stripped off Lavender's canteens and ammo, all the heavy things, and Rat Kiley said the obvious, the guy's dead, and Mitchell Sanders used his radio to report one U.S. KIA and to request a chopper. Then they wrapped Lavender in his poncho. They carried him out to a dry paddy, established security, and sat smoking the dead man's dope until the chopper came. Lieutenant Cross kept to himself. He pictured Martha's smooth young face, thinking he loved her more than anything, more than his men, and now Ted Lavender was dead because he loved her so much and could not stop thinking about her. When the dust-off arrived, they carried Lavender aboard. Afterward they burned Than Khe. They marched until dusk, then dug their holes, and that night Kiowa kept explaining how you had to be there, how fast it was, how the poor guy just dropped like so much concrete. Boom-down, he said. Like cement.

In addition to the three standard weapons—the M-60, M-16, and M-79—they carried whatever presented itself, or whatever seemed appropriate as a means of killing or staying alive. They carried catch-as-catch-can. At various times, in various situations, they carried M-14s and CAR-15s and Swedish Ks and grease guns and captured AK-47s and Chi-Coms and RPGs and Simonov carbines and black-market Uzis and .38-caliber Smith & Wesson handguns and 66 mm LAWs and shotguns and silencers and blackjacks and bayonets and C-4 plastic explosives. Lee Strunk carried a slingshot; a weapon of last resort, he called it. Mitchell Sanders carried brass knuckles. Kiowa carried his grandfather's feathered hatchet. Every third or fourth man carried a Claymore antipersonnel mine—3.5 pounds with its firing device. They all carried fragmentation grenades—fourteen ounces each. They all carried at least one M-18 colored smoke grenade—twenty-four ounces. Some carried CS or teargas grenades. Some carried white-phosphorus grenades. They carried all they could bear, and then some, including a silent awe for the terrible power of the things they carried.

In the first week of April, before Lavender died, Lieutenant Jimmy Cross received a good-luck charm from Martha. It was a simple pebble, an ounce at most. Smooth to the touch, it was a milky-white color with flecks of orange and violet, oval-shaped, like a miniature egg. In the accompanying letter, Martha wrote that she had found the pebble on the Jersey shoreline, precisely where the land touched water at high tide, where things came together but also separated. It was this separate-but-together quality, she wrote, that had inspired her to pick up the pebble and to carry it in her breast pocket for several days, where it seemed weightless, and then to send it through the mail, by air, as a token of her truest feelings for him. Lieutenant Cross found this romantic. But he wondered what her truest feelings were, exactly, and what she meant by separate-but-together. He wondered how the tides and waves had come into play on that afternoon along the Jersey shoreline when Martha saw the pebble and bent down to rescue it from geology. He imagined bare feet. Martha was a poet, with the poet's sensibilities, and her feet would be brown and bare, the toenails unpainted, the eyes chilly and somber like the ocean in March, and though it was painful, he wondered who had been with her that afternoon. He imagined a pair of shadows moving along the strip of sand where things came together but also separated. It was phantom jealousy, he knew, but he couldn't help himself. He loved her so much. On the march, through the hot days of early April, he carried the pebble in his mouth, turning it with his tongue, tasting sea salts and moisture. His mind wandered. He had difficulty keeping his attention on the war. On occasion he would yell at his men to spread out the column, to keep their eyes open, but then he would slip away into daydreams, just pretending, walking barefoot along the Jersey shore, with Martha, carrying nothing. He would feel himself rising. Sun and waves and gentle winds, all love and lightness.

What they carried varied by mission.

When a mission took them to the mountains, they carried mosquito netting, machetes, canvas tarps, and extra bug juice.

If a mission seemed especially hazardous, or if it involved a place they knew to be bad, they carried everything they could. In certain heavily mined AOs, where the land was dense with Toe Poppers and Bouncing Betties, they took turns humping a twenty-eight-pound mine detector. With its headphones and big sensing plate, the equipment was a stress on the lower back and shoulders, awkward to handle, often useless because of the shrapnel in the earth, but they carried it anyway, partly for safety, partly for the illusion of safety.

On ambush, or other night missions, they carried peculiar little odds and ends. Kiowa always took along his New Testament and a pair of moccasins for silence. Dave Jensen carried night-sight vitamins high in carotin. Lee Strunk carried his slingshot; ammo, he claimed, would never be a problem. Rat Kiley carried brandy and M&M's. Until he was shot, Ted Lavender carried the starlight scope, which weighed 6.3 pounds with its aluminum carrying case. Henry Dobbins carried his girlfriend's panty hose wrapped around his neck as a comforter. They all carried ghosts. When dark came, they would move out single file across the meadows and paddies to their ambush coordinates, where they would quietly set up the Claymores and lie down and spend the night waiting.

Other missions were more complicated and required special equipment. In mid-April, it was their mission to search out and destroy the elaborate tunnel complexes in the Than Khe area south of Chu Lai. To blow the tunnels, they carried one-pound blocks of pentrite high explosives, four blocks to a man, sixty-eight pounds in all. They carried wiring, detonators, and battery-powered clackers. Dave Jensen carried earplugs. Most often, before blowing the tunnels, they were ordered by higher command to search them, which was considered bad news, but by and large they just shrugged and carried out orders. Because he was a big man, Henry Dobbins was excused from tunnel duty. The others would draw numbers. Before Lavender died there were seventeen men in the platoon, and whoever drew the number seventeen would strip off his gear and crawl in headfirst with a flashlight and Lieutenant Cross's .45-caliber pistol. The rest of them would fan out as security. They would sit down or kneel, not facing the hole, listening to the ground beneath them, imagining cobwebs and ghosts, whatever was down there—the tunnel walls squeezing in—how the flashlight seemed impossibly heavy in the hand and how it was tunnel vision in the very strictest sense, compression in all ways, even time, and how you had to wiggle in—ass and elbows—a swallowed-up feeling—and how you found yourself worrying about odd things—will your flashlight go dead? Do rats carry rabies? If you screamed, how far would the sound carry? Would your buddies hear it? Would they have the courage to drag you out? In some respects, though not many, the waiting was worse than the tunnel itself. Imagination was a killer.

On April 16, when Lee Strunk drew the number seventeen, he laughed and muttered something and went down quickly. The morning was hot and very still. Not good, Kiowa said. He looked at the tunnel opening, then out across a dry paddy toward the village of Than Khe. Nothing moved. No clouds or birds or people. As they waited, the men smoked and drank Kool-Aid, not talking much, feeling sympathy for Lee Strunk but also feeling the luck of the draw. You win some, you lose some, said Mitchell Sanders, and sometimes you settle for a rain check. It was a tired line and no one laughed.

Henry Dobbins ate a tropical chocolate bar. Ted Lavender popped a tranquilizer and went off to pee.

After five minutes, Lieutenant Jimmy Cross moved to the tunnel, leaned down, and examined the darkness. Trouble, he thought—a cave-in maybe. And then suddenly, without willing it, he was thinking about Martha. The stresses and fractures, the quick collapse, the two of them buried alive under all that weight. Dense, crushing love. Kneeling, watching the hole, he tried to concentrate on Lee Strunk and the war, all the dangers, but his love was too much for him, he felt paralyzed, he wanted to sleep inside her lungs and breathe her blood and be smothered. He wanted her to be a virgin and not a virgin, all at once. He wanted to know her. Intimate secrets—why poetry? Why so sad? Why that grayness in her eyes? Why so alone? Not lonely, just alone—riding her bike across campus or sitting off by herself in the cafeteria. Even dancing, she danced alone—and it was the aloneness that filled him with love. He remembered telling her that one evening. How she nodded and looked away. And how, later, when he kissed her, she received the kiss without returning it, her eyes wide open, not afraid, not a virgin's eyes, just flat and uninvolved.

Lieutenant Cross gazed at the tunnel. But he was not there. He was buried with Martha under the white sand at the Jersey shore. They were pressed together, and the pebble in his mouth was her tongue. He was smiling. Vaguely, he was aware of how quiet the day was, the sullen paddies, yet he could not bring himself to worry about matters of security. He was beyond that. He was just a kid at war, in love. He was twenty-two years old. He couldn't help it.

A few moments later Lee Strunk crawled out of the tunnel. He came up grinning, filthy but alive. Lieutenant Cross nodded and closed his eyes while the others clapped Strunk on the back and made jokes about rising from the dead.

Worms, Rat Kiley said. Right out of the grave. Fuckin' zombie.

The men laughed. They all felt great relief.

Spook City, said Mitchell Sanders.

Lee Strunk made a funny ghost sound, a kind of moaning, yet very happy, and right then, when Strunk made that high happy moaning sound, when he went *Ahhooooo*, right then Ted Lavender was shot in the head on his way back from peeing. He lay with his mouth open. The teeth were broken. There was a swollen black bruise under his left eye. The cheekbone was gone. Oh shit, Rat Kiley said, the guy's dead. The guy's dead, he kept saying, which seemed profound—the guy's dead. I mean really.

The things they carried were determined to some extent by superstition. Lieutenant Cross carried his good-luck pebble. Dave Jensen carried a rabbit's foot. Norman Bowker, otherwise a very gentle person, carried a thumb that had been presented to him as a gift by Mitchell Sanders.

The thumb was dark brown, rubbery to the touch, and weighed four ounces at most. It had been cut from a VC corpse, a boy of fifteen or sixteen. They'd found him at the bottom of an irrigation ditch, badly burned, flies in his mouth and eyes. The boy wore black shorts and sandals. At the time of his death he had been carrying a pouch of rice, a rifle, and three magazines of ammunition.

You want my opinion, Mitchell Sanders said, there's a definite moral here.

He put his hand on the dead boy's wrist. He was quiet for a time, as if counting a pulse, then he patted the stomach, almost affectionately, and used Kiowa's hunting hatchet to remove the thumb.

Henry Dobbins asked what the moral was.

Moral?

You know. *Moral.*

Sanders wrapped the thumb in toilet paper and handed it across to Norman Bowker. There was no blood. Smiling, he kicked the boy's head, watched the flies scatter and said, It's like with that old TV show—Paladin. Have gun, will travel.

Henry Dobbins thought about it.

Yeah, well, he finally said. I don't see no moral.

There it *is*, man.

Fuck off.

They carried USO stationery and pencils and pens. They carried Sterno, safety pins, trip flares, signal flares, spools of wire, razor blades, chewing tobacco, liberated joss sticks and statuettes of the smiling Buddha, candles, grease pencils, *The Stars and Stripes,* fingernail clippers, Psy Ops leaflets, bush hats, bolos, and much more. Twice a week, when the resupply choppers came in, they carried hot chow in green Mermite cans and large canvas bags filled with iced beer and soda pop. They carried plastic water containers, each with a two-gallon capacity. Mitchell Sanders carried a set of starched tiger fatigues for special occasions. Henry Dobbins carried Black Flag insecticide. Dave Jensen carried empty sandbags that could be filled at night for added protection. Lee Strunk carried tanning lotion. Some things they carried in common. Taking turns, they carried the big PRC-77 scrambler radio, which weighed thirty pounds with its battery. They shared the weight of memory. They took up what others could no longer bear. Often, they carried each other, the wounded or weak. They carried infections. They carried chess sets, basketballs, Vietnamese-English dictionaries, insignia of rank, Bronze Stars and Purple Hearts, plastic cards imprinted with the Code of Conduct. They carried diseases, among them malaria and dysentery. They carried lice and ringworm and leeches and paddy algae and various rots and molds. They carried the land itself—Vietnam, the place, the soil—a powdery orange-red dust that covered their boots and fatigues and faces. They carried the sky. The whole atmosphere, they carried it, the humidity, the monsoons, the stink of fungus and decay, all of it, they carried gravity. They moved like mules. By daylight they took sniper fire, at night they were mortared, but it was not battle, it was just the endless march, village to village, without purpose, nothing won or lost. They marched for the sake of the march. They plodded along slowly, dumbly, leaning forward against the heat, unthinking, all blood and bone, simple grunts, soldiering with their legs, toiling up the hills and down into the paddies and across the rivers and up again and down, just humping, one step and then the next and then another, but no volition, no will, because it was automatic, it was anatomy, and the war was entirely a matter of posture and carriage, the hump was everything, a kind of inertia, a kind of emptiness, a dullness of desire and intellect and conscience and hope and human sensibility. Their principles were in their feet. Their calculations were biological. They had no sense of strategy or mission. They searched the villages without knowing what to look for, not caring, kicking over jars of rice, frisking children and old men, blowing tunnels, sometimes setting fires and sometimes not, then forming up and moving on to the next village, then other villages, where it would always be the same. They carried their own lives. The pressures were enormous. In the heat of early afternoon, they would remove their helmets and flak jackets, walking bare, which was dangerous but which helped ease the strain. They would often discard things along the route of march. Purely for comfort, they would throw away rations, blow their Claymores and grenades, no matter, because by nightfall the resupply choppers would arrive with more of the same, then a day or two later still more, fresh watermelons and crates of ammunition and sunglasses and woolen sweaters—the resources were stunning—sparklers for the Fourth of July, colored eggs for Easter. It was the great American war chest—the fruits of science, the smokestacks, the canneries, the arsenals at Hartford, the Minnesota forests, the machine shops, the vast fields of corn and wheat—they carried like freight trains; they carried it on their backs and shoulders—and for all the ambiguities of Vietnam, all the mysteries and unknowns, there was at least the single abiding certainty that they would never be at a loss for things to carry.

After the chopper took Lavender away, Lieutenant Jimmy Cross led his men into the village of Than Khe. They burned everything. They shot chickens and dogs, they trashed the village well, they called in artillery and watched the wreckage, then they marched for several hours through the hot afternoon, and then at dusk, while Kiowa explained how Lavender died, Lieutenant Cross found himself trembling.

He tried not to cry. With his entrenching tool, which weighed five pounds, he began digging a hole in the earth.

He felt shame. He hated himself. He had loved Martha more than his men, and as a consequence Lavender was now dead, and this was something he would have to carry like a stone in his stomach for the rest of the war.

All he could do was dig. He used his entrenching tool like an ax, slashing, feeling both love and hate, and then later, when it was full dark, he sat at the bottom of his foxhole and wept. It went on for a long while. In part, he was grieving for Ted Lavender, but mostly it was for Martha, and for himself, because she belonged to another world, which was not quite real, and because she was a junior at Mount Sebastian College in New Jersey, a poet and a virgin and uninvolved, and because he realized she did not love him and never would.

Like cement, Kiowa whispered in the dark. I swear to God—boom-down. Not a word.

I've heard this, said Norman Bowker.

A pisser, you know? Still zipping himself up. Zapped while zipping.

All right, fine. That's enough.

Yeah, but you had to see it, the guy just—

I *heard,* man. Cement. So why not shut the fuck *up?*

Kiowa shook his head sadly and glanced over at the hole where Lieutenant Jimmy Cross sat watching the night. The air was thick and wet. A warm, dense fog had settled over the paddies and there was the stillness that precedes rain.

After a time Kiowa sighed.

One thing for sure, he said. The Lieutenant's in some deep hurt. I mean that crying jag—the way he was carrying on—it wasn't fake or anything, it was real heavy-duty hurt. The man cares.

Sure, Norman Bowker said.

Say what you want, the man does care.

We all got problems.

Not Lavender.

No, I guess not, Bowker said. Do me a favor, though.

Shut up?

That's a smart Indian. Shut up.

Shrugging, Kiowa pulled off his boots. He wanted to say more, just to lighten up his sleep, but instead he opened his New Testament and arranged it beneath his head as a pillow. The fog made things seem hollow and unattached. He tried not to think about Ted Lavender, but then he was thinking how fast it was, no drama, down and dead, and how it was hard to feel anything except surprise. It seemed unchristian. He wished he could find some great sadness, or even anger, but the emotion wasn't there and he couldn't make it happen. Mostly he felt pleased to be alive. He liked the smell of the New Testament under his cheek, the leather and ink and paper and glue, whatever the chemicals were. He liked hearing the sounds of night. Even his fatigue, it felt fine, the stiff muscles and the prickly awareness of his own body, a floating feeling. He enjoyed not being dead. Lying there, Kiowa admired Lieutenant Jimmy Cross's capacity for grief. He wanted to share the man's pain, he wanted to care as Jimmy Cross cared. And yet when he closed his eyes, all he could think was Boom-down, and all he could feel was the pleasure of having his boots off and the fog curling in around him and the damp soil and the Bible smells and the plush comfort of night.

After a moment Norman Bowker sat up in the dark.

What the hell, he said. You want to talk, *talk*. Tell it to me.

Forget it.

No, man, go on. One thing I hate, it's a silent Indian.

For the most part they carried themselves with poise, a kind of dignity. Now and then, however, there were times of panic, when they squealed or wanted to squeal but couldn't, when they twitched and made moaning sounds and covered their heads and said Dear Jesus and flopped around on the earth and fired their weapons blindly and cringed and sobbed and begged for the noise to stop and went wild and made stupid promises to themselves and to God and to their mothers and fathers, hoping not to die. In different ways, it happened to all of them. Afterward, when the firing ended, they would blink and peek up. They would touch their bodies, feeling shame, then quickly hiding it. They would force themselves to stand. As if in slow motion, frame by frame, the world would take on the old logic—absolute silence, then the wind, then sunlight, then voices. It was the burden of being alive. Awkwardly, the men would reassemble themselves, first in private, then in groups, becoming soldiers again. They would repair the leaks in their eyes. They would check for casualties, call in dust-offs, light cigarettes, try to smile, clear their throats and spit and begin cleaning their weapons. After a time someone would shake his head and say, No lie, I almost shit my pants, and someone else would laugh, which meant it was bad, yes, but the guy had obviously not shit his pants, it wasn't that bad, and in any case nobody would ever do such a thing and then go ahead and talk about it. They would squint into the dense, oppressive sunlight. For a few moments, perhaps, they would fall silent, lighting a joint and tracking its passage from man to man, inhaling, holding in the humiliation. Scary stuff, one of them might say. But then someone else would grin or flick his eyebrows and say, Roger-dodger, almost cut me a new asshole, *almost*.

There were numerous such poses. Some carried themselves with a sort of wistful resignation, others with pride or stiff soldierly discipline or good humor or macho zeal. They were afraid of dying but they were even more afraid to show it.

They found jokes to tell.

They used a hard vocabulary to contain the terrible softness. *Greased,* they'd say. *Offed, lit up, zapped while zipping.* It wasn't cruelty, just stage presence. They were actors and the war came at them in 3-D. When someone died, it wasn't quite dying, because in a curious way it seemed scripted, and because they had their lines mostly memorized, irony mixed with tragedy, and because they called it by other names, as if to encyst and destroy the reality of death itself. They kicked corpses. They cut off thumbs. They talked grunt lingo. They told stories about Ted Lavender's supply of tranquilizers, how the poor guy didn't feel a thing, how incredibly tranquil he was.

There's a moral here, said Mitchell Sanders.

They were waiting for Lavender's chopper, smoking the dead man's dope.

The moral's pretty obvious, Sanders said, and winked. Stay away from drugs. No joke, they'll ruin your day every time.

Cute, said Henry Dobbins.

Mind-blower, get it? Talk about wiggy—nothing left, just blood and brains.

They made themselves laugh.

There it is, they'd say, over and over, as if the repetition itself were an act of poise, a balance between crazy and almost crazy, knowing without going. There it is, which meant be cool, let it ride, because oh yeah, man, you can't change what can't be changed, there it is, there it absolutely and positively and fucking well *is.*

They were tough.

They carried all the emotional baggage of men who might die. Grief, terror, love, longing—these were intangibles, but the intangibles had their own mass and specific gravity, they had tangible weight. They carried shameful memories. They carried the common secret of cowardice barely restrained, the instinct to run or freeze or hide, and in many respects this was the heaviest burden of all, for it could never be put down, it required perfect balance and perfect posture. They carried their reputations. They carried the soldier's greatest fear, which was the fear of blushing. Men killed, and died, because they were embarrassed not to. It was what had brought them to the war in the first place, nothing positive, no dreams of glory or honor, just to avoid the blush of dishonor. They died so as not to die of embarrassment. They crawled into tunnels and walked point and advanced under fire. Each morning, despite the unknowns, they made their legs move. They endured. They kept humping. They did not submit to the obvious alternative, which was simply to close the eyes and fall. So easy, really. Go limp and tumble to the ground and let the muscles unwind and not speak and not budge until your buddies picked you up and lifted you into the chopper that would roar and dip its nose and carry you off to the world. A mere matter of falling, yet no one ever fell. It was not courage, exactly; the object was not valor. Rather, they were too frightened to be cowards.

By and large they carried these things inside, maintaining the masks of composure. They sneered at sick call. They spoke bitterly about guys who had found release by shooting off their own toes or fingers. Pussies, they'd say. Candyasses. It was fierce, mocking talk, with only a trace of envy or awe, but even so, the image played itself out behind their eyes.

They imagined the muzzle against flesh. They imagined the quick, sweet pain, then the evacuation to Japan, then a hospital with warm beds and cute geisha nurses.

They dreamed of freedom birds.

At night, on guard, staring into the dark, they were carried away by jumbo jets. They felt the rush of takeoff. *Gone!* they yelled. And then velocity, wings and engines, a smiling stewardess—but it was more than a plane, it was a real bird, a big sleek silver bird with feathers and talons and high screeching. They were flying. The weights fell off, there was nothing to bear. They laughed and held on tight, feeling the cold slap of wind and altitude, soaring, thinking *It's over, I'm gone!*—they were naked, they were light and free—it was all lightness, bright and fast and buoyant, light as light, a helium buzz in the brain, a giddy bubbling in the lungs as they were taken up over the clouds and the war, beyond duty, beyond gravity and mortification and global entanglements—*Sin loi!* they yelled, *I'm sorry, motherfuckers, but I'm out of it, I'm goofed, I'm on a space cruise, I'm gone!*—and it was a restful, disencumbered sensation, just riding the light waves, sailing that big silver freedom bird over the mountains and oceans, over America, over the farms and great sleeping cities and cemeteries and highways and the Golden Arches of McDonald's. It was flight, a kind of fleeing, a kind of falling, falling higher and higher, spinning off the edge of the earth and beyond the sun and through the vast, silent vacuum where there were no burdens and where everything weighed exactly nothing. *Gone!* they screamed, *I'm sorry but I'm gone!* And so at night, not quite dreaming, they gave themselves over to lightness, they were carried, they were purely borne.

On the morning after Ted Lavender died, First Lieutenant Jimmy Cross crouched at the bottom of his foxhole and burned Martha's letters. Then he burned the two photographs. There was a steady rain falling, which made it difficult, but he used heat tabs and Sterno to build a small fire, screening it with his body, holding the photographs over the tight blue flame with the tips of his fingers.

He realized it was only a gesture. Stupid, he thought. Sentimental, too, but mostly just stupid.

Lavender was dead. You couldn't burn the blame.

Besides, the letters were in his head. And even now, without photographs, Lieutenant Cross could see Martha playing volleyball in her white gym shorts and yellow T-shirt. He could see her moving in the rain.

When the fire died out, Lieutenant Cross pulled his poncho over his shoulders and ate breakfast from a can.

There was no great mystery, he decided.

In those burned letters Martha had never mentioned the war, except to say, Jimmy, take care of yourself. She wasn't involved. She signed the letters "Love," but it wasn't love, and all the fine lines and technicalities did not matter.

The morning came up wet and blurry. Everything seemed part of everything else, the fog and Martha and the deepening rain.

It was a war, after all.

Half smiling, Lieutenant Jimmy Cross took out his maps. He shook his head hard, as if to clear it, then bent forward and began planning the day's march. In ten minutes, or maybe twenty, he would rouse the men and they would pack up and head west, where the maps showed the country to be green and inviting. They would do what they had always done. The rain might add some weight, but otherwise it would be one more day layered upon all the other days.

He was realistic about it. There was that new hardness in his stomach.

No more fantasies, he told himself.

Henceforth, when he thought about Martha, it would be only to think that she belonged elsewhere. He would shut down the daydreams. This was not Mount Sebastian, it was another world, where there were no pretty poems or midterm exams, a place where men died because of carelessness and gross stupidity. Kiowa was right. Boom-down, and you were dead, never partly dead.

Briefly, in the rain, Lieutenant Cross saw Martha's gray eyes gazing back at him.

He understood.

It was very sad, he thought. The things men carried inside. The things men did or felt they had to do.

He almost nodded at her, but didn't.

Instead he went back to his maps. He was now determined to perform his duties firmly and without negligence. It wouldn't help Lavender, he knew that, but from this point on he would comport himself as a soldier. He would dispose of his good-luck pebble. Swallow it, maybe, or use Lee Strunk's slingshop, or just drop it along the trail. On the march he would impose strict field discipline. He would be careful to send out flank security, to prevent straggling or bunching up, to keep his troops moving at the proper pace and at the proper interval. He would insist on clean weapons. He would confiscate the remainder of Lavender's dope. Later in the day, perhaps, he would call the men together and speak to them plainly. He would accept the blame for what had happened to Ted Lavender. He would be a man about it. He would look them in the eyes, keeping his chin level, and he would issue the new SOPs in a calm, impersonal tone of voice, an officer's voice, leaving no room for argument or discussion. Commencing immediately, he'd tell them, they would no longer abandon equipment along the route of march. They would police up their acts. They would get their shit together, and keep it together, and maintain it neatly and in good working order.

He would not tolerate laxity. He would show strength, distancing himself.

Among the men there would be grumbling, of course, and maybe worse, because their days would seem longer and their loads heavier, but Lieutenant Cross reminded himself that his obligation was not to be loved but to lead. He would dispense with love; it was not now a factor. And if anyone quarreled or complained, he would simply tighten his lips and arrange his shoulders in the correct command posture. He might give a curt little nod. Or he might not. He might just shrug and say Carry on, then they would saddle up and form into a column and move out toward the villages west of Than Khe.

David Michael Kaplan

1946 –

Comfort: Short Stories by David Michael Kaplan (1987) was greeted by critics as the "auspicious beginning of a most promising career." A native of Pennsylvania, Kaplan has lived in many other parts of the United States—the Northeast, Far West, Middle Atlantic, and Midwest. He has been a member of the Iowa Writers' Workshop and was the winner of writing fellowships from Yaddo and the Fine Arts Work Center in Provincetown, Massachusetts. His stories, which have appeared in such magazines as *The Atlantic*, have been named winners in the P.E.N. Syndicated Fiction Project and chosen for *Best American Short Stories.*

The range of subject, character, and situation in Kaplan's short fiction is extraordinarily broad. "Doe Season" can by itself give only a suggestion of this diversity, but it provides impressive evidence of Kaplan's skill with language and his moving, penetrating insight into human experience.

Doe Season

They were always the same woods, she thought sleepily as they drove through the early morning darkness—deep and immense, covered with yesterday's snowfall which had frozen overnight. They were the same woods that lay behind her house, *and they stretch all the way to here,* she thought, *for miles and miles, longer than I could walk in a day, or a week even, but they are still the same woods.* The thought made her feel good: it was like thinking of God; it was like thinking of the space between here and the moon; it was like thinking of all the foreign countries from her geography book where even now, Andy knew, people were going to bed, while they—she and her father and Charlie Spoon and Mac, Charlie's eleven-year-old son—were driving deeper into the Pennsylvania countryside, to go hunting.

They had risen long before dawn. Her mother, yawning and not trying to hide her sleepiness, cooked them eggs and French toast. Her father smoked a cigarette and flicked ashes into his saucer while Andy listened, wondering *Why doesn't he come?* and *Won't he ever come?,* until at last a car pulled into the graveled drive and honked. "That will be Charlie Spoon," her father said; he always said "Charlie Spoon," even though his real name was Spreun, because Charlie was, in a sense, shaped like a spoon, with a large head and a narrow waist and chest.

Andy's mother kissed her and her father and said, "Well, have a good time" and "Be careful." Soon they were outside in the bitter dark, loading gear by the back-porch light, their breath steaming. The woods behind the house were then only a black streak against the wash of night.

Andy dozed in the car and woke to find that it was half-light. Mac—also sleeping—had slid against her. She pushed him away and looked out the window. Her breath clouded the glass, and she was cold; the car's heater didn't work right. They were riding over gentle hills, the woods on both sides now—the same woods, she knew, because she had been watching the whole way, even while she slept. They had been in her dreams, and she had never lost sight of them.

Charlie Spoon was driving. "I don't understand why she's coming," he said to her father. "How old is she anyway—eight?"

"Nine," her father replied. "She's small for her age."

"So—nine. What's the difference? She'll just add to the noise and get tired besides."

"No, she won't," her father said. "She can walk me to death. And she'll bring good luck, you'll see. Animals—I don't know how she does it, but they come right up to her. We go walking in the woods, and we'll spot more raccoons and possums and such than I ever see when I'm alone."

Charlie grunted.

"Besides, she's not a bad little shot, even if she doesn't hunt yet. She shoots the .22 real good."

"Popgun," Charlie snorted. "And target shooting ain't deer hunting."

"Well, she's not gonna be shooting anyway, Charlie," her father said. "Don't worry. She'll be no bother."

"I still don't know why she's coming," Charlie said.

"Because she wants to, and I want her to. Just like you and Mac. No difference."

Charlie turned onto a side road and after a mile or so slowed down. "That's it!" he cried. He stopped, backed up, and entered a narrow dirt road almost hidden by trees. Five hundred yards down, the road ran parallel to a fenced-in field. Charlie parked in a cleared area deeply rutted by frozen tractor tracks. The gate was locked. *In the spring,* Andy thought, *there will be cows here, and a dog that chases them,* but now the field was unmarked and bare.

"This is it," Charlie Spoon declared. "Me and Mac was up here just two weeks ago, scouting it out, and there's deer. Mac saw the tracks."

"That's right," Mac said.

"Well, we'll just see about that," her father said, putting on his gloves. He turned to Andy. "How you doing, honeybun?"

"Just fine," she said.

Andy shivered and stamped as they unloaded: first the rifles, which they unsheathed and checked, sliding the bolts, sighting through scopes, adjusting the slings; then the gear, their food and tents and sleeping bags and stove stored in four backpacks—three big ones for Charlie Spoon and her father and Mac, and a day pack for her.

"That's about your size," Mac said, to tease her.

She reddened and said, "Mac, I can carry a pack big as yours any day." He laughed and pressed his knee against the back of hers, so that her leg buckled. "Cut it out," she said. She wanted to make an iceball and throw it at him, but she knew that her father and Charlie were anxious to get going, and she didn't want to displease them.

Mac slid under the gate, and they handed the packs over to him. Then they slid under and began walking across the field toward the same woods that ran all the way back to her home, where even now her mother was probably rising again to wash their breakfast dishes and make herself a fresh pot of coffee. *She is there, and we are here:* the thought satisfied Andy. There was no place else she would rather be.

Mac came up beside her. "Over there's Canada," he said, nodding toward the woods.

"Huh!" she said. "Not likely."

"I don't mean *right* over there. I mean further up north. You think I'm dumb?"

Dumb as your father, she thought.

"Look at that," Mac said, pointing to a piece of cow dung lying on a spot scraped bare of snow. "A frozen meadow muffin." He picked it up and sailed it at her. "Catch!"

"Mac!" she yelled. His laugh was as gawky as he was. She walked faster. He seemed different today somehow, bundled in his yellow-and-black-checkered coat, a rifle in hand, his silly floppy hat not quite covering his ears. They all seemed different as she watched them trudge through the snow—Mac and her father and Charlie Spoon—bigger, maybe, as if the cold landscape enlarged rather than diminished them, so that they, the only figures in that landscape, took on size and meaning just by being there. If they weren't there, everything would be quieter, and the woods would be the same as before. *But they are here,* Andy thought, looking behind her at the boot prints in the snow, *and I am too, and so it's all different.*

"We'll go down to the cut where we found those deer tracks," Charlie said as they entered the woods. "Maybe we'll get lucky and get a late one coming through."

The woods descended into a gully. The snow was softer and deeper here, so that often Andy sank to her knees. Charlie and Mac worked the top of the gully while she and her father walked along the base some thirty yards behind them. "If they miss the first shot, we'll get the second," her father said, and she nodded as if she had known this all the time. She listened to the crunch of their boots, their breathing, and the drumming of a distant woodpecker. And the crackling. In winter the woods crackled as if everything were straining, ready to snap like dried chicken bones.

We are hunting, Andy thought. The cold air burned her nostrils.

They stopped to make lunch by a rock outcropping that protected them from the wind. Her father heated the bean soup her mother had made for them, and they ate it with bread already stiff from the cold. He and Charlie took a few pulls from a flask of Jim Beam while she scoured the plates with snow and repacked them. Then they had coffee with sugar and powdered milk, and her father poured her a cup, too. "We won't tell your momma," he said, and Mac laughed. Andy held the cup the way her father did, not by the handle but around the rim. The coffee tasted smoky. She felt a little queasy, but she drank it all.

Charlie Spoon picked his teeth with a fingernail. "Now, you might've noticed one thing," he said.

"What's that?" her father asked.

"You might've noticed you don't hear no rifles. That's because there ain't no other hunters here. We've got the whole damn woods to ourselves. Now, I ask you—do I know how to find 'em?"

"We haven't seen deer yet, neither."

"Oh, we will," Charlie said, "but not for a while now." He leaned back against the rock. "Deer're sleeping, resting up for the evening feed."

"I seen a deer behind our house once, and it was afternoon," Andy said.

"Yeah, honey, but that was *before* deer season," Charlie said, grinning. "They know something now. They're smart that way."

"That's right," Mac said.

Andy looked at her father—had she said something stupid?

"Well, Charlie," he said, "if they know so much, how come so many get themselves shot?"

"Them's the ones that don't *believe* what they know," Charlie replied. The men laughed. Andy hesitated, and then laughed with them.

They moved on, as much to keep warm as to find a deer. The wind became even stronger. Blowing through the treetops, it sounded like the ocean, and once Andy thought she could smell salt air. But that was impossible; the ocean was *hundreds* of miles away, farther than Canada even. She and her parents had gone last summer to stay for a week at a motel on the New Jersey shore. That was the first time she'd seen the ocean, and it frightened her. It was huge and empty, yet always moving. Everything lay hidden. If you walked in it, you couldn't see how deep it was or what might be below; if you swam, something could pull you under and you'd never be seen again. Its musky, rank smell made her think of things dying. Her mother had floated beyond the breakers, calling to her to come in, but Andy wouldn't go farther than a few feet into the surf. Her mother swam and splashed with animal-like delight while her father, smiling shyly, held his white arms above the waist-deep water as if afraid to get them wet. Once a comber rolled over and sent them both tossing, and when her mother tried to stand up, the surf receding behind, Andy saw that her mother's swimsuit top had come off, so that her breasts swayed free, the nipples like two dark eyes. Embarrassed, Andy looked around: except for two women under a yellow umbrella farther up, the beach was empty. Her mother stood up unsteadily, regained her footing. Taking what seemed the longest time, she calmly refixed her top. Andy lay on the beach towel and closed her eyes. The sound of the surf made her head ache.

And now it was winter; the sky was already dimming, not just with the absence of light, but with a mist that clung to the hunters' faces like cobwebs. They made camp early. Andy was chilled. When she stood still, she kept wiggling her toes to make sure they were there. Her father rubbed her arms and held her to him briefly, and that felt better. She unpacked the food while the others put up the tents.

"How about rounding us up some firewood, Mac?" Charlie asked.

"I'll do it," Andy said. Charlie looked at her thoughtfully and then handed her the canvas carrier.

There wasn't much wood on the ground, so it took her a while to get a good load. She was about a hundred yards from camp, near a cluster of high, lichen-covered boulders, when she saw through a crack in the rock a buck and two does walking gingerly, almost daintily, through the alder trees. She tried to hush her breathing as they passed not more than twenty yards away. There was nothing she could do. If she yelled, they'd be gone; by the time she got back to camp, they'd be gone. The buck stopped, nostrils quivering, tail up and alert. He looked directly at her. Still she didn't move, not one muscle. He was a beautiful buck, the color of late-turned maple leaves. Unafraid, he lowered his tail, and he and his does silently merged into the trees. Andy walked back to camp and dropped the firewood.

"I saw three deer," she said. "A buck and two does."

"Where?" Charlie Spoon cried, looking behind her as if they might have followed her into camp.

"In the woods yonder. They're gone now."

"Well, hell!" Charlie banged his coffee up against his knee.

"Didn't I say she could find animals?" her father said, grinning.

"Too late to go after them," Charlie muttered. "It'll be dark in a quarter hour. Damn!"

"Damn," Mac echoed.

"They just walk right up to her," her father said.

"Well, leastwise this proves there's deer here." Charlie began snapping long branches into shorter ones. "You know, I think I'll stick with you," he told Andy, "since you're so good at finding deer and all. How'd that be?"

"Okay, I guess," Andy murmured. She hoped he was kidding: no way did she want to hunt with Charlie Spoon. Still, she was pleased he had said it.

Her father and Charlie took one tent, she and Mac the other. When they were in their sleeping bags, Mac said in the darkness, "I bet you really didn't see no deer, did you?"

She sighed. "I did, Mac. Why would I lie?"

"How big was the buck?"

"Four point. I counted."

Mac snorted.

"You just believe what you want, Mac," she said testily.

"Too bad it ain't buck season," he said. "Well, I got to go pee."

"So pee."

She heard him turn in his bag. "You ever see it?" he asked.

"It? What's 'it'?"

"It. A pecker."

"Sure," she lied.

"Whose? Your father's?"

She was uncomfortable. "No," she said.

"Well, whose, then?"

"Oh, I don't know! Leave me be, why don't you?"

"Didn't see a deer, didn't see a pecker," Mac said teasingly.

She didn't answer right away. Then she said, "My cousin Lewis. I saw his."

"Well, how old's he?"

"One and a half."

"Ha! A baby! A baby's is like a little worm. It ain't a real one at all."

If he says he'll show me his, she thought, *I'll kick him. I'll just get out of my bag and kick him.*

"I went hunting with my daddy and Versh and Danny Simmons last year in buck season," Mac said, "and we got ourselves one. And we hog-dressed the thing. You know what that is, don't you?"

"No," she said. She was confused. What was he talking about now?

"That's when you cut him open and take out all his guts, so the meat don't spoil. Makes him lighter to pack out, too."

She tried to imagine what the deer's guts might look like, pulled from the gaping hole. "What do you do with them?" she asked. "The guts?"

"Oh, just leave 'em for the bears."

She ran her finger like a knife blade along her belly.

"When we left them on the ground," Mac said, "they smoked. Like they were cooking."

"Huh," she said.

"They cut off the deer's pecker, too, you know."

Andy imagined Lewis's pecker and shuddered. "Mac, you're disgusting."

He laughed. "Well, I gotta go pee." She heard him rustle out of his bag. "Broo!" he cried, flapping his arms. "It's cold!"

He makes so much noise, she thought, *just noise and more noise.*

Her father woke them before first light. He warned them to talk softly and said that they were going to the place where Andy had seen the deer, to try to cut them off on their way back from their night feeding. Andy couldn't shake off her sleep. Stuffing her sleeping bag into its sack seemed to take an hour, and tying her boots was the strangest thing she'd ever done. Charlie Spoon made hot chocolate and oatmeal with raisins. Andy closed her eyes and, between beats of her heart, listened to the breathing of the forest. *When I open my eyes, it will be lighter,* she decided. But when she did, it was still just as dark, except for the swaths of their flashlights and the hissing blue flame of the stove. *There has to be just one moment when it all changes from dark to light,* Andy thought. She had missed it yesterday, in the car; today she would watch more closely.

But when she remembered again, it was already first light and they had moved to the rocks by the deer trail and had set up shooting positions—Mac and Charlie Spoon on the up-trail side, she and her father behind them, some six feet up on a ledge. The day became brighter, the sun piercing the tall pines, raking the hunters, yet providing little warmth. Andy now smelled alder and pine and the slightly rotten odor of rock lichen. She rubbed her hand over the stone and considered that it must be very old, had probably been here before the giant pines, *before anyone was in these woods at all.* A chipmunk sniffed on a nearby branch. She aimed an imaginary rifle and pressed the trigger. The chipmunk froze, then scurried away. Her legs were cramping on the narrow ledge. Her father seemed to doze, one hand in his parka, the other cupped lightly around the rifle. She could smell his scent of old wool and leather. His cheeks were speckled with gray-black whiskers, and he worked his jaws slightly, as if chewing a small piece of gum.

Please let us get a deer, she prayed.

A branch snapped on the other side of the rock face. Her father's hand stiffened on the rifle, startling her—*He hasn't been sleeping at all,* she marveled—and then his jaw relaxed, as did the lines around his eyes, and she heard Charlie Spoon call, "Yo, don't shoot, it's us." He and Mac appeared from around the rock. They stopped beneath the ledge. Charlie solemnly crossed his arms.

"I don't believe we're gonna get any deer here," he said drily.

Andy's father lowered his rifle to Charlie and jumped down from the ledge. Then he reached up for Andy. She dropped into his arms and he set her gently on the ground.

Mac sidled up to her. "I knew you didn't see no deer," he said.

"Just because they don't come when you want 'em to don't mean she didn't see them," her father said.

Still, she felt bad. Her telling about the deer had caused them to spend the morning there, cold and expectant, with nothing to show for it.

They tramped through the woods for another two hours, not caring much about noise. Mac found some deer tracks, and they argued about how old they were. They split up for a while and then rejoined at an old logging road that deer might use, and followed it. The road crossed a stream, which had mostly frozen over but in a few spots still caught leaves and twigs in an icy swirl. They forded it by jumping from rock to rock. The road narrowed after that, and the woods thickened.

They stopped for lunch, heating up Charlie's wife's corn chowder. Andy's father cut squares of applesauce cake with his hunting knife and handed them to her and Mac, who ate his almost daintily. Andy could faintly taste knife oil on the cake. She was tired. She stretched her leg; the muscle that had cramped on the rock still ached.

"Might as well relax," her father said, as if reading her thoughts. "We won't find deer till suppertime."

Charlie Spoon leaned back against his pack and folded his hands across his stomach. "Well, even if we don't get a deer," he said expansively, "it's still great to be out here, breathe some fresh air, clomp around a bit. Get away from the house and the old lady." He winked at Mac, who looked away.

"That's what the woods are all about, anyway," Charlie said. "It's where the women don't want to go." He bowed his head toward Andy. "With your exception, of course, little lady." He helped himself to another piece of applesauce cake.

"She ain't a woman," Mac said.

"Well, she damn well's gonna be," Charlie said. He grinned at her. "Or will you? You're half a boy anyway. You go by a boy's name. What's your real name? Andrea, ain't it?"

"That's right," she said. She hoped that if she didn't look at him, Charlie would stop.

"Well, which do you like? Andy or Andrea?"

"Don't matter," she mumbled. "Either."

"She's always been Andy to me," her father said.

Charlie Spoon was still grinning. "So what are you gonna be, Andrea? A boy or a girl?"

"I'm a girl," she said.

"But you want to go hunting and fishing and everything, huh?"

"She can do whatever she likes," her father said.

"Hell, you might as well have just had a boy and be done with it!" Charlie exclaimed.

"That's funny," her father said, and chuckled. "That's just what her momma tells me."

They were looking at her, and she wanted to get away from them all, even from her father, who chose to joke with them.

"I'm going to walk a bit," she said.

She heard them laughing as she walked down the logging trail. She flapped her arms; she whistled. *I don't care how much noise I make,* she thought. Two grouse flew from the underbrush, startling her. A little farther down, the trail ended in a clearing that enlarged into a frozen meadow; beyond it the woods began again. A few moldering posts were all that was left of a fence that had once enclosed the field. The low afternoon sunlight reflected brightly off the snow, so that Andy's eyes hurt. She squinted hard. A gust of wind blew across the field, stinging her face. And then, as if it had been waiting for her, the doe emerged from the trees opposite and stepped cautiously into the field. Andy watched: it stopped and stood quietly for what seemed a long time and then ambled across. It stopped again about seventy yards away and began to browse in a patch of sugar grass uncovered by the wind. Carefully, slowly, never taking her eyes from the doe, Andy walked backward, trying to step into the boot prints she'd already made. When she was far enough back into the woods, she turned and walked faster, her heart racing. *Please let it stay,* she prayed.

"There's a doe in the field yonder," she told them.

They got their rifles and hurried down the trail.

"No use," her father said. "We're making too much noise any way you look at it."

"At least we got us the wind in our favor," Charlie Spoon said, breathing heavily.

But the doe was still there, grazing.

"Good Lord," Charlie whispered. He looked at her father. "Well, whose shot?"

"Andy spotted it," her father said in a low voice. "Let her shoot it."

"What!" Charlies eyes widened.

Andy couldn't believe what her father had just said. She'd only shot tin cans and targets; she'd never even fired her father's .30-30, and she'd never killed anything.

"I can't," she whispered.

"That's right, she can't," Charlie Spoon insisted. "She's not old enough and she don't have a license even if she was!"

"Well, who's to tell?" her father said. "Nobody's going to know but us." He looked at her. "Do you want to shoot it, punkin?"

Why doesn't it hear us? she wondered. *Why doesn't it run away?* "I don't know," she said.

"Well, I'm sure as hell gonna shoot it," Charlie said. Her father grasped Charlie's rifle barrel and held it. His voice was steady.

"Andy's a good shot. It's her deer. She found it, not you. You'd still be sitting on your ass back in camp." He turned to her again. "Now—do you want to shoot it, Andy? Yes or no."

He was looking at her; they were all looking at her. Suddenly she was angry at the deer, who refused to hear them, who wouldn't run away even when it could. "I'll shoot it," she said. Charlie turned away in disgust.

She lay on the ground and pressed the rifle stock against her shoulder bone. The snow was cold through her parka; she smelled oil and wax and damp earth. She pulled off one glove with her teeth. "It sights just like the .22," her father said gently. "Cartridge's already chambered." As she had done so many times before, she sighted down the scope; now the doe was in the reticle. She moved the barrel until the cross hairs lined up. Her father was breathing beside her.

"Aim where the chest and legs meet, or a little above, punkin," he was saying calmly. "That's the killing shot."

But now, seeing it in the scope, Andy was hesitant. Her finger weakened on the trigger. Still, she nodded at what her father said and sighted again, the cross hairs lining up in exactly the same spot—the doe had hardly moved, its brownish gray body outlined starkly against the blue-backed snow. *It doesn't know,* Andy thought. *It just doesn't know.* And as she looked, deer and snow and faraway trees flattened within the circular frame to become like a picture on a calendar, not real, and she felt calm, as if she had been dreaming everything—the day, the deer, the hunt itself. And she, finger on the trigger, was only a part of that dream. "Shoot!" Charlie hissed.

Through the scope she saw the deer look up, ears high and straining.

Charlie groaned, and just as he did, and just at the moment when Andy knew—*knew*—the doe would bound away, as if she could feel its haunches tensing and gathering power, she pulled the trigger. Later she would think, *I felt the recoil, I smelled the smoke, but I don't remember pulling the trigger.* Through the scope the deer seemed to shrink into itself, and then slowly knelt, hind legs first, head raised as if to cry out. It trembled, still straining to keep its head high, as if that alone would save it; failing, it collapsed, shuddered, and lay still.

"Whoee!" Mac cried.

"One shot! One shot!" her father yelled, clapping her on the back. Charlie Spoon was shaking his head and smiling dumbly.

"I told you she was a great little shot!" her father said. "I told you!" Mac danced and clapped his hands. She was dazed, not quite understanding what had happened. And then they were crossing the field toward the fallen doe, she walking dreamlike, the men laughing and joking, released now from the tension of silence and anticipation. Suddenly Mac pointed and cried out, "Look at that!"

The doe was rising, legs unsteady. They stared at it, unable to comprehend, and in that moment the doe regained its feet and looked at them, as if it, too, were trying to understand. Her father whistled softly. Charlie Spoon unslung his rifle and raised it to his shoulder, but the doe was already bounding away. His hurried shot missed, and the deer disappeared into the woods.

"Damn, damn, damn," he moaned.

"I don't believe it," her father said. "That deer was dead."

"Dead, hell!" Charlie yelled. "It was gutshot, that's all. Stunned and gutshot. Clean shot, my ass!"

What have I done? Andy thought.

Her father slung his rifle over his shoulder. "Well, let's go. She can't get too far."

"Hell, I've seen deer run ten miles gutshot," Charlie said. He waved his arms. "We may never find her!"

As they crossed the field, Mac came up to her and said in a low voice, "Gutshoot a deer, you'll go to hell."

"Shut up, Mac," she said, her voice cracking. It was a terrible thing she had done, she knew. She couldn't bear to think of the doe in pain and frightened. *Please let it die,* she prayed.

But though they searched all the last hour of daylight, so that they had to recross the field and go up the logging trail in a twilight made even deeper by thick, smoky clouds, they didn't find the doe. They lost its trail almost immediately in the dense stands of alderberry and larch.

"I am cold, and I am tired," Charlie Spoon declared. "And if you ask me, that deer's in another county already."

"No one's asking you, Charlie," her father said.

They had a supper of hard salami and ham, bread, and the rest of the applesauce cake. It seemed a bother to heat the coffee, so they had cold chocolate instead. Everyone turned in early.

"We'll find it in the morning, honeybun," her father said, as she went to her tent.

"I don't like to think of it suffering." She was almost in tears.

"It's dead already, punkin. Don't even think about it." He kissed her, his breath sour and his beard rough against her cheek.

Andy was sure she wouldn't get to sleep; the image of the doe falling, falling, then rising again, repeated itself whenever she closed her eyes. Then she heard an owl hoot and realized that it had awakened her, so she must have been asleep after all. She hoped the owl would hush, but instead it hooted louder. She wished her father or Charlie Spoon would wake up and do something about it, but no one moved in the other tent, and suddenly she was afraid that they had all decamped, wanting nothing more to do with her. She whispered, "Mac, Mac," to the sleeping bag where he should be, but no one answered. She tried to find the flashlight she always kept by her side, but couldn't, and she cried in panic, "Mac, are you there?" He mumbled something, and immediately she felt foolish and hoped he wouldn't reply.

When she awoke again, everything had changed. The owl was gone, the woods were still, and she sensed light, blue and pale, light where before there had been none. *The moon must have come out,* she thought. And it was warm, too, warmer than it should have been. She got out of her sleeping bag and took off her parka—it was that warm. Mac was asleep, wheezing like an old man. She unzipped the tent and stepped outside.

The woods were more beautiful than she had ever seen them. The moon made everything ice-rimmed glimmer with a crystallized, immanent light, while underneath that ice the branches of trees were as stark as skeletons. She heard a crunching in the snow, the one sound in all that silence, and there, walking down the logging trail into their camp, was the doe. Its body, like everything around her, was silvered with frost and moonlight. It walked past the tent where her father and Charlie Spoon were sleeping and stopped no more than six feet from her. Andy saw that she had shot it, yes, had shot it cleanly, just where she thought she had, the wound a jagged, bloody hole in the doe's chest.

A heart shot, she thought.

The doe stepped closer, so that Andy, if she wished, could have reached out and touched it. It looked at her as if expecting her to do this, and so she did, running her hand, slowly at first, along the rough, matted fur, then down to the edge of the wound, where she stopped. The doe stood still. Hesitantly, Andy felt the edge of the wound. The torn flesh was sticky and warm. The wound parted under her touch. And then, almost without her knowing it, her fingers were within, probing, yet still the doe didn't move. Andy pressed deeper, through flesh and muscle and sinew, until her whole hand and more was inside the wound and she had found the doe's heart, warm and beating. She cupped it gently in her hand. *Alive,* she marveled. *Alive.*

The heart quickened under her touch, becoming warmer and warmer until it was hot enough to burn. In pain, Andy tried to remove her hand, but the wound closed about it and held her fast. Her hand was burning. She cried out in agony, sure they would all hear and come help, but they didn't. And then her hand pulled free, followed by a steaming rush of blood, more blood than she ever could have imagined—it covered her hand and arm, and she saw to her horror that her hand was steaming. She moaned and fell to her knees and plunged her hand into the snow. The doe looked at her gently and then turned and walked back up the trail.

In the morning, when she woke, Andy could still smell the blood, but she felt no pain. She looked at her hand. Even though it appeared unscathed, it felt weak and withered. She couldn't move it freely and was afraid the others would notice. *I will hide it in my jacket pocket,* she decided, *so nobody can see.* She ate the oatmeal that her father cooked and stayed apart from them all. No one spoke to her, and that suited her. A light snow began to fall. It was the last day of their hunting trip. She wanted to be home.

Her father dumped the dregs of his coffee. "Well, let's go look for her," he said.

Again they crossed the field. Andy lagged behind. She averted her eyes from the spot where the doe had fallen, already filling up with snow.

Mac and Charlie entered the woods first, followed by her father. Andy remained in the field and considered the smear of gray sky, the nearby flock of crows pecking at unyielding stubble. *I will stay here,* she thought, *and not move for a long while.* But now someone—Mac—was yelling. Her father appeared at the woods' edge and waved for her to come. She ran and pushed through a brake of alderberry and larch. The thick underbrush scratched her face. For a moment she felt lost and looked wildly about. Then, where the brush thinned, she saw them standing quietly in the falling snow. They were staring down at the dead doe. A film covered its upturned eye, and its body was lightly dusted with snow.

"I told you she wouldn't get too far," Andy's father said triumphantly. "We must've just missed her yesterday. Too blind to see."

"We're just damn lucky no animal got to her last night," Charlie muttered.

Her father lifted the doe's foreleg. The wound was blood-clotted, brown, and caked like frozen mud. "Clean shot," he said to Charlie. He grinned. "My little girl."

Then he pulled out his knife, the blade gray as the morning. Mac whispered to Andy, "Now watch this," while Charlie Spoon lifted the doe from behind by its forelegs so that its head rested between his knees, its underside exposed. Her father's knife sliced thickly from chest to belly to crotch, and Andy was running from them, back to the field and across, scattering the crows who cawed and circled angrily. And now they were all calling to her—Charlie Spoon and Mac and her father—crying *Andy, Andy* (but that wasn't her name, she would no longer be called that); yet louder than any of them was the wind blowing through the treetops, like the ocean where her mother floated in green water, also calling *Come in, come in,* while all around her roared the mocking of the terrible, now inevitable, sea.

Jayne Anne Phillips

1952 –

Following two short story collections issued quietly by small presses, Jayne Anne Phillips's *Black Tickets* had major national impact when it appeared from a large commercial publisher in 1979. A native of West Virginia, Phillips was educated at West Virginia University and the University of Iowa. She lives now near Boston. Other of her books are the novel *Machine Dreams* (1984) and *Fast Lanes* (1984/87), more short stories.

The main themes or concerns of Phillips's fiction are said to be the rootlessness and disorientation of the '60s and '70s generation of Americans. The "richly sensuous language" of her prose has received special praise. She is tending now to work in longer forms than the more poetic, extremely compressed pieces that characterized her earlier work; whether she will return to produce more impressive "short shorts" remains to be seen. With "Cheers" one may test Phillips's observations that in such pieces she was experimenting with writing about "perception" and that in "that kind of compression . . . images carry a great deal of weight, and tell a great deal"—plus, also, her general contention that "good writing is intrinsically political."

Cheers

The sewing woman lived across the tracks, down past Arey's Feed Store. Row of skinny houses on a mud alley. Her rooms smelled of salted grease and old newspaper. Behind the ironing board she was thin, scooping up papers that shuffled open in her hands. Her eyebrows were arched sharp and painted on.

She made cheerleading suits for ten-year-olds. Threading the machine, she clicked her red nails on the needle and pulled my shirt over my head. In the other room the kids watched *Queen for a Day*. She bent over me. I saw each eyelash painted black and hard and separate. Honey, she said. Turn around this way. And on the wall there was a postcard of orange trees in Florida. A man in a straw hat reached up with his hand all curled. Beautiful Bounty said the card in wavy red letters.

I got part of it made up, she said, fitting the red vest. You girls are bout the same size as mine. All you girls are bout the same. She pursed her red lips and pinched the cloth together. Tell me somethin Honey. How'd I manage all these kids an no man. On television there was loud applause for the queen, whose roses were sharp and real. Her machine buzzed like an animal beside the round clock. She frowned as she pressed the button with her foot, then furled the red cloth out and pulled me to her. Her pointed white face was smudged around the eyes. I watched the pale strand of scalp in her hair. There, she said.

When I left she tucked the money in her sweater. She had pins between her teeth and lipstick gone grainy in the cracks of her mouth. I had a red swing skirt and a bumpy *A* on my chest. Lord, she said. You do look pretty.

Louise Erdrich

1954 –

Louise Erdrich's books include a volume of poetry, *Jacklight* (1984), and three books of fiction: *Love Medicine* (1984), *Beet Queen* (1986), and *Tracks* (1988). Called "novels" on the title page, all three of the latter can also be seen as interconnected short stories—"sections" or "parts" of each book having appeared earlier as separate stories in various periodicals. Similarly, the novels are themselves interrelated, part of a projected tetralogy about members of the Ojibway Indian Nation.

Erdrich's mother, Rita Gourneau Erdrich, was a Chippewa Indian; her father, German-born, worked for the Bureau of Indian Affairs. Born in Little Falls, Minnesota, she grew up in Wahpeton, North Dakota, near the Turtle Mountain Reservation. She holds degrees from Dartmouth College and Johns Hopkins University. She lives now in New Hampshire.

In making fictional use of her Indian heritage, Erdrich employs multiple points of view and a complex mixture of character and narrator. From one perspective, she presents documentaries; from another, lyrical legend and mythology. Few short stories have a more startling beginning than the first five words of "Fleur." Our engagement and mystification begin here and, as good fiction ensures, endure significantly beyond the conclusion of our reading of the work.

Fleur

The first time she drowned in the cold and glassy waters of Lake Turcot, Fleur Pillager was only a girl. Two men saw the boat tip, saw her struggle in the waves. They rowed over to the place she went down, and jumped in. When they dragged her over the gunwales, she was cold to the touch and stiff, so they slapped her face, shook her by the heels, worked her arms back and forth, and pounded her back until she coughed up lake water. She shivered all over like a dog, then took a breath. But it wasn't long afterward that those two men disappeared. The first wandered off, and the other, Jean Hat, got himself run over by a cart.

It went to show, my grandma said. It figured to her, all right. By saving Fleur Pillager, those two men had lost themselves.

The next time she fell in the lake, Fleur Pillager was twenty years old and no one touched her. She washed onshore, her skin a dull dead gray, but when George Many Women bent to look closer, he saw her chest move. Then her eyes spun open, sharp black riprock, and she looked at him. "You'll take my place," she hissed. Everybody scattered and left her there, so no one knows how she dragged herself home. Soon after that we noticed Many Women changed, grew afraid, wouldn't leave his house, and would not be forced to go near water. For his caution, he lived until the day that his sons brought him a new tin bathtub. Then the first time he used the tub he slipped, got knocked out, and breathed water while his wife stood in the other room frying breakfast.

Men stayed clear of Fleur Pillager after the second drowning. Even though she was good-looking, nobody dared to court her because it was clear that Misshepeshu, the waterman, the monster, wanted her for himself. He's a devil, that one, love-hungry with desire and maddened for the touch of young girls, the strong and daring especially, the ones like Fleur.

Our mothers warn us that we'll think he's handsome, for he appears with green eyes, copper skin, a mouth tender as a child's. But if you fall into his arms, he sprouts horns, fangs, claws, fins. His feet are joined as one and his skin, brass scales, rings to the touch. You're fascinated, cannot move. He casts a shell necklace at your feet, weeps gleaming chips that harden into mica on your breasts. He holds you under. Then he takes the body of a lion or a fat brown worm. He's made of gold. He's made of beach moss. He's a thing of dry foam, a thing of death by drowning, the death a Chippewa cannot survive.

Unless you are Fleur Pillager. We all knew she couldn't swim. After the first time, we thought she'd never go back to Lake Turcot. We thought she'd keep to herself, live quiet, stop killing men off by drowning in the lake. After the first time, we thought she'd keep the good ways. But then, after the second drowning, we knew that we were dealing with something much more serious. She was haywire, out of control. She messed with evil, laughed at the old women's advice, and dressed like a man. She got herself into some half-forgotten medicine, studied ways we shouldn't talk about. Some say she kept the finger of a child in her pocket and a powder of unborn rabbits in a leather thong around her neck. She laid the heart of an owl on her tongue so she could see at night, and went out, hunting, not even in her own body. We know for sure because the next morning, in the snow or dust, we followed the tracks of her bare feet and saw where they changed, where the claws sprang out, the pad broadened and pressed into the dirt. By night we heard her chuffing cough, the bear cough. By day her silence and the wide grin she threw to bring down our guard made us frightened. Some thought that Fleur Pillager should be driven off the reservation, but not a single person who spoke like this had the nerve. And finally, when people were just about to get together and throw her out, she left on her own and didn't come back all summer. That's what this story is about.

During that summer, when she lived a few miles south in Argus, things happened. She almost destroyed that town.

When she got down to Argus in the year of 1920, it was just a small grid of six streets on either side of the railroad depot. There were two elevators, one central, the other a few miles west. Two stores competed for the trade of the three hundred citizens, and three churches quarreled with one another for their souls. There was a frame building for Lutherans, a heavy brick one for Episcopalians, and a long narrow shingled Catholic church. This last had a tall slender steeple, twice as high as any building or tree.

No doubt, across the low, flat wheat, watching from the road as she came near Argus on foot, Fleur saw that steeple rise, a shadow thin as a needle. Maybe in that raw space it drew her the way a lone tree draws lightning. Maybe, in the end, the Catholics are to blame. For if she hadn't seen that sign of pride, that slim prayer, that marker, maybe she would have kept walking.

But Fleur Pillager turned, and the first place she went once she came into town was to the back door of the priest's residence attached to the landmark church. She didn't go there for a handout, although she got that, but to ask for work. She got that too, or the town got her. It's hard to tell which came out worse, her or the men or the town, although the upshot of it all was that Fleur lived.

The four men who worked at the butcher's had carved up about a thousand carcasses between them, maybe half of that steers and the other half pigs, sheep, and game animals like deer, elk, and bear. That's not even mentioning the chickens, which were beyond counting. Pete Kozka owned the place, and employed Lily Veddar, Tor Grunewald, and my stepfather, Dutch James, who had brought my mother down from the reservation the year before she disappointed him by dying. Dutch took me out of school to take her place. I kept house half the time and worked the other in the butcher shop, sweeping floors, putting sawdust down, running a hambone across the street to a customer's bean pot or a package of sausage to the corner. I was a good one to have around because until they needed me, I was invisible. I blended into the stained brown walls, a skinny, big-nosed girl with staring eyes. Because I could fade into a corner or squeeze beneath a shelf, I knew everything, what the men said when no one was around, and what they did to Fleur.

Kozka's Meats served farmers for a fifty-mile area, both to slaughter, for it had a stock pen and a chute, and to cure the meat by smoking it or spicing it in sausage. The storage locker was a marvel, made of many thicknesses of brick, earth insulation, and Minnesota timber, lined inside with sawdust and vast blocks of ice cut from Lake Turcot, hauled down from home each winter by horse and sledge.

A ramshackle board building, part slaughterhouse, part store, was fixed to the low, thick square of the lockers. That's where Fleur worked. Kozka hired her for her strength. She could lift a haunch or carry a pole of sausages without stumbling, and she soon learned cutting from Pete's wife, a string-thin blonde who chain-smoked and handled the razor-sharp knives with nerveless precision, slicing close to her stained fingers. Fleur and Fritzie Kozka worked afternoons, wrapping their cuts in paper, and Fleur hauled the packages to the lockers. The meat was left outside the heavy oak doors that were only opened at 5:00 each afternoon, before the men ate supper.

Sometimes Dutch, Tor, and Lily ate at the lockers, and when they did I stayed too, cleaned floors, restoked the fires in the front smokehouses, while the men sat around the squat cast-iron stove spearing slats of herring onto hardtack bread. They played long games of poker or cribbage on a board made from the planed end of a salt crate. They talked and I listened, although there wasn't much to hear since almost nothing ever happened in Argus. Tor was married, Dutch had lost my mother, and Lily read circulars. They mainly discussed about the auctions to come, equipment, or women.

Every so often, Pete Kozka came out front to make a whist, leaving Fritzie to smoke cigarettes and fry raised doughnuts in the back room. He sat and played a few rounds but kept his thoughts to himself. Fritzie did not tolerate him talking behind her back, and the one book he read was the New Testament. If he said something, it concerned weather or a surplus of sheep stomachs, a ham that smoked green or the markets for corn and wheat. He had a good-luck talisman, the opal-white lens of a cow's eye. Playing cards, he rubbed it between his fingers. That soft sound and the slap of cards was about the only conversation.

Fleur finally gave them a subject.

Her cheeks were wide and flat, her hands large, chapped, muscular. Fleur's shoulders were broad as beams, her hips fishlike, slippery, narrow. An old green dress clung to her waist, worn thin where she sat. Her braids were thick like the tails of animals, and swung against her when she moved, deliberately, slowly in her work, held in and half-tamed, but only half. I could tell, but the others never saw. They never looked into her sly brown eyes or noticed her teeth, strong and curved and very white. Her legs were bare, and since she padded around in beadwork moccasins they never saw that her fifth toes were missing. They never knew she'd drowned. They were blinded, they were stupid, they only saw her in the flesh.

And yet it wasn't just that she was a Chippewa, or even that she was a woman, it wasn't that she was good-looking or even that she was alone that made their brains hum. It was how she played cards.

Women didn't usually play with men, so the evening that Fleur drew a chair up to the men's table without being so much as asked, there was a shock of surprise.

"What's this," said Lily. He was fat, with a snake's cold pale eyes and precious skin, smooth and lily-white, which is how he got his name. Lily had a dog, a stumpy mean little bull of a thing with a belly drum-tight from eating pork rinds. The dog liked to play cards just like Lily, and straddled his barrel thighs through games of stud, rum poker, vingt-un. The dog snapped at Fleur's arm that first night, but cringed back, its snarl frozen, when she took her place.

"I thought," she said, her voice soft and stroking, "you might deal me in."

There was a space between the heavy bin of spiced flour and the wall where I just fit. I hunkered down there, kept my eyes open, saw her black hair swing over the chair, her feet solid on the wood floor. I couldn't see up on the table where the cards slapped down, so after they were deep in their game I raised myself up in the shadows, and crouched on a sill of wood.

I watched Fleur's hands stack and ruffle, divide the cards, spill them to each player in a blur, rake them up and shuffle again. Tor, short and scrappy, shut one eye and squinted the other at Fleur. Dutch screwed his lips around a wet cigar.

"Gotta see a man," he mumbled, getting up to go out back to the privy. The others broke, put their cards down, and Fleur sat alone in the lamplight that glowed in a sheen across the push of her breasts. I watched her closely, then she paid me a beam of notice for the first time. She turned, looked straight at me, and grinned the white wolf grin a Pillager turns on its victims, except that she wasn't after me.

"Pauline there," she said, "how much money you got?"

We'd all been paid for the week that day. Eight cents was in my pocket.

"Stake me," she said, holding out her long fingers. I put the coins in her palm and then I melted back to nothing, part of the walls and tables. It was a long time before I understood that the men would not have seen me no matter what I did, how I moved. I wasn't anything like Fleur. My dress hung loose and my back was already curved, an old woman's. Work had roughened me, reading made my eyes sore, caring for my mother before she died had hardened my face. I was not much to look at, so they never saw me.

When the men came back and sat around the table, they had drawn together. They shot each other small glances, stuck their tongues in their cheeks, burst out laughing at odd moments, to rattle Fleur. But she never minded. They played their vingt-un, staying even as Fleur slowly gained. Those pennies I had given her drew nickels and attracted dimes until there was a small pile in front of her.

Then she hooked them with five-card draw, nothing wild. She dealt, discarded, drew, and then she sighed and her cards gave a little shiver. Tor's eye gleamed, and Dutch straightened in his seat.

"I'll pay to see that hand," said Lily Veddar.

Fleur showed, and she had nothing there, nothing at all.

Tor's thin smile cracked open, and he threw his hand in too.

"Well, we know one thing," he said, leaning back in his chair, "the squaw can't bluff."

With that I lowered myself into a mound of swept sawdust and slept. I woke up during the night, but none of them had moved yet, so I couldn't either. Still later, the men must have gone out again, or Fritzie come out to break the game, because I was lifted, soothed, cradled in a woman's arms and rocked so quiet that I kept my eyes shut while Fleur rolled me into a closet of grimy ledgers, oiled paper, balls of string, and thick files that fit beneath me like a mattress.

The game went on after work the next evening. I got my eight cents back five times over, and Fleur kept the rest of the dollar she'd won for a stake. This time they didn't play so late, but they played regular, and then kept going at it night after night. They played poker now, or variations, for one week straight, and each time Fleur won exactly one dollar, no more and no less, too consistent for luck.

By this time, Lily and the other men were so lit with suspense that they got Pete to join the game with them. They concentrated, the fat dog sitting tense in Lily Veddar's lap, Tor suspicious, Dutch stroking his huge square brow, Pete steady. It wasn't that Fleur won that hooked them in so, because she lost hands too. It was rather that she never had a freak hand or even anything above a straight. She only took on her low cards, which didn't sit right. By chance, Fleur should have gotten a full or flush by now. The irritating thing was she beat with pairs and never bluffed, because she couldn't, and still she ended up each night with exactly one dollar. Lily couldn't believe, first of all, that a woman could be smart enough to play cards, but even if she was, that she would then be stupid enough to cheat for a dollar a night. By day I watched him turn the problem over, his hard white face dull, small fingers probing at his knuckles, until he finally thought he had Fleur figured out as a bit-time player, caution her game. Raising the stakes would throw her.

More than anything now, he wanted Fleur to come away with something but a dollar. Two bits less or ten more, the sum didn't matter, just so he broke her streak.

Night after night she played, won her dollar, and left to stay in a place that just Fritzie and I knew about. Fleur bathed in the slaughtering tub, then slept in the unused brick smokehouse behind the lockers, a windowless place tarred on the inside with scorched fats. When I brushed against her skin I noticed that she smelled of the walls, rich and woody, slightly burnt. Since that night she put me in the closet I was no longer afraid of her, but followed her close, stayed with her, became her moving shadow that the men never noticed, the shadow that could have saved her.

August, the month that bears fruit, closed around the shop, and Pete and Fritzie left for Minnesota to escape the heat. Night by night, running, Fleur had won thirty dollars, and only Pete's presence had kept Lily at bay. But Pete was gone now, and one payday, with the heat so bad no one could move but Fleur, the men sat and played and waited while she finished work. The cards sweat, limp in their fingers, the table was slick with grease, and even the walls were warm to the touch. The air was motionless. Fleur was in the next room boiling heads.

Her green dress, drenched, wrapped her like a transparent sheet. A skin of lakeweed. Black snarls of veining clung to her arms. Her braids were loose, half-unraveled, tied behind her neck in a thick loop. She stood in steam, turning skulls through a vat with a wooden paddle. When scraps boiled to the surface, she bent with a round tin sieve and scooped them out. She'd filled two dishpans.

"Ain't that enough now?" called Lily. "We're waiting." The stump of a dog trembled in his lap, alive with rage. It never smelled me or noticed me above Fleur's smoky skin. The air was heavy in my corner, and pressed me down. Fleur sat with them.

"Now what do you say?" Lily asked the dog. It barked. That was the signal for the real game to start.

"Let's up the ante," said Lily, who had been stalking this night all month. He had a roll of money in his pocket. Fleur had five bills in her dress. The men had each saved their full pay.

"Ante a dollar then," said Fleur, and pitched hers in. She lost, but they let her scrape along, cent by cent. And then she won some. She played unevenly, as if chance was all she had. She reeled them in. The game went on. The dog was stiff now, poised on Lily's knees, a ball of vicious muscle with its yellow eyes slit in concentration. It gave advice, seemed to sniff the lay of Fleur's cards, twitched and nudged. Fleur was up, then down, saved by a scratch. Tor dealt seven cards, three down. The pot grew, round by round, until it held all the money. Nobody folded. Then it all rode on one last card and they went silent. Fleur picked hers up and blew a long breath. The heat lowered like a bell. Her card shook, but she stayed in.

Lily smiled and took the dog's head tenderly between his palms.

"Say, Fatso," he said, crooning the words, "you reckon that girl's bluffing?"

The dog whined and Lily laughed. "Me, too," he said, "let's show." He swept his bills and coins into the pot and then they turned their cards over.

Lily looked once, looked again, then he squeezed the dog up like a fist of dough and slammed it on the table.

Fleur threw her arms out and drew the money over, grinning that same wolf grin that she'd used on me, the grin that had them. She jammed the bills in her dress, scooped the coins up in waxed white paper that she tied with string.

"Let's go another round," said Lily, his voice choked with burrs. But Fleur opened her mouth and yawned, then walked out back to gather slops for the one big hog that was waiting in the stock pen to be killed.

The men sat still as rocks, their hands spread on the oiled wood table. Dutch had chewed his cigar to damp shreds, Tor's eye was dull. Lily's gaze was the only one to follow Fleur. I didn't move. I felt them gathering, saw my stepfather's veins, the ones in his forehead that stood out in anger. The dog had rolled off the table and curled in a knot below the counter, where none of the men could touch it.

Lily rose and stepped out back to the closet of ledgers where Pete kept his private stock. He brought back a bottle, uncorked and tipped it between his fingers. The lump in his throat moved, then he passed it on.

They drank, quickly felt the whiskey's fire, and planned with their eyes things they couldn't say out loud.

When they left, I followed. I hid out back in the clutter of broken boards and chicken crates beside the stock pen, where they waited. Fleur could not be seen at first, and then the moon broke and showed her, slipping cautiously along the rough board chute with a bucket in her hand. Her hair fell, wild and coarse, to her waist, and her dress was a floating patch in the dark. She made a pig-calling sound, rang the tin pail lightly against the wood, froze suspiciously. But too late. In the sound of the ring Lily moved, fat and nimble, stepped right behind Fleur and put out his creamy hands. At his first touch, she whirled and doused him with the bucket of sour slops. He pushed her against the big fence and the package of coins split, went clinking and jumping, winked against the wood. Fleur rolled over once and vanished in the yard.

The moon fell behind a curtain of ragged clouds, and Lily followed into the dark muck. But he tripped, pitched over the huge flank of the pig, who lay mired to the snout, heavily snoring. I sprang out of the weeds and climbed the side of the pen, stuck like glue. I saw the sow rise to her neat, knobby knees, gain her balance, and sway, curious, as Lily stumbled forward. Fleur had backed into the angle of rough wood just beyond, and when Lily tried to jostle past, the sow tipped up on her hind legs and struck, quick and hard as a snake. She plunged her head into Lily's thick side and snatched a mouthful of his shirt. She lunged again, caught him lower, so that he grunted in pained surprise. He seemed to ponder, breathing deep. Then he launched his huge body in a swimmer's dive.

The sow screamed as his body smacked over hers. She rolled, striking out with her knife-sharp hooves, and Lily gathered himself upon her, took her foot-long face by the ears and scraped her snout and cheeks against the trestles of the pen. He hurled the sow's tight skull against an iron post, but instead of knocking her dead, he merely woke her from her dream.

She reared, shrieked, drew him with her so that they posed standing upright. They bowed jerkily to each other, as if to begin. Then his arms swung and flailed. She sank her black fangs into his shoulder, clasping him, dancing him forward and backward through the pen. Their steps picked up pace, went wild. The two dipped as one, box-stepped, tripped each other. She ran her split foot through his hair. He grabbed her kinked tail. They went down and came up, the same shape and then the same color, until the men couldn't tell one from the other in that light and Fleur was able to launch herself over the gates, swing down, hit gravel.

The men saw, yelled, and chased her at a dead run to the smokehouse. And Lily too, once the sow gave up in disgust and freed him. That is where I should have gone to Fleur, saved her, thrown myself on Dutch. But I went stiff with fear and couldn't unlatch myself from the trestles or move at all. I closed my eyes and put my head in my arms, tried to hide, so there is nothing to describe but what I couldn't block out, Fleur's hoarse breath, so loud it filled me, her cry in the old language, and my name repeated over and over among the words.

The heat was still dense the next morning when I came back to work. Fleur was gone but the men were there, slack-faced, hung over. Lily was paler and softer than ever, as if his flesh had steamed on his bones. They smoked, took pulls off a bottle. It wasn't noon yet. I worked awhile, waiting shop and sharpening steel. But I was sick, I was smothered, I was sweating so hard that my hands slipped on the knives, and I wiped my fingers clear of the greasy touch of the customers' coins. Lily opened his mouth and roared once, not in anger. There was no meaning to the sound. His boxer dog, sprawled limp beside his foot, never lifted its head. Nor did the other men.

They didn't notice when I stepped outside, hoping for a clear breath. And then I forgot them because I knew that we were all balanced, ready to tip, to fly, to be crushed as soon as the weather broke. The sky was so low that I felt the weight of it like a yoke. Clouds hung down, witch teats, a tornado's green-brown cones, and as I watched one flicked out and became a delicate probing thumb. Even as I picked up my heels and ran back inside, the wind blew suddenly, cold, and then came rain.

Inside, the men had disappeared already and the whole place was trembling as if a huge hand was pinched at the rafters, shaking it. I ran straight through, screaming for Dutch or for any of them, and then I stopped at the heavy doors of the lockers, where they had surely taken shelter. I stood there a moment. Everything went still. Then I heard a cry building in the wind, faint at first, a whistle and then a shill scream that tore through the walls and gathered around me, spoke plain so I understood that I should move, put my arms out, and slam down the great iron bar that fit across the hasp and lock.

Outside, the wind was stronger, like a hand held against me. I struggled forward. The bushes tossed, the awnings flapped off storefronts, the rails of porches rattled. The odd cloud became a fat snout that nosed along the earth and sniffled, jabbed, picked at things, sucked them up, blew them apart, rooted around as if it was following a certain scent, then stopped behind me at the butcher shop and bored down like a drill.

I went flying, landed somewhere in a ball. When I opened my eyes and looked, stranger things were happening.

A herd of cattle flew through the air like giant birds, dropping dung, their mouths opened in stunned bellows. A candle, still lighted, blew past, and tables, napkins, garden tools, a whole school of drifting eyeglasses, jackets on hangers, hams, a checkerboard, a lampshade, and at last the sow from behind the lockers, on the run, her hooves a blur, set free, swooping, diving, screaming as everything in Argus fell apart and got turned upside down, smashed, and thoroughly wrecked.

Days passed before the town went looking for the men. They were bachelors, after all, except for Tor, whose wife had suffered a blow to the head that made her forgetful. Everyone was occupied with digging out, in high relief because even though the Catholic steeple had been torn off like a peaked cap and sent across five fields, those huddled in the cellar were unhurt. Walls had fallen, windows were demolished, but the stores were intact and so were the bankers and shop owners who had taken refuge in their safes or beneath their cash registers. It was a fair-minded disaster, no one could be said to have suffered much more than the next, at least not until Fritzie and Pete came home.

Of all the businesses in Argus, Kozka's Meats had suffered worst. The boards of the front building had been split to kindling, piled in a huge pyramid, and the shop equipment was blasted far and wide. Pete paced off the distance the iron bathtub had been flung—a hundred feet. The glass candy case went fifty, and landed without so much as a cracked pane. There were other surprises as well, for the back rooms where Fritzie and Pete lived were undisturbed. Fritzie said the dust still coated her china figures, and upon her kitchen table, in the ashtray, perched the last cigarette she'd put out in haste. She lit it up and finished it, looking through the window. From there, she could see that the old smokehouse Fleur had slept in was crushed to a reddish sand and the stockpens were completely torn apart, the rails stacked helter-skelter. Fritzie asked for Fleur. People shrugged. Then she asked about the others and, suddenly, the town understood that three men were missing.

There was a rally of help, a gathering of shovels and volunteers. We passed boards from hand to hand, stacked them, uncovered what lay beneath the pile of jagged splinters. The lockers, full of the meat that was Pete and Fritzie's investment, slowly came into sight, still intact. When enough room was made for a man to stand on the roof, there were calls, a general urge to hack through and see what lay below. But Fritzie shouted that she wouldn't allow it because the meat would spoil. And so the work continued, board by board, until at last the heavy oak doors of the freezer were revealed and people pressed to the entry. Everyone wanted to be the first, but since it was my stepfather lost, I was let go in when Pete and Fritzie wedged through into the sudden icy air.

Pete scraped a match on his boot, lit the lamp Fritzie held, and then the three of us stood still in its circle. Light glared off the skinned and hanging carcasses, the crates of wrapped sausages, the bright and cloudy blocks of lake ice, pure as winter. The cold bit into us, pleasant at first, then numbing. We must have stood there a couple of minutes before we saw the men, or more rightly, the humps of fur, the iced and shaggy hides they wore, the bearskins they had taken down and wrapped around themselves. We stepped closer and tilted the lantern beneath the flaps of fur into their faces. The dog was there, perched among them, heavy as a doorstop. The three had hunched around a barrel where the game was still laid out, and a dead lantern and an empty bottle, too. But they had thrown down their last hands and hunkered tight, clutching one another, knuckles raw from beating at the door they had also attacked with hooks. Frost stars gleamed off their eyelashes and the stubble of their beards. Their faces were set in concentration, mouths open as if to speak some careful thought, some agreement they'd come to in each other's arms.

Power travels in the bloodlines, handed out before birth. It comes down through the hands, which in the Pillagers were strong and knotted, big, spidery, and rough, with sensitive fingertips good at dealing cards. It comes through the eyes, too, belligerent, darkest brown, the eyes of those in the bear clan, impolite as they gaze directly at a person.

In my dreams, I look straight back at Fleur, at the men. I am no longer the watcher on the dark sill, the skinny girl.

The blood draws us back, as if it runs through a vein of earth. I've come home and, except for talking to my cousins, live a quiet life. Fleur lives quiet too, down on Lake Turcot with her boat. Some say she's married to the waterman, Misshepeshu, or that she's living in shame with white men or windigos, or that she's killed them all. I'm about the only one here who ever goes to visit her. Last winter, I went to help out in her cabin when she bore the child, whose green eyes and skin the color of an old penny made more talk, as no one could decide if the child was mixed blood or what, fathered in a smokehouse, or by a man with brass scales, or by the lake. The girl is bold, smiling in her sleep, as if she knows what people wonder, as if she hears the old men talk, turning the story over. It comes up different every time and has no ending, no beginning. They get the middle wrong too. They only know that they don't know anything.

Michael Martone

1955 –

A graduate of Indiana University and of The Writing Seminars at Johns Hopkins University, Michael Martone has taught fiction writing at Johns Hopkins, Iowa State, and Harvard. He is the author of two collections of short stories, *Alive and Dead in Indiana* (1984) and *Safety Patrol* (1988), and was the contributing editor of a nonfiction anthology, *A Place of Sense: Essays in Search of the Midwest* (1988). The "Prose Poems" subtitle of his *Return to Powers* (1985) is descriptive also of his early chapbook publication *At a Loss* (1977).

Newsweek's review of *Alive and Dead in Indiana* characterized this book as "very exciting" and its stories as "very short, very fine, exceedingly complex." Martone has said that he thinks of himself "as a short story writer," and that when he approaches the task of writing stories, he thinks of them as poems. Thus far he has made shortness, a sense of place, and an impressive if various first-person speaking voice hallmarks of his fiction.

"The Mayor of the Sister City Speaks to the Chamber of Commerce in Klamath Falls, Oregon" was the 1986 winner of The World's Best Short Short Story Contest sponsored by the Creative Writing Program of the English Department of Florida State University, and was subsequently first published in *Sundog: The Southeast Review* (Fall, 1986, 7:2). In this short short Martone has created an experience of great power, a bomb of meaning whose shock waves expand with time and travel on and on in the reader's mind.

The Mayor of the Sister City Speaks to the Chamber of Commerce in Klamath Falls, Oregon

"It was after the raid on Tokyo. We children were told to collect scraps of cloth. Anything we could find. We picked over the countryside; we stripped the scarecrows. I remember this remnant from my sister's *obi.* Red silk suns bounced like balls. And these patches were quilted together by the women in the prefecture. The seams were waxed as if to make the stitches rainproof. Instead they held air, gasses, and the rags billowed out into balloons, the heavy heads of chrysanthemums. The balloons bobbed as the soldiers attached the bombs. And then they rose up to the high wind, so many, like planets, heading into the rising sun and America. . . . "

I had stopped translating before he reached this point. I let his words fly away. It was a luncheon meeting. I looked down at the tables. The white napkins looked like mountain peaks of a range hung with clouds. We were high above them on the stage. I am *yonsei,* the fourth American generation. Four is an unlucky number in Japan. The old man, the mayor, was trying to say that the world was knit together with threads we could not see, that the wind was a bridge between people. It was a hot day. I told these beat businessmen about children long ago releasing the bright balloons, how they disappeared ages and ages ago. And all of them looked up as if to catch the first sight of the balloons returning to earth, a bright scrap of joy.

Verderber, Rudolph F.
The Challenge Of Effective
Speaking

DATE DUE	BORROWER'S NAME	ROOM NUMBER
APR 5 '90	[illegible] APR 12 [illegible]	

DATE DUE	BORROWER'S NAME	ROOM NUMBER